Cat 25.19

The Complete Works of
*WASHINGTON
IRVING*

Richard Dilworth Rust
General Editor

LETTERS OF
JONATHAN OLDSTYLE, GENT.

SALMAGUNDI

Washington Irving
1805

WASHINGTON IRVING

LETTERS OF JONATHAN OLDSTYLE, GENT.

SALMAGUNDI;

or The Whim-whams and Opinions of Launcelot Langstaff, Esq. & Others

Edited by
Bruce I. Granger and
Martha Hartzog

Twayne Publishers

Boston

1977

Published by Twayne Publishers

A Division of G. K. Hall & Co.

Copyright © 1977 by

G. K. Hall & Co.

All Rights Reserved

The Complete Works of Washington Irving

Volume VI

CENTER FOR EDITIONS OF
AMERICAN AUTHORS
AN APPROVED TEXT
MODERN LANGUAGE
ASSOCIATION OF AMERICA
®

Library of Congress Cataloging in Publication Data

Irving, Washington, 1783–1859.
Letters of Jonathan Oldstyle, gent.; Salmagundi.

(The complete works of Washington Irving; v. 6)
Includes bibliographical references.
I. Irving, Washington, 1783–1859. Salmagundi. 1977.
II. Title. III. Title: The whim-whams and opinions of
Launcelot Langstaff, Esq. & others.
PS2072.L4 1977   818'.2'07   77–6806
ISBN 0–8057–8509–4

Manufactured in the United States of America

DEDICATION

This edition is dedicated to Henry A. Pochmann who until his death on January 13, 1973, was its prime mover and General Editor, responsible for the first three volumes to appear, *Journals and Notebooks I, Journals and Notebooks III,* and *Mahomet and His Successors,* the last of which was produced by him as a model of editorial excellence. As effective leader of the enterprise, he brought to it a lifelong devotion to Irving scholarship and a commitment to editorial precision which was both guide and inspiration to all the rest of us who had the privilege of working under his direction.

GENERAL INTRODUCTION

In the preface to his *Dictionary of the English Language,* Dr. Johnson provided the dictum that explains the present re-editing of Washington Irving's writings: "The chief glory of every people arises from its authors." This is, too, the fitting motto for the Center for Editions of American Authors, belatedly but earnestly seeking to correct the anomalous situation that permitted the American people to be content for more than a century to read their major authors in incomplete and corrupt so called "standard" editions.

In some respects Irving fared better than several of his compeers. Winning the distinction of being the "first" in many areas of literary activity, he also achieved, by his own foresight and the cooperation of an enterprising publisher, the honor of being the first American man of letters to have his writings collected, revised, and edited by himself, in what then passed for a complete, uniform, authorized edition.

The "Author's Revised Edition" published by G. P. Putnam in 1848–1851 originally put the "Father of American Literature" in a favored position, barely ahead of Cooper (whose twelve-volume edition of 1848–1850, however, was far from complete), but two decades and more before the other major nineteenth-century authors were enshrined in "complete" or "collected" editions, when the Houghton Mifflin firm sought to consolidate their authors' and their own position about the turn of the century. A score of years before Irving's contemporaries became the subjects of "official" biographies, Pierre Munro Irving, with his four-volume biography (1863–1864), set the style, tone, and scope for others to follow in preparing so-called authoritative lives of the major American authors.

In this case, nevertheless, being first proved an uncertain blessing; for while Pierre M. Irving quoted liberally from his uncle's journals and letters, their separate collection lagged far behind what was being done for Irving's contemporaries, presumably on the assumption that the samplings provided by the official biography were sufficient for most purposes. So they were until the demands of twentieth-century scholarship encouraged a first generation of serious Irving students to supply some of the more significant lacunae in Irving's journals and notebooks and special collections of his letters.

Good as these were, they followed various methods of transcription and standards of editing. They also left large gaps—in the journals, some two dozen manuscripts or volumes; of the letters, hundreds which had remained uncollected, unedited, and unlocated. To rectify this unfortunate situation, a half-dozen students met informally during the sessions of the 1959 Modern Language Association convention and projected a complete edition of Irving's journals and letters to be prepared uniformly in accord with modern editorial standards. When the Center for Editions of American Authors was formed, the project was included among the editions sponsored by the Center, and expanded to twenty-eight volumes—five of journals, four of letters, eighteen of works, and a bibliography.

However wide the cast and fine the mesh, we are prepared to accept the likelihood that some manuscripts have eluded our net. Accordingly, in anticipation that some fugitive journals, notebooks, and letters, as well as stray bits of Irving's writings may come to light after the relevant volumes have already been published, a place is reserved for them in the last volume of each of the three series—journals, letters, and works; and in an effort at least to record, if not reproduce, anything that appears even after all these are published, a special place is reserved for them in the final bibliographical volume.

In the pursuit of this cooperative enterprise the associated editors incurred debts to many individuals and institutions for ready access to manuscripts, for rare copies of Irving's books, and for personal assistance. At the head of this long list stands The New York Public Library, whose officers and staff supplied from their unrivalled Berg, Hellman, Seligman, and other special collections, the bulk of primary documents without which the edition could not have been launched at all—thus repaying a more than century-old debt to Washington Irving, who, as much as any other man, was responsible for the founding of the Library, who became its first President in 1849, and who served regularly and faithfully in that capacity until his death a decade later. The C. Waller Barrett Collection in the Alderman Library of the University of Virginia, the Yale, Harvard, Columbia, and Pennsylvania university libraries were no less ready to make their holdings available, and the Miriam Lutcher Stark Library of the University of Texas freely supplied materials unavailable elsewhere from its superb collection of books originally assembled by Stanley T. Williams. We also relied heavily on documents preserved in the Library of Congress and the National Archives in Washington, D. C., on the ever-growing collection of Irvingiana in the library of Sleepy Hollow Restorations in Tarrytown, New York, as well as on extant records of Irving's publishers, including John Murray of 50 Albemarle Street, London. To these, and to hundreds of other libraries, institutions, and individuals, the editors owe debts that can be acknowledged only in the prefaces and notes to individual volumes. Finally, we gratefully acknowledge our indebtedness to the Center for

Editions of American Authors of the Modern Language Association of America for editorial guidance and sponsorship, and to the National Endowment for the Humanities, which shared fully and generously with the editors' own universities, the indispensable needed financial support for the entire undertaking.

HENRY A. POCHMANN
H. L. KLEINFIELD

ACKNOWLEDGMENTS

We are indebted to many persons and institutions. We offer grateful thanks to the Center for Editions of American Authors for financial support derived chiefly from the National Endowment for the Humanities, and to the New York Public Library and the Alderman Library at the University of Virginia for making available their manuscripts bearing on *Salmagundi*. Our special thanks goes to Henry A. Pochmann for his unfailing wisdom and encouragement. We are indebted to numerous other libraries and several individuals, named in the Textual Commentaries, who supplied us with copies essential for the collations.

Bruce Granger would like to thank the American Philosophical Society and the Faculty Research Committee of the University of Oklahoma for helping defray travel and clerical expenses and for money to pay for hourly help for the sight collations. Especial thanks are owing to those students at the University of Oklahoma who helped in the typing and the collation: Norma Jane Bumgarner, Janet Constantinides, Ronald Johns, William Robert, Sally Robinson, David Rowland, James Stewart; and to the staff of the University of Oklahoma Library for cheerful responses to many requests.

Martha Hartzog would like to thank William B. Todd for his encouragement and example. He has, in all things bibliographical, been the perfect teacher. Special mention should be made of Elisabeth Eccles, whose questions and suggestions greatly improved the Textual Commentary to *Salmagundi*. Thanks also to Alfred Rose, David Randall, Edwin Bowden, and June Moll.

B. I. G.
M. H.

University of Oklahoma
University of Texas

STATEMENT OF DIVISION OF LABOR

The introduction, the establishment of the text of *Oldstyle*, the preparation of the textual commentary and lists, and the historical and explanatory notes to *Oldstyle* were the primary responsibility of Bruce Granger. The historical and explanatory notes to *Salmagundi* were also prepared by Bruce Granger. The establishment of the text of *Salmagundi* and the preparation of the textual commentary and lists to *Salmagundi* were the primary responsibility of Martha Hartzog. Throughout the preparation of this edition, however, the two editors continually consulted and assisted each other.

CONTENTS

EDITORIAL APPENDIX

ILLUSTRATIONS

FRONTISPIECE

Portrait of Washington Irving at 22

John Vanderlyn (1776–1852) did a crayon drawing of Washington Irving at Paris in the summer of 1805. This portrait, whose present location is unknown, was recorded in Irving's memorandum book for August 12, 1805. This print was made from the *Rutgers University Library Journal,* IX (June 1946).

WOODCUTS

INTRODUCTION

Letters of Jonathan Oldstyle, Gent. and *Salmagundi; or, The Whim-Whams and Opinions of Launcelot Langstaff, Esq. & Others* are essay serials which appeared at a time when the tradition of the periodical essay in America was drawing to a close and would be assimilated shortly into other forms of prose, notably the sketch and the tale. At its inception in the early years of the eighteenth century the English periodical essay was social in point of view and moral in purpose. And so it long remained in America, though by the end of the century a shift had occurred. During the Revolution patriot writers often cast their political satire against the Loyalists and the British in essay form; later, during the administrations of John Adams and Jefferson, many essayists, ignoring the neutrality which Addison had at least urged, adopted a Federalist or Republican stance. Moreover, as the eighteenth century advanced, some American essayists tended to instruct their audiences less and divert them more, until finally one hears the *Salmagundi* authors promising to teach parents "how to govern their children, girls how to get husbands, and old maids how to do without them."

Joseph Addison, who was chiefly responsible for fixing the manner and the matter of the periodical essay, chose to address the London merchants, professional men, and gentry who read the *Tatler, Spectator,* and *Guardian* in a gentlemanly middle style. The formal conventions that were incorporated into this new tradition had, most of them, a long and respectable history: dream vision, moral dialogue, beast fable, genealogy and adventures, transformation, fictitious letter, mock-advertisement, aptronym, and (later in the century) foreign visitor and oriental tale. The matter ranged through manners and morality, philosophical reflection, character, criticism, and humor.[1]

Precisely because it was addressed in the first instance to a middle-class public, the tradition soon caught hold in America. In the fall of 1721 thirteen numbers of a student periodical, the *Telltale,* circulated in manuscript at Harvard.[2] In the same year Benjamin Franklin's older brother, James, and the wits associated with him began composing essays for his newly founded paper, the *New-England Courant.* Over-

---

1. Ernest Claude Coleman, "The Influence of the Addisonian Essay in America Before 1810" (Ph.D. diss., University of Illinois, 1936), p. 16.
2. See W. C. Lane, *Publications of the Colonial Society of Massachusetts* 12 (1909), 220–31.

night the periodical essay became a regular feature of the colonial newspaper. In the 1750s the colonial magazines began to carry original essays, and, starting in the 1790s, essay serials were gathered and made available in book form.

The convention which more than any other distinguishes and gives coherence to the essay serial is the persona, a fictitious character possessing dramatic identity distinct from his creator. An early character, and easily the most famous, is Addison's Spectator, whose curiosity steadily impels him to make observations about town-and-country society. American writers from the time of Benjamin Franklin modified the character of the spectator out of regard for their immediate audience. Whereas Mr. Spectator is a university graduate who has made the Grand Tour and claims never to have "espoused any Party with Violence," Franklin's Silence Dogood is a half-educated widow from the provinces who swears mortal enmity "to arbitrary Government and unlimited Power." Except for this first American spectator, the memorable essay serials present a gallery of men, most of them unmarried. The most fully drawn character in this gallery is Francis Hopkinson's Old Bachelor (*Pennsylvania Magazine*, March, 1775–June, 1776), who admits to an ambivalent attitude toward the married state: "I *find* so many reasons to wish I was a married man, and see so many reasons to rejoice I am not, that I am like the pendulum of a clock, hanging in suspence, and perpetually vibrating between two opinions." Jonathan Oldstyle and the several bachelors in *Salmagundi*—Launcelot Langstaff, Anthony Evergreen, Will Wizard, Pindar Cockloft—are late examples of the conventional Old Bachelor so popular throughout the eighteenth century.[3]

That the *Salmagundi* authors, William and Washington Irving and James Kirke Paulding, read and were influenced by the English essayists Steele, Addison, Johnson, and Goldsmith is well known. Less well known, but just as important in determining the matter and the manner of the *Oldstyle* letters and *Salmagundi* papers, is the achievement of American essayists like Franklin, Hopkinson, Philip Freneau, Joseph Dennie, and Charles Brockden Brown. Of immediate importance were the writings published in certain magazines at the turn of the nineteenth century. Dennie's *Port Folio*, which appeared weekly in the period 1801–1807, included not only essay serials like "The Lay Preacher" but departments of art, drama, fashion, fiction, music, poetry, politics, and travel as well. John Howard Payne's *Thespian Mirror* (1805–1806) carried a theatrical register of New York productions, biographical sketches of contemporary actors and actresses, selections from British

---

3. See Bruce Granger, "The Whim-Whamsical Bachelors in *Salmagundi*," *Costerus* 2 (1972), 63–69.

and American writings on drama, and dramatic anecdotes. Brown's *Literary Magazine and American Register* (1803–1807) published original essays on such topics as female dress, marriage, and punning. At the beginning of 1807 there appeared five numbers of *The Town*,[4] a short-lived magazine which helped precipitate the first number of *Salmagundi* and which makes it clear that the *Salmagundi* authors set out to parody the tradition of the periodical essay rather than take it seriously. Will Wizard's essay on "Theatrics" and Anthony Evergreen's on the "New-York Assembly" in the first number of *Salmagundi* and Anthony's essay on "Fashions" in the third number are satirical responses to *The Town's* serious criticisms of a recent performance of *Macbeth* at the Park Theater, an account of a recent gathering of the City Assembly, and a note on London female fashion.

In the period following the Revolution, New York City gradually developed a self-consciousness that enabled it to outdistance Philadelphia in the early years of the nineteenth century and become for a time the literary capital of the country. Even before the turn of the century literary clubs arose which "aimed at promoting friendship and good conversation, intellectual development, literary cultivation, through frequent meetings devoted to debate and oratory, reading aloud, original compositions in poetry and prose, all presided over by the keen and candid critic."[5] Two of Washington Irving's older brothers, William and Peter, were active in the Calliopean Society. On December 7, 1790, William debated the negative side of the question, "Whether it would be beneficial to the public to oblige men after attaining the age of 28 years to enter into the State of Matrimony under the penalty of a heavy tax," and lost; three months later Peter responded in the negative to the quesion, "Has the invention of fire arms been productive of benefit or disadvantageous to mankind," and won.[6] William Irving (1766–1821), a prominent merchant whom Paulding characterized as "a man of great wit, genius, and originality,"[7] became president of the Calliopean Society in 1791. Dr. Peter Irving (1772–1838) was elected first vice-president the next year. William Dunlap remembered him as one of the gentlemen who in 1796 "were regular frequenters of the New-York theatre, enjoyed

4. January 1, 3, 7, 9, 12, 1807. The only known file is in the New York State Library at Albany.

5. Eleanor Scott, "Early Literary Clubs in New York City," *American Literature* 5 (March, 1933), 16.

6. "Proceedings of the Calliopean Society Founded for the express purpose of improving Education" (November 20, 1788–March 10, 1795); manuscript in the New-York Historical Society.

7. William I. Paulding, *Literary Life of James K. Paulding* (New York, 1867), p. 29.

its productions as men of education and lovers of literature, and wished
to correct the abuses existing in the costume, demeanour, and general
conduct, of the actors on the stage."[8]

James Kirke Paulding (1778–1860) was bound to the Irving family
not only by literary interests but also by marriage; his sister Julia
married William Irving in 1793, and the couple took James into their
home when he came to New York from Westchester County as a young
man of eighteen or nineteen. Remembering Goldsmith's *Letters from
a Citizen of the World* as the book that "possibly gave a direction to
my whole life,"[9] Paulding was early attracted to a career in letters.
"Oh—may all the glory and success attend the noble art of scribbling!"
he wrote a friend on August 14, 1802. "What would become of me
without the solace it affords?"[10] It is likely that he wrote for Peter Irving's
Morning Chronicle (1802–1805).[11] From the time he contributed to
Salmagundi there existed a tension in his style between satire and
sentimentality.

Washington Irving (1783–1859), whose acquaintance with Paulding
ripened into friendship at least as early as the time of their association
on the *Morning Chronicle*, wrote with greater geniality and always
with an "eye to the *picturesque*."[12] In his earliest journals, written during
the four years separating *Oldstyle* and *Salmagundi*, his prose style
matured rapidly. It is Nathalia Wright's considered judgment that
whereas the New York journal (1803) "foreshadows his later writing:
general fluency, with particular tendencies toward a pictorial technique
in describing landscapes and toward low-keyed satire of pretense and
pomposity," the style of the European journal (1804–1806) is "decidedly
more confident. . . . not only the type of scenic description in *The Sketch
Book* but its whole range of literary genres—reverie, scenic description,
character sketch, narrative, historical account—are found in the journal."[13]
Invective too, though it all but disappeared in later works, marks his
early style. Martin Roth argues convincingly that Washington Irving
contributed twelve satirical pieces, and possibly as many as forty-five,
to Peter Irving's *The Corrector*, a New York newspaper of March–April,

8. William Dunlap, *History of the American Theatre* (New York, 1832), I, 373.
9. Paulding, *Literary Life of James K. Paulding*, p. 26.
10. James Kirke Paulding, *The Letters of James Kirke Paulding*, ed. Ralph M.
Aderman (Madison, 1962), p. 17.
11. Among the pieces which can possibly be attributed to him are "The Eccentric Man," October 22, 1802; "Woman:—An Apologue," October 28, 1802; and
"The Stroke of Death," November 9, 1802.
12. Washington Irving, *Journals and Notebooks*, Vol. I, ed. Nathalia Wright
(Madison, 1969), p. 433.
13. *Journals and Notebooks*, I, xxviii, xxxiv, xxxv.

1804 that supported Aaron Burr in his unsuccessful bid for the governorship of New York.[14] Even though Irving would contribute political essays to *Salmagundi* which closely resemble these *Corrector* pieces in tone and topic—for example, the Mustapha letters in Nos. XI and XVI and "On Greatness" in No. XV—he was speaking from the heart when he wrote on February 2, 1807, "I have rather shunned than sought political notoriety."[15] For all his traveling and long sojourns abroad, Irving always identified himself with New York, the city of his birth. "The bay; the rivers & their wild & woody shores; the haunts of my boyhood, both on land and water, absolutely have a witchery over my mind, he wrote Henry Brevoort from Paris on December 16, 1824. "I thank God for my having been born in so beautiful a place among such beautiful scenery."[16] The only one of the *Salmagundi* authors who remained a bachelor, he realized the dream of being able "to return home, nestle down comfortable . . . and have wherewithal to shelter me from the storms and buffetings of this uncertain world,"[17] when in 1836 he moved into Sunnyside, north of the city.

Drawn together by a love of literature and the desire for conviviality were a group of young New Yorkers which included William, Peter, Ebenezer, and Washington Irving, Peter and Gouverneur Kemble, Paulding, Henry Brevoort, Henry Ogden, David Porter, and Richard McCall. Gouverneur Kemble opened Mount Pleasant, an old family country place on the banks of the Passaic between Newark and Belleville, to this group, known by such names as the "Nine Worthies," the "Lads of Kilkenny," the "Ancient and Honorable Order," and the "Ancient Club of New-York." When in the city the club would sometimes "riot at Dyde's" (99.4), a public house near the Park Theater. *Salmagundi* grew spontaneously from the activities of this club, Mount Pleasant serving as model for Cockloft Hall.

Letters of Jonathan Oldstyle, Gent. (1802–1803), *Salmagundi* (1807–1808), and *A History of New York* (1809) comprise the first stage in Irving's literary career, being separated by a decade and more from *The Sketch Book* and succeeding books. What helps give coherence to this stage is the evolving character of the Old Bachelor. Jonathan Oldstyle, who discourses on fashion and the theater, becomes split into several

14. *Washington Irving's Contributions to "The Corrector,"* Minnesota Monographs in the Humanities, No. 3, ed. Martin Roth (Minneapolis, 1968). The contributions attributed with certainty to Irving are nos. 6, 8, 14, 15, 16, 19, 23, 25, 28, 30, 32, 34.

15. Pierre M. Irving, *The Life and Letters of Washington Irving* (New York, 1862–1864), I, 175; hereafter cited as PMI.

16. *Letters of Washington Irving to Henry Brevoort*, ed. George S. Hellman (New York, 1918), p. 396.

17. *Ibid.*, p. 207.

figures. From Oldstyle to Langstaff, Evergreen, and Wizard to Diedrich Knickerbocker, this persona grows more and more whim-whamsical. *Salmagundi* foreshadows the *History* in other respects. The same air of mystery surrounds Diedrich that surrounds the Little Man in Black, whose story Langstaff tells. Irving's "Stranger in Pennsylvania," and even more immediately "Chronicles on the City of Gotham," also antici- pate the matter and the manner of the *History*. In this first stage Irving's predilection for burlesque is everywhere present; for example, the description of Will Wizard's partner at a ball as "a young lady of most voluminous proportions, that quivered at every skip; and being braced up in the fashionable style, with whalebone, stay-tape and buckram, looked like an apple-pudding tied in the middle, or, taking her flaming dress into consideration, like a bed and bolsters rolled up in a suit of red curtains" (126.14–18) is of a piece with the burlesque similes in the *History*. Only occasionally do these early writings point clearly to the later, though in his *Salmagundi* writings (notably in the Will Wizard and Cockloft essays) Irving commingles the picturesque and the whimsi- cal as he frequently does in *The Sketch Book* and later books. Other affinities between these early and Irving's mature writings merit exhaus- tive study.

LETTERS OF
JONATHAN OLDSTYLE
GENT.

LETTER I

Printed in *The Morning Chronicle*, November 15, 1802.

Mr. Editor,

If the observations of an odd old fellow are not wholly superfluous, I would thank you to shove them into a spare corner of your paper.

It is a matter of amusement to an uninterested spectator like myself, to observe the influence fashion has on the dress and deportment of its votaries, and how very quick they fly from one extreme to the other.

A few years since, the rage was; very high crowned hats with very narrow brims, tight neckcloth, tight coat, tight jacket, tight small clothes, and shoes loaded with enormous silver buckles: the hair craped, plaited, queued and powdered:—in short, an air of the greatest spruceness and tightness diffused over the whole person.

The ladies, with their tresses neatly turned up over an immense cushion; waist a yard long, braced up with stays into the smallest compass, and encircled by an enormous hoop: so that the fashionable belle resembled a walking bottle.

Thus dressed, the lady was seen, with the most bewitching languor, reclining on the arm of an extremely attentive beau, who, with a long cane, decorated with an enormous tassel, was carefully employed in removing every stone, stick or straw that might impede the progress of his tottering companion, whose high-heel'd shoes just brought the points of her toes to the ground.

What an alteration has a few years produced!—We now behold our gentleman, with the most studied carelessness, and almost slovenliness of dress; large hat, large coat, large neckcloth, large pantaloons, large boots, and hair scratch'd into every careless direction, lounging along the streets in the most apparent listlessness and vacuity of thought; staring with an unmeaning countenance at every passenger, or leaning upon the arm of some kind fair one for support, with the other hand cramm'd into his breeches pocket. Such is the picture of a modern beau: in his dress stuffing himself up to the dimensions of a Hercules, in his manners affecting the helplessness of an invalid.

The belle who has to undergo the fatigue of dragging along this sluggish animal, has chosen a character the very reverse: emulating in her dress and actions all the airy lightness of a sylph, she trips along with the greatest vivacity. Her laughing eye, her countenance enlivened with affability and good humor, inspire with kindred animation every beholder, except the torpid being by her side, who is either affecting

3

the fashionable sang-froid, or is wrapt up in profound contemplation of—himself.

Heavens! how changed are the manners since I was young!—then, how delightful to contemplate a ball-room: such bowing, such scraping, such complimenting; nothing but copperplate speeches to be heard on both sides; no walking but in minuet measure; nothing more common than to see half a dozen gentlemen knock their heads together in striving who should first recover a lady's fan or snuff-box that had fallen.

But now, our youths no longer aim at the character of *pretty gentlemen:* their greatest ambition is to be called lazy dogs—careless fellows—&c. &c. Dressed up in the mammoth style, our buck saunters into the ball-room in a surtout, hat under arm, cane in hand; strolls round with the most vacant air; stops abruptly before such lady as he may choose to honor with his attention; entertains her with the common *slang* of the day, collected from the conversation of hostlers, footmen, porters, &c. until his string of smart sayings is run out, and then lounges off, to entertain some other fair one with the same unintelligible jargon.

Surely, Mr. Editor, puppyism must have arrived to a *climax:* it *must* turn; to carry it to a greater extent seems to me impossible.

                                                    JONATHAN OLDSTYLE.

LETTER II

Printed in *The Morning Chronicle*, November 20, 1802.

Mr. Editor,

Encouraged by the ready insertion you gave my former communication, I have taken the liberty to intrude on you a few more remarks.

Nothing is more intolerable to an old person than innovation on old habits. The customs that prevailed in our youth become dear to us as we advance in years; and we can no more bear to see them abolished, than we can to behold the trees cut down under which we have sported in the happy days of infancy.

Even I myself, who have floated down the stream of life with the tide; who have humored it in all its turnings; who have conformed, in a great measure, to all its fashions—cannot but feel sensible of this prejudice. I often sigh when I draw a comparison between the present and past: and though I cannot but be sensible that, in general, times are altered for the better, yet there is something even in the *imperfections* of the manners which prevailed in my youthful days that is inexpressibly endearing.

There is nothing that seems more strange and preposterous to me than the manner in which modern marriages are conducted. The parties keep the matter as secret as if there was something disgraceful in the connexion. The lady positively denies that any thing of the kind is to happen; will laugh at her intended husband, and even lay bets against the event, the very day before it is to take place. They sneak into matrimony as quietly as possible, and seem to pride themselves on the cunning and ingenuity they have displayed in their manœuvres.

How different is this from the manners of former times!—I recollect when my *aunt Barbara* was addressed by *'squire Stylish:* nothing was heard of during the whole courtship but consultations and negociations between her friends and relatives: the matter was considered and reconsidered, and at length the time set for a final answer. Never, Mr. Editor, shall I forget the awful solemnity of the scene. The whole family of the Oldstyles assembled in formal conclave: my aunt Barbara, dressed out as fine as hands could make her—high cushion, enormous cap, long waist, prodigious hoop, ruffles that reached to the end of her fingers, and a gown of flame colored brocade, figured with poppies, roses and sun-flowers. Never did she look so sublimely handsome. The 'squire entered the room with a countenance suited to the solemnity of the occasion. He was arrayed in a full suit of scarlet velvet, his coat decorated with a profusion of large silk buttons, and the skirts stiffened with a yard or two of buckram; a long pig-tail'd wig, well powdered, adorned his head, and stockings of deep blue silk, rolled over the knees, graced his extremities; the flaps of his vest reached to his knee-buckles; and the ends of his cravat, tied with the most precise neatness, twisted through every button-hole. Thus accoutred, he gravely walked into the room, with his ivory-headed ebony cane in one hand, and gently swaying his three-cornered beaver with the other.—The gallant and fashionable appearance of the 'squire, the gracefulness and dignity of his deportment, occasioned a general smile of complacency through the room: my aunt Barbara modestly veiled her countenance with her fan; but I observed her contemplating her admirer with great satisfaction through the sticks.

The business was opened with the most formal solemnity, but was not long in agitation. The Oldstyles were moderate—their articles of capitulation few: the 'squire was gallant, and acceded to them all. In short, the blushing Barbara was delivered up to his embraces with due ceremony. Then, Mr. Editor—then were the happy times: such oceans of arrack—such mountains of plumb-cake—such feasting and congratulating—such fiddling and dancing—ah me! who can think of those days, and not sigh when he sees the degeneracy of the present: no eating of cake nor throwing of stockings—not a single skin filled with wine on the joyful occasion—nor a single pocket edified by it but the parson's.

It is with the greatest pain I see those customs dying away, which served to awaken the hospitality and friendship of my ancient com-rades—that strewed with flowers the path to the altar, and shed a ray of sunshine on the commencement of the matrimonial union.

The deportment of my aunt Barbara and her husband, was as decorous after marriage as before—*her* conduct was always regulated by *his*—her sentiments ever accorded with his opinions—she was always eager to tie on his neckcloth of a morning—to tuck a napkin under his chin at meal-times—to wrap him up warm of a winter's day, and to spruce him up as smart as possible of a Sunday. The squire was the most attentive and polite husband in the world: would hand his wife in and out of church, with the greatest ceremony—drink her health at dinner with particular emphasis, and ask her advice on every subject—though I must confess he invariably adopted his own—nothing was heard of from both sides but dears, sweet loves, doves, &c. The squire could never stir out of a winter's day, without his wife calling after him from the window, to button up his waistcoat carefully. Thus all things went on smoothly, and my relations *Stylish* had the name, and, as far as I know, deserved it, of being the most happy and loving couple in the world.

A modern married pair will, no doubt, laugh at all this: they are accustomed to treat one another with the utmost carelessness and neglect. No longer does the wife tuck the napkin under her husband's chin—nor the husband attend to heaping her plate with dainties—no longer do I see those little amusing fooleries in company, where the lady would pat her husband's cheek, and he chuck her under the chin: when dears and sweets, were as plenty as cookies on a new year's day. The wife now considers herself as totally independent—will advance her own opinions, without hesitation, though directly opposite to his— will carry on accounts of her own, and will even have secrets of her own with which she refuses to entrust him.

Who can read these facts and not lament, with me, the degeneracy of the present times—what husband is there but will look back with regret, to the happy days of female subjection.

JONATHAN OLDSTYLE.

LETTER III

Printed in *The Morning Chronicle*, December 1, 1802.

Mr. EDITOR,

There is no place of public amusement of which I am so fond as the theatre. To enjoy this with the greater relish I go but seldom; and I find there is no play, however poor or ridiculous from which I cannot derive some entertainment.

I was very much taken with a play-bill of last week, announcing in large capitals

THE BATTLE OF HEXHAM, *or days of old.*

Here said I to myself will be something grand—*days of old!*—my fancy fired at the words. I pictured to myself all the gallantry of chivalry; here, thought I, will be a display of court manners and true politeness; the play will no doubt be garnished with tilts and tournaments: and as to those *banditti* whose names make such a formidable appearance on the bills, they will be hung up, every mother's son, for the edification of the gallery.

With such impressions I took my seat in the pit, and was so impatient that I could hardly attend to the music, though I found it very good.

The curtain rose. Out walked the queen with great majesty, she answered my ideas, she was dressed well, she looked well, and she acted well. The queen was followed by a pretty gentleman, who from his winking and grinning I took to be the court fool. I soon found out my mistake. He was a courtier *"high in trust,"* and either general, colonel, or something of *martial* dignity.

They talked for some time, though I could not understand the drift of their discourse, so I amused myself with eating pea-nuts.

In one of the scenes I was diverted with the stupidity of a corporal and his men, who sung a dull song, and talked a great deal about nothing: though I found by their laughing, there was a great deal of fun in the corporal's remarks.

What this scene had to do with the rest of the piece, I could not comprehend: I suspect it was a part of some other play thrust in here *by accident.*

I was then introduced to a cavern where there were several hard looking fellows, sitting round a table carousing. They told the audience they were banditti. They then sung a *gallery song*, of which I could understand nothing but two lines:

"The Welchman had lik'd to've been chok'd by a mouse,

"But he pulled him out by the tail!"

8

Just as they had ended this elegant song their banquet was disturbed by the *melodious sound* of a horn, and in march'd a *portly gentleman,* who I found was their captain. After this worthy gentleman had fumed his hour out: after he had slapped his breast and drawn his sword half a dozen times, the act ended.

In the course of the play I learnt that there had been, or was, or would be, a battle; but how, or when, or where I could not understand. The banditti once more made their appearance, and frighted the wife of the portly gentleman, who was dressed in man's clothes, and was seeking her husband. I could not enough admire the dignity of her deportment, the sweetness of her countenance, and the unaffected gracefulness of her action; but who the captain really was, or why he ran away from his spouse, I could not understand. However, they seemed very glad to find one another again; and so at last the play ended by the falling of the curtain.

I wish the manager would use a *drop scene* at the close of the acts: we might then always ascertain the termination of the piece by the *green* curtain. On this occasion I was indebted to the polite bows of the actors for this pleasing information. I cannot say that I was entirely satisfied with the play, but I promised myself ample entertainment in the after-piece, which was called *The Tripolitan Prize.* Now, thought I, we shall have some *sport* for our money: we will no doubt see a few of those Tripolitan scoundrels spitted like turkeys for our amusement. Well, sir, the curtain rose—the trees waved in front of the stage, and the sea rolled in the rear. All things looked very pleasant and smiling. Presently I heard a bustling behind the scenes—here thought I comes a fierce band of Tripolitans with whiskers as long as my arm.—No such thing—they were only a party of village masters and misses taking a walk for exercise, and very pretty behaved young gentry they were, I assure you; but it was cruel in the manager to dress them in *buckram,* as it deprived them entirely of the use of their limbs. They arranged themselves very orderly on each side of the stage; and sang something doubtless very affecting, for they all looked pitiful enough. By and by came up a most tremenduous storm: the lightning flash'd, the thunder roar'd, the rain descended in torrents; however, our pretty rustics stood gaping quietly at one another, till they must have been wet to the skin. I was surprised at their torpidity, till I found they were each one afraid to move first, through fear of being laughed at for their aukwardness. How they got off I do not recollect, but I advise the manager, in a similar case, to furnish every one with a *trap door,* through which to make his exit. Yet this would deprive the audience of much amusement: for nothing can be more laughable than to see a body

of guards with their spears, or courtiers with their long robes *get* across
the stage at our theatre.

Scene pass'd after scene. In vain I strained my eyes to catch a
glimpse of a Mahometan phiz. I once heard a great bellowing behind
the scenes, and expected to see a strapping Musselman come bouncing
in; but was miserably disappointed, on distinguishing his voice, to find
out by his *swearing*, that he was only a *Christian*. In he came—an
American navy officer. Worsted stockings—olive velvet small clothes—
scarlet vest—pea-jacket, and *gold laced hat*—dressed quite *in character*.
I soon found out by his talk, that he was an American prize master: that,
returning thro' the *Mediterranean* with his Tripolitan prize, he was
driven by a storm on the *coast of England!*

The honest gentleman seemed from his actions to be rather intoxi-
cated: which I could account for in no other way than his having drank
a great deal of salt water as he swam ashore.

Several following scenes were taken up with hallooing and huzzaing
between the captain, his crew, and the gallery:—with several amusing
tricks of the captain and his son, a very funny, mischievous little fellow.
Then came the cream of the joke: the captain wanted to put to sea, and
the young fellow, who had fallen desperately in love, to stay ashore.
Here was a contest between love and honor—such piping of eyes,
such blowing of noses, such slapping of pocket holes! But *old Junk*
was inflexible.—What! an American tar desert his duty! (three cheers
from the gallery) impossible!—American tars forever!! True blue will
never stain!! &c. &c. (a continual thundering among the gods).

Here was a scene of distress—here was bathos. The author seemed
as much puzzled how to dispose of the young tar as old Junk was. It
would not do to leave an American seaman on foreign ground; nor
would it do to separate him from his mistress.

Scene the last opened—it seems that another Tripolitan cruiser had
bore down on the prize as she lay about a mile off shore.—How a
Barbary corsair had got in this part of the world—whether she had
been driven there by the same storm, or whether she was cruising
about to pick up a few English first rates, I could not learn. However,
here she was—again were we conducted to the sea shore, where we
found all the village gentry, in their buckram suits, ready assembled
to be entertained with the rare show, of an American and Tripolitan
engaged yard arm and yard arm. The battle was conducted with proper
decency and decorum, and the Tripolitan very politely gave in—as it
would be indecent to conquer in the face of an American audience.

After the engagement, the crew came ashore, joined with the captain
and gallery in a few more huzzas, and the curtain fell. How old Junk,
his son, and his son's sweetheart settled it, I could not discover.

I was somewhat puzzled to understand the meaning and necessity of this engagement between the ships, till an honest old countryman at my elbow, said he supposed *this* was the *battle of Hexham*; as he recollected no fighting in the first piece.—With this explanation I was perfectly satisfied.

My remarks upon the audience I shall postpone to another opportunity.

JONATHAN OLDSTYLE.

LETTER IV

Printed in *The Morning Chronicle*, December 4, 1802.

MR. EDITOR,

My last communication mentioned my visit to the theatre; the remarks it contained were chiefly confined to the play and the actors: I shall now extend them to the audience, who, I assure you, furnish no inconsiderable part of the entertainment.

As I entered the house, some time before the curtain rose, I had sufficient leisure to make some observations. I was much amused with the waggery and humor of the gallery, which, by the way, is kept in *excellent* order by the constables who are stationed there. The noise in this part of the house is somewhat similar to that which prevailed in Noah's ark; for we have an imitation of the whistles and yells of every kind of animal.—This, in some measure, compensates for the want of music, (as the gentlemen of our orchestra are very economic of their favors). Some how or another the anger of the gods seemed to be aroused all of a sudden, and they commenced a discharge of apples, nuts & ginger-bread, on the heads of the honest folks in the pit, who had no possibility of retreating from this new kind of thunder-bolts. I can't say but I was a little irritated at being saluted aside of my head with a rotten pippin, and was going to shake my cane at them; but was prevented by a decent looking man behind me, who informed me it was useless to threaten or expostulate. They are only *amusing themselves* a little at our expence, said he, sit down quietly and bend your back to it. My kind neighbor was interrupted by a hard green apple that hit him between the shoulders—he made a wry face, but knowing it was all in joke, bore the blow like a philosopher. I soon saw the wisdom of this determination,—a stray thunder-bolt happened to light on the head of a little sharp-faced Frenchman, dress'd in a white coat and small cock'd hat, who sat two or three benches ahead of me, and seemed to be an irritable little animal: Monsieur was terribly exasperated; he jumped upon his seat, shook his fist at the gallery, and swore violently in bad English. This was all nuts to his merry persecutors, their attention was wholly turned on him, and he formed their *target* for the rest of the evening.

I found the ladies in the boxes, as usual, studious to please; their charms were set off to the greatest advantage; each box was a little battery in itself, and they all seemed eager to out do each other in the havoc they spread around. An arch glance in one box was rivalled

Interior of the Park Theater, New York, 1805. A reproduction of this woodcut from *Appleton's Journal*, Nov. 23, 1872, may be found in the New York Public Library Theater Collection at Lincoln Center, with the explanation "Copied from an Old Woodcut used as a Frontispiece to the Rejected Address of the Opening." This print was made from a reproduction in Oral Sumner Coad and Edwin Mim, Jr., *The American Stage* (New Haven, 1929), p. 52.

by a smile in another, that smile by a simper in a third, and in a fourth, a most bewitching languish carried all before it.

I was surprised to see some persons reconnoitering the company through spy-glasses; and was in doubt whether these machines were used to remedy deficiencies of vision, or whether this was another of the eccentricities of fashion. Jack Stylish has since informed me that glasses were lately all *the go;* though hang it, says Jack, it is quite *out* at present; we used to mount glasses in *great snuff,* but since so many *tough jockies* have followed the lead, the bucks have all *cut* the custom. I give you, Mr. Editor, the account in my dashing cousin's own language. It is from a vocabulary I don't well understand.

I was considerably amused by the queries of the countryman mentioned in my last, who was now making his first visit to the theatre. He kept constantly applying to me for information, and I readily communicated, as far as my own ignorance would permit.

As this honest man was casting his eye round the house, his attention was suddenly arrested. And pray, who are these? said he, pointing to a cluster of young fellows. These I suppose are the critics, of whom I have heard so much. They have, no doubt, got together to communicate their remarks, and compare notes; these are the persons through whom the audience exercise their judgments, and by whom they are told, when they are to applaud or to hiss. Critics! ha, ha, my dear sir, they trouble themselves as little about the elements of criticism as they do about other departments of science or belles lettres. These are the beaus of the present day, who meet here to lounge away an idle hour, and play off their little impertinencies for the entertainment of the public. They no more regard the merits of a play, or of the actors, than my cane. They even *strive* to appear inattentive; and I have seen one of them perch'd upon the front of the box with his back to the stage, sucking the head of his stick, and staring vacantly at the audience, insensible to the most interesting specimens of scenic representation: though the tear of sensibility was trembling in every eye around him.

I have heard that some have even gone so far in search of amusement, as to propose a game or two of cards, in the theatre, during the performance: the eyes of my neighbor sparkled at this information; his cane shook in his hand; the word, *puppies,* burst from his lips. Nay, said I, I don't give this for absolute fact: my cousin Jack was, I believe, *quizzing* me (as he terms it) when he gave me the information. But you seem quite indignant, said I to the decent looking man in my rear. It was from him the exclamation came; the honest *countryman* was gazing in gaping wonder on some new attraction. Believe me, said I, if you had them daily before your eyes, you would get quite used to them. Used to them! replied he, how is it possible for people of sense to relish such conduct. Bless you, my friend, people of sense have nothing to do with it; they merely endure it in silence. These young gentlemen live in an indulgent age. When I was a young man, such tricks and fopperies were held in proper contempt. Here I went a little too far; for upon better recollection I must own that a lapse of years has produced but little alteration in this department of folly and impertinence. But do the ladies admire these manners? truly I am not as conversant in female circles as formerly; but I should think it a poor compliment to my fair country women, to suppose them pleased with the stupid stare and cant phrases with which these votaries of fashion, add affected to real ignorance.

Our conversation was here interrupted by the ringing of a bell. Now for the play, said my companion. No, said I, it is only for the musicians. Those worthy gentlemen then came crawling out of their holes, and began with very solemn and important phizes, strumming and tuning their instruments in the usual style of discordance, to the great *entertainment* of the audience. What tune is that? asked my neighbor, covering his ears. This, said I, is no tune; it is only a pleasing *symphony*, with which we are regaled as a preparative. For my part, though I admire the effect of contrast, I think they might as well play it in their cavern under the stage. The bell rung a second time; and then began the tune in reality; but I could not help observing that the countryman was more diverted with the queer grimaces, and contortions of countenance exhibited by the musicians, than their melody.

What I heard of the music, I liked very well (though I was told by one of my neighbors that the same pieces have been played every night for these three years;) but it was often overpowered by the gentry in the gallery, who vociferated loudly for *Moll in the wad, Tally ho the grinders*, and several other *airs* more suited to their tastes.

I observed that every part of the house has its different department. The good folks of the gallery have all the trouble of ordering the music (their directions, however, are not more frequently followed than they deserve.) The mode by which they issue their mandates is stamping, hissing, roaring, whistling, and, when the musicians are refractory, groaning in cadence. They also have the privilege of demanding a *bow* from *John* (by which name they designate every servant at the theatre, who enters to move a table or snuff a candle;) and of detecting those cunning dogs who peep from behind the curtain.

By the bye, my honest country friend was much puzzled about the curtain itself. He wanted to know why that *carpet* was hung up in the theatre. I assured him it was no carpet, but a very fine curtain. And what, pray, may be the meaning of that gold head with the nose cut off that I see in front of it? The meaning—why really I can't tell exactly—tho' my cousin Jack stylish says there is a great deal of meaning in it. But surely you like the *design* of the curtain? The design—why really I can see no design about it, unless it is to be brought down about our ears by the weight of those gold heads and that heavy *cornice* with which it is garnished. I began now to be uneasy for the credit of our curtain, and was afraid he would perceive the mistake of the painter in putting a *harp* in the middle of the curtain, and calling it a *mirror*; but his attention was *happily* called away by the *candle-grease* from the chandelier, over the centre of the pit, dropping on his clothes. This he loudly complained of, and declared his coat was *bran-new*. How, my friend, said I, we must put up with a few trifling inconveniencies when in the pursuit of pleasure. True said he:—but I think I pay pretty dear for it:—first to give six shillings at the door, and then to have my head battered with rotten apples, and my coat spoiled by candle-grease: by and by I shall have my other clothes dirtied by sitting down, as I perceive every body mounted on the benches. I wonder if they could not see as well if they were all to stand upon the floor.

Here I could no longer defend our customs, for I could scarcely breathe while thus surmounted by a host of strapping fellows standing with their dirty boots on the seats of the benches. The little Frenchman who thus found a temporary shelter from the missive compliments of his gallery friends, was the only person benefited. At last the bell again rung, and the cry of down, down—hats off, was the signal for the commencement of the play.

If, Mr. Editor, the garrulity of an old fellow is not tiresome, and you chuse to give this *view of a New-York theatre*, a place in your paper, you may, perhaps, hear further from your friend,

JONATHAN OLDSTYLE.

LETTER V

Printed in *The Morning Chronicle*, December 11, 1802.

[We have to apologize to our friend *Old Style* for the omission of his communication these two or three days back. We shall in future be more punctual.]

Mr. EDITOR,

I shall now conclude my remarks on the theatre, which I am afraid you will think are spun out to an unreasonable length; for this I can give no other excuse, than that it is the privilege of old folks to be tiresome, and so I shall proceed.

I had chosen a seat in the pit, as least subject to annoyance from a habit of talking loud that has lately crept into our theatres, and which particularly prevails in the boxes. In old times people went to the theatre for the sake of the play and acting; but I now find it begins to answer the purpose of a coffee-house, or fashionable lounge, where many indulge in loud conversation, without any regard to the pain it inflicts on their more attentive neighbors. As this conversation is generally of the most trifling kind, it seldom repays the latter for the inconvenience they suffer, of not hearing one half of the play.

I found, however, that I had not much bettered my situation; but that every part of the house has its share of evils. Besides those I had already suffered, I was yet to undergo a new kind of torment. I had got in the neighborhood of a very obliging personage, who had seen the play before, and was kindly anticipating every scene, and informing those about him what was to take place; to prevent, I suppose, any *disagreeable* surprise to which they would otherwise have been liable. Had there been any thing of a plot to the play, this might have been a serious inconvenience; but as the piece was entirely *innocent* of every thing of the kind, it was not of so much importance. As I generally contrive to extract amusement from every incident that happens, I now entertained myself with remarks on the self-important air with which he delivered his information, and the distressed and impatient looks of his unwilling auditors. I also observed that he made several mistakes in the course of his communications: "Now you'll see," *said he,* "the queen, in all her glory, surrounded with her courtiers, fine as fiddles, and ranged on each side of the stage, like rows of pewter dishes." On the contrary, we were presented with the portly gentleman and his *ragged regiment* of banditti. Another time he promised us a regale from the fool; but we were presented with a *very fine speech* from the queen's *grinning counsellor.*

My country neighbor was exceedingly delighted with the performance,

16

though he did not half the time understand what was going forward. He sat staring with open mouth at the portly gentleman, as he strode across the stage, and in furious rage drew his sword on the *white lion.* "By George but that's a brave fellow," said he when the act was over, "that's what you call first rate acting, I suppose."

Yes, said I, it is what the critics of the present day admire, but it is not altogether what I like; you should have seen an actor of the *old school* do this part; he would have given it to some purpose; you'd have had such ranting and roaring, and stamping and storming; to be sure this honest man gives us a *bounce* now and then in the true old style, but in the main he seems to prefer walking on plain ground to strutting on the *stilts* used by the tragic heroes of my day.

This is the chief of what passed between me and my companion during the play and entertainment, except an observation of his, that it would be well if the manager was to *drill* his nobility and gentry now and then, to enable them to go through their evolution with more grace and spirit. This put me in mind of something my cousin Jack said to the same purpose, though he went too far in his zeal for reformation. He declared, "he wished sincerely, one of the critics of the day would take all the *slab shabs* of the theatre in a body (like *cats in a bag*) and *twig* the whole bunch." I can't say but I like Jack's idea well enough, though it is rather a severe one.

He might have remarked another fault that prevails among our performers (though I don't know whether it occurred this evening) of dressing for the same piece in the fashions of different ages and countries, so that while one actor is strutting about the stage in the cuirass and helmet of Alexander, another dressed up in a gold-laced coat and a bag-wig, with a chapeau de bras under his arm, is taking snuff in the fashion of one or two centuries back, and perhaps a third figuring with Suwarrow boots, in the true style of modern buckism.

But what, pray, has become of the noble marquis of Montague, and earl of Warwick? (said the countryman, after the entertainments were concluded). Their names make a great appearance on the bill, but I do not recollect having seen them in the course of the evening.

Very true—I had quite forgot those worthy personages, but I suspect they have been behind the scene, smoking a pipe with our other friends, *incog.* the Tripolitans. We must not be particular now-a-days, my friend. When we are presented with a Battle of Hexham *without fighting,* and a Tripolitan after-piece without even a *Mahometan whisker,* we need not be surprised at having an *invisible* marquis or two thrown into the bargain.

"But what is your opinion of the house," said I, "don't you think it a very substantial, *solid-looking* building, both inside and out? Observe what a fine effect the dark colouring of the wall has upon the white faces of the audience, which glare like the stars in a dark night. And then what can be more pretty than the paintings on the front of the boxes; those little masters and misses sucking their thumbs and making mouths at the audience?"

Very fine, upon my word—and what, pray, is the use of that chandelier, as you call it, that is hung up among the clouds, and has showered down its favors on my coat?

Oh, that is to illumine the heavens and to set off, to advantage, the little perriwig'd cupids, tumbling head over heels, with which the painter has decorated the *dome*. You see we have no need of the chandelier below, as here, the house is *perfectly well* illuminated: but I think it would have been a great saving of candle-light, if the manager had ordered the painter, among his other pretty designs, to paint a moon up there, or if he was to hang up that sun with whose *intense light* our eyes were greatly annoyed in the beginning of the after-piece.

But don't you think, after all, there is rather a—sort of a—kind of a *heavyishness* about the house; don't you think it has a little of an *under groundish* appearance.

To this I could make no answer. I must confess I have often thought myself the house had a *dungeon-like* look; so I proposed to him to make our exit, as the candles were putting out, and we should be left in the dark. Accordingly, groping our way through the dismal *subterraneous* passage that leads from the pit, and passing through the ragged bridewell looking anti-chamber, we once more emerged into the purer air of the park, when bidding my honest countryman good night, I repaired home considerably pleased with the amusements of the evening.

Thus, Mr. Editor, have I given you an account of the chief incidents that occurred in my visit to the theatre. I have shewn you a few of its accommodations and its imperfections. Those who visit it more frequently may be able to give you a better statement.

I shall conclude with a few words of advice for the benefit of every department of it.

I would recommend,

To the actors—less etiquette—less fustian—less buckram.

To the orchestra—new music and more of it.

To the pit—patience—clean benches and umbrellas.

To the boxes—less affectation—less noise—less coxcombs.

To the gallery—less grog and better constables—and,

To the whole house—inside and out, a total reformation.—And so much for the theatre.

JONATHAN OLDSTYLE.

LETTER VI

Printed in *The Morning Chronicle*, January 17, 1803.

[The following communication from our correspondent, OLDSTYLE, and his friend, will, we hope, induce a number to attend the *benefit* performance this evening, and see the diverting farce alluded to in the latter part of Mr. Quoz's letter.]

TO THE EDITOR OF THE MORNING CHRONICLE

SIR,

As I was sitting quietly by my fire side the other morning, nursing my wounded shin, and reading to my cousin, Jack Stylish, a chapter or two from Chesterfield's Letters, I received the following epistle from my friend Andrew Quoz: who, hearing that I talked of paying the actors a visit, and shaking my cane over their heads, has written the following letter, part of which is strongly in their defence.

To JONATHAN OLDSTYLE, Gent.

MY DEAR FRIEND,

I perceive by the late papers you have been entertaining the town with remarks on the theatre. As you do not seem from your writings to be much of an adept in the Thespian arcana, permit me to give you a few hints for your information.

The theatre, you observe, begins to answer all the purposes of a coffee-house. Here you are right: it is the polite lounge, where the idle and curious resort, to pick up the news of the fashionable world; to meet their acquaintances, and to shew themselves off to advantage. As to the dull souls who go for the sake of the play, why if their attention is interrupted by the conversation of their neighbors, they must bear it with patience—it is a custom authorized by fashion. Persons who go for the purpose of chatting with their friends are not to be deprived of their amusement: *they have paid their dollar*, and have a right to entertain themselves as well as they can. As to those who are annoyed by their talking, why they need not listen to it—*let them mind their own business.*

You were surprized at so many persons using opera glasses; & wished to know whether they were all near sighted. Your cousin, Jack Stylish, has not explained that matter sufficiently—for though many *mount* glasses because it is *the go*, yet I am told that several do it to enable them to distinguish the countenances of their friends across our scantily illumined theatre. I was considerably amused the other evening with an honest

19

tar who had stationed himself in front of the gallery, with an air of affected foppishness, & was reconnoitering the house thro' a pocket telescope. I could not but like his notion, for really the gods are so elevated among the clouds, that unless they are unusually strong of vision, I can't tell how they manage to discern with the naked eye what is passing in the little painted world below them.

I think you complain of the deficiency of the music; and say that we want a greater variety and more of it. But you must know that, though this might have been a grievance in old times, when people attended to the musicians, it is a thing of but little moment at present.— Our orchestra is kept principally for form sake. There is such a continual noise and bustle between the acts that it is difficult to hear a note; and if the musicians were to get up a new piece of the finest melody, so nicely tuned are the ears of their auditors, that I doubt whether nine hearers out of ten would not complain, on leaving the house, that they had been *bored* with the same old pieces they have heard these two or three years back. Indeed, many who go to the theatre carry their own music with them; and we are so often delighted with the crying of children by way of glee, and such coughing and sneezing from various parts of the house, by way of chorus—not to mention the regale of a sweet symphony from a sweep or two in the gallery—and occasionally a full piece, in which nasal, vocal, *whistling and thumping* powers are admirably exerted and blended, that what want we of an orchestra?

In your remarks on the actors, my dear friend let me beg of you to be cautious. I would not for the world that you should *degenerate* into a critic. The critics, my dear Jonathan, are the very pests of society: they rob the actor of his reputation; the public of their amusement: they open the eyes of their readers to a full perception of the faults of our performers, they reduce our feelings to a state of miserable refinement, and destroy entirely all the enjoyments in which our coarser sensations delighted. I can remember the time when I could hardly keep my seat thro' laughing at the wretched buffoonery, the merry-andrew tricks, and the unnatural grimaces played off by one of our theatric Jack Puddings: when I was struck with awful admiration at the roaring and ranting of a buskined hero; and hung with rapture on every word, while he was "tearing a passion to tatters—to very rags!" I remember the time when he who could make the queerest mouth, roll his eyes, and twist his body with the most hideous distortions, was surest to please. Alas! how changed the times, or rather how changed the tastes. I can now sit with the gravest countenance and look without a smile on all such *mimicry*: their skipping, their squinting, their shrugging, their snuffling, delight not me; and as to their ranting and roaring,

"I'd rather hear a brazen candlestick turned,
    "Or a dry wheel grate on the axle tree,"
than any such fustian efforts to obtain a shallow gallery applause.

Now though I confess these critics have reformed the manners of the actors as well as the tastes of the audience; so that these absurdities are almost banished from the New-York stage; yet do I think they have employed a most unwarrantable liberty.

A critic, my dear sir, has no more right to expose the faults of an actor, than he has to detect the deceptions of a juggler, or the impositions of a quack. All trades must live; and, as long as the public are satisfied to admire the tricks of the juggler, to swallow the drugs of the quack, or to applaud the fustian of the actor, whoever attempts to undeceive them, does but curtail the pleasures of the latter, and deprive the former of their bread.

Ods-bud, hath not an actor eyes and shall he not *wink*?—hath not an actor teeth and shall he not grin?—feet and shall he not stamp?—lungs and shall he not roar?—breast and shall he not slap it?—hair and shall he not *club* it? Is he not fed with plaudits from the gods? delighted with thumpings from the groundlings? annoyed by hisses from the boxes?

If you censure his follies, does he not complain? If you take away his bread will he not starve? If you starve him will he not die? And if you kill him will not his wife and seven small infants, six at her back and one at her breast, rise up and cry vengeance against you? Ponder these things seriously my friend Oldstyle, and you will agree with me that, as the actor is the most meritorious and faultless, so is the critic the most cruel and sanguinary character in the world. "As I will shew you more fully in my next." Your loving friend,

ANDREW QUOZ.

From the tenor and conclusion of these remarks of my friend Mr. Andrew Quoz, they may not improperly be called the "Rights of Actors;" his arguments are, I confess, very forcible, but, as they are entirely *new* to me, I shall not hastily make up my mind. In the mean time, as my leg is much better, I believe I shall hobble to the theatre on Monday evening, borrow a seat in a side-box, and observe how the actors conduct themselves.

JONATHAN OLDSTYLE.

LETTER VII

Printed in *The Morning Chronicle*, January 22, 1803.

SIR,

I mentioned in my last my intention of visiting the theatre on Monday night. I accordingly reached there with the assistance of Jack Stylish, who procured me in one of the boxes an uncomfortable and dirty seat, which, however, I found as good as any of my neighbors. In the pit I was determined never again to venture. The little Frenchman mentioned in my former remarks had adopted the same resolution; for on casting my eyes around the theatre, I recognized his sharp phiz and pinched up cocked hat, peering over the ledge of the Shakspeare. The poor little fellow had not changed his place for the better; a brawny Irishman was leaning with arms akimbo on his shoulders, and coolly surveying the audience, unmindful of the writhings and expostulations of the irritated little Gaul, whose chin was pressed hard upon the front of the box, and his small black eyes twinkling with fury and suffocation. How he disengaged himself I don't know, for my attention was just then called away by a different object, and on turning round some time afterwards, little Monsieur had disappeared.

I found every thing wore its old appearance. The same *silence, order* and *regularity* prevailed as on my former visit. The central chandelier hung unmolested in the heaven, setting off to advantage the picture of Mr. Anybody, with which it is adorned, and shedding a melancholy ray into that den in which (if we may judge from the sounds that issue thence) so many troubled spirits are confined.

I had marched into the theatre through rows of tables heaped up with delicacies of every kind—here a pyramid of apples or oranges invited the playful palate of the dainty; while there a regiment of mince pies and custards promised a more substantial regale to the hungry. I entered the box, and looked round with astonishment—not a grinder but had its employment. The crackling of nuts and the craunching of apples saluted my ears on every side. Surely, thought I, never was an employment followed up with more assiduity than that of gormandizing; already it pervades every public place of amusement; nay, it even begins to steal into our churches, where many a mouthful is munched in private; and few have any more objection to eat than laugh in *their sleeves*.

The eating mania prevails through every class of society; not a soul but has caught the infection. Eating clubs are established in every street and alley, and it is impossible to turn a corner without hearing the hissing of frying pans, winding the savory steams of roast and boiled, or seeing some hungry genius bolting raw oysters in the middle of the street. I expect we shall shortly carry our knives and forks, like the Chinese do their chop sticks, in our pockets.

I was interrupted in my meditations by Jack Stylish, who proposed that we might take a peep into the *lounging room*, the dashing appearance of which Jack described in high terms; I willingly agreed to his proposal.

The room perfectly answered my expectations, and was a piece with the rest of the theatre: the high finish of the walls, the windows fancifully decorated with red baize and painted canvass, and the *sumptuous* wooden benches placed around it had a most inviting appearance.

I drew the end of one of them near to an elegant stove that stood in the centre of the room, and seating myself on it, stretched my lame leg over a chair; placing my hands on the head of my cane, and resting my chin upon them, I began to amuse myself by reconnoitering the company, and snuffing up the delightful perfume of French brandy, Holland gin, and Spanish segars.

I found myself in a circle of young gentry, who appeared to have something in agitation by their winking and nodding: at the same time I heard a confused whispering around me, and could distinguish the words smoke his wig—twig his silver buckles—old quiz—cane—cock'd hat—queer phiz—and a variety of others, by which I soon found I was in bad quarters. Jack Stylish seemed equally uneasy as myself, for though he is fond of fun himself, yet I believe the young dog has too much love for his old relation, to make him the object of his mirth. To get me away, he told me my friend Quoz was at the lower end of the room, and seemed by his looks anxious to speak with me, we accordingly joined him, and finding that the curtain was about rising, we adjourned to the box together.

In our way I exclaimed against the indecorous manner of the young men of the present day; the impertinent remarks on the company in which they continually indulge; and the cant phrases with which their shallow conversation is generally interlarded. Jack observed that I had popp'd among a set of *hard boys*; yes, master Stylish said I, turning round to him abruptly, and I observed by your winks and grins that you are better acquainted with them than I could wish. Let me tell you honest friend, if ever I catch you indulging in such despicable fopperies, and hankering after the company of these disrespectful youngsters, be assured that I will discard you from my affections entirely. By this time we had reached our box: so I left my cousin Jack to digest what I had just said; and I hope it may have weight with him; though I fear, from the thoughtless gaiety of his disposition, and his knowledge of the strong hold he has in my foolish old heart, my menaces will make but little impression.

We found the play already commenced. I was particularly delighted with the appearance and manners of one of the female performers. What ease, what grace, what elegance of deportment—this is not acting, cousin Jack, said I—this is reality.

After the play, this lady again came forward and delivered a ludicrous epilogue. I was extremely sorry to find her step so far out of that graceful line of character in which she is calculated to shine; and I perceived by the countenances around me that the sentiment was universal.

Ah, said I, how much she forgets what is due to her dignity. That charming countenance was never made to be so unworthily distorted: nor that graceful person and carriage to represent the awkward movements of hobbling decrepitude—take this word of advice fair lady, from an old man and a *friend*: Never, if you wish to retain that character for elegance you so deservedly possess—never degrade yourself by assuming the part of a mimic.

The curtain rose for the after-piece. Out skipped a *jolly Merry Andrew*. Aha! said I, here is the *Jack-pudding*. I see he has forgot his broomstick and grid-iron; he'll compensate for these wants, I suppose, by his wit and humor. But where is his master, the Quack? He'll be here presently, said Jack Stylish; he's a queer old codger; his name's Puffaway: here's to be a rare roasting match, and this quizical looking fellow turns the spit. The Merry Andrew now began to deal out his speeches with great rapidity; but, on a sudden, pulling off a black hood that covered his face, who should I recognize but my old acquaintance, the *portly gentleman*.

I started back with astonishment. *Sic transit gloria mundi!* exclaimed I, with a melancholy shake of the head. Here is a *dreary,* but true picture of the vicissitudes of life—one night paraded in regal robes, surrounded with a *splendid train* of nobility; the next, degraded to a poor *Jack-pudding,* and without even a *grid-iron* to help himself. What think you of this, my friend *Quoz?* said I; think you an actor has any right to sport with the *feelings* of his audience, by presenting them with such *distressing* contrasts. Honest Quoz, who is of the melting mood, shook his head ruefully, and said nothing. I, however, saw the tear of *sympathy* tremble in his eye, and honored him for his *sensibility.*

The *Merry Andrew* went on with his part, and my pity increased as he progressed; when all of a sudden he exclaimed, "And as to *Oldstyle,* I wish him to old nick." My blood mounted into my cheeks at this insolent mention of my name. And what think you of *this,* friend Quoz? exclaimed I, vehemently, I presume this is one of your "rights of actors."

I suppose we are now to have the stage a vehicle for lampoons and slanders; on which, our fellow citizens are to be caricatured by the clumsy hand of every dauber who can hold a brush!

Let me tell you, Mr. Andrew Quoz, I have known the time when such insolence would have been hooted from the stage.

After some persuasion I resumed my seat, and attempted to listen patiently to the rest of the afterpiece; but I was so disgusted with the Merry Andrew, that in spite of all his skipping, and jumping, and turning on his heel, I could not yield him a smile.

Among the other *original* characters of the dramatis personæ, we were presented with an ancient maiden; and entertained with jests and remarks from the buffoon and his associates, containing equal *wit* and *novelty*. But jesting apart, I think these attempts to injure female happiness, at once cruel and unmanly. I have ever been an enthusiast in my attachment to the fair sex. I have ever thought them possessed of the strongest claims on our admiration, our tenderness and our protection. But when to these are added still stronger claims—when we see them aged and infirm, solitary and neglected, without a partner to support them down the descent of life—cold indeed must be that heart, and unmanly that spirit, that can point the shafts of ridicule at their defenceless bosoms—that can poison the few drops of comfort heaven has poured into their cup.

The form of my sister Dorothy presented itself to my imagination; her hair silvered by time; but her face unwrinkled by sorrow or care.

She "hath borne her faculties so meekly," that age has marked no traces on her forehead: amiable sister of my heart! cried I, who hast jogged with me through so many years of existence, is this to be the recompense of all thy virtues; art thou who never, in thought or deed, injured the feelings of another, to have thy own massacred, by the jeering insults of those to whom thou shouldst look for honor and protection?

Away with such despicable trumpery—such shallow, worn-out attempts to obtain applause from the unfeeling. I'll no more of it; come along friend Quoz, if we stay much longer, I suppose we shall find our courts of justice insulted, and attempts to ridicule the characters of private persons. Jack Stylish entreated me to stay and see the addition the manager had made to his live stock, of an ass, a goose, and a monkey. Not I, said I, I'll see no more. I accordingly hobbled off with my friend Mr. Andrew Quoz, Jack declaring he would stay behind and see the end of the joke. On our way home, I asked friend Quoz, how he could justify such clumsy attempts at personal satire. He seemed, however, rather reserved in his answers, and informed me he would write his sentiments on the subject.

The next morning Jack Stylish related to me the conclusion of the piece. How several actors went into a wheel one after another, and after a little grinding, were converted into asses, geese and monkies, except the *Merry Andrew*, who was found such a *tough jockey*, that the wheel could not digest him, so he came out as much a Jack-pudding as ever.

JONATHAN OLDSTYLE.

LETTER VIII

Printed in *The Morning Chronicle*, February 8, 1803.

[The following communication was received sometime since, but accidently mislaid.]

TO THE EDITOR OF THE MORNING CHRONICLE.

SIR,

I had just put on my spectacles and mended my pen, to give you an account of a visit I made some time since, with friend Quoz and my sister Dorothy, to a ball, when I was interrupted by the following letter from the former.

My friend Quoz, who is what the world calls a *knowing man*, is extremely fond of giving his opinion in every affair. He displays in this epistle more than usual knowledge of his subject, and seems to exert all his argumentative talents to enforce the importance of his advice. I give you his letter without further comment, and shall postpone my description of the ball to another opportunity.

————

To JONATHAN OLDSTYLE, Gent.

My Dear Friend,

I once more address you on a subject that I fear will be found irksome, and may chafe that testy disposition (forgive my freedom) with which you are afflicted. Exert, however, the good humor of which at bottom I know you to have a plentiful stock, and hear me patiently through: It is the anxious fear I entertain of your sinking into the gloomy abyss of criticism, on the brink of which you are at present tottering, that urges me to write.

I would set before you the rights and wrongs of an *actor*, and by painting, in strong colors, the peculiarity of his situation, call your good sense into action.

The world, my friend Oldstyle, has ever been prone to consider the theatrical profession in a degraded point of view. What first gave rise to this opinion, I am at a loss to conceive; but I consider it as the reliques of one of those ancient prejudices which the good sense of the world is daily discarding; and I flatter myself it will in a little time be totally exploded. Why the actor should be considered inferior in point of respectability to the poet, the painter, or any other person who exerts his talents in delineating character, or in exhibiting the various operations of the human mind, I cannot imagine. I know you, friend Oldstyle, to be a man of too liberal sentiments not to be superior

27

to these little prejudices, and also one who regards an actor, provided
his private character be good, with equal respect as the member of
any other profession. Yet you are not quite aware of the important
privileges solely attached to the dramatic performer. These I will
endeavor to point out.

The works of a poet or painter you may freely criticise—nay, they
offer them for that purpose—they listen attentively to your observations,
and profit by your censures. But beware how you exercise such conduct
towards an actor—he needs no instruction—his own *impartial* judgment
is sufficient to detect and amend all his imperfections. Attempt to correct
his errors and you ruin him at once—he'll *starve* to spite you—he is like
a decayed substance, that crumbles at the touch.

No, sir—when an actor is on the stage he is in his own house—it is
his castle—he then has you in his power—he may there *bore* you with
his buffoonery, or insult you with his pointed remarks, with perfect
impunity. You, my friend, who are rather apt to be dissatisfied, may
call it hard treatment to be thus annoyed, and yet compensate the
annoyer for his trouble. You may say, that as you pay an equivalent
for your amusement, you should have the liberty of directing the actor
in his attempts; and, as the Chinese does his ear-tickler, tell him when
his instrument offends, and how he over-does himself in the operation.
This is an egregious mistake: you are obliged to him for his *condescension*
in exerting his talents for your instruction; and as to your money, why
he only takes it to lessen *in part* the weight of your obligation.

An actor is, as I before observed, competent to judge of his own
abilities—he may undertake whatever character he pleases—tragedy—
comedy—or pantomime—however ill adapted his audience may think
him to sustain it. He may rant and roar, and wink and grin, and fret
and fume his hour upon the stage, and "who shall say him nay?" He
is paid by the manager for using his lungs and limbs, and the more
he exerts them the better does he fulfil the engagement, and the harder
does he *work* for his living—and who shall deprive him of his *"hard-
earned* bread?"

How many an honest, lazy genius has been flogged by these unfeeling
critics into a cultivation of his talents and attention to his profession!—
how have they doomed him to hard study and unremitting exertion!
—how have they prejudiced the public mind, so that what might once
have put an audience in convulsions of laughter, now excites nothing
but a slight pattering from the hands of the little shavers who are
rewarded with seats in the gallery for their trouble in keeping the boxes.
Oh! Mr. Oldstyle, it cuts me to the soul to see a poor actor stamp and
storm, and slap his forehead, his breast, his pocket-holes, all in vain:
to see him throw himself into some attitude of distraction or despair,

and there wait in fruitless expectation the applauses of his friends in the gallery. In such cases I always take care and clap him myself, to enable him to quit his posture, and resume his part with credit.

You was much irritated the other evening, at what you termed an ungenerous and unmanly attempt to bring forward an ancient maiden in a ridiculous point of view. But I don't see why that should be made a matter of complaint. Has it not been done time out of mind? Is it not sanctioned by daily custom in private life? Is not the character of aunt Tabitha, in the farce, the same we have laughed at in hundreds of dramatic pieces? Since, then, the author has but travelled in the same *beaten track* of character so many have trod before him, I see not why he should be blamed as severely as if he had all the *guilt of originality* upon his shoulders.

You may say that it is cruel to sport with the feelings of any class of society: that *folly* affords sufficient field for wit and satire to work upon, without resorting to misfortune for matter of ridicule: that female sensibility should ever be sacred from the lash of sarcasm, &c. &c. But this is all stuff, all cant.

If an author is too indolent or too stupid, to seek new sources for remark, he is surely excuseable in employing the ideas of others, for his own use and benefit. But I find I have digressed, imperceptibly, into the "rights of *authors*," so let us return to our subject.

An actor when he "holds the mirror up to nature," may by his manœuvres, twist and turn it so, as to represent the object in any shape he pleases—nay, even give a caricature where the author intended a resemblance; he may blur it with his breath, or soil it with his dirty fingers, so that the object may have a colouring from the glass in which it is viewed, entirely different from its natural appearance. To be plain, my friend, an actor has a right whenever he thinks his author not sufficiently explicit to assist him by his own *wit* and *abilities;* and if by these means the character should become quite different from what was originally intended, and in fact belong more to the *actor* than the *author*, the actor deserves high credit for his ingenuity. And even tho' his additions are *quaint*, and fulsome, yet his *intention* is highly praise worthy, and deserves ample encouragement.

Only think, my dear sir, how many snug little domestic arrangements are destroyed by the officious interference of these ever dissatisfied critics. The honest *king of Scotland*, who used to dress for market and theatre at the same time, and wear with his kelt and plaid his half boots and black breeches, looking half king, half cobler, has been obliged totally to dismiss the former from his royal service; yet I am happy to find, so obstinate is his attachment to *old habits*, that all their efforts have not been sufficient to dislodge him from the strong hold he has in the latter. They may force him from the boots—but nothing shall drive him out of the breeches.

Consider, my friend, the puerile nature of such remarks. Is it not derogating from the elevated character of a Critic, to take notice of clubb'd wigs, red coats, black breeches and half boots! Fie, fie upon it! I blush for the Critics of the day, who consider it a matter of importance whether a Highlander should appear in breeches and boots, or a Otaheitan in the dress of a New-York coxcomb. Trust me, friend Old-style, it is to the *manner*, not the *appearance* of an actor, we are to look: and as long as he performs his part well (to use the words of my friend Sterne), "it shall not be enquired whether he did it in a black coat or a red."

Believe me, friend Oldstyle, few of our modern critics can shew any substantial claim to the character they assume. Let me ask them one question—have they ever been in Europe? Have they ever seen a Garrick, a Kemble or a Siddons? If they have not, I can assure you (upon the words of two or three of my friends, *the actors*) they have no right to the title of critics.

They may talk as much as they please about judgment and taste, and feeling, but that is all nonsense. It has lately been determined (*at the theatre*) that any one who attempts to decide upon such ridiculous principles, is an arrant *goose*, and deserves to be *roasted*.

Having thus, friend Oldstyle, endeavored, in a feeble manner, to shew you a few of the rights of an actor, and of his wrongs; having mentioned his constant and *disinterested* endeavors to please the public; and how much better he knows what will please them than they do themselves; having also depicted the cruel and persecuting nature of a critic; the continual restraint he lays on the harmless irregularity of the performer, and the relentless manner in which he obliges him to attend sedulously to his professional duty, through fear of censure, let me entreat you to pause!—Open your eyes to the precipice on which you are tottering, and hearken to the earnest warnings of your loving friend,

ANDREW QUOZ.

My friend Quoz certainly writes with *feeling:* every line evinces that *acute sensibility* for which he has ever been remarked.

I am, however, perfectly at a loss to conceive on what grounds he suspects me of a disposition to turn Critic. My remarks hitherto have rather been the result of immediate impression than of critical examination. With my friend, Mr. Andrew Quoz, I begin to doubt the motives of our New-York Critics; especially since I have, in addition to these arguments, the assurances of two or three doubtless *disinterested* actors, and an editor, who Mr. Quoz tells me is remarkable for his *candor* and *veracity*, that the Critics are the most 'presumptuous,' 'arrogant,' 'malevolent,' 'illiberal,' 'ungentleman-like,' 'malignant,' 'rancorous,' 'villainous,' 'ungrateful,' 'crippled,' 'invidious,' 'detracting,' 'fabricating,' 'personal,' 'dogmatical,' 'illegitimate,' 'tyrannical,' 'distorting,' 'spindle-shanked moppets, designing villains, and upstart ignorants.'

These, I say, and many other equally *high polished* appellations, have awakened doubts in my mind respecting the sincerity and justice of the Critics; and lest my pen should unwittingly draw upon me the suspicion, of having a hankering after criticism, I now wipe it carefully—lock it safely up, and promise not to draw it forth again, till some new department of folly calls for my attention.

JONATHAN OLDSTYLE.

LETTER IX

Printed in *The Morning Chronicle*, April 23, 1803.

SIR,

I was calmly enjoying my toast and coffee some mornings ago, with my sister Dorothy and Jack Stylish, when we were surprized by the abrupt entrance of my friend, Mr. Andrew Quoz. By the particular expression of his *knowing phiz*, as cousin Jack calls it, I immediately perceived he was labouring with some important intelligence.

In one hand he held the Morning Chronicle, and with the fore-finger of the other pointed to a particular paragraph. I hastily put on my spectacles, and seized the paper with eager curiosity. Judge my surprize, Mr. Editor, on reading an act of our legislature, pronouncing any citizen of this state who shall send, bear, or accept a challenge, either verbal or written, disqualified from holding any office of honor or confidence, or of voting at any election within this state, &c. &c.

The paper fell from my hands—I turned my eyes to friend Andrew in mute astonishment. Quoz put his finger to his nose, and winking significantly, cried, "What do you think of this, my friend Jonathan?"

"Here is a catastrophe," exclaimed I, in a melancholy tone. "Here is a damper for the mettlesome youths of the age. Spirit of chivalry, whither hast thou flown! Shade of Don Quixote, dost thou not look down with contempt on the degeneracy of the times!"

My sister Dorothy caught a sympathetic spark of enthusiasm—deep read in all the volumes of ancient romance, and delighted with their glowing descriptions of the heroic age, she had learned to admire the gallantry of former days, and mourned to see the last spark of chivalric fire thus rudely extinguished.

Alas! my brother, said she, to what a deplorable state are our young men reduced! how piteous must be their situation—with sensibilities so *easily injured*, and bosoms so *tremblingly alive* to the calls of honor and etiquette!

Indeed, my dear Dorothy, said I, I feel most deeply for their melancholy situation. Deprived in these dull, monotonous, peaceable times, of all opportunities of evincing, in the hardy contest of the tented field, that heroic flame that burns within their breasts, they were happy to vent the lofty fumings of their souls in the more domestic and *less dangerous* encounters of the duel—like the warrior in the fable, who, deprived of the pleasure of slaughtering armies, contented himself with cutting down cabbages.

Here a solemn pause ensued. I called to mind all the tales I had heard or read of ancient knights; their amours, their quarrels, and their combats; how, on a fair summer's morning, the knight of the Golden Goose met the knight of the Fiery Fiddle; how the knight of the Fiery Fiddle exclaimed in lofty tones, "whoever denies that Donna Fiddleosa is the most peerless beauty in the universe, must brave the strength of this arm!" how they both engaged with dreadful fury; and, after fighting till sunset, the knight of the Fiery Fiddle fell a martyr to his constancy; murmuring in melodious accents, with his latest breath, the beloved name of Fiddleosa.

From these ancient engagements, I descended to others more modern in their dates, but equally important in their origins. I recalled the genuine politeness and polished ceremony with which duels were conducted in my youthful days, when that gentlemanly weapon, the *small sword*, was in highest vogue. A challenge was worded with the most particular complaisance; and one that I have still in my possession, ends with the words, "*your friend and affectionate servant Nicholas Stubbs.*" When the parties met on the field, the same decorum was observed; they pulled off their hats, wished one another a good day, and helped to draw off each other's coats and boots, with the most respectful civility. Their fighting too was so handsomely conducted: no aukward movements; no eager and angry pushes; all cool, elegant and graceful. Every thrust had its *sa-sa*; and a *ha-hah* lunged you gently through the body. Then nothing could equal the tenderness and attention with which a wounded antagonist was treated: his adversary, after wiping his sword deliberately, kindly supported him in his arms, examined his pulse, and enquired, with the most affectionate solicitude, "how he felt himself now?"—Thus every thing was conducted in a well-bred, gentlemanly manner.

Our present customs I can't say I much admire—a *twelve inch barrell pistol* and *ounce ball*, are blunt, unceremonious affairs, and prevent that display of grace and elegance allowed by the small sword; besides, there is something so awkward in having the muzzle of a pistol staring one full in the face, that I should think it might be apt to make some of our youthful heroes feel rather disagreeable, unless, as I am told has been sometimes the case, the duel was fought by twilight.

The ceremony of loading, priming, cocking, &c. has not the most soothing effects on a person's feelings; and I am told that some of our warriors have been known to tremble and make wry faces during these preparations—though this has been attributed, and doubtless with much justice, to the violence of their wrath and fierceness of their courage.

I had thus been musing for some time, when I broke silence at last by hinting to friend Quoz some of my objections to the mode of fighting with pistols.

Truly, my friend Oldstyle, said Quoz, I am surprised at your ignorance of modern customs: trust me, I know of no amusement that is, generally speaking, more harmless. To be sure, there may now and then a couple of determined fellows take the field who resolve to do the thing in good earnest; but in general our fashionable duellists are content with only one discharge; and then, either they are poor shots, or their triggers pull hard, or they shut the wrong eye, or some other cause intervenes, so that it is ten, aye, twenty chances to one in their favour.

Here I begged leave to differ from friend Andrew. I am well convinced, said I, of the valour of our young men, and that they determine, when they march forth to the field, either to conquer or die; but it generally happens that their seconds are of a more peaceable mind, and interpose after the first shot; but I am informed that they come often very near being killed, having bullet holes through their hats and coats, which, like Falstaff's hack'd sword, are strong proofs of the serious nature of their encounters.

My sister Dorothy, who is of a humane and benevolent disposition, would no doubt detest the idea of duels, did she not regard them as the last gleams of those days of chivalry, to which she looks back with a degree of romantic enthusiasm. She now considered them as having received their death-blow; for how can even the challenges be conveyed, said she, when the very messengers are considered as principals in the offence?

Nothing more easy, said friend Quoz:—a man gives me the lie—very well: I tread on his toes in token of challenge—he pulls my nose by way of acceptance: thus you see the challenge is safely conveyed without a third party.—We then settle the mode in which satisfaction is to be given; as for instance, we draw lots which of us must be slain to satisfy the demands of honor. Mr. A. or Mr. B. my antagonist, is to fall: well, madam, he stands below in the street; I run up to the garret window, and drop a brick upon his head: If he survives well and good; if he falls, why nobody is to blame, it was purely accidental. Thus the affair is settled, according to the common saying, to our mutual satisfaction.

Jack Stylish observed, that as to Mr. Quoz's project of dropping bricks on people's heads, he considered it a vulgar substitute: for his part, he thought that it would be well for the legislature to amend their law respecting duels, and licence them under proper restrictions—That no persons should be allowed to fight without taking out a regular license from what might be called the *Blood and Thunder Office*—That they should be obliged to give two or three weeks notice of the intended combat in the newspapers—That the contending parties should fight till one of them fell—and that the public should be admitted to *the show*.

This he observed, would in some degree, be reviving the *spectacles* of antiquity, when the populace were regaled with the combats of gladiators. We have at present no games resembling those of the ancients; except now and then, a bull or bear bait, and this would be a valuable addition to the list of our refined amusements.

I listened to their discourse in silence: yet I cannot but think, Mr. Editor, that this plan is entitled to some attention. Our young men fight ninety-nine times out of a hundred, through *fear* of being branded with the epithet of *coward;* and since they fight to please the world, the world being thus interested in their encounter, should be permitted to attend and judge in person of their conduct.

As I think the subject of importance, I take the liberty of requesting a corner in the Morning Chronicle, to submit it to the consideration of the public.

JONATHAN OLDSTYLE.

EDITORIAL APPENDIX

Textual Commentary, Discussions, and Lists by

Bruce I. Granger

SYMBOLS AND ABBREVIATIONS

ARE	Author's Revised Edition (Putnam, 1848–1850).
BAL	Jacob Blanck, *Bibliography of American Literature* (New Haven, 1969).
]	Left-facing bracket sets off reading adopted in the Twayne edition from those rejected.
[ ]	Brackets in the text of *Salmagundi* are represented as italicized in the Substantive and Accidental transcriptions.
DA	*A Dictionary of Americanisms*, ed. Mitford M. Matthews (Chicago, 1951).
DAE	*A Dictionary of American English*, ed. Sir William A. Craigie and James R. Hulbert (Chicago, 1938).
EDD	*The English Dialect Dictionary*, ed. Joseph Wright (Oxford, 1923).
fn	footnote
PP	Paragraph
PMI	Pierre M. Irving, *The Life and Letters of Washington Irving* (New York, 1862).
STW	Stanley T. Williams, *The Life of Washington Irving* (New York, 1935).
Typo	Typographical error
T	Twayne edition: used in the editorial emendations.
Walker	*A Critical Pronouncing Dictionary and Expositor of the English Language* (London, 1797).
Webster	*A Compendious Dictionary of the English Language* (Hartford and New Haven, 1806).
WI	Washington Irving

HISTORICAL NOTE

The New York *Morning Chronicle,* a pro-Burrite daily founded October 9, 1802, and subsidized by Aaron Burr, sought to establish a position between James Cheetham's *American Citizen,* a Jeffersonian paper pledged to support the Clinton party, and William Coleman's *Evening Post,* Hamilton's Federalist paper in New York. The editor, Peter Irving, at once announced: "The interests of LITERATURE will be blended with those of Commerce and Politics.... The sportive effusions of wit and humor... will receive a welcome and grateful insertion... but malignity, detraction and scurrilous abuse, shall never be permitted to stain its pages." Aware that the *Chronicle* had "found its way into a world of turmoil and vexation," Peter declared it "his purpose to publish a fair and independent paper," though he confessed that he had "embraced a situation foreign to his pursuits and habits: one, to the duties of which he is sensible that his talents are not sufficiently competent." Although he tried to steer a smooth course between the *American Citizen* and the *Evening Post,* even so apparently innocent an incident as Jonathan Oldstyle's observations in Letter VII on John Hodgkinson's performance in *The Wheel of Truth* angered both Cheetham and Coleman and produced a critical flurry. (See Explanatory Note at 27.1.) "Peter Irving was replaced by Henry Stanley as editor of the *Morning Chronicle* in December, 1805. Aaron Burr, who had raised him up, was no longer able to help him."[1]

In much the way that young Benjamin Franklin began his literary career by publishing the *Dogood* papers in his brother James's *New-England Courant,* nineteen-year-old Washington Irving published his first writings (though not surreptitiously) in the *Morning Chronicle.* "An inviting opportunity here presented itself," noted a later editor of the *Oldstyle* letters, "for trying the scarcely fledged wings of our juvenile author: and a two-fold benefit could be conferred—credit to himself, and relief to the care-worn and harassed editor, whose political conflicts did not allow him leisure to woo the muses to his aid; and he knew, that without some contributions from the Pierian district, his paper, even in this 'bank-note-world,' would soon decline, for the want of contributions of a more substantial quality."[2] And as Franklin broke

1. *Peter Irving's Journal,* ed. Leonard B. Beach and Others (New York, 1943), p. 9.
2. *Letters of Jonathan Oldstyle, Gent.* (New York: William Clayton, 1824), p. v.

off the *Dogood* papers when his "small Fund of Sense for such Performances was pretty well exhausted,"[3] young Irving broke off abruptly
after the ninth letter. The fact that Jonathan Oldstyle does not fulfill the
promise he makes at the beginning of Letter VIII to describe in a subsequent letter the ball he visited with Quoz and Dorothy is proof enough
that Irving was not then planning to discontinue the series.

The nine letters of Jonathan Oldstyle were first published in the
Morning Chronicle, November 15, 20, December 1, 4, 11, 1802, and
January 17, 22, February 8, April 23, 1803. Because this is the only publication which carries all nine letters and because Washington Irving is
not positively known to have revised them for any later printing, the
Morning Chronicle version has been chosen as copy-text;[4] the only com-
plete file is at the New-York Historical Society. The copy-text was
emended after being collated with four later printings: Letters II–IX
reprinted in the *Chronicle Express*, a semiweekly country edition of the
Morning Chronicle, in 1802–1803; the first American edition (New
York: William Clayton, 1824), where the title *Letters of Jonathan Oldstyle, Gent.* appears for the first time; the first English edition (London:
Effingham Wilson, 1824); and Letters I–V which appear in *Spanish
Papers and Other Miscellanies*, ed. Pierre M. Irving (New York, 1866),
II, 11–33. Full discussion of the textual history and collational pattern
followed will be found in the Textual Commentary, pp. 50–55.

On January 29, 1804, Aaron Burr sent his daughter Theodosia the
Oldstyle letters, clipped from the pages of the *Morning Chronicle*, with
an apology. These, he wrote, "would not, perhaps, merit so high an
honour as that of being perused by your—eyes and touched by your fair
hands, but that [they are] the production of a youth of about nineteen,
the youngest brother of Dr. Peter Irving of New York."[5] Faint praise
indeed! When the first English edition appeared in 1824, an anonymous
reviewer protested the unfairness of reprinting these letters without the
author's consent. "They are not without merit as to the style," he declared, "but, in other respects, they present, for the most part, only a
mass of common-places, dressed out in all the pomp with which unim-
portant subjects are usually loaded by a very young writer, who imagines
that he displays his intelligence by 'holding his farthing rushlight to
the sun,' and endeavours to be very witty upon topics on which humour

3. *The Autobiography of Benjamin Franklin*, ed. Leonard W. Labaree et al.
(New Haven, 1964), p. 68.
4. "Copy-text" is the text accepted as the basis for an edition in all respects
except those specific instances in which emendation is required.
5. *Memoirs of Aaron Burr, with Miscellaneous Selections of His Correspondence*,
ed. M. L. Davis (New York, 1837), II, 274; cited in *Letters of Jonathan Oldstyle,
Gent.*, intro. Stanley T. Williams (New York, 1941), p. v.

has long since been exhausted."[6] John Neal characterized the letters as "boyish theatrical criticisms ... from the rubbish of old printing-offices. ... Nevertheless, there is a touch of Irving's quality in these papers—paltry as they are: A little of that happy, sly humour; that grave pleasantry, (wherein he resembles Goldsmith, so much); that quiet, shrewd, good-humoured sense of the ridiculous, which, altogether, in our opinion, go to make up the chief excellence of Geoffrey [Crayon]—that, which will outlive the fashion of this day; and set him apart, after all, from every writer in our language."[7] In 1832 William Dunlap called them "pleasant effusions" and proceeded to quote liberally from Jonathan's theatrical criticism in Letters III–VII.[8] Shortly after Irving's death Evert A. Duyckinck wrote that the *Oldstyle* letters "are noticeable for the early [formation?] of the writer's happy style."[9]

Letters I–V, as has been said, appeared in the second volume of Putnam's 1866 edition of *Spanish Papers and Other Miscellanies*, entitled "Biographies and Miscellanies." These five *Oldstyle* letters were subsequently reprinted in the second volume of *Spanish Papers* in such various Putnam impressions as the Geoffrey Crayon Edition (1867), the Spuyten Duyvil Edition (1881), and two Hudson Editions (1856–1889, 1902); the 1897 Knickerbocker Edition reprinted these five letters in the second volume of *Salmagundi*. The 1867 English edition of Bell and Daldy, entitled *Biographies and Miscellaneous Papers*, reprinted the first five *Oldstyle* letters from Putnam's 1866 edition of *Spanish Papers*, and subsequent English issues of this work were based on this 1867 London edition. Thus, although Irving thought poorly of this youthful work, five of the nine *Oldstyle* letters remained in print throughout the nineteenth century.

6. *Monthly Critical Gazette* 1 (June, 1824), 94.
7. *Blackwood's Edinburgh Magazine* 18 (January, 1825), 60–61.
8. *History of the American Theatre*, II, 172–83.
9. "Memoranda of the Literary Career of Washington Irving by Evert Duyckinck," p. 12; manuscript in the New York Public Library.

EXPLANATORY NOTES

The numbers before all notes indicate page and line respectively. Chapter numbers, chapter or section titles, epigraphs, author's chapter or section summaries, text quotations, and footnotes are included in the line count. Only running heads and rules added by the printer to separate the running head from the text are omitted from the count. The quotation from the text, to the left of the bracket, is the matter under discussion.

References to four dictionaries are abbreviated as follows: *DA–A Dictionary of Americanisms*, ed. Mitford M. Matthews (Chicago, 1951); *DAE–A Dictionary of American English*, ed. Sir William A. Craigie and James R. Hulbert (Chicago, 1938); *EDD–The English Dialect Dictionary*, ed. Joseph Wright (Oxford, 1923); and *OED–The Oxford English Dictionary*, ed. James A. H. Murray and Others (Oxford, 1961).

3.11   craped] Made wavy and curly (*OED*).

4.3   Heavens! how changed are the manners since I was young!] *The Oracle* of 1804 declared: "What a routine we have had of everything disgusting, in the name of Fashion! Slouched hats, jockey waistcoats, half-boots, leather breeches, cropped heads, unpowdered hair... the present race of Bucks without blood, Beaux without taste, and Gentlemen without manners!" And *The Universal Magazine* of 1810 announced: "The manners of the men have undergone a complete revolution, particularly as they regard the fair sex.... An indifference to the convenience and accommodation of the softer sex has taken place in our public assemblies.... the extreme of the fashion is little short of brutal rudeness" (quoted in C. Willett and Phillis Cunnington, *Handbook of English Costume in the Nineteenth Century* [London, 1959], pp. 12–13).

4.5   copperplate] A polished plate of copper on which a design is engraved or etched for printing (*OED*). Copperplate engravings were much in fashion during the eighteenth and early nineteenth centuries (*DA*). Here apparently the term means rigid and conventional.

4.20   JONATHAN OLDSTYLE] This aptronym for the old bachelor, a persona that recurs constantly in the Anglo-American periodical essay from the time of Addison, is so conventional as probably to have occurred instinctively to the young Irving. "Oliver Oldschool" was the appellation under which Joseph Dennie wrote in the *Port Folio,* beginning in 1801; in Letter V Jonathan Oldstyle longs to see a part played by "an actor of the *old school*" (17.7–8). One of the characters in William Dunlap's *Where is He?* is "Major Oldstyle"; Irving may well have seen the performance at the Park Theater in December, 1801. See George C. D. Odell, *Annals of the New York Stage* (New York, 1927), II, 127–28. Early nineteenth-century readers would still have remembered that in 1752, by an act of Parliament, England and her colonies changed from Old Style (Julian) to New Style (Gregorian) by dropping eleven days out of the calendar.

8.5   the theatre] The only theater in New York City at this time was the Park Theater on Park Row near Broadway, which opened its doors January 29, 1798. It faced the park where a new City Hall was under construction. "A contemporary account of the opening described the pit as 'remarkably commodious,' and praised the three semi-circular rows of boxes, unsupported by the customary pillars which heretofore had proved such a 'common and great obstacle to the view.' The gallery was 'thrown back of the upper front boxes.' The stage was also described as 'remarkably commodious,' and the scenery [was] superior to 'everything of the kind heretofore seen in America.' The perfection of the architect's plan ... was not attained for a number of years, if at all." Oral Sumner Coad and Edwin Mims, Jr., *The American Stage* (New Haven, 1929), p. 51.

8.10   THE BATTLE OF HEXHAM] *The Battle of Hexham; or, Days of Old* (1798) by George Colman the Younger is a romantic comedy set in the time of the War of the Roses. The Battle of Hexham ended in the total defeat of the Lancastrian party, after which Henry VI's wife, Queen Margaret, fled with her son into the forest. It is here that most of the action in the play takes place. In a performance at the Park Theater on November 24, 1802, one which Irving may well have attended, the captain of the robbers, Gondibert, was played by John Hodgkinson (1767?–1805), the greatest American actor of the day. John Bernard described him as "tall and well-proportioned,

though inclining to be corpulent, with a face of great
mobility, that showed the minutest change of feeling, while
his voice, full and flexible, could only be likened to an
instrument that his passions played upon at pleasure." *Retrospections of America, 1797–1811* (New York, 1887), pp.
257–58. Gondibert's wife, Adeline, was played by Elizabeth Johnson, a celebrated English actress whom all New
York fell in love with during her engagement at the Park.
The "pretty gentleman" who follows the queen is apparently a reference to La Varenne, Seneschal of Normandy
(act 1, sc. 3). At Henry VI's camp, before the battle, a
corporal sings a song urging his men to fight "for the
cause of the jolly Red Rose" (act 2, sc. 2). In a cave in
Hexham Forest after the battle, several robbers are discovered drinking and singing; Irving quotes from the
last stanza of their song about a Welsh thief who loved
toasted cheese: "Usquebaugh burnt the Irishman, / The
Scot was drown'd in ale; / The Welshman had like t' have
been choked with a mouse, / But he pull'd her out by the
tail" (act 2, sc 1).

9.21   *The Tripolitan Prize*] *The Tripolitan Prize; or, American
Tars on an English Shore* was the afterpiece to *The Battle
of Hexham* at the Park Theater on November 24, 1802.
It was advertised as "A comic Opera, in 2 acts," altered
from Samuel James Arnold's *The Veteran Tar* (1801),
"never performed here." In this patriotic play, performed
at a time when the United States was at war with Tripoli,
John Hodgkinson was cast in the role of the navy officer,
Tom Sturdy.

10.25   the gods] The gallery gods, i.e., those seated high in the
gallery close to the sky-painted ceiling.

13.9   *jockies*] A contemptuous term for men of the common people
(*OED*).

14.28   *Moll in the wad*] "A much admired duett. Sung in Larry's
return. New York, Printed & sold at J. Hewitt's Musical
repository." Oscar G. T. Sonneck, *A Bibliography of
Early Secular American Music* (Washington, D. C., 1945),
p. 265.

14.28–29 *Tally ho the grinders*] Possibly a reference to "TALLY HO.
Sung by Mrs. Pownall. New York, Printed & sold by G.
Gilfert & co." Sonneck, *A Bibliography of Early Secular
American Music,* p. 421.

15.7–8 *harp ... mirror*] "The curtain of blue mohair, fringed in gold," writes Oral Sumner Coad, "contained in the center a lyre and the motto: 'To hold the Mirror up to Nature.' " *William Dunlap* (New York, 1917), p. 65.

17.3   the *white lion*] The Earl of Warwick in *The Battle of Hexham*, played by Mr. Prigmore. William Dunlap, *History of the American Theatre* (New York, 1832), II, 172.

17.20   *slab shabs*] Apparently in the sense of low, mean-spirited fellows (*OED*).

17.21   *twig*] Administer a slight but not unduly severe reproof (*EDD*).

17.30   Suwarrow boots] A type of cavalry boot, named for the Russian field marshall, A. V. Suvorov (1729–1800) (*DA*).

17.31   marquis of Montague] The Marquis of Montague appears in *The Battle of Hexham*, claiming a victory for the House of York (act 1, sc. 5).

18.11   *dome*] Above the tier of the second boxes, said the *Commercial Advertiser* of December 4, 1798, "arises a vaulted cieling or dome. . . . The surface is an azure scene, interspersed with floating clouds, between which celestial forms are visable. . . . Over the stage and each range of boxes hangs a canopy of green and gold. This assemblage of splendid and graceful objects is made to strike the eye with uncommon force by means of a glass chandelier, containing sixteen lights, depending from the centre of the dome and by fifteen lustres, disposed around it." Stanley T. Williams, *The Life of Washington Irving* (New York, 1935, I, 39.

18.37   new music] A writer in the *New-York Mirror* 10 (No. 31, February 2, 1833), 246, declared that this suggestion "has never been attended to even to the present day." In a letter which follows, "The Tune in Book Number Six" recalls "being of a lively disposition" at the Park Theater thirty-six years ago. In time, however, the tune came to be "played on all occasions, farce or melo-drama, tragedy, comedy, or pantomime," so that now "I am a by-word in the pit. People insult me by eating apples, and crack jokes and peanuts on me with a total forgetfulness of my original charms. The managers, and not I, are to blame for my long sojourn and constant repetition in the orchestra."

18.38   clean benches] "Philo Dramaticus," lauding Jonathan for his strictures, attributes the foul state of the boxes to the custom the gentlemen have "of standing on the seats with dirty boots, and to the parings of apples and oranges, and the shells of pea-nuts, which they distribute plentifully around them." *Morning Chronicle*, February 1, 1803.

18.41   a total reformation] Early in February, 1803, the Park Theater was closed for a short time. "During the recess," reported the *Morning Chronicle* of February 23, in its review of the reopening two days earlier, "the backs of the boxes have been re-colored with a lighter blue, and the benches newly covered. These are the only improvements that could be made in so short a space of time." See Odell, *Annals*, II, 172–73. In the summer of 1807 the interior was extensively remodeled, a fact noted by Will Wizard in *Salmagundi* No. XIV.

19.8–9   nursing my wounded shin] "We have received a note from our correspondent Jonathan Oldstyle. The old gentleman seems in quite a testy humor. ... He also states that he has been confined to his house since the famous Battle of Hexham, in which engagement he received a broken shin, in a skirmish with some impudent boys, who assailed him for his check of admittance during the interval between the play and farce." *Morning Chronicle*, January 15, 1803.

19.11   Andrew Quoz] Although variously identified as Peter Irving, James Kirke Paulding, and Henry Brevoort, it seems probable that Andrew Quoz was modeled on Elias Hicks (1771–1845), nephew to the Quaker preacher of that name. He was associated with Peter Irving in early efforts in dramatic criticism. See Dunlap, *History of the American Theatre*, I, 373. Obviously Irving regarded this "venerable friend" with both respect and affection and here uses him as defender of the "rights of actors." Irving "addressed him in 1804 at the office of the Morning Chronicle in a series of gossipy letters, signing himself on one occasion: 'Your friend until Death.'" *Letters of Jonathan Oldstyle, Gent.*, intro. Stanley T. Williams (New York, 1941), p. xiv, note.

20.37   "tearing a passion to tatters—to very rags!"] Said of the players in *Hamlet* (Act 3, sc. 2, lines 9–10).

21.1–2   "I'd ... tree,"] *Henry IV*, Part I, act 3, sc. 1, lines 131–32.

21.15–23   hath not an actor eyes] A parody of Shylock's speech which begins, "Hath not a Jew Eyes?" *Merchant of Venice*, act 3, sc. 1, lines 51–62.

21.18   *club*] A club was a club-shaped tail or knot in which men's hair was tied at the back—a late eighteenth-century fashion.

22.11   the Shakspeare] The Shakespeare box occupied the front of the second tier directly in front of the stage at the Park Theater. It was abolished when improvements to the interior were made in 1807. See Odell, *Annals*, II, 291.

24.3   the play] Sir John Vanbrugh's *The Provoked Husband* (1728), performed as the first play on the bill at the Park Theater, January 14, 1803, with Elizabeth Johnson in the role of Lady Townly. The "ludicrous epilogue," spoken by Lady Townly, is typical of the moral sentiment that brought many an eighteenth-century English comedy to a close.

24.19   the after-piece] James Fennell's *The Wheel of Truth* was the second play on the bill at the Park Theater, January 14, 1803. Harlequin (the *"jolly Merry Andrew"*) was played by Hodgkinson; the "ancient maiden" was Tabitha. The *Morning Chronicle* for January 14, 1803, described this farce as "a piece of patch-work thrown together with considerable whim" wherein Harlequin is made manager of the Wheel of Truth, a machine "for trying characters, and reducing [men] to their real forms." Among the pretenders to a young lady who are put into the wheel are a fop, a quack doctor, and a critic; they come out as a monkey, an ass, and a goose. When Harlequin enters the wheel, he remains unaltered, being the only "actor who can stand the test of truth," and is rewarded with the hand of the young lady.

25.25   "hath borne her faculties so meekly,"] Adapted from *Macbeth*, act 1, sc. 7, line 17.

27.1   *Letter VIII*] Andrew Quoz's aspersions on theater critics in Letter VI (20.25–21.27) and Jonathan's irritation with *The Wheel of Truth* in Letter VII (24.19–26.6) touched off a critical flurry in the New York press which involved the author Fennell, the actor Hodgkinson, and the editors William Coleman and James Cheetham. Although Fennell claimed to be sole author of this play, Hodgkinson was suspected of having introduced the character Littlewit as an actor's revenge on drama critics. Cheetham defended Hodgkinson against Coleman's attack upon him, calling his opponent "Mr. *Cole*-man or more properly Mr. *Black*-man" (*American Citizen*, February 3, 1803). When Hodgkinson finally declared, "I had no agency whatever in the production of the 'Wheel of Truth,'" Coleman replied, "I have done you an injustice in attributing to you some considerable share in its authorship" (*New-York Evening-*

Post, February 7, 1803). *Oldstyle* No. VIII appeared the
next day, wherein Irving, deploring the critical bickering
over *The Wheel of Truth,* has Jonathan "begin to doubt
the motives of our New-York Critics" (30.40–41).

29.23   "holds the mirror up to nature,"] *Hamlet,* act 3, sc. 2, lines
20–21.

30.11   Sterne] In *Tristram Shandy,* bk. 4, chap. 8, Uncle Toby tells
Corporal Trim, "God Almighty is so good and just a governor of the world, that if we have but done our duties in it,—
it will never be enquired into, whether we have done
them in a red coat or a black one."

30.16   Garrick] David Garrick (1717–1779), famous English actor.

30.16   Kemble...Siddons] A reference to three members of a
famous English acting family: John Philip Kemble (1751–
1823), best known in heroic roles; Charles Kemble (1775–
1854), noted at this time for his talent in comedy; and
Sarah Kemble Siddons (1755–1831), the most celebrated
actress of the day. In the autumn of 1805 Irving saw all
three perform at Covent Garden, in *The Merchant of
Venice, Henry IV,* Part I, Rowe's *The Fair Penitent,* and
Otway's *Venice Preserved.* See *Journals and Notebooks,*
Vol. I, ed. Nathalia Wright (Madison, 1969), 456–57,
565, 566.

32.12   an act of our legislature] On April 2, 1803, the New York
legislature passed a law imposing penalties for dueling.
Accordingly, all citizens of the State of New York who
gave or accepted a challenge to fight a duel or who acted
as seconds were "disqualified from holding any office of
honour, profit or trust, and voting at any election within
this state, for the term of twenty years." See *Laws of the
State of New-York* (Albany: George Webster, 1804), III,
334–35. The English traveler, John Lambert, observed soon
after: "Duels are very frequent and fatal throughout the
States, and all attempts to prevent them have hitherto
failed. At New York, a law was passed to prohibit the
sending of challenges, and the fighting of duels, under
severe penalties; but it answered no other end than to
produce a smart piece of satire on the subject of duels"
(*Travels through Canada, and the United States of North
America, in the Years 1806, 1807, & 1808* [London, 1810],
II, 113).

32.37   like the warrior in the fable] While no precise source for
this Quixotic fable has been found, Irving developed it

in the 1809 *History of New York,* bk. 5, chap. 7, wherein the braggart soldier General Jacobus Von Poffenburgh, whenever "he found his martial spirit waxing hot within him," "would prudently sally forth into the fields, and lugging out his   trusty sabre . . . would lay about him most lustily, decapitating cabbages by platoons."

33.2–3   knight of the Golden Goose] Probably fictitious.

TEXTUAL COMMENTARY

Letters of Jonathan Oldstyle, Gent. is an essay serial in nine parts, published first in newspaper and later in book form. Prior to the Twayne edition no complete and uniform text of the *Oldstyle* letters had been published subsequent to their original appearance in 1802–1803. The genealogy of the text with an identifying symbol for each edition is illustrated in the following chart.

Textual History Tree

1Aa
Letters I–IX originally published in the New York *Morning Chronicle*, 1802–1803. Copy-text.

1Ab
Letters II–IX reprinted within a few days in the New York *Chronicle Express*, 1802–1803.

2A
Letters of Jonathan Oldstyle, Gent. By the Author of The Sketch Book. With a Biographical Notice. New York: William H. Clayton, 1824. (*BAL* 10112)

1E
Letters of Jonathan Oldstyle, Gent. By the Author of The Sketch Book. With a Biographical Notice. London: Effingham Wilson, 1824.

3A
Letters I–V, in *Spanish Papers and Other Miscellanies, Hitherto Unpublished or Uncollected. By Washington Irving.* New York: G. P. Putnam, 1866. II, 11–33. (*BAL* 10201)

NY 1941
Letters of Jonathan Oldstyle, Gent. Facsimile Text Society. New York: Columbia University Press, 1941.

1Aa: New York, Morning Chronicle, 1802–1803.
No manuscript of *Letters of Jonathan Oldstyle* is known to survive. The work was first published as nine untitled and unnumbered letters to the editor of the New York *Morning Chronicle* (i.e., Peter Irving),

signed "Jonathan Oldstyle," in the issues of November 15, 1802, p. 3; November 20, 1802, p. 2; December 1, 1802, pp. 2–3; December 4, 1802, pp. 2–3; December 11, 1802, p. 3; January 17, 1803, p. 2; January 22, 1803, p. 2; February 8, 1803, p. 2; and April 23, 1803, pp. 2–3. The *Morning Chronicle* also carried a letter addressed to Jonathan Oldstyle, signed "Philo Dramaticus," February 1, 1803 (see Explanatory Notes on 18.38), but there is no reason to attribute it to Washington Irving. Because the *Morning Chronicle* is the only publication which carried all nine *Oldstyle* letters, this printing was chosen as copy-text; the only file containing the nine issues in which these letters appeared is held by the New-York Historical Society.[1]

1Ab: New York, Chronicle Express, 1802–1803.

Within a few days of their original appearance all but the first of the *Oldstyle* letters (3.1–4.20) and the first paragraph of the second letter (5.4–5) were reprinted in the New York *Chronicle Express*, a semiweekly country edition of the *Morning Chronicle*, in the issues of November 25, December 2, 6, 13, 1802, and January 20, 24, February 10, April 25, 1803. The only file of the *Chronicle Express* containing the issues in which these eight letters appeared is located at the New-York Historical Society. It is not clear whether the first letter was omitted deliberately or simply overlooked; whichever the case, with the first letter missing it became necessary to delete the first paragraph of the second letter: "*Mr. Editor*, Encouraged by the ready insertion you gave my former communication, I have taken the liberty to intrude on you a few more remarks." The *Chronicle Express* text, probably supervised by Irving, deleted the first and faulty version of a paragraph in the final letter inadvertently printed twice in the copy-text, corrected three other printer's errors, and made six substantive revisions. In all other respects it follows closely the reading of the copy-text.

2A: New York, William H. Clayton, 1824 (BAL 10112).

Early in the year 1824,[2] at a time when the success of *The Sketch Book* and *Bracebridge Hall* was helping establish Irving's literary repu-

---

1. For other libraries holding short runs and scattered issues of the *Morning Chronicle*, see Clarence S. Brigham, *History and Bibliography of American Newspapers 1690–1820* (Worcester, Mass., 1947), I, 668. Although Brigham lists the New York Public Library as owning the nine issues in which the *Oldstyle* letters appeared, three of these issues are in fact missing from that set: December 4, 1802 (containing Letter IV), December 11, 1802 (Letter V), and April 23, 1803 (Letter IX).

2. Jacob Blanck, comp., *Bibliography of American Literature*, V (New Haven and London, 1969), 23, says that the title-page of the 1824 New York edition was deposited on February 19, 1824.

tation on both sides of the Atlantic, the New York printer William H. Clayton published the *Oldstyle* letters in pamphlet form, with the notation: "To the new generation of readers produced by the lapse of twenty-two years, we trust that their republication will be peculiarly acceptable" (pp. iii–iv). Clayton must have used the *Chronicle Express* text as printer's copy since the first letter and the first paragraph of the second letter are missing. Also missing, because inappropriate to book publication, are the editorial introductions to the sixth and eighth letters (19.3–5, 27.3). Clayton was the first to give the *Oldstyle* letters the now familiar title, *Letters of Jonathan Oldstyle, Gent.*; he numbered them I–VIII, apparently unaware of the existence of the first letter. Irving not only did not supervise the publication of this the first American edition in book form, but withheld approval altogether. As Pierre M. Irving, his uncle's literary executor, later explained, "The Oldstyle papers were collected and given anew to the world, without his knowledge or consent, and a good deal to his regret, as he considered them rather crude and boyish."[3] In this edition punctuation was regularized to make it conform with Clayton's house style. In all, fifty-three substantive and fifty-four accidental revisions were introduced into the text.

1E: London, Effingham Wilson, 1824.

The first English edition was published in April 1824.[4] It follows closely the substantives of 2A, Clayton's American edition, and differs in accidentals at only five points. Irving learned of this piracy at John Murray's home in London on Saturday afternoon, May 29, "between sips of strong coffee." "Murray offered to publish a corrected or revised edition, but Irving's obvious embarrassment over the subject and his serious protests describing the *Letters* as 'juvenile writings' caused the host to abandon the idea at once."[5]

3A: New York, G. P. Putnam, 1866 (BAL 10201).

Irving excluded *Letters of Jonathan Oldstyle, Gent.* from the 1848–1850 revised edition of his writings published by George Putnam. He died in 1859. In 1866 Pierre M. Irving included the first five *Oldstyle* letters in *Spanish Papers and Other Miscellanies*, thereby restoring Letter I which had been omitted from all intermediate editions; but

3. *The Life and Letters of Washington Irving* (New York, 1862–1864), I, 47–48.
4. Blanck, *American Bibliography*, V, 24, says that the first English edition was advertised April 12, 1824, and the second and third editions on April 24 and May 22, 1824.
5. *Washington Irving and the House of Murray*, ed. Ben Harris McClary (Knoxville, Tenn., 1969), p. 53.

Letters VI–IX were not included, "in deference to the wishes of the author, who marked them as 'not to be reprinted,' when there was question of including the pamphlet of Oldstyle papers in a collective edition of his writings."[6] Pierre M. Irving corrected three printer's errors in Letter I. Letters II–V follow the substantives and accidentals of 2A, with one notable exception (15.11). Letter IV is misdated "Dec. 3."

London, Bell and Daldy, 1867 (BAL 10378).

The first five *Oldstyle* letters were reprinted from 3A in an English edition entitled *Biographies and Miscellaneous Papers.* In this English reprint the type has been reset from 3A and the text house-styled to make it conform with British practice, a fact seen most clearly in the spelling (e.g., "humoured," 5.12; "honour," 10.21; "neighbour," 13.35). Otherwise the text coincides with that of 3A. This 1867 English edition is so far removed from the copy-text (and the lost manuscript) that it is not included in the Textual History Tree.

NY 1941: New York, Columbia University Press, 1941.

In 1941, Stanley T. Williams reprinted the 1824 New York edition (2A) in facsimile, prefacing it with the *Morning Chronicle* text of Letter I. The edition that emerges is unsatisfactory in that the stylistic eccentricities of Letter I, an important feature of Irving's early prose, clash with the house-styled tone of Letters II–IX.

Collation and Emendation of the Text

In the absence of a manuscript the first printing of *Letters of Jonathan Oldstyle, Gent.* was chosen as copy-text: the file of the New York *Morning Chronicle* for 1802–1803 (designated 1Aa). Later printings include: the *Chronicle Express* reprinting of Letters II–IX in 1802–1803 (1Ab), the 1824 New York edition (2A), the 1824 London edition (1E), and the 1866 New York edition of Letters I–V (3A). These printings of the *Oldstyle* letters have been collated in the following pattern:

1. Sight collation of two copies of the copy-text, 1Aa: the only complete set at the New-York Historical Society with the incomplete set at the New York Public Library which lacks issues containing Letters IV, V, and IX.
2. Sight collation of 1Aa with 1Ab, the only complete set of 1Ab being at the New-York Historical Society.
3. Sight collation of 1Aa with three later editions: 2A, 1E, 3A.

6. *Spanish Papers and Other Miscellanies* (New York, 1866), II, 10.

Lateral collation of the two copies of 1Aa failed to turn up any variants. Vertical collation of 1Aa with 1Ab revealed five substantive and four accidental variants. Four of the five substantives (13.5, 14.2, 14.36, 19.32) and the four accidentals (15.10, 31.3, 31.3, 33.29–35) were adopted. Although the *Chronicle Express* had a smaller page than the *Morning Chronicle*, a comparison of 1Aa and 1Ab by paragraph and line reveals that type was not reset for 1Ab. Three of the four adopted substantive revisions are so nearly of a length with their originals in 1Aa that only one line of type had to be reset for each; and in the case of the other one, only two lines. Three of the four accidentals only require the substitution of en quads. The fourth involves the deletion of the first and faulty version of a paragraph in the final letter printed twice in the copy-text (33.29–35). Further proof that type was not reset is the fact that 1Ab reproduces eighteen of the printer's errors present in 1Aa. It seems evident that Irving or his brother, Peter, rather than the printer, made the corrections for 1Ab; this would be in accord with his practice later of correcting proofs for substantives but being negligent about accidentals.

Three later editions, 2A, 1E, 3A, underwent extensive house-styling. Accidental variants in these editions which correct printer's errors in 1Aa were examined closely and thirty-six of them adopted: thirty-two from 2A, three from 3A, and one from 1E (17.32–33). At two points (13.34, 20.16) the editor, faced with having to choose among several variants, emended on his own authority. All told, vertical collation of 1Aa with 1Ab, 2A, 1E, and 3A turned up 122 important variants, sixty-two substantives and sixty accidentals; of this number five substantives and forty accidentals were adopted. No substantive variant was adopted unless it had the authority of 1Ab. Except at 17.32–33, where emendation was made for clarity's sake, all the accidental variants in 2A, 1E, and 3A that were adopted to correct printer's errors.

In order to preserve the texture of the *Oldstyle* letters, Irving's earliest known prose work, inconsistencies and idiosyncrasies within the text have been retained except where they obscure the meaning. The great majority of these eccentricities are accidentals, although at one point (22.6) idiom is involved. Four eccentric spellings in 1Aa—"tremenduous" (9.34), "anti-chamber" (18.25), "quizical" (24.24), "*barrell*" (33.29)— have been retained. Probably the most idiosyncratic feature of the *Oldstyle* letters, one that all but disappeared in later editions as a result of successive American and British house-stylings, are Irving's uses and omissions of the comma, which impart a special flavor to this early work without leading to downright obscurity. He often uses commas instead of semicolons to separate clauses not themselves connected by coordinating conjunctions (12.24, 23.27, 24.43), even when

the longest pause in an involved sentence is not immediately apparent
to the reader (8.20, 12.34). He separates a compound subject from its
predicate by a comma (14.11). On the other hand, he omits commas
customarily used in direct discourse (23.34, 23.37, 24.16, 25.33, 34.43),
and commas that set off nonrestrictive modifiers (8.6) and appositives
(17.37).

The editor hopes that the Twayne edition of *Letters of Jonathan
Oldstyle, Gent.* stays close enough to the lost manuscript to preserve
the flavor and rhythm of the young Irving's prose, but that he has
edited out of the copy-text unintended obscurities and obvious printer's
errors.

DISCUSSIONS OF ADOPTED READINGS

In these discussions of decisions to emend or not to emend, the symbols to designate texts used earlier in the Textual Commentary are again employed:

1Aa	Letters I–IX, New York *Morning Chronicle*, 1802–1803. Copy-text
1Ab	Letters II–IX, New York *Chronicle Express*, 1802–1803
2A	Clayton's New York edition (1824)
1E	Wilson's London edition (1824)
3A	Putnam's New York edition (1866)
T	Twayne edition

The page and line figures are keyed in each case to a word or words in the text to which the discussion or comment refers. A bracket separates the key word or words from the comment that follows.

8.39   had lik'd to've] There is no reason to adopt the reading in later editions, "lik'd to have"; the 1808 London edition of *The Battle of Hexham*, the one consulted, reads "had like t' have."

9.34   tremenduous] The *OED* lists "tremenduous" as an alternate spelling. The word is so spelled in *Salmagundi* (87.23).

13.34   game or two] In view of "or two of cards" in 1Aa (altered to "game of cards" in 1Ab and subsequent editions), it is very likely that Irving's MS read "game or two of cards."

13.37   don't] The omitted apostrophe in 1Aa appears to be a printer's error, and is added in accord with Irving's usual practice. Even in his journals, where he wrote carelessly, he frequently uses the apostrophe, though almost never in "oclock."

13.37   Jack] The comma following "Jack" in 1Aa is not in accord with Irving's practice and is deleted for the reader's comfort.

14.36   which name] This reading in 1Ab clears up the ambiguous reference of "which" in 1Aa.

14.42   what, pray, may] Here the compositor mistakenly enclosed "may" in commas, instead of "pray."

15.10   loudly] In 1Aa the printer set the "u" upside down, so as to make it appear to be an "n." See also 31.3 "malevolent," where the "m" is upside down and looks almost like a "w."

15.20 surmounted] 1Aa "surmounted" rather than "surrounded" (as in 1Ab, 2A, 1E, and 3A) is retained because Jonathan is literally surmounted by "a host of strapping fellows standing with their dirty boots on the seats of the benches" around him. The "little Frenchman" in *Oldstyle* No. VII is similarly discomfited (22.11–16).

17.32–33 Warwick? (said . . . concluded). Their] The accidentals in 1E have been adopted for clarity's sake, but the substantives in 1Aa-b are retained.

19.32 wished] The "I wished" of 1Aa is either an unintentional auctorial error or a printer's gratuitous addition (probably the latter), for it is not Jonathan Oldstyle but the friend whom Jonathan addresses who "wished to know . . . ."

20.16 *bored*] The printer's error in 1Aa-b has been corrected by the editor (T). The revision in 2A and 1E is rejected as lacking auctorial assent.

22.21 chandelier] The normal spelling of this word (as emended in 2A and 1E) has been adopted to bring it into accord with 18.6 and 18.12. Since "chandaleir" is not found in any dictionary and since Irving twice spelled the word "chandelier," this one "chandaleir" seems clearly a miscue, either Irving's or the printer's. It should be noted, however, that in the early journals Irving spells the word "chandalier." *Journals and Notebooks*. Vol. I, ed. Nathalia Wright (Madison, 1969), p. 60.

23.6 terms; I willingly] There is a long enough blank space in 1Aa-b to accommodate the personal pronoun "I" which seems to have been dropped by the printer in 1Aa-b, but was restored in 2A and 1E.

24.16 *friend*:] Although "*friend*" is the last word on the line in 1Aa-b and there is no space for a mark of punctuation, a colon (or comma) is clearly called for.

33.29–35 Our . . . twilight.] This paragraph of ten lines is printed twice in 1Aa, with the following accidental variants in the second version: "*barrel*" becomes "*barrell*" (33.29); "sword. Beside," becomes "sword; besides" (33.31); "aukward" becomes "awkward" (33.32); and "mazzle" becomes "muzzle" (33.32). Since "mazzle" is clearly a printer's error and since 1Ab deletes the first version of this paragraph and prints only the second, the editor has adopted the second and rejected the first.

LIST OF EMENDATIONS

In this list of changes in the copy-text, the symbols to designate texts used earlier (page 56) are again employed:

1Aa	Letters I–IX, New York *Morning Chronicle*, 1802–1803. Copy-text
1Ab	Letters II–IX, New York *Chronicle Express*, 1802–1803
2A	Clayton's New York edition (1824)
1E	Wilson's London edition (1824)
3A	Putnam's New York edition (1866)
T	Twayne edition

These notes identify all emendations of the copy-text. The numbers before each note indicate the page and line. Only running heads and rules added by the printer to separate running heads from the text are omitted from the line count.

The reading to the left of the bracket is the portion of the text under consideration and represents an accepted reading that differs from the copy-text. The source of the reading is identified by symbol after the bracket.

The reading after the semicolon is the rejected reading of the copy-text and any other text in which that reading occurs; if other alternatives are also available, they are recorded following that reading.

The swung (wavy) dash ~ represents the same word or words that appear before the bracket, and is used in recording punctuation variants; the caret ∧ indicates that a mark of punctuation is omitted. T signifies that a decision to emend or not to emend has been made on the authority of the editor of the Twayne edition. Some of these editorial decisions are explained among the Discussions of Adopted Readings, which include decisions to emend as well as some decisions not to emend. Discussion is identified by an asterisk *.

3.10	neckcloth] 3A; neckloth 1Aa
3.29	unmeaning] 3A; umeaning 1Aa
3.34	dragging] 3A; draging 1Aa
5.14	prejudice.] 2A, 1E, 3A; ~∧ 1Aa-b
9.4	slapped] 2A, 3A; slap'd 1Aa-b; slapp'd 1E
10.11	the] 2A, 1E, 3A; the the 1Aa-b

12.37	little] 2A, 1E, 3A; litle 1Aa-b
13.5	remedy] 1Ab, 2A, 1E, 3A; render 1Aa
13.17	And pray, who are these? said he,] 2A, 1E; And, pray, who are these, said he? 1Aa-b; "And pray, who are these?" said he, 3A
*13.34	game or two] T; or two 1Aa; game 1Ab, 2A, 1E, 3A
*13.37	don't] 2A, 1E, 3A; dont 1Aa-b
*13.37	Jack] 2A, 1E; Jack, 1Aa-b, 3A
13.40–41	came; the . . . attraction. Believe] 2A; came, (the . . . attraction) believe 1Aa-b; came: . . . attraction. Believe 1E; came; . . . attraction. "Believe 3A
14.2	in] 1Ab, 2A, 1E, 3A; with 1Aa
*14.36	which name] 1Ab, 2A, 1E, 3A; which 1Aa
*14.42	what, pray, may] 2A, 1E, 3A; what pray, may, 1Aa-b
14.43	can't] 2A, 1E, 3A; cant 1Aa-b
*15.10	loudly] 1Ab, 2A, 1E, 3A; londly 1Aa
17.21	bunch."] 2A, 1E, 3A; bunch. 1Aa-b
*17.32–33	Warwick? (said . . . concluded). Their] 1E; Warwick, (said . . . concluded) their 1Aa-b; Warwick? (said . . . concluded.) Their 2A; Warwick?" said . . . concluded. Their 3A
17.43–18.5	out? . . . audience?"] 2A, 1E, 3A; out?" . . . audience. 1Aa-b
18.17	don't] 2A, 1E, 3A; dont 1Aa-b
18.18	*heavyishness*] 2A, 1E, 3A; *heavyshiness* 1A-b
18.18	don't] 2A, 1E, 3A; dont 1Aa-b
*19.32	wished] 1Ab; I wished 1Aa; wish 2A, 1E
19.35	because] 2A, 1E; becauss 1Aa-b
19.36	scantily] 2A, 1E; scantlyy 1Aa-b
20.1	of] 2A, 1E; off 1Aa-b
*20.16	*bored*] T; *borod* 1Aa-b; bored to death, 2A, 1E
20.42	squinting,] 2A, 1E; ~. 1Aa-b
*22.21	chandelier] 2A, 1E; chandaleir 1Aa-b
*23.6	terms; I willingly] 2A, 1E; terms, willingly 1Aa-b
24.15	decrepitude] 2A, 1E; decripitude 1Aa-b
*24.16	*friend*:] 2A, 1E; ~ₐ 1Aa-b
25.17	still] 2A, 1E; stil 1Aa-b
26.1	morning] 2A, 1E; morcing 1Aa-b
30.8	Trust me,] 2A, 1E; Trust, me, 1Aa-b
30.9	it] 2A, 1E; is 1Aa-b
30.14	ask] 2A, 1E; ask, 1Aa-b
30.35	friend] 2A, 1E; friond 1Aa-b
31.3	'malevolent,'] 1Ab, 2A, 1E; 'ɯalevolent,' 1Aa

31.3	'illiberal,'] 1Ab, 2A, 1E; 'illiberal;' 1Aa
32.21	Quixote] 2A, 1E; Quixotte 1Aa-b
32.22	times!"] 2A, 1E; times! 1Aa-b
33.17	*Stubbs."*] 2A, 1E; *Stubbs*‸" 1Aa-b
33.18	off] 2A, 1E; of 1Aa-b
*33.29–35	Our . . . twilight.] 1Ab, 2A, 1E, 3A; Our . . . twilight. Our . . . twilight. 1Aa

LIST OF REJECTED SUBSTANTIVES

In this list, which provides a historical record of substantive variants that were not adopted for the Twayne text, the following symbols are used to designate the sources of the readings:

1Aa	Letters I–IX, New York *Morning Chronicle*, 1802–1803. Copy-text
1Ab	Letters II–IX, New York *Chronicle Express*, 1802–1803
2A	Clayton's New York edition (1824)
1E	Wilson's London edition (1824)
3A	Putnam's New York edition (1866)

3.25	studied] 1Aa; studious 3A
5.15	past] 1Aa-b; the past 2A, 1E, 3A
5.33	formal] 1Aa-b; awful 2A, 1E, 3A
6.38	of from] 1Aa-b; from 2A, 1E, 3A
°8.39	had lik'd to've] 1Aa-b; lik'd to have 2A, 1E, 3A
9.8	frighted] 1Aa-b; frightened 2A, 1E, 3A
9.27	fierce band of] 1Aa-b; band of fierce 2A, 1E, 3A
9.32	sang] 1Aa-b; sung 2A, 1E, 3A
°9.34	tremenduous] 1Aa-b; tremendous 2A, 1E, 3A
9.35	descended] 1Aa-b; fell 2A, 1E, 3A
9.38	through] 1Aa-b; for 2A, 1E, 3A
10.27	how] 1Aa-b; to know how 2A, 1E, 3A
10.33–34	cruising about] 1Aa-b; cruising 2A, 1E, 3A
12.27	in] 1Aa-b; a 2A, 1E, 3A
13.8	mount] 1Aa-b; mount our 2A, 1E, 3A
13.24	or] 1Aa-b; and 2A, 1E, 3A
13.27	a play, or] 1Aa-b; the play, nor 2A, 1E, 3A
13.29	upon] 1Aa-b; on 2A, 1E, 3A
13.37	said] 1Aa-b; says 2A, 1E, 3A
14.4	fopperies] 1Aa-b; follies 2A, 1E, 3A
14.14	Those] 1Aa-b; These 2A, 1E, 3A
14.39	country] 1Aa-b; *omitted* 2A, 1E, 3A
15.11	How] 1Aa-b, 2A, 1E; Pooh 3A
°15.20	surmounted] 1Aa; surrounded 1Ab, 2A, 1E, 3A
15.23	friends] 1Aa-b; friend 2A, 1E, 3A

16.29	incident] 1Aa-b; thing 2A, 1E, 3A
17.16	evolution] 1Aa-b; evolutions 2A, 1E, 3A
17.20	in a body] 1Aa-b; *omitted* 2A, 1E, 3A
17.29–30	figuring with] 1Aa-b; figures in 2A, 1E, 3A
17.36	scene] 1Aa-b; scenes 2A, 1E, 3A
18.3	on] 1Aa-b; in 2A, 1E, 3A
18.8	on] 1Aa-b; upon 2A, 1E, 3A
18.25	anti-chamber] 1Aa-b; ante-chamber 2A, 1E, 3A
19.32	were] 1Aa-b; are 2A, 1E
19.36	illumined] 1Aa-b; illuminated 2A, 1E
20.16	these] 1Aa-b; *omitted* 2A, 1E
21.3	obtain] 1Aa-b; attain 2A, 1E
22.6	me in] 1Aa-b; for me in 2A, 1E
22.13	arms] 1Aa-b; his arms 2A, 1E
22.18	round] 1Aa-b; around 2A, 1E
22.19	little] 1Aa-b; *omitted* 2A, 1E
22.22	heaven] 1Aa-b; heavens 2A, 1E
22.30	round] 1Aa-b; around 2A, 1E
23.23	as] 1Aa-b; with 2A, 1E
23.33	generally] 1Aa-b; continually 2A, 1E
23.39	be assured that] 1Aa-b; *omitted* 2A, 1E
25.16	on] 1Aa-b; to 2A, 1E
25.30	jeering] 1Aa-b; jarring 2A, 1E
27.30	a] 1Aa-b; *omitted* 2A, 1E
28.29	him] 1Aa-b; *omitted* 2A, 1E
28.43	into] 1Aa-b; in 2A, 1E
30.20	that 1Aa-b; this 2A, 1E
30.32	warnings] 1Aa-b; warning 2A, 1E
32.17	to] 1Aa-b; on 2A, 1E
32.24–25	their glowing descriptions] 1Aa-b; the glowing description 2A, 1E

LIST OF COMPOUND WORDS
HYPHENATED
AT END OF LINE

List I includes all compound and possible compound words that are hyphenated at the end of the line in the copy-text. In deciding whether to retain the hyphen or to print the word as a single-word compound (without the hyphen), the editor has made his decision on the use of each compound word elsewhere in the copy-text. Each word is listed in its editorially accepted form after the page and line numbers of its appearance in the T text.

List II presents all compounds, or possible compounds, that are hyphenated or separated as two words at the end of the line in the T text. They are listed in the form in which they would have appeared in the T text had they come in mid-line.

LIST I

16.14	coffee-house
17.39	after-piece

LIST II

6.3	knee-buckles
12.19	thunderbolts
13.40	*countryman*
24.32	*Jack-pudding*
28.32	*hard-earned*
31.5	spindle-shanked

SALMAGUNDI

SALMAGUNDI;

OR, THE
WHIM-WHAMS AND OPINIONS
OF
LAUNCELOT LANGSTAFF, ESQ.
AND OTHERS.

In hoc est hoax, cum quiz et jokesez,
Et smokem, toastem, roastem folkesez,
Fee, faw, fum.   *Psalmanazar.*

With baked, and broil'd, and stew'd, and toasted,
And fried, and boil'd, and smoak'd, and roasted,
We treat the town.

NO. I]   *Saturday, January* 24, 1807.

AS every body knows, or ought to know, what a Salmagundi is, we shall spare ourselves the trouble of an explanation—besides, we despise trouble as we do every thing that is low and mean, and hold the man who would incur it unnecessarily, as an object worthy our highest pity and contempt. Neither will we puzzle our heads to give an account of ourselves, for two reasons; first, because it is nobody's business; secondly, because if it was, we do not hold ourselves bound to attend to any body's business but our own, and even *that* we take the liberty of neglecting when it suits our inclination. To these we might add a third, that very few men *can* give a tolerable account of themselves, let them try ever so hard; but this reason we candidly avow, would not hold good with ourselves.

There are, however, two or three pieces of information which we bestow gratis on the public, chiefly because it suits our own pleasure and convenience that they should be known, and partly because we do not wish that there should be any ill will between us at the commencement of our acquaintance.

Our intention is simply to instruct the young, reform the old, correct the town and castigate the age; this is an arduous task, and therefore we undertake it with confidence. We intend for this purpose to present a striking picture of the town; and as every body is anxious to see his own phiz on canvas, however stupid or ugly it may be, we have no doubt but that the whole town will flock to our exhibition. Our picture will necessarily include a vast variety of figures, and should any gentleman or lady, be displeased with the inveterate truth of their likenesses, they may ease their spleen by laughing at those of their neighbors—this being what *we* understand by POETICAL JUSTICE.

Like all true and able editors, we consider ourselves infallible, and therefore with the customary diffidence of our brethren of the quill, we shall take the liberty of interfering in all matters either of a public or private nature. We are critics, amateurs, dillitanti, and cognoscenti; and as we know "by the pricking of our thumbs," that every opinion which we may advance in either of those characters will be correct, we are determined, though it may be questioned, contradicted, or even controverted, yet it shall never be revoked.

We beg the public particularly to understand, that we solicit no patronage. We are determined on the contrary, that the patronage shall be entirely on our side. We have nothing to do with the pecuniary concerns of the paper, its success will yield us neither pride nor profit— nor will its failure occasion to us either loss or mortification. We advise the public therefore, to purchase our numbers merely for their own sakes—if they do not, let them settle the affair with their consciences and posterity.

To conclude, we invite all editors of newspapers and literary journals, to praise us heartily in advance, as we assure them that we intend to deserve their praises. To our next door neighbor "TOWN," we hold out a hand of amity, declaring to him that, after ours, his paper will stand the best chance for immortality. We proffer an exchange of civilities; he shall furnish us with notices of epic poems and tobacco—and we in return will enrich him with original speculations on all manner of subjects: together with "the rummaging of my grandfather's mahogany chest of drawers," "the life and amours of mine uncle John," "anecdotes of the cockloft family," and learned quotations from that unheard of writer of folios, *Linkum Fidelius.*

PUBLISHER'S NOTICE.

This work will be published and sold by D. Longworth. It will be printed on hot-prest vellum paper, as that is held in highest estimation for buckling up young ladies' hair—a purpose to which similar works are usually appropriated: it will be a small neat duodecimo size, so that when enough numbers are written, it may form a volume sufficiently portable to be carried in old ladies' pockets and young ladies' work bags.

LAUNCELOT LANGSTAFF, Esq.
FROM THE ORIGINAL DRAWING.

Woodcut by Alexander Anderson (1775–1870), the first American wood engraver, for the second American edition of *Salmagundi* (D. Longworth: New York. 1814).

As the above work will not come out at stated periods, notice will be given when another number will be published. The price will depend on the size of the number, and must be paid on its delivery. The publisher professes the same sublime contempt for money as his authors. The liberal patronage bestowed by his discerning fellow-citizens on various works of taste which he has published, has left him no *inclination* to ask for further favors at their hands, and he publishes this work in the mere hope of requiting their bounty.

It was not originally the intention of the authors to insert the above address in the work; but, unwilling that a *morceau* so precious should be lost to posterity, they have been induced to alter their minds. This will account for any repetition of idea that may appear in the introductory essay.

FROM THE ELBOW-CHAIR OF

LAUNCELOT LANGSTAFF, ESQ.

We were a considerable time in deciding whether we should be at the pains of introducing ourselves to the public. As we care for nobody, and as we are not yet at the bar, we do not feel bound to hold up our hands and answer to our names.

Willing, however, to gain at once that frank, confidential footing, which we are certain of ultimately possessing in this, doubtless, "best of all possible cities;" and, anxious to spare its worthy inhabitants the trouble of making a thousand *wise* conjectures, not one of which would be worth a "tobacco-stopper;" we have thought it in some degree a necessary exertion of charitable condescension to furnish them with a slight clue to the truth.

Before we proceed further, however, we advise every body, man, woman, and child, that can read, or get any friend to read for them, to purchase this paper:—not that we write for money; for, in common with all philosophical wiseacres, from Solomon downwards, we hold it in supreme contempt. The public are welcome to buy this work, or not, just as they choose. If it be purchased freely, so much the better for the public, and the publisher—we gain not a stiver. If it be not purchased we give fair warning, we shall burn all our essays, critiques, and epigrams, in one promiscuous blaze; and, like the books of the sybils, and the alexandrian library, they will be lost forever to posterity. For the sake, therefore, of our publisher, for the sake of the Public, and for the sake of the Public's children, to the nineteenth generation, we advise them to purchase our paper. We beg the respectable old matrons of this city, not to be alarmed at the appearance we make;—we are none of those outlandish geniuses who swarm in New-York, who live by their wits, or rather by the little wit of their neighbors; and who spoil the genuine honest american tastes of their daughters, with french slops and friccazeed sentiment.

We have said we do not write for money—neither do we write for fame;—we know too well the variable nature of public opinion, to build our hopes upon it—we *care* not what the public think of us, and we suspect before we reach the tenth number, they will not *know* what to think of us. In two words—we write for no other earthly purpose but to please ourselves—and this we shall be sure of doing; for we are all three of us determined beforehand to be pleased with what we write. If, in the course of this work, we edify, and instruct, and amuse the public, so much the better for the public;—but we frankly acknowledge that so soon as we get tired of reading our own works, we shall discontinue them, without the least remorse, whatever the public may think of it.—While we continue to go on, we will go on merrily—if we moralize, it shall be but seldom; and, on all occasions, we shall be more solicitous to make our readers laugh than cry; for we are laughing philosophers, and clearly of opinion, that wisdom, true wisdom, is a plump, jolly dame, who sits in her arm chair, laughs right merrily at the farce of life—and takes the world as it goes.

We intend particularly to notice the conduct of the fashionable world—nor in this shall we be governed by that carping spirit with which narrow-minded book-worm cynics squint at the little extravagancies of the ton; but with that liberal toleration which actuates every man of fashion.—While we keep a more than Cerberus watch over the guardian rules of female delicacy and decorum—we shall not discourage any little sprightliness of demeanor or innocent vivacity of character. Before we advance one line further, we must let it be understood as our firm opinion, void of all prejudice or partiality, that the ladies of New-York are the fairest, the finest, the most accomplished, the most bewitching, the most ineffable beings, that walk, creep, crawl, swim, fly, float, or vegetate in any or all of the four elements; and that they only want to be cured of certain whims, eccentricities, and unseemly conceits, by our superintending cares, to render them absolutely perfect. They will, therefore, receive a large portion of those attentions directed to the fashionable world;—nor will the gentlemen, who *doze* away their time in the circles of the *haut-ton*, escape our currying. We mean those stupid fellows, who sit stock-still upon their chairs, without saying a word, and then complain how damned stupid it was, at miss ———'s party.

This department will be under the peculiar direction and control of ANTHONY EVERGREEN, gent. to whom all communications on this subject are to be addressed. This gentleman, by being experienced in the routine

of balls, tea-parties, and assemblies, is eminently qualified for the task
he has undertaken. He is a kind of patriarch in the fashionable world,
and has seen generation after generation pass away into the silent tomb
of matrimony, while he remains unchangeably the same. He can recount
the amours and courtships of the fathers, mothers, uncles and aunts,
and even grandames, of all the belles of the present day, provided their
pedigrees extend so far back, without being lost in obscurity. As, however, treating of pedigrees is rather an ungrateful task, in this city,
and as we mean to be perfectly good-natured, he has promised to be
cautious in this particular. He recollects perfectly the time when young
ladies use to go sleigh-riding, at night, without their mammas, or grand-
mammas, in short, without being matronized at all, and can relate a
thousand pleasant stories about Kissing-bridge. He likewise remembers
the time when ladies paid tea-visits at three in the afternoon, and
returned before dark, to see that the house was shut up and the servants
on duty. He has often played cricket in the orchard, in the rear of old
Vauxhall, and remembers when the Bull's-head was quite out of town.
Though he has slowly and gradually given into modern fashions, and
still flourishes in the *beaumonde,* yet he seems a little prejudiced in
favor of the dress and manners of the *old school,* and his chief commen-
dation of a new mode is, "that is the same good old fashion we had before the war." It has cost us much trouble to make him confess that a cotillion is superior to a minuet, or an unadorned crop to a pig-tail and
powder. Custom and fashion have, however, had more effect on him
than all our lectures, and he tempers so happily the grave and cere-
monious gallantry of the old school with the "hail fellow" familiarity
of the new, that we trust, on a little acquaintance, and making allowance for his old-fashioned prejudices, he will become a very considerable favorite with our readers;—if not, the worse for themselves, as
they will have to endure his company.

In the territory of criticism, WILLIAM WIZARD, esq. has undertaken
to preside, and though we may all dabble in it a little by turns, yet we
have willingly ceded to him all discretionary powers in this respect.
Though Will has not had the advantage of an education at Oxford, or
Cambridge, or even at Edinburgh, or Aberdeen, and though he is but
little versed in hebrew, yet we have no doubt he will be found fully
competent to the undertaking. He has improved his taste by a long
residence abroad, particularly at Canton, Calcutta, and the gay and
polished court of Hayti. He has also had an opportunity of seeing the
best singing girls, and tragedians of China, and is a great connoisseur
in mandarine dresses, and porcelaine. He is likewise promised the assistance of a gentleman, lately from London, who was born and bred
in that centre of science and *bon-gout,* the vicinity of Fleet-market,

where he has been edified man and boy, these six-and-twenty years, with the harmonious jingle of bow-bells. His taste therefore has attain'd to such an exquisite pitch of refinement, that there are few exhibitions of any kind which do not put him in a fever. He has assured Will, that if mr. COOPER emphasises *"and"* instead of *"but"*—or mrs. OLDMIXON pins her kerchief a hairs breadth awry—or mrs. DARLEY offers to dare to look less than the "daughter of a senator of Venice"—the standard of a senator's daughter being exactly six feet—they shall all hear of it in good time. We have, however, advised WILL WIZARD, to keep his friend in check, lest by opening the eyes of the public to the wretchedness of the actors by whom they have hitherto been entertained, he might cut off one source of amusement from our fellow-citizens. We hereby give notice that we have taken the whole corps, from the manager in his mantle of gorgeous copper-lace, to honest *John*, in his green coat and black breeches, under our wing, and woe be unto him who injures a hair of their heads. As we have no design against the patience of our fellow-citizens, we shall not *dose* them with copious draughts of theatrical criticism; we well know that they have already been well physicked with them of late: our theatrics shall take up but a small part of our paper; nor shall they be altogether confined to the stage, but extend from time to time, to those incorrigible offenders against the peace of society, the stage-critics; who not unfrequently create the fault they find, in order to yield an opening for their witticisms—censure an actor for a gesture he never made, or an emphasis he never gave; and, in their attempts to show off *new readings,* make the sweet swan of Avon cackle like a goose. If any one shall feel himself offended by our remarks, let him attack us in return—we shall not wince from the combat. If his passes are successful, we will be the first to cry out a hit! a hit! and we doubt not we shall frequently lay ourselves open to the weapons of our assailants. But let them have a care, how they run a tilting with us—they have to deal with stubborn foes, who can bear a world of pummeling; we will be relentless in our vengeance, and will fight "till from our bones the flesh be hackt."

What other subjects we shall include in the range of our observations, we have not determined, or rather we shall not trouble ourselves to detail. The public have already more information concerning us than we intended to impart. We owe them no favors, neither do we ask any. We again advise them for their own sakes, to read our papers when they come out. We recommend to all mothers to purchase them for their daughters, who will be taught the true line of propriety, and the most adviseable method of managing their beaux. We advise all daughters to purchase them for the sake of their mothers, who shall be initiated into the arcana of the bon-ton, and cured of all those rusty old notions which they acquired during the last century: parents shall be taught how to govern their children, girls how to get husbands, and old maids how to do without them.

As we do not measure our wits by the yard or the bushel, and as they do not flow periodically nor constantly, we shall not restrict our paper as to size, or the time of its appearance. It will be published whenever we have sufficient matter to constitute a number, and the size of the number shall depend on the stock in hand. This will best suit our negligent habits, and leave us that full liberty and independence which is the joy and pride of our souls. As we have before hinted, that we do not concern ourselves about the pecuniary matters of our paper, we leave its price to be regulated by our publisher; only recommending him for his own interest, and the honor of his authors, not to sell their invaluable productions too cheap.

Is there any one who wishes to know more about us?—let him read SALMAGUNDI, and grow wise apace. Thus much we will say—there are three of us, "Bardolph, Peto, and I; all townsmen good and true"—many a time and oft have we three amused the town, without its knowing to whom it was indebted; and many a time have we seen the midnight lamp twinkle faintly on our studious phizes, and heard the morning salutation of "past three o'clock," before we sought our pillows. The result of these midnight studies is now offered to the public; and little as we care for the opinion of this exceedingly stupid world, we shall take care, as far as lies in our careless natures, to fulfil the promises made in this introduction;—if we do not, we shall have so many examples to justify us, that we feel little solicitude on that account.

Theatrics.
containing the quintessence of modern criticism.
BY WILLIAM WIZARD, ESQ.

MACBETH was performed to a very crowded house, and much to *our* satisfaction. As, however, our neighbor Town has been very voluminous already in his criticisms on this play, we shall make but few remarks. Having never seen KEMBLE in this character, we are absolutely at a loss to say whether MR. COOPER performed it well or not. We think, however, that there was an error in his *costume*, as the learned Linkum Fidelius is of opinion, that in the time of Macbeth the scots did not wear sandals, but wooden shoes. Macbeth also was noted for wearing his jacket open, that he might play the scotch fiddle more conveniently—that being an hereditary accomplishment in the Glamis family.

We have seen this character performed in China, by the celebrated *Chow-Chow*, the Roscius of that great empire, who in the dagger scene always electrified the audience, by blowing his nose like a trumpet. Chow-Chow, in compliance with the opinion of the sage Linkum Fidelius, performed Macbeth in wooden shoes. This gave him an opportunity of producing great effect, for on first seeing the air-drawn dagger, he always cut a prodigious high caper, and kicked his shoes into the pit at the heads of the critics, whereupon the audience were marvelously delighted, flourished their hands, and stroaked their whiskers three times, and the matter was carefully recorded in the next number of a paper called the *flim flam* (*english*-town)

We were much pleased with MRS. VILLIERS, in lady MACBETH; but we think she would have given greater effect to the night-scene, if, instead of holding the candle in her hand, or setting it down on the table (which is sagaciously censured by neighbor Town) she had stuck it in her night-cap. This would have been extremely picturesque, and would have marked more strongly the derangement of her mind.

Mrs. Villiers, however, is not by any means large enough for the character; lady Macbeth having been, in our opinion, a woman of extraordinary size, and of the race of the giants, notwithstanding what she says of her "little hand," which being said in her sleep, passes for nothing. We should be happy to see this character in the hands of the lady who played *Glumdalca*, queen of the giants, in Tom Thumb; she is exactly of imperial dimensions, and, provided she is well shaved, of a most interesting physiognomy: as she appears likewise to be a lady of some nerve, I dare engage she will read a letter about witches vanishing in air, and such *common occurences*, without being unnaturally surprised, to the annoyance of honest "Town."

We are happy to observe that Mr. Cooper profits by the instructions of friend Town, and does not dip the daggers in blood so deep as formerly, by a matter of an inch or two. This was a violent outrage upon our immortal bard. We rather differ with Mr. Town in his *reading* of the words "this is a *sorry sight*." We are of opinion the force of the sentence should be thrown on the word *sight*, because Macbeth, having been shortly before most confoundedly humbugged with an aerial dagger, was in doubts whether the daggers actually in his hands, were real, or whether they were not mere shadows, or, as the old english *may* have termed it, **syghtes**. (this at any rate will establish our skill in *new readings*). Though we differ in this respect from our neighbor Town, yet we heartily agree with him in censuring Mr. Cooper for omitting that passage so remarkable for "beauty of imagery, &c." beginning with "and pity like a naked new-born babe, &c." It is one of those passages of Shakspeare, which should always be retained, for the purpose of showing how sometimes that great poet could talk like a buzzard; or, to speak more plainly, like the famous mad poet, Nat Lee.

As it is the first duty of a friend to advise—and as we profess and do actually feel a friendship for honest "Town," we warn him never, in his criticisms, to meddle with a lady's "petticoats," or to quote Nick Bottom. In the first instance, he may "catch a tartar;" and in the second, the asses head may rise up in judgment against him, and when it is once afloat, there is no knowing where some unlucky hand may place it. We would not, for all the money in our pockets, see Town flourishing his critical quill under the auspices of an asses head, like the great Franklin in his *Monterio Cap*.

NEW-YORK ASSEMBLY.
BY ANTHONY EVERGREEN, GENT.

The Assemblies this year have gained a great accession of beauty. Several brilliant stars have arisen from the east and from the north, to brighten the firmament of fashion; among the number, I have discovered *another planet*, which rivals even Venus in lustre, and I claim equal honor with Herschell for my discovery. I shall take some future opportunity to describe this planet, and the numerous satellites which revolve around it.

At the last assembly the company began to make some show about *eight*, but the most fashionable delayed their appearance until about *nine*—nine being the number of the *muses*, and therefore the best possible hour for beginning to exhibit the *graces*. (This is meant for a pretty play upon words, and I assure my readers that I think it very tolerable).

Poor WILL HONEYCOMB, whose memory I hold in special consideration, even with his half century of experience, would have been puzzled to point out the humor of a lady by her prevailing colors, for the "rival queens" of fashion, Mrs. TOOLE and madame BOUCHARD, appeared to have exhausted their wonderful inventions in the different disposition, variation and combination of tints and shades. The *philosopher* who maintained that black was white, and that *of course* there was no such color as white, might have given some color to his theory on this occasion, by the absence of poor forsaken white muslin. I was, however, much pleased to see that red maintains its ground against all other colors, because red is the color of mr. Jefferson's *****, Tom Paine's nose, and my slippers.

Let the grumbling smellfungi of this world, who cultivate taste among books, cobwebs and spiders, rail at the extravagance of the age; for my part I was delighted with the magic of the scene, and as the ladies tripped through the mazes of the dance, sparkling, and glowing and dazzling, I, like the honest chinese, thanked them heartily for the jewels

and finery, with which they loaded themselves, merely for the entertainment of bystanders—and blessed my stars that I was a bachelor.

The gentlemen were considerably numerous, and being as usual equipt
in their appropriate *black uniforms*, constituted a sable regiment, which
contributed not a little to the brilliant gaiety of the ball-room. I must
confess I am indebted for this remark to our friend the cockney, mr.
'SBIDLIKENS-FLASH, or *'Sbidlikens*, as he is called for shortness. He is a
fellow of infinite verbosity—stands in high favor with himself,—and
like Caleb Quotem, is "up to every thing." I remember when a comfortable plump-looking citizen led into the room a fair damsel, who
looked for all the world like the personification of a rainbow:—'Sbidlikens
observed, that it reminded him of a fable, which he had read somewhere, of the marriage of an honest pains-taking snail, who had once
walked six feet in an hour for a wager, to a butterfly, whom he used
to gallant by the elbow, with the aid of much puffing and exertion. On
being called upon to tell where he had come across this story, 'Sbidlikens
absolutely refused to answer.

It would but be repeating an old story, to say that the ladies of New-
York dance well;—and well may they, since they learn it scientifically,
and begin their lessons before they have quit their swaddling clothes.
The immortal DUPORT has usurped despotic sway over all the female
heads and heels in this city;—hornbooks, primers and pianos are neglected, to attend to his positions; and poor CHILTON, with his pots and
kettles, and chemical crockery, finds him a more potent enemy than the
whole collective force of the "North-river society." 'Sbidlikens insists
that this dancing mania will inevitably continue as long as a dancing-
master will charge the fashionable price of *five-and-twenty dollars* a
quarter, and all the other accomplishments are so vulgar as to be attain-
able at "half the money"—but I put no faith in 'Sbidlikens' candor in this
particular. Among his infinitude of endowments, he is but a poor
proficient in dancing; and though he often flounders through a cotillion,
yet he never cut a pigeon-wing in his life.

In my mind, there's no position more positive and unexceptionable
than that most frenchmen, dead or alive, are born dancers. I came
pounce upon this discovery at the assembly, and I immediately noted it
down in my register of indisputable facts—the public shall know all
about it. As I never dance cotillions, holding them to be monstrous
distortors of the human frame, and tantamount in their operations, to
being broken and dislocated on the wheel, I generally take occasion,
while they are going on, to make my remarks on the company. In the
course of these observations, I was struck with the energy and eloquence
of sundry limbs, which seemed to be flourishing about, without appertaining to any body. After much investigation and difficulty, I at length

"Set 'em lively".

WALTZ DANCE.

Woodcut by Alexander Anderson (1775–1870), the first American wood engraver, for the second American edition of *Salmagundi* (D. Longworth: New York, 1814).

traced them to their respective owners, whom I found to be all french-men—to a man. Art may have meddled somewhat in these affairs, but Nature certainly did more. I have since been considerably employed in calculations on this subject, and by the most accurate computation I have determined, that a frenchman passes at least three-fifths of his time between the heavens and the earth, and partakes eminently of the nature of a gossamer or soap-bubble. One of these jack-o-lanthorn heroes, in taking a *figure*, which neither Euclid, nor Pythagoras himself, could demonstrate, unfortunately wound himself—I mean his foot—his better part—into a lady's cobweb muslin robe; but perceiving it at the instant, he set himself a spinning the other way, like a top; unravelled his step, without omitting one angle or curve, and extricated himself, without breaking a thread of the lady's dress! he then sprung up like a sturgeon, crossed his feet four times, and finished this wonderful evolu-tion by quivering his left leg, as a cat does her paw, when she has accidentally dipped it in water. No man "of woman born," who was not a frenchman, or a mountebank, could have done the like.

Among the new faces, I remarked a blooming nymph, who has brought a fresh supply of roses from the country to adorn the wreath of beauty, where lilies too much predominate. As I wish well to every sweet face under heaven, I sincerely hope her roses may survive the frosts and dissipations of winter; and lose nothing by a comparison with the loveliest offerings of the spring. 'Sbidlikens, to whom I made similar remarks, assured me that they were very just, and very prettily exprest, and that the lady in question was a prodigious fine piece of *flesh and blood*. Now could I find it in my heart to baste these cocknies like their own roast-beef—they can make no distinction between a fine woman and a fine horse.

I would praise the sylph-like grace with which another young lady acquitted herself in the dance, but that she excels in far more valuable accomplishments. Who praises the rose for its beauty, even though it *is* beautiful?

The company retired at the customary hour to the supper-room, where the tables were laid out with their *usual* splendor and profusion. My friend 'Sbidlikens, with the native forethought of a cockney, had care-fully stowed his pocket with cheese and crackers, that he might not be tempted again to venture his limbs in the crowd of hungry fair ones who throng the supper-room door:—his precaution was unnecessary, for the company entered the room with surprising order and decorum. No gowns were torn—no ladies fainted—no noses bled—nor was there any need of the interference of either managers or peace officers.

SALMAGUNDI NO. II

NO. II]   *Wednesday, February 4, 1807.*

FROM THE ELBOW-CHAIR OF
LAUNCELOT LANGSTAFF, ESQ.

IN the conduct of an epic poem, it has been the custom from time immemorial, for the poet occasionally to introduce his reader to an intimate acquaintance with the heroes of his story, by showing him into their tents, and giving him an opportunity of observing them in their night-gown and slippers. However, I despise the servile genius that would descend to follow a precedent, though furnished by Homer himself, and consider him as on a par with the cart that follows at the heels of the horse, without ever taking the lead; yet at the present moment my whim is opposed to my opinion, and whenever this is the case, my opinion generally surrenders at discretion. I am determined, therefore, to give the town a peep into our divan; and I shall repeat it as often as I please, to show that I intend to be sociable.

The other night, Will Wizard and Evergeen called upon me, to pass away a few hours in social chat, and hold a kind of council of war. To give a zest to our evening, I uncorked a bottle of London particular, which has grown old with myself, and which never fails to excite a smile in the countenances of my old cronies, to whom alone it is devoted. After some little time the conversation turned on the effect produced by our first number: every one had his budget of information, and I assure my readers that we laughed most unceremoniously at their expense;—they will excuse us for our merriment—tis a way we've got. Evergreen, who is equally a favorite and companion of young and old, was particularly satisfactory in his details, and it was highly amusing to hear how different characters were tickled with different passages. The old folks were delighted to find there was a bias in our junto towards the "gold old times;" and he particularly noticed a worthy old gentleman of his acquaintance, who had been somewhat a beau in his day, whose eyes brightened at the bare mention of Kissing-bridge. It recalled to his recollection several of his youthful exploits, at that celebrated pass, on which he seemed to dwell with great pleasure and self-complacency:—he hoped, he said, that the bridge might be preserved for the benefit of posterity, and as a monument of the gallantry of their grandfathers; and even hinted at the expediency of erecting a toll gate there, to collect the forfeits of the ladies. But the most flattering testimony of approbation, which our work has received, was from an old lady who never laughed but once in her life, and that was at the conclusion of the last war. She was detected by friend Anthony in the very fact of laughing most obstreperously at the description of the little dancing frenchman. Now it glads my very heart to find our effusions have such a pleasing effect. I venerate the aged, and joy whenever it is in my power to scatter a few flowers in their path.

The young people were particularly interested in the account of the assembly. There was some difference of opinion respecting the *new planet,* and the blooming nymph from the country; but as to the compliment paid to the fascinating little sylph who danced so gracefully— every lady modestly took that to herself.

Evergreen mentioned also that the young ladies were extremely anxious to learn the true mode of managing their beaux, and miss DIANA WEARWELL, who is as chaste as an icicle, has seen a few superfluous winters pass over her head, and boasts of having slain her thousands, wished to know how old maids were to do without husbands—not that she was very curious about the matter, she "only asked for information." Several ladies expressed their earnest desire that we would not spare those *wooden* gentlemen, who perform the parts of *mutes,* or stalking horses, in their drawing rooms; and their mothers were equally anxious that we would show no quarter to those lads of spirit, who now and then *cut* their bottles to enliven a tea-party with the humors of the dinner table.

Will Wizard was not a little chagrined at having been mistaken for a gentleman, "who is no more like me," said Will, "than I like Hercules."—"I was well assured," continued Will, "that as our characters were drawn from nature, the originals would be found in every society. And so it has happened—every little circle has its 'Sbidlikens; and the cockney, intended merely as the representative of his *species,* has dwindled into an insignificant individual, who having recognized his own likeness, has foolishly appropriated to himself a picture for which he never sat. Such, too, has been the case with DING-DONG, who has kindly undertaken to be my representative—not that I care much about the matter, for it must be acknowledged that the animal is a good-natured animal enough— and what is more, a fashionable animal—and this is saying more than to call him a *conjuror.* But, I am much mistaken, if he can claim any affinity to the *Wizard* family.—Surely every body knows Ding-dong, the gentle Ding-dong, who pervades all space, who is here and there and every where; no tea-party can be complete without Ding-dong—and his appearance is sure to occasion a smile. Ding-dong has been the occasion of much wit in his day; I have even seen many puny whipsters attempt to be dull at his expense, who were as much inferior to him as the gad-fly is to the ox, that he buzzes about. Does any witling want to distress the company with a miserable pun?—nobody's name presents sooner than Ding-dong's; and it has been played upon with equal skill and equal entertainment to the bye-standers as Trinity-bells. Ding-dong is profoundly devoted to the ladies, and highly entitled to their regard; for I know no man who makes a better bow, or talks less to the purpose than Ding-dong. Ding-dong has acquired a prodigious fund of knowledge, by reading Dilworth when a boy; and the other day, on being asked who was the author of Macbeth, answered, without the least hesitation—Shakspeare!—Ding-dong has a quotation for every day of the year, and every hour of the day, and every minute of the hour, but he often commits petty larcenies on the poets—plucks the grey hairs of old Chaucer's head, and claps them on the chin of Pope; and filches Johnson's wig, to cover the bald pate of Homer;—but his blunders pass undetected by one half of his hearers. Ding-dong it is true, though he has long wrangled at our bar, cannot boast much of his legal knowledge, nor does his forensic eloquence entitle him to rank with a Cicero or a Demosthenes; but bating his professional deficiencies, he is a man of most delectable discourse, and can hold forth for an hour upon the color of a ribbon or the construction of a workbag. Ding-dong is now in his fortieth year, or perhaps a little more—rivals all the little beaux in town, in his attentions to the ladies—is in a state of rapid improvement; and there is no doubt but that by the time he arrives at years of discretion, he will be a very accomplished agreeable young fellow."—I advise all clever, good-for-nothing, "learned and authentic" gentlemen, to take care how they *wear this cap,* however well it fits; and to bear in mind, that our characters are not individuals, but species: if after this warning, any person chooses to represent mr. Ding-dong, the sin is at his own door—we wash our hands of it.

We all sympathised with Wizard, that he should be mistaken for a person so very different; and I hereby assure my readers, that William Wizard is no other person in the whole world *but* William Wizard; so I beg I may hear no more conjectures on the subject. Will, is in fact, a wiseacre by inheritance. The Wizard family has long been celebrated for knowing more than their neighbors, particularly concerning their neighbors' affairs. They were antiently called Josselin, but Will's great uncle, by the father's side, having been accidentally burnt for a *witch* in Connecticut, in consequence of blowing up his own house in a philosophical experiment, the family, in order to perpetuate the recollection of this memorable circumstance, assumed the name and arms of Wizard, and have borne them ever since.

In the course of my customary morning's walk, I stopped in at a book-store, which is noted for being the favorite haunt of a number of literati, some of whom rank high in the opinion of the world, and others rank equally high in their own. Here I found a knot of queer fellows listening to one of their company, who was reading our paper; I particularly noticed mr. ICHABOD FUNGUS among the number.

Fungus is one of those fidgeting, meddling quidnuncs, with which this unhappy city is pestered: one of your "Q in a corner fellows," who speaks volumes with a wink—conveys most portentous information, by laying his finger beside his nose,—and is always smelling a rat in the most trifling occurrence. He listened to our work with the most frigid gravity—every now and then gave a mysterious shrug—a *humph*—or a screw of the mouth; and on being asked his opinion at the conclusion, said, he did not know what to think of it;—he hoped it did not mean any thing against the Government—that no lurking treason was couched in all this talk. These were dangerous times—times of plot and conspiracy;—he did not at all like those stars after mr. Jefferson's name, they had an air of concealment. DICK PADDLE, who was one of the group, undertook our cause. Dick is known to the world, as being a most knowing genius, who can see as far as any body—into a millstone; maintains, in the teeth of all argument, that a spade *is* a spade; and will labor a good half hour by St. Paul's clock, to establish a self-evident fact. Dick assured old Fungus, that those stars merely stood for mr. Jefferson's red *what-d'ye-callums*; and that so far from a conspiracy against their peace and prosperity, the authors, whom he knew very well, were only expressing their high respect for them. The old man shook his head, shrugged his shoulders, gave a mysterious lord Burleigh nod, said he hoped it might be so; but he was by no means satisfied with this attack upon the president's breeches, as "thereby *hangs a tale.*"

MR. WILSON'S CONCERT.

BY ANTHONY EVERGREEN, GENT.

In my register of indisputable facts I have noted it conspicuously, that all modern music is but the mere dregs and draining of the ancient, and that all the spirit and vigor of harmony has entirely evaporated in the lapse of ages. Oh! for the chant of the naiades, and the dryades, the shell of the tritons, and the sweet warblings of the mermaids of ancient days! where now shall we seek the Amphion, who built walls with a turn of his hurdy-gurdy, the Orpheus who made stones to whistle about his ears, and trees hop in a country dance, by the mere quavering of his fiddle-stick! ah! had I the power of the former, how soon would I build up the new City-Hall, and save the cash and credit of the corporation; and how much sooner would I build myself a snug house in Broadway—nor would it be the first time a house has been obtained there for a song. In my opinion, the scotch bag-pipe is the only instrument that rivals the ancient lyre, and I am surprised it should be almost the only one entirely excluded from our concerts.

Talking of concerts reminds me of that given a few nights since by mr. WILSON; at which I had the misfortune of being present. It was attended by a numerous company, and gave great satisfaction, if I may be allowed to judge from the frequent *gapings* of the audience; though I will not risk my credit as a connoisseur, by saying whether they proceeded from wonder, or a violent inclination to doze. I was delighted to find, in the mazes of the crowd, my particular friend SNIVERS, who had put on his cognoscenti phiz—he being according to his own account a profound adept in the science of music. He can tell a crochet at first sight, and like a true englishman, is delighted with the plumb-pudding rotundity of a semi-breve; and, in short, boasts of having incontinently climbed up Paff's musical tree, which hangs every day upon the poplar, from the fundamental-concord, to the fundamental major discord, and so on from branch to branch, until he reached the very top, where he sung "Rule Britannia," clapped his wings, and then—came down again. Like all true transatlantic judges, he suffers most horribly at our musical entertainments, and he assures me that what with the confounded scraping, and scratching, and grating of our fiddlers, he thinks the sitting out one of our concerts tantamount to the punishment of that unfortunate saint, who was frittered in two with a hand-saw.

The concert was given in the tea-room, at the City-Hotel; an apartment admirably calculated by its dingy walls, beautifully marbled with smoke, to show off the dresses and complexions of the ladies, and by the flatness of its ceiling to repress those impertinent reverberations of the music, which, whatever others may foolishly assert, are, as Snivers says, "no better than repetitions of old stories."

Mr. Wilson gave me infinite satisfaction by the gentility of his demeanor, and the roguish looks he now and then cast at the ladies; but we fear his excessive *modesty* threw him into some little confusion, for he absolutely *forgot himself,* and in the whole course of his entrances and exits, never once made his bow to the audience. On the whole, however, I think he has a fine voice, sings with great taste, and is a very *modest* good-looking little man; but I beg leave to repeat the advice so often given by the illustrious tenants of the theatrical sky-parlor, to the gentlemen who are charged with the "nice conduct" of chairs and tables,—"make a bow, Johnny—Johnny make a bow!"

I cannot, on this occasion, but express my surprise that certain amateurs should be so frequently at concerts, considering what agonies they suffer while a piece of music is playing. I defy any man of common humanity, and who has not the heart of a Choctaw, to contemplate the countenance of one of these unhappy victims of a fiddle-stick, without feeling a sentiment of compassion. His whole visage is distorted; he rolls up his eyes, as M'Sychophant says, "like a duck in thunder," and the music seems to operate upon him like a fit of the cholic; his very bowels seem to sympathize at every twang of the cat-gut, as if he heard at that moment the wailings of the helpless animal that had been sacrificed to harmony. Nor does the hero of the orchestra seem less affected: as soon as the signal is given, he seizes his fiddle-stick, makes a most horrible grimace, scowls fiercely upon his music-book, and grins every little trembling crochet and quaver out of countenance. I have sometimes particularly noticed a hungry looking gaul, who torments a huge bass viol, and who is doubtless the original of the famous "Raw-head-and-bloody-bones," so potent in frightening naughty children.

The person who played the french horn was very excellent in his way, but Snivers could not relish his performance, having sometime since heard a gentleman amateur in Gotham play a solo on his *proboscis,* or nozzle, in a style infinitely superior;—Snout, the bellows-mender, never tuned his wind instrument more musically; nor did the celebrated "knight of the burning lamp," ever yield more exquisite entertainment with his nose; this gentleman had latterly ceased to exhibit this prodigious accomplishment, having, it was whispered, hired out his snout to a ferryman, who had lost his conch-shell—the consequence was, that he did not *show his nose* in company so frequently as before.

SITTING late the other evening in my elbow-chair, indulging in that kind of indolent meditation, which I consider the perfection of human bliss, I was roused from my reverie by the entrance of an old servant in the COCKLOFT livery, who handed me a letter, containing the following address from my cousin, and old college chum, PINDAR COCKLOFT.

Honest ANDREW as he delivered it, informed me that his master, who resides a little way from town, on reading a small pamphlet in a neat yellow cover, rubbed his hands with symptoms of great satisfaction, called for his favorite chinese ink-stand, with two sprawling mandarins for its supporters, and wrote the letter which he had the honor to present me.

As I foresee my cousin will one day become a great favorite with the public, and as I know him to be somewhat punctilious as it respects etiquette, I shall take this opportunity to gratify the old gentleman, by giving him a proper introduction to the fashionable world. The Cockloft family, to which I have the comfort of being related, has been fruitful in old bachelors and humorists, as will be perceived when I come to treat more of its history. My cousin Pindar is one of its most conspicuous members—he is now in his fifty-eighth year—is a bachelor, partly through choice, and partly through chance, and an oddity of the first water. Half his life has been employed in writing odes, sonnets, epigrams and elegies, which he seldom shows to any body but myself, after they are written; and all the old chests, drawers, and chair-bottoms in the house, teem with his productions.

In his younger days, he figured as a dashing blade in the great world; and no young fellow of the town wore a longer pig-tail, or carried more buckram in his skirts. From sixteen to thirty he was continually in love, and during that period, to use his own words, he be-scribbled more paper than would serve the theatre for snow-storms a whole season. The evening of his thirtieth birth-day, as he sat by the fire-side, as much in love as ever was man in this world, and writing the name of his mistress in the ashes, with an old tongs that had lost one of its legs, he was seized with a whim-wham that he was an old fool to be in love at his time of life. It was ever one of the Cockloft characteristics, to *strike* to whim, and had Pindar stood out on this occasion he would have brought the reputation of his mother in question. From that time, he gave up all particular attentions to the ladies, and though he still loves their company, he has never been known to exceed the bounds of common courtesy in his intercourse with them. He was the life and ornament of our family circle in town, until the epoch of the french revolution, which sent so many *unfortunate* dancing-masters from their country to polish and enlighten our hemisphere. This was a sad time for Pindar, who had taken a genuine Cockloft prejudice against every thing french, ever since he was brought to death's door by a *ragout*: he groaned at Ca Ira, and the Marseilles Hymn had much the same effect upon him, that sharpening a knife on a dry whetstone has upon some people—it set his teeth chattering. He might in time have been reconciled to these rubs, had not the introduction of french cockades on the hats of our citizens absolutely thrown him into a fever: the first time he saw an instance of this kind, he came home with great precipitation, packed up his trunk, his old fashioned writing-desk, and his chinese inkstand, and made a kind of growling retreat to Cockloft Hall, where he has resided ever since.

My cousin Pindar is one of a mercurial disposition—a humorist without ill-nature—he is of the true gun-powder temper—one flash and all is over. It is true, when the wind is easterly, or the gout gives him a gentle twinge, or he hears of any new successes of the french, he will become a little splenetic; and heaven help the man, and more particularly the woman, that crosses his humor at that moment—she is sure to receive no quarter. These are the most sublime moments of Pindar. I swear to you, dear ladies and gentlemen, I would not lose one of these splenetic bursts, for the best wig in my wardrobe, even though it were proved to be the identical wig worn by the sage Linkum Fidelius, when he demonstrated before the whole university of Leyden, that it *was* possible to make bricks without straw. I have seen the old gentleman, blaze forth such a volcanic explosion of wit, ridicule, and satire, that I was almost tempted to believe him inspired. But these sallies only lasted for a moment, and passed like summer clouds over the benevolent sunshine which ever warmed his heart, and lighted up his countenance.

Time, though it has dealt roughly with his person, has passed lightly over the graces of his mind, and left him in full possession of all the sensibilities of youth. His eye kindles at the relation of a noble or generous action, his heart melts at the story of distress, and he is still a warm admirer of the fair. Like all *old bachelors* however, he looks back with a fond and lingering eye on the period of his *boyhood*, and would sooner suffer the pangs of matrimony, than acknowledge that the world or any thing in it, is half so clever, as it was in those good old times that are "gone by."

I believe I have already mentioned, that with all his good qualities he is a humorist, and a humorist of the highest order. He has some of the most intolerable whim-whams I ever met with in my life, and his oddities are sufficient to eke out a hundred tolerable originals. But I will not enlarge on them—enough has been told to excite a desire to know more; and I am much mistaken, if in the course of half a dozen of our numbers, he dont tickle, plague, please and perplex the whole town, and completely establish his claim to the Laureatship he has solicited, and with which we hereby invest him, recommending him and his effusions to public reverence and respect.

LAUNCELOT LANGSTAFF.

TO LAUNCELOT LANGSTAFF, ESQ.

DEAR LAUNCE,

    As I find you have taken the quill,
To put our gay town, and its fair under drill,
I offer my hopes for success to your cause,
And sent you unvarnish'd my mite of applause.
  Ah, Launce, this poor town has been woefully *fashed;*
Has long been be-frenchman'd, be-cockney'd, be-trashed;
And our ladies be-devil'd, bewilder'd astray,
From the rules of their grandames have wander'd away.
No longer that modest demeanor we meet,
Which whilom the eyes of our fathers did greet;—
No longer be-mobbled, be-ruffled, be-quill'd,

Be-powder'd, be-hooded, be-patch'd and be-frill'd;—
No longer our fair ones their grograms display,
And stiff in brocade, strut "like castles" away.
   Oh, how fondly my soul forms departed has traced,
When our ladies in stays, and in boddice well laced,
When bishop'd, and cushion'd, and hoop'd to the chin,
Well callash'd without, and well bolster'd within;
All cased in their buckrams, from crown down to tail,
Like O'Brallagan's mistress, were shaped like a pail.
   Well—peace to those fashions—the joy of *our* eyes—
Tempora mutantur,—new follies will rise;
Yet, "like joys that are past," they still crowd on the mind,
In moments of thought, as the soul looks behind.
   Sweet days of our boyhood, gone by, my dear Launce,
Like the shadows of night, or the forms in a trance:
Yet oft we retrace those bright visions again,
Nos mutamur, tis true—but those visions remain.
I recal with delight, how my bosom would creep;
When some delicate foot from its chamber would peep,
And when I a neat stocking'd ankle could spy,
—By the sages of old, I was rapt to the sky!
All then was retiring—was modest—discreet;—
The beauties, all shrouded, were left to conceit;
To the visions which fancy would form in her eye
Of graces that snug in soft ambush would lie.
And the heart, like the poets, in thought would pursue
The elysium of bliss, which was veil'd from its view.
   We are *old fashion'd* fellows, our nieces all say:
Old fashion'd, indeed, coz—and swear it they may—
For I freely confess that it yields me no pride,
To see them all blaze what their mothers would hide;
To see them, all shiv'ring, some cold winter's day,
So lavish their beauties and graces display,
And give to each foppling that offers his hand,
Like Moses from Pisgah—a peep at the land.
   But a truce with complaining—the object in view
Is to offer my help in the work you pursue;
And as your effusions and labors sublime,
May need, now and then, a few touches of rhyme,
I humbly solicit, as cousin and friend,
A quiddity, quirk, or remonstrance to send:
Or should you a Laureat want in your plan,
By the muff of my grandmother, I am your man!

You must know I have got a *poetical mill,*
Which with odd lines, and couplets, and triplets I fill;
And a poem I grind, as from rags white and blue
The paper mill yields you a sheet fair and new.
I can grind down an ode, or an epic that's long,
Into sonnet, acrostic, conundrum or song:
As to dull Hudibrastic, so boasted of late,
The doggrel discharge of some muddle brain'd pate,
I can grind it by wholesale—and give it its point,
With billingsgate dish'd up in rhymes out of joint.
    I have read all the poets—and got them by heart,
Can slit them, and twist them, and take them apart;
Can cook up an ode out of patches and shreds,
To muddle my readers, and bother their heads.
Old Homer, and Virgil, and Ovid I scan,
Anacreon, and Sappho, (who changed to a swan;)—
Iambics and sapphics I grind at my will,
And with ditties of love every noddle can fill.
    Oh, 'twould do your heart good, Launce, to see my mill grind
Old stuff into verses, and poems refined;—
Dan Spencer, Dan Chaucer, those poets of old,
Though cover'd with dust, are yet true sterling gold;
I can grind off their tarnish, and bring them to view,
New model'd, new mill'd, and improved in their hue.
    But I promise no more—only give me the place,
And I warrant I'll fill it with credit and grace;
By the living! I'll figure and cut you a dash
—As bold as Will Wizard, or 'SBIDLIKENS-FLASH!

                                        PINDAR COCKLOFT.

                      ADVERTISEMENT.

PERHAPS the most fruitful source of mortification to a merry writer,
who for the amusement of himself and the public, employs his leisure
in sketching odd characters from imagination, is, that he cannot flourish
his pen, but every Jack-pudding imagines it is pointed directly at himself:—he cannot, in his gambols, throw a fool's cap among the crowd,
but every queer fellow insists upon putting it on his own head; or chalk
an outlandish figure, but every outlandish genius is eager to write his
own name under it. However we may be mortified, that these men
should each individually think himself of sufficient consequence to
engage our attention, we should not care a rush about it, if they did
not get into a passion, and complain of having been ill-used.

It is not in our hearts to hurt the feelings of one single mortal, by holding him up to public ridicule, and if it were, we lay it down as one of our indisputable facts, that no man can be made ridiculous but by his own folly. As however we are aware that when a man by chance gets a thwack in the crowd, he is apt to suppose the blow was intended exclusively for himself, and so fall into unreasonable anger, we have determined to let these crusty gentry know what kind of satisfaction they are to expect from us. We are resolved not to fight, for three special reasons—first, because fighting is at all events extremely troublesome and inconvenient, particularly at this season of the year;—second, because if either of us should happen to be killed, it would be a great loss to the public, and rob them of many a good laugh we have in store for their amusement;—and third, because if we should chance to kill our adversary, as is most likely, for we can every one of us split balls upon razors and snuff candles,—it would be a loss to our publisher, by depriving him of a good customer. If any gentleman casuist will give three as good reasons *for* fighting, we promise him a complete set of Salmagundi for nothing.

But though we do not fight in our own proper persons, let it not be supposed that we will not give ample satisfaction to all those who may choose to demand it—for this would be a mistake of the first magnitude and lead very valiant gentlemen perhaps into what is called a *quandary*. It would be a thousand and one pities, that any honest man, after taking to himself the cap and bells which we *merely* offered to his acceptance, should not have the privilege of being cudgeled into the bargain. We pride ourselves upon giving satisfaction in every department of our paper; and to fill that of fighting, have engaged two of those strapping heroes of the Theatre, who figure in the retinues of our ginger-bread kings and queens—now hurry an old stuff petticoat on their backs, and strut senators of Rome, or aldermen of London—and now be-whisker their muffin faces with burnt cork, and swagger right valiant warriors, armed cap-a-pee, in buckram. Should, therefore, any great little man about town, take offence at our good-natured villainy, though we intend to offend nobody under heaven—he will please to apply at any hour after twelve o'clock, as our champions will then be off duty at the Theatre, and ready for any thing. They have promised to fight "with or without balls"—to give two tweaks of the nose for one—to submit to be kicked, and to cudgel their applicant most heartily in return;—this being what we understand by "the *satisfaction* of *a gentleman*."

SALMAGUNDI NO. III

Friday, February 13, 1807.

FROM MY ELBOW-CHAIR.

As I delight in every thing novel and eccentric, and would at any time give an old coat for a new idea, I am particularly attentive to the manners and conversation of strangers, and scarcely ever a traveller enters this city whose appearance promises any thing original, but by some means or another, I form an acquaintance with him. I must confess I often suffer manifold afflictions from the intimacies thus contracted: my curiosity is frequently punished by the stupid details of a blockhead, or the shallow verbosity of a coxcomb. Now I would prefer at any time to travel with an ox-team through a Carolina sand-flat, than plod through a heavy unmeaning conversation with the former, and as to the latter, I would sooner hold sweet converse with the wheel of a knife grinder, than endure his monotonous chattering. In fact the strangers who flock to this most pleasant of all earthly cities, are generally mere birds of passage, whose plumage is often gay enough, I own; but their notes, "heaven save the mark," are as unmusical as those of that classic night bird, whom the antients humorously selected as the emblem of wisdom. Those from the south, it is true, entertain me with their horses, equipages, and puns; and it is excessively pleasant to hear a couple of these *four in hand* gentlemen, detail their exploits over a bottle. Those from the east, have often induced me to doubt the existence of the wise men of yore, who are said to have flourished in that quarter; and as for those from parts beyond seas—oh! my masters, ye shall hear more from me anon. Heaven help this unhappy town!— hath it not goslings enow of its own hatching and rearing that it must be overwhelmed by such an inundation of ganders from other climes? I would not have any of my courteous and gentle readers suppose that I am running *a muck*, full tilt, cut and slash upon all foreigners indiscriminately. I have no national antipathies, though related to the Cockloft family. As to honest John Bull, I shake him heartily by the hand, assuring him that I love his jolly countenance, and moreover am lineally descended from him; in proof of which I alledge my invincible predilection for roast beef and pudding. I therefore look upon all his children as my kinsmen; and I beg when I tickle a cockney I may not be understood as trimming an englishman, they being very distinct animals, as I shall clearly demonstrate in a future number. If any one wishes to know my opinion of the irish and scotch, he may find it in the characters of those two nations, drawn by the first advocate of the age. But the french I must confess are my favorites, and I have taken more pains to argue my cousin Pindar out of his antipathy to them, than I ever did about any other thing. When, therefore, I choose to hunt a monsieur for my own particular amusement, I beg it may not be asserted that I intend him as a representative of his countrymen at large. For from this—I love the nation, as being a nation of right merry fellows, possessing the true secret of being happy; which is nothing more than thinking of nothing, talking about any thing, and laughing at every thing. I mean only to tune up those little thing-o-mys, who represent nobody but themselves; who have no national trait about them but their language, and who hop about our town in swarms like little toads after a shower.

Among the few strangers whose acquaintance has entertained me, I particularly rank the magnanimous MUSTAPHA RUB-A-DUB KELI KHAN, a most illustrious Captain of a Ketch, who figured some time since, in our fashionable circles, at the head of a ragged regiment of tripolitan prisoners. His conversation was to me a perpetual feast—I chuckled with inward pleasure at his whimsical mistakes and unaffected observations on men and manners; and I rolled each odd conceit "like a sweet morsel under my tongue."

Whether Mustapha was captivated by my iron-bound physiognomy, or flattered by the attentions which I paid him, I won't determine; but I so far gained his confidence, that at his departure, he presented me with a bundle of papers, containing among other articles, several copies of letters, which he had written to his friends in Tripoli.—The following is a translation of one of them. The original is in arabic-greek, but by the assistance of Will Wizard, who understands all languages, not excepting that manufactured by Psalmanazar, I have been enabled to accomplish a tolerable translation. We should have found little difficulty in rendering it into english, had it not been for Mustapha's confounded pot-hooks and trammels.

LETTER FROM MUSTAPHA RUB-A-DUB KELI KHAN,
Captain of a Ketch,
To ASEM HACCHEM, principal slave-driver to
his highness the Bashaw of Tripoli.

THOU wilt learn from this letter, most illustrious disciple of Mahomet, that I have for some time resided in New-York, the most polished, vast and magnificent city of the United States of America. But what to me are its delights! I wander a captive through its splendid streets, I turn a heavy eye on every rising day that beholds me banished from my country. The christian husbands here lament most bitterly any short absence from home, though they leave but one wife behind to lament their departure—what then must be the feelings of thy unhappy kinsman, while thus lingering at an immeasurable distance from three-and-twenty of the most lovely and obedient wives in all Tripoli! Oh Allah! shall thy servant never again return to his native land, nor behold his beloved wives, who beam on his memory beautiful as the rosy morn of the east, and graceful as Mahomet's camel!

Yet beautiful, oh most puissant slave-driver, as are my wives, they are far exceeded by the women of this country. Even those who run about the streets with bare arms and necks, (*et cætera*) whose habiliments are too scanty to protect them either from the inclemency of the seasons, or the scrutinizing glances of the curious, and who it would seem belong to nobody, are lovely as the Houris that people the elysium of true believers. If then, such as run wild in the highways, and whom nobody cares to appropriate, are thus beauteous; what must be the charms of those who are shut up in the seraglios, and never permitted to go abroad! surely the region of beauty, the valley of the graces can contain nothing so inimitably fair!

But, notwithstanding the charms of these infidel women, they are apt to have one fault, which is extremely troublesome and inconvenient. Wouldst thou believe it, Asem, I have been positively assured by a famous dervise (or doctor as he is here called) that at least one-fifth part of them—have souls! incredible as it may seem to thee, I am the more inclined to believe them in possession of this monstrous superfluity, from my own little experience, and from the information which I have derived from others. In walking the streets I have actually seen an exceeding good looking woman with soul enough to box her husband's ears to his heart's content, and my very whiskers trembled with indignation at the abject state of these wretched infidels. I am told, moreover, that some of the women have soul enough to usurp the breeches of the men, but these I suppose are married and kept close, for I have not, in my rambles, met with any so extravagantly accoutred; others, I am informed, have soul enough to swear:—yea! by the beard of the great Omar, who prayed three times to each of the one hundred and twenty-four thousand prophets of our most holy faith, and who never swore but once in his life—they actually swear!

Get thee to the mosque, good Asem! return thanks to our most holy prophet, that he has been thus mindful of the comfort of all true musselmen, and has given them wives with no more souls than cats and dogs, and other necessary animals of the household.

Thou will doubtless be anxious to learn our reception in this country, and how we were treated by a people whom we have been accustomed to consider as unenlightened barbarians.

On landing we were waited upon to our lodgings, I suppose according to the directions of the municipality, by a vast and respectable escort of boys and negroes, who shouted and threw up their hats, doubtless to do honor to the magnanimous Mustapha, captain of a ketch; they were somewhat ragged and dirty in their equipments, but this we attributed to their republican simplicity. One of them, in the zeal of admiration, threw an old shoe, which gave thy friend rather an ungentle salutation on one side of the head, whereat I was not a little offended, until the interpreter informed us that this was the customary manner in which great men were honored in this country; and that the more distinguished they were, the more were they subjected to the attacks and peltings of the mob. Upon this I bowed my head three times, with my hands to my turban, and made a speech in arabic-greek, which gave great satisfaction, and occasioned a shower of old shoes, hats, and so forth, that was exceedingly refreshing to us all.

Thou wilt not as yet expect that I should give thee an account of the laws and politics of this country—I will reserve them for some future letter, when I shall be more experienced in their complicated and seemingly contradictory nature.

This empire is governed by a grand and most puissant bashaw, whom they dignify with the title of President. He is chosen by persons, who are chosen by an assembly elected by the people—hence the mob is called the *sovereign people*—and the country, *free*; the body politic doubtless resembling a vessel, which is best governed by its tail. The present bashaw is a very plain old gentleman—something they say of a humorist, as he amuses himself with impaling butterflies and pickling tadpoles; he is rather declining in popularity, having given great offence by wearing red breeches, and tying his horse to a post. The people of the United States have assured me that they themselves are the most enlightened nation under the sun; but thou knowest that the barbarians of the desart, who assemble at the summer solstice, to shoot their arrows at that glorious luminary, in order to extinguish his burning rays, make precisely the same boast;—which of them have the superior claim, I shall not attempt to decide.

I have observed, with some degree of surprize, that the men of this country do not seem in haste to accommodate themselves even with the *single* wife, which alone the laws permit them to marry; this backwardness is probably owing to the misfortune of their absolutely having no female *mutes* among them. Thou knowest how invaluable are these silent companions;—what a price is given for them in the east, and what entertaining wives do they make! what delightful entertainment arises from beholding the silent eloquence of their signs and gestures! but a wife possessed both of a tongue and a soul—monstrous! monstrous! Is it astonishing that these unhappy infidels should shrink from a union with a woman so preposterously endowed?

Thou hast doubtless read in the works of Abul Faraj, the arabian historian, the tradition which mentions that the muses were once upon the point of falling together by the ears about the admission of a *tenth* among their number, until she assured them, by signs, that she was dumb, whereupon they received her with great rejoicing. I should, perhaps, inform thee that there are but *nine* christian muses, (who were formerly pagans, but have since been converted) and that in this country we never hear of a tenth, unless some crazy poet wishes to pay an hyperbolical compliment to his mistress; on which occasion it goes hard but she figures as a tenth muse, or fourth grace, even though she should be more illiterate than a Hottentot, and more ungraceful than a dancing-bear! Since my arrival in this country, I have not met with less than a hundred of these supernumerary muses and graces—and may Allah preserve me from ever meeting with any more!

When I have studied this people more profoundly, I will write thee again; in the mean time watch over my household, and do not beat my beloved wives, unless you catch them with their noses out at the window. Tho' far distant, and a slave, let me live in thy heart, as thou livest in mine:—think not, oh friend of my soul, that the splendors of this luxurious capitol, its gorgeous palaces, its stupenduous mosques, and the beautiful females who run wild in herds about its streets, can obliterate thee from my remembrance. Thy name shall still be mentioned in the five-and-twenty prayers which I offer up daily; and may our great prophet, after bestowing on thee all the blessings of this life, at length, in a good old age, lead thee gently by the hand, to enjoy the dignity of bashaw of three tails in the blissful bowers of Eden.

MUSTAPHA.

Fashions,

BY ANTHONY EVERGREEN, GENT.

The following article is furnished me by a young lady of unquestionable taste, and who is the oracle of fashion and frippery. Being deeply initiated into all the mysteries of the toilet, she has promised me from time to time, a similar detail.

MRS. TOOLE has for some time reigned unrivalled in the fashionable world, and had the supreme direction of caps, bonnets, feathers, flowers, and tinsel. She has dressed and undressed our ladies just as she pleased; now loading them with velvet and wadding, now turning them adrift upon the world, to run shivering through the streets with scarcely a covering to their—backs; and now obliging them to drag a long train at their heels, like the tail of a paper kite. Her despotic sway, however, threatens to be limited. A dangerous rival has sprung up in the person of MADAME BOUCHARD, an intrepid little woman, fresh from the headquarters of fashion and folly, and who has burst like a second Bonaparte upon the fashionable world. Mrs. Toole, notwithstanding, seems determined to dispute her ground bravely for the honor of old England. The ladies have begun to arrange themselves under the banner of one or other of these heroines of the needle, and everything portends open war. Madame Bouchard marches gallantly to the field, flourishing a flaming red robe for a standard, "flouting the skies;" and mrs. Toole, no ways dismayed, sallies out under cover of a forest of artificial flowers, like Malcolm's host. Both parties possess great merit, and both deserve the victory. Mrs. Toole charges the highest, but madame Bouchard makes the lowest curtsey. Madame Bouchard is a little short lady—nor is there any hope of her growing any larger; but then she is perfectly genteel— and so is mrs. Toole. Mrs. Toole lives in Broadway, and madame Bouchard in Courtlandt-street; but madame atones for the inferiority of her *stand,* by making two curtseys to mrs. Toole's one, and talking french like an angel. Mrs. Toole is the best looking—but madame Bouchard wears a most bewitching little scrubby wig.—Mrs. Toole is the tallest—but madame Bouchard has the longest nose.—Mrs. Toole is fond of roast beef—but madame is loyal in her adherence to onions: in short, so equally are the merits of the two ladies balanced, that there is no judging which will "kick the beam." It however seems to be the prevailing opinion, that madame Bouchard will carry the day, because she wears a wig, has a long nose, talks french, loves onions, and does not charge above ten times as much for a thing as it is worth.

Under the direction of these High Priestesses of the beau-monde, the following is the fashionable morning dress for walking.

If the weather be very cold, a thin muslin gown, or frock is most adviseable, because it agrees with the season, being perfectly cool. The neck, arms, and particularly the elbows bare, in order that they may be agreeably painted and mottled by mr. JOHN FROST, nose-painter-general, of the color of castile-soap. Shoes of kid, the thinnest that can possibly be procured—as they tend to promote colds and make a lady look interesting—(*i.e. grizzly*). Picnic silk stockings, with lace clocks, flesh-colored are most fashionable, as they have the appearance of bare legs—*nudity* being all the rage. The stockings carelessly bespattered with mud, to agree with the gown, which should be bordered about three inches deep with the most fashionable colored mud that can be found: the ladies permitted to hold up their trains, after they have swept two or three streets, in order to show—the clocks of their stockings. The shawl, scarlet, crimson, flame, orange, salmon, or any other combustible or brimstone color, thrown over one shoulder like an indian blanket, with one end dragging on the ground.

N. B. If the ladies have not a red shawl at hand, a red petticoat turned topsy-turvy over the shoulders, would do just as well. This is called being dressed *à la drabble*.

When the ladies do not go abroad of a morning, the usual chimney-corner dress is a dotted, spotted, striped, or cross-barred gown—a yellowish, whitish, smokish, dirty colored shawl, and the hair curiously ornamented with little bits of newspaper, or pieces of a letter from a dear friend. This is called the "Cinderella dress."

The receipt for a full dress, is as follows: take of spider net, crape, sattin, gymp, cat-gut, gauze, whalebone, lace, bobbin, ribbons, and artificial flowers, as much as will rig out the congregation of a village church: to these add as many spangles, beads, and gew-gaws, as would be sufficient to turn the heads of all the fashionable fair ones of Nootka-sound. Let mrs. Toole, or madame Bouchard patch all these articles together, one upon another, dash them plentifully over with stars, bugles, and tinsel, and they will altogether form a dress, which hung upon a lady's back, cannot fail of supplying the place of beauty, youth and grace, and of reminding the spectator of that celebrated region of finery, called *Rag Fair*.

> Dat veniam corvis, vexat censura Columbas.
>
> JUV.
>
> A, *was an archer and shot at a frog,*
> *But missing his aim shot into a bog.*
>
> LINK. FID. vol. CIII. chap. CLV.

One of the greatest sources of amusement incident to our humorous knight-errantry, is to ramble about and hear the various conjectures of the town respecting our worships, whom every body pretends to know as well as Falstaff did prince Hal at Gads-hill. We have sometimes seen a sapient sleepy fellow on being tickled with a straw, make a furious effort, and fancy he had fairly caught a gnat in his clutches; so, that many-headed monster the public, who with all its heads is, we fear, sadly off for brains, has after long hovering, come souse down, like a king-fisher, on the authors of Salmagundi, and caught them as certainly as the aforesaid honest fellow caught the gnat.

Would that we were rich enough to give every one of our numerous readers a cent, as a reward for their ingenuity! not that they have really conjectured within a thousand leagues of the truth, but that we consider it a great stretch of ingenuity even to have guessed wrong—and that we hold ourselves much obliged to them for having taken the trouble to guess at all.

One of the most tickling, dear, mischievous pleasures of this liife is to laugh in one's sleeve—to sit snug in a corner unnoticed and unknown, and hear the wise men of Gotham, who are profound judges (of horseflesh), pronounce from the style of our work, who are the authors. This listening incog. and receiving a hearty praising over another man's back, is a situation so celestially whimsical that we have done little else than laugh in our sleeves ever since our first number was publisht.

The town has at length allayed the titilations of curiosity, by fixing on two young gentlemen of literary talents—that is to say, they are equal to the composition of a news-paper squib, a hodge-podge criticism, or some such trifle, and may occasionally raise a smile by their effusions; but pardon us, sweet sirs, if we modestly doubt your capability of supporting the atlean burthen of Salmagundi, or of keeping up a laugh for a whole fortnight, as we have done, and intend to do, until the whole town becomes a community of laughing philosophers like ourselves. We have no intention, however, of undervaluing the abilities of these two young men whom we verily believe, according to common acceptation, young men *of promise*.

Were we ill-natured, we might publish something that would get our representatives into difficulties; but far be it from us to do any thing to the injury of persons to whom we are under such obligations. While they stand before us, we, like little Teucer, behind the sevenfold shield of Ajax, can launch unseen our sportive arrows, which we trust will never inflict a wound, unless like his, they fly, "heaven directed," to some conscience struck bosom.

Another marvellous great source of pleasure to us, is the abuse our work has received from several wooden gentlemen, whose censures we covet more than ever we did any thing in our lives. The moment we declared open war against folly and stupidity, we expected to receive no quarter, and to provoke a confederacy of all the blockheads in town. For it is one of our indisputable facts, that so sure as you catch a gander by the tail, the whole flock, geese, goslings, one and all, have a fellow-feeling on the occasion, and begin to cackle and hiss like so many devils bewitched. As we have a profound respect for these antient and respectable birds, on the score of their once saving the capitol, we hereby declare, that we mean no offence whatever by comparing them to the aforesaid confederacy. We have heard in our walks such criticisms on Salmagundi, as almost induced a belief that folly had here, as in the east, her moments of inspired idiotism. Every silly-royster has, as if by an instinctive sense of anticipated danger, joined in the cry, and condemned us without mercy. All is thus as it should be. It would have mortified us very sensibly had we been disappointed in this particular, as we should then have been apprehensive that our shafts had fallen to the ground, innocent of the "blood or brains" of a single numskull. Our efforts have been crowned with wonderful success. All the queer fish, the grubs, the flats, the noddies, and the live oak and timber gentlemen, are pointing their empty guns at us; and we are threatened with a most puissant confederacy of the "pigmies and cranes," and other "light militia," backed by the heavy armed artillery of dullness and stupidity. The veriest dreams of our most sanguine moments are thus realized. We have no fear of the censures of the wise, the good, or the fair; for they will ever be sacred from our attacks. We reverence the wise, love the good, and adore the fair; we declare ourselves champions in their cause—in the cause of morality—and we throw our gauntlet to all the world besides.

While we profess and feel the same indifference to public applause as at first, we most earnestly invite the attacks and censures of all the wooden warriors of this sensible city, and especially of that distinguished and learned body, heretofore celebrated under the appellation of "The North-river Society." The thrice valiant and renowned Don Quixote, never made such work amongst the wool-clad warriors of Trapoban, or the puppets of the itinerant showman, as we promise to make amongst these fine fellows; and we pledge ourselves to the public in general, and the Albany skippers, in particular, that the North-river shall not be set on fire this winter at least, for we shall give the authors of that nefarious scheme, ample employment for some time to come.

"———— *How now, mooncalf!*"

We have been congratulating ourselves exceedingly on having, at length, attracted the notice of a ponderous genius of this city, Dr. Christopher Costive, L. L. D. &c. who has spoken of us in such a manner that we are ten times better pleased than ever we were before. It shall never be said of us, that we have been out-done in the way of complimenting, and we therefore assure Dr. Christopher Costive that, for a Yankee doodle song, about "Sister Tabitha," "our Cow," and "dandy," and "sugar-candy," and all these jokes of truely *Eastern saltness,* we know no man more "cute" than himself.

If Dr. Costive should find fault with having nothing but whipt syllabub from us, we promise him that, if circumstances render it necessary, we will occasionally give it a little variety by whipping him up in it as completely as ever a dish of ass's milk was whipt up in this world. Our friend seems rather vociferous in his demand for a dish of "flummery," and as such a dish is not in our bill of fare, we immediately requested our publisher to procure us one that would suit our friend's appetite. He has brought us "Democracy Unveiled, or Tyranny stripped of the garb of Patriotism," by Christopher Costive, L. L. D. &c. &c. &c. &c. &c. &c. &c. We can now promise our friend to serve him up a plentiful dish of flummery from his own shop, whenever he thinks fit to demand it, and garnished with a little Salmagundi for sauce. We hope he will not behave like his prototype, Dr. Lampedo, and gag at his own "patent draught."

Our respected friend appears a little worried that we do not write for money. Now this looks ill of Dr. Costive—not that we thereby mean to insinuate that Dr. Costive is an ill-looking personage: on the contrary, we think him a great poet, a very great poet, the greatest poet of the age, and, considering the excessive gravity of his person, we are the more astonished at the sublime flights of his fat fancy. To convince him that we are disposed to befriend him, all in our power, we take this opportunity to inform our numerous readers that there *is* such a man as Dr. Christopher Costive, and that he publishes a *weakly* paper, called the "Weekly Inspector," some where in this city; and that he writes *for money*. We, therefore, advise "every body, man, woman, and child, that can read, or get any body to read for them, to purchase *his* paper," where they will find the true "bubble and squeak," and "topsy-turvy," which Dr. Costive will at any time exchange *for money*.

Upon the whole, we consider him a very modest, decent, good-looking *big* man, who writes *for money*; being but "half a fish and half a monster."

PROCLAMATION,
from the MILL *of* PINDAR COCKLOFT, *esq.*

To all the young belles who enliven our scene,
From ripe five-and-forty, to blooming fifteen;
Who racket at routs, and who rattle at plays,
Who visit, and fidget, and dance out their days;
Who conquer all hearts, with a shot from the eye,
Who freeze with a frown, and who thaw with a sigh;—
To all those bright youths who embellish the age,
Whether young boys or old boys, or numskull or sage;
Whether DULL DOGS, who cringe at their mistresses' feet,
Who sigh and who whine, and who try to look sweet;
Whether TOUGH DOGS, who squat down stock-still in a row,

And play wooden gentlemen stuck up for show;
Or SAD DOGS, who glory in *running their rigs,*
Now dash in their sleighs, and now whirl in their gigs;
Who riot at Dyde's on imperial champaign,
And then scour our city—the peace to maintain;
To whoe'er it concerns, or may happen to meet,
By these presents their worships I lovingly greet.
Now KNOW YE, that I, PINDAR COCKLOFT, Esquire,
Am Laureat, appointed at special desire;—
A censor, self-dubb'd, to admonish the fair,
And tenderly take the town under my care.

   I'm a ci-devant beau, cousin Launcelot has said—
A remnant of habits long vanish'd and dead:
But still, though my heart dwells with rapture sublime,
On the fashions and customs which reign'd in my prime;
I yet can perceive—and still candidly praise,
Some maxims and manners of these "latter days;"—
Still own that some wisdom and beauty appears,
Though almost entomb'd in the rubbish of years.

   No fierce nor tyrannical cynic am I,
Who frown on each foible I chance to espy;
Who pounce on a novelty, just like a kite,
And tear up a victim through malice or spite;
Who expose to the scoffs of an ill-natur'd crew,
A trembler for starting a whim that is new.
No, no—I shall cautiously hold up my glass,
To the sweet little blossoms who heedlessly pass;—
My remarks not too pointed to wound or offend,
Nor so vague as to miss their benevolent end:
Each innocent fashion shall have its full sway;
New modes shall arise to astonish Broadway;
Red hats and red shawls still illumine the town,
And each belle, like a bonfire, blaze up and down.

   Fair spirits, who brighten the gloom of our days,
Who cheer this dull scene with your heavenly rays,
No mortal can love you more firmly and true,
From the crown of the head, to the sole of the shoe.
I'm old fashion'd, tis true,—but still runs in my heart,
That affectionate stream, to which youth gave the start;
More calm in its current,—yet potent in force;
Less ruffled by gales,—but still stedfast in course.
Though the lover enraptured no longer appears—
Tis the guide and the guardian enlighten'd by years.

All ripen'd, and mellow'd, and soften'd by time,
The asperities polish'd which chafed in my prime,
I am fully prepared for that delicate end,
The fair one's instructor, companion and friend.
—And should I perceive you in fashion's gay dance,
Allured by the frippery-mongers of France,
Expose your weak frames to a wintery sky,
To be nipp'd by its frosts, to be torn from the eye;
My soft admonitions shall fall on your ear—
Shall whisper those parents to whom you are dear—
Shall warn you of hazards you heedlessly run,
And sing of those fair ones whom *Frost* has undone;—
Bright suns, that would scarce on our horizon dawn,
Ere *shrouded* from sight, they were early withdrawn:
Gay sylphs, who have floated in circles below,
As pure in their souls, and as transient as snow;
Sweet roses, that bloom'd and decay'd to my eye,
And of forms that have flitted and pass'd to the sky.

But as to those brainless pert bloods of our town,
Those sprigs of the ton who run decency down;
Who lounge, and who lout, and who booby about,
No knowledge within, and no manners without;
Who stare at each beauty with insolent eyes;
Who rail at those morals their fathers would prize;
Who are loud at the play,—and who impiously dare
To come in their cups to the routs of the fair;—
I shall hold up my mirror, to let them survey
The figures they cut as they dash it away:
Should my good-humored verse no amendment produce,
Like scare-crows, at least, they shall still be of use:
I shall stitch them in effigy up in my rhyme,
And hold them aloft through the progress of time,
As figures of fun to make the folks laugh,
Like that b——h of an angel erected by Paff,
"Vhat shtops," as he says, "all de peoples vhat come
"Vhat shmiles on dem all, and vhat peats on de trum."

SALMAGUNDI NO. IV

Tuesday, February 24, 1807.

FROM MY ELBOW-CHAIR

Perhaps there is no class of men to which the curious and literary are more indebted than travellers—I mean travel-mongers, who write whole volumes about themselves, their horses and their servants, interspersed with anecdotes of inn-keepers—droll sayings of stage-drivers, and interesting memoirs of the lord knows who. They will give you a full acccount of a city, its manners, customs, and manufactures, though perhaps all their knowledge of it was obtained by a peep from their inn-windows, and an interesting conversation with the landlord or the waiter. America has had its share of these buzzards; and in the name of my countrymen I return them profound thanks for the compliments they have lavished upon us, and the variety of particulars concerning our own country, which we should never have discovered without their assistance.

Influenced by such sentiments, I am delighted to find that the Cockloft Family, among its other whimsical and monstrous productions, is about to be enriched with a genuine travel-writer. This is no less a personage than Mr. JEREMY COCKLOFT, the only son and darling pride of my cousin, Mr. CHRISTOPHER COCKLOFT. I should have said Jeremy Cockloft *the younger*, as he so styles himself by way of distinguishing him from IL SIGNORE JEREMO COCKLOFTICO, a gouty old gentleman who flourished about the time that Pliny the elder was smoked to death with the fire and brimstone of Vesuvius, and whose travels, if he ever wrote any, are now lost forever to the world. Jeremy is at present in his one-and-twentieth year, and a young fellow of wonderful quick parts, if you will trust to the word of his father, who having begotten him, should be the best judge of the matter. He is the oracle of the family, dictates to his sisters on every occasion, though they are some dozen or more years older than himself—and never did son give mother better advice than Jeremy.

As old Cockloft was determined his son should be both a scholar and a gentleman, he took great pains with his education, which was completed at our university, where he became exceedingly expert in quizzing his teachers and playing billiards. No student made better squibs and crackers to blow up the chemical professor; no one chalked more ludicrous caricatures on the walls of the college; and none were more adroit in shaving pigs and climbing lightening rods. He moreover learned all the letters of the greek alphabet, could demonstrate that water never "of its own accord" rose above the level of its source, and that air was certainly the principle of life, for he had been entertained with the humane experiment of a cat, worried to death in an air-pump. He once shook down the ash-house by an artificial earthquake, and nearly blew his sister Barbara and her cat, out of the window with thundering powder. He likewise boasts exceedingly of being thoroughly acquainted with the composition of Lacedemonian black broth, and once made a pot of it which had well nigh poisoned the whole family, and actually threw the cook-maid into convulsions. But above all, he values himself upon his logic, has the old college conundrum of the cat with three tails at his fingers' ends, and often hampers his father with his syllogisms, to the great delight of the old gentleman, who considers the major, minor, and conclusion, as almost equal in argument to the pulley, the wedge, and the lever in mechanics. In fact, my cousin Cockloft was once nearly annihilated with astonishment, on hearing Jeremy trace the derivation of Mango from Jeremiah King—as Jeremiah King, Jerry King! Jerking, Girkin! Cucumber, Mango! In short, had Jeremy been a student at Oxford or Cambridge, he would, in all probability, have been promoted to the dignity of a *senior wrangler*. By this sketch, I mean no disparagement to the abilities of other students of our college, for I have no doubt that every commencement ushers into society, luminaries full as brilliant as *Jeremy Cockloft, the younger.*

Having made a very pretty speech on graduating, to a numerous assemblage of old folks and young ladies, who all declared that he was a very fine young man, and made very handsome gestures: Jeremy was seized with a great desire to see, or rather to be seen by the world; and as his father was anxious to give him every possible advantage, it was determined Jeremy should visit foreign parts. In consequence of this resolution, he has spent a matter of three or four months in visiting strange places, and in the course of his travels has tarried some few days at the splendid metropolis' of Albany and Philadelphia.

Jeremy has travelled as every modern man of sense should do, that is, he judges of things by the sample next at hand—if he has ever any doubt on a subject, always decides against the city where he happens to sojourn, and invariably takes *home* as the standard by which to direct his judgment.

Going into his room the other day, when he happened to be absent, I found a manuscript volume laying on his table, and was overjoyed to find it contained notes and hints for a book of travels which he intends publishing. He seems to have taken a late fashionable travel-monger for his model, and I have no doubt his work will be equally instructive and amusing with that of his prototype. The following are some extracts, which may not prove uninteresting to my readers.

MEMORANDUMS
For a Tour, to be entitled
"THE STRANGER IN NEW-JERSEY;
OR, COCKNEY TRAVELLING."
BY JEREMY COCKLOFT, the Younger.

CHAPTER I.

The man in the moon*—preparations for departure—hints to travellers about packing their trunks†—straps, buckles and bed-cords—case of pistols, *a la cockney*—five trunks, three bandboxes—a cocked hat,—and a medicine-chest, *a la francaise*—parting advice of my two sisters—quere, why old maids are so particular in their cautions against naughty women—Description of Powles-Hook ferry-boats—might be converted into gun boats, and defend our port equally well with Albany sloops—BROM, the black ferryman—Charon—River Styx—ghosts—Major Hunt—good story—ferryage nine-pence—city of Harsimus—built on the spot where the folk once danced on their stumps, while the devil fiddled—quere, why do the Harsimites talk dutch?—story of the Tower of Babel, and confusion of tongues—get into the stage—driver a wag—famous fellow for running stage races—killed three passengers and crippled nine in the course of his practice—philosophical reasons why stage drivers love grog—causeway—ditch on each side for folk to tumble into—famous place for *skilly-pots;* Philadelphians call 'em tarapins—roast them under the ashes as we do potatoes—quere, may not this be the reason that the Philadelphians are all turtle heads?—Hackensack bridge—good painting of a blue horse jumping over a mountain—wonder who it was painted by—mem. to ask the *Baron de Gusto* about it on my return—Rattle-snake hill, so called from abounding with butterflies—salt marsh, *surmounted* here and there by a solitary hay-stack—more tarapins—wonder why the Philadelphians dont establish a fishery here, and get a patent for it—bridge over the Passaic—rate of toll—description of toll boards—toll man had but one eye—story how it *is possible* he *may* have lost the other—pence table, &c.‡—

CHAP. II.

Newark—noted for its fine breed of fat musquitoes—sting through the thickest boot§—story about *Gallynipers*—Archy Gifford and his man

* *vide* Carr's Stranger in Ireland.
† *vide* Weld.
‡ *vide* Carr.
§ *vide* Weld.

Caliban—jolly fat fellows—a knowing traveller always judges of every
thing by the inn-keepers and waiters*—set down Newark people all fat
as butter—learned dissertation on Archy Gifford's green coat, with philosophical reasons why the Newarkites wear red worsted night-caps, and
turn their noses to the south when the wind blows—Newark Academy
full of windows—sunshine excellent to make little boys grow—Elizabeth-
Town—fine girls—vile musquitoes—plenty of oysters—quere, have oysters
any feeling?—good story about the fox catching them by his tail—ergo,
foxes might be of great use in the pearl fishery—landlord member of the
Legislature—treats every body who has a vote—mem. all the inn-
keepers members of Legislature in New-Jersey—Bridge-Town, vulgarly
called *Spank-Town*, from a story of a quondam parson and his wife—
real name, according to Linkum Fidelius, Bridge-Town, from *bridge*,
a contrivance to get dry shod over a river or brook; and *town*, an appellation given in America to the accidental assemblage of a church, a
tavern, and a blacksmith's shop—Linkum as right as my left leg—Rahway-
River—good place for gun-boats—wonder why Mr. Jefferson dont send
a *river fleet* there, to protect the hay vessels?—Woodbridge—landlady
mending her husband's breeches—sublime apostrophe to conjugal affection and the fair sex†—Woodbridge famous for its crab fishery—sentimental correspondence between a crab and a lobster—digression to
Abelard and Eloisa—mem. when the moon is in *Pisces* she plays the
devil with the crabs.

CHAP. III.

Brunswick—oldest town in the state—division line between two coun-
ties in the middle of the street—posed a lawyer with the case of a man
standing with one foot in each county—wanted to know in which he
was *domicil*—lawyer couldn't tell for the soul of him—mem. all the New-
Jersey lawyers *nums*—Miss Hay's boarding-school—young ladies not
allowed to eat mustard—and why?—fat story of a mustard pot, with a
good saying of Ding-dong's—Vernon's tavern—fine place to sleep, if the
noise would let you—another Caliban!—Vernon *slew* eyed—people of
Brunswick, of course, all squint—Drake's tavern—fine old blade—wears
square buckles in his shoes—tells bloody long stories about last war—
people, of course, all do the same—Hook'em Snivy, the famous fortune
teller, born here—cotemporary with mother Shoulders—particulars of his
history—died one day—lines to his memory, *which found their way into*

---

* *vide* Carr. *vide* Moore. *vide* Weld. *vide* Parkinson. *vide* Priest. *vide* Linkum Fidelius, and *vide* Messrs. Tag, Rag, and Bobtail.
† *vide* The Sentimental Kotzebue.

*my pocket-book**—melancholy reflections on the death of great men—beautiful epitaph on myself.

CHAP. IV.

Princeton—college—professors wear boots!—students famous for their love of a jest—set the college on fire, and burnt out the professors; an excellent joke, but not worth repeating—mem. American students very much addicted to burning down colleges—reminds me of a good story, nothing at all to the purpose—two societies in the college—good notion—encourages emulation, and makes little boys fight—students famous for their eating and erudition—saw two at the tavern, who had just got their allowance of spending-money—laid it all out in a supper—got fuddled, and d——d the professors for nincoms. N. B. Southern gentlemen.— Church-yard—apostrophe to grim death—saw a cow feeding on a grave— metempsychosis—who knows but the cow may have been eating up the soul of one of my ancestors—made me melancholy and pensive for fifteen minutes—man planting cabbages†—wondered how he could plant them so straight—method of mole catching—and all that—quere, whether it would not be a good notion to ring their noses as we do pigs—mem. to propose it to the American Agricultural Society—get a premium per- haps—commencement—students give a ball and supper—company from New-York, Philadelphia and Albany—great contest which spoke the best english—albanians vociferous in their demand for sturgeon—philadel- phians gave the preference to racoon,‡ and splac-nuncs—gave them a long dissertation on the phlegmatic nature of a goose's gizzard—students can't dance—always set off with the wrong foot foremost—Duport's opin- ion on that subject—Sir Christopher Hatton the first man who ever turned out his toes in dancing—great favorite with queen Bess on that account—Sir Walter Raleigh—good story about his smoking—his descent into New-Spain—El Dorado—Candid—Dr. Pangloss—Miss Cunegunde— earthquake at Lisbon—Baron of Thundertentronck—jesuits—monks—Car- dinal Woolsey—Pope Joan—Tom Jefferson—Tom Paine, and Tom the ———— whew! N. B. Students got drunk as usual.

CHAP. V.

Left Princeton—country finely diversified with sheep and haystacks§— saw a man riding alone in a waggon! why the deuce didn't the block-

* *vide* Carr and *Blind Bet!*
† *vide* Carr.
‡ *vide* Priest.
§ *vide* Carr.

head ride in a chair? fellow must be a fool;—particular account of the
construction of waggons, carts, wheelbarrows and quail-traps—saw
a large flock of crows—concluded there must be a dead horse in the
neighborhood—mem. country remarkable for crows—won't let the horses
die in peace—anecdote of a jury of crows—stopped to give the horses
water—good looking man came up, and asked me if I had seen his
wife? heavens! thought I, how strange it is that this virtuous man should
ask *me* about his wife—story of Cain and Abel—stage-driver took a *swig*—
mem. set down all the people as drunkards—old house had moss on the
top—swallows built in the roof—better place than old men's beards—story
about that—derivation of words, *kippy, kippy, kippy* and *shoo-pig**—
negro driver could not write his own name—languishing state of literature in this country†—philosophical inquiry of 'Sbidlikens, why the
americans are so much inferior to the mobility of Cheapside and Shore-
ditch, and why they do not eat plum-pudding on Sundays—superfine
reflections about any thing.

CHAP. VI.

Trenton—built above the head of navigation to encourage commerce—
capital of the state—only wants a castle, a bay, a mountain, a sea, and
a volcano, to bear a strong resemblance to the bay of Naples—‡supreme
court sitting—fat chief justice—used to get asleep on the bench after
dinner—gave judgment, I suppose like Pilate's wife, from his dreams—
reminded me of Justice Bridlegoose deciding by a throw of a die, and
of the oracle of the holy bottle—attempted to kiss the chamber-maid—
boxed my ears till they rung like our theatre bell—girl had lost one tooth—
mem. all the american ladies prudes, and have bad teeth—Anacreon
Moore's opinion on the matter—State-house—fine place to see the sturgeons jump up—quere, whether sturgeons jump up by an impulse of
the tail, or whether they bounce up from the bottom by the elasticity of
their noses—Linkum Fidelius of the latter opinion—I too—sturgeon's nose
capital for tennis-balls—learnt that at school—went to a ball—negro
wench principal musician!—N. B. People of America have no fiddlers
but females!—origin of the phrase "fiddle of your heart"—reasons why
men fiddle better than the women—expedient of the amazons who were
expert at the bow—waiter at the city-tavern—good story of his—nothing
to the purpose—never mind—fill up my book like Carr—make it sell.—

* *vide* Carr's learned derivation of *gee* and *whoa.*
† Moore.
‡ Carr.

Saw a democrat get into the stage followed by his dog*—N. B. This town
remarkable for dogs and democrats—superfine sentiment†—good story
from Joe Miller—ode to a piggin of butter—pensive meditations on a
mouse-hole—make a book as clear as a whistle!

FROM MY ELBOW-CHAIR.

I have observed a particular intimacy for these few days past, between
that dry wag WILL WIZARD and my cousin PINDAR. The latter has taken
his winter quarters at old COCKLOFT's, in the corner room opposite mine,
in order to be at hand and overlook the town. They hardly gave themselves time, on Sunday last, to wait for the family toast of "our absent
friends" before they adjourned to Pindar's chamber. In the course of an
hour my cousin's enormous mandarine inkstand was sent down to be
replenished;—I began to be seriously alarmed, for I thought if they
had exhausted its contents without exhausting their subject, there was
no knowing where it would end.

On returning to tea, my cousin Pindar was observed to rub his hands,
a sure sign that something tickled his fancy; he however maintained
as mysterious a countenance as a seventh ward politician. As to Will
Wizard, he took longer strides than usual, his inflexible phiz had an
uncommonly knowing air, and a sagacious wink occasionally betrayed
that he had more in his head than he chose to communicate. The whole
family (who in truth are much given to *wonder* at every thing) were
sadly puzzled to conjecture what their two precious noddles had been
bothering about.

In the evening, after I had retreated to my citadel, the elbow-chair,
I was surprized by the abrupt entrance of these two worthies. My cousin
opened the budget at once: he declared that it was as necessary for a
modern poet to have an assistant, as for Don Quixote to have a Sancho—
that it was the fashion for poets, now a-days, to write so ineffably obscure, that every line required a page of notes to explain its meaning,
and render its "darkness visible"—that a modern poem could no more
succeed without notes, than a paper kite could fly without a tail. In
a word, Pegasus had become a most mulish animal, and would not budge
a foot, unless he lumbered along a cart-load of quotations and explanations, and illustrations at his heels: he had therefore prevailed on Will
Wizard to assist him occasionally as annotator and illustrator. As a
specimen of their united labors, he handed me the following compli-
mentary ode to that king of the buzzards, Dr. CHRISTOPHER COSTIVE, in-

* Moore.
† Carr.

forming me that he had plenty more on hand whenever occasion required it. I had been rather surprized lately at the doctor's meddling with us, as he was sure of gaining more kicks than coppers in return; but I am told an ass loves to have his muzzle scratched with nettles. On expressing my surprise, Will informed me that it was all a sham battle; that he was very intimate with the doctor, and could relate a thousand diverting anecdotes concerning him; and that the doctor finding we were in want of a butt, had generously volunteered himself as our target. I wish him joy of his bargain.

In the following poem it will be observed that, while my cousin Pindar tunes his pipe on the top of the page, Will Wizard, worries away at his thorough bass below. The notes of a modern poem being like the sound of a french horn, bassoon, kettle drum, and bass-viol in our orchestra, which make such a confounded racket, that they entirely drown the song; and no man, who has not the sublime ear of a connoisseur, can tell what the devil tune they're playing.

FLUMMERY
FROM THE MILL (1) OF PINDAR COCKLOFT, ESQ.
Being a Poem with Notes, or rather Notes with a
Poem, (2) *in the manner of*
DOCTOR (3) CHRISTOPHER COSTIVE.
"Prick me Bull-calf till he roars." (4)
Falstaff.

THE greatest (5) poet of our day,
From State of Maine to Louisiana; (6)
The hero who did 'sist upon't,
He wouldn't be deputy to Mr. Hunt; (7)
Who rear'd a gallows for each elf, and
Did for *hangman* his own self stand. (8)
And made folks think it very odd, he
Should turn *Jack Ketch* to every body,
This modern mounter of Pegasus,
This clumsy jolter of Jackasses (9)
Who, now the poets dray horse starts on,
Anon, the gibbet hurdle carts on,
Now o'er a poem dozes happy,
And next expertly draws the cap; he
Who cares not though the world should know it
That he's half hangman, half a poet. (10)
Who gibbetted the knaves so knowing,
That kept Democracy a going,

WILL WIZARD,

Woodcut by Alexander Anderson (1775–1870), the first American wood engraver, for the second American edition of *Salmagundi* (D. Longworth: New York, 1814).

Hung his *fac simile* famed Toney (11)
Pasquin, the friend of Mr. Honé.
Who drags like snail his filthy slime
Through many a ragged hobbling rhyme,
Then calls his billingsgate—sarcastic!
His drabbling doggrel—hudibrastic!
[Good lack, my friends, 'twould make you soon (12) laugh,
To see this jolter-headed moon-calf,
From Hudibras his honors steal
And break Sam Butler on the wheel.] (13)
With other things that I might tell ye on
Performed by this rump-fed hellion (14)
—But not o'er long to dwell upon't,
This man as big as an elephant. (15)
This *sweetest* witling of the age, (16)
This hero, hangman, critic, sage, (17)
This poet of five hundred pound (18)
Has come to grace our hapless town.
And when he entered, every goose
Began to cackle like the deuce;
The asses brayed to one another—
Twas plain—the creatures smelt a brother.

NOTES, BY WILLIAM WIZARD, ESQ.

1 *Mill*] As we are not a little anxious to cultivate the intimacy so happily commenced between the Doctor and ourselves, we feel bound in candor to confess the charge made against us, of having borrowed from him some of the phrazes and ideas of our last number; and we justify ourselves by attributing it to our high regard for his talents: for what can be a greater proof of friendship, now a days, than borrowing? if we were his enemies, we might justify it by the old maxim of "foiling the devil with his own weapons." As to the "mill," which the Doctor so vociferously claims, honest Pindar acknowledges that he borrowed the idea from the Doctor's writings in general, for he never dipped in them without thinking of our nocturnal music-grinder, who continually grinds over and over the same sleepy tune of, "Oh, hard is my fate."

2 *Notes with a Poem*] Whatever merit may appear in this Poem, my friend Cockloft must own that it is entirely owing to his close adherence to his *big* prototype, Dr. Costive. The rhymes are generally *borrowed* from the Doctor's own works, possessing all that quaintness, cuteness and clumsiness, for which he is remarkable. As the lesser thing should always depend upon the greater, we have rather inverted the usual title of such

works, and made the poem minor. We recommend the Doctor's mode of *compiling* a book to all the nums of the day—as an example, we instance his "Terrible Tractoration," of which as few buy, and still fewer read it, (a proof that the town are not quite such fools as the Doctor would make them) we shall say little. This book was smothered in notes, like a goose in onions—some ill-natured cynics have asserted that what little whim the work contained, lay entirely in the notes, which we are sorry to say were not written by the Doctor;—his poem might therefore be said to resemble the *leg of a stool*, dress'd up with *savory sauce;* or, as the Doctor will understand it better, that famous dish called *pumpkin-pie*, where, though the *pumpkin* gives the *name* to the dish, yet the great skill of the cook is to hide the twang of it as much as possible with *spice* and *sugar.*

3 *Doctor*] The Doctor, we are told, was not bred a physician; nor was he indebted for his appellation to a gratuitous donation from any university, as Doctor of Laws—he was humorously so dubbed by his neighbors in Vermont, on account of having once benevolently physick'd a sick horse—his works bear testimony to his drenching abilities; and we may justly apply to him an unlucky epigram, written on a brother quack in physic and poetry:

> "For *physic and farces*
> *His equal there scarce is;—*
> *His* farces *are* physic,—
> *His* physic *a* farce *is."*

4. *Prick bull-calf, &c.*] We had not the least expectation that our notice of Doctor Costive, in the last number, would have put him into such an indecent passion. Bless us how he has roared! and like Falstaff not only roared but "ran and roared"—

> ———"unpack'd his heart with words,
> And fell a cursing—like a very drab!
> A scullion!"

He has given us a most woeful *scolding* through some eight or nine columns, and plainly proved that our work was not worth a fig, because "Salmagundi" had been heretofore given as a title to another work—Launcelot Langstaff was evidently copied from Isaac Bickerstaff, because they both ended with *staff*—"Whim whams" was the same as "Flim Flams"—"Will Wizard" was taken from—the lord knows where, "*Wintry*" was accidentally misspelled or misprinted *Wintery*, and "*Weakly*" was borrowed from his own *Weakly* productions—Oh Midas, Midas, how thine ears do loom through the fog of thy writings—When a man of the Doctor's gumption can write nine columns against our work and discover no greater faults, we may well be vain—were we to criticize our own writings, they would stand a much poorer chance. In spite of the Doctor's crustiness we still love him in our hearts—he may scold like an old woman, but we know it all arises from that excessive irritability common to all men who have "written a book" and particularly a book of doggrel rhymes.—We again assure him of our perfect good will towards himself and his most amiable offspring, that delectable pair of twin brothers, Terrible Tractoration and Democracy Unveiled.— May the whole world in general and posterity in particular know the proper distinction between Hudibrastic and Doggerel, and acquit the Doctor from the imputation meanly levelled against him by sundry nincoms of imitating Hudibras—We are sorry that he should ever have been thought capable of descending to be a copyist, and we challenge the whole world to deny that the Doctor's verse is doggerel, genuine broken winded, rickety doggerel, whatever his enemies may insist to the contrary. The Doctor's waggery, however, like that of many other double headed wits, seems often to have been taken by the wrong end. On the first appearance of his Terrible Tractoration, the critics were absolutely at a loss, such was the delicacy of his wit, to say whether he was the champion or opponent of Perkinism—Thus the Critical Review for 1803, "His real object cannot always be ascertained—we *think* him however the friend of the Tractors." Either the doctor or the critic must have been a dunder head—we charitably suppose the critic. The Doctor afterwards, like "John-a-Gudgeon" in the "pleaders guide" explained, and his explanation proved so perfectly satisfactory that there were very few of the reviewers but could tell, or at least *guess* at his object. The fact was the doctor, good inoffensive soul, did not mean to attack any thing—except common sense—We recommend this work as a soporific specimen of the doctor's skill in *balderdash.*

5 *Greatest poet.*] *Great* is sometimes a positive, sometimes a figurative term—as we say a *great man*, a *great mountain*, or when speaking of the Doctor, a *great man mountain*—having no allusion here to the mountain which brought forth a mouse. When, however, we speak of the Doctor as a *great* man, or *great* poet, we mean to be understood that he is some six feet six inches high—three feet across the shoulders, nine round the paunch—that he weighs about half a ton, and is withal most clumsily hung together.

6 *Louisiana.*] Though we plume ourselves on adhering closely to the Doctor's rhymes, yet we have taken the liberty of differing a little in the pronunciation of this word—the Doctor gives it in the true eastern dialect, Lousy-anee—but to give it *a-la-costive—*

"Which late, tis said, in weather rainy,
Was melted in Louisiana."

Again: for when the Doctor gets hold of a good rhyme, he is a "woundy toad" for harping on it.

> But please his highness ship, I wont
> Be deputy to Mr. Hunt:
> No—were it offered 'twould be vain, he
> Wont catch me in Louisiana. (or Lousy anee.)

These two latter lines are truly as musical, as marrow-bones and cleavers, and remind us of that sweet couplet, by the Doctor's rival, the inimitable SEARSON.

> From this seat I pass'd to Alexandria,
> And am pleased through rural scenes to wander.
>
> SEAR. Mount Ver.

If our reader wishes for more specimens of the Doctor's knack at rhyming, we'll give him the oft repeated tags of 'rogues and demagogues,' 'brewing and ruin,' 'wildering & children' 'women & common' 'trimming and women' 'well-knows and fellows,' 'comparison and harrass'd-em;' together with an occasional mixture of those attic eastern jingles of 'dandy and handy' and 'sugar-candy.' The Doctor and Searson's poetic contest is similar to one that whilom took place between two honest tars (we beg the gentle Joe Miller's pardon for *borrowing* an anecdote) one gave as *prize couplet;*

> As she slips she slides along,
> A faithful friend is hard to find.

but the other *rhymster* beat him all hollow by singing out,

> "My quart pot holds a gallon,
> By zounds!"

7 *Deputy to Mr. Hunt*] Mr. Hunt was a *little* man and a young man, the Doctor, although of the same age, feeling the *immensity* of his qualifications refuses to second such a governor, urging his *size*, and like Billy Bugby, alledging that what he wanted in years he made up in *bulk;* and if he lacked in brains, he atoned for all in *garbage.*

8 *Did for hangman, &c.*] How the Doctor ever came to stumble on this unhappy idea, we are at a loss to imagine—it is an odd "whim-wham," for a fellow to dub himself with the humorous epithet of *hangman.* "We would not have his enemies say so." Whether the doctor has a *hanging look* or no, we leave others to determine. We are certain he is in no danger of the gallows himself;—but we warn him to take care how he visits Connecticut—he may chance to be burnt for a witch. We give the doctor's own claim to his *Tyburn title.*

> Now since ye are a ruffian crew,
> As honest Jack Ketch ever knew;
> No threats nor growling shall prohibit
> My hanging you on satire's gibbet.   vide Costive

9 *This clumsy jolter of jackasses.*] As this line partakes of the true costive obscurity, we beg leave to explain. There is no intention of call-

ing the Doctor a jackass, we only mean that he makes an ass of Pegasus, and even when on poor Pegasus (so degraded) he is but a miserable rider. His trotting, pacing, nigglety-nagglety lines, put us often in mind of that pious but quaint expression about the "devil riding rough shod over a soul."

10 *Half a poet.*] Oh fie, friend Cockloft, this savors of sheer envy. Were there any doubts of the Doctors being a whole poet—aye, and a *big* poet, the following verse would set them at rest. It shows that he is a complete jockey on Pegasus; and when the poor nag wont pace, he'll cudgel him as soundly as he does his own brains.

> Yes, we were 'raptured when he said
> We're all republican, all fed-
> Ral fellow-citizens, Americans,
> And hoped we'd done with factions' hurricanes!
>
> *Costive*

Is this poetic frenzy, (alias idiotism) or is it turgid stupidity? truly it is as smooth as a pine log causeway; it confirms the Doctor's right to his *sir-name*, and can only be matched by a stave from the Doctor's cotemporary bard, and rival *rhymster*, Searson—videlicet.

> *From house to house, soon took my departure,*
> *And to the garden look'd for sweet nature.*
> *The fishing very great at Mount Vernon,*
> *When there with other scenes I look'd upon.*
> *This pleasing seat hath its prospects so high,*
> *That one would think 'twas for astronomy,*
> *'Twould answer for an observatory.*

The reader will perceive the similarity in taste, style, and ear of these rival poets. I have their works bound up together, and Minshull's into the bargain. It shall go hard but that they shall all descend the gutter of immortality together.

11 *His fac simile famed Toney*] The Doctor's abusing poor Toney Pasquin, brought forcibly to our recollection the vulgar cant saying about the pot and the kettle. Perhaps no two of the *great* poets of the day, are more alike, in most particulars, than Doctor Costive and honest Tony. The Doctor is a true poetic blackguard—and so is Toney. The Doctor is an adept in the Billingsgate vocabulary—so is Tony. The Doctor has bespattered many a poor devil who never offended him—so has Toney. The doctor has written a book—so has Toney. It may be said of each of them—

> *"We will not rake the dunghill for his crimes,*
> *Who knows the man will never read his rhymes."*

The only particular in which they disagree is, that Toney has been

occasionally convicted of saying a good thing—the gentle stupidity of
the doctor being entirely innocent of any thing of the kind.
      "Oh here's another pumpion, the cramm'd son of a starved
   usurer, Cacafogo. Both their brains buttered cannot make
   two spoonsful."   *Rule a Wife.*
   12 *Soon*] This word is entirely unnecessary to the sense, and is
dragged in for no other purpose whatever, but to eke out the line, in
humbler *imitation* of a dull, but honest expedient, frequently made use
of by the illustrious Searson, and his great rival, Doctor Costive.
   13 *And break, &c.*] It has for some time been a trick with many a
sleepy scribbler, beside the Doctor, though now it has grown rather
notorious, to break their crabbed lines with a "fist or stick" or crow-bar,
and then term their *chopped hay* Hudibrastic—thus is poetry daily put on
the rack; and thus is poor Butler crucified every hour!
   14 *Rump-fed hellion*] Lest the Doctor should here again accuse us
of *borrowing*, a thing, by the by, we strongly suspect him of, as we
think we can discover that many of his thoughts, and certainly some of
his rhymes, are *borrowed* from the immortal Searson and the inimitable
Minshull, we acknowledge that we are indebted for this line to Shakspeare. Whether the term *rump-fed* applies to the doctor or not, we cannot exactly tell; but if we were not afraid of swelling our notes, we
would, following the example of the Doctor in his Democracy Unveiled,
give our readers an account of the famous *rump* parliament—and truly
'twould be as much in point as most of the notes in that celebrated work.
   Hellion. "A deputy scullion employed in regions below "to cook up
the broth"—Link. Fid.—The doctor, good man, has employed himself,
while on earth, as far as his *weakly* powers would go, in stewing up
many a woeful kettle of fish.—
                  "Double, double, toil and trouble,
                  "Fire burn, and caldron bubble."
Shakspeare must certainly have had the Doctor's weekly mess of
bubble and *squeak* in view, when he wrote the above.
   15 *As big as an elephant*] There is more truth than poetry in this
comparison. The following curious anecdote was told me by the Doctor
himself, when I breakfasted with him the other morning:—The elephant
which travelled lately through our country, was shown in New England;—
two simple country girls, desirous of seeing what kind of a beast it was,
applied for admittance. On entering the room, the doctor, who was
stooping to tie his shoe-string with his back towards them, was for a
moment taken for the elephant!—they declared it was a clumsy creature—
"they could not make head nor tail of it." No wonder, poor things, the
critics were as much puzzled themselves, as we have already shown.
   16 *Sweetest witling*] A poetic licence, the Doctor certainly being

none of the sweetest of personages. Many a fair flower, however, springs out of a dung-hill—and the Doctor is not the first poet who has written a *sweet* song in "marvelous dirty linen."

17 *This hero hangman, &c.*]
> *All hush'd in mute attention sit,*
> *To hear this critic, poet, wit,*
> *Philosopher, all, all at once,*
> *And to complete them, all this* DUNCE.
>
>   LLOYD.

18 *Five hundred pounds*] i. e. five hundred pounds weight; or in true avoirdupoise, 4 cwt. 1 qu. 24 lbs.

GENERAL REMARK.

We have endeavored to copy the Doctor's style and manner as correctly as possible throughout this charming poem: the *rhymes* are chiefly "filched" from his own *labors,* and jingle as harmoniously as sleigh bells— like him we have sometimes risen, and sometimes descended, with all his leaden profundity. Some poets sip in the heliconian stream, others dabble in it. The Doctor exceeds them all—he has a true poetic DIVING BELL—plunges boldly to the bottom, and there drabbles in the mud like a flounder. In the *gallows* part of his poem, the doctor may truly be said to *rise;* and in our touch on the Hellion, we have certainly almost equalled those profound sinkings of his genius, where the Doctor even descends *below himself.* We conclude with *borrowing* a speech from old Shakspeare—"Give me thy hand," Doctor, "I am sorry I beat thee; but while thou livest, keep a good tongue in thy head."

NOTICE.

While in a "state militant," waging war with folly and stupidity, and assailed on all sides by a combination of nincoms and numsculls, we are gratified to find that our careless effusions have received the approbation of men and wit and genius. We have expressed heretofore our contempt for the applause of *the million,* but we confess ourselves ambitious of the praises of *the few;* we have read therefore with infinite self-congratulation the encomiums passed on our productions by the learned and liberal editor of the "People's Friend." The attacks of that *billingsgate droll* Dr. Costive, and his whole *North-River fraternity,* could not give us greater delight. We also publish with pride the following card from the authors of "THE ECHO," a work which we have commended to a conspicuous post in our library; and we do hereby shake its authors by the hand as a set of right merry wags, choice spirits, and what we think better than all, genuine humorists.

CARD.

"The authors of "THE ECHO" send a copy of it to the writers of "SALMAGUNDI," which they request them to accept, as a mark of the pleasure they have received from their cervantic effusions."

Now we are in the humour of card writing, we would acknowledge the reception of several effusions in prose and verse, which, though they do great credit to the writers, and would doubtless be both pleasing and instructing to the public, yet do not come exactly within the intention of our work, the authors therefore will excuse our not publishing them.

We have likewise received a note written in a french hand, but in villainous bad english. Will Wizard has been at much pains to decypher it, but in vain, it is as unintelligible as an herculanean manuscript. He has discovered however that it is a vindication of dancing, together with a long eulogy on the *pas de chat*.

As a considerable part of this paper is taken up with a stupid subject, viz. the Doctor, and as we do not wish that our readers should pay for "flummery" merely, we have directed our publisher to give them eight pages extra: this will account for the unusual size of the present number. We confess we *borrowed* this idea among many others from the Doctor, who lately finding that his readers were dissatisfied with the *contents* of his *weakly* paper, endeavored to put them in good humor by doubling its *bulk*; this he waggishly enough terms *doubling the dose*—oh the droll dog!

SALMAGUNDI NO. V

NO. V]   *Saturday, March 7, 1807.*
                FROM MY ELBOW-CHAIR.

THE following letter of my friend Mustapha appears to have been written some time subsequent to the one already published. Were I to judge from its contents, I should suppose it was suggested by the splendid review of the twenty fifth of last November, when a pair of colors was presented, at the City-Hall, to the regiments of artillery: and when a huge dinner was devoured by our corporation, in honorable remembrance of the evacuation of this city. I am happy to find that the laudable spirit of military emulation which prevails in our city has attracted the attention of a stranger of Mustapha's sagacity—by military emulation I mean that spirited rivalry in the size of a hat, the length of a feather, and the gingerbread finery of a sword belt; this being what I understand by *military foppery*.

LETTER

From MUSTAPHA RUB-A-DUB KELI KHAN, to
ABDALLAH EB'N AL RAHAB, surnamed the
SNORER, military centinel at the gate of his
highness' palace.

THOU hast heard, oh Abdallah, of the great magician, MULEY FUZ, who could change a blooming land, blessed with all the elysian charms of hill and dale, of glade and grove, of fruit and flower into a desart, frightful, solitary and forlorn; who with a wave of his wand could transform even the disciples of Mahomet into grinning apes and chattering monkeys. Surely, thought I to myself this morning, the dreadful Muley has been exercising his infernal enchantments on these unhappy infidels. Listen, oh Abdallah, and wonder. Last night I committed myself to tranquil slumber, encompassed with all the monotonous tokens of peace, and this morning I awoke enveloped in the noise, the bustle, the clangor, and the shouts of war. Every thing was changed as if by magic. An immense army had sprung up, like mushrooms, in a night, and all the coblers, tailors, and tinkers of the city had mounted the nodding plume; had become, in the twinkling of an eye, helmetted heroes and war-worn veterans.

Alarmed at the beating of drums, the braying of trumpets and the shouting of the multitude, I dressed myself in haste, sallied forth and followed a prodigious crowd of people to a place called the Battery. This is so denominated, I am told, from having once been defended with formidable *wooden* bulwarks, which in the course of a hard winter were *thriftly* pulled to pieces by an *economic* corporation, to be distributed for fire-wood among the poor; this was done at the hint of a cunning old engineer, who assured them it was the only way in which their fortifications would ever be able to keep up a *warm fire*. ECONOMY, my friend, is the watch-word of this nation; I have been studying for a month past to divine its meaning, but truly am as much perplexed as ever. It is a kind of national starvation, an experiment how many comforts and necessaries the body politic can be deprived of before it perishes. It has already arrived to a lamentable degree of debility, and promises to share the fate of the arabian philosopher, who proved that he could live without food, but unfortunately died just as he had brought his experiment to perfection.

On arriving at the battery, I found an *immense* army of SIX HUNDRED MEN, drawn up in a true mussulman crescent. At first, I supposed this was in compliment to myself, but my interpreter informed me that it was done merely for want of room, the corporation not being able to afford them sufficient to display in a straight line. As I expected a display of some grand evolutions and military manoevres, I determined to remain a tranquil spectator, in hopes that I might possibly collect some hints which might be of service to his highness.

This great body of men I perceived was under the command of a small *bashaw*, in yellow and gold, with white nodding plumes, and most formidable whiskers, which, contrary to the tripolitan fashion, were in the neighborhood of his ears instead of his nose. He had two attendants called aid-de-camps, (or *tails*) being similar to a bashaw with two tails. The bashaw, though commander in chief, seemed to have little more to do than myself—he was a spectator within the lines and I without—he was clear of the rabble and I was encompassed by them, this was the only difference between us, except that he had the best opportunity of showing his clothes. I waited an hour or two with exemplary patience, expecting to see some grand military evolutions or a sham battle exhibited, but no such thing took place; the men stood stock still, supporting their arms, groaning under the fatigues of war, and now and then sending out a foraging party to levy contributions of beer and a favorite beverage which they denominate *grog*. As I perceived the crowd very active in examining the line, from one extreme to the other, and as I could see no other purpose, for which these sunshine warriors should be exposed so long to the merciless attacks of wind and weather, I of course concluded that this must be *the review*.

In about two hours the army was put in motion, and marched through some narrow streets, where the *economic corporation* had carefully provided a soft carpet of mud, to a magnificent castle of painted brick decorated with grand pillars of pine boards. By the ardor which brightened in each countenance, I soon perceived that this castle was to undergo a vigorous attack. As the ordnance of the castle was perfectly silent, and as they had nothing but a straight street to advance through, they made their approaches with great courage and admirable regularity, until within about a hundred feet of the castle, a pump opposed a formidable obstacle in their way, and put the whole army to a nonplus. The circumstance was sudden and unlooked-for—the commanding officer ran over all the military tactics with which his head was crammed, but none offered any expedient for the present awful emergency. The pump maintained its post, and so did the commander; there was no knowing which was most at a stand. The commanding officer ordered his men to wheel and take it in flank—the army accordingly wheeled, and came full butt against it in rear exactly as they were before:—"wheel to the left!" cried the officer; they did so, and again, as before, the inveterate pump intercepted their progress. "Right about, face!" cried the officer; the men obeyed, but bungled—they *faced back to back*. Upon this the bashaw with two tails, with great coolness, undauntedly, ordered his men to push right forward, pell-mell, pump or no pump—they gallantly

obeyed; after unheard-of acts of bravery the pump was carried without
the loss of a man, and the army firmly entrenched itself under the very
walls of the castle. The bashaw had then a council of war with his
officers; the most vigorous measures were resolved on. An advance guard
of musicians were ordered to attack the castle without mercy. Then
the whole band opened a most tremendous battery of drums, fifes,
tambourines, and trumpets, and kept up a thundering assault, as if
the castle, like the walls of Jericho, spoken of in the jewish chronicles,
would tumble down at the blowing of rams' horns. After some time a
parley ensued. The grand bashaw of the city appeared on the battlements
of the castle, and as far as I could understand from circumstances, dared
the little bashaw of two tails to single combat;—this thou knowest was in
the style of antient chivalry:—the little bashaw dismounted with great
intrepidity, and ascended the battlements of the castle, where the
great bashaw waited to receive him, attended by numerous dignitaries
and worthies of his court, one of whom bore the splendid banners of
the castle. The battle was carried on intirely by *words*, according to the
universal custom of this country, of which I shall speak to thee more
fully hereafter. The grand bashaw made a furious attack in a speech of
considerable length; the little bashaw by no means appalled, retorted
with great spirit. The grand bashaw attempted to rip him up with an
argument, or stun him with a solid fact; but the little bashaw parried
them both with admirable adroitness, and run him clean through and
through with syllogism. The grand bashaw was overthrown, the banners
of the castle yielded up to the little bashaw, and the castle surrendered
after a vigorous defence of three hours—during which the besiegers
suffered great extremity from muddy streets and a drizzling atmosphere.

On returning to dinner I soon discovered that as usual I had been
indulging in a great mistake. The matter was all clearly explained to me
by a fellow lodger, who on ordinary occasions moves in the humble
character of a tailor, but in the present instance figured in a high military
station denominated *corporal*. He informed me that what I had mistaken
for a castle was the splendid palace of the municipality, and that the
supposed attack was nothing more than the delivery of a flag, given by
the authorities, to the army for its magnanimous defence of the town
for upwards of twenty years past, (that is, ever since the last war!)
Oh, my friend, surely every thing in this country is on a great scale!—
The conversation insensibly turned upon the military establishment of
the nation, and I do assure thee, that my friend the taylor, though being
according to a national proverb, but the ninth part of a man, yet
acquitted himself on military concerns as ably as the grand bashaw of
the empire himself. He observed that their rulers had decided that wars
were very useless and expensive, and ill-befitting an economic philosophic

nation; they had therefore made up their minds never to have any wars, and consequently there was no need of soldiers or military discipline. As, however, it was thought highly ornamental to a city to have a number of men drest in fine clothes and *feathers*, strutting about the streets on a holiday—and as the women and children were particularly fond of such *raree shows*, it was ordered that the tailors of the different cities throughout the empire should, forthwith, go to work, and cut out and manufacture soldiers as fast as their sheers and needles would permit.

These soldiers have no pecuniary pay, and their only recompense for the immense services which they render their country in their voluntary parades, is the plunder of smiles, and winks, and nods which they extort from the ladies. As they have no opportunity, like the vagrant arabs, of making inroads on their neighbors, and as it is necessary to keep up their military spirit, the town is therefore, now and then, but particularly on two days of the year, given up to their ravages. The arrangements are contrived with admirable address, so that every officer from the bashaw down to the drum-major, (the chief of the eunuchs, or musicians) shall have his share of that invaluable booty, the *admiration of the fair*. As to the soldiers, poor animals, they, like the privates in all great armies, have to bear the brunt of danger and fatigue, while their officers receive all the glory and reward. The narrative of a parade day will exemplify this more clearly.

The chief bashaw, in the plenitude of his authority orders a grand review of the *whole army*, at two o'clock. The bashaw *with two tails*, that he may have an opportunity of vaporing about as greatest man on the field, orders the army to assemble at twelve. The kiaya, or *colonel*, as he is called, (that is, commander of one hundred and twenty men) orders his regiment or tribe to collect *one mile at least* from the place of parade, at eleven. Each captain (or *fag rag* as we term them) commands his squad to meet at ten, at least *a half mile* from the regimental parade— and to close all, the chief of the eunuchs orders his infernal concert of fifes, trumpets, cymbals and kettle drums to assemble at ten! from that moment the city receives no quarter. All is noise, hooting, hubbub and combustion. Every window, door, crack and loop-hole, from the garret to the cellar, is crowded with the fascinating fair, of all ages and of all complexions. The mistress smiles through the windows of the drawing-room; the chubby chambermaid lolls out of the attic casement, and a host of sooty wenches roll their white eyes, and grin and chatter from the cellar-door. Every nymph seems anxious to yield voluntarily, that tribute which the heroes of their country demand. First struts the chief eunuch, or drum-major, at the head of his sable band, magnificently arrayed in tarnished scarlet. Alexander himself could not have spurned the earth more superbly. A host of ragged boys shout in his train, and inflate the bosom of the warrior with ten-fold self-complacency. After he has rattled his kettle drums through the town, and swelled and swaggered like a turkey-cock before all the dingy Floras, and Dianas, and Junoes, and Didoes of his acquaintance, he repairs to his place of destination, loaded with a rich booty of smiles and approbation. Next comes the FAG-RAG, or captain, at the head of his mighty band, consisting of one lieutenant, one ensign, (or mute) four sergeants, four corporals, one drummer, one fifer, and if he has any privates so much the better for himself. In marching to the regimental parade he is sure to paddle through the street or lane which is honored with the residence of his mistress or intended, whom he resolutely lays under a heavy contribution. Truly it is delectable to behold these heroes as they march along, cast side glances at the upper windows, to collect the smiles, the nods, and the winks, which the enraptured fair ones lavish profusely on the magnanimous defenders of their country.

The Fag-rags having conducted their squads to their respective regiments, then comes the turn of the colonel, (a bashaw with *no tails*) for all eyes are now directed to him, and the Fag-rags, and the eunuchs and the kettle-drummers, having had their hour of notoriety, are confounded and lost in the military crowd. The colonel sets his whole regiment in motion; and, mounted on a mettlesome charger, frisks and fidgets, and capers, and plunges in front, to the great entertainment of the multitude, and the great hazard of himself and his neighbors. Having displayed himself, his trappings, his horse, and his *horsemanship*, he at length arrives at the place of general rendezvous, blessed with the universal admiration of his country women. I should, perhaps, mention a squadron of hardy veterans, most of whom have seen a deal of service during the nineteen or twenty years of their existence, and who, most gorgeously equipped in tight green jackets and breeches, trot, and amble, and gallop, and scamper, like little devils through every street and nook and corner and poke hole of the city, to the great dread of all old people, and sage matrons with young children. This is truly sublime! This is what I call making a mountain out of a mole-hill. Oh, my friend, on what a *great scale* is every thing in this country. It is in the style of the wandering arabs of the desert *El-Tih*. Is a village to be attacked, or a hamlet to be plundered, the whole desert, for weeks before hand, is in a buz—such marching and counter-marching, ere they can concentrate their ragged forces! and the consequence is, that before they can bring their troops into action, *the whole enterprise is blown.*

The army being all happily collected on the battery, though, perhaps, two hours after the time appointed, it is now the turn of the bashaw, with two tails, to distinguish himself. Ambition, my friend, is implanted alike in every heart, it pervades each bosom, from the bashaw to the drum-major. This is a sage truism, and I trust, therefore, it will not be disputed. The bashaw fired with that thirst for glory, inseperable from the noble mind, is anxious to reap a full share of the laurels of the day, and bear off his portion of female plunder. The drums beat, the fifes whistle, the standards wave proudly in the air. The signal is given!— thunder roars the cannon!—away goes the bashaw, and away go the *tails*! The review finished, evolutions and military manœuvres are generally dispensed with for three excellent reasons; first, because the army knows very little about them; second, because as the country has determined to remain always at peace, there is no necessity for them to know any thing about them; and third, as it is growing late, the bashaw must dispatch, or it will be too dark for him to get his quota of the plunder. He of course orders the whole army to march; and now, my friend, now comes the tug of war—now is the city completely sacked. Open fly the battery-gates, forth sallies the bashaw with his two tails, surrounded by a shouting body-guard of boys and negroes! Then pour forth his legions, potent as the pismires of the desert! The customary salutations of the country commence, those tokens of joy and admiration which so much annoyed me on first landing: the air is darkened with old hats, shoes, and dead cats, they fly in showers like the arrows of the parthians. The soldiers, no ways disheartened, like the intrepid followers of Leonidas, march gallantly under their shade. On they push, splash-dash, mud or no mud. Down one lane, up another—the martial music resounds through every street—the fair ones throng to their windows—the soldiers look every way but straight forward. "Carry arms!" cries the bashaw—"tantara ra-ra," brays the trumpet—"rub-a-dub," roars the drum—"hurraw," shout the ragamuffins. The bashaw smiles with exultation—every Fag-rag feels himself a hero—"none but the brave deserve the fair!" Head of the immortal Amrou, on what a great scale is every thing in this country!

Aye, but you'll say, is not this unfair that the officers should share all the sports while the privates undergo all the fatigue? truly, my friend, I indulged the same idea, and pitied from my heart, the poor fellows who had to drabble through the mud and the mire, toiling under pondrous cocked hats, which seemed as unwieldy, and cumbrous, as the shell which the snail lumbers along on his back. I soon found out, however, that they have their quantum of notoriety. As soon as the army is dismissed, the city swarms with little scouting parties, who fire off their guns at every corner, to the great delight of all the women and children in their vicinity; and woe unto any dog, or pig, or hog, that falls in the way of these magnanimous warriors—they are shewn no quarter. Every gentle swain repairs to pass the evening at the feet of his dulcinea, to play "the soldier tired of war's alarms," and to captivate her with the glare of his regimentals, excepting some ambitious heroes, who strut to the theatre, flame away in the front boxes, and hector every old apple woman in the lobbies.

Such, my friend, is the gigantic genius of this nation, and its faculty of swelling up nothings into importance. Our bashaw of Tripoli, will review his troops of some thousands, by an early hour in the morning. Here a review of six hundred men is made the mighty work of a day! With us a bashaw of *two tails* is never appointed to a command of less than ten thousand men; but here we behold every grade from the bashaw, down to the drum-major, in a force of less than one tenth of the number. By the beard of Mahomet, but every thing here is *indeed* on a great scale!

BY ANTHONY EVERGREEN, GENT.

I was not a little surprized the other morning at a request from Will Wizard that I would accompany him that evening to Mrs. ————'s Ball. The request was simple enough in itself, it was only singular as coming from Will;—of all my acquaintance, Wizard is the least calculated and disposed for the society of ladies—not that he dislikes their company; on the contrary, like every man of pith and marrow, he is a professed admirer of the sex; and had he been born a poet, would undoubtedly have bespattered and be-rhymed some hard named goddess, until she became as famous as Petrarch's Laura, or Waller's Sacharissa; but Will is such a confounded bungler at a bow, has so many odd bachelor habits, and finds it so troublesome to be gallant, that he generally prefers smoking his segar, and telling his story among cronies of his own gender —and thundering long stories they are, let me tell you—set Will once a-going about China, or Crim Tartary, or the Hottentots, and heaven help the poor victim who has to endure his prolixity—he might better be tied to the tail of a Jack-o-lantern. In one word—Will talks like a traveller. Being well acquainted with his character, I was the more alarmed at his inclination to visit a party, since he has often assured me, that he considered it as equivalent to being stuck up for three hours in a steam-engine. I even wondered how he had received an invitation—this he soon accounted for. It seems Will, on his last arrival from Canton, had made a present of a case of tea, to a lady for whom he had once entertained a sneaking kindness, when at grammar school; and she in return had invited him to come and drink some of it—a cheap way enough of paying off little obligations. I readily acceded to Will's proposition, expecting much entertainment from his eccentric remarks; and as he has been absent some few years, I anticipated his surprize at the splendor and elegance of a modern rout.

On calling for Will in the evening, I found him full dressed, waiting for me. I contemplated him with absolute dismay—as he still retained a spark of regard for the lady who once reigned in his affections, he had been at unusual pains in decorating his person, and broke upon my sight arrayed in the true style that prevailed among our beaux some years ago. His hair was turned up and tufted at the top, frizzed out at the ears, a profusion of powder puffed over the whole, and a long plaited club swung gracefully from shoulder to shoulder, describing a pleasing semicircle of powder and pomatum. His claret colored coat was decorated with a profusion of gilt buttons, and reached to his calves. His white casimere small clothes were so tight that he seemed to have grown up in them; and his ponderous legs, which are the thickest part of his body, were beautifully clothed in sky-blue silk stockings, once considered so becoming. But above all, he prided himself upon his waistcoat of China silk, which might almost have served a good housewife for a short gown; and he boasted that the roses and tulips upon it were the work of *Nang-Fou*, daughter of the great *Chin-Chin-Fou*, who had fallen in love with the graces of his person, and sent it to him as a parting present—he assured me she was a remarkable beauty with sweet obliquity of eyes, and a foot no larger than the thumb of an alderman;—he then dilated most copiously on his silver sprigged Dicky, which he assured me was quite the rage among the dashing young mandarins of Canton.

I hold it an ill-natured office to put any man out of conceit with himself; so, though I would willingly have made a little alteration in my friend Wizard's picturesque costume, yet I politely complimented him on his rakish appearance.

On entering the room I kept a good look out on Will, expecting to see him exhibit signs of surprize; but he is one of those knowing fellows who are never surprized at any thing, or at least will never acknowledge it. He took his stand in the middle of the floor, playing with his great steel watch-chain, and looking round on the company, the furniture and the pictures, with the air of a man "who had seen d——d finer things in his time;" and to my utter confusion and dismay, I saw him cooly pull out his villanous old japanned tobacco-box, ornamented with a bottle, a pipe, and a scurvy motto, and help himself to a quid in the face of all the company.

I knew it was all in vain to find fault with a fellow of Will's socratic turn, who is never to be put out of humor with himself; so, after he had given his box its prescriptive rap and returned it to his pocket, I drew him to a corner, where we might observe the company, without being prominent objects ourselves.

"And pray who is that stylish figure," said Will, "who blazes away in red like a volcano, and who seems wrapped in flames like a fiery dragon?" that, cried I, is MISS LAURELIA DASHAWAY—she is the highest flash of the ton—has much whim and more eccentricity, and has reduced many an unhappy gentleman to stupidity by her charms—you see she holds out the red flag in token of "no quarter." "Then keep me safe out of the sphere of her attractions," cried Will, "I would not e'en come in contact with her train, lest it should scorch me like the tail of a comet.—But who, I beg of you, is that amiable youth who is handing along a young lady, and at the same time contemplating his sweet person in a mirror as he passes?" His name, said I, is BILLY DIMPLE—he is a universal smiler, and would travel from Dan to Beersheba, and smile on every body as he passed. Dimple is a slave to the ladies—a hero at tea parties, and is famous at the *pirouet* and the pigeon-wing—a fiddle-stick is his idol, and a dance his elysium. "A very pretty young gentleman, truly," cried Wizard, "he reminds me of a cotemporary beau at Hayti. You must know that the maganimous Dessalines gave a great ball to his court one fine sultry summer's evening; Dessy and me were great cronies—hand and glove—one of the most condescending, great men I ever knew. Such a display of black and yellow beauties! such a show of madras handkerchiefs, red beads, cocks tails and pea-cocks feathers!— it was, as here, who should wear the highest top-knot, drag the longest tails, or exhibit the greatest variety of combs, colors and gew-gaws. In the middle of the rout, when all was buzz, slip-slop, clack and perfume, who should enter but TUCKY SQUASH! The yellow beauties blushed blue, and the black ones blushed as red as they could, with pleasure; and there was a universal agitation of fans—every eye brightened and whitened to see Tucky, for he was the pride of the court, the pink of courtesy. the mirror of fashion, the adoration of all the sable fair ones of Hayti. Such breadth of nose, such exuberance of lip! his shins had the true cucumber curve—his face in dancing shone like a kettle; and, provided you kept to windward of him in summer, I do not know a sweeter youth in all Hayti than Tucky Squash. When he laughed, there appeared from ear to ear a chevaux-de-frize of teeth, that rivalled the shark's in whiteness; he could whistle like a northwester—play on a three-stringed fiddle like Apollo;—and as to dancing, no Long-Island negro could shuffle you "double trouble," or "hoe corn and dig potatoes" more scientifically— in short, he was a second Lothario, and the dusky nymphs of Hayti, one and all, declared him a perpetual Adonis. Tucky walked about, whistling to himself, without regarding any body; and his *nonchalance* was irresistible."

I found Will had got neck and heels into one of his travellers stories, and there is no knowing how far he would have run his parallel between Billy Dimple and Tucky Squash, had not the music struck up, from an adjoining apartment, and summoned the company to the dance. The sound seemed to have an inspiring effect on honest Will, and he procured the hand of an old acquaintance for a country dance. It happened to be the fashionable one of "the Devil among the Tailors," which is so vociferously demanded at every ball and assembly: and many a torn gown, and many an unfortunate toe did rue the dancing of that night; for Will thundered down the dance like a coach and six, sometimes right, sometimes wrong, now running over half a score of little frenchmen, and now making sad inroads into ladies cobweb muslins and spangled tails. As every part of Will's body partook of the exertion, he shook from his capacious head such volumes of powder, that like pious Eneas on his first interview with queen Dido, he might be said to have been enveloped in a cloud. Nor was Will's partner an insignificant figure in the scene. She was a young lady of most voluminous proportions, that quivered at every skip; and being braced up in the fashionable style, with whalebone, stay-tape and buckram, looked like an apple-pudding tied in the middle, or, taking her flaming dress into consideration, like a bed and bolsters rolled up in a suit of red curtains. The dance finished—I would gladly have taken Will off, but no—he was now in one of his happy moods, and there was no doing any thing with him. He insisted on my introducing him to miss SOPHY SPARKLE, a young lady unrivalled for playful wit and innocent vivacity, and who, like a brilliant, adds lustre to the front of fashion. I accordingly presented him to her, and began a conversation in which, I thought, he might take a share; but no such thing. Will took his stand before her, straddling like a Colossus, with his hands in his pockets, and an air of the most profound attention, nor did he pretend to open his lips for some time, until, upon some lively sally of hers, he electrified the whole company with a most intolerable burst of laughter. What was to be done with such an incorrigible fellow?—to add to my distress, the first word he spoke was to tell Miss Sparkle that something she said reminded him of a circumstance that happened to him in China—and at it he went, in the true traveller style—described the chinese mode of eating rice with chopsticks—entered into a long eulogium on the succulent qualities of boiled birds nests, and I made my escape at the very moment when he was on the point of squatting down on the floor, to show how the little chinese *Joshes* sit cross-legged.

TO THE LADIES.
FROM THE MILL OF
PINDAR COCKLOFT, ESQ.

THOUGH jogging down the hill of life,
Without the comfort of a wife;—

And though I ne'er a helpmate chose,
To stock my house and mend my hose;
With care my person to adorn,
And spruce me up on Sunday morn;—
Still do I love the gentle sex,
And still with cares my brain perplex,
To keep the fair ones of the age
Unsullied as the spotless page;
All pure, all simple, all refined,
The sweetest solace of mankind.

I hate the loose insidious jest,
To beauties modest ear addrest,
And hold that frowns should never fail
To check each smooth, but fulsome tale:—
But he whose impious pen should dare
Invade the morals of the fair;
To taint that purity divine
Which should each female heart enshrine;
Though soft his vicious strains should swell,
As those which erst from Gabriel fell,
Should yet be held aloft to shame
And foul dishonor shade his name.

Judge then, my friends, of my surprize,
The ire that kindled in my eyes,
When I relate, that t'other day,
I went a morning call to pay,
On two young nieces, just come down
To take the *polish* of the town;
By which I mean no more nor less
Than *a la francaise* to *undress;*
To whirl the modest waltz's rounds,
Taught by Duport for *snug ten pounds.*
To thump and thunder through a song,
Play *fortes* soft and *dolce's* strong;
Exhibit loud *piano* feats,
Caught from that crotchet hero, Meetz;
To drive the rose bloom from the face
And fix the lily in its place;
To doff the white, and in its stead
To bounce about in brazen red.

While in the parlor I delay'd
Till they their persons had array'd,
A dapper volume caught my eye,
That on the window chanced to lie.
A book's a friend—I always choose
To turn its pages and peruse—
It proved those poems known to fame
For praising every cyprian dame—
The bantlings of a dapper youth,
Renown'd for *gratitude* and *truth;*
A little pest, hight TOMMY MOORE,
Who hopp'd and skipp'd our country o'er;
Who sipp'd our tea and lived on sops,
Revell'd on syllabubs and slops,
And when his brain, of cobweb fine,
Was fuddled with five drops of wine,
Would all his puny loves rehearse,
And many a maid debauch—in verse.

Surprized to meet in open view
A book of such lascivious hue,
I chid my nieces—but they say,
'Tis all the *passion* of the day—
That many a fashionable belle
Will with enraptured accents dwell,
On the sweet *morceaux* she has found
In this delicious, curs'd, compound!

Soft do the tinkling numbers roll,
And lure to vice the unthinking soul;
They tempt by softest sounds away;
They lead entranced the heart astray,
And satan's doctrine sweetly sing
As with a seraph's heavenly string;
Such sounds, so good old Homer sung,
Once warbled from the Siren's tongue—
Sweet melting tones were heard to pour
Along Ausonia's sun-gilt shore—
Seductive strains in æther float,
And every wild deceitful note
That could the yielding heart assail,
Were wafted on the breathing gale—
And every gentle accent bland
To tempt Ulysses to their strand.

And can it be this book so base,
Is laid on every window case?
Oh! fair ones, if you will profane
Those breasts where heaven itself should reign,
And throw those pure recesses wide,
Where peace and virtue should reside,
To let the holy pile admit
A guest unhallowed and unfit;
Pray, like the frail ones of the night,
Who hide their wanderings from the light,
So let *your* errors secret be,
And hide, at least, your fault from me:—
Seek some bye corner to explore
The smooth polluted pages o'er:
There drink the insidious poison in;
There *slily* nurse your souls for sin;
And while that purity you blight,
Which stamps you messengers of light;
And sap those mounds the gods bestow,
To keep you spotless here below;
Still, in compassion to *our* race,
Who joy, not only in the face
But in that more exalted part,
The sacred temple of the heart;
Oh! hide forever from our view,
The fatal mischief you pursue—
Let MEN your praises still exalt,
And none but ANGELS mourn your fault.

SALMAGUNDI NO. VI

Friday, March 20, 1807.

FROM MY ELBOW-CHAIR.

THE Cockloft family, of which I have made such frequent mention, is of great antiquity, if there be any truth in the genealogical tree which hangs up in my cousin's library. They trace their descent from a celebrated roman knight, cousin to the progenitor of his majesty of Britain, who left his native country, on occasion of some disgust, and coming into Wales,

became a great favorite of prince Madoc, and accompanied that famous
Argonaut in the voyage which ended in the discovery of this continent.
Though a member of the family, I have sometimes ventured to doubt
the authenticity of this portion of their annals, to the great vexation of
cousin Christopher, who is looked up to as the head of our house, and
who, though as orthodox as a bishop, would sooner give up the whole
decalogue than lop off a single limb of the family tree. From time
immemorial, it has been the rule for the Cocklofts to marry one of their
own name; and as they always bred like rabbits, the family has increased
and multiplied like that of Adam and Eve. In truth their number is
almost incredible, and you can hardly go into any part of the country
without starting a warren of genuine Cocklofts. Every person of the least
observation or experience, must have observed, that where this practice
of marrying cousins and second cousins prevails in a family, every member, in the course of a few generations, becomes queer, humorous and
original; as much distinguished from the common race of mongrels as
if he was of a different species. This has happened in our family, and
particularly in that branch of it of which mr. Christopher Cockloft, or to
do him justice, Christopher Cockloft, esq. is the head. Christopher is, in
fact, the only married man of the name who resides in town; his family
is small, having lost most of his children when young, by the excessive
care he took to bring them up like vegetables. This was one of his first
whim-whams, and a confounded one it was, as his children might have
told had they not fallen victims to his experiment before they could talk.
He had got, from some quack philosopher or other, a notion that there
was a complete analogy between children and plants, and that they ought
both to be reared alike. Accordingly he sprinkled them every morning
with water, laid them out in the sun, as he did his geraniums, and if
the season was remarkably dry, repeated this wise experiment three or
four times of a morning. The consequence was, the poor little souls died
one after the other, except Jeremy and his two sisters, who, to be sure,
are a trio of as odd, *runty*, mummy looking originals as ever Hogarth
fancied in his most happy moments. Mrs. Cockloft, the larger if not the
better half of my cousin, often remonstrated against this vegetable
theory, and even brought the parson of the parish, in which my cousin's
country house is situated, to her aid—but in vain: Christopher persisted
and attributed the failure of his plan to its not having been exactly conformed to. As I have mentioned mrs. Cockloft, I may as well say a
little more about her while I am in the humor. She is a lady of wonderful
notability, a warm admirer of shining mahogany, clean hearths, and
her husband, who she considers the wisest man in the world, bating Will
Wizard and the parson of our parish; the last of whom is her oracle on
all occasions. She goes constantly to church every Sunday and Saints-day,

and insists upon it that no man is entitled to ascend a pulpit unless he has been ordained by a bishop;—nay, so far does she carry her orthodoxy, that all the argument in the world will never persuade her that a presby-- terian, or baptist, or even a calvinist has any possible chance of going to heaven. Above every thing else, however. she abhors paganism, can scarcely refrain from laying violent hands on a Pantheon when she meets with it, and was very nigh going into hysterics, when my cousin insisted one of his boys should be christened after our laureat, because the parson of the parish had told her that Pindar was the name of a pagan writer, famous for his love of boxing matches, wrestling, and horse racing. To sum up all her qualifications in the shortest possible way, mrs. Cockloft is in the true sense of the phrase, a good sort of a woman; and I often congratulate my cousin on possessing her. The rest of the family con- sists of Jeremy Cockloft, the younger, who has already been mentioned, and the two miss Cocklofts, or rather the *young ladies*, as they have been called by the servants, time out of mind; not that they are really young, the younger being somewhat on the shady side of thirty, but it has ever been the custom to call every member of the family young under fifty. In the south-east corner of the house, I hold quiet possession of an old fashioned apartment, where myself and my elbow-chair are suffered to amuse ourselves undisturbed, save at meal times. This apart- ment old Cockloft has facetiously denominated cousin Launce's paradise, and the good old gentleman has two or three favorite jokes about it, which are served up as regularly as the standing family dish of beef- steaks and onions, which every day maintains its station at the foot of the table. in defiance of mutton, poultry, or even venison itself.

Though the family is apparently small, yet like most old establishments of the kind it does not want for honorary members. It is the city rendezvous of the Cocklofts, and we are continually enlivened by the company of half a score of uncles, aunts, and cousins in the fortieth remove, from all parts of the country, who profess a wonderful regard for cousin Christopher, and overwhelm every member of his household, down to the cook in the kitchen, with their attentions. We have for three weeks past been greeted with the company of two worthy old spinsters, who came down from the country to settle a law suit. They have done little else but retail stories of their village neighbors, knit stockings, and take snuff all the time they have been here; the whole family are bewil- dered with church-yard tales of sheeted ghosts, white horses without heads, and with large goggle eyes in their buttocks; and not one of the old servants dare budge an inch after dark without a numerous company at his heels. My cousin's visitors, however, always return his hospitality with due gratitude, and now and then remind him of their fraternal re- gard, by a present of a pot of apple sweet-meats, or a barrel of sour cider

at christmas. Jeremy displays himself to great advantage among his country relations, who all think him a prodigy, and often stand astounded in
"gaping wonderment," at his *natural* philosophy. He lately frightened a
simple old uncle almost out of his wits by giving it as his opinion that the
earth would one day be scorched to ashes by the eccentric gambols of
the famous comet, so much talked of, and positively asserting that this
world revolved round the sun, and that the moon was certainly inhabited.

The family mansion bears equal marks of antiquity with its inhabitants.
As the Cocklofts are remarkable for their attachment to every thing
that has remained long in the family, they are bigoted towards their old
edifice, and I dare say would sooner have it crumble about their ears
than abandon it. The consequence is, it has been so patched up and
repaired, that it has become as full of whims and oddities as its tenants,
requires to be nursed and humored like a gouty old codger of an alderman, and reminds one of the famous ship in which a certain admiral
circumnavigated the globe, which was so patched and timbered, in
order to preserve so great a curiosity, that at length not a particle of the
original remained. Whenever the wind blows, the old mansion makes a
most perilous groaning, and every storm is sure to make a day's work
for the carpenter, who attends upon it as regularly as the family physician.
This predilection for every thing that has been long in the family shows
itself in every particular. The domestics are all grown grey in the service
of our house. We have a little old crusty grey-headed negro, who has
lived through two or three generations of the Cocklofts, and of course
has become a personage of no little importance in the household. He
calls all the family by their christian names; tells long stories about how
he dandled them on his knee when they were children; and is a complete
Cockloft chronicle for the last seventy years. The family carriage was
made in the last french war, and the old horses were most indubitably
foaled in Noah's ark, resembling marvellously, in gravity of demeanor,
those sober animals which may be seen any day of the year in the
streets of Philadelphia, walking their snails' pace, a dozen in a row, and
harmoniously jingling their bells. Whim-whams are the inheritance of
the Cocklofts, and every member of the household is a humorist *sui
generis,* from the master down to the footman. The very cats and dogs
are humorists, and we have a little runty scoundrel of a cur, who, whenever the church bells ring, will run to the street door, turn up his nose
in the wind, and howl most piteously. Jeremy insists that this is owing
to a peculiar delicacy in the organization of his ears, and supports his
position by many learned arguments which nobody can understand; but
I am of opinion that it is a mere Cockloft whim-wham which the little
cur indulges, being descended from a race of dogs which has flourished
in the family ever since the time of my grandfather. A propensity to

save every thing that bears the stamp of family antiquity, has accumulated an abundance of trumpery and rubbish, with which the house is incumbered from the cellar to the garret, and every room, and closet, and corner, is crammed with three legged chairs, clocks without hands, swords without scabbards, cocked hats, broken candlesticks, and looking glasses with frames carved into fantastic shapes of feathered sheep, woolly birds, and other animals that have no name except in books of heraldry. The ponderous mahogany chairs in the parlor, are of such unwieldly proportions that it is quite a serious undertaking to gallant one of them across the room, and sometimes make a most equivocal noise when you set down in a hurry; the mantlepiece is decorated with little lacquered earthen shepherdesses, some of which are without toes, and others without noses, and the fire-place is garnished out with dutch tiles, exhibiting a great variety of scripture pieces, which my good old soul of a cousin takes infinite delight in explaining.—Poor Jeremy hates them as he does poison, for while a younker, he was obliged by his mother to learn the history of a tile every Sunday morning before she would permit him to join his play-mates; this was a terrible affair for Jeremy, who, by the time he had learned the last, had forgotten the first, and was obliged to begin again. He assured me the other day, with a round college oath, that if the *old house* stood out till he inherited it, he would have these tiles taken out, and ground into powder, for the perfect hatred he bore them.

My cousin Christopher enjoys unlimited authority in the mansion of his forefathers; he is truly what may be termed a hearty old blade, has a florid, sunshine countenance, and if you will only praise his wine, and laugh at his long stories, himself and his house, are heartily at your service. The first condition is indeed easily complied with, for to tell the truth, his wine is excellent; but his stories being not of the best, and often repeated, are apt to create a disposition to yawn, being in addition to their other qualities, most unfeelingly long. His prolixity is the more afflicting to me, since I have all his stories by heart; and when he enters upon one, it reminds me of Newark causeway, where the traveller sees the end at the distance of several miles. To the great misfortune of all his acquaintance, cousin Cockloft is blessed with a most provoking retentive memory, and can give day and date, and name and age, and circumstance, with the most unfeeling precision. These, however, are but trivial foibles, forgotten, or remembered, only with a kind of tender respectful pity by those who know with what a rich redundant harvest of kindness and generosity his heart is stored. It would delight you to see with what social gladness he welcomes a visitor into his house; and the poorest man that enters his door never leaves it without a cordial invitation to sit down, and drink a glass of wine. By the honest farmers around his country-seat, he is looked up to with love and reverence—they never pass him by, without his inquiring after the welfare of their families, and receiving a cordial shake of his liberal hand. There are but two classes of people who are thrown out of the reach of his hospitality, and these are frenchmen and democrats. The old gentleman considers it treason against the majority of good breeding, to speak to any visitor with his hat on; but the moment a democrat enters his door, he forthwith bids his man Pompey bring his hat, puts it on his head, and salutes him with an appalling "Well, sir, what do you want with me?"

He has a profound contempt for frenchmen, and firmly believes, that they eat nothing but frogs and soup-maigre in their own country. This unlucky prejudice is partly owing to my great aunt PAMELA, having been, many years ago, run away with by a french count, who turned out to be the son of a generation of barbers—and partly to a little vivid spark of toryism which burns in a secret corner of his heart. He was a loyal subject of the crown, has hardly yet recovered the shock of independence; and though he does not care to own it, always does honor to his majesty's birth-day, by inviting a few cavaliers, like himself, to dinner, and gracing his table with more than ordinary festivity. If by chance the revolution is mentioned before him, my cousin shakes his head; and you may see, if you take good note, a lurking smile of contempt in the corner of his eye, which marks a decided disapprobation of the sound. He once, in the fulness of his heart, observed to me that green peas were a month later than they were under the old government. But the most eccentric manifestation of loyalty he ever gave was making a voyage to Halifax, for no other reason under heaven, but to hear his majesty prayed for in church, as he used to be here formerly. This he never could be brought fairly to acknowledge; but it is a certain fact I assure you. It is not a little singular that a person so much given to long story-telling, as my cousin, should take a liking to another of the same character; but so it is with the old gentleman—his prime favorite and companion is Will Wizard, who is almost a member of the family, and will set before the fire, with his feet on the massy andirons, and smoke his cigarr, and screw his phiz, and spin away tremendous long stories of his travels, for a whole evening, to the great delight of the old gentleman and lady, and especially of the *young ladies*, who, like Desdemona, do "seriously incline," and listen to him with innumerable "O dears," "is it possibles," "goody graciouses," and look upon him as a second Sinbad the sailor.

The miss Cocklofts, whose pardon I crave for not having particularly introduced them before, are a pair of delectable damsels, who, having purloined and locked up the family-bible, pass for just what age they please to plead guilty to. BARBARA the eldest, has long since resigned the character of a belle, and adopted that staid, sober, demure, snuff-taking air, becoming her years and discretion. She is a good natured soul, whom I never saw in a passion but once, and that was occasioned by seeing an old favorite beau of hers, kiss the hand of a pretty blooming girl; and in truth, she only got angry because as she very properly said, it was spoiling the child. Her sister MARGERY, or MAGGIE, as she is familiarly termed, seemed disposed to maintain her post as a belle, until a few months since, when accidentally hearing a gentleman observe that she broke very fast, she suddenly left off going to the assembly, took a cat into high favor, and began to rail at the forward pertness of young misses. From that moment I set her down for an old maid; and so she is, "by the hand of my body." The *young ladies* are still visited by some half a dozen of veteran beaux, who grew and flourished in the *haut ton,* when the miss Cocklofts were quite children; but have been brushed rather rudely by the hand of time, who, to say the truth, can do almost any thing but make people young. They are, notwithstanding, still warm candidates for female favor, look venerably tender, and repeat over and over the same honeyed speeches, and sugared sentiments to the little belles, that they poured so profusely into the ears of their mothers. I beg leave here to give notice that by this sketch, I mean no reflection on *old bachelors;* on the contrary, I hold that next to a fine lady, the *ne plus ultra,* an old bachelor to be the most charming being upon earth, in as much as by living in "single blessedness," he of course does just as he pleases; and if he has any genius, must acquire a plentiful stock of whims, and oddities, and whalebone habits, without which I esteem a man to be mere beef without mustard, good for nothing at all, but to run on errands for ladies, take boxes at the theatre, and act the part of a screen at tea-parties, or a walking-stick in the streets. I merely speak of these *old boys* who infest public walks, pounce upon ladies from every corner of the street, and like old Tommy Fizgig, worry and frisk, and amble, and caper before, behind, and round about the fashionable belles, like old ponies in a pasture, and strive to supply the absence of youthful whim, and hilarity, by grimaces and grins, and artificial vivacity. I have sometimes seen one of these "reverend youths," endeavoring to elevate his wintry passions into something like love, by basking in the sunshine of beauty, and it did remind me of an old moth attempting to fly through a pane of glass towards a light, without ever approaching near enough to warm itself, or scorch its wings.

Never, I firmly believe, did there exist a family that went more by tangents than the Cocklofts. Every thing is governed by whim; and if one member starts a new freak, away all the rest follow on like wild geese in a string. As the family, the servants, the horses, cats and dogs, have all grown old together, they have accommodated themselves to each others habits completely; and though every body of them is full of odd points, angles, rhomboids, and ins and outs, yet some how or other, they harmonize together like so many straight lines, and it is truly a grateful and refreshing sight to see them agree so well. Should one, however, get out of tune, it is like a cracked fiddle, the whole concert is ajar, you perceive a cloud over every brow in the house, and even the old chairs seem to creak affetuosso. If my cousin, as he is rather apt to do, betray any symptoms of vexation or uneasiness, no matter about what, he is worried to death with inquiries, which answer no other end but to demonstrate the good will of the inquirer, and put him in a passion; for every body knows how provoking it is to be cut short in a fit of the *blues*, by an impertinent question about what is the matter, when a man can't tell himself. I remember a few months ago, the old gentleman came home in quite a *squall*, kicked poor Cæsar, the mastiff, out of his way, as he came through the hall, threw his hat on the table with most violent emphasis, and pulling out his box, took three huge pinches of snuff, and threw a fourth into the cat's eyes as he sat purring his astonishment by the fire-side. This was enough to set the body politic going—mrs. Cockloft began my dearing it as fast as tongue could move—the *young ladies* took each a stand at an elbow of his chair—Jeremy marshalled in the rear—the servants came tumbling in— the mastiff put up an enquiring nose; and even grimalkin, after he had cleaned his whiskers and finished sneezing, discovered indubitable signs of sympathy. After the most affectionate inquiries on all sides, it turned out that my cousin, in crossing the street, had got his silk stockings bespattered with mud by a coach, which it seems belonged to a dashing gentleman who had formerly supplied the family with hot rolls and muffins! Mrs. Cockloft thereupon turned up her eyes, and the *young ladies* their noses; and it would have edified a whole congregation to hear the conversation which took place concerning the insolence of upstarts, and the vulgarity of would-be gentlemen and ladies, who strive to emerge from low life, by dashing about in carriages to pay a visit two doors off, giving parties to people who laugh at them, and *cutting* all their old friends.

Theatrics.

BY WILLIAM WIZARD, ESQ.

I WENT a few evenings since to the theatre, accompanied by my friend, Snivers the cockney, who is a man deeply read in the history of Cinderella, Valentine and Orson, Blue Beard, and all those recondite works so necessary to enable a man to understand the modern drama. Snivers is one of those intolerable fellows who will never be pleased

with any thing until he has turned and twisted it divers ways, to
see if it corresponds with his notions of congruity, and as he is none
of the quickest in his ratiocinations, he will sometimes come out
with his approbation, when every body else have forgotten the cause
which excited it. Snivers is, moreover, a great critic, for he finds fault
with every thing—this being what I understand by *modern criticism*.
He, however, is pleased to acknowledge that our theatre is not so
despicable, all things considered, and really thinks Cooper one of our
best actors. As the house was crowded, we were complimented with
seats in Box No. 2, a sad little rantipole place, which is the strong hold
of a set of rare wags, and where the poor actors undergo the most
merciless tortures of verbal criticism. The play was OTHELLO, and,
to speak my mind freely, I think I have seen it performed much worse
in my time. The actors, I firmly believe, did their best, and whenever
this is the case, no man has a right to find fault with them, in my
opinion. Little RUTHERFORD, the roscius of the Philadelphia theatre,
looked as big as possible, and what he wanted in size, he made up
in frowning—I like frowning in tragedy, and if a man but keeps his
forehead in proper wrinkle, talks big, and takes long strides on the
stage, I always set him down as a great tragedian, and so does my
friend Snivers.

Before the first act was over, Snivers began to flourish his critical
wooden sword like a harlequin. He first found fault with Cooper
for not having made himself as black as a negro, "for," said he, "that
Othello was an arrant black, appears from several expressions of the
play, as for instance, 'thick lips,' 'sooty bosom,' and a variety of others.
I am inclined to think," continued he, "that Othello was an egyptian
by birth, from the circumstance of the handkerchief given to his
mother by a native of that country, and, if so, he certainly was as
black as my hat, for Herodotus has told us that the egyptians had
flat noses and frizzled hair, a clear proof that they were all negroes."
He did not confine his strictures to this single error of the actor, but
went on to run him down in toto. In this he was seconded by a
red hot philadelphian, who proved, by a string of most eloquent
logical puns, that Fennel was unquestionably in every respect a
better actor than Cooper. I knew it was vain to contend with him,
since I recollected a most obstinate trial of skill these two great
Roscii had last spring in Philadelphia. Cooper brandished his blood-
stained dagger at the theatre—Fennel flourished his snuff-box, and
shook his wig at the Lyceum, and the unfortunate philadelphians
were a long time at a loss to decide which deserved the palm. The
literati were inclined to give it to Cooper, because his name was the
most fruitful in puns; but then, on the other side, it was contended

that Fennel was the best greek scholar. Scarcely was the town of
Strasburgh in a greater hub bub about the courteous stranger's nose,
and it was well that the doctors of the university did not get into the
dispute, else it might have become a battle of folioes. At length, after
much excellent argument had been expended on both sides, recourse
was had to Cocker's Arithmetic and a carpenter's rule, the rival
candidates were both measured by one of their most steady-handed
critics, and by the most exact measurement it was proved that mr.
Fennel was the greatest actor by three inches and a quarter. Since
this demonstration of his inferiority, Cooper has never been able to
hold up his head in Philadelphia.

In order to change a conversation, in which my favorite suffered
so much, I made some inquiries of the philadelphian concerning the
two heroes of his theatre, Wood and Cain, but I had scarcely
mentioned their names, when, whack! he threw a whole handful
of puns in my face; twas like a bowl of cold water. I turned on my
heel, had recourse to my tobacco-box, and said no more about Wood
and Cain; nor will I ever more, if I can help it, mention their names
in the presence of a philadelphian. Would that they could leave off
punning! for I love every soul of them with a cordial affection, warm
as their own generous hearts, and boundless as their hospitality.

During the performance, I kept an eye on the countenance of my
friend, the cockney, because having come all the way from England,
and having se'en Kemble once, on a visit which he made from the
Button manufactory to Lunnun, I thought his phiz might serve as a
kind of thermometer to direct my manifestations of applause or disapprobation. I might as well have looked at the backside of his
head, for I could not, with all my peering, perceive by his features
that he was pleased with any thing—except himself. His hat was
twitched a little on one side, as much as to say, "demme, I'm your
sorts!" he was sucking the end of a little stick, he was "gemman"
from head to foot; but as to his face, there was no more expression
in it than in the face of a chinese lady on a tea-cup. On Cooper's
giving one of his gun-powder explosions of passion, I exclaimed, "fine.
very fine!" "Pardon me," said my friend Snivers, "this is damnable!—
the gesture, my dear sir, only look at the gesture? how horrible! do
you not observe that the actor slaps his forehead, whereas, the passion
not having arrived at the proper height, he should only have slapped
his—pocket flap? this figure of rhetoric is a most important stage trick,
and the proper management of it is what peculiarly distinguishes the
great actor from the mere plodding mechanical buffoon. Different
degrees of passion require different slaps, which we critics have reduced to a perfect manual, improving upon the principle adopted by

Frederic of Prussia, by deciding that an actor, like a soldier, is a mere machine, as thus—the actor, for a minor burst of passion, merely slaps his pocket-hole—good!—for a major burst, he slaps his breast—very good! but for a burst maximus, he whacks away at his forehead, like a brave fellow—this is excellent!—nothing can be finer than an exit slapping the forehead from one end of the stage to the other." "Except," replied I, "one of those slaps on the breast, which I have sometimes admired in some of our fat heroes and heroines, which make their whole body shake and quiver like a pyramid of jelly."

The philadelphian had listened to this conversation with profound attention, and appeared delighted with Snivers' mechanical strictures; twas natural enough in a man who chose an actor as he would a grenadier. He took the opportunity of a pause, to enter into a long conversation with my friend, and was receiving a prodigious fund of information concerning the true mode of emphasising conjunctions, shifting scenes, snuffing candles, and making thunder and lightning, better than you can get every day from the sky, as practised at the royal theatres, when, as ill luck would have it, they happened to run their heads full butt against a *new reading*. Now this was a *stumper*, as our friend Paddle would say, for the philadelphians are as inveterate new reading hunters as the cocknies, and for aught I know, as well skilled in finding them out. The philadelphian thereupon met the cockney on his own ground, and at it they went, like two inveterate curs at a bone. Snivers quoted Theobold, Hanmer, and a host of learned commentators, who have pinned themselves on the sleeve of Shakspeare's immortality, and made the old bard, like General Washington, in General Washington's life, a most diminutive figure in his own book—his opponent chose Johnson for his bottle-holder, and thundered him forward like an elephant to bear down the ranks of the enemy. I was not long in discovering that these two precious judges had got hold of that unlucky passage of Shakspeare, which like a straw has tickled and puzzled and confounded many a somniferous buzzard of past and present time. It was the celebrated wish of Desdemona, that heaven had made her such a man as Othello. Snivers insisted that "the gentle Desdemona" merely wished for such a man for a husband, which in all conscience was a modest wish enough, and very natural in a young lady, who might possibly have had a predilection for flat noses, like a certain philosophical great man of our day. The philadelphian contended with all the vehemence of a member of congress, moving the house to have "whereas," or "also," or "nevertheless" struck out of a bill; that the young lady wished heaven had made her a man instead of a woman, in order that she might have an opportunity of seeing the "anthropophagi, and the men whose heads do grow beneath their

shoulders;" which was a very natural wish, considering the curiosity of
the sex. On being referred to, I incontinently decided in favor of the
honorable member who spoke last, inasmuch as I think it was a very
foolish, and therefore very *natural* wish for a young lady to make before
a man she wished to marry. It was, moreover, an indication of the
violent inclination she felt to *wear the breeches*, which was afterwards,
in all probability, gratified, if we may judge from the title of "our captain's captain," given her by Cassio, a phrase which, in my opinion,
indicates that Othello was, at that time, most ignominiously *hen pecked*.
I believe my argument staggered Snivers himself, for he looked confoundedly queer, and said not another word on the subject.

A little while after, at it he went again on another tack, and began
to find fault with Cooper's manner of dying—"it was not natural," he said,
for it had lately been demonstrated by a learned doctor of physic, that
when a man is mortally stabbed, he ought to take a flying leap of at
least five feet, and drop down "dead as a salmon in a fishmonger's
basket."—Whenever a man in the predicament above mentioned, departed
from this fundamental rule, by falling flat down, like a log, and rolling
about for two or three minutes, making speeches all the time: the
said learned doctor maintained that it was owing to the waywardness
of the human mind, which delighted in flying in the face of nature, and
dying in defiance of all her established rules.—I replied "for my part,
I held that every man had a right of dying in whatever position he
pleased, and that the mode of doing it depended altogether on the
peculiar character of the person going to die. A persian could not die
in peace unless he had his face turned to the east;—a mahometan would
always choose to have his towards Mecca; a frenchman might prefer
this mode of throwing a somerset; but mynheer Van Brumblebottom, the
Roscius of Rotterdam, always chose to thunder down on his seat of
honor whenever he receive a mortal wound. Being a man of ponderous
dimensions, this had a most electrifying effect, for the whole theatre
"shook like Olympus at the nod of Jove." The Philadelphian was immediately inspired with a pun, and swore that mynheer must be great
in a dying scene, since he knew how to make the most of his *latter
end.*"

It is the inveterate cry of stage critics that an actor does not perform
the character naturally, if, by chance he happens not to die exactly as
they would have him. I think the exhibition of a play at Pekin would suit
them exactly, and I wish, with all my heart, they would go there and see
one: nature is there imitated with the most scrupulous exactness in every
trifling particular. Here, an unhappy lady or gentleman who happens
unluckily to be poisoned or stabbed, is left on the stage to writhe and
groan, and make faces at the audience, until the poet pleases he should

die, while the honest folks of the *dramatis personæ*, bless their hearts! all croud round and yield most potent assistance, by crying and lamenting most vociferously! the audience, tender souls, pull out their white pocket handkerchiefs, wipe their eyes, blow their noses, and swear it is natural as life, while the poor actor is left to die without common christian comfort. In China, on the contrary, the first thing they do is to run for the doctor and *Tchoonc*, or notary. The audience are entertained throughout the fifth act, with a learned consultation of physicians, and if the patient must die, he does it *secundum artem*, and always is allowed time to make his will. The celebrated Chow-Chow, was the completest hand I ever saw at killing himself, he always carried under his robe a bladder of bull's blood, which, when he gave the mortal stab, spirted out to the infinite delight of the audience. Not that the ladies of China are more fond of the sight of blood than those of our own country, on the contrary, they are remarkably sensitive in this particular, and we are told by the great Linkum Fidelius, that the beautiful Ninny Consequa, one of the ladies of the emperor's seraglio, once fainted away on seeing a favorite slave's nose bleed, since which time refinement has been carried to such a pitch, that a buskined hero is not allowed to run himself through the body in the face of the audience. The immortal Chow-Chow, in conformity to this absurd prejudice, whenever he plays the part of Othello, which is reckoned his master-piece, always keeps a bold front, stabs himself slily behind, and is dead before any body suspects that he has given the mortal blow.

P. S. Just as this was going to press, I was informed by Evergreen that Othello had not been performed here the lord knows when; no matter, I am not the first that has criticised a play without seeing it, and this critique will answer for the last performance, if that was a dozen years ago.

SALMAGUNDI NO. VII

no. VII]   *Saturday, April 4, 1807.*

LETTER

From Mustapha Rub-a-dub Keli Khan,
To Asem Hacchem *principal slave-driver to his
highness the Bashaw of Tripoli.*

I promised in a former letter, good Asem, that I would furnish thee with a few hints respecting the nature of the government by which

I am held in durance.—Though my inquiries for that purpose have been industrious, yet I am not perfectly satisfied with their results, for thou mayest easily imagine that the vision of a captive is overshadowed by the mists of illusion and prejudice, and the horizon of his speculations must be limited indeed.

I find that the people of this country are strangely at a loss to determine the nature and proper character of their government. Even their dervises are extremely in the dark as to this particular, and are continually indulging in the most preposterous disquisitions on the subject; some have insisted that it savors of an *aristocracy;* others maintain that it is a *pure* democracy; and a third set of theorists declare absolutely that it is nothing more nor less than a *mobocracy.* The latter, I must confess, though still wide in error, have come nearest to the truth. You of course must understand the meaning of these different words, as they are derived from the ancient greek language, and bespeak loudly the verbal poverty of these poor infidels, who cannot utter a learned phrase without laying the dead languages under contribution. A man, my dear Asem, who talks good sense in his native tongue, is held in tolerable estimation in this country; but a fool, who clothes his feeble ideas in a foreign or antique garb, is bowed down to, as a literary prodigy. While I conversed with these people in plain english, I was but little attended to, but the moment I prosed away in greek, every one looked up to me with veneration as an oracle.

Although the dervises differ widely in the particulars above-mentioned, yet they all agree in terming their government one of the most *pacific* in the known world. I cannot help pitying their ignorance, and smiling at times to see into what ridiculous errors those nations will wander who are unenlightened by the precepts of Mahomet, our divine prophet, and uninstructed by the five hundred and forty-nine books of wisdom of the immortal Ibrahim Hassan al Fusti. To call this nation pacific! most preposterous! it reminds me of the title assumed by the Sheck of that murderous tribe of wild arabs, who desolate the valleys of Belsaden, who styles himself *star of courtesy—beam of the mercy seat!*

The simple truth of the matter is, that these people are totally ignorant of their own true character; for, according to the best of my observation, they are the most warlike, and I must say, the most savage nation that I have as yet discovered among all the barbarians. They are not only at war (in their own way) with almost every nation on earth, but they are at the same time engaged in the most complicated knot of civil wars that ever infested any poor unhappy country on which ALLA has denounced his malediction!

To let thee at once into a secret, which is unknown to these people themselves, their government is a pure unadulterated LOGOCRACY or *government of words.* The whole nation does every thing *viva voce,* or, by word of mouth, and in this manner is one of the most military nations in existence. Every man who has, what is here called, the *gift of the gab,* that is, a plentiful stock of verbosity, becomes a soldier outright, and is forever in a militant state. The country is intirely defended *vi et lingua,* that is to say, by *force of tongues.* The account which I lately wrote to our friend the snorer, respecting the immense army of six hundred men, makes nothing against this observation; that formidable body being kept up, as I have already observed, only to amuse their fair country women by their splendid appearance and nodding plumes, and are, by way of distinction, denominated the *"defenders of the fair."*

In a logocracy thou well knowest there is little or no occasion for fire arms, or any such destructive weapons. Every offensive or defensive measure is enforced by *wordy battle,* and *paper war;* he who has the longest tongue, or readiest quill, is sure to gain the victory—will carry horror, abuse, and *ink-shed* into the very trenches of the enemy, and without mercy or remorse, put men, women, and children, to the point of the—pen!

There are still preserved in this country some remains of that gothic spirit of knight-errantry, which so much annoyed the faithful in the middle ages of the Hejira. As, notwithstanding their martial disposition, they are a people much given to commerce and agriculture, and must necessarily at certain seasons be engaged in these employments, they have accommodated themselves by appointing knights, or constant warriors, incessant brawlers, similar to those, who, in former ages, swore eternal enmity to the followers of our divine prophet.—These knights denominated editors or SLANG-WHANGERS are appointed in every town, village and district, to carry on both foreign and internal warfare, and may be said to keep up a constant firing "in words." Oh, my friend, could you but witness the enormities sometimes committed by these tremendous slang-whangers, your very turban would rise with horror and astonishment. I have seen them extend their ravages even into the kitchens of their opponents, and annihilate the very cook with a blast; and I do assure thee, I beheld one of these warriors attack a most venerable bashaw, and at one stroke of his pen lay him open from the waist-band of his breeches to his chin!

There has been a civil war carrying on with great violence for some time past, in consequence of a conspiracy among the higher classes, to dethrone his highness, the present bashaw, and place another in his stead. I was mistaken when I formerly asserted to thee that this disaffection arose from his wearing *red breeches.* It is true the nation have long held that color in great detestation in consequence of a dispute they had some twenty years since with the barbarians of the british islands. The color, however, is again rising into favor, as the ladies have transferred it to their heads from the bashaw's—body. The true reason, I am told, is that the bashaw absolutely refuses to believe in the deluge, and in the story of Balaam's ass:—maintaining that this animal was never yet permitted to talk except in a genuine logocracy, where it is true his voice may often be heard, and is listened to with reverence as "the voice of the sovereign people." Nay, so far did he carry his obstinacy that he absolutely invited a professed *anti-deluvian* from the gallic empire, who illuminated the whole country with his principles— and his *nose*. This was enough to set the nation in a blaze—every slang-whanger resorted to his tongue or his pen; and for seven years have they carried on a most inhuman war, in which volumes of words have been expended, oceans of ink have been shed; nor has any mercy been shown to age, sex, or condition. Every day have these slang-whangers made furious attacks upon each other, and upon their respective adherents, discharging their heavy artillery, consisting of large sheets, loaded with scoundrel! villain! liar! rascal! numskull! nincompoop! dunderhead! wiseacre! blockhead! jackass! And I do swear by my beard, though I know thou wilt scarcely credit me, that in some of these skirmishes the grand bashaw himself has been woefully pelted! Yea, most ignominiously pelted!—and yet have these talking desperadoes escaped without the bastinado!

Every now and then, a slang-whanger, who has a longer head, or rather a *longer tongue,* than the rest, will elevate his piece and discharge a shot quite across the ocean, levelled at the head of the Emperor of France, the king of England; or, (wouldst thou believe it, oh, Asem) even at his sublime highness the bashaw of Tripoli! these long pieces are loaded with single ball or langrage, as tyrant! usurper! robber! tyger! monster! And thou mayest well suppose, they occasion great distress and dismay in the camps of the enemy, and are marvellously annoying to the crowned heads at which they are directed. The slang-whanger, though perhaps the mere champion of a village, having fired off his shot, struts about with great self-congratulation, chuckling at the prodigious bustle he must have occasioned, and seems to ask of every stranger, "Well, sir, what do they think of me in Europe."* This

NOTE, BY WILLIAM WIZARD, ESQ.

*The sage Mustapha, when he wrote the above paragraph, had probably in his eye the following anecdote, related either by Linkum Fidelius, or Josephus Millerius, vulgarly called Joe Miller—of facetious memory.

The captain of a slave-vessel, on his first landing on the coast of Guinea, observed under a palm-tree, a negro chief sitting most majestically on a stump, while two women, with wooden spoons, were administering his favorite pottage of boiled rice, which, as his imperial majesty was a little greedy, would part of

is sufficient to show you the manner in which these bloody, or rather *windy* fellows fight; it is the only mode allowable in a *Logocracy* or government of words. I would also observe that their civil wars have a thousand ramifications.

While the fury of the battle rages in the metropolis, every little town and village has a distinct broil, growing like excrescences out of the grand national altercation, or rather agitating within it, like those complicated pieces of mechanism where there is a "wheel within a wheel."

But in nothing is the verbose nature of this government more evident, than in its grand national divan, or congress, where the laws are framed; this is a blustering windy assembly where every thing is carried by noise, tumult and debate; for thou must know, that the members of this assembly do not meet together to find out wisdom in the multitude of counsellors, but to wrangle, call each other hard names and hear *themselves talk*. When the congress opens, the bashaw first sends them a long message (i.e. a huge mass of words—*vox et preterea nihil*) all meaning nothing; because it only tells them what they perfectly know already. Then the whole assembly are thrown into a ferment, and have a *long talk*, about the quantity of words that are to be returned in answer to this message; and here arise many disputes about the correction and alteration of "*if so bes*," and "*how so evers*." A month, perhaps, is spent in thus determining the precise number of words the answer shall contain, and then another, most probably, in concluding whether it shall be carried to the bashaw on foot, on horseback, or in coaches. Having settled this weighty matter, they next fall to work upon the message itself, and hold as much chattering over it as so many magpies over an addled egg. This done, they divide the message into small portions, and deliver them into the hands of little juntos of *talkers*, called committees: these juntos have each a world of talking about their respective paragraphs, and return the results to the grand divan, which forthwith falls to and *re-talks* the matter over more earnestly than ever. Now after all, it is an even chance that the subject of this prodigious arguing, quarrelling, and talking, is an affair of no importance, and ends intirely in smoke. May it not then be said, the whole nation have been talking to

---

it escape the place of destination, and run down his chin. The watchful attendants were particularly careful to intercept these scape grace particles, and return them to their proper port of entry. As the captain appoached, in order to admire this curious exhibition of royalty, the great chief clapped his hands to his sides, and saluted his visitor with the following pompous question, "Well, sir! what do they say of me in England?"

no purpose? the people, in fact, seem to be somewhat conscious of this propensity to talk, by which they are characterized, and have a favorite proverb on the subject, viz. "all talk and no cider;" this is particularly applied when their congress (or assembly of all the sage chatterers of the nation) have chattered through a whole session, in a time of great peril and momentous event, and have done nothing but exhibit the length of their tongues and the emptiness of their heads. This has been the case more than once, my friend; and to let thee into a secret, I have been told in confidence, that there have been absolutely several old women smuggled into congress from different parts of the empire, who having once got on the breeches, as thou mayst well imagine, have taken the lead in debate, and overwhelmed the whole assembly with their garrulity; for my part, as times go, I do not see why old women should not be as eligible to public councils as old men, who possess their dispositions—they certainly are eminently possessed of the qualifications requisite to govern in a logocracy.

Nothing, as I have repeatedly insisted, can be done in this country without talking, but they take so long to talk over a measure, that by the time they have determined upon adopting it, the period has elapsed, which was proper for carrying it into effect. Unhappy nation—thus torn to pieces by intestine talks! never, I fear, will it be restored to tranquility and silence. Words are but breath—breath is but air; and air put in motion is nothing but wind. This vast empire, therefore, may be compared to nothing more nor less than a mighty windmill, and the orators, and the chatterers, and the slang-whangers, are the breezes that put it in motion; unluckily, however, they are apt to blow different ways, and their blasts counteracting each other—the mill is perplexed, the wheels stand still, the grist is unground, and the miller and his family starved.

Every thing partakes of the windy nature of the government. In case of any domestic grievance, or an insult from a foreign foe, the people are all in a buzz—town meetings are immediately held, where the quid-nuncs of the city repair, each like an Atlas, with the cares of the whole nation upon his shoulders, each resolutely bent upon saving his country, and each swelling and strutting like a turkey-cock, puffed up with words, and wind, and nonsense. After bustling, and buzzing, and bawling for some time, and after each man has shown himself to be indubitably the greatest personage in the meeting, they pass a string of resolutions (i.e. *words*) which were *previously prepared* for the purpose; these resolutions are whimsically denominated the *sense* of the meeting, and are sent off for the instruction of the reigning bashaw, who receives them graciously, puts them into his red breeches pocket, forgets to read them—and so the matter ends.

As to his highness, the present bashaw, who is at the very top of the logocracy, never was a dignitary better qualified for his station. He is a man of superlative ventosity, and comparable to nothing but a huge bladder of wind. He *talks* of vanquishing all opposition by the force of reason and philosophy; throws his gauntlet at all the nations of the earth and defies them to meet him—on the field of argument!—Is the national dignity insulted, a case in which his highness of Tripoli would immediately call forth his forces—the bashaw of America—utters a *speech*. Does a foreign invader molest the commerce in the very mouth of the harbors, an insult which would induce his highness of Tripoli to order out his fleets—his highness of America—utters a *speech*. Are the *free* citizens of America dragged from on board the vessels of their country and forcibly detained in the war ships of another power—his highness— utters a *speech*. Is a peaceable citizen killed by the marauders of a foreign power, on the very shores of his country—his highness—utters a *speech*. Does an alarming insurrection break out in a distant part of the empire—his highness—utters a *speech!*—nay, more, for here he shows his "energies"—he most intrepidly dispatches a courier on horseback, and orders him to ride one hundred and twenty miles a day, with a most formidable army of *proclamations*, (i.e. a collection of words) packed up in his saddle-bags. He is instructed to show no favor nor affection, but to charge the thickest ranks of the enemy, and to speechify and batter by words the conspiracy and the conspirators out of existence. Heavens, my friend, what a deal of blustering is here! it reminds me of a dunghill cock in a farm-yard, who, having accidentally in his scratchings found a worm, immediately begins a most vociferous cackling—calls around him his *hen-hearted* companions, who run chattering from all quarters to gobble up the poor little worm that happened to turn under his eye. Oh Asem! Asem! on what a prodigious great scale is every thing in this country!

Thus, then, I conclude my observations. The infidel nations have each a separate characteristic trait, by which they may be distinguished from each other:—the spaniards, for instance, may be said to *sleep* upon every affair of importance—the italians to *fiddle* upon everything—the french to *dance* upon every thing—the germans to *smoke* upon every thing— the british islanders to *eat* upon every thing,—and the *windy* subjects of the american logocracy to *talk* upon every thing.

Ever thine,
Mustapha.

FROM THE MILL OF
PINDAR COCKLOFT, ESQ.

How oft, in musing mood, my heart recals,
From grey-beard father Time's oblivious halls,

The modes and maxims of my early day,
Long in those dark recesses stow'd away:
Drags once more to the cheerful realms of light
Those buckram fashions long since lost in night;
And makes, like Endor's witch, once more to rise
My grogram grandames to my raptured eyes!
  Shades of my fathers! in your pasteboard skirts,
Your broidered waistcoats and your plaited shirts,
Your formal bag-wigs—wide-extended cuffs,
Your five inch chitterlings and nine inch ruffs.
Gods! how ye strut, at times, in all your state,
Amid the visions of my thoughtful pate!
I see ye move the solemn *minuet* o'er,
The modest foot scarce rising from the floor;
No thundering *rigadoon* with boisterous prance,
No *pigeon-wing* disturb your *contra dance*.
But silent as the gentle Lethe's tide
Adown the festive maze ye peaceful glide!
  Still in my mental eye each dame appears—
Each modest beauty of departed years;
Close by mama I see her stately march,
Or set, in all the majesty of starch;—
When for the dance a stranger seeks her hand,
I see her doubting, hesitating, stand,
Yield to his claim with most fastidious grace,
And sigh for her *intended* in his place!
  Ah golden days! when every gentle fair
On sacred sabbath conn'd with pious care
Her holy bible, or her prayer-book o'er,
Or studied honest Bunyan's drowsy lore.
Travell'd with him the PILGRIM's PROGRESS through,
And storm'd the famous town of MAN-SOUL too—
Beat *eye* and *ear-gate* up with thundring jar,
And fought triumphant through the HOLY WAR;
Or if, perchance, to lighter works inclined,
They sought the *novels* to relax the mind,
Twas GRANDISON's politely formal page,
Or CLELIA or PAMELA were the rage.
  No plays were then—theatrics were unknown—
A learned pig—a dancing monkey shown—
The feats of Punch—a cunning juggler's slight,
Were sure to fill each bosom with delight.
An honest, simple, humdrum race we were,

Undazzled yet by fashion's wildering glare;
Our manners unreserved, devoid of guile,
We knew not then the modern monster *style*,
Style, that with pride each empty bosom swells,
Puffs boys to manhood, little girls to *belles*.
  Scarce from the nursery freed, our gentle fair
Are yielded to the dancing-master's care;
And e'er the head one mite of sense can gain,
Are introduced mid folly's frippery train.
A stranger's grasp no longer gives alarms,
Our fair surrender to their very arms,
And in the insidious *Waltz* (1) will swim and twine,
And whirl and languish tenderly divine!
Oh, how I hate this loving, hugging dance,
This imp of Germany—brought up in France;
Nor can I see a niece its windings trace,
But all the honest blood glows in my face.
"Sad, sad refinement this," I often say,
"Tis modesty indeed refined away!
"Let France its whim, its sparkling wit supply,
"The easy grace that captivates the eye,
"But curse their waltz—their loose lascivious arts,
"That smooth our manners, to corrupt our hearts!" (2)
  Where now those books, from which in days of yore
Our mothers gained their literary store?
Alas! stiff-skirted Grandison gives place
To novels of a new and *rakish* race;
And honest Bunyan's pious dreaming lore,
To the lascivious rhapsodies of MOORE.
  And, last of all, behold the mimic Stage
Its morals lend to *polish* off the age,
With flismy farce, a comedy miscall'd,
Garnish'd with vulgar cant, and proverbs bald,
With puns most puny, and a plenteous store
Of smutty jokes, to catch a gallery roar.
Or see, more fatal, graced with every art,
To charm and captivate the female heart,
The false, "the gallant, gay Lothario" smiles, (3)
And loudly boasts his base seductive wiles,—
In glowing colors paints Calista's wrongs,
And with voluptuous scenes the tale prolongs.
When COOPER lends his fascinating powers,
Decks vice itself in bright alluring flowers,

Pleased with his manly grace, his youthful fire,
Our fair are lured the villain to admire;
While humbler virtue, like a stalking horse,
Struts clumsily and croaks in honest MORSE.
  Ah, hapless days! when trials thus combin'd,
In pleasing garb assail the female mind;
When every smooth insidious snare is spread
To sap the morals and delude the head!
Not Shadrach, Meshach and Abed-nego,
To prove their faith and virtue here below,
Could more an angel's helping hand require,
To guide their steps uninjured through the fire;
Where had but heaven its guardian aid deny'd,
The holy trio in the proof had died.
If, then, *their* manly vigor sought supplies
From the bright stranger in celestial guise,
Alas! can we from feebler nature's claim,
To brave seduction's ordeal, free from blame;
To pass through fire unhurt like golden ore,
Though ANGEL MISSIONS bless the earth no more!

NOTES, BY WILLIAM WIZARD, ESQ.

1 *Waltz*] As many of the retired matrons of this city, unskilled in "gestic lore," are doubtless ignorant of the movements and figures of this modest exhibition, I will endeavor to give some account of it, in order that they may learn what odd capers their daughters sometimes cut when from under their guardian wings.

On a signal being given by the music, the gentleman seizes the lady round her waist—the lady, scorning to be outdone in courtesy, very politely takes the gentleman round the neck, with one arm resting against his shoulder to prevent encroachments. Away then they go, about and about and about—"about what, sir?"—about the room, madam, to be sure. The whole economy of this dance consists in turning round and round the room in a certain measured step; and it is truly astonishing that this continued revolution does not set all their heads swimming like a top; but I have been positively assured that it only occasions a gentle sensation which is marvelously agreeable. In the course of this circumnavigation, the dancers, in order to give the charm of variety, are continually changing their relative situations—now the gentleman, meaning no harm in the world, I assure you, madam, carelessly flings his arm about the lady's neck, with an air of celestial impudence, and anon, the lady, meaning as little harm as the gentleman, takes him round the waist with most ingenuous, modest languishment, to the great delight of numerous spectators and amateurs, who generally form a ring, as the mob do about a pair of amazons pulling caps, or a couple of fighting mastiffs.

After continuing this divine interchange of hands, arms, *et cetera*, for half an hour or so, the lady begins to tire, and with "eyes upraised," in most bewitching languor petitions her partner for a little more support. This is always given without hesitation. The lady leans gently on his shoulder, their arms intertwine in a thousand seducing mischievous curves—dont be alarmed, madam—closer and closer they approach each other, and in conclusion, the parties being overcome with extatic fatigue, the lady seems almost sinking into the gentleman's arms, and then—"Well, sir! and what then?"—lord, madam, how should I know!

2] My friend Pindar, and in fact, our whole junto have been accused of an unreasonable hostility to the french nation; and I am informed by a parisian correspondent, that our first number played the very devil in the court of St. Cloud. His Imperial majesty got into a most outrageous passion, and being withal, a waspish little gentleman, had nearly kicked his bosom friend, Tallyrand, out of the cabinet, in the paroxisms of his wrath. He insisted upon it that the nation was assailed in its most vital part; being, like Achilles, extremely sensitive to any attacks upon the *heel.* When my correspondent sent off his dispatches, it was still in doubt what measures should be adopted; but it was strongly suspected that vehement representations would be made to our government. Willing, therefore, to save our executive from any embarrassment on the subject, and above all, from the disagreeable alternative of sending an *apology* by the HORNET, we do assure, mr. Jefferson, that there is nothing farther from our thoughts than the subversion of the gallic empire, or any attack on the interests, tranquility, or reputation of the nation at large, which we seriously declare possesses the highest rank in our estimation. Nothing less than the national welfare could have induced us to trouble ourselves with this explanation; and in the name of the junto, I once more declare, that when we toast a frenchman, we merely mean one of these *inconnus,* who swarmed to this country, from the kitchens and barbers shops of Nantz, Bordeaux and Marseilles—played games of *leap-frog,* at all our balls and assemblies—set this unhappy town *hopping mad*—and passed themselves off on our tender-hearted damsels for *unfortunate noblemen*—ruined in the revolution! such only, can wince at the lash, and accuse us of severity; and we should be mortified in the extreme if they did not feel our well intended castigation.

3 *Fair Penitent*] The story of this play, if told in its native language, would exhibit a scene of guilt and shame, which no modest ear could

listen to without shrinking with disgust; but arrayed as it is in all the splendor of harmonious, rich, and polished verse, it steals into the heart like some gay luxurious smooth-faced villain, and betrays it insensibly to immorality and vice; our very sympathy is enlisted on the side of guilt, and the piety of Altamont, and the gentleness of Lavinia, are lost in the splendid debaucheries of the "gallant gay Lothario" and the blustering, hollow repentance of the fair Calista, whose sorrow reminds us of that of Pope's Heloise—"I mourn the lover, not lament the fault." Nothing is more easy than to banish such plays from our stage. Were our ladies, instead of crowding to see them again and again repeated, to discourage their exhibition by absence, the stage would soon be indeed the school of morality, and the number of "Fair Penitents," in all probability diminish.

SALMAGUNDI NO. VIII

NO. VIII]   Saturday, April 18, 1807.

BY ANTHONY EVERGREEN, GENT.

"In all thy humors, whether grave or mellow,
Thou'rt such a touchy, testy, pleasant fellow;
Hast so much wit, and mirth, and spleen about thee,
There is no living with thee—nor without thee."

"NEVER, in the memory of the oldest inhabitant has there been known a more backward spring." This is the universal remark among the almanac quidnuncs, and weather wiseacres of the day; and I have heard it at least fifty-five times from old mrs. Cockloft, who, poor woman, is one of those walking almanacs that foretel every snow, rain, or frost by the shooting of corns, a pain in the bones, or an "ugly stitch in the side." I do not recollect, in the whole course of my life, to have seen the month of March indulge in such untoward capers, caprices and coquetries as it has done this year: I might have forgiven these vagaries, had they not completely knocked up my friend Langstaff, whose feelings are ever at the mercy of a weather-cock, whose spirits rise and sink with the mercury of a barometer, and to whom an east wind is as obnoxious as a sicilian *sirocco*. He was tempted some time since, by the fineness of the weather, to dress himself with more than ordinary care, and take his morning stroll; but before he had half finished his

peregrination he was utterly discomfited, and driven home by a tremenduous squall of wind, hail, rain and snow, or as he testily termed
it "a most villanous congregation of vapors."

This was too much for the patience of friend Launcelot; he declared
he would humor the weather no longer in its whim-whams, and according to his immemorial custom on these occasions, retreated in high
dudgeon to his elbow-chair, to lie in of the spleen, and rail at nature
for being so fantastical:—"confound the jade," he frequently exclaims,
"what a pity nature had not been of the masculine instead of the femi-
nine gender, the almanac makers might then have calculated with some
degree of certainty."

When Langstaff invests himself with the spleen, and gives audience
to the blue devils from his elbow chair, I would not advise any of his
friends to come within gunshot of his citadel, with the benevolent
purpose of administering consolation or amusement; for he is then as
crusty and crabbed as that famous coiner of false money, Diogenes himself. Indeed his room is at such times inaccessable, and old Pompey is
the only soul that can gain admission or ask a question with impunity:
the truth is, that on these occasions, there is not a straws difference
between them, for Pompey is as grum and grim and cynical as his
master.

Launcelot has now been above three weeks in this desolate situation,
and has therefore had but little to do in our last number. As he could
not be prevailed on to give any account of himself in our introduction,
I will take the opportunity of his confinement, while his back is turned,
to give a slight sketch of his character—fertile in whim-whams and
bachelorisms, but rich in many of the sterling qualities of our nature.
Annexed to this article, our readers will perceive a striking likeness of
my friend, which was taken by that cunning rogue Will Wizard, who
peeped through the key-hole, and sketched it off, as honest Launcelot
sat by the fire, wrapped up in his flannel *robe de chambre,* and indulging in a mortal fit of the *hyp.* Now take my word for it, gentle reader,
this is the most auspicious moment in which to touch off the phiz of a
genuine humorist.

Of the antiquity of the Langstaff family I can say but little, except
that I have no doubt it is equal to that of most families who have the
privilege of making their own pedigree, without the impertinent inter-
position of a college of heralds. My friend Launcelot is not a man
to *blazon* any thing; but I have heard him talk with great complacency
of his ancestor, Sir ROWLAND, who was a dashing buck in the days of
Hardiknute, and broke the head of a gigantic dane, at a game of quarter-
staff, in presence of the whole court. In memory of this gallant exploit,
Sir Rowland was permitted to take the name of Langstoffe, and to assume

as a crest to his arms, a hand grasping a cudgel. It is however a foible so ridiculously common in this country, for people to claim consanguinity with all the great personages of their own name in Europe, that I should put but little faith in this family boast of friend Langstaff, did I not know him to be a man of most unquestionable veracity.

The whole world knows already that my friend is a batchelor, for he is, or pretends to be, exceedingly proud of his personal independence, and takes care to make it known in all companies where strangers are present. He is forever vaunting the precious state of "single blessedness," and was not long ago considerably startled by a proposition of one of his great favorites, miss Sophy Sparkle, "that old batchelors should be taxed as luxuries." Launcelot immediately hied him home and wrote a tremendous long representation in their behalf, which I am resolved to publish, if it is ever attempted to carry the measure into operation. Whether he is sincere in these professions, or whether his present situation is owing to choice or disappointment, he only can tell; but if he ever does tell, I will suffer myself to be shot by the first lady's eye that can twang an arrow. In his youth he was forever in love; but it was his misfortune to be continually crossed and rivalled by his bosom friend and contemporary beau, Pindar Cockloft, esq., for as Langstaff never made a confidant on these occasions, his friend never knew which way his affections pointed, and so, between them both, the lady generally slipped through their fingers.

It has ever been the misfortune of Launcelot, that he could not for the soul of him restrain a *good thing*; and this fatality has drawn upon him the ill-will of many whom he would not have offended for the world. With the kindest heart under heaven, and the most benevolent disposition towards every being around him, he has been continually betrayed by the mischievous vivacity of his fancy, and the good-humored waggery of his feelings, into satirical sallies, which have been treasured up by the invidious, and retailed out with the bitter sneer of malevolence, instead of the playful hilarity of countenance which originally sweetened and tempered and disarmed them of their sting. These misrepresentations have gain'd him many reproaches and lost him many a friend.

This unlucky characteristic played the mischief with him in one of his love affairs. He was, as I have before observed, often opposed in his gallantries by that formidable rival, Pindar Cockloft, esq.—and a most formidable rival he was, for he had Apollo, the nine muses, together with all the joint tenants of Olympus, to back him, and every body knows what important confederates they are to a lover. Poor Launcelot stood no chance—the lady was cooped up in the poets' corner of every weekly paper, and at length Pindar attacked her with a *sonnet* that took up a whole column, in which he enumerated at least a dozen cardinal virtues, together with innumerable others of inferior consideration. Launcelot saw his case was desperate, and that unless he sat down forthwith, be-cherubim'd and be-angel'd her to the skies, and put every virtue under the sun in requisition, he might as well go hang himself, and so make an end of the business. At it, therefore, he went, and was going on very swimmingly, for, in the space of a dozen lines, he had enlisted under her command at least three score and ten substantial, house-keeping virtues, when unluckily for Launcelot's reputation as a poet, and the lady's as a saint, one of those confounded *good thoughts* struck his laughter-loving brain—it was irresistable—away he went full sweep before the wind, cutting and slashing, and tickled to death with his own fun: the consequence was, that by the time he had finished, never was poor lady so most ludicrously lampooned, since lampooning came into fashion. But this was not half—so hugely was Launcelot pleased with this frolic of his wits, that nothing would do but he must show it to the lady, who, as well she might, was mortally offended and forbid him her presence. My friend was in despair, but through the interference of his generous rival, was permitted to make his apology, which however most unluckily happened to be rather worse than the original offence; for, though he had studied an eloquent compliment, yet, as ill-luck would have it, a most preposterous whim-wham knocked at his peri-cranium, and inspired him to say some consummate *good things,* which all put together amounted to a downright *hoax,* and provoked the lady's wrath to such a degree that sentence of eternal banishment was awarded against him.

Launcelot was inconsolable, and determined in the true style of novel heroics, to make the tour of Europe, and endeavor to lose the recollection of this misfortune amongst the gaieties of France, and the classic charms of Italy; he accordingly took passage in a vessel and pursued his voyage prosperously, as far as Sandy-Hook, where he was seized with a violent fit of sea-sickness, at which he was so affronted that he put his port-manteau into the first pilot-boat, and returned to town, completely cured of his love, and his rage for travelling.

I pass over the subsequent amours of my friend Langstaff, being but little acquainted with them; for, as I have already mentioned, he never was known to make a confidant of any body. He always affirmed a man must be a fool to fall in love, but an ideot to boast of it—ever denomi-nated it the *villanous passion*—lamented that it could not be cudgelled out of the human heart—and yet could no more live without being in love with somebody or other than he could without whim-whams.

My friend Launcelot is a man of excessive irritability of nerve, and I am acquainted with no one so susceptible of the petty "miseries of human life;" yet its keener evils and misfortunes he bears without shrinking, and however they may prey in secret on his happiness, he never complains. This was strikingly evinced in an affair where his heart was deeply and irrevocably concerned, and in which his success was ruined by one for whom he had long cherished a warm friendship. The circumstances cut poor Langstaff to the very soul; he was not seen in company for months afterwards, and for a long time he seemed to retire within himself, and battle with the poignancy of his feelings; but not a murmur or a reproach was heard to fall from his lips, though at the mention of his friend's name, a shade of melancholy might be observed stealing across his face, and his voice assumed a touching tone that seemed to say he remembered his treachery "more in sorrow than in anger." This affair has given a slight tinge of sadness to his disposition, which, however, does not prevent his entering into the amusements of the world; the only effect it occasions is, that you may occasionally observe him at the end of a lively conversation sink for a few minutes into an apparent forgetfulness of surrounding objects, during which time he seems to be indulging in some melancholy retrospection.

Langstaff inherited from his father a love of literature, a disposition for *castle building*, a mortal enmity to noise, a sovereign antipathy to cold weather and brooms, and a plentiful stock of whim-whams. From the delicacy of his nerves he is peculiarly sensible to discordant sounds; the rattling of a wheelbarrow is "horrible," the noise of children "drives him distracted," and he once left excellent lodgings merely because the lady of the house wore high-heeled shoes, in which she clattered up and down stairs, till, to use his own emphatic expression "they made life loathsome" to him. He suffers annual martyrdom from the razor-edged zephyrs of our "balmy spring," and solemnly declares that the boasted month of May has become a perfect "vagabond." As some people have a great antipathy to cats, and can tell when one is locked up in a closet, so Launcelot declares his feelings always announce to him the neighborhood of a broom, a household implement which he abominates above all others. Nor is there any living animal in the world that he holds in more utter abhorrence than what is usually termed a *notable housewife*, a pestilent being who he protests is the bane of good fellowship, and has a heavy charge to answer for the many offences committed against the ease, comfort and social enjoyments of sovereign man. He told me, not long ago, that he had rather see one of the weird sisters flourish through his key-hole on a broomstick, than one of the servant maids enter the door with a *besom*.

My friend Launcelot is ardent and sincere in his attachments, which are confined to a chosen few, in whose society he loves to give free scope to his whimsical imagination; he, however, mingles freely with the world, though more as a spectator than an actor, and without an anxiety or hardly a care to please, is generally received with welcome and listened to with complacency. When he extends his hand, it is in a free, open, liberal style, and when you shake it you feel his honest heart throb in its pulsations. Though rather fond of gay exhibitions, he does not appear so frequently at balls and assemblies, since the introduction of the drum, trumpet and tamborine, all of which he abhors on account of the rude attacks they make on his organs of hearing—in short, such is his antipathy to noise, that though exceedingly patriotic; yet he retreats every fourth of July to Cockloft Hall, in order to get out of the way of the hub-bub and confusion, which made so considerable a part of the pleasure of that splendid anniversary.

I intend this article as a mere sketch of Langstaff's multifarious character—his innumerable whim-whams will be exhibited by himself, in the course of this work, in all their strange varieties; and the machinery of his mind, more intricate than the most subtle piece of clock-work, be fully explained. And trust me, gentlefolk, his are the whim-whams of a courteous gentleman, full of excellent qualities; honorable in his disposition, independent in his sentiments, and of unbounded good nature, as may be seen through all his works.

On Style.

BY WILLIAM WIZARD, ESQ.

STYLE, *a manner of writing; title; pin of a dial; the pistil of plants.*   *Johnson.*

STLYE, *is* —————————— *style.*   *Link. Fed.*

Now I would not give a straw for either of the above definitions, though I think the latter is by far the most satisfactory; and I do wish sincerely every modern numskull who takes hold of a subject he knows nothing about, would adopt honest Linkum's mode of explanation. Blair's lectures on the subject have not thrown a whit more light on the subject of my inquiries—they puzzled me just as much as did the learned and laborious expositions and illustrations of the worthy professor of our college, in the middle of which I generally had the ill luck to fall asleep.

This same word *style,* though but a diminutive word, assumes to itself more contradictions, and significations, and eccentricities, than any monosyllable in the language is legitimately entitled to. It is an arrant little humourist of a word, and full of whim-whams, which occasions me to like it hugely; but it puzzled me most wickedly on my first return from a long residence abroad; having crept into fashionable use during my absence; and had it not been for friend Evergreen, and that thrifty sprig of knowledge, Jeremy Cockloft the younger, I should have remained to this day ignorant of its meaning.

Though it would seem that the people of all countries are equally vehement in the pursuit of this phantom style, yet, in almost all of them, there is a strange diversity in opinion as to what constitutes its essence; and every different class, like the pagan nations, adore it under a different form. In England, for instance, an honest cit packs up himself, his family and his style in a buggy or tim-whiskey, and rattles away on sunday with his fair partner blooming beside him like an eastern bride, and two chubby children, squatting like chinese images at his feet. A baronet requires a chariot and pair—a lord must needs have a barouche and four;—but a duke—oh! a duke cannot possibly lumber his style along under a coach and six, and half a score of footmen into the bargain. In china, a puissant mandarine loads at least three elephants with style, and an overgrown sheep, at the Cape of Good-Hope, trails along his tail and his style on a wheel-barrow. In Egypt, or at Constantinople, style consists in the quantity of fur and fine clothes a lady can put on without danger of suffocation—here it is otherwise, and consists in the quantity she can put off without the risk of freezing. A chinese lady is thought prodigal of her charms, if she exposes the tip of her nose, or the ends of her fingers to the ardent gaze of bye-standers: and I recollect that all Canton was in a buzz in consequence of the great belle, miss Nang-fou's, peeping out of the window with her face uncovered! Here the style is to show not only the face, but the neck, shoulders, &c.; and a lady never presumes to hide them except when she is *not at home* and not sufficiently *undress'd* to see company.

This style has ruined the peace and harmony of many a worthy household; for no sooner do they set up for style, but instantly all the honest old comfortable *sans ceremonie* furniture is discarded, and you stalk cautiously about, amongst the uncomfortable splendour of grecian chairs, egyptian tables, turkey carpets, and etruscan vases. This vast improvement in furniture demands an increase in the domestic establishment; and a family that once required two or three servants for convenience, now employ half a dozen for style.

BELLBRAZEN, late favourite of my unfortunate friend Dessalines, was one of these patterns of style, and whatever freak she was seized with, however preposterous, was implicitly followed by all who would be considered as admitted in the stylish arcana. She was once seized with a whim-wham that tickled the whole court. She could not lay down to take an afternoon's loll, but she must have one servant to scratch her head, two to tickle her feet, and a fourth to fan her delectable person while she slumbered. The thing *took*—it became the *rage*, and not a sable bell in all Hayti, but what insisted upon being fanned, and scratched, and tickled in the true imperial style. Sneer not at this picture, my most excellent townswomen, for who among you but are daily following fashions equally absurd!

Style, according to Evergreen's account, consists in certain fashions, or certain eccentricities, or certain manners of certain people, in certain situations, and possessed of a certain share of fashion or importance. A red cloak, for instance, on the shoulders of an old market-woman is regarded with contempt, it is vulgar, it is odious:—fling, however, its usurping rival, a red shawl, over the fine figure of a fashionable belle, and let her flame away with it in Broadway, or in a ball-room, and it is immediately declared to be the *style*.

The modes of attaining this *certain situation* which entitles its holder to style, are various and opposite: the most ostensible is the attainment of wealth, the possession of which changes at once the pert airs of vulgar ignorance, into fashionable ease and elegant vivacity. It is highly amusing to observe the gradations of a family aspiring to style, and the devious windings they pursue in order to attain it. While beating up against wind and tide they are the most complaisant beings in the world—they keep "booing and booing," as M'Sychophant says, until you would suppose them incapable of standing upright; they kiss their hands to every body who has the least claim to style—their familiarity is intolerable, and they absolutely overwhelm you with their friendship and loving kindness. But having once gained the envied pre-eminence, never were beings in the world more changed. They assume the most intolerable caprices; at one time address you with importunate sociability, at another, pass you by with silent indifference, sometimes sit up in their chairs in all the majesty of dignified silence, and at another time bounce about with all the obstreperous, ill-bred noise of a little hoyden just broke loose from a boarding-school.

Another feature which distinguishes these new made fashionables, is the inveteracy with which they look down upon the honest people who are struggling to climb up to the same envied height. They never fail to salute them with the most sarcastic reflections; and like so many worthy hod-men clambering a ladder, each one looks down with a sneer upon his next neighbor below, and makes no scruple of shaking the dust off his shoes into his eyes. Thus by dint of perseverence merely, they come to be considered as established denizens of the great world; as in some barbarous nations an oyster-shell is of sterling value, and a copper washed counter will pass current for genuine gold.

In no instance, have I seen this grasping after style more whimsically exhibited than in the family of my old acquaintance, TIMOTHY GIBLET. I recollect old Giblet when I was a boy, and he was the most surly curmudgeon I ever knew. He was a perfect scare-crow to the *small fry* of the day, and inherited the hatred of all these unlucky little shavers; for never could we assemble about his door of an evening to play and make a little hub-bub, but out he sallied from his nest like a spider, flourish'd his formidable horsewhip, and dispersed the whole crew in the twinkling of a lamp. I perfectly remember a bill he sent in to my father for a pane of glass I had accidentally broken, which came well nigh getting me a sound flogging; and I remember, as perfectly, that the next night I revenged myself by breaking half a dozen. Giblet was as arrant a grub-worm as ever crawled; and the only rules of right and wrong he cared a button for, were the rules of multiplication and addition, which he practiced much more successfully than he did any of the rules of religion or morality. He used to declare they were the true *golden rules*, and he took special care to put Cocker's arithmetic in the hands of his children, before they had read ten pages in the bible or the prayer-book. The practice of these favourite maxims was at length crowned with the harvest of success; and after a life of incessant self-denial, and starvation, and after enduring all the pounds, shillings and pence miseries of a miser, he had the satisfaction of seeing himself worth a *plum*, and of dying just as he had determined to enjoy the remainder of his days, in contemplating his great wealth and accumulating mortgages.

His children inherited his money, but they buried the disposition, and every other memorial of their father, in his grave. Fired with a noble thirst for *style*, they instantly emerged from the retired lane in which themselves, and their accomplishments had hitherto been buried, and they blazed, and they whizzed, and they cracked about town, like a nest of squibs and devils in a firework. I can liken their sudden *eclat* to nothing but that of the locust, which is hatched in the dust, where it increases and swells up to maturity, and after feeling for a moment the vivifying rays of the sun, bursts forth a mighty insect, and flutters, and rattles, and buzzes from every tree. The little warblers who have long cheered the woodlands with their dulcet notes, are stunned by the discordant racket of these upstart intruders, and contemplate, in contemptuous silence, their tinsel and their noise.

Having once started, the Giblets were determined that nothing should stop them in their career, until they had run their full course, and arrived at the very tip-top of *style*. Every tailor, every shoe-maker, every coachmaker, every milliner, every mantuamaker, every paper-hanger, every piano teacher, and every dancing-master in the city were enlisted in their service; and the willing wights most courteously answered their call, and fell to work to build up the fame of the Giblets as they had done that of many an aspiring family before them. In a little time the young ladies could dance the waltz, thunder Iodoiska, murder french, kill time, and commit violence on the face of nature in a landscape in water-colours, equal to the best lady in the land; and the young gentlemen were seen lounging at corners of streets, and driving tandem; heard talking loud at the theatre, and laughing in church, with as much ease and grace and *modesty*, as if they had been gentlemen all the days of their lives.

And the Giblets arrayed themselves in scarlet, and in fine linen, and seated themselves in high-places, but nobody noticed them except to honour them with a little contempt. The Giblets made a prodigious splash in their own opinion; but nobody extolled them except the tailors and the milliners who had been employed in manufacturing their paraphernalia. The Giblets thereupon being like Caleb Quotem, determined to have "a place at the review," fell to work more fiercely than ever—they gave dinners, and they gave balls, they hired cooks, they hired fiddlers, they hired confectioners, and they would have kept a newspaper in pay, had they not been all bought up at that time for the election. They invited the dancing men and the dancing women, and the gormandizers and the epicures of the city, to come and make merry at their expense; and the dancing men, and the dancing women, and the epicures, and the gormandizers, did come, and they did *make merry* at their expense; and they eat, and they drank, and they capered, and they danced, and they—laughed at their entertainers.

Then commenced the hurry and the bustle, and the mighty nothingness of fashionable life;—such rattling in coaches! such flaunting in the streets! such slamming of box doors at the theatre! such a tempest of bustle and unmeaning noise where-ever they appeared! the Giblets were seen here and there and every where—they visited every body they knew, and every body they did not know, and there was no getting along for the Giblets. Their plan at length succeeded. By dint of dinners, of feeding and frolicking the town, the Giblet family worked themselves into notice, and enjoyed the ineffable pleasure of being forever pestered by visitors, who cared nothing about them, of being squeezed, and smothered, and par-boiled at nightly balls, and evening tea-parties—they were allowed the privilege of forgetting the very few old friends they once possessed—they turned their noses up in the wind at every thing that was not genteel, and their superb manners and sublime affectation, at length left it no longer a matter of doubt that the Giblets were perfectly in the *style*.

"....... *Being, as it were, a small contentmente in a never contenting subjecte; a bitter pleasaunte taste of a sweete seasoned*

*sower; and, all in all, a more than ordinaire rejoycing, in an
extraordinairie sorrowe of delyghts!"*

Linkum Fidelius.

We have been considerably edified of late by several letters of advice
from a number of sage correspondents, who really seem to know more
about our work than we do ourselves. One warns us against saying any
thing more about SNIVERS, who is a very particular friend of the writer, and
who has a singular disinclination to be laughed at. This correspondent
in particular inveighs against personalities, and accuses us of ill nature
in bringing forward old Fungus and Billy Dimple, as figures of fun
to amuse the public. Another gentleman, who states that he is a near
relation of the Cockloft's, proses away most soporifically on the impro-
priety of ridiculing a respectable old family, and declares that if we
make them and their whim-whams the subject of any more essays, he
shall be under the necessity of applying to our theatrical champions
for satisfaction. A third, who by the crabbedness of the hand-writing
and a few careless inaccuracies in the spelling, appears to be a lady,
assures us that the miss Cockloft's, and miss Diana Wearwell, and miss
Dashaway, and mrs. ————, Will Wizard's quondam flame, are so
much obliged to us for our notice, that they intend in future to take
no notice of us at all, but leave us out of all their tea-parties, for which
we make them one of our best bows, and say, "thank you, ladies."

We wish to heaven these good people would attend to their own
affairs, if they have any to attend to, and let us alone. It is one of the most
provoking things in the world that we cannot tickle the public a little,
merely for our own private amusement, but we must be crossed and
jostled by these meddling incendiaries, and in fact, have the whole
town about our ears. We are much in the same situation with an
unlucky blade of a cockney, who having mounted his bit of blood to
enjoy a little innocent recreation, and display his horsemanship along
Broadway, is worried by all those little yelping curs that infest our
city, and who never fail to sally out and growl, and bark, and snarl,
to the great annoyance of the Birmingham equestrian.

Wisely was it said by the sage Linkum Fidelius, "howbeit, moreover,
neverthelesse, this thrice wicked towne is charged up to the muzzle with
all manner of ill-natures and uncharitablenesses, and is, moreover,
exceedinglie naughte." This passage of the erudite Linkum was applied
to the city of Gotham, of which he was once lord mayor, as appears by
his picture hung up in the hall of that ancient city—but his observation fits this best of all possible cities "to a hair." It is a melancholy
truth that this same New-York, though the most charming, pleasant,
polished and praise-worthy city under the sun, and in a word, the *bonne*

bouche of the universe, is most shockingly ill-natured and sarcastic, and wickedly given to all manner of backslidings—for which we are very sorry indeed. In truth, for it must come out like murder one time or other, the inhabitants are not only ill-natured, but manifestly unjust: no sooner do they get one of our random sketches in their hands, but instantly they apply it most unjustifiably to some "dear friend," and then accuse us vociferously of the personality which originated in their own officious *friendship!* Truly it is an ill-natured town, and most earnestly do we hope it may not meet with the fate of Sodom and Gomorrah of old.

As, however, it may be thought incumbent upon us to make some apology for these mistakes of the town, and as our good-nature is truly exemplary, we would certainly answer this expectation, were it not that we have an invincible antipathy to making apologies. We have a most profound contempt for any man who cannot give three good reasons for an unreasonable thing, and will therefore condescend, as usual, to give the public three special reasons for never apologizing—first, an apology implies that we are accountable to some body or another for our conduct—now as we do not care a fiddle-stick, as authors, for either public opinion or private ill-will, it would be implying a falsehood to apologize:—second, an apology would indicate that we had been doing what we ought not to have done. Now as we never did, nor ever intend to do any thing wrong, it would be ridiculous to make an apology:— third, we labor under the same incapacity in the art of apologizing that lost Langstaff his mistress—we never yet undertook to make an apology without committing a new offence, and making matters ten times worse than they were before, and we are, therefore, determined to avoid such predicaments in future.

But though we have resolved never to apologize, yet we have no particular objection to explain, and if this is all that's wanted, we will go about it directly:—*allons*, gentlemen!—before, however, we enter upon this serious affair, we take this opportunity to express our surprize and indignation at the incredulity of some people. Have we not, over and over, assured the town that we are three of the best natured fellows living? And is it not astonishing that having already given seven convincing proofs of the truth of this assurance, they should still have any doubts on the subject? but as it is one of the impossible things to make a knave believe in honesty, so, perhaps, it may be another to make this most sarcastic, satirical and tea-drinking city believe in the existence of good-nature. But to our explanation.—Gentle reader! for we are convinced that none but gentle or genteel readers can relish our excellent productions—if thou art in expectation of being perfectly satisfied with what we are about to say, thou mayest as well "whistle lillebullero" and skip quite over what follows, for never wight was more disappointed than thou wilt be most assuredly.—But to the explanation: we care just as much about the public and its wise conjectures, as we do about the man in the moon and his whim-whams, or the criticisms of the lady who sits majestically in her elbow-chair in the lobster, and who, belying her sex, as we are credibly informed, never says any thing worth listening to. We have launched our bark, and we will steer to our destined port with undeviating perseverence, fearless of being shipwrecked by the way. *Good-nature* is our steersman, *reason* our ballast, *whim* the breeze that wafts us along, and MORALITY our leading star.

SALMAGUNDI NO. IX

NO. IX]   *Saturday, April 25, 1807.*

FROM MY ELBOW-CHAIR.

IT in some measure jumps with my humour to be "melancholy and gentleman-like" this stormy night, and I see no reason why I should not indulge myself for once.—Away, then, with joke, with fun and laughter for a while; let my soul look back in mournful retrospect, and sadden with the memory of my good aunt CHARITY—who died of a frenchman!

Stare not, oh most dubious reader, at the mention of a complaint so uncommon; grievously hath it afflicted the ancient family of the Cocklofts, who carry their absurd antipathy to the french so far, that they will not suffer a clove of garlic in the house: and my good old friend Christopher was once on the point of abandoning his paternal country mansion of Cockloft-hall, merely because a colony of frogs had settled in a neighbouring swamp. I verily believe he would have carried his whim-wham into effect, had not a fortunate drought obliged the enemy to strike their tents, and, like a troop of wandering arabs, to march off towards a moister part of the country.

My aunt Charity departed this life in the fifty-ninth year of her age, though she never grew older after twenty-five. In her teens, she was, according to her own account, a celebrated beauty—though I never could meet with any body that remembered when she was handsome; on the contrary, Evergreen's father, who used to gallant her in his youth, says she was as knotty a little piece of humanity as he ever saw; and that, if she had been possessed of the least sensibility, she would like poor old *Acco*, have most certainly run mad at her own figure and face, the first time she contemplated herself in a looking-glass. In the good old times that saw my aunt in the hey-day of youth, a fine lady was a most formidable animal, and required to be approached with the same awe and devotion that a tartar feels in the presence of his Grand Lama. If a gentleman offered to take her hand, except to help her into a carriage, or lead her into a drawing-room, such frowns! such a rustling of brocade and taffeta! her very paste shoe-buckles sparkled with indignation, and for a moment assumed the brilliancy of diamonds: In those days the person of a belle was sacred; it was unprofaned by the sacrilegious grasp of a stranger—simple souls!—they had not the *waltz* among them yet!

My good aunt prided herself on keeping up this buckram delicacy, and if she happened to be playing at the old-fashioned game of forfeits, and was fined a kiss, it was always more trouble to get it than it was worth; for she made a most gallant defence, and never surrendered until she saw her adversary inclined to give over his attack. Evergreen's father says he remembers once to have been on a sleighing party with her, and when they came to Kissing-bridge, it fell to his lot to levy contributions on miss Charity Cockloft; who, after squalling at a hideous rate, at length jumped out of the sleigh plump into a snow-bank, where she stuck fast like an icicle, until he came to her rescue. This latonian feat cost her a rheumatism, which she never thoroughly recovered.

It is rather singular that my aunt, though a great beauty, and an heiress withal, never got married. The reason she alledged was that she never met with a lover who resembled sir Charles Grandison, the hero of her nightly dreams and waking fancy; but I am privately of opinion that it was owing to her never having had an offer. This much is certain, that for many years previous to her decease, she declined all attentions from the gentlemen, and contented herself with watching over the welfare of her fellow-creatures. She was, indeed, observed to take a considerable lean towards methodism, was frequent in her attendance at love-feasts, read Whitfield and Westley, and even went so far as once to travel the distance of five-and-twenty miles, to be present at a camp meeting. This gave great offence to my cousin Christopher and his good lady, who, as I have already mentioned, are rigidly orthodox; and had not my aunt Charity been of a most pacific disposition, her religious whim-wham would have occasioned many a family altercation. She was, indeed, as good a soul as the Cockloft family ever boasted; a lady of unbounded loving kindness, which extended to man, woman and child, many of whom she almost killed with good-nature. Was any acquaintance sick? in vain did the wind whistle and the storm beat; my aunt would waddle through mud and mire, over the whole town, but what she would visit them. She would sit by them for hours together with the most persevering patience, and tell a thousand melancholy stories of human misery, *to keep up their spirits*. The whole catalogue of *yerb* teas was at her fingers' ends, from formidable wormwood down to gentle *balm;* and she would descant by the hour on the healing qualities of hoarhound, catnip, and penny-royal. Woe be to the patient that came under the benevolent hand of my aunt Charity, he was sure, willy nilly, to be drenched with a deluge of decoctions; and full many at time has my cousin Christopher borne a twinge of pain in silence, through fear of being condemned to suffer the martyrdom of her materia-medica. My good aunt had, moreover, considerable skill in astronomy, for she could tell when the sun rose and set every day in the year; and no woman in the whole world was able to pronounce, with more certainty, at what precise minute the moon changed. She held the story of the moon's being made of green cheese, as an abominable slander on her favourite planet; and she had made several valuable discoveries in solar eclipses, by means of a bit of burnt glass, which entitled her at least to an honorary admission in the american philosophical society. *Hutchin's improved* was her favourite book; and I shrewdly suspect that it was from this valuable work she drew most of her sovereign remedies for colds, coughs, corns and consumptions.

But the truth must be told; with all her good qualities my aunt Charity was afflicted with one fault, extremely rare among her gentle sex—it was curiosity. How she came by it, I am at a loss to imagine, but it played the very vengeance with her and destroyed the comfort of her life. Having an invincible desire to know every body's character, business, and mode of living, she was forever prying into the affairs of her neighbours, and got a great deal of ill will from people towards whom she had the kindest disposition possible. If any family on the opposite side of the street gave a dinner, my aunt would mount her spectacles, and sit at the window until the company were all housed, merely that she might know who they were. If she heard a story about any of her acquaintance, she would, forthwith, set off full sail and never rest until, to use her usual expression, she had got "to the bottom of it," which meant nothing more than telling it to every body she knew.

I remember one night my aunt Charity happened to hear a most precious story about one of her good friends, but unfortunately too late to give it immediate circulation. It made her absolutely miserable; and she hardly slept a wink all night, for fear her bosom-friend, mrs. SIPKINS, should get the start of her in the morning and blow the whole affair. You must know there was always a contest between these two ladies, who should first give currency to the good-natured things said about every body, and this unfortunate rivalship at length proved fatal to their long and ardent friendship. My aunt got up full two hours that morning before her usual time; put on her pompadour taffeta gown, and sallied forth to lament the misfortune of her dear friend.—Would you believe it!—wherever she went mrs. Sipkins had anticipated her; and, instead of being listened to with uplifted hands and open-mouthed wonder, my unhappy aunt was obliged to sit down quietly and listen to the whole affair, with numerous additions, alterations and amendments!—Now this was too bad; it would almost have provoked Patient Grizzle or a saint— it was too much for my aunt, who kept her bed for three days after- wards, with a cold as she pretended; but I have no doubt it was owing to this affair of mrs. Sipkins, to whom she never would be reconciled.

But I pass over the rest of my aunt Charity's life, checquered with the various calamities and misfortunes and mortifications, incident to those worthy old gentlewomen who have the domestic cares of the whole community upon their minds; and I hasten to relate the melan- choly incident that hurried her out of existence in the full bloom of anti- quated virginity.

In their frolicsome malice the fates had ordered that a french boarding-house, or *Pension Francaise*, as it was called, should be estab- lished directly opposite my aunt's residence. Cruel event! unhappy aunt Charity!—it threw her into that alarming disorder denominated the *fidgets*; she did nothing but watch at the window day after day, but without becoming one whit the wiser at the end of a fortnight than she was at the beginning; she thought that *neighbour Pension* had a monstrous large family, and some how or other they were all men! she could not imagine what business *neighbour Pension* followed to support so numerous a household, and *wondered* why there was always such a scraping of fiddles in the parlour, and such a smell of onions from neighbour Pension's kitchen; in short, neighbour Pension was continually uppermost in her thoughts and incessantly on the outer edge of her tongue. This was, I believe, the very first time she had ever fail'd "to get at the bottom of a thing," and the disappointment cost her many a sleepless night I warrant you. I have little doubt, however, that my aunt would have ferreted neighbour Pension out, could she have spoken or understood french, but in those times people in general could make themselves understood in plain english; and it was always a standing rule in the Cockloft family, which exists to this day, that not one of the females should learn french.

My aunt Charity had lived at her window for some time in vain, when one day as she was keeping her usual look-out, and suffering all the pangs of unsatisfied curiosity, she beheld a little meagre, weazel- faced frenchman, of the most forlorn, diminutive and pitiful proportions, arrive at neighbour Pension's door. He was dressed in white, with a little pinched up cocked hat; he seemed to shake in the wind, and every blast that went over him whistled through his bones and threatened instant annihilation. This embodied spirit of famine was followed by three carts, lumbered with crazy trunks, chests, band-boxes, *bidets*, medicine-chests, parrots and monkeys, and at his heels ran a yelping pack of little black nosed pug dogs. This was the one thing wanting to fill up the measure of my aunt Charity's afflictions; she could not conceive, for the soul of her, who this mysterious little apparition could be that made so great a display; what he could possibly do with so much baggage, and particularly with his parrots and monkeys; or how so small a carcase could have occasion for so many trunks of clothes. Honest soul! she had never had a peep into a frenchman's wardrobe, that *depot* of old coats, hats and breeches, of the growth of every fashion he has followed in his life.

From the time of this fatal arrival my poor aunt was in a quandary—all her inquirites were fruitless; no one could expound the history of this mysterious stranger; she never held up her head afterwards,—drooped daily, took to her bed in a fortnight, and in "one little month" I saw her quietly deposited in the family vault—being the seventh Cockloft that has died of a whim-wham!

Take warning, my fair country women! and you, oh ye excellent ladies—whether married or single, who pry into other people's affairs and neglect those of your own household—who are so busily employed in observing the faults of others that you have no time to correct your own—remember the fate of my dear aunt Charity, and eschew the evil spirit of curiosity.

FROM MY ELBOW-CHAIR.

I find, by perusal of our last number, that WILL WIZARD and EVERGREEN, taking advantage of my confinement, have been playing some of their confounded gambols. I suspected these rogues of some malpractices, in consequence of their queer looks and knowing winks whenever I came down to dinner, and of their not showing their faces at old Cockloft's for several days after the appearance of their precious effusions. Whenever these two waggish fellows lay their heads together, there is always sure to be hatched some notable piece of mischief, which, if it tickles nobody else, is sure to make its authors merry. The public will take notice that, for the purpose of teaching these my associates better manners, and punishing them for their high misdemeanours, I have by virtue of my authority suspended them from all interference in Salmagundi, until they show a proper degree of repentance, or I get tired of supporting the burthen of the work myself. I am sorry for

Will, who is already sufficiently mortified, in not daring to come to the old house and tell his long stories and smoke his cygarr; but Evergreen being an old beau, may solace himself in his disgrace by trimming up all his old finery and making love to the little girls.

At present my right hand man is cousin Pindar, whom I have taken into high favour. He came home the other night all in a blaze like a sky-rocket—whisked up to his room in a paroxysm of poetic inspiration, nor did we see any thing of him until late the next morning, when he bounced upon us at breakfast

"Fire in each eye—and paper in each hand."

This is just the way with Pindar: he is like a volcano, will remain for a long time silent without emitting a single spark, and then all at once burst out in a tremendous explosion of rhyme and rhapsody.

As the letters of my friend Mustapha seem to excite considerable curiosity, I have subjoined another. I do not vouch for the justice of his remarks, or the correctness of his conclusions; they are full of the blunders and errors into which strangers continually indulge, who pretend to give an account of this country, before they well know the geography of the street in which they live. The copies of my friend's papers being confused and without date, I cannot pretend to give them in systematic order—in fact they seem now and then to treat of matters which have occurred since his departure: whether these are sly interpolations of that meddlesome wight Will Wizard; or whether honest Mustapha was gifted with the spirit of prophecy or second sight, I neither know—nor in fact do I care. The following seems to have been written when the tripolitan prisoners were so much annoyed by the ragged state of their wardrobe. Mustapha feelingly depicts the embarrassments of his situation, traveller like, makes an easy transition from his breeches to the seat of government, and incontinently abuses the whole administration; like a sapient traveller I once knew, who damned the french nation *in toto*—because they eat sugar with green peas.

LETTER

From MUSTAPHA RUB-A-DUB KELI KHAN, captain of a ketch,
to ASEM HACCHEM, principal slave-driver
to his highness the bashaw of Tripoli.

Sweet, oh, ASEM! is the memory of distant friends! like the mellow ray of a departing sun it falls tenderly yet sadly on the heart. Every hour of absence from my native land rolls heavily by, like the sandy wave of the desert, and the fair shores of my country rise blooming to my imagination, clothed in the soft illusive charms of distance. I sigh—yet no one listens to the sigh of the captive; I shed the bitter tear of recollection, but no one sympathizes in the tear of the turban'd stranger! Think not, however, thou brother of my soul, that I complain of the horrors of my situation;—think not that my captivity is attended with the labours, the chains, the scourges, the insults that render slavery, with us, more dreadful than the pangs of hesitating, lingering death. Light, indeed, are the restraints on the personal freedom of thy kinsman; but who can enter into the afflictions of the mind;—who can describe the agonies of the heart? they are mutable as the clouds of the air, they are countless as the waves that divide me from my native country.

I have, of late, my dear Asem, laboured under an inconvenience singularly unfortunate, and am reduced to a dilemma most ridiculously embarrassing. Why should I hide it from the companion of my thoughts, the partner of my sorrows and my joys? Alas! Asem, thy friend Mustapha, the sublime and invincible *captain of a ketch*, is sadly in want of a pair of breeches! Thou will doubtless smile, oh most grave mussulman, to hear me indulge in such ardent lamentations about a circumstance so trivial, and a want apparently so easy to be satisfied; but little canst thou know of the mortifications attending my necessities, and the astonishing difficulty of supplying them. Honoured by the smiles and attentions of the beautiful ladies of this city, who have fallen in love with my whiskers and my turban; courted by the bashaws and the great men, who delight to have me at their feasts; the honour of my company eagerly solicited by every fiddler who gives a concert; think of my chagrin at being obliged to decline the host of invitations that daily overwhelm me, merely for want of a pair of breeches! Oh Allah! Allah! that thy disciples could come into the world all be-feathered like a bantam, or with a pair of leather breeches like the wild deer of the forest! Surely, my friend, it is the destiny of man to be forever subjected to petty evils, which, however trifling in appearance, prey in silence on his little pittance of enjoyment, and poison those moments of sunshine, which might otherwise be consecrated to happiness.

The want of a garment thou wilt say is easily supplied, and thou mayest suppose need only be mentioned, to be remedied at once by any tailor of the land: little canst thou conceive the impediments which stand in the way of my comfort; and still less art thou acquainted with the prodigious *great scale* on which every thing is transacted in this country. The nation moves most majestically slow and clumbsy in the most trivial affairs, like the unwieldy elephant, which makes a formidable difficulty of picking up a straw! When I hinted my necessities to the officer who has charge of myself and my companions, I expected to have them forthwith relieved, but he made an amazing long face, told me that we were prisoners of state, that we must therefore be clothed at the expense of government; that as no provision had been made by congress for an emergency of the kind, it was impossible to furnish me with a pair of breeches, until all the sages of the nation had been convened to *talk* over the matter, and debate upon the expediency of granting my request. Sword of the immortal Khalid, thought I, but this is great!—this is truly sublime! All the sages of an immense *logocracy* assembled together to talk about my breeches! Vain mortal that I am—I cannot but own I was somewhat reconciled to the delay which must necessarily attend this method of clothing me, by the consideration that if they made the affair a national act, my "name must of course be embodied in history," and myself and my breeches flourish to immortality in the annals of this mighty empire!

"But pray," said I, "how does it happen that a matter so insignificant should be erected into an object of such importance as to employ the representative wisdom of the nation, and what is the cause of their talking so much about a trifle?" "Oh," replied the officer, who acts as our slave-driver, "it all proceeds from *economy*. If the government did not spend ten times as much money in debating whether it was proper to supply you with breeches, as the breeches themselves would cost, the people who govern the bashaw and his divan would straightway begin to complain of their liberties being infringed; the national finances squandered: not a hostile slang-whanger, throughout the logocracy, but would burst forth like a barrel of combustion; and ten chances to one but the bashaw and the sages of his divan would all be turned out of office together. My good mussulman," continued he, "the administration have the good of the people too much at heart to trifle with their pockets; and they would sooner assemble and *talk* away ten thousand dollars, than expend fifty silently out of the treasury; such is the wonderful spirit of *economy*, that pervades every branch of this government." "But," said I, "how is it possible they can spend money in talking— surely words cannot be the current coin of this country?" "Truely," cried he, smiling, "your question is pertinent enough, for words indeed often supply the place of cash among us, and many an honest debt is paid in promises; but the fact is, the grand bashaw and the members of congress, or grand talkers of the nation, either receive a yearly salary or are paid *by the day.*" "By the nine-hundred tongues of the great beast in Mahomet's vision but the murder is out—it is no wonder these honest men talk so much about nothing, when they are paid for *talking,* like day laborers:" "you are mistaken," said my driver, "it is nothing but *economy!*"

I remained silent for some minutes, for this inexplicable word *economy* always discomfits me, and when I flatter myself I have grasped it, it slips through my fingers like a jack-o'lantern. I have not, nor perhaps ever shall acquire, sufficient of the philosophic policy of this government, to draw a proper distinction between an individual and a nation. If a man was to throw away a pound in order to save a beggarly penny, and boast at the same time of his economy, I should think him on a par with the fool in the fable of Alfanji, who, in skinning a flint worth a farthing, spoiled a knife worth fifty times the sum, and thought he had acted wisely. The shrewd fellow would doubtless have valued himself much more highly on his *economy*, could he have known that his example would one day be followed by the bashaw of America. and sages of his divan.

This economic disposition, my friend, occasions much fighting of the spirit, and innumerable contests of the tongue in this talking assembly. Wouldst thou believe it? they were actually employed for a whole week in a most strenuous and eloquent debate about patching up a hole in the wall of the room appropriated to their meetings! A vast profusion of nervous argument and pompous declamation was expended on the occasion. Some of the orators, I am told, being rather waggishly inclined, were most stupidly jocular on the occasion; but their waggery gave great offence, and was highly reprobated by the more *weighty* part of the assembly, who hold all wit and humour in abomination, and thought the business in hand much too solemn and serious to be treated lightly. It is supposed by some that this affair would have occupied a whole winter, as it was a subject upon which several gentlemen spoke who had never been known to open their lips in that place except to say *yes* and *no*. These silent members are by way of distinction denominated *orator mums*, and are highly valued in this country on account of their great talents for silence—a qualification extremely rare in a logocracy.

In the course of debate on this momentous question, the members began to wax warm, and grew to be exceeding wroth with one another, because their opponents most obstinately refused to be convinced by their arguments—or rather their *words*. The hole in the wall came well nigh producing a civil war of words throughout the empire; for, as usual in all public questions, the whole country was divided, and the *holeans* and the *anti-holeans*, headed by their respective slang-whangers, were marshalled out in array, and menaced deadly warfare. Fortunately for the public tranquility, in the hottest part of the debate, when two rampant virginians, brim-full of logic and philosophy, were measuring tongues, and syllogistically cudgelling each other out of their unreasonable notions, the president of the divan, a knowing old gentleman, one night slyly sent a mason with a hod of mortar, who, in the course of a few minutes, closed up the hole and put a final end to the argument. Thus did this wise old gentleman, by hitting on a most simple expedient, in all probability, save his country as much money as would build a gun-boat, or pay a hireling slang-whanger for a whole volume of *words*. As it happened, only a few thousand dollars were expended in paying these men, who are denominated, I suppose in derision, legislators.

Another instance of their economy I relate with pleasure, for I really begin to feel a regard for these poor barbarians. They talked away the best part of a whole winter before they could determine *not* to expend a few dollars in purchasing a sword to bestow on an illustrious warrior: yes, Asem, on that very hero who frightened all our poor old women and young children at Derne, and fully proved himself a greater man than the mother that bore him. Thus, my friend, is the whole collective wisdom of this mighty logocracy employed in somniferous debates about the most trivial affairs, like I have sometimes seen a herculean mountebank exerting all his energies in balancing a straw upon his nose. Their sages behold the minutest object with the microscopic eyes of a pismire; mole-hills swell into mountains, and a grain of mustard-seed will set the whole ant-hill in a hub-bub. Whether this indicates a capacious vision, or a diminutive mind, I leave thee to decide; for my part I consider it as another proof of the *great scale* on which every thing is transacted in this country.

I have before told thee that nothing can be done without consulting the sages of the nation, who compose the assembly called the congress. This prolific body may not improperly be termed the "mother of inventions;" and a most fruitful mother it is let me tell thee, though its children are generally abortions. It has lately laboured with what was deemed the conception of a mighty navy.—All the old women and the good wives that assist the bashaw in his emergencies hurried to head quarters to be busy, like midwives, at the delivery.—All was anxiety, fidgetting and consultation; when, after a deal of groaning and struggling, instead of formidable first rates and gallant frigates, out crept a litter of sorry little gun-boats! These are most pitiful little vessels, partaking vastly of the character of the grand bashaw, who has the credit of begetting them—being flat shallow vessels that can only sail before the wind—must always keep in with the land—are continually foundering or running ashore; and in short, are only fit for *smooth water*. Though intended for the defence of the maritime cities, yet the cities are obliged to *defend them*; and they require as much nursing as so many rickety little bantlings. They are, however, the darling pets of the grand bashaw, being the children of his dotage, and, perhaps from their diminutive size and palpable weakness, are called the "infant navy of America." The act that brought them into existence was almost deified by the majority of the people as a grand stroke of *economy*.—By the beard of Mahomet, but this word is truly inexplicable!

To this economic body therefore was I advised to address my petition, and humbly to pray that the august assembly of sages would, in the plenitude of their wisdom and the magnitude of their powers, munificently bestow on an unfortunate captive, a pair of cotton breeches! "Head of the immortal Amrou," cried I, "but this would be presumptuous to a degree—what! after these worthies have thought proper to leave their country naked and defenceless, and exposed to all the political storms that rattle without, can I expect that they will lend a helping hand to comfort the *extremities* of a solitary captive?" my exclamation was only answered by a smile, and I was consoled by the assurance that, so far from being neglected, it was every way probable my breeches might occupy a whole session of the divan, and set several of the longest heads together by the ears. Flattering as was the idea of a whole nation being agitated about my breeches, yet I own I was somewhat dismayed at the idea of remaining *in querpo*, until all the national grey-beards should have made a speech on the occasion, and given their consent to the measure. The embarrassment and distress of mind which I experienced was visible in my countenance, and my guard, who is a man of infinite good-nature, immediately suggested, as a more expeditious plan of supplying my wants—a benefit at the theatre. Though profoundly ignorant of his meaning, I agreed to his proposition, the result of which I shall disclose to thee in another letter.

Fare thee well, dear Asem;—in thy pious prayers to our great prophet, never forget to solicit thy friend's return; and when thou numberest up the many blessings bestowed on thee by all bountiful Allah, pour forth thy gratitude that he has cast thy nativity in a land where there is no assembly of legislative chatterers—no great Bashaw, who bestrides a gunboat for a hobby-horse—where the word *economy* is unknown—and where an unfortunate captive is not obliged to call upon the whole nation, to cut him out a pair of breeches.

ever thine,

MUSTAPHA.

FROM THE MILL OF
PINDAR COCKLOFT, ESQ.

THOUGH entered on that sober age,
When men withdraw from fashion's stage,
And leave the follies of the day,
To shape their course a graver way;
Still those gay scenes I loiter round,
In which my youth sweet transport found:
And though I feel their joys decay,
And languish every hour away,—

Yet like an exile doomed to part,
From the dear country of his heart,
From the fair spot in which he sprung,
Where his first notes of love were sung,
Will often turn to wave the hand,
And sigh his blessing on the land,
Just so my lingering watch I keep—
Thus oft I take my farewel peep.

And, like that pilgrim, who retreats
Thus lagging from his parent seats,
When the sad thought pervades his mind,
That the fair land he leaves behind
Is ravaged by a foreign foe,
Its cities waste—its temples low,
And ruined all those haunts of joy
That gave him rapture when a boy;
Turns from it with averted eye,
And while he heaves the anguish'd sigh,
Scarce feels regret that the loved shore
Shall beam upon his sight no more;—
Just so it grieves my soul to view,
While breathing forth a fond adieu,
The innovations pride has made—
The fustian, frippery and parade,
That now usurp with mawkish *grace*
Pure tranquil pleasure's wonted place!

Twas *joy* we look'd for in my prime—
That idol of the olden time;
When all our pastimes had the art
To please, and not mislead, the heart.
Style cursed us not,—that modern flash—
That love of racket and of trash;
Which scares at once all feeling joys,
And drowns delight in empty noise;
Which barters friendship, mirth and truth,
The artless air—the bloom of youth,
And all those gentle sweets that swarm
Round nature in her simplest form,
For cold display—for hollow state—
The trappings of the *would be great.*

Oh! once again those days recal,
When heart met heart in fashion's hall;
When every honest guest would flock

To add his pleasure to the stock,
More fond his transports to express,
Than show the tinsel of his dress!
These were the times that clasped the soul
In gentle friendship's soft controul;
Our fair ones, unprofaned by art,
Content to gain *one* honest heart,
No train of sighing swains desired—
Sought to be *loved* and not *admired*.
But now tis form—not love unites—
Tis show—not pleasure that invites.
Each seeks the ball to play the queen,
To flirt, to conquer—to be *seen*;
Each grasps at universal sway,
And reigns the idol of the day;
Exults amid a thousand sighs,
And triumphs when a lover dies.
Each belle a rival belle surveys,
Like deadly foe with hostile gaze;
Nor can her "dearest friend" caress,
Till she has slyly scann'd her dress;
Ten conquests in one year will make,
And six *eternal friendships* break!

How oft I breathe the inward sigh,
And feel the dew-drop in my eye,
When I behold some beauteous frame,
Divine in every thing but name,
Just venturing, in the tender age,
On Fashion's late new fangled stage!
Where soon the guileless heart shall cease
To beat in artlessness and peace;
Where all the flowers of gay delight
With which youth decks its prospects bright,
Shall wither mid the cares—the strife—
The cold realities of life!

Thus lately, in my careless mood,
As I the world of fashion view'd,
While celebrating *great and small*,
That grand *solemnity*—a ball,
My roving vision chanced to light
On two sweet forms, divinely bright;
Two sister nymphs, alike in face,
In mein, in loveliness and grace;

Twin rose-buds, bursting into bloom,
In all their brilliance and perfume;
Like those fair forms that often beam
Upon the eastern poets dream;
For Eden had each lovely maid
In native innocence arrayed,—
And heaven itself had almost shed
Its sacred halo round each head!
   They seemed, just entering hand in hand,
To cautious tread this fairy land;
To take a timid hasty view,
Enchanted with a scene so new.
The modest blush, untaught by art,
Bespoke their purity of heart;
And every timorous act unfurl'd
Two souls unspotted by the world.
   Oh, how these strangers joy'd my sight,
And thrill'd my bosom with delight!
They brought the visions of my youth
Back to my soul in all their truth,
Recalled fair spirits into day,
That time's rough hand had swept away!
Thus the bright natives from above,
Who come on messages of love,
Will bless, at rare and distant whiles,
Our sinful dwelling by their smiles!
   Oh! my romance of youth is past,
Dear airy dreams too bright to last!
Yet when such forms as these appear,
I feel your soft remembrance here;
For, ah! the simple poet's heart,
On which fond love once play'd its part,
Still feels the soft pulsations beat,
As loth to quit their former seat.
Just like the harp's melodious wire,
Swept by a bard with heavenly fire,
Though ceased the loudly swelling strain,
Yet sweet vibrations long remain.
   Full soon I found the lovely pair
Had sprung beneath a mother's care,
Hard by a neighbouring streamlet's side,
At once its ornament and pride.
The beauteous parent's tender heart

Had well fulfill'd its pious part;
And, like the holy man of old,
As we're by sacred writings told,
Who, when he from his pupil sped,
Pour'd two-fold blessings on his head,—
So this fond mother had imprest
Her early virtues in each breast,
And as she found her stock enlarge,
Had stampt new graces on her charge.
　　The fair resigned the calm retreat,
Where first their souls in concert beat,
And flew on expectation's wing,
To sip the joys of life's gay spring;
To sport in fashion's splendid maze,
Where friendship fades, and love decays.
So two sweet wild flowers, near the side
Of some fair river's silver tide,
Pure as the gentle stream that laves
The green banks with its lucid waves,
Bloom beauteous in their native ground,
Diffusing heavenly fragrance round:
But should a venturous hand transfer
These blossoms to the gay parterre,
Where, spite of artificial aid,
The fairest plants of nature fade;
Though they may shine supreme awhile,
Mid *pale ones* of the stranger soil,
The tender beauties soon decay,
And their sweet fragrance dies away.
　　Blest spirits! who enthron'd in air,
Watch o'er the virtues of the fair,
And with angelic ken survey,
Their windings through life's chequer'd way;
Who hover round them as they glide
Down fashion's smooth deceitful tide,
And guard them o'er that stormy deep
Where Dissipation's tempests sweep:
Oh, make this inexperienced pair
The objects of your tenderest care.
Preserve them from the languid eye,
The faded cheek—the long drawn sigh;
And let it be your constant aim
To keep the fair ones *still the same*:

Two sister hearts, unsullied, bright
As the first beam of lucid light,
That sparkled from the youthful sun,
When first his jocund race begun.
So when these hearts shall burst their shrine,
To wing their flight to realms divine,
They may to radiant mansions rise
Pure as when first they left the skies.

SALMAGUNDI NO. X

NO. X]   *Saturday, May* 16, 1807.

FROM MY ELBOW-CHAIR.

The long interval which has elapsed since the publication of our last number, like many other remarkable events, has given rise to much conjecture and excited considerable solicitude. It is but a day or two since I heard a knowing young gentleman observe, that he suspected Salmagundi would be a nine days wonder, and had even prophesied that the ninth would be our last effort. But the age of prophecy, as well as that of chivalry, is past; and no reasonable man should now venture to fortel aught but what he is determined to bring about himself:— he may then, if he please, monopolize prediction, and be honored as a prophet even in his own country.

Though I hold whether we write, or not write, to be none of the public's business, yet as I have just heard of the loss of three thousand votes at least to the Clintonians, I feel in a remarkable dulcet humour thereupon, and will give some account of the reasons which induced us to resume our useful labours—or rather our amusements; for, if writing cost either of us a moment's labour, there is not a man but what would hang up his pen, to the great detriment of the world at large, and of our publisher in particular, who has actually bought himself a pair of trunk breeches, with the profits of our writings!!

He informs me that several persons having called last Saturday for No. X, took the disappointment so much to heart that he really apprehended some terrible catastrophe; and one good-looking man in particular, declared his intention of quitting the country if the work was not continued. Add to this, the town has grown quite melancholy in the last fortnight; and several young ladies have declared in my hearing that if another number did not make its appearance soon, they would be obliged to amuse themselves with teasing their beaux, and making them miserable. Now I assure my readers there was no flattery in this, for they no more suspected me of being Launcelot Langstaff, than they suspect me of being the emperor of China, or the man in the moon.

I have also received several letters complaining of our indolent procrastination; and one of my correspondents assures me that a number of young gentlemen, who had not read a book through since they left school, but who have taken a wonderful liking to our paper, will certainly relapse into their old habits, unless we go on.

For the sake, therefore, of all these good people, and most especially for the satisfaction of the ladies, every one of whom we would love, if we possibly could, I have again wielded my pen, with a most hearty determination to set the whole world to rights, to make cherubims and seraphs of all the fair ones of this enchanting town, and raise the spirits of the poor federalists, who, in truth, seem to be in a sad taking, ever since the American Ticket met with the accident of being so unhappily *dished*.

TO LAUNCELOT LANGSTAFF, ESQ.

SIR,

I felt myself hurt and offended by mr. Evergreen's terrible phillipic against modern music in No. II of your work, and was under serious apprehension that his strictures might bring the art which I have the honor to profess, into contempt. The opinions of yourself and fraternity appear indeed to have a wonderful effect upon the town. I am told the ladies are all employed in reading Bunyan and Pamela, and the waltz has been entirely forsaken ever since the winter balls have closed. Under these apprehensions I should have addressed you before, had I not been sedulously employed, while the theatre continued open, in supporting the astonishing variety of the orchestra, and in composing a new chime or Bob-major for Trinity-church, to be rung during the summer, beginning with *ding-dong di-do*, instead of *di-do ding-dong*. The citizens, especially those who live in the neighborhood of that harmonious quarter, will no doubt be infinitely delighted with this novelty.

But to the object of this communication.—So far, sir, from agreeing with mr. Evergreen in thinking that all modern music is but the mere dregs and drainings of the antient, I trust, before this letter is concluded, I shall convince you and him that some of the late Professors of this enchanting art have completely distanced the paltry efforts of the antients, and that I in particular have at length brought it almost to absolute perfection.

The greeks, simple souls! were astonished at the powers of Orpheus, who made the woods and rocks dance to his lyre—of Amphion who converted crotchets into bricks, and quavers into mortar—and of Arion who won upon the compassion of the fishes. In the fervency of admiration, their poets fabled that Apollo had lent them his lyre, and inspired them with his own spirit of harmony. What then would they have said had they witnessed the wonderful effects of my skill? Had they heard me in the compass of a single piece, describe in glowing notes one of the most sublime operations of nature, and not only make inanimate objects dance, but even speak, and not only speak, but speak in strains of exquisite harmony?

Let me not, however, be understood to say that I am the sole author of this extraordinary improvement in the art, for I confess I took the hint of many of my discoveries from some of those meritorius productions that have lately come abroad and made so much noise under the title of *overtures*. From some of these, as, for instance, Lodoiska, and the battle of Marengo, a gentleman, or a captain in the city militia, or an amazonian young lady, may indeed acquire a tolerable idea of military tactics, and become very well experienced in the firing of musketry, the roaring of cannon, the rattling of drums, the whistling of fifes, braying of trumpets, groans of the dying, and trampling of cavalry, without ever going to the wars;—but it is more especially in the art of imitating inimitable things, and giving the language of every passion and sentiment of the human mind, so as entirely to do away the necessity of speech, that I particularly excel the most celebrated musicians of antient and modern times.

I think, sir, I may venture to say there is not a sound in the whole compass of nature which I cannot imitate and even improve upon—nay, what I consider the perfection of my art, I have discovered a method of expressing, in the most striking manner, that undefinable, indescribable silence which accompanies the falling of snow.

In order to prove to you that I do not arrogate to myself what I am unable to perform, I will detail to you the different movements of a grand piece which I pride myself upon exceedingly, called the Breaking up of the Ice in the North-river.

The piece opens with a gentle andante affetuoso, which ushers you into the assembly-room, in the state-house at Albany, where the speaker addresses his farewel speech, informing the members that the ice is about breaking up, and thanking them for their great services and good behaviour in a manner so pathetic as to bring tears into their eyes.—Flourish of Jacks a donkies.—Ice cracks—Albany in a hubbub—air, "Three children sliding on the ice, all on a summer's day."—Citizens quarrelling in dutch—chorus of a tin trumpet, a cracked fiddle, and a hand-saw!—allegro moderato.—*Hard frost*—this if given with proper spirit has a charming effect, and sets every body's teeth chattering.—Symptoms of snow—consultation of old women who complain of pains in the bones and *rheumatics*—air, "There was an old woman tossed up in a blanket, &c." —allegro staccato—waggon breaks into the ice—people all run to see what is the matter—air, *siciliano*—"Can you row the boat ashore, Billy boy, Billy boy"—andante—frost fish froze up in the ice—air—"Ho, why dost thou shiver and shake, Gaffer Gray, and why does thy nose look so blue?"—Flourish of two-penny trumpets and rattles—consultation of the North-river society—determine to set the North river on fire, as soon as it will burn—air—"O, what a fine kettle of fish."

Part II.—GREAT THAW.—This consists of the most *melting* strains, flowing so smoothly, as to occasion a great overflowing of scientific rapture—air—"One misty moisty morning."—The house of assembly breaks up—air—"The owls came out and flew about"—Assemblymen embark on their way to New-York—air—"The ducks and the geese they all swim over, fal, de ral, &c.—Vessel sets sail—chorus of mariners— "Steer her up, and let her gang." After this a rapid movement conducts you to New-York—the North-river society hold a meeting at the corner of Wall-street, and determine to delay burning till all the assemblymen are safe home, for fear of consuming some of their own members who belong to that respectable body.—Return again to the *capital.*—Ice floats down the river—lamentation of skaiters—air, affetuoso—"I sigh and lament me in vain, &c."—Albanians cutting up sturgeon—air—"O the roast beef of *Albany.*"—Ice runs against Polopoy's island, with a terrible crash.—This is represented by a fierce fellow travelling with his fiddle-stick over a huge bass viol, at the rate of one hundred and fifty bars a minute, and tearing the music to rags—this being what is called *execution.*—The great body of ice passes West-Point, and is saluted by three or four dismounted cannon, from Fort Putnam.—"Jefferson's march" —by a full band—air—"Yankee doodle, with seventy-six variations, never before attempted, except by the celebrated eagle, which flutters his wings over the copper-bottomed angel at messrs. Paff's in Broadway.—Ice passes New-York—conch-shell sounds at a distance—ferryman calls o-v-e-r—people run down Courtlandt-street—ferryboat sets sail—air— accompanied by the conch-shell—"We'll all go over the ferry."—Rondeau —giving a particular account of BROM the Powles-Hook admiral, who is supposed to be closely connected with the North-river society.—The society make a grand attempt to fire the stream, but are utterly defeated by a remarkable high tide, which brings the plot to light—drowns up-wards of a thousand rats, and occasions twenty robins to break their necks.*—Society not being discouraged. apply to "Common Sense," for

*Vide—Solomon Lang.

his lantern—Air—"Nose, nose, jolly red nose."—Flock of wild geese fly over the city—old wives chatter in the fog—cocks crow at Communipaw —drums beat on Governor's island.—The whole to conclude with *the blowing up of Sands' powder-house.*

Thus, sir, you perceive what wonderful powers of expression have been hitherto locked up in this enchanting art—a whole history is here told without the aid of speech, or writing; and provided the hearer is in the least acquainted with music he cannot mistake a single note. As to the blowing up of the powder-house, I look upon it as a chef d'ouvre, which I am confident will delight all modern amateurs, who very properly estimate music in proportion to the noise it makes, and delight in thundering, cannon and earthquakes.

I must confess, however, it is a difficult part to manage, and I have already broken six pianoes in giving it the proper force and effect. But I do not despair, and am quite certain that by the time I have broken eight or ten more, I shall have brought it to such perfection, as to be able to teach any young lady of tolerable ear, to thunder it away to the infinite delight of papa and mamma, and the great annoyance of those vandals, who are so barbarous as to prefer the simple melody of a scots air, to the sublime effusions of modern musical doctors.

In my warm anticipation of future improvement, I have sometimes almost convinced myself that music will in time be brought to such a climax of perfection, as to supercede the necessity of speech and writing, and every kind of social intercourse be conducted by flute and fiddle. The immense benefits that will result from this improvement must be plain to every man of the least consideration. In the present unhappy situation of mortals, a man has but one way of making himself perfectly understood—if he loses his speech, he must inevitably be dumb all the rest of his life; but having once learned this new musical language, the loss of speech will be a mere trifle not worth a moment's uneasiness. Not only this, mr. L. but it will add much to the harmony of domestic intercourse, for it is certainly much more agreeable to hear a lady give lectures on the piano, than *viva voce*, in the usual discordant measure. This manner of discoursing may also, I think, be introduced with great effect into our national assemblies, where every man, instead of wagging his tongue, should be obliged to flourish a fiddle-stick, by which means, if he said nothing to the purpose, he would at all events "discourse most eloquent music," which is more than can be said of most of them at present. They might also sound their own trumpets, without being obliged to a hireling scribbler for an immortality of nine days, or subjected to the censure of egotism.

But the most important result of this discovery is, that it may be applied to the establishment of that great desideratum, in the learned world, a universal language. Wherever this science of music is cultivated, nothing more will be necessary than a knowledge of its alphabet, which being almost the same every where, will amount to a universal medium of communication. A man may thus, with his violin under his arm, a piece of rosin and a few bundles of catgut, fiddle his way through the world, and never be at a loss to make himself understood.

I am, &c.

DEMY SEMIQUAVER.

P. S. I forgot to mention that I intend to publish my piece by subscription, and dedicate it to the North-River Society. D. S.

THE STRANGER IN PENNSYLVANIA

BY JEREMY COCKLOFT, THE YOUNGER

CHAPTER I.

Cross the Delaware—knew I was in Pennsylvania, because all the people were fat and looked like the statue of William Penn—Bristol—very remarkable for having nothing in it worth the attention of the traveller—saw Burlington on the opposite side of the river—fine place for pigeon-houses—and why?—Pennsylvania famous for barns—cattle in general better lodged than the farmers—barns appear to be built, as the old roman peasant planted his trees, "for posterity and the immortal gods." Saw several fine bridges of two or three arches built over dry places—wondered what could be the use of them—reminded me of the famous bridge at Madrid, built over no water—Chamouny—floating bridge made of pine logs fastened together by ropes of walnut bark—strange that the people who have such a taste for bridges should not have taken advantage of this river, to indulge in their favorite kind of architecture! —expressed my surprise to a fellow passenger, who observed to me with great gravity, "that nothing was more natural than that people who build bridges over dry places should neglect them where they are really necessary"—could not, for the head of me, see to the bottom of the man's reasoning—about half an hour after it struck me that he had been quizzing me a little—didn't care much about that—revenge myself by mentioning him in my book. Village of Washington—very pleasant, and remarkable for being built on each side of the road—houses all cast in the same mould—have a very quakerish appearance, being built of stone, plastered and white-washed, and green doors, ornamented with brass knockers, kept very bright—saw several genteel young ladies scouring them—which was no doubt the reason for their brightness. Breakfasted at the Fox-Chase—recommend this house to all gentlemen travelling for information, as the land-lady makes the best buckwheat-cakes in the whole world; and because it bears the same name with a play, written by a young gentleman of Philadelphia, which, notwithstanding its very considerable merit, was received at that city with indifference and neglect, because it had no puns in it. Frankfort *in the mud*—very picturesque town, situate on the edge of a pleasant swamp—or meadow as they call it—houses all built of turf, cut in imitation of stone—poor substitute—took in a couple of Princeton students, who were going on to the southward, to tell their papas, (or rather their mammas) what fine manly little boys they were, and how nobly they resisted the authority of the trustees—both pupils of Godwin and Tom Paine—talked about the rights of man, the social compact, and the perfectability of boys—hope their parents will whip them when they get home, and send them back to college without any spending money. Turnpike gates—direction to keep to the right, as the law directs—very good advice, in my opinion; but one of the students swore he had no idea of submitting to this kind of oppression, and insisted on the driver's taking the left passage, in order to show the world we were not to be imposed upon by such arbitrary rules—driver, who, I believe, had been a student at Princeton himself, shook his head like a professor, and said it would not do. Entered Philadelphia through the suburbs—four little markets in a herd—one turned into a school for young ladies—mem. young ladies early in the market here—pun—good.

CHAPTER II.

Very ill—confined to my bed with a violent fit of the *pun* mania—strangers always experience an attack of the kind on their first arrival, and undergo a *seasoning* as europeans do in the West-Indies. In my way from the stage-office to Renshaw's I was accosted by a good-looking young gentleman from New-Jersey, who had caught the infection—he took me by the button and informed me of a contest that had lately taken place between a tailor and shoemaker about I forget what;—SNIP was pronounced a fellow of great *capability*, a man of gentlemanly *habits*, who would doubtless *suit* every body. The shoemaker *bristled* up at this, and *waxed* exceeding wroth—swore the tailor was but a *half-souled* fellow, and that it was easy to *shew* he was never *cut-out* for a gentleman. The *choler* of the tailor was up in an instant, he swore by his thimble that he would never *pocket* such an insult, but would *baste* any man who dared to repeat it.—Honest CRISPIN was now worked up to his proper *pitch*, and was determined to yield the tailor no *quarters;*—he vowed he would lose his *all* but what he would gain his *ends*. He resolutely held on to the *last*, and on his threatening to *back-strap* his adversary, the tailor was obliged to *sheer* off, declaring, at the same

time, that he would have him *bound over*. The young gentleman, having
finished his detail, gave a most obstreperous laugh, and hurried off to
tell his story to somebody else—*Licentia punica*, as Horace observes—it
did my business—I went home, took to my bed, and was two days
confined with this singular complaint.

Having, however, looked about me with the argus eyes of a traveller,
I have picked up enough in the course of my walk from the stage
office, to the hotel, to give a full and impartial account of this remarkable city. According to the good old rule, I shall begin with the etymology
of its name, which according to Linkum Fidelius. Tom. LV. is clearly
derived, either from the name of its first founder, viz. PHILO DRIPPING-
PAN, or the singular taste of the aborigines, who flourished there, on his
arrival. Linkum, who is as shrewd a fellow as any theorist or F. S. A. for
peeping with a dark lantern into the lumber garret of antiquity, and
lugging out all the trash which was left there for oblivion, by our wiser
ancestors, supports his opinion by a prodigious number of ingenious
and inapplicable arguments; but particularly rests his position on the
known fact, that Philo Dripping-pan was remarkable for his predilection
to eating, and his love of what the learned dutch call *doup*. Our
erudite author likewise observes that the citizens are to this day, noted
for their love of "a sop in the pan," and their portly appearance, "except,
indeed," continues he, "the young ladies, who are perfectly genteel in
their dimensions"—this, however, he ill naturedly enough attributes to
their eating pickles, and drinking vinegar.

The philadelphians boast much of the situation and plan of their
city, and well may they, since it is undoubtedly, as fair and square, and
regular, and right angled, as any mechanical genius could possibly have
made it. I am clearly of opinion that this hum drum regularity has a
vast effect on the character of its inhabitants and even on their looks,
"for you will observe," writes Linkum, "that they are an honest, worthy,
square, good-looking, well-meaning, regular, uniform, straight forward,
clockwork, clear-headed, one-like-another, salubrious, upright, kind of
people, who always go to work methodically, never put the cart before
the horse, talk like a book, walk mathematically, never turn but in right
angles, think syllogistically, and pun theoretically, according to the
genuine rules of Cicero, and Dean Swift;—whereas the people of
New-York—God help them—tossed about over hills and dales, through
lanes and alleys, and crooked streets—continually mounting and descending, turning and twisting—whisking off at tangents, and left-angle-tri-
angles, just like their own queer, odd, topsy-turvy rantipole city, are
the most irregular, crazy headed, quicksilver, eccentric, whim-whamsical
set of mortals that ever were jumbled together in this uneven, villanous
revolving globe, and are the very antipodeans to the philadelphians."

The streets of Philadelphia are wide and strait, which is wisely ordered, for the inhabitants having generally crooked noses, and most commonly travelling hard after them, the good folks would undoubtedly soon *go to the wall,* in the crooked streets of our city. This fact of the crooked noses has not been hitherto remarked by any of our american travellers, but must strike every stranger of the least observation. There is, however, one place which I would recommend to all my fellow-citizens, who may come after me as a promenade—I mean Dock-street—the only street in Philadelphia that bears any resemblance to New-York—how tender, how exquisite are the feelings awakened in the breast of a traveller, when his eye encounters some object which reminds him of his far distant country! The pensive new-yorker, having drank his glass of porter, and smoked his cygarr after dinner, (by the way I would recommend Sheaff, as selling the best in Philadelphia) may here direct his solitary steps and indulge in that mellow tenderness in which the sentimental Kotzebue, erst delighted to wallow—he may recal the romantic scenery and grace-ful windings of Maiden-lane, and Pearl-street, trace the tumultuous gutter in its harmonious meanderings, and almost fancy he beholds the moss-crowned roof of the Bear-market, or the majestic steeple of St Paul's towering to the clouds.—Perhaps too, he may have left behind him some gentle fair one, who, all the live-long evening, sits pensively at the window, leaning on her elbows, and counting the lingering, lame and broken-winded moments that so tediously lengthen the hours which separate her from the object of her contemplations!—delightful Lethe of the soul—sunshine of existence—wife and children poking up the cheer-ful evening fire—paper windows, mud walls, love in a cottage—sweet sensibility—and all that.

Every body has heard of the famous bank of Pennsylvania, which, since the destruction of the tomb of Mausolus, and the colossus of Rhodes, may fairly be estimated as one of the wonders of the world. My landlord thinks it unquestionably the finest building upon earth. The honest man has never seen the theatre in New-York, or the new brick church at the head of Rector-street, which when finished, will, beyond all doubt, be infinitely superior to the Pennsylvania barns, I noted before.

Philadelphia is a place of great trade and commerce—not but that it would have been much more so, that is had it been built on the scite of New-York: but as New York has engrossed its present situation, I think Philadelphia must be content to stand where it does at present—at any rate it is not Philadelphia's fault nor is it any concern of mine, so I shall not make myself uneasy about the affair. Besides, to use Trim's argu-ment, were that city to stand where New-York does, it might perhaps have the misfortune to be called New-York and not Philadelphia, which

would be quite another matter, and this portion of my travels had undoubtedly been smothered before it was born—which would have been
a thousand pities indeed.

Of the manufactures of Philadelphia, I can say but little, except that
the people are famous for an excellent kind of confectionary, made from
the drainings of sugar. The process is simple as any in mrs. Glass's
excellent and useful work, (which I hereby recommend to the fair
hands of all young ladies, who are not occupied in reading Moore's
poems)—you buy a pot—put your molasses in your pot—(if you can beg,
borrow, or steal your molasses it will come much cheaper than if you
buy it)—boil your molasses to a proper consistency; but if you boil it
too much, it will be none the better for it—then pour it off and let it cool,
or draw it out into little pieces about nine inches long, and put it by for
use. This manufacture is called by the bostonians *lasses-candy*, by the
new-yorkers, *cock-a-nee-nee*—but by the polite philadelphians, by a
name utterly impossible to pronounce.

The Philadelphia ladies, are some of them beautiful, some of them
tolerably good looking, and some of them, to say the truth, are not at all
handsome. They are, however, very agreeable in general, except those
who are reckoned witty, who, if I might be allowed to speak my mind,
are very disagreeable, particularly to young gentlemen, who are travelling
for information. Being fond of tea-parties, they are a little given to
criticism—but are in general remarkably discreet, and very industrious,
as I have been assured by some of my friends. Take them all in all,
however, they are much inferior to the ladies of New-York, as plainly
appears, from several young gentlemen having fallen in love with some
of our belles, after resisting all the female attractions of Philadelphia.
From this inferiority, I except one, who is the most amiable, the most
accomplished, the most bewitching, and the most of every thing that
constitutes the divinity of woman—mem—*golden apple!*

The amusements of the philadelphians are dancing, punning, tea-parties,
and theatrical exhibitions. In the first, they are far inferior to the young
people of New-York, owing to the misfortune of their mostly preferring
to idle away time in the cultivation of the head instead of the heels.
It is a melancholy fact that an infinite number of young ladies in
Philadelphia, whose minds are elegantly accomplished in literature, have
sacrificed to the attainment of such trifling acquisitions, the pigeon-wing,
the waltz, the cossack dance, and other matters of equal importance.
On the other hand they excel the new-yorkers in punning, and in the
management of tea-parties. In N York you never hear, except from
some young gentleman just returned from a visit to Philadelphia, a
single attempt at punning, and at a tea-party, the ladies in general, are
disposed close together, like a setting of jewels, or pearls round a

locket, in all the majesty of good behaviour—and if a gentleman wishes
to have a conversation with one of them, about the backwardness of the
spring, the improvements in the theatre, or the merits of his horse, he
is obliged to march up in the face of such vollies of eye-shot! such a
formidable artilery of glances!—if he escapes annihilation, he should cry
out a miracle! and never encounter such dangers again. I remember to
have once heard a very valiant british officer, who had served with great
credit for some years in the train bands, declare with a veteran oath,
that sooner than encounter such deadly peril, he would fight his way
clear through a London mob, though he were pelted with brick-bats
all the time. Some ladies who were present at this declaration of the
gallant officer, were inclined to consider it a great compliment, until
one, more knowing than the rest, declared with a little piece of a sneer,
"that they were very much obliged to him for likening the company to a
London mob, and their glances to brick-bats:"—the officer looked blue,
turned on his heel, made a fine retreat and went home, with a determination to quiz the american ladies as soon as he got to London.

SALMAGUNDI NO. XI

no. XI]   Tuesday, June 2, 1807.

LETTER
From MUSTAPHA RUB-A-DUB KELI KHAN, captain of a ketch,
to ASEM HACCHEM, principal slave-driver
to his highness the bashaw of Tripoli.

The deep shadows of midnight gather around me—the footsteps of the
passenger have ceased in the streets, and nothing disturbs the holy
silence of the hour, save the sound of distant drums, mingled with the
shouts, the bawlings, and the discordant revelry of his majesty, the
sovereign mob. Let the hour be sacred to friendship, and consecrated
to thee, oh thou brother of my inmost soul!
    Oh Asem! I almost shrink at the recollection of the scenes of con-
fusion, of licentious disorganization, which I have witnessed during the
last three days. I have beheld this whole city, nay this whole state,
given up to the tongue and the pen, to the puffers, the bawlers, the
babblers and the *slang-whangers*. I have beheld the community con-
vulsed with a civil war, (or *civil talk*) individuals verbally massacred,
families annihilated by whole sheets full, and slang-whangers coolly
bathing their pens in ink, and rioting in the slaughter of their thousands.

I have seen, in short, that awful despot, *the people,* in the moment of unlimited power, wielding newspapers in one hand, and with the other scattering mud and filth about, like some desperate lunatic relieved from the restraints of his strait waistcoat. I have seen beggers on horeback, ragamuffins riding in coaches, and swine seated in places of honour —I have seen liberty, I have seen equality, I have seen fraternity!—I have seen that great political puppet-show—AN ELECTION.

A few days ago the friend, whom I have mentioned in some of my former letters, called upon me to accompany him to witness this grand ceremony, and we forthwith sallied out to *the polls,* as he called them. Though for several weeks before this splendid exhibition, nothing else had been talked of, yet I do assure thee I was entirely ignorant of its nature; and when, on coming up to a church, my companion informed me we were at the poll, I supposed that an election was some great religious ceremony, like the fast of Ramazan, or the great festival of Haraphat, so celebrated in the East.

My friend, however, undeceived me at once, and entered into a long dissertation on the nature and object of an election, the substance of which was nearly to this effect: "You know," said he, "that this country is engaged in a violent internal warfare, and suffers a variety of evils from civil dissentions. An election is the grand trial of strength, the decisive battle when the Belligerents draw out their forces in martial array; when every leader burning with warlike ardour, and encouraged by the shouts and acclamations of tatterdemalians, buffoons, dependents, parasites, toad-eaters, scrubs, vagrants, mumpers, ragamuffins, bravoes and beggers, in his rear, and puffed up by his bellows-blowing slang-whangers, waves gallantly the banners of faction, and presses forward TO OFFICE AND IMMORTALITY!"

"For a month or two previous to the critical period which is to decide this important affair, the whole community is in a ferment. Every man of whatever rank or degree, such is the wonderful patriotism of the people, disinterestedly neglects his business, to devote himself to his country—and not an insignificant fellow, but feels himself inspired on this occasion, with as much warmth in favour of the cause he has espoused, as if all the comfort of his life, or even his life itself, was dependent on the issue. Grand councils of war are, in the first place, called by the different powers, which are dubbed general meetings, where all the head workmen of the party collect, and arrange the order of battle—appoint the different commanders, and their subordinate instruments, and furnish the funds indispensible for supplying the expenses of the war. Inferior councils are next called in the different classes or wards, consisting of young cadets, who are candidates for offices, idlers who come there from mere curiosity, and orators who appear for the

NO. XI   191

purpose of detailing all the crimes, the faults or the weaknesses of
their opponents, and *speaking the sense of the meeting*, as it is called—
for as the meeting generally consists of men whose quota of sense, taken
individually, would make but a poor figure, these orators are appointed
to collect it all in a lump, when I assure you it makes a very formidable
appearance, and furnishes sufficient matter to spin an oration of two
or three hours.

"The orators who declaim at these meetings are, with a few exceptions,
men of most profound and perplexed eloquence; who are the oracles
of barber's shops, market places and porter houses; and who you may
see every day at the corner of the streets, taking honest men prisoners
by the button, and talking their ribs quite bare without mercy and
without end. These orators, in addressing an audience, generally mount a
chair, a table, or an empty beer barrel, (which last is supposed to
afford considerable inspiration) and thunder away their combustible
sentiments at the heads of the audience, who are generally so busily
employed in smoking, drinking, and hearing themselves talk, that they
seldom hear a word of the matter. This, however, is of little moment;
for as they come there to agree at all events to a certain set of resolutions, or articles of war, it is not at all necessary to hear the speech,
more especially as few would understand it if they did. Do not suppose,
however, that the minor persons of the meeting are entirely idle.
Besides smoking, and drinking, which are generally practised, there
are few who do not come with as great a desire to talk as the orator
himself—each has his little circle of listeners, in the midst of whom
he sets his hat on one side of his head, and deals out matter of fact
information, and draws self-evident conclusions, with the pertinacity
of a pedant, and to the great edification of his gaping auditors. Nay, the
very urchins from the nursery, who are scarcely emancipated from the
dominion of birch, on these occasions, strut pigmy great men—bellow
for the instruction of grey bearded ignorance, and, like the frog in
the fable, endeavour to puff themselves up to the size of the great
object of their emulation—the principal orator."

"But head of Mahomet," cried I, "is it not preposterous to a degree,
for those puny whipsters to attempt to lecture age and experience? they
should be sent to school to learn better." "Not at all," replied my friend;
"for as an election is nothing more than a war of words, the man
that can wag his tongue with the greatest elasticity, whether he
speaks to the purpose or not, is entitled to lecture at ward meetings
and polls, and instruct all who are inclined to listen to him—You may
have remarked a ward meeting of politic dogs, where, although the great
dog is, ostensibly, the leader and makes the most noise, yet every little
scoundrel of a cur has something to say, and in proportion to his insig-

nificance, fidgets and worries, and puffs about mightily, in order to
obtain the notice and approbation of his betters. Thus it is with these
little beardless bread and butter politicians, who, on this occasion,
escape from the jurisdiction of their mamas, to attend to the affairs of
the nation. You will see them engaged in dreadful wordy contest with
old cartmen, coblers and tailors, and plume themselves not a little, if
they should chance to gain a victory.—Aspiring spirits!—how interesting
are the first dawnings of political greatness!—An election, my friend, is
a nursery or hot-bed of genius in a logocracy—and I look with enthusiasm
on a troop of these liliputian partizans, as so many chatterers, and orators, and puffers, and slang-whangers in embryo, who will one day, take
an important part in the quarrels, and wordy wars of their country.

"As the time for fighting the decisive battle approaches, appearances
become more and more alarming—committees are appointed, who hold
little encampments, from whence they send out small detachments of
tatlers, to reconnoitre, harrass and skirmish with the enemy, and, if
possible, ascertain their numbers; every body seems big with the mighty
event that is impending—the orators they gradually swell up beyond
their usual size—the little orators, they grow greater and greater—the
secretaries of the ward committees strut about, looking like wooden
oracles—the puffers put on the airs of mighty consequence; the slang-
whangers deal out direful innuendoes, and threats of doughty import,
and all is buzz, murmur, suspense and sublimity!

"At length the day arrives. The storm that has been so long gathering,
and threatening in distant thunders bursts forth in terrible explosion.
All business is at an end—the whole city is in a tumult—the people are
running helter skelter, they know not whither, and they know not why.
The hackney coaches rattle through the streets with thundering vehemence, loaded with recruiting serjeants who have been prowling in
cellars and caves, to unearth some miserable minion of poverty and ignorance, who will barter his vote for a glass of beer, or a ride in a coach
with such *fine gentlemen*!—The buzzards of the party scamper from poll
to poll, on foot or on horeback—and they twaddle from committee to
committee, and buzz, and chafe, and fume, and talk big, and—*do nothing*
—like the vagabond drone, who wastes his time in the laborious idleness
of *see-saw-song*, and busy nothingness."

I know not how long my friend would have continued his detail, had
he not been interrupted by a squabble which took place between two
old continentals, as they were called. It seems they had entered into
an argument on the respective merits of their cause, and not being able
to make each other clearly understood, resorted to what are called
knock-down arguments, which form the superlative degree of the
argumentum ad hominem; but are, in my opinion, extremely incon-

sistent with the true spirit of a genuine logocracy. After they had beaten each other soundly, and set the whole mob together by the ears, they came to a full explanation, when it was discovered that they were both of the same way of thinking—whereupon they shook each other heartily by the hand, and laughed with great glee at their *humourous* misunderstanding.

I could not help being struck with the exceeding great number of ragged, dirty looking persons, that swaggered about the place, and seemed to think themselves the bashaws of the land. I inquired of my friend if these people were employed to drive away the hogs, dogs, and other intruders that might thrust themselves in and interrupt the ceremony? "By no means," replied he; "these are the representatives of the sovereign people, who come here to make governors, senators and members of assembly, and are the source of all power and authority in this nation." "Preposterous," said I, "how is it possible that such men can be capable of distinguishing between an honest man and a knave, or even if they were, will it not always happen that they are led by the nose by some intriguing demagogue, and made the mere tools of ambitious political jugglers?—Surely it would be better to trust to providence, or even chance, for governors, than resort to the discriminating powers of an ignorant mob.—I plainly perceive the consequence.—A man, who possesses superior talents, and that honest pride which ever accompanies this possession, will always be sacrificed to some creeping insect who will prostitute himself to familiarity with the lowest of mankind, and like the idolatrous egyptian, worship the wallowing tenants of filth and mire."

"All this is true enough," replied my friend, "but after all you cannot say but that this is a free country, and that the people can get drunk cheaper here, particularly at elections, than in the despotic countries of the east." I could not, with any degree of propriety or truth, deny this last assertion, for just at that moment a patriotic brewer arrived with a load of beer, which, for a moment, occasioned a cessation of argument.— The great crowd of buzzards, puffers, and old continentals of all *parties*, who throng to the polls, to persuade, to cheat, or to force the freeholders into the right way, and to maintain the *freedom of suffrage*, seemed for a moment to forget their antipathies, and joined, heartily, in a copious libation of this patriotic, and argumentative beverage.

These *beer barrels*, indeed seem to be most able logicians, well stored with that kind of sound argument, best suited to the comprehension, and most relished by the mob, or sovereign people, who are never so tractable as when operated upon by this convincing liquor, which, in fact, seems to be imbrued with the very spirit of logocracy. No sooner does it begin its operation, than the tongue waxes exceeding valourous, and becomes impatient for some mighty conflict. The puffer puts himself at the head of his body guard of buzzards, and his legion of ragamuffins, and woe then to every unhappy adversary who is uninspired by the deity of the beer-barrel—he is sure to be talked, and argued into complete insignificance.

While I was making these observations, I was surprised to observe a bashaw, high in office, shaking a fellow by the hand, that looked rather more ragged, than a scare-crow, and inquiring with apparent solicitude concerning the health of his family; after which he slipped a little folded paper into his hand and turned away. I could not help applauding his humility in shaking the fellow's hand, and his benevolence in relieving his distresses, for I imagined the paper contained something for the poor man's necessities; and truly he seemed verging towards the last stage of starvation. My friend, however, soon undeceived me by saying that this was an elector, and the bashaw had merely given him the list of candidates, for whom he was to vote. "Ho! ho!" said I, "then he is a particular friend of the bashaw?" "By no means," replied my friend, "the bashaw will pass him without notice, the day after the election, except, perhaps, just to drive over him with his coach."

My friend then proceeded to inform me that for some time before, and during the continuance of an election, there was a most *delectable courtship* or intrigue, carried on between the great bashaws, and *mother mob*. That *mother mob* generally preferred the attentions of the rabble, or of fellows of her own stamp, but would sometimes condescend to be treated to a feasting, or any thing of that kind, at the bashaw's expense; nay, sometimes when she was in a good humour, she would condescend to toy with them in her rough way—but woe be to the bashaw who attempted to be familiar with her, for she was the most pestilent, cross, crabbed, scolding, thieving, scratching, toping, wrong-headed, rebellious, and abominable termagant that ever was let loose in the world, to the confusion of honest gentlemen bashaws.

Just then, a fellow came round and distributed among the crowd a number of hand-bills, written by the *ghost of Washington*, the fame of whose illustrious actions, and still more illustrious virtues, has reached even the remotest regions of the east, and who is venerated by this people as the Father of his country. On reading this paltry paper, I could not restrain my indignation. "Insulted hero," cried I, "is it thus thy name is profaned, thy memory disgraced, thy spirit drawn down from heaven to administer to the brutal violence of party rage!—It is thus the necromancers of the east, by their infernal incantations, sometimes call up the shades of the just, to give their sanction to frauds, to lies, and to every species of enormity." My friend smiled at my warmth, and observed, that raising ghosts, and not only raising them but making them speak, was one of the miracles of election. "And believe me," continued he, "there is good reason for the ashes of departed heroes being disturbed on these occasions, for such is the *sandy* foundation of our government, that there never happens an election of an alderman, or a collector, or even a constable, but we are in imminent danger of losing our liberties, and becoming a province of France, or tributary to the British islands." "By the hump of Mahomet's camel," said I, "but this is only another striking example of the prodigious great scale on which every thing is transacted in this country."

By this time I had become tired of the scene; my head ached with the uproar of voices, mingling in all the discordant tones of triumphant exclamation, nonsensical argument, intemperate reproach, and drunken absurdity.—The confusion was such as no language can adequately describe, and it seemed as all the restraints of decency, and all the bands of law had been broken and given place to the wide ravages of licentious brutality. These, thought I, are the orgies of liberty, these are the manifestations of the spirit of independence, these are the symbols of man's sovereignty! Head of Mahomet! with what a fatal and inexorable despotism do empty names and ideal phantoms exercise their dominion over the human mind! The experience of ages has demonstrated, that in all nations, barbarous or enlightened, the mass of the people, the *mob*, must be slaves, or they will be tyrants—but their tyranny will not be long—some ambitious leader, having at first condescended to be their slave, will at length become their master; and in proportion to the vileness of his former servitude, will be the severity of his subsequent tyranny.—Yet, with innumerable examples staring them in the face, the people still bawl out liberty, by which they mean nothing but freedom from every species of legal restraint, and a warrant for all kinds of licentiousness: and the bashaws and leaders, in courting the mob, convince them of their power, and by administering to their passions, for the purposes of ambition, at length learn by fatal experience, that he who worships the beast that carries him on its back, will sooner or later be thrown into the dust and trampled under foot by the animal who has learnt the secret of its power, by this very adoration.

ever thine,

MUSTAPHA.

FROM MY ELBOW-CHAIR

MINE UNCLE JOHN.

To those whose habits of abstraction may have let them into some of the secrets of their own minds, and whose freedom from daily toil, has

left them at leisure to analyze their feelings, it will be nothing new to
say that the present is peculiarly the season of remembrance. The
flowers, the zephyrs, and the warblers of spring, returning after their
tedious absence, bring naturally to our recollection past times and
buried feelings; and the whispers of the full-foliaged grove, fall on the
ear of contemplation, like the sweet tones of far distant friends, whom
the rude jostles of the world have severed from us, and cast far beyond
our reach. It is at such times, that casting backward many a lingering
look we recal, with a kind of sweet-souled melancholy, the days of our
youth and the jocund companions who started with us the race of life,
but parted midway in the journey to pursue some winding path that
allured them with a prospect more seducing—and never returned to us
again. It is then, too, if we have been afflicted with any heavy sorrow,
if we have ever lost (and who has not!)—an old friend, or chosen companion, that his shade will hover around us—the memory of his virtues
press on the heart, and a thousand endearing recollections, forgotten
amidst the cold pleasures and midnight dissipations of winter, arise to
our remembrance.

These speculations bring to my mind MY UNCLE JOHN, the history
of whose loves and disappointments, I have promised to the world.
Though I must own myself much addicted to forgetting my promises,
yet as I have been so happily reminded of this, I believe I must pay
it at once, "and there an end." Lest my readers—good-natured souls
that they are! should, in the ardour of peeping into millstones, take my
uncle for an old acquaintance, I here inform them, that the old gentleman died a great many years ago, and it is impossible they should
ever have known him:—I pity them—for they would have known a good-
natured, benevolent man, whose example might have been of service.

The last time I saw my uncle John, was fifteen years ago, when I
paid him a visit at his old mansion. I found him reading a newspaper;—
for it was election time, and he was always a warm federalist, and had
made several converts to the true political faith in his time—particularly
one old tenant who always just before the election became a violent
anti——— in order that he might be convinced of his errors by my uncle,
who never failed to reward his conviction by some substantial benefit.

After we had settled the affairs of the nation, and I had paid my
respects to the old family chronicles in the kitchen—an indispensible
ceremony—the old gentleman exclaimed, with heart-felt glee, "Well, I
suppose you are for a trout-fishing—I have got every thing prepared;—
but first you must take a walk with me to see my improvements." I
was obliged to consent, though I knew my uncle would lead me a most
villanous dance, and in all probability treat me to a quagmire, or a
tumble into a ditch.—If my readers choose to accompany me in this

expedition, they are welcome—if not, let them stay at home like lazy fellows—and sleep—or be hanged.

Though I had been absent several years, yet there was very little alteration in the scenery, and every object retained the same features it bore when I was a schoolboy; for it was in this spot that I grew up in the fear of ghosts, and in the breaking of many of the ten commandments. The brook, or *river* as they would call it in Europe, still murmured with its wonted sweetness through the meadow, and its banks were still tufted with dwarf willows, that bent down to the surface. The same echo inhabited the valley, and the same tender air of repose, pervaded the whole scene. Even my good uncle was but little altered, except that his hair was grown a little greyer, and his forehead had lost some of its former smoothness. He had, however, lost nothing of his former activity; and laughed heartily at the difficulty I found in keeping up with him as he stumped through bushes, and briers and hedges, talking all the time about his improvements, and telling what he would do with such a spot of ground, and such a tree. At length after showing me his stone fences, his famous two year old bull, his new invented cart, which was to go before the horse, and his Eclipse colt, he was pleased to return home to dinner.

After dining and returning thanks—which with him was not a cere- mony merely, but an offering from the heart—my uncle opened his trunk, took out his fishing-tackle, and without saying a word sallied forth with some of those truly alarming steps which Daddy Neptune once took when he was in a great hurry to attend to the affair of the siege of Troy. Trout-fishing was my uncle's favourite sport; and though I always caught two fish to his one, he never would acknowledge my superiority, but puzzled himself often and often, to account for such a singular phenomenon.

Following the current of the brook for a mile or two, we retraced many of our old haunts, and told a hundred adventures which had befallen us at different times. It was like snatching the hour-glass of time, inverting it, and rolling back again the sands that had marked the lapse of years. At length the shadows began to lengthen, the south-wind gradually settled into a perfect calm, and the sun threw his rays through the trees on the hill-top, in golden lustre, and a kind of sabbath still- ness pervaded the whole valley, indicating that the hour was fast approaching which was to relieve for awhile, the farmer from his rural labour, the ox from his toil, the school urchin from his primer, and bring the loving ploughman home to the feet of his blooming dairy-maid.

Ae we were watching in silence the last rays of the sun, beaming their farewel radiance on the high hills at a distance, my uncle exclaimed, in a kind of half desponding tone, while he rested his arm over an old tree that had fallen—"I know not how it is, my dear Launce, but such an evening, and such a still quiet scene as this, always make me a little sad, and it is at such a time I am most apt to look forward with regret to the period when this farm on which "I have been young but now am old," and every object around me that is endeared by long acquaintance—when all these and I must shake hands and part. I have no fear of death, for my life has afforded but little temptation to wickedness; and when I die, I hope to leave behind me more substantial proofs of virtue than will be found in my epitaph, and more lasting memorials than churches built, or hospitals endowed, with wealth wrung from the hard hand of poverty, by an unfeeling landlord, or unprincipled knave;—but still, when I pass such a day as this and contemplate such a scene, I cannot help feeling a latent wish to linger yet a little longer in this peaceful asylum, to enjoy a little more sunshine in this world, and to have a few more fishing matches with my boy." As he ended, he raised his hand a little from the fallen tree, and dropping it languidly by his side, turned himself towards home. The sentiment, the look, the action, all seemed to be prophetic.—And so they were—for when I shook him by the hand and bade him farewel the next morning—it was for the last time!

He died a bachelor, at the age of sixty-three, though he had been all his life trying to get married, and always thought himself on the point of accomplishing his wishes. His disappointments were not owing either to the deformity of his mind or person; for in his youth he was reckoned handsome, and I myself can witness for him that he had as kind a heart as ever was fashioned by heaven;—neither were they owing to his poverty—which sometimes stands in an honest man's way;—for he was born to the inheritance of a small estate which was sufficient to establish his claim to the title of "one well to do in the world." The truth is, my uncle had a prodigious antipathy to doing things in a hurry— "A man should consider," said he to me once—"that he can always get a wife, but cannot always get rid of her. For my part," continued he, "I am a young fellow with the world before me, (he was but about forty!) and am resolved to look sharp, weigh matters well, and know what's what before I marry:—in short, Launce, *I dont intend to do the thing in a hurry depend upon it.*" On this whim-wham, he proceeded: he began with young girls and ended with widows. The girls he courted until they grew old maids, or married out of pure apprehension of incurring certain penalties hereafter; and the widows not having quite as much patience, generally, at the end of a year while the good man thought himself in the high road to success, married some *harum-*

scarum young fellow, who had not such an antipathy *to doing things in a hurry*.

My uncle would have inevitably sunk under these repeated disappointments—for he did not want sensibility—had he not hit upon a discovery which set all to rights at once. He consoled his vanity—for he was a little vain, and soothed his pride, which was his master passion—by telling his friends and very significantly, while his eye would flash triumph, *"that he might have had her."* Those who know how much of the bitterness of disappointed affection arises from wounded vanity and exasperated pride, will give my uncle credit for this discovery.

My uncle had been told by a prodigious number of married men, and had read in an innumerable quantity of books, that a man could not possibly be happy except in the marriage state; so he determined at an early age to marry, that he might not lose his only chance for happiness. He accordingly forthwith paid his addresses to the daughter of a neighbouring gentleman farmer, who was reckoned the beauty of the whole world—a phrase by which the honest country people mean nothing more than the circle of their acquaintance, or that territory of land which is within sight of the smoke of their own hamlet.

This young lady, in addition to her beauty, was highly accomplished, for she had spent five or six months at a boarding-school in town, where she learned to work pictures in satin and paint sheep, that might be mistaken for wolves, to hold up her head, set straight in her chair, and to think every species of useful acquirement beneath her attention. When she returned home, so completely had she forgotten every thing she knew before, that on seeing one of the maids milching a cow, she asked her father, with an air of most enchanting ignorance, "what that odd looking thing was doing to that queer animal?" The old man shook his head at this, but the mother was delighted at these symptoms of gentility, and so enamoured of her daughter's accomplishments, that she actually got framed a picture worked in satin by the young lady. It represented the Tomb Scene in Romeo and Juliet: Romeo was dressed in an orange-coloured cloak, fastened round his neck, with a large golden clasp, a white satin tamboured waistcoat, leather breeches, blue silk stockings, and white topt boots. The amiable Juliet shone in a flame coloured gown, most gorgeously bespangled with silver stars, a high-crowned muslin cap that reached to the top of the tomb;—on her feet she wore a pair of short-quartered high-heeled shoes, and her waist was the exact fac simile of an inverted sugarloaf. The head of the "noble county Paris" looked like a chimney-sweeper's brush that had lost its handle; and the cloak of the good Friar hung about him as gracefully as the armour of a Rhinoceros. The good lady considered this picture as a splendid proof of her daughter's accomplishments, and hung it up in the best parlour, as an honest tradesman does his certificate of admission into that enlightened body, yclept the Mechanic Society.

With this accomplished young lady then did my uncle John become deeply enamoured, and as it was his first love he determined to bestir himself in an extraordinary manner. Once at least in a fortnight, and generally on a Sunday evening, he would put on his leather breeches (for he was a great beau) mount his grey horse Pepper, and ride over to see miss Pamela, though she lived upwards of a mile off, and he was obliged to pass close by a church-yard, which at least a hundred creditable persons would swear was haunted! Miss Pamela could not be insensible to such proofs of attachment, and accordingly received him with considerable kindness; her mother always left the room when he came, and my uncle had as good as made declaration, by saying one evening very significantly "that he believed he should soon change his condition," when some how or other, he got a tremendous *flea in his ear*, began to think he was *doing things in too great a hurry*, and that it was high time to consider: so he considered near a month about it, and there is no saying how much longer he might have spun the thread of his doubts had he not been roused from this state of indecision, by the news that his mistress had married an attorney's apprentice, who she had seen the Sunday before at church, where he had excited the applauses of the whole congregation, by the invincible gravity with which he listened to a Dutch sermon. The young people in the neighbourhood laughed a good deal at my uncle on the occasion, but he only shrugged his shoulders, looked mysterious and replied, *"Tut, boys! I might have had her."**

*NOTE, BY WILLIAM WIZARD ESQ.

Our publisher, who is busily engaged in printing a celebrated work, which is perhaps more generally read in this city than any other book, (not excepting the bible)—I mean the New-York Directory—has begged so hard that we will not overwhelm him with too much of a good thing, that we have, with Langstaff's approbation, cut short the residue of uncle John's amours. In all probability it will be given in a future number, whenever Launcelot is in the humour for it—he is such an odd—but, mum—for fear of another suspension.

SALMAGUNDI NO. XII

NO. XII]   Saturday, June 27, 1807.

FROM MY ELBOW-CHAIR.

"Tandem vincitur."

TANDEM *conquers!* LINK. FID.

Some men delight in the study of plants, in the dissection of a leaf, or the contour and complexion of a tulip;—others are charmed with the beauties of the feathered race, or the varied hues of the insect tribe. A naturalist will spend hours in the fatiguing pursuit of a butterfly, and a man of the ton will waste whole years in the chase of a fine lady. I feel a respect for their avocations, for my own are somewhat similar. I love to open the great volume of human character—to me the examination of a beau is more interesting than that of a Daffodil or Narcissus, and I feel a thousand times more pleasure in catching a new view of human nature, than in kidnapping the most gorgeous butterfly—even *an Emperor of Morocco* himself.

In my present situation I have ample room for the indulgence of this taste, for perhaps there is not a house in this city more fertile in subjects for the anatomist of human character, than my cousin Cockloft's. Honest Christopher, as I have before mentioned, is one of those hearty old cavaliers who pride themselves upon keeping up the good, honest, unceremonious hospitality of old times. He is never so happy as when he has drawn about him a knot of sterling-hearted associates, and sits at the head of his table dispensing a warm, cheering welcome to all. His countenance expands at every glass and beams forth emanations of hilarity, benevolence and good fellowship, that inspire and gladden every guest around him. It is no wonder, therefore, that such excellent social qualities should attract a host of friends and guests; in fact, my cousin is almost overwhelmed with them, and they all uniformly pronounce Old Cockloft to be one of the finest old fellows in the world. His wine also always comes in for a good share of their approbation; nor do they forget to do honor to mrs. Cockloft's cookery, pronouncing it to be modelled after the most approved recipes of Heliogabulus and mrs. Glasse. The variety of company thus attracted is particularly pleasing to me; for being considered a privileged person in the family, I can sit in a corner, indulge in my favourite amusement of observation, and retreat to my elbow-chair, like a bee to his hive, whenever I have collected sufficient food for meditation.

Will Wizard is particularly efficient in adding to the stock of originals which frequent our house, for he is one of the most inveterate hunters of oddities I ever knew, and his first care, on making a new acquaintance, is to gallant him to old Cockloft's, where he never fails to receive the freedom of the house in a pinch from his gold box. Will has, without exception, the queerest, most eccentric and indescribable set of intimates that ever man possessed; how he became acquainted with them I cannot conceive, except by supposing there is a secret attraction or unintelligible sympathy that unconsciously draws together oddities of every soil.

Will's great crony for some time was TOM STRADDLE, to whom he really took a great liking. Straddle had just arrived in an importation of hardware, fresh from the city of Birmingham, or rather as the most learned english would call it, *Brummagem*, so famous for its manufactories of gimblets, pen-knives and pepper-boxes, and where they make buttons and beaux enough to inundate our whole country. He was a young man of considerable standing in the manufactory at Birmingham, sometimes had the honour to hand his master's daughter into a timwhiskey, was the oracle of the tavern he frequented on Sundays, and could beat all his associates (if you would take his word for it) in boxing, beer drinking, jumping over chairs, and imitating cats in a gutter and opera singers. Straddle was, moreover, a member of a Catch-club, and was a great hand at ringing bob-majors; he was, of course, a complete connoissieur in music, and entitled to assume that character at all performances in the art. He was likewise a member of a Spouting-club, had seen a company of strolling actors perform in a barn, and had even, like Abel Drugger, "enacted" the part of Major Sturgeon with considerable applause; he was consequently a profound critic, and fully authorised to turn up his nose at any american performances. He had twice partaken of annual dinners given to the head manufacturers of Birmingham, where he had the good fortune to get a taste of turtle and turbot, and a smack of champaign and burgundy, and he had *heard* a vast deal of the roast-beef of Old England; he was therefore epicure sufficient to d——n every dish and every glass of wine he tasted in America, though at the same time he was as voracious an animal as ever crossed the atlantic. Straddle had been splashed half a dozen times by the carriages of nobility, and had once the superlative felicity of being kicked out of doors by the footman of a noble duke—he could, therefore, talk of nobility and despise the untitled plebeians of America. In short, Straddle was one of those dapper, bustling, florid, round, self-important *"gemmen"* who bounce upon us half beau half button-maker, undertake to give us the true polish of the *bon-ton*, and endeavour to inspire us with a proper and dignified contempt of our native country.

Straddle was quite in raptures when his employers determined to send him to America as an agent. He considered himself as going among a nation of barbarians, where he would be received as a prodigy; he anticipated with a proud satisfaction the bustle and confusion his arrival would occasion, the crowd that would throng to gaze at him as he walked or rode through the streets; and had little doubt but that he should occasion as much curiosity as an indian-chief or a turk in the streets of Birmingham. He had heard of the beauty of our women, and chuckled at the thought of how completely he should eclipse their unpolished beaux, and the number of despairing lovers that would mourn the hour of his arrival. I am even informed by Will Wizard that he put good store of beads, spike-nails and looking glasses in his trunk to win the affections of the fair ones, as they paddled about in their bark canoes—the reason Will gave for this error of Straddle's respecting our ladies was, that he had read in Guthrie's Geography that the aborigines of America were all savages, and not exactly understanding the word aborigines, he applied to one of his fellow apprentices, who assured him that it was the latin word for inhabitants. Now Straddle knew that the savages were fond of beads, spike-nails and looking glasses, and therefore filled his trunk with them.

Wizard used to tell another anecdote of Straddle, which always put him in a passion—Will swore that the captain of the ship told him that when Straddle heard they were off the banks of Newfoundland, he insisted upon going on shore, there to gather some good cabbages, of which he was excessively fond; Straddle, however, denied all this, and declared it to be a mischievous *quiz* of Will Wizard, who indeed often made himself merry at his expense. However this may be, certain it is he kept his tailor and shoemaker constantly employed for a month before his departure, equipped himself with a smart crooked stick about eighteen inches long, a pair of breeches of most unheard of length, a little short pair of Hoby's white-topped boots, that seemed to stand on tip-toe to reach his breeches, and his hat had the true trans-atlantic declination towards his right ear. The fact was, nor did he make any secret of it—he was determined to *"astonish the natives a few!"*

Straddle was not a little disappointed on his arrival, to find the americans were rather more civilized than he had imagined;—he was suffered to walk to his lodgings unmolested by a crowd, and even unnoticed by a single individual—no love-letters came pouring in upon him; no rivals lay in wait to assassinate him; his very dress excited no attention, for there were many fools dressed equally ridiculously with himself. This was mortifying indeed to an aspiring youth, who had come out with the idea of *astonishing* and *captivating.* He was equally unfortunate in his pretentions to the character of critic, connoisseur and boxer; he condemned our whole dramatic corps, and every thing appertaining to the theatre; but his critical abilities were ridiculed—he found fault with old Cockloft's dinner, not even sparing his wine, and was never invited to the house afterwards;—he scoured the streets at night, and was cudgelled by a sturdy watchman;—he hoaxed an honest mechanic, and was soundly kicked: Thus disappointed in all his attempts at notoriety, Straddle hit on the expedient which was resorted to by the *Giblets*—he determined to take the town by storm. He accordingly bought horses and equipages, and forthwith made a furious dash at *style* in a *gig and tandem*.

As Straddle's finances were but limited, it may easily be supposed that his fashionable career infringed a little upon his consignments, which was indeed the case, for to use a true cockney phrase, *Brummagem suffered*. But this was a circumstance that made little impression upon Straddle, who was now a lad of spirit, and lads of spirit always despise the sordid cares of keeping another man's money. Suspecting this circumstance, I never could witness any of his exhibitions of *style*, without some whimsical association of ideas. Did he give an entertainment to a host of guzzling friends, I immediately fancied them gormandizing heartily at the expense of poor Birmingham, and swallowing a consignment of hand-saws and razors. Did I behold him dashing through Broadway in his gig, I saw him, "in my mind's eye" driving tandem on a nest of tea-boards; nor could I ever contemplate his cockney exhibitions of horsemanship, but my mischievous imagination would picture him spurring a cask of hardware, like rosy Bacchus bestriding a beer barrel, or the little gentleman who be-straddles the world in the front of Hutchin's Almanack.

Straddle was equally successful with the *Giblets*, as may well be supposed; for though pedestrian merit may strive in vain to become fashionable in *Gotham*, yet a candidate in an equipage is always recognized, and like Philip's ass, laden with gold, will gain admittance every where. Mounted in his curricle or his gig, the candidate is like a statue elevated on a high pedestal, his merits are discernable from afar, and strike the dullest optics.—Oh! Gotham, Gotham! most enlightened of cities!—how does my heart swell with delight when I behold your sapient inhabitants lavishing their attention with such wonderful discernment!

Thus Straddle became quite a man of *ton*, and was caressed, and courted, and invited to dinners and balls. Whatever was absurd or ridiculous in him before, was now declared to be the *style*. He criticised our theatre, and was listened to with reverence. He pronounced our musical entertainments barbarous; and the judgment of Apollo himself would not have been more decisive. He abused our dinners; and the god of eating, if there be any such deity, seemed to speak through his organs. He became at once a man of taste, for he put his malediction on every thing; and his arguments were conclusive, for he supported every assertion *with a bet*. He was likewise pronounced by the learned in the fashionable world, a young man of great research and deep observation; for he had sent home as natural curiosities, an ear of indian corn, a pair of moccasons, a belt of wampum, and a four leaved clover. He had taken great pains to enrich this curious collection with an Indian, and a *cataract*, but without success. In fine, the people talked of Straddle, and his equipage, and Straddle talked of his horses, until it was impossible for the most critical observer to pronounce, whether Straddle or his horses were most admired, or whether Straddle admired himself or his horses most.

Straddle was now in the zenith of his glory. He swaggered about parlours and drawing rooms with the same unceremonious confidence he used to display in the taverns at Birmingham. He accosted a lady as he would a bar maid; and this was pronounced a certain proof that he had been used to better company in Birmingham. He became the great man of all the taverns between New-York and Haerlem, and no one stood a chance of being accommodated, until Straddle and his horses were perfectly satisfied. He d——d the landlords and waiters, with the best air in the world, and accosted them with true gentlemanly familiarity. He staggered from the dinner table to the play, entered the box like a tempest, and staid long enough to be *bored* to death, and to *bore* all those who had the misfortune to be near him. From thence he dashed off to a ball, time enough to flounder through a cotillon, tear half a dozen gowns, commit a number of other depredations, and make the whole company sensible of his infinite condescension in coming amongst them. The people of Gotham thought him a prodigious fine fellow; the young bucks cultivated his acquaintance with the most persevering assidulity, and his *retainers* were sometimes complimented with a seat in his curricle, or a ride on one of his fine horses. The belles were delighted with the attentions of such a fashionable gentleman, and struck with astonishment at his learned distinctions between *wrought scissors*, and those of *cast-steel*; together with his profound dissertations on buttons and horse flesh. The rich merchants courted his acquaintance because he was an *englishman*, and their wives treated him with great deference, because he had come from beyond seas. I cannot help here observing that your salt water is a marvellous great sharpener of mens wits, and I intend to recommend it to some of my acquaintance in a particular essay.

Straddle continued his brilliant career for only a short time. His prosperous journey over the turn-pike of fashion, was checked by some

of those stumbling-blocks in the way of aspiring youth, called creditors
—or duns—a race of people who, as a celebrated writer observes, "are
hated by gods and men." Consignments slackened, whispers of distant
suspicion floated in the dark, and those pests of society, the tailors and
shoemakers, rose in rebellion against Straddle. In vain were all his
remonstrances, in vain did he prove to them that though he had given
them no money, yet he had given them more *custom*, and as many
promises as any young man in the city. They were inflexible, and the
signal of danger being given, a host of other persecutors pounced upon
his back. Straddle saw there was but one way for it; he determined
to do the thing genteelly, to go *to smash* like a hero, and dashed into
the limits in high style, being the fifteenth gentleman I have known to
drive tandem to the—*ne plus ultra*—the d——l.

Unfortunate Straddle! may thy fate be a warning to all young
gentlemen who come out from Birmingham to *astonish the natives!*—
I should never have taken the trouble to delineate his character, had he
not been a genuine cockney, and worthy to be the representative of his
numerous tribe. Perhaps my simple countrymen may hereafter be able
to distinguish between the real english gentleman, and individuals of
the cast I have heretofore spoken of, as mere mongrels, springing at
one bound from contemptible obscurity at home, to day light and
splendour in this good natured land. The true born, and true bred
english gentleman, is a character I hold in great respect; and I love
to look back to the period when our forefathers flourished in the same
generous soil, and hailed each other as brothers. But the *cockney!*—
when I contemplate him as springing too from the same source, I feel
ashamed of the relationship, and am tempted to deny my origin. In
the character of Straddle is traced the complete outline of a true cockney,
of english growth, and a descendant of that individual facetious character
mentioned by Shakespeare, "*who, in pure kindness to his horse, buttered
his hay.*"

THE STRANGER AT HOME; OR, A TOUR IN BROADWAY

BY JEREMY COCKLOFT *the younger.*

. . . . . *Peregre rediit.*

He is returned home from abroad.

DICTIONARY.

PREFACE.

Your learned traveller begins his travels at the commencement of his
journey; others begin theirs at the end; and a third class begin any
how and any where, which I think is the true way. A late facetious

writer begins what he calls, "a Picture of New-York," with a particular description of Glen's Falls, from whence with admirable dexterity he makes a digression to the celebrated Mill Rock, on Long-Island! now this is what I like; and I intend in my present tour to digress as often and as long as I please. If, therefore, I choose to make a hop, skip, and jump to China, or New-Holland, or Terra Incognita, or Communipaw, I can produce a host of examples to justify me even in books that have been praised by the english reviewers, whose *fiat* being all that is necessary to give books a currency in this country, I am determined, as soon as I finish my edition of travels in seventy-five volumes, to transmit it forthwith to them for judgment. If these trans-atlantic censors praise it, I have no fear of its success in this country, where *their* approbation gives, like the tower stamp, a fictitious value, and makes tinsel and wampum pass current for classick gold.

CHAPTER I.

Battery—flag-staff kept by Louis Keaffee—Keaffee maintains two spy-glasses by subscriptions—merchants pay two shillings a-year to look through them at the signal poles on Staten-Island—a very pleasant prospect; but not so pleasant as that from the hill of Howth—quere, ever been there?—Young *seniors* go down to the flag-staff to buy peanuts and beer, after the fatigue of their morning studies, and sometimes to play at ball, or some other innocent amusement—digression to the Olympic, and Isthmian games, with a description of the Isthmus of Corinth, and that of Darien: to conclude with a dissertation on the indian custom of offering a whiff of tobacco smoke to their great spirit Areskou.—Return to the battery—delightful place to indulge in the luxury of sentiment.—How various are the mutations of this world! but a few days, a few hours—at least not above two hundred years ago, and this spot was inhabited by a race of aborigines, who dwelt in bark huts, lived upon oysters, and indian corn, danced buffalo dances, and were lords "of the fowl and the brute"—but the spirit of time, and the spirit of brandy, have swept them from their antient inheritance: and as the white wave of the ocean by its ever toiling assiduity, gains on the brown land, so the white man, by slow and sure degrees has gained on the brown savage, and dispossessed him of the land of his forefathers.—Conjectures on the first peopling of America—different opinions on that subject, to the amount of near one hundred—opinion of Augustine Torniel—that they are the descendants of Shem and Japheth, who came by the way of Japan to America—Juffridius Petri, says they came from Friezeland—mem. cold journey.—Mons. Charron says they are descended from the gauls—bitter enough.—A Milius from the Celtæ—Kircher

from the egyptians—L'Compte from the phenicians—Lescarbot from the
canaanites, alias the anthropophagi—Brerewood from the tartars—Grotius
from the norwegians—and Linkum Fidelius, has written two folio volumes to prove that America was first of all peopled either by the antipodeans, or the cornish miners, who he maintains, might easily have
made a subterraneous passage to this country, particularly the antipodeans, who, he asserts, can get along under ground, as fast as moles—
quere, which of these is in the right, or are they all wrong?—For my
part, I dont see why America had not as good a right to be peopled at
first, as any little contemptible country of Europe, or Asia; and I am
determined to write a book at my first leisure, to prove that Noah
was born here—and that so far is America from being indebted to any
other country for inhabitants, that they were every one of them peopled
by colonies from her!—mem. battery a very pleasant place to walk
on a sunday evening—not quite genteel though—every body walks
there, and a pleasure, however genuine, is spoiled by general participation—the fashionable ladies of New-York, turn up their noses if you ask
them to walk on the battery on sunday—quere, have they scruples of
conscience, or scruples of delicacy?—neither—they have only scruples of
gentility, which are quite different things.

CHAPTER II.

Custom-house—origin of duties on merchandize—this place much
frequented by merchants—and why?—different classes of merchants—
importers—a kind of nobility—Wholesale merchants—have the privilege
of going to the city assembly!—Retail traders cannot go to the assembly—
Some curious speculations on the vast distinction betwixt selling tape by
the piece or by the yard.—Wholesale merchants look down upon
the retailers, who in return look down upon the green grocers, who look
down upon the market women, who don't care a straw about any of
them.—Origin of the distinction of ranks—Dr. Johnson once horribly
puzzled to settle the point of precedence between a louse and a flea . . .
good hint enough to humble purse-proud arrogance. . . . Custom house
partly used as a lodging house for the pictures belonging to the academy
of arts . . . . couldn't afford the statues house room, most of them in the
cellar of the City hall . . . poor place for the gods and goddesses, . . .
after Olympus . . . Pensive reflections on the ups and downs of life . . .
Apollo, and the rest of the sett, used to cut a great figure in days of
yore.—Mem. . . . every dog has his day . . . sorry for Venus though, poor
wench, to be cooped up in a cellar with not a single grace to wait on
her! . . . Eulogy on the gentlemen of the academy of arts, for the
great spirit with which they began the undertaking, and the perseverance

with which they have pursued it... It is a pity however, they began at
the wrong end... maxim... If you want a bird and a cage, always buy
the cage first... hem!... a word to the wise!

CHAPTER III.

Bowling green... fine place for pasturing cows... a perquisite of
the late corporation... formerly ornamented with a statue of George the
3d.... people pulled it down in the war to make bullets... great pity, as
it might have been given to the academy... it would have become a
cellar as well as any other.... The pedestal still remains, because, there
was no use in pulling *that* down, as it would cost the corporation money,
and not sell for any thing... mem... a penny saved is a penny got.
... If the pedestal must remain, I would recommend that a statue of
somebody, or something be placed on it, for truly it looks quite melancholy and forlorn.... Broadway... great difference in the gentility of
streets... a man who resides in Pearl-street, or Chatham-row, derives no
kind of dignity from his domicil, but place him in a certain part of
Broadway... any where between the battery and Wall-street, and he
straightway becomes entitled to figure in the beau-monde, and strut as
a person of prodigious consequence!... Quere, whether there is a degree
of purity in the air of that quarter which changes the gross particles of
vulgarity, into gems of refinement and polish?... A question to be asked
but not to be answered.... New brick church!... what a pity it is the
corporation of Trinity church are so poor!... if they could not afford
to build a better place of worship, why did they not go about with a
subscription?... even I would have given them a few shillings rather
than our city should have been disgraced by such a pitiful specimen
of economy.... Wall-street.... City-hall, famous place for catch-poles,
deputy sheriffs, and young lawyers, which last attended the courts,
not because they have business there, but because they have no business any where else. My blood always curdles when I see a catchpole,
they being a species of vermin, who feed and fatten on the common
wretchedness of mankind, who trade in misery, and in becoming the
executioners of the law, by their oppression and villainy, almost counter-
balance all the benefits which are derived from its salutary regulations.
... Story of Quevedo, about a catchpole possessed by a devil, who in
being interrogated, declared that he did not come there voluntarily, but
by compulsion, and that a decent devil would never of his own free
will enter into the body of a catchpole... instead therefore of doing
him the injustice to say that here was a catchpole be-devilled, they
should say it was a devil be-catchpoled... that being in reality the truth.
... Wonder what has become of the old crier of the court, who used to

make more noise in preserving silence than the audience did in breaking
it.... If a man happened to drop his cane, the old hero would sing out
silence! in a voice that emulated the "wide-mouthed thunder"....
On inquiring, found he had retired from business to enjoy *otium cum
dignitate*, as many a great man had done before.... Strange that wise
men, as they are thought, should toil through a whole existence merely
to enjoy a few moments of leisure at last! ... why don't they begin to be
easy at first, and not purchase a moments pleasure with an age of pain?
...mem...posed some of the jockeys...eh!

CHAP. IV.

Barber's Pole—three different orders of *shavers* in New-York—those
who shave *pigs*, N. B.—Freshmen and Sophomores—those who cut
beards, and those who *shave notes of hand*—the last are the most respectable, because in the course of a year, they make more money and
that *honestly*, than the whole corps of other *shavers*, can do in half a
century—besides, it would puzzle a common barber to ruin any man,
except by cutting his throat; whereas, your higher order of *shavers*, your
true blood suckers of the community, seated snugly behind the curtain in
watch for prey, live on the vitals of the unfortunate, and grow rich on the
ruin of thousands.—Yet this last class of *barbers* are held in high respect
in the world—they never offend against the decencies of life, go often
to church, look down on honest poverty walking on foot, and call
themselves gentlemen—yea, men of honour!—Lottery offices—another
set of Capital Shavers! licensed gambling houses good things enough
though, as they enable a few *honest industrious gentlemen* to humbug
the people—according to law—besides, if the people will be such
fools, whose fault is it but their own if they get *bit?*—Messrs. Paff...
beg pardon for putting them in such bad company, because they are a
couple of fine fellows—mem.—to recommend Michael's antique snuff box
to all amateurs *in the art*.—Eagle singing Yankey-doodle—N. B.—Buffon,
Pennant, and the rest of the naturalists all *naturals*, not to know the
eagle was a singing bird—Linkum Fidelius knew better, and gives a
long description of a bald eagle that serenaded him once in Canada—
digression—particular account of the canadian indians—story about
Areskou learning to make fishing nets of a spider—don't believe it
though, because, according to Linkum, and many other learned authorities, Areskou is the same as *Mars*, being derived from his greek name
of *Ares*, and if so he knew well enough what *a net* was without consult-
a spider—story of Arachne being changed into a spider as a reward for
having hanged herself—derivation of the word spinster from spider—
Colophon, now Altobosco, the birth place of Arachne, remarkable for

a famous breed of spiders to this day—mem.—nothing like a little scholarship—make the *ignoramus'* viz. the majority of my readers, stare like wild pigeons—return to New-York by a short cut—meet a dashing belle, in a thick white veil—tried to get a peep at her face... saw she squinted a little... thought so at first... never saw a face covered with a veil that was worth looking at... saw some ladies holding a conversation across the street about going to church next Sunday ... talked so loud they frightened a cartman's horse, who ran away, and overset a basket of gingerbread with a little boy under it... mem. I dont much see the use of speaking trumpets now-a-days.

CHAP. V.

Bought a pair of gloves—dry-good stores the genuine schools of politeness—true parisian manners there—got a pair of gloves and a pistareen's worth of bows for a dollar—dog cheap!—Courtlandt-street corner—famous place to see the belles go by—quere, ever been shopping with a lady?—some account of it—ladies go into all the shops in the city to buy a pair of gloves—good way of spending time, if they have nothing else to do.—Oswego-Market—looks very much like a triumphal arch—some account of the manner of erecting them in ancient times—digression to the *arch*-duke Charles, and some account of the ancient germans.—N. B. quote Tacitus on this subject.—Particular description of market-baskets, butchers' blocks and wheelbarrows—mem. queer things run upon one wheel!—Saw a cartman driving full-tilt through Broadway—run over a child—good enough for it—what business had it to be in the way?—Hint concerning the laws against pigs, goats, dogs and cartmen—grand apostrophe to the sublime science of jurisprudence—comparison between legislators and tinkers—quere, whether it requires greater ability to mend a law than to mend a kettle?—inquiry into the utility of making laws that are broken a hundred times in a day with impunity—my lord Coke's opinion on the subject—my lord a very great man—so was lord Bacon—good story about a criminal named Hog claiming relationship with him.—Hogg's porter-house—great haunt of Will Wizard—Will put down there one night by a sea captain, in an argument concerning the aera of the Chinese empire, Whang-po;—Hogg's a capital place for hearing the same stories, the same jokes and the same songs every night in the year—mem. except Sunday nights—fine school for young politicians too —some of the longest and thickest heads in the city come there to settle the nation.—Scheme of *Ichabod Fungus* to restore the balance of Europe—digression—some account of the balance of Europe—comparison between it, and a pair of scales, with the emperor Alexander in one and the emperor Napoleon in the other—fine fellows—both of a weight, can't

tell which will kick the beam . . . mem. dont care much either . . . nothing
to me . . . *Ichabod* very unhappy about it . . . thinks Napoleon has an eye
on this country . . . capital place to pasture his horses, and provide for
the rest of his family . . . . Dey-street . . . ancient dutch name of it,
signifying murders'-valley—formerly the site of a great peach orchard
. . . my grandmother's history of the famous *Peach war* . . . arose from an
indian stealing peaches out of this orchard . . . good cause as need be
for a war . . . just as good as the balance of power . . . Anecdote of a
war between two italian states about a bucket . . . introduce some capital
new *truisms* about the folly of mankind, the ambition of kings, potentates
and princes, particularly Alexander, Caesar, Charles the XIIth, Napoleon,
little king Pepin and the great Charlemagne . . . . Conclude with an ex-
hortation to the present race of sovereigns to keep the king's peace, and
abstain from all those deadly quarrels which produce battle, murder
and sudden death . . . Mem. ran my nose against lamp-post . . . conclude
in great dudgeon.

FROM MY ELBOW-CHAIR.

Our cousin Pindar after having been confined for some time past with
a fit of the gout, which is a kind of keep-sake in our family, has again
set his mill going, as my readers will perceive. On reading his piece
I could not help smiling at the high compliments which, contrary to
his usual style, he has lavished on the dear sex. The old gentleman
unfortunately observing my merriment, stumped out of the room with
great vociferation of crutch, and has not exchanged three words with
me since. I expect every hour to hear that he has packed up his move-
ables, and, as usual in all cases of disgust, retreated to his old country
house.

Pindar, like most of the old Cockloft heroes, is wonderfully susceptible
to the genial influence of warm weather. In winter he is one of the most
crusty old bachelors under heaven, and is *wickedly* addicted to sarcastic
reflections of every kind, particularly on the little enchanting foibles,
and whim-whams of women. But when the spring comes on, and the
mild influence of the sun releases nature from her icy fetters, the ice of
his bosom dissolves into a gentle current, which reflects the bewitching
qualities of the fair, as, in some mild clear evening when nature reposes
in silence, the stream bears in its pure bosom, all the starry magnificence
of heaven. It is under the controul of this influence he has written his
piece, and I beg the ladies in the plentitude of their harmless conceit
not to flatter themselves, that because the good Pindar has suffered them
to escape his censures, he had nothing more to censure. It is but sunshine and zephyrs, which have wrought this wonderful change, and I

am much mistaken, if the first North-easter don't convert all his good
nature into most exquisite spleen.

FROM THE MILL OF
PINDAR COCKLOFT, ESQ.

How often I cast my reflections behind,
And call up the days of past youth to my mind!
When folly assails in habiliaments new,
When fashion obtrudes some fresh whim-wham to view
When the foplings of fashion bedazzle my sight,
Bewilder my feelings—my senses benight;
I retreat in disgust from the world of the day,
To commune with the world that has mouldered away
To converse with the shades of those friends of my love
Long gathered in peace to the angels above.
In my rambles thro' life should I meet with annoy
From the bold beardless stripling—the turbid pert boy
One reared in the mode lately reckoned *genteel,*
Which neglecting the head, aims to perfect the heel,
Which completes the sweet fopling while yet in his teens,
And fits him for fashion's light changeable scenes;
Proclaims him *a man* to the near and the far,
Can he dance a cotillion or smoke a cygarr.
And tho' brainless and vapid as vapid can be,
To routs and to parties pronounces him free;—
Oh, I think on the beaux that existed of yore,
On those rules of the ton that exist now no more!
I recal with delight how each yonker at first
In the cradle of science and virtue was nursed;
—How the graces of person and graces of mind,
The polish of learning and fashion combined,
Till soft'ned in manners and strength'ned in head,
By the classical lore of the living and dead,
Matured in person till manly in size,
He then was presented a beau to our eyes!
My nieces of late have made frequent complaint
That they suffer vexation and painful constraint,
By having their circles too often distrest
By some three or four goslings just fledg'd in the nest,
Who propp'd by the credit their fathers sustain,
Alike tender in years, and in person and brain,
But plenteously stock'd with that substitute *brass,*

For true wits and critics would anxiously pass.
They complain of that empty sarcastical slang,
So common to all the coxcombical gang,
Who the fair with their shallow experience vex,
By thrumming forever their *weakness of sex;*
And who boast to themselves when they talk with proud air
Of MAN's mental ascendancy over the fair.
   Twas thus the young owlet, produced in the nest,
Where the eagle of Jove her young eaglets had prest
Pretended to boast of his royal descent,
And vaunted that force which to eagles is lent;
Tho' fated to shun with his dim visual ray,
The cheering delights, and the brilliance of day;
To forsake the fair regions of aether and light,
For dull moping caverns of darkness and night:
Still talked of that eagle like strength of the eye,
Which approaches unwinking the pride of the sky;
Of that wing which unwearied can hover and play
In the noon-tide effulgence and torrent of day.
   Dear girls, the sad evils of which ye complain,
Your sex *must* endure from the feeble and vain.
Tis the common place jest of the nursery scape-goat,
Tis the common place ballad that croaks from his throat.
He knows not that nature—that polish decrees,
That women should always endeavour to please:
That the law of their system has early imprest
The importance of fitting themselves to each guest;
And, of course, that full oft, when ye trifle and play,
Tis to gratify triflers who strut in your way.
The child might as well of its mother complain,
As wanting true wisdom and soundness of brain.
Because that, at times, while it hangs on her breast,
She with "lulla-by-baby" beguiles it to rest.
Tis its weakness of mind that induces the strain,
For wisdom to *infants* is prattled in vain.
   Tis true at odd times, when in frolicksome fit,
In the midst of his gambols, the mischievous wit
May start some light foible that clings to the fair,
Like cobwebs that fasten to objects most rare—
In the play of his fancy will sportively say
Some delicate censure that pops in his way.
He may smile at your fashions, and frankly express
His dislike of a dance, or a flaming red dress;

Yet he blames not your want of man's physical force,
Nor complains though ye cannot in latin discourse.
He delights in the language of nature ye speak
Tho' not so refined as true classical greek.
He remembers that providence never designed
Our females like suns to bewilder and blind;
But like the mild star of pale evening serene,
Whose radiance illumines, yet softens the scene,
To light us with cheering and welcoming ray,
Along the rude path when the sun is away.
Nor e'er would he wish those fair beings to find
In places for *Di majorum gentium* designed;
But as *Dii penates* performing their part—
Receiving and claiming the vows of the heart—
Recalling affections long given to roam,
To centre at last in the bosom of HOME.
  I own in my scribblings I lately have named
Some faults of our fair which I gently have blamed
But be it forever by all understood
My censures were only pronounced for their good.
I delight in the sex, tis the pride of my mind
To consider them gentle, endearing, refin'd,
As our solace below in the journey of life
To smooth its rough passes—to soften its strife:
As objects intended our joys to supply
And to lead us in love to the temples on high.
How oft have I felt when two lucid blue eyes
As calm and as bright as the gems of the skies,
Have beam'd their soft radiance into my soul,
Impress'd with an awe like an angel's controul!
  Yes, fair ones, by this is forever defin'd,
The fop from the man of refinement and mind;
The latter believes ye in bounty were given
As a bond upon earth of our union with heaven:
And, if ye are weak and are frail in his view,
Tis to call forth fresh warmth, and his fondness renew.
Tis his joy to support these defects of your frame,
And his love at your weakness redoubles its flame,
He rejoices the gem is so rich and so fair,
And is proud that it claims his protection and care.

SALMAGUNDI NO. XIII

NO. XIII]   *Friday, August* 14, 1807.

FROM MY ELBOW-CHAIR.

I was not a little perplexed, a short time since, by the eccentric conduct of my knowing coadjutor, Will Wizard. For two or three days, he
was completely in a quandary. He would come into old Cockloft's
parlour ten times a day, swinging his ponderous legs along with his
usual vast strides, clap his hands into his sides, contemplate the little
shepherdesses on the mantle-piece for a few minutes, whistling all the
while, and then sally out full sweep, without uttering a word. To be
sure a *pish,* or a *pshaw* occasionally escaped him; and he was observed
once to pull out his enormous tobacco box, drum for a moment upon its
lid with his knuckles, and then return it into his pocket without taking
a quid—'twas evident Will was full of some mighty idea—not that his
restlessness was any way uncommon; for I have often seen Will throw
himself almost into a fever of heat and fatigue—doing nothing. But his
inflexible taciturnity set the whole family, as usual, a wondering, as Will
seldom enters the house without giving one of his "one thousand and
one" stories. For my part, I began to think that the late *fracas* at Canton
had alarmed Will for the safety of his friends Kinglun, Chinqua and
Consequa; or, that something had gone wrong in the alterations of the
theatre—or that some new outrage at Norfolk had put him in a worry—
in short, I did not know what to think; for Will is such an universal
busy-body, and meddles so much in every thing going forward, that
you might as well attempt to conjecture what is going on in the north
star, as in his precious pericranium. Even mrs. Cockloft who (like a
worthy woman as she is) seldom troubles herself about any thing in
this world—saving the affairs of her household, and the correct deportment of her female friends—was struck with the mystery of Will's
behaviour. She happened, when he came in and went out the tenth
time, to be busy darning the bottom of one of the old red damask chairs,
and notwithstanding this is to her an affair of vast importance, yet,
she could not help turning round and exclaiming "I *wonder* what can be
the matter with mr. Wizard?"—"Nothing" replied old Christopher,
"only we shall have an eruption soon." The old lady did not understand
a word of this—neither did she care—she had expressed her wonder;
and that, with her, is always sufficient.

I am so well acquainted with Will's peculiarities, that I can tell,
even by his whistle, when he is about an essay for our paper, as cer-

tainly as a weather wiseacre knows that it is going to rain, when he sees a pig run squeaking about with his nose in the wind. I therefore, laid my account with receiving a communication from him before long, and sure enough, the evening before last I distinguished his free-mason knock at my door. I have seen many wise men in my time, philosophers, mathematicians, astronomers, politicians, editors, and almanack makers, but never did I see a man look half as wise as did my friend Wizard on entering the room. Had Lavater beheld him at that moment, he would have set him down to a certainty, as a fellow who had just discovered the longitude, or the philosopher's stone.

Without saying a word, he handed me a roll of paper, after which he lighted his cygarr, sat down, crossed his legs, folded his arms, and elevating his nose to an angle of about forty-five degrees, began to smoke like a steam-engine—Will delights in the picturesque. On opening his budget, and perceiving the motto, it struck me that Will had brought me one of his confounded chinese manuscripts, and I was forthwith going to dismiss it with indignation, but accidentally seeing the name of our oracle, the sage Linkum, (of whose inestimable folioes we pride ourselves upon being the sole possessors,) I began to think the better of it and looked round at Will to express my approbation. I shall never forget the figure he cut at that moment! He had watched my countenance, on opening his manuscript, with the argus eyes of an author, and perceiving some tokens of disapprobation, began, according to custom, to puff away at his cygarr with such vigour, that in a few minutes he had entirely involved himself in smoke, except his nose and one foot which were just visible, the latter wagging with great velocity. I believe I have hinted before—at least I ought to have done so—that Will's nose is a very goodly nose; to which it may be as well to add, that in his voyages under the tropics, it has acquired a copper complexion, which renders it very brilliant and luminous. You may imagine what a sumptuous appearance it made, projecting boldly, like the celebrated *promontorium nasidium* at Samos, with a light-house upon it, and surrounded on all sides with smoke and vapour. Had my gravity been like the chinese philosopher's "within one degree of absolute frigidity," here would have been a trial for it.—I could not stand it, but burst into such a laugh, as I do not indulge in above once in a hundred years—this was too much for Will—he emerged from his cloud, threw his cygarr into the fire-place, and strode out of the room pulling up his breeches, muttering something which, I verily believe, was nothing more or less than a horrible long chinese malediction.

He however left his manuscript behind him, which I now give to the world. Whether he is serious on the occasion, or only bantering, no one I believe can tell; for whether in speaking or writing, there is such an invincible gravity in his demeanour and style that even I, who have studied him as closely as an antiquarian studies an old manuscript or inscription, am frequently at a loss to know what the rogue would be at. I have seen him indulge in his favourite amusement of *quizzing* for hours together, without any one having the least suspicion of the matter, until he would suddenly twist his phiz into an expression that baffles all description, thrust his tongue in his cheek and *blow up* in a laugh almost as loud as a shout of the romans on a certain occasion, which honest Plutarch avers frightened several crows to such a degree that they fell down stone dead into the Campus Martius. Jeremy Cockloft the younger, who, like a true modern philosopher, delights in experiments that are of no kind of use, took the trouble to measure one of Will's risible explosions, and declared to me that, according to accurate measurement, it contained thirty feet square of solid laughter—what will the professors say to this?

PLANS FOR DEFENDING OUR HARBOUR.
BY WILLIAM WIZARD, ESQ.

Long-fong te-ko buzz tor-pe-do,
Fudge ———   CONFUCIUS.
We'll blow the villains all sky high;
But do it with econo——my.   LINK. FID.

Surely never was a town more subject to mid-summer fancies and dog-day whim-whams, than this most excellent of cities:—Our notions, like our diseases, seem all epidemick; and no sooner does a new disorder or a new freak seize one individual but it is sure to run through all the community. This is particularly the case when the summer is at the hottest, and every body's head is in a vertigo, and his brain in a ferment—'tis absolutely necessary then the poor souls should have some bubble to amuse themselves with, or they would certainly run mad. Last year the *poplar worm* made its appearance most fortunately for our citizens, and every body was so much in horror of being poisoned and devoured, and so busied in making humane experiments on cats and dogs, that we got through the summer quite comfortably—the cats had the worst of it—every mouser of them was shaved, and there was not a whisker to be seen in the whole sisterhood. This summer every body has had full employment in planning fortifications for our harbour. Not a cobler or tailor in the city but has left his awl and his thimble, become an engineer outright, and aspired so magnanimously to the building of forts and destruction of navies! Heavens! as my friend Mustapha would say, on what great scale is every thing in this country!

Among the various plans that have been offered, the most conspicuous is one devised and exhibited, as I am informed, by that notable confederacy, THE NORTH RIVER SOCIETY.

Anxious to redeem their reputation from the foul suspicions that have for a long time overclouded it, these aquatic incendiaries have come forward at the present alarming juncture, and announced a most potent discovery, which is to guarantee our port from the visits of any foreign marauders. The society have, it seems, invented a cunning machine, shrewdly y'clep'd a *Torpedo*, by which the stoutest line of battle ship, even a *santissima trinidada* may be caught napping, and *decomposed* in a twinkling—a kind of sub-marine powder magazine to *swim* under water, like an aquatic mole, or water rat, and destroy the enemy in the moments of unsuspicious security.

This straw tickled the noses of all our dignitaries wonderfully—for, to do our government justice, it has no objection to injuring and exterminating its enemies in any manner—provided the thing can be done *economically.*

It was determined the experiment should be tried, and an old brig was purchased (for not more than twice its value,) and delivered over into the hands of its tormenters, the North River Society, to be tortured, and battered, and annihilated, *secundum artem*. A day was appointed for the occasion, when all the good citizens of the wonder loving city of Gotham were invited to the blowing up; like the fat inn-keeper in Rabelais, who requested all his customers to come on a certain day and see him burst.

As I have almost as great a veneration as the good mr. Walter Shandy, for all kinds of experiments that are ingeniously ridiculous, I made very particular mention of the one in question at the table of my friend Christopher Cockloft, but it put the honest old gentleman in a violent passion. He condemned it in toto, as an attempt to introduce a dastardly, and exterminating mode of warfare. "Already have we proceeded far enough" said he, "in the science of destruction; war is already invested with sufficient horrors and calamities—let us not increase the catalogue—let us not by these deadly artifices provoke a system of insidious and indiscriminate hostility, that shall terminate in laying our cities desolate, and exposing our women, our children, and our infirm, to the sword of pitiless recrimination." Honest old cavalier!— it was evident he did not reason as a true politcian—but he felt as a christian and philanthropist, and that was, perhaps, just as well.

It may be readily supposed, that our citizens did not refuse the invitation of the society to the *blow up*—it was the first *naval* action ever exhibited in our port; and the good people all crowded to see the british navy blown up in effigy. The young ladies were delighted with the novelty of the show, and declared that if war could be conducted in this manner, it would become a fashionable amusement, and the destruction of a fleet be as pleasant as a ball or a tea party. The old folk were equally pleased with the spectacle—because it cost them nothing. Dear souls, how hard was it they should be disappointed! the brig most obstinately refused to be *decomposed*—the dinners grew cold, and the puddings were overboiled, throughout the renowned city of Gotham, and its sapient inhabitants, like the honest strasburghers, (from whom most of them are doubtless descended) who went out to see the courteous stranger and his nose, all returned home, after having threatened to pull down the flag-staff, by way of taking satisfaction for their disappointment.—By the way, there is not an animal in the world more discriminating in its vengeance than a free born *mob*.

In the evening I repaired to friend Hogg's, to smoke a sociable cygarr, but had scarcely entered the room when I was taken prisoner by my friend, mr. Ichabod Fungus, who I soon saw was at his usual trade of prying into mill-stones. The old gentleman informed me that the brig had actually blown up, after a world of manoeuvreing, and had nearly blown up the society with it—he seemed to entertain strong doubts as to the objects of the society in the invention of these infernal machines—hinted a suspicion of their wishing to set the river on fire, and that he should not be surprized on waking one of these mornings, to find the Hudson in a blaze. "Not that I disapprove of the plan," said he, "provided it has the end in view which they profess—no, no, an excellent plan of defence—no need of batteries, forts, frigates, and gun-boats:—observe, sir, all that's necessary is that the ships must come to anchor in a convenient place—watch must be asleep, or so complacent as not to disturb any boats paddling about them—fair wind and tide—no moonlight—machines well-directed—mustn't *flash in the pan*—bang's the word, and the vessel's blown up in a moment!" "Good," said I, "you remind me of a lubberly chinese who was flogged by an honest captain of my acquaintance, and who on being advised to retaliate, exclaimed—"Hi yah! spose two men hold fast him captain, den very mush me bamboo he!"

The old gentleman grew a little crusty, and insisted that I did not understand him—all that was requisite to render the effect certain, was that the enemy should enter into the project, or in other words, be *agreeable to the measure*, so that if the machine did not come to the ship, the ship should go to the machine, by which means he thought the success of the machine would be inevitable—provided it struck fire. "But do not you think," said I, doubtingly, "that it would be rather difficult to persuade the enemy into such an agreement? some people have an invincible antipathy to being blown up"—"not at all, not at all," replied he, triumphantly—"got an excellent notion for that—do with them as we have done with the brig; *buy* all the vessels we mean to destroy, and blow 'em up as best suits our convenience. I have thought deeply on that subject and have calculated to a certainty, that if our funds hold out, we may in this way distroy the whole british navy—by contract."

By this time all the quidnuncs of the room had gathered around us, each pregnant with some mighty scheme for the salvation of his country. One pathetically lamented that we had no such men among us as the famous Toujoursdort and Grossitout, who, when the celebrated captain Tranchemont, made war against the city of Kalacahabalaba, utterly discomfited the great king Big-staff, and blew up his whole army by sneezing. Another imparted a sage idea which seems to have occupied more heads than one—that is, that the best way of fortifying the harbour was to ruin it at once; choak the channel with rocks and blocks; strew it with *chevaux-de-frises* and torpedoes; and make it like a nursery-garden, full of men-traps and spring-guns. No vessel would then have the temerity to enter our harbour—we should not even dare to navigate it ourselves. Or if no cheaper way could be devised, let Governor's-Island be raised by levers and pulleys—floated with empty casks, &c. towed down to the Narrows, and dropped plump in the very mouth of the harbour!—"But," said I, "would not the prosecution of these whim-whams be rather expensive and dilatory?"—"Pshaw!" cried the other—"what's a million of money to an experiment—the true spirit of our economy requires that we should *spare no expense* in discovering the *cheapest* mode of defending ourselves; and then if all these modes should fail, why you know the worst we have to do is to return to the old-fashioned hum-drum mode of forts and batteries." "By which time," cried I, "the arrival of the enemy may have rendered their erection superfluous."

A shrewd old gentleman, who stood listening by with a mischievously equivocal look, observed that the most effectual mode of repulsing a fleet from our ports would be to administer them a proclamation from time to time, *till it operated.*

Unwilling to leave the company without demonstrating my patriotism and ingenuity, I communicated a plan of defence, which in truth was suggested long since by that infallible oracle MUSTAPHA, who had as clear a head for cobweb weaving, as ever dignified the shoulders of a projector. He thought the most effectual mode would be to assemble all the slang-whangers, great and small, from all parts of the state, and marshall them at the battery, where they should be exposed, point blank, to the enemy, and form a tremendous body of scolding infantry, similar to the *poissards* or doughty champions of Billingsgate. They should be exhorted to fire away without pity or remorse, in sheets, half-sheets, columns, hand-bills or squibs—great canon, little canon, pica, german-text, stereotype—and to run their enemies through and through with sharp pointed italics. They should have orders to show no quarter— to blaze away in their loudest epithets—*"miscreants!" "murderers!" "bar- barians!" "pirates!" "robbers!"* "BLACKGUARDS!" and to do away all fear of consequences they should be guaranteed from all dangers of pillory, kicking, cuffing, nose-pulling, whipping-post, or prosecution for libels. If, continued Mustapha, you wish men to fight well and valiantly, they must be allowed those weapons they have been used to handle. Your countrymen are notoriously adroit in the management of the tongue and the pen, and conduct all their battles by speeches or newspapers. Adopt, therefore, the plan I have pointed out, and rely upon it, that let any fleet, however large, be but once assailed by this battery of slang-whangers, and if they have not entirely lost the sense of hearing, or a regard for their own characters and feelings, they will, at the very first fire, slip their cables and retreat with as much precipitation as if they had unwarily entered into the atmosphere of the *Bohan upas*. In this manner may your wars be conducted with proper economy; and it will cost no more to drive off a fleet than to write *up* a party or write down a bashaw of three tails.

The sly old gentleman, I have before mentioned, was highly delighted with this plan, and proposed, as an improvement, that mortars should be placed on the battery, which, instead of throwing shells and such trifles, might be charged with newspapers, Tammany addresses, &c. by way of red-hot shot, which would undoubtedly be very potent in blowing up any powder magazine they might chance to come in contact with. He concluded by informing the company, that in the course of a few evenings he would have the honour to present them with a scheme for loading certain vessels with newspapers, resolutions of numerous and respectable meetings, and other combustibles, which vessels were to be blown directly in the midst of the enemy by the bellows of the slang-whangers, and he was much mistaken if they would not be more fatal than fire-ships, bomb-ketches, gun-boats, or even torpedoes.

These are but two or three specimens of the nature and efficacy of the innumerable plans with which this city abounds. Every body seems charged to the muzzle with gun-powder—every eye flashes fire-works and torpedoes, and every corner is occupied by knots of inflammatory projectors, not one of whom but has some preposterous mode of destruc- tion which he has proved to be infallible by a previous experiment in a *tub of water!*

Even Jeremy Cockloft has caught the infection, to the great annoyance of the inhabitants of Cockloft-hall, whither he retired to make his ex- periments undisturbed. At one time all the mirrors in the house were unhung—their collected rays thrown into the hot-house, to try Archimedes' plan of burning-glasses; and the honest old gardener was almost knocked down by what he mistook for a stroke of the sun, but which turned out to be nothing more than a sudden attack of one of these tremendous *jack-o'lanterns*. It became dangerous to walk through the court-yard for fear of an explosion: and the whole family was thrown into absolute distress and consternation, by a letter from the old house-keeper to mrs. Cockloft, informing her of his having blown up a favorite chinese gander, which I had brought from Canton, as he was majestically sailing in the duck-pond.

"In the multitude of counsellors there is safety"—if so, the defenceless city of Gotham has nothing to apprehend;—but much do I fear that so many excellent and infallible projects will be presented, that we shall be at a loss which to adopt, and the peaceable inhabitants fare like a famous projector of my acquaintance, whose house was unfortunately plundered while he was contriving a patent lock to secure the door.

FROM MY ELBOW-CHAIR.

A RETROSPECT,
OR, "WHAT YOU WILL."

Lolling in my Elbow-Chair this fine summer noon, I feel myself insensibly yielding to that genial feeling of indolence the season is so well fitted to inspire. Every one, who is blessed with a little of the delicious languor of disposition that delights in repose, must often have sported among the faëry scenes, the golden visions, the voluptuous reveries, that swim before the imagination at such moments—and which so much resemble those blissful sensations a mussulman enjoys after his favourite indulgence of opium, which Will Wizard declares can be compared to nothing but "swimming in an ocean of peacocks' feathers." In such a mood, every body must be sensible it would be idle and unprofitable for a man to send his wits a gadding on a voyage of discovery into futurity; or even to trouble himself with a laborious investigation of what is actually passing under his eye. We are, at such times, more disposed to resort to the pleasures of memory, than to those of the imagination; and like the way-faring traveller, reclining for a moment on his staff, had rather contemplate the ground we have travelled, than the region which is yet before us.

I could here amuse myself and stultify my readers with a most elaborate and ingenious parallel between authors and travellers; but in this balmy season which makes men stupid and dogs mad, and when doubtless many of our most strenuous admirers have great difficulty in keeping awake through the day, it would be cruel to saddle them with the formidable difficulty of putting two ideas together and drawing a conclusion, or in the learned phrase, forging *syllogisms in Baroco*—a terrible undertaking for the Dog Days! To say the truth, my observations were only intended to prove that this, of all others, is the most auspicious moment, and my present, the most favourable mood for indulging in a retrospect. Whether, like certain great personages of the day, in attempting to prove one thing, I have exposed another; or whether like certain other great personages, in attempting to prove a great deal, I have proved nothing at all, I leave to my readers to decide, provided they have the power and inclination so to do; but a RETROSPECT will I take notwithstanding.

I am perfectly aware that in doing this I shall lay myself open to the charge of imitation, than which a man might better be accused of downright house-breaking, for it has been a standing rule with many of my illustrious predecessors, occasionally, and particularly at the conclusion of a volume, to look over their shoulder and chuckle at the miracles they had atchieved. But as I before professed, I am determined to hold myself intirely independent of all manner of opinions and criticisms, as the only method of getting on in this world in any thing like a straight line. True it is, I may sometimes seem to angle a little for the good opinion of mankind, by giving them excellent reasons for doing unreasonable things; but this is merely to show them, that although I may occasionally go wrong, it is not for want of knowing how to go right: and here I will lay down a maxim, which will for ever intitle me to the gratitude of my inexperienced readers—namely, that a man always gets more credit in the eyes of this naughty world for sinning wilfully, than for sinning through sheer ignorance.

It will doubtless be insisted by many ingenious cavillers, who will be meddling with what does not at all concern them, that this retrospect should have been taken at the commencement of our second volume—it is usual, I know—moreover it is natural. So soon as a writer has once accomplished a volume, he forthwith becomes wonderfully increased in altitude—he steps upon his book as upon a pedestal, and is elevated in proportion to its magnitude. A duodecimo makes him one inch taller; an octavo, three inches; a quarto, six;—but he who, like mynheer, has written a book "as tick as a cheese" looks down upon his follew creatures from such a fearful height, that, ten to one, the poor man's head is turned for ever afterwards. From such a lofty situation, therefore, it is natural an author should cast his eyes behind, and having reached the first landing place on the stairs of immortality, may reasonably be allowed to plead his privilege to look back over the height he has ascended. I have deviated a little from this venerable custom, merely that our retrospect might fall in the Dog Days—of all days in the year most congenial to the indulgence of a little self-sufficiency, inasmuch as people have then little to do but to retire within the sphere of self, and make the most of what they find there.

Let it not be supposed, however, that we think ouselves a whit the wiser or better since we have finished our volume than we were before; on the contrary, we seriously assure our readers that we were fully possessed of all the wisdom and morality it contains at the moment we commenced writing. It is the world which has grown wiser—not us; we have thrown our mite into the common stock of knowledge—we have shared our morsel with the ignorant multitude; and so far from elevating ourselves above the world, our sole endeavour has been to raise the world to our own level—and make it as wise as we, its disinterested benefactors.

To a moral writer like myself, who, next to his own comfort and entertainment, has the good of his fellow-citizens at heart, a retrospect is but a sorry amusement. Like the industrious husbandman, he often contemplates in silent disappointment his labours wasted on a barren soil, or the seed he has carefully sown, choaked by a redundancy of worthless weeds. I expected long ere this to have seen a complete reformation in manners and morals, atchieved by our united efforts. My fancy echoed to the applauding voices of a retrieved generation; I anticipated, with proud satisfaction, the period, not far distant, when our work would be introduced into the *Academies* with which every lane and alley of our cities abounds; when our precepts would be gently inducted into every unlucky urchin by force of birch, and my iron-bound physiognomy, as taken by Will Wizard, be as notorious as that of Noah Webster, junr. esq. or his no less renowned predecessor the illustrious Dilworth of spelling-book immortality. But, well-a-day! to let my readers into a profound secret—the expectations of man are like the varied hues that tinge the distant prospect—never to be realised, never to be enjoyed but in perspective. Luckless Launcelot! that the humblest of the many air castles thou hast erected should prove a "baseless fabrick!" Much does it grieve me to confess, that after all our lectures, precepts, and excellent admonitions, the people of New-York are nearly as much given to backsliding and ill-nature as ever; they are just as much abandoned to dancing and tea-drinking: and as to scandal, Will Wizard informs me that by a rough computation, since the last cargo of gunpowder-tea from Canton, no less than eighteen characters have been blown up, besides a number of others that have been woefully shattered.

The ladies still labour under the same scarcity of muslins, and delight in flesh-coloured silk stockings; it is evident, however, that our advice has had very considerable effect on them, as they endeavour to act as opposite to it as possible—this being what Evergreen calls *female independence*. As to Straddles, they abound as much as ever in Broadway, particularly on Sundays; and Wizard roundly asserts that he supped in company with a knot of them a few evenings since, when they *liquidated* a whole Birmingham consignment, in a batch of imperial champaign. I have furthermore, in the course of a month past, detected no less than three Giblet families making their first onset towards style and gentility, in the very manner we have heretofore reprobated. Nor have our utmost efforts been able to check the progress of that alarming epidemic, the rage for punning, which, though doubtless originally intended merely to ornament and enliven conversation by little sports of fancy, threatens to overrun and poison the whole, like the baneful ivy which destroys the useful plant it first embellished. Now I look upon an habitual punster as a depredator upon conversation; and I have remarked sometimes one of these offenders, sitting silent on the watch for an hour together, until some luckless wight, unfortunately for the ease and quiet of the company, dropped a phrase susceptible of a double meaning,— when—pop,—our punster would dart out like a veteran mouser from her covert, seize the unlucky word, and after worrying and mumbling at it until it was capable of no further marring, relapse again into silent watchfulness, and lie in wait for another opportunity. Even this might be borne with, by the aid of a little philosophy: but, the worst of it is, they are not content to manufacture puns and laugh heartily at them themselves; but they expect we should laugh with them—which I consider as an intolerable hardship, and a flagrant imposition on good nature. Let these gentlemen fritter away conversation with impunity, and deal out their wits in sixpenny bits if they please, but I beg I may have the choice of refusing currency to their small change. I am seriously afraid, however, that our junto is not quite free from the infection, nay, that it has even approached so near as to menace the tranquility of my elbow-chair: for, Will Wizard, as we were in caucus the other night, absolutely electrified Pindar and myself with a most palpable and perplexing pun—had it been a torpedo, it could not have more discomposed the fraternity. Sentence of banishment was unanimously decreed, but on his confessing that like many celebrated wits, he was merely retailing other men's wares on commission, he was for that once forgiven, on condition of refraining from such diabolical practices in future. Pindar is particularly outrageous against punsters; and quite astonished and put me to a nonplus a day or two since, by asking abruptly "whether I thought a punster could be a good christian?" He followed up his question triumphantly by offering to prove, by sound logic and historical fact, that the roman empire owed its decline and fall to a pun; and that nothing tended so much to demoralize the french nation, as their abominable rage for *jeux de mots*.

But what, above every thing else, has caused me much vexation of spirit, and displeased me most with this stiff-necked nation, is that in spite of all the serious and profound censures of the sage Mustapha, in his various letters—they *will talk!*—they will still wag their tongues, and chatter like very slang-whangers! This is a degree of obstinacy incomprehensible in the extreme; and is another proof, how alarming is the force of habit, and how difficult it is to reduce beings, accustomed to talk, to that state of silence which is the very acme of human wisdom.

We can only account for these disappointments in our moderate and reasonable expectations, by supposing the world so deeply sunk in the mire of delinquency, that not even Hercules, were he to put his shoulder to the axletree, would be able to extricate it. We comfort ourselves, however, by the reflection, that there are, at least, three good men left in this degenerate age, to benefit the world by example, should precept ultimately fail. And borrowing, for once, an example from certain sleepy writers, who, after the first emotions of surprise at finding their invaluable effusions neglected or despised, console themselves with the idea that 'tis a stupid age, and look forward to posterity for redress—we bequeath our first volume to future generations—and much good may it do them. Heaven grant they may be able to read it! for, if our fashionable mode of education continues to improve, as of late, I am under serious apprehensions that the period is not far distant, when the discipline of the dancing master will supersede that of the grammarian; crochets and quavers supplant the alphabet, and the heels, by an antipodean manoeuvre, obtain entire pre-eminence over the head. How does my heart yearn for poor dear posterity, when this work shall become as unintelligible to our grandchildren, as it seems to be to their grandfathers and grandmothers.

In fact (for I love to be candid) we begin to suspect that many people read our numbers, merely for their amusement, without paying any attention to the serious truths conveyed in every page. Unpardonable want of penetration! not that we wish to restrict our readers in the article of laughing, which we consider as one of the dearest prerogatives of man, and the distinguishing characteristic which raises him above all other animals: let them laugh therefore if they will, provided they profit at the same time, and do not mistake our object. It is one of our indisputable facts, that it is easier to laugh ten follies out of countenance than to coax, reason, or flog a man out of one. In this odd singular and indescribable age, which is neither the age of gold, silver, iron, brass, chivalry, or *pills* (as sir John Carr asserts) a grave writer who attempts to attack folly with the heavy artillery of moral reasoning, will fare like Smollet's honest pedant, who clearly demonstrated by angles &c., after the manner of Euclid, that it was wrong to do evil—and was laughed at for his pains. Take my word for it, a little well applied ridicule, like Hannibal's application of vinegar to rocks, will do more with certain hard heads and obdurate hearts, than all the logic or demonstrations in Longinus or Euclid. But the people of Gotham, wise souls! are so much accustomed to see morality approach them clothed in formidable wigs and sable garbs, "with leaden eye that loves the ground," that they can never recognize her when, drest in gay attire, she comes tripping towards them with smiles and sunshine in her countenance.—Well, let the rogues remain in happy ignorance, for "ignorance is bliss," as the poet says;—and I put as implicit faith in poetry as I do in the almanack or the newapaper—we *will* improve them, without their being the wiser for it, and they shall become better in spite of their teeth, and without their having the least suspicion of the reformation working within them.

Among all our manifold grievances, however, still some small, but vivid rays of sunshine occasionally brighten along our path, cheering our steps, and inviting us to persevere.

The publick have paid some little regard to a few articles of our advice—they have purchased our numbers freely—so much the better for our publisher—they have read them attentively—so much the better for themselves. The melancholy fate of my dear aunt Charity has had a wonderful effect, and I have now before me a letter from a gentleman who lives opposite to a couple of old ladies, remarkable for the interest they took in his affairs—his apartments were absolutely in a state of blockade, and he was on the point of changing his lodgings or capitulating, until the appearance of our ninth number, which he immediately sent over with his compliments—the good old ladies took the hint, and have scarcely appeared at their window since. As to the *wooden gentlemen*, our friend miss Sparkle assures me, they are wonderfully improved by our criticisms, and sometimes venture to make a remark or attempt a pun in company, to the great edification of all who happen to understand them. As to red shawls, they are intirely discarded from the fair shoulders of our ladies—ever since the last importation of finery—nor has any lady, since the cold weather, ventured to expose her elbows to the admiring gaze of scrutinizing passengers. But there is one victory we have atchieved which has given us more pleasure than to have written down the whole administration. I am assured from unquestionable authority, that our young ladies, doubtless in consequence of our weighty admonitions, have not once indulged in that intoxicating, inflammatory, and whirligig dance, the *waltz*—ever since hot weather commenced. True it is, I understand an attempt was made to exhibit it by some of the sable fair ones at the last *african ball*, but it was highly disapproved of by all the respectable elderly ladies present.

These are sweet sources of comfort to atone for the many wrongs and misrepresentations heaped upon us by the world—for even *we* have experienced its ill nature. How often have we heard ourselves reproached for the insidious applications of the uncharitable!—how often have we been accused of emotions which never found an entrance into our bosoms!—how often have our sportive effusions been wrested to serve the purposes of particular enmity and bitterness!—Meddlesome spirits! little do they know our dispositions; we "lack gall" to wound the feelings of a single innocent individual; we can even forgive *them* from the very bottom of our souls—may they meet as ready a forgiveness from their own consciences! Like true and independent bachelors, having no domestic cares to interfere with our general benevolence, we consider it incumbent upon us to watch over the welfare of society; and although we are indebted to the world for little else than left-handed favours, yet we feel a proud satisfaction in requiting evil with good, and the sneer of illiberality with the unfeigned smile of good-humour. With these mingled motives of selfishness and philanthrophy we commenced our work, and if we cannot solace ourselves with the consciousness of having done much good, yet there is still one pleasing consolation left, which the world can neither give nor take away. There are moments—lingering moments of listless indifference and heavy-hearted despondency—when our best hopes and affections slipping, as they sometimes will, from their hold on those objects to which they usually cling for support, seem abandoned on the wide waste of cheerless existence, without a place to cast anchor—without a shore in view to excite a single wish, or to give a momentary interest to comtemplation. We look back with delight upon many of these moments of mental gloom, whiled away by the cheerful exercise of our pen, and consider every such triumph over the spleen, as retarding the furrowing hand of time, in its insidious encroachments on our brows. If, in addition to our own amusements, we have, as we jogged carelessly laughing along, brushed away one tear of dejection, and called forth a smile in its place; if we have brightened the pale countenance of a single child of sorrow; we shall feel almost as much joy and rejoicing as a slang-whanger does when he bathes his pen in the heart's-blood of a patron and factor; or sacrifices one more illustrious victim on the altar of *party animosity.*

TO READERS AND CORRESPONDENTS.

It is our misfortune to be frequently pestered, in our peregrinations about this learned city, by certain critical gad-flies, who buzz around and merely attack the skin, without ever being able to penetrate the body. The reputation of our promising *protégé*, Jeremy Cockloft the younger, has been assailed by these skin-deep critics; they have questioned his claims to originality, and even hinted that the ideas for his New-Jersey Tour were borrowed from a late work entitled "MY POCKETBOOK." As there is no literary offence more despicable in the eyes of the trio than *borrowing*, we immediately called Jeremy to an account; when he proved, by the dedication of the work in question, that it was first published in *London* in March 1807—and that his "Stranger in New-Jersey" had made its appearance on the 24th of the preceding February.

We were on the point of acquitting Jeremy with honour, on the ground that it was impossible, *knowing* as he is, to borrow from a foreign work *one month before* it was in existence, when Will Wizard suddenly took up the cudgels for the critics, and insisted that nothing was more probable, for he recollected reading of an ingenious dutch author, who plainly convicted the *antients* of stealing from his labours!—So much for *criticism*.

We have received a host of friendly and admonitory letters from different quarters, and among the rest a very loving epistle from Georgetown, Columbia, signed *Teddy M'Gundy*, who addresses us by the name of Saul M'Gundy, and insists that we are descended from the same irish progenitors, and nearly related. As friend Teddy seems to be an honest merry rogue, we are sorry that we cannot admit his claims to kindred; we thank him, however, for his good will, and should he ever be inclined to *favour* us with another epistle, we will hint to him, and at the same time to our other numerous correspondents, that their communications will be infinitely more acceptable if they will just recollect Tom Shuffleton's advice, "pay the post-boy, Muggins."

SALMAGUNDI NO. XIV

NO. XIV]   *Saturday, September* 19, 1807.

FROM MUSTAPHA RUB-A-DUB KELI KHAN,
To ASEM HACCHEM, *principal slave-driver to his highness the Bashaw of Tripoli.*

Health and joy to the friend of my heart!—May the angel of peace ever watch over thy dwelling, and the star of prosperity shed its benignant lustre on all thy undertakings. Far other is the lot of thy captive friend—his brightest hopes extend but to a lengthened period of weary captivity, and memory only adds to the measure of his griefs, by holding up a mirror which reflects with redoubled charms the hours of past felicity. In midnight slumbers my soul holds sweet converse with the tender objects of its affections—it is then the exile is restored to his country—it is then the wide waste of waters that rolls between us disappears, and I clasp to my bosom the companion of my youth. I awake, and find it is but a vision of the night—the sigh will rise—the tear of dejection will steal adown my cheek—I fly to my pen, and strive to forget myself and my sorrows in conversing with my friend.

In such a situation, my good Asem, it cannot be expected that I should be able so wholly to abstract myself from my own feelings, as to give thee a full and systematick account of the singular people among whom my disastrous lot has been cast. I can only find leisure from my own individual sorrows, to entertain thee occasionally with some of the most prominent features of their character, and now and then a solitary picture of their most preposterous eccentricities.

I have before observed that among the distinguishing characteristicks of the people of this logocracy, is their invincible love of talking; and that I could compare the nation to nothing but a mighty wind-mill. Thou art doubtless at a loss to conceive how this mill is supplied with grist; or, in other words, how it is possible to furnish subjects to supply the perpetual motion of so many tongues.

The genius of the nation appears in its highest lustre in this particular, in the discovery, or rather the application, of a subject which seems to supply an inexhaustible mine of words. It is nothing more, my friend, than POLITICKS, a word, which I declare to thee, has perplexed me almost as much as the redoubtable one of *economy*. On consulting a dictionary of this language, I found it denoted the science of government, and the relations, situations and dispositions of states and empires.—Good, thought I, for a people who boast of governing themselves, there could not be a more important subject of investigation. I therefore listened attentively, expecting to hear from "the most enlightened people under the sun," (for so they modestly term themselves) sublime disputations on the science of legislation, and precepts of political wisdom, that would not have disgraced our great prophet and legislator himself—but alas, Asem! how continually are my expectations disappointed! how dignified a meaning does this word bear in the dictionary—how despicable its common application! I find it extending to every contemptible discussion of local animosity, and every petty altercation of insignificant individuals. It embraces alike all manner of concerns, from the organization of a divan, the election of a bashaw, or the levying of an army, to the appointment of a constable, the personal disputes of two miserable slang-whangers, the cleaning of the streets, or the economy of a dirt cart. A couple of politicians will quarrel with the most vociferous pertinacity, about the character of a bum-bailiff, whom nobody cares for, or the deportment of a little great man, whom nobody knows—and this is called talking *politicks;*—nay, it is but a few days since, that I was annoyed by a debate between two of my fellow lodgers, who were magnanimously employed in condemning a luckless wight to infamy, because he chose to wear a *red coat,* and to entertain certain erroneous opinions some thirty years ago. Shocked at their illiberal and vindictive spirit, I rebuked them for thus indulging in slander and uncharitablenesses, about the colour of a coat, which had doubtless for many years been worn out, or the belief in errors, which in all probability had been long since atoned for and abandoned; but they justified themselves by alledging that they were only engaged in *politicks,* and exerting that liberty of speech, and freedom of discussion, which was the glory and safeguard of their national independence. "Oh Mahomet!" thought I, "what a country must that be, which builds its political safety on ruined characters and the persecution of individuals!"

Into what transports of surprize and incredulity am I continually betrayed, as the character of this eccentrick people gradually developes itself to my observations. Every new research encreases the perplexities in which I am involved, and I am more than ever at a loss where to place them in the scale of my estimation. It is thus the philosopher, in pursuing truth through the labyrinth of doubt, error and misrepresentation, frequently finds himself bewildered in the maze of contradictory experience, and almost wishes he could quietly retrace his wandering steps, steal back into the path of honest ignorance, and jog on once more in contented indifference.

How fertile in these contradictions is this extensive logocracy! Men of different nations, manners and languages, live in this country in the most perfect harmony, and nothing is more common than to see individuals, whose respective governments are at variance, taking each other by the hand and exchanging the offices of friendship. Nay, even on the subject of religion, which, as it affects our dearest interests, our earliest opinions and prejudices, some warmth and heart-burnings might be excused, which even in *our* enlightened country is so fruitful in difference between man and man—even religion occasions no dissension among these people, and it has even been discovered by one of their *sages,* that believing in one God or twenty Gods, "neither breaks a man's leg, nor picks his pocket." The idolatrous persian may here bow down before his everlasting fire, and prostrate himself towards the glowing east. The chinese may adore his *Fo'* or his *Josh*—the egyptian his stork,—and the mussulman practise unmolested the divine precepts of our immortal prophet. Nay, even the forlorn, abandoned atheist, who lays down at night without committing himself to the protection of heaven, and rises in the morning without returning thanks for his safety—

who hath no deity but his own will—whose soul, like the sandy desart, is barren of every flower of hope, to throw a solitary bloom over the dead level of sterility, and soften the wide extent of desolation—whose darkened views extend not beyond the horizon that bounds his cheerless existence—to whom no blissful perspective opens beyond the grave;— even he is suffered to indulge in his desperate opinions, without exciting one other emotion than pity or contempt. But this mild and tolerating spirit reaches not beyond the pale of religion:—once differ in *politicks*, in mere theories, visions and chimeras, the growth of interest, of folly, or madness, and deadly warfare ensues; every eye flashes fire, every tongue is loaded with reproach, and every heart is filled with gall and bitterness.

At this period several unjustifiable and serious injuries on the part of the barbarians of the british island, have given new impulse to the tongue and the pen, and occasioned a terrible wordy fever. Do not suppose, my friend, that I mean to condemn any proper and dignified expression of resentment for injuries. On the contrary, I love to see a word before a blow: for "in the fulness of the heart the tongue moveth." But my long experience has convinced me, that people who talk the most about taking satisfaction for affronts, generally content themselves with talking, instead of revenging the insult: like the street women of this country, who, after a prodigious scolding, quietly sit down and fan themselves cool as fast as possible. But to return—the rage for talking has now, in consequence of the aggressions I alluded to, increased to a degree far beyond what I have observed heretofore. In the gardens of his highness of Tripoli, are fifteen thousand bee-hives, three hundred peacocks, and a prodigious number of parrots and baboons—and yet I declare to thee, Asem, that their buzzing and squalling and chattering is nothing, compared to the wild uproar and war of words now raging within the bosom of this mighty and distracted *logocracy*. *Politicks* pervade every city, every village, every temple, every porter house—the universal question is, "what is the news?"—This is a kind of challenge to political debate, and as no two men think exactly alike, tis ten to one but before they finish, all the *polite* phrases in the language are exhausted, by way of giving fire and energy to argument. What renders this talking fever more alarming is, that the people appear to be in the unhappy state of a patient whose palate nauseates the medicine best calculated for the cure of his disease, and seem anxious to continue in the full enjoyment of their chattering epidemick. They alarm each other by direful reports and fearful apprehensions, like I have seen a knot of old wives in this country, entertain themselves with stories of ghosts and goblins, until their imaginations were in a most agonizing panick. Every day begets some new tale big with agitation, and the busy *goddess* rumour (to speak in the poetick language of the *christians*) is constantly in motion. She mounts her rattling stage-waggon, and gallops about the country, freighted with a load of "hints" "informations" "extracts of letters from respectable gentlemen" "observations of respectable corres-pondents," and "unquestionable authorities," which her high priests, the slang-whangers, retail to their sapient followers, with all the solem-nity and all the authenticity of oracles. True it is, the unfortunate slang-whangers are sometimes at a loss for food to supply this insatiable appe-tite for intelligence, and are not unfrequently reduced to the necessity of manufacturing dishes suited to the taste of the times, to be served up as morning and evening repasts to their disciples.

When the hungry politician is thus full charged with important infor-mation, he sallies forth to give due exercise to his tongue, and tell all he knows to every body he meets. Now it is a thousand to one, that every person he meets is just as wise as himself, charged with the same articles of information, and possessed of the same violent inclination to give it vent, for in this country every man adopts some particular slang-whanger as the standard of his judgment, and reads every thing he writes, if he reads nothing else—which is doubtless the reason why the people of this logocracy are so marvelously *enlightened*. So away they tilt at each other with their borrowed lances, advancing to the combat with the opinions and speculations of their respective slang-whangers which in all probability, are diametrically opposite—here then arises as fair an opportunity for a battle of words as heart could wish; and thou mayest rely upon it, Asem, they do not let it pass unimproved. They *sometimes* begin with argument, but in process of time, as the tongue begins to wax wanton, other auxiliaries become necessary—re-crimination commences, reproach follows close at its heels—from political abuse they proceed to personal, and thus often is a friendship of years trampled down by this contemptible enemy; this gigantic dwarf of POLITICKS, the mongrel issue of grovelling ambition and aspiring ignorance!

There would be but little harm indeed in all this, if it ended merely in a broken head; for this might soon be healed, and the scar, if any remained, might serve as a warning ever after against the indulgence of political intemperance—at the worst, the loss of such heads as these would be a gain to the nation.—But the evil extends far deeper; it threatens to impair all social intercourse, and even to sever the sacred union of family and kindred. The convivial table is disturbed, the cheerful fire-side is invaded, the smile of social hilarity is chased away—the bond of social love is broken by the everlasting intrusion of this fiend of conten-tion, who lurks in the sparkling bowl, crouches by the fire-side, growls in the friendly circle, infests every avenue to pleasure; and like the scowling Incubus, sits on the bosom of society, pressing down and smothering every throe and pulsation of liberal philanthropy.

But thou wilt perhaps ask, "What can these people dispute about? one would suppose that being all *free* and *equal*, they would harmonize as brothers; children of the same parent, and equal heirs of the same inheritance." This theory is most exquisite, my good friend, but in practice it turns out the very dream of a madman. Equality, Asem, is one of the most consummate scoundrels that ever crept from the brain of a political juggler. A fellow who thrusts his hand into the pocket of honest industry, or enterprising talent, and squanders their hard earned profit on profligate idleness or indolent stupidity. There will always be an inequality among mankind, so long as a portion of it is enlightened and industrious, and the rest idle and ignorant. The one will acquire a larger share of wealth, and its attendant comforts, refinements, and luxuries of life, and the influence and power which those will always possess who have the greatest ability of administering to the necessities of their fellow creatures. These advantages will inevitably excite envy, and envy as inevitably begets ill-will—hence arises that eternal warfare which the lower orders of society are waging against those who have raised themselves by their own merits, or have been raised by the merits of their ancestors, above the common level. In a nation possessed of quick feelings and impetuous passions, this hostility might engender deadly broils, and bloody commotions; but here it merely vents itself in high sounding words, which lead to continual breaches of decorum; or in the insidious assassination of character, and a restless propensity among the base to blacken every reputation which is fairer than their own.

I cannot help smiling sometimes to see the solicitude with which the people of *America* (so called from the country having been first discovered by *Christopher Columbus*) battle about them when any election takes place; as if *they* had the least concern in the matter, or were to be benefitted by an exchange of bashaws—they really seem ignorant, that none but the *bashaws and their dependants* are at all interested in the event, and that the people at large will not find their situation altered in the least. I formerly gave thee an account of an election, which took place under my eye. The result has been, that the *people*, as some of the slang-whangers say, have obtained a glorious triumph, which however, is flatly denied by the opposite slang-whangers, who insist that *their* party is composed of the true sovereign people, and that the others are all jacobins, frenchmen, and *irish rebels*. I ought to apprize thee, that the last is a term of great reproach here, which perhaps thou wouldst not otherwise imagine, considering that it is not many years since this very people were engaged in a revolution; the failure of which would have subjected them to the same ignominious epithet, and a participation in which, is now the highest recommendation to publick confidence. By Mahomet, but it cannot be denied that the *consistency* of this people, like every thing else appertaining to them is on a prodigious *great scale!* To return, however, to the event of the election.— The people triumphed—and much good has it done them. I, for my part, expected to see wonderful changes, and most magical metamorphoses. I expected to see the people all rich, that they would be all gentlemen bashaws, riding in their coaches, and faring sumptuously every day; emancipated from toil, and revelling in luxurious ease. Wilt thou credit me, Asem, when I declare to thee, that every thing remains exactly in the same state as it was before the last wordy campaign? except a few noisy retainers who have crept into office, and a few noisy patriots on the other side, who have been kicked out, there is not the least difference. The labourer still toils for his daily support; the beggar still lives on the charity of those who have any charity to bestow, and the only *solid* satisfaction the multitude have reaped, is that they have got a *new governor* (or bashaw) whom they will praise, idolize, and exalt for a while, and afterwards, notwithstanding the sterling merits he really possesses, in compliance with immemorial custom, they will abuse, calumniate, and trample under foot.

Such, my dear Asem, is the way in which the wise people, of "the most enlightened country under the sun," are amused with straws, and puffed up with mighty conceits: like a certain fish I have seen here, which having his belly tickled for a short time, will swell and puff himself up to twice his usual size, and become a mere bladder of wind and vanity.

The blessing of a true mussulman light on thee, good Asem,—ever while thou livest, be true to thy prophet, and rejoice, that though the boasting *political chatterers* of this logocracy cast upon thy countrymen the ignominious epithet of slaves; yet, thou livest in a country where the people, instead of being at the mercy of a tyrant with a *million of heads*, have nothing to do but submit to the will of a bashaw of *only three tails.*

ever thine,

MUSTAPHA.

COCKLOFT HALL.

BY LAUNCELOT LANGSTAFF, ESQ.

Those who pass their time immured in the smoky circumference of the city, amid the rattling of carts, the brawling of the multitude, and the variety of unmeaning and discordant sounds that prey insensibly upon the nerves, and beget a weariness of the spirits, can alone understand and feel that expansion of the heart, that physical renovation which a citizen experiences when he steals forth from his dusty prison, to breathe the free air of heaven, and enjoy the unsophisticated face of nature. Who that has rambled by the side of one of our majestic rivers, at the hour of sun-set, when the wildly romantick scenery around is softened and tinted by the voluptuous mist of evening; when the bold and swelling outlines of the distant mountain seem melting into the glowing horizon, and a rich mantle of refulgence is thrown over the whole expanse of the heavens, but must have felt how abundant is nature in sources of pure enjoyment; how luxuriant in all that can enliven the senses or delight the imagination. The jocund zephyr full freighted with native fragrance, sues sweetly to the senses; the chirping of the thousand varieties of insects with which our woodlands abound, forms a concert of simple melody; even the barking of the farm dog, the lowing of the cattle, the tinkling of their bells, and the strokes of the woodman's axe from the opposite shore, seem to partake of the softness of the scene and fall tunefully upon the ear; while the voice of the villager, chaunting some rustick ballad, swells from a distance, in the semblance of the very musick of harmonious love.

At such times I feel a sensation of a sweet tranquility—a hallowed calm is diffused over my senses; I cast my eyes around and every object is serene, simple, and beautiful; no warring passion, no discordant string there vibrates to the touch of ambition, self-interest, hatred or revenge— I am at peace with the whole world, and hail all mankind as friends and brothers.—Blissful moments! ye recal the careless days of my boyhood, when mere existence was happiness, when hope was certainty, this world a paradise, and every woman a ministering angel!—Surely man was designed for a tenant of the universe, instead of being pent up in these dismal cages, these dens of strife, disease and discord. We were created to range the fields, to sport among the groves, to build castles in the air, and have every one of them realized!

A whole legion of reflections like these, insinuated themselves into my mind, and stole me from the influence of the cold realities before me, as I took my accustomed walk, a few weeks since, on the Battery. Here watching the splendid mutations of one of our summer skies, which emulated the boasted glories of an italian sun-set, I all at once discovered that it was but to pack up my portmanteau; bid adieu for a while to my elbow-chair, and in a little time I should be transported from the region of smoke and noise and dust, to the enjoyment of a far sweeter prospect and a brighter sky. The next morning I was off full tilt to Cockloft-Hall, leaving my man Pompey to follow at his leisure with my baggage. I love to indulge in rapid transitions, which are prompted by the quick impulse of the moment—tis the only mode of guarding against that intruding and deadly foe to all parties of pleasure—anticipation.

Having now made good my retreat, until the black frosts commence, it is but a piece of civility due to my readers, who I trust are, ere this, my friends, to give them a proper introduction to my present residence. I do this as much to gratify them as myself, well knowing a reader is always anxious to learn how his author is lodged, whether in a garret or a cellar, a hovel or a palace—at least an author is generally vain enough to think so; and an author's vanity ought sometimes to be gratified—poor vagabond! it is often the only gratification he ever tastes in this world!

COCKLOFT-HALL is the country residence of the family, or rather the paternal mansion, which, like the mother country, sends forth whole colonies to populate the face of the earth. Pindar whimsically denominates it the *family hive*, and there is at least as much truth as humour in my cousin's epithet—for many a redundant swarm has it produced. I dont recollect whether I have at any time mentioned to my readers (for I seldom look back on what I have written) that the fertility of the Cocklofts is proverbial. The female members of the family are most incredibly fruitful; and to use a favourite phrase of old Cockloft, who is excessively addicted to backgammon, they seldom fail "to throw doublets every time." I myself have known three or four very industrious young men reduced to great extremities, with some of these capital breeders—heaven smiled upon their union, and enriched them with a numerous and hopeful offspring—who eat them out of doors.

But to return to the hall.—It is pleasantly situated on the bank of a sweet pastoral stream, not so near town as to invite an inundation of unmeaning, idle acquaintance, who come to lounge away an afternoon, nor so distant as to render it an absolute deed of charity or friendship to perform the journey. It is one of the oldest habitations in the country, and was built by my cousin Christopher's grandfather, who was also mine by the mother's side, in his latter days, to form, as the old gentleman expressed himself, "a snug retreat, where he meant to sit himself down *in his old days* and be comfortable *for the rest of his life.*" He was at this time a few years over fourscore; but this was a common saying of his, with which he usually closed his airy speculations. One would have thought from the long vista of years through which he contemplated many of his projects, that the good man had forgot the age of the patriarchs had long since gone by, and calculated upon living a century longer at least. He was for a considerable time in doubt, on the question of roofing his house with shingles or slate—shingles would not last *above thirty* years; but then they were much cheaper than slates. He settled the matter by a kind of compromise, and determined to build

with shingles first; "and when they are worn out," said the old gentleman, triumphantly, "twill be time enough for us to replace them with
more durable materials:" But his contemplated improvements surpassed
every thing; and scarcely had he a roof over his head, when he discovered
a thousand things to be arranged before he could "sit down comfortably." In the first place every tree and bush on the place, was cut down
or grubbed up by the roots because they were not placed to his mind;
and a vast quantity of oaks, chesnuts and elms, set out in clumps and
rows, and labyrinths, which he observed in about *five-and-twenty or
thirty years* at most, would yield a very tolerable shade, and moreover,
shut out all the surrounding country; for he was determined he said, to
have all his views on his own land, and be beholden to no man for a
prospect. This, my learned readers will perceive, was something very
like the idea of Lorenzo de Medici, who gave as a reason for preferring
one of his seats above all the others, "that all the ground within view of
it, was his own:" now, whether my grandfather ever heard of the Medici,
is more than I can say; I rather think however from the characteristic
originality of the Cocklofts that it was a whim-wham of his own begetting. Another odd notion of the old gentleman, was to blow up a large
bed of rocks for the purpose of having a fish-pond, although the river
ran at about one hundred yards distance from the house, and was well
stored with fish—but there was nothing he said like having things to
oneself. So at it he went with all the ardour of a projector, who has just
hit upon some splendid and useless whim-wham. As he proceeded, his
views enlarged; he would have a summer-house built on the margin of
the fish-pond; he would have it surrounded with elms and willows; and
he would have a cellar dug under it, for some incomprehensible purpose,
which remains a secret to this day. "In a few years," he observed, "it
would be a delightful piece of wood and water, where he might ramble
on a summer's noon, smoke his pipe and enjoy himself in his old days"—
thrice honest old soul!—he died of an apoplexy in his ninetieth year,
just as he had begun to blow up the fish-pond.

Let no one ridicule the whim-whams of my grandfather:—If—and of
this there is no doubt, for wise men have said it—if life is but a dream,
happy is he who can make the most of the illusion.

Since my grandfather's death, the hall has passed through the hands
of a succession of true old cavaliers, like himself, who gloried in observing the golden rules of hospitality, which, according to the Cockloft principle, consist in giving a guest the freedom of the house, cram-
ming him with beef and pudding, and if possible, laying him under the
table with prime port, claret or London particular. The mansion appears
to have been consecrated to the jolly god, and teems with monuments
sacred to conviviality. Every chest of drawers, clothes-press and cabinet

is decorated with enormous china punch-bowls, which mrs. Cockloft
has paraded with much ostentation, particularly in her favourite red
damask bed-chamber, and in which a projector might with great satisfaction practise his experiments on fleets, diving-bells, and sub-marine
boats.

I have before mentioned cousin Christopher's profound veneration
for antique furniture; in consequence of which the old hall is furnished
in much the same style with the house in town. Old fashioned bed-
steads, with high testers, massy clothes-presses, standing most majestically on eagles' claws, and ornamented with a profusion of shining brass
handles, clasps and hinges, and around the grand parlour are solemnly
arranged a sett of high-backed leather-bottomed, massy mahogany
chairs, that always remind me of the formal long-waisted belles who
flourished in stays and buckram, about the time they were in fashion.

If I may judge from their height it was not the fashion for gentlemen
in those days to loll over the back of a lady's chair, and whisper in her
ear what—might be as well spoken aloud—at least they must have been
patagonians to have effected it. Will Wizard declares that he saw a
little fat german gallant attempt once to whisper miss Barbara Cockloft in this manner, but being unluckily caught by the chin, he dangled
and kicked about for half a minute, before he could find terra firma—
but Will is much addicted to hyperbole, by reason of his having been a
great traveller.

But what the Cocklofts most especially pride themselves upon, is the
possession of several family portraits, which exhibit as honest a square
set of portly well fed looking gentlemen, and gentlewomen as ever grew
and flourished under the pencil of a dutch painter. Old Christopher, who
is a complete genealogist, has a story to tell of each, and dilates with
copious eloquence on the great services of the general in large sleeves,
during the old french war, and on the piety of the lady in blue velvet,
who so attentively peruses her book, and was once so celebrated for a
beautiful arm: But much as I reverence my illustrious ancestors, I find
little to admire in their biography, except my cousin's excellent memory,
which is most provokingly retentive of every uninteresting particular.

My allotted chamber in the hall is the same that was occupied in days
of yore by my honoured uncle John. The room exhibits many memorials
which recal to my remembrance the solid excellence and amiable
eccentricities of that gallant old lad. Over the mantlepiece hangs the
portrait of a young lady, dressed in a flaring long-waisted blue silk gown,
be-flowered, and be-furbelowed, and be-cuffed in a most abundant manner—she holds in one hand a book, which she very complaisantly neglects,
to turn and smile on the spectator; in the other, a flower, which I hope,
for the honor of dame nature, was the sole production of the painter's

imagination; and a little behind her is something tied to a blue ribbon, but whether a little dog, a monkey, or a pigeon, must be left to the judgment of future commentators. This little damsel, tradition says, was my uncle John's third flame, and he would infallibly have run away with her, could he have persuaded her into the measure; but at that time, ladies were not quite so easily run away with as Columbine; and my uncle failing in the point, took a lucky thought, and with great gallantry run off with her picture, which he conveyed in triumph to Cockloft-hall, and hung up in his bed-chamber as a monument of his enterprising spirit. The old gentleman prided himself mightily on this chivalrick manoeuvre; always chuckled, and pulled up his stock when he contemplated the picture, and never related the exploit without winding up with—"I might, indeed, have carried off the original, had I chose to dangle a little longer after her chariot-wheels—for, to do the girl justice, I believe she had a liking for me, but I always scorned to coax, my boy—always—'twas my way." My uncle John was of a happy temperament—I would give half I am worth for his talent at self-consolation.

The miss Cocklofts have made several spirited attempts to introduce modern furniture into the hall, but with very indifferent success. Modern *style* has always been an object of great annoyance to honest Christopher, and is ever treated by him with sovereign contempt, as an upstart intruder. It is a common observation of his, that your old-fashioned substantial furniture bespeaks the respectability of one's ancestors, and indicates that the family has been used to hold up its head for more than the present generation; whereas the fragile appendages of modern style seemed to be emblems of mushroom gentility, and to his mind predicted that the family dignity would moulder away and vanish with the finery thus put on of a sudden. The same whim-wham makes him averse to having his house surrounded with poplars, which he stigmatizes as mere upstarts, just fit to ornament the shingle palaces of modern gentry, and characteristick of the establishments they decorate. Indeed, so far does he carry his veneration for all the antique trumpery, that he can scarcely see the venerable dust brushed from its resting place on the old-fashioned testers, or a grey-bearded spider dislodged from his antient inheritance, without groaning; and I once saw him in a transport of passion, on Jeremy's knocking down a mouldering martin-coop with his tennis-ball, which had been set up in the latter days of my grandfather. Another object of his peculiar affection is an old english cherry-tree, which leans against a corner of the hall, and whether the house supports it, or it supports the house, would be, I believe, a question of some difficulty to decide.

It is held sacred by friend Christopher, because he planted and reared it himself, and had once well nigh broke his neck, by a fall from one of its branches. This is one of his favourite stories; and there is reason to believe, that if the tree was out of the way, the old gentleman would forget the whole affair—which would be a great pity. The old tree has long since ceased bearing, and is exceedingly infirm—every tempest robs it of a limb, and one would suppose, from the lamentations of my old friend, on such occasions, that he had lost one of his own. He often contemplates it in a half-melancholy, half-moralizing humour— "together" he says "have we flourished, and together shall we wither away—a few years, and both our heads will be laid low; and, perhaps my mouldering bones, may one day or other, mingle with the dust of the tree I have planted." He often fancies, he says, that it rejoices to see him when he revisits the hall, and that its leaves assume a brighter verdure, as if to welcome his arrival. How whimsically are our tenderest feelings assailed! At one time the old tree had obtruded a withered branch before miss Barbara's window, and she desired her father to order the gardener to saw it off. I shall never forget the old man's answer, and the look that accompanied it. "What" cried he, "lop off the limbs of my cherry tree in its old age?—why do you not cut off the grey locks of your poor old father?"

Do my readers yawn at this long family detail?—they are welcome to throw down our work, and never resume it again. I have no care for such ungratified spirits, and will not throw away a thought on one of them—full often have I contributed to their amusement, and have I not a right for once to consult my own? Who is there that does not fondly turn at times, to linger round those scenes which were once the haunt of his boyhood ere his heart grew heavy, and his head waxed grey— and to dwell with fond affection on the friends who have twined themselves round his heart—mingled in all his enjoyments—contributed to all his felicities? If there be any, who cannot relish these enjoyments, let them despair—for they have been so soiled in their intercourse with the world, as to be incapable of tasting some of the purest pleasures, that survive the happy period of youth.

To such as have not yet lost the rural feeling, I address this simple family picture—and in the honest sincerity of a warm heart, I invite them to turn aside from bustle, care and toil, to tarry with me for a season in the hospitable mansion of the Cocklofts.

I was really apprehensive, on reading the following effusion of Will Wizard, that he still retained that pestilent hankering after *puns* of which we lately convicted him. He however declares, that he is fully authorized by the example of the most popular criticks and wits of the present age, whose manner and matter he has closely, and he flatters himself, successfully, copied in the subsequent essay.

THEATRICAL INTELLIGENCE.
BY WILLIAM WIZARD, ESQ.

The uncommon healthiness of the season (occasioned, as several learned physicians assure me, by the universal prevalence of the influenza) has encouraged the chieftain of our dramatick corps to marshal his forces, and commence the campaign at a much earlier day than usual. He has been induced to take the field thus suddenly, I am told, by the invasion of certain foreign marauders, who pitched their tents at Vauxhall-Garden during the warm months, and taking advantage of his army being disbanded and dispersed in *summer quarters*, committed sad depredations upon the borders of his territories—carrying off a considerable portion of his winter harvest, and *murdering* some of his most distinguished characters.

It is true, these hardy invaders have been reduced to great extremity by the late heavy rains, which injured and destroyed much of their camp equipage, besides spoiling the best part of their wardrobe. Two cities, a triumphal car, and a new moon for Cinderella, together with the barber's boy, who was employed every night to powder and make it shine white, have been entirely washed away, and the sea has become very wet and mouldy, insomuch that great apprehensions are entertained that it will never be dry enough for use. Add to this, the noble county Paris had the misfortune to tear his corduroy breeches in the scuffle with Romeo (by reason of the tomb being very wet, which occasioned him to slip) and he, and his noble rival, possessing but one poor pair of sattin ones between them, were reduced to considerable shifts to keep up the dignity of their respective houses. In spite of these disadvantages, and untoward circumstances, they continued to enact most intrepidly, performing with much ease and confidence, inasmuch as they were seldom pestered with an audience to criticise and put them out of countenance. It is rumored that the last heavy shower has absolutely *dissolved* the company, and that our manager has nothing further to apprehend from that quarter.

The theatre opened on Wednesday last with great *eclat*, (as we criticks say) and almost vied in brilliancy with that of my superb friend Consequa in Canton, where the castles were all ivory, the sea mother of pearl, the skies gold and silver leaf, and the outside of the boxes *inlaid* with scallop shell-work. Those who want a better description of the theatre, may as well go and see it, and then they can judge for themselves. For the gratification of a highly respectable class of readers, who love to see every thing on paper, I had indeed prepared a circumstantial and truly incomprehensible account of it, such as your traveller always fills his book with, and which I defy the most intelligent architect, even the great sir Christopher Wren, to understand. I had jumbled cornices, and pilasters, and pillars, and capitals, and trigliphs, and modules, and plinths, and volutes, and perspectives, and fore-shortenings, helter-skelter, and had set all the orders of architecture, doric, ionic, corinthian, &c. together by the ears, in order to work out a satisfactory description; but the manager, having sent me a polite note, requesting that I would not take off the sharp edge (as he whimsically expresses it) of publick curiosity, thereby diminishing the receipts of his house, I have willingly consented to oblige him, and have left my description at the store of our publisher, where any person may see it—provided he applies at a proper hour.

I cannot refrain here from giving vent to the satisfaction I received from the excellent performances of the different actors, one and all, and particularly the gentlemen who shifted the scenes, who acquitted themselves throughout with great celerity, dignity, pathos, and effect. Nor must I pass over the peculiar merits of my friend JOHN, who gallanted off the chairs and tables in the most dignified and circumspect manner. Indeed I have had frequent occasion to applaud the correctness with which this gentleman fulfills the parts allotted him, and consider him as one of the best general performers in the company. My friend the cockney, who Evergreen whimsically dubs my *Tender*, found considerable fault with the manner in which *John* shoved a huge rock from behind the scenes, maintaining that he should have put his left foot forward, and pushed it with his right hand, that being the method practised by his contemporaries of the royal theatres, and universally approved by their best criticks. He also took exception to *John's* coat, which he pronounced too short by a foot at least—particularly when he turned his back to the company. But I look upon these objections in the same light as new readings, and insist that *John* shall be allowed to manoeuvre his chairs and tables, shove his rocks, and wear his skirts in that style which his genius best effects. My hopes in the rising merit of this *favourite actor* daily increase; and I would hint to the manager the propriety of giving him a benefit, advertising in the usual style of play-bills, as a "springe to catch woodcocks," that between the play and farce *John* will MAKE A BOW—for that night only!

I am told that no pains have been spared to make the exhibitions of this season as splendid as possible. Several expert rat-catchers have been sent into different parts of the country to catch white mice for the grand pantomime of CINDERELLA. A nest full of little squab Cupids have been taken in the neighbourhood of Communipaw; they are as yet but half fledged, of the true *Holland* breed, and it is hoped will be able to fly about by the middle of October; otherwise they will be suspended about the stage by the waistband, like little alligators in an apothecaries shop, as the pantomime must positively be performed by that time. Great pains and expense have been incurred in the importation of one of the most portly pumpkins in New-England; and the publick may be assured there is now one on board a vessel from New-Haven, which will contain Cinderella's coach and six with perfect ease, were the white mice even ten times as large.

Also several barrels of hail, rain, brimstone, and gunpowder are in store for *melo-drames*, of which a number are to be played off this winter. It is furthermore whispered me that the great *thunder drum* has been new braced, and an expert performer on that instrument engaged, who will thunder in plain english, so as to be understood by the most illiterate hearer. This will be infinitely preferable to the miserable italian thunderer employed last winter by mr. Ciceri, who performed in such an unnatural and outlandish tongue, that none but the scholars of Signior Da Ponte could understand him. It will be a further gratification to the patriotic audience to know that the present thunderer is a fellow countryman, born at Dunderbarrack, among the echoes of the highlands—and that he thunders with peculiar emphasis and pompous enunciation, in the true style of a fourth of July orator.

In addition to all these additions, the manager has provided an entire new snow-storm the very sight of which will be quite sufficient to draw a shawl over every naked bosom in the theatre—the snow is perfectly fresh having been manufactured last August

N. B. The outside of the theatre has been ornamented with a new chimney!!

SALMAGUNDI NO. XV

NO. XV]   *Thursday, October 1, 1807.*

SKETCHES FROM NATURE.
BY ANTHONY EVERGREEN, GENT.

The brisk north-westers which prevailed not long since, had a powerful effect in arresting the progress of belles, beaux and wild-pigeons, in their fashionable northern tour, and turning them back to the more balmy region of the south. Among the rest I was encountered, full butt, by a blast, which set my teeth chattering, just as I doubled one of the frowning bluffs of the Mohawk mountains, in my route to Niagara, and facing about incontinently, I forthwith scud before the wind, and a few days since arrived at my old quarters in New-York. My first care on returning from so long an absence, was to visit the worthy family of the Cocklofts, whom I found safe burrowed in their country mansion. On inquiring for my highly respected coadjutor, Langstaff, I learned with great concern that he had relapsed into one of his eccentrick fits of the spleen, ever since the era of a turtle dinner, given by old Cockloft to some of the neighbouring squires, wherein the old gentleman had achieved a glorious victory in laying honest Launcelot fairly under the table. Langstaff, although fond of the social board and cheerful glass, yet abominates any excess, and has an invincible aversion to *getting mellow*, considering it a wilful outrage on the sanctity of imperial *mind*, a senseless abuse of the body, and an unpardonable, because a voluntary, prostration of both mental and personal dignity. I have heard him moralize on the subject, in a style that would have done honour to Michael Cassio himself; but I believe, if the truth were known, this antipathy rather arises from his having, as the phrase is, but a weak head, and nerves so extremely sensitive, that he is sure to suffer severely from a frolick, and will groan and make resolutions against it for a week afterwards. He therefore took this waggish exploit of old Christopher's, and the consequent quizzing which he underwent, in high dudgeon, had kept aloof from company for a fortnight, and appeared to be meditating some deep plan of retaliation upon his mischievous old crony. He had, however, for the last day or two, shown some symptoms of convalescence; had listened, without more than half a dozen twitches of impatience, to one of Christopher's unconscionable long stories, and even was seen to smile, for the one hundred and thirtieth time, at a venerable joke, originally borrowed from Joe Miller; but which by dint of long occupancy, and frequent repetition, the old gentleman now firmly believes happened to himself somewhere in New-England.

As I am well acquainted with Launcelot's haunts, I soon found him out. He was lolling on his favourite bench rudely constructed at the foot of an old tree, which is full of fantastical twists, and with its spreading branches forms a canopy of luxuriant foliage. This tree is a kind of chronicle of the short reigns of his uncle John's mistresses, and its trunk is sorely wounded with carvings of true lovers knots, hearts, darts, names, and inscriptions—frail memorials of the variety of fair dames who captivated the wandering fancy of that old cavalier in the days of his youthful romance. Launcelot holds this tree in particular regard, as he does every thing else connected with the memory of his good uncle John. He was reclining, in one of his usual brown studies, against its trunk, and gazing pensively upon the river that glided just by, washing the drooping branches of the dwarf willows that fringed its bank. My appearance roused him—he grasped my hand with his usual warmth, and with a tremulous but close pressure, which spoke that his heart entered into the salutation. After a number of affectionate inquiries and felicitations, such as friendship, not form, dictated, he seemed to relapse into his former flow of thought, and to resume the chain of ideas my appearance had broken for a moment.

"I was reflecting," said he, "my dear Anthony, upon some observations I made in our last number, and considering whether the sight of objects once dear to the affections, or of scenes where we have passed different happy periods of early life, really occasions most enjoyment or most regret. Renewing our acquaintance with well-known but long separated objects, revives, it is true, the recollection of former pleasures and touches the tenderest feelings of the heart, like the flavour of a delicious beverage will remain upon the palate long after the cup has parted from the lips. But on the other hand, my friend, these same objects are too apt to awaken us to a keener recollection of what *we were*, when they erst delighted us, and to provoke a mortifying and melancholy contrast with what we are at present. They act in a manner as milestones of existence, showing us how far we have travelled in the journey of life—how much of our weary but fascinating pilgrimage is accomplished. I look round me, and my eye fondly recognizes the fields I once sported over, the river in which I once swam, and the orchard I intrepidly robbed in the halcyon days of boyhood. The fields are still green, the river still rolls unaltered and undiminished, and the orchard is still flourishing and fruitful—it is I only am changed. The thoughtless flow of mad-cap spirits that nothing could depress—the elasticity of nerve that enabled me to bound over the field, to stem the stream, and climb the tree—the "sunshine of the breast" that beamed an illusive charm over every object, and created a paradise around me—where are they?— The thievish lapse of years has stolen them away, and left in return nothing but grey hairs, and a repining spirit." My friend Launcelot concluded his harangue with a sigh, and as I saw he was still under the influence of a whole legion of the *blues*, and just on the point of sinking into one of his whimsical, and unreasonable fits of melancholy abstraction, I proposed a walk—he consented, and slipping his left arm in mine, and waving in the other a gold-headed thorn cane, bequeathed him by his uncle John, we slowly rambled along the margin of the river.

Langstaff, though possessing great vivacity of temper, is most woefully subject to these "thick coming fancies;" and I do not know a man whose animal spirits do insult him with more jiltings, and coquetries, and slippery tricks. In these moods he is often visited by a whim-wham which he indulges in common with the Cocklofts. It is that of looking back with regret, conjuring up the phantoms of good old times, and decking them out in imaginary finery, with the spoils of his fancy, like a good lady widow, regretting the loss of the "poor dear man," for whom, while living, she cared not a rush. I have seen him and Pindar, and old Cockloft, amuse themselves over a bottle with their youthful days, until by the time they had become what is termed *merry*, they were the most miserable beings in existence. In a similar humour was Launcelot at present, and I knew the only way was to let him moralize himself out of it.

Our ramble was soon interrupted by the appearance of a personage of no little importance at Cockloft-hall—for, to let my readers into a family secret, friend Christopher is notoriously hen-pecked by an old negro, who has *whitened* on the place, and is his master's almanack and counsellor. My readers, if haply they have sojourned in the country and become conversant in rural manners, must have observed, that there is scarce a little hamlet but has one of these old weather-beaten wiseacres of negroes, who ranks among the great characters of the place. He is always resorted to as an oracle to resolve any question about the weather, fishing, shooting, farming and horse-doctoring; and on such occasions will slouch his remnant of a hat on one side, fold his arms, roll his white eyes and examine the sky, with a look as knowing as Peter Pindar's magpie, when peeping into a marrow-bone. Such a sage curmudgeon is *Old Caesar*, who acts as friend Cockloft's prime minister, or grand vizier, assumes, when abroad, his master's style and title, to wit, *Squire Cockloft*, and is, in effect, absolute lord and ruler of the soil.

As he passed us, he pulled off his hat, with an air of something more than respect,—it partook, I thought, of affection. "There, now, is another memento of the kind I have been noticing," said Launcelot; "Caesar was a bosom friend and chosen playmate of cousin Pindar and myself, when we were boys. Never were we so happy as when stealing away on a holiday to the hall, we ranged about the fields with honest Caesar. He was particularly adroit in making our quail-traps and fishing rods, was always the ring-leader in all the schemes of frolicksome mischief per-petrated by the urchins of the neighbourhood, considered himself on an equality with the best of us, and many a hard battle have I had with him, about a division of the spoils of an orchard, or the title to a bird's nest. Many a summer evening do I remember when, huddled together on the steps of the hall door, Caesar, with his stories of ghosts, goblins, and witches, would put us all in a panick, and people every lane, and church-yard, and solitary wood, with imaginary beings. In process of time, he became the constant attendant and *Man Friday* of cousin Pindar, whenever he went a *sparking* among the rosy country girls of the neighbouring farms; and brought up his rear at every rustick dance, when he would mingle in the sable group that always thronged the door of merriment, and it was enough to put to the rout a host of splenetick imps, to see his mouth gradually dilate from ear to ear, with pride and exultation, at seeing how neatly master Pindar footed it over the floor. Caesar was likewise the chosen confidant and special agent of Pindar in all his love affairs, until, as his evil stars would have it, on being entrusted with the delivery of a poetick billetdoux, to one of his patron's sweethearts, he took an unlucky notion to send it to his own sable dulcinea, who, not being able to read it, took it to her mistress—and so the whole affair was blown; Pindar was univerally roasted, and Caesar discharged forever from his confidence.

"Poor Caesar!—he has now grown old like his young masters; but he still remembers old times, and will, now and then, remind me of them as he lights me to my room, and lingers a little while to bid me a good night—believe me, my dear Evergreen, the honest simple old creature has a warm corner in my heart—I dont see, for my part, why a body may not like a negro, as well as a white man!"

By the time these biographical anecdotes were ended, we had reached the stable, into which we involuntarily strolled, and found Caesar busily employed in rubbing down the horses, an office he would not entrust to any body else; having contracted an affection for every beast in the stable, from their being descendants of the old race of animals, his youthful contemporaries. Caesar was very particular in giving us their pedigrees, together with a panegyrick on the swiftness, bottom, blood, and spirit of their sires. From these he digressed into a variety of anecdotes in which Launcelot bore a conspicuous part, and on which the old negro dwelt with all the garrulity of age. Honest Langstaff stood leaning with his arm over the back of his favorite steed, old *Killdeer,* and I could perceive he listened to Caesar's simple details with that fond attention with which a feeling mind will hang over the narratives of boyish days. His eye sparkled with animation, a glow of youthful fire stole across his pale visage—he nodded with smiling approbation at every sentence—chuckled at every exploit—laughed heartily at the story of his once having smoked out a country singing-school with brimstone and assafoetida—and slipping a piece of money into old Caesar's hand to buy himself a new tobacco-box, he seized me by the arm and hurried out of the stable brimfull of good nature. "Tis a pesilent old rogue for talking, my dear fellow," cried he, "but you must not find fault with him— the creature means well." I knew at the very moment that he made this apology, honest Caesar could not have given him half the satisfaction, had he talked like a Cicero or a Solomon.

Launcelot returned to the house with me in the best possible humour:— the whole family, who in truth love and honour him from their very souls, were delighted to see the sun-beams once more play in his countenance. Every one seemed to vie who should talk the most, tell the longest stories and be most agreeable; and Will Wizard, who had accompanied me in my visit, declared, as he lighted his cygarr, which had gone out forty times in the course of one of his oriental tales—that he had not passed so pleasant an evening since the birth-night ball of the beauteous empress of Hayti.

[The following essay was written by my friend Langstaff, in one of the paroxysms of his splenetick complaint; and, for aught I know, may have been effectual in restoring him to good humour—A mental discharge of the kind has a remarkable tendency toward sweetening the temper—and Launcelot is at this moment one of the best natured men in existence.

A. EVERGREEN.]

ON GREATNESS.

BY LAUNCELOT LANGSTAFF, ESQ.

——'Αχιλλεὸς ωρτο.

THE HERO ROSE.   *Pope.*

We have, more than once in the course of our work, been most jocosely familiar with great personages; and, in truth, treated them with as little ceremony, respect, and consideration, as if they had been our most particular friends. Now, we would not suffer the mortification of having our readers even suspect us of an intimacy of the kind; assuring them we are extremely choice in our intimates, and uncommonly circumspect in avoiding connexion with all doubtful characters, particularly pimps, bailiffs, lottery-brokers, chevaliers of industry, and *great men*. The world in general is pretty well aware of what is to be understood by the former classes of delinquents; but as the latter has never, I believe, been specifically defined, and as we are determined to instruct our readers to the extent of our abilities, and their limited comprehension, it may not be amiss here, to let them know what we understand by a *great man*.

First, therefore, let us (editors and kings are always plural) premise, that there are two kinds of greatness—one conferred by *heaven*—the exalted nobility of the soul—the other, a spurious distinction engendered by the mob, and lavished upon its favourites. The former of these distinctions we have always contemplated with reverence; the latter, we will take this opportunity to strip naked before our unenlightened readers: so that if by chance any of them are held in ignominious thraldom by this base circulation of false coin, they may forthwith emancipate themselves from such inglorious delusion.

It is a fictitious value given to individuals by publick caprice, as bankers give an impression to a worthless slip of paper, thereby gaining it a currency for infinitely more than its intrinsick value. Every nation has its peculiar coin, and peculiar great men; neither of which will, for the most part, pass current out of the country where they are stamped. Your true mob-created great man, is like a note of one of the little New-England banks, and his value depreciates in proportion to the distance from home. In England, a great man is he who has most ribbonds and gew-gaws on his coat, most horses to his carriage, most slaves in his retinue, or most toad-eaters at his table; in France, he who can most dexterously flourish his heels above his head—*Duport* is most incontestably the greatest man in France, when the emperor is absent. The greatest man in China, is he who can trace his ancestry up to the moon; and in this country our great men may generally *hunt down* their pedigree until it burrows into the dirt like a rabbit. To be concise, our great men are those who are most expert at crawling on all-fours, and have the happiest facility in dragging and winding themselves along in the dirt like very reptiles. This may seem a paradox to many of my readers, who, with great good nature be it hinted, are too stupid to look beyond the mere surface of our invaluable writings, and often pass over the knowing allusion, and poignant meaning, that is slily couching beneath. It is for the benefit of such helpless ignorants, who have no other creed but the opinion of the mob, that I shall trace, as far as it is possible to follow him in his progress from insignificance—the rise, progress, and completion of a LITTLE GREAT MAN.

In a *logocracy* (to use the sage Mustapha's phrase) it is not absolutely necessary to the formation of a great man, that he should be either wise or valiant, upright, or honourable. On the contrary, daily experience shows, that these qualities rather impede his preferment; inasmuch as they are prone to render him too inflexibly erect, and are directly at variance with that willowy *suppleness*, which enables a man to wind and twist through all the nooks and turns, and dark winding passages that lead to greatness. The grand requisite for climbing the rugged hill of popularity—the summit of which is the seat of power—is to be useful. And here once more, for the sake of our readers, who are of course not so wise as ourselves, I must explain what we understand by *usefulness.* The horse, in his native state, is wild, swift, impetuous, full of majesty, and of a most generous spirit. It is then the animal is noble, exalted, and *useless.* But entrap him, manacle him, cudgel him, break down his lofty spirit, put the curb into his mouth, the load upon his back, and reduce him into servile obedience to the bridle and the lash, and it is then he becomes *useful.* Your jackass is one of the most *useful* animals in existence. If my readers do not now understand what I mean by usefulness, I give them all up for most absolute *nincoms.*

To rise in this country a man must first *descend*. The aspiring politician, may be compared to that indefatigable insect, called the *Tumbler*; (pronounced by a distinguished personage to be the only industrious animal in Virginia,) which buries itself in filth, and works ignobly in the dirt until it forms a little ball, which it rolls laboriously along, (like Diogenes his tub) sometimes head, sometimes tail foremost, pilfering from every rut and mud hole, and increasing its ball of greatness by the contributions of the kennel. Just so the candidate for greatness—he plunges into that mass of obscenity the *mob*, labours in dirt and oblivion, and makes unto himself the rudiments of a popular name from the admiration and praises of rogues, ignoramuses and blackguards. His name once started, onward he goes, struggling, and puffing, and pushing it before him, collecting new tributes from the dregs and offals of the land, as he proceeds, until having gathered together a mighty mass of popularity, he mounts it in triumph, is hoisted into office, and becomes a *great man*, and a ruler in the land—all this will be clearly illustrated by a sketch of a worthy of the kind, who sprung up under my eye, and was hatched from pollution by the broad rays of popularity, which, like the sun, can "breed maggots in a dead dog."

TIMOTHY DABBLE was a young man of very promising talents—for he wrote a fair hand, and had thrice won the silver medal at a country academy—he was also an orator, for he talked with emphatick volubility, and could argue a full hour, without taking either side, or advancing a single opinion—he had still farther requisites for eloquence—for he made very handsome gestures, had dimples in his cheeks when he smiled, and enunciated most harmoniously through his nose. In short, nature had certainly marked him out for a great man; for though he was not tall, yet he added at least half an inch to his stature by elevating his head, and assumed an amazing expression of dignity by turning up his nose and curling his nostrils, in a style of conscious superiority. Convinced by these unequivocal appearances, Dabble's friends in full caucus, one and all, declared that he was undoubtedly born to be a great man, and it would be his own fault if he were not one. Dabble was tickled with an opinion which coincided so happily with his own—for vanity, in a confidential whisper, had given him the like intimation—and he reverenced the judgment of his friends, because they thought so highly of himself—accordingly he sat out with a determination to become a great man, and to start in the scrub-race for honour and renown. How to attain the desired prizes was however the question. He knew by a kind of instinctive feeling, which seems peculiar to grovelling minds, that honour, and its better part—profit, would never seek *him* out; that they would never knock at his door and crave admittance, but must be courted, and toiled after, and *earned*. He therefore strutted forth into the highways, the market-places, and the assemblies of the people—ranted like a true cockerel orator about virtue, and patriotism, and liberty, and equality, and *himself*. Full many a political wind-mill did he battle with; and full many a time did he talk himself out of breath and his hearers out of their patience. But Dabble found to his vast astonishment, that there was not a notorious political pimp at a ward meeting but could out-talk him; and what was still more mortifying, there was not a notorious political pimp, but was more noticed and caressed than himself. The reason was simple enough, while he harangued about *principles*, the others ranted about *men*; where he reprobated a political error, they blasted a political character—they were, consequently, the most *useful*: for the great object of our political disputes is, not who shall have the *honour* of emancipating the community from the leading-strings of delusion, but who shall have the *profit* of holding the strings, and leading the community by the nose.

Dabble was likewise very loud in his professions of integrity, incorruptibility, and disinterestedness, words which, from being filtered and refined through newspapers and election handbills, have lost their original signification, and in the political dictionary, are synonymous with empty pockets, itching palms, and interested ambition. He, in addition to all this, declared that he would support none but honest men—but unluckily as but few of these offered themselves to be supported, Dabble's services were seldom required. He pledged himself never to engage in party schemes or party politicks, but to stand up solely for the broad interests of his country—so he stood alone, and what is the same thing, he stood still; for, in this country, he who does not side with either party, is like a body in a *vacuum* between two planets, and must for ever remain motionless.

Dabble was immeasurably surprised that a man so honest, so disinterested, and so sagacious withal—and one too, who had the good of his country so much at heart, should thus remain unnoticed and unapplauded. A little worldly advice whispered in his ear by a shrewd old politician, at once explained the whole mystery. "He who would become great," said he, "must serve an apprenticeship to greatness, and rise by regular gradation, like the master of a vessel, who commences by being scrub and cabin-boy. He must fag in the train of great men, echo all their sentiments, become their toad-eater and parasite— laugh at all their jokes, and above all, endeavour to make *them* laugh; if you only now and then make a great man laugh your fortune is made. Look but about you, youngster, and you will not see a single little great man of the day, but has his miserable herd of retainers, who yelp at his heels, come at his whistle, worry whoever he points his finger at, and think themselves fully rewarded by sometimes snapping up a crumb that falls from the great man's table. Talk of patriotism and virtue, and incorruptibility!—tut, man!—they are the very qualities that scare munificence, and keep patronage at a distance. You might as well attempt to entice crows with red rags and gunpowder. Lay all these scarecrow virtues aside, and let this be your maxim, that a candidate for political eminence is like a dried herring—he never becomes *luminous* until he is *corrupt.*"

Dabble caught with hungry avidity these congenial doctrines, and turned into his pre-destined channel of action with the force and rapidity of a stream which has for awhile been restrained from its natural course. He became what nature had fitted him to be—his tone softened down from arrogant self-sufficiency, to the whine of fawning solicitation. He mingled in the *caucuses* of the sovereign people, adapted his dress to a similitude of dirty raggedness, argued most logically with those who were of his own opinion, and slandered with all the malice of impotence, exalted characters whose orbit he despaired ever to approach—just as that scoundred midnight thief, the owl, hoots at the blessed light of the sun, whose glorious lustre he dares never contemplate. He likewise applied himself to discharging faithfully the honourable duties of a partizan—he poached about for private slanders, and ribald anecdotes—he folded handbills—he even wrote one or two himself, which he carried about in his pocket and read to every body—he became a secretary at ward-meetings, set his hand to divers resolutions of patriotick import, and even once went so far as to make a speech, in which he proved that patriotism was a virtue—the *reigning bashaw* a great man—that this was a free country, and he himself an arrant and incontestible buzzard!

Dabble was now very frequent and devout in his visits to those temple of politicks, popularity and smoke, the ward porter-houses; those true dens of equality, where all ranks, ages, and talents, are brought down to the dead level of rude familiarity. 'Twas here his talents expanded, and his genius swelled up into its proper size, like the loathsome toad, which shrinking from balmy airs, and jocund sunshine, finds his congenial home in caves and dungeons, and there nourishes his venom, and bloats his deformity. 'Twas here he revelled with the swinish multitude in their debauches on patriotism and porter; and it became an even chance whether Dabble would turn out a great man, or a great drunkard. But Dabble in all this kept steadily in his eye the only deity he ever worshipped—his interest. Having by this familiarity ingratiated himself with the mob, he became wonderfully potent and industrious at elections, knew all the dens and cellars of profligacy and intemperance, brought more negroes to the polls, and knew to a greater certainty where votes could be bought for beer, than any of his contemporaries. His exertions in the cause, his persevering industry, his degrading compliance, his unresisting humility, his steadfast dependence, at length caught the attention of one of the leaders of the party, who was pleased to observe that Dabble was a very *useful* fellow, who would *go all lengths*. From that moment his fortune was made—he was hand and glove with orators and slang-whangers, basked in the sunshine of great mens' smiles, and had the honour, sundry times, of shaking hands with dignitaries, and drinking out of the same pot with them at a porter-house!!

I will not fatigue myself with tracing this catterpillar in his slimy progress from worm to butterfly: suffice it to say that Dabble bowed and bowed, and fawned, and sneaked, and smirked, and libelled, until one would have thought perseverence itself would have settled down into despair. There was no knowing how long he might have lingered at a distance from his hopes, had he not luckily got *tarred and feathered* for some of his electioneering manoeuvres—this was the making of him!— Let not my readers stare—tarring and feathering here is equal to pillory and cropped ears in England, and either of these kinds of martyrdom will ensure a *patriot* the sympathy and support of his faction. His partizans (for even he had his partizans) took his case into considera-tion—he had been kicked and cuffed, and disgraced, and dishonoured in the cause—he had licked the dust at the feet of the mob——he was a faithful drudge, slow to anger, of invincible patience, of incessant assiduity—a thorough going tool, who could be curbed, and spurred, and directed at pleasure;—in short he had all the important qualifications for *a little great man*, and he was accordingly ushered into office amid the acclamations of the party. The leading men complimented his useful-ness, the multitude his republican simplicity, and the slang-whangers vouched for his patriotism. Since his elevation he has discovered indubitable signs of having been destined for a great man. His nose has acquired an additional elevation of several degrees, so that now he appears to have bidden adieu to this world, and to have set his thoughts altogether *on things above;* and he has swelled and inflated himself to such a degree that his friends are under apprehensions that he will one day or other explode and blow up like a *torpedo.*

SALMAGUNDI NO. XVI

NO. XVI]   *Thursday, October* 15, 1807.

STYLE AT BALLSTON.
BY WILLIAM WIZARD, ESQ.

Notwithstanding Evergreen has never been abroad, nor had his understanding enlightened, or his views enlarged by that marvellous sharpener
of the wits, a salt-water voyage; yet he is tolerably shrewd, and correct,
in the limited sphere of his observations; and now and then astounds
me with a right pithy remark, which would do no discredit even to a
man who had made the grand tour.

In several late conversations at Cockloft-Hall, he has amused us
exceedingly by detailing sundry particulars concerning that notorious
slaughter-house of time, Ballston Springs, where he spent a considerable part of the last summer. The following is a summary of his
observations.

Pleasure has passed through a variety of significations at Ballston.
It originally meant nothing more than a relief from pain and sickness;
and the patient who had journeyed many a weary mile to the Springs,
with a heavy heart, and emaciated form, called it pleasure when he threw
by his crutches, and danced away from them with renovated spirits and
limbs jocund with vigour. In process of time pleasure underwent a
refinement and appeared in the likeness of a sober unceremonious
country-dance, to the flute of an amateur, or the three-stringed fiddle
of an itinerant country musician. Still every thing bespoke that happy
holiday which the spirits ever enjoy, when emancipated from the
shackles of formality, ceremony and modern politeness: things went on
cheerily, and Ballston was pronounced a charming hum-drum careless
place of resort, where every one was at his ease, and might follow
unmolested the bent of his humour—provided his wife was not there—
when, lo! all of a sudden *Style* made its baneful appearance in the
semblance of a gig and tandem, a pair of leather breeches, a liveried
footman and a cockney!—since that fatal era pleasure has taken an
entire new signification, and at present means nothing but STYLE.

The worthy, fashionable, dashing, good-for-nothing people of every
state, who had rather suffer the martyrdom of a crowd, than endure the
monotony of their own homes, and the stupid company of their own
thoughts, flock to the Springs—not to enjoy the pleasures of society,
or benefit by the qualities of the waters, but to exhibit their equipages
and wardrobes, and to excite the admiration, or what is much more

satisfactory, the *envy* of their fashionable competitors. This of course awakens a spirit of noble emulation between the eastern, middle and southern states, and every lady hereupon finding herself charged in a manner with the whole weight of her country's dignity and *style*, dresses, and dashes, and sparkles without mercy, at her competitors from other parts of the union. This kind of rivalship naturally requires a vast deal of preparation and prodigious quantities of supplies. A sober citizen's wife will break half a dozen milliners' shops, and sometimes starve her family a whole season, to enable herself to make the Springs campaign in *style*—she repairs to the seat of war with a mighty force of trunks and bandboxes, like so many ammunition chests, filled with caps, hats, gowns, ribbons, shawls, and all the various artillery of fashionable warfare. The lady of a southern planter will lay out the whole annual produce of a rice plantation in silver and gold muslins, lace veils, and new liveries, carry a hogshead of tobacco on her head, and trail a bale of sea-island cotton at her heels—while a lady of Boston or Salem will wrap herself up in the nett proceeds of a cargo of whale oil, and tie on her hat with a quintal of codfish.

The planters' ladies, however, have generally the advantage in this contest; for, as it is an incontestable fact, that whoever comes from the West or East Indies, or Georgia, or the Carolinas, or in fact any warm climate, is immensely rich, it cannot be expected that a simple cit of the north can cope with them in *style*. The planter, therefore, who drives four horses abroad, and a thousand negroes at home, and who flourishes up to the Springs followed by half a score of black-a-moors in gorgeous liveries, is unquestionably superiour to the northern merchant, who plods on in a carriage and pair; which being nothing more than is quite *necessary*, has no claim whatever to *style*. He, however, has his consolation in feeling superiour to the honest cit, who dashes about in a simple gig—he in return sneers at the country squire, who jogs along with his scrubby long-eared poney and saddle bags; and the squire, by way of taking satisfaction, would make no scruple to run over the unobtrusive pedestrian, were it not that the last, being the most independent of the whole, might chance to break his head by way of retort.

The great misfortune is, that this *style* is supported at such an expense as sometimes to encroach on the rights and privileges of the pocket, and occasion very awkward embarrassments to the tyro of fashion. Among a number of instances, Evergreen mentions the fate of a dashing blade from the south, who made his *entré* with a tandem and two out-riders, by the aid of which he attracted the attention of all the ladies, and caused a coolness between several young couples, who, it was thought before his arrival, had a considerable kindness for each other.

In the course of a fortnight his tandem disappeared!—the class of good folk who seem to have nothing to do in this world but pry into other people's affairs—began to stare!—in a little time longer an outrider was missing—this increased the alarm, and it was consequently whispered that he had eaten the horses, and drank the negro—(N. B. Southern gentlemen are very apt to do this on an emergency.)—Serious apprehensions were entertained about the fate of the remaining servant, which were soon verified, by his actually vanishing—and in "one little month" the dashing carolinian modestly took his departure in the *Stage-Coach!*—universally regretted by the friends who had generously released him from his cumbrous load of *style*.

Evergreen, in the course of his detail, gave very melancholy accounts of an alarming famine which raged with great violence at the Springs. Whether this was owing to the incredible appetites of the company, or the scarcity which prevailed at the inns, he did not seem inclined to say, but he declares, that he was for several days in imminent danger of starvation, owing to his being a little too dilatory in his attendance at the dinner-table. He relates a number of "moving accidents," which befel many of the polite company in their zeal to get a good seat at dinner, on which occasion a kind of scrub-race always took place, wherein a vast deal of jockeying and unfair play was shown, and a variety of squabbles and unseemly altercations occured. But when arrived at the scene of action, it was truly an awful sight to behold the confusion, and to hear the tumultuous uproar of voices crying out, some for one thing, and some for another, to the tuneful accompanyment of knives and forks, rattling with all the energy of hungry impatience.—The feast of the Centaurs and the Lapithae was nothing when compared with a dinner at the *Great House*. At one time, an old gentleman, whose natural irascibility was a little sharpened by the gout, had scalded his throat, by gobbling down a bowl of hot soup in a vast hurry, in order to secure the first fruits of a roasted partridge, before it was snapped up by some hungry rival; when, just as he was whetting his knive and fork preparatory for a descent on the promised land, he had the mortification to see it transferred, bodily, to the plate of a squeamish little damsel, who was taking the waters for debility and loss of appetite. This was too much for the patience of old Crusty; he longed his fork into the partridge, whipt it into his dish, and cutting off a wing of it,—"There, miss, there's more than you can eat—Oons! what should such a little chalky-faced puppet as you do with a whole partridge!"—At another time a mighty sweet disposed old dowager, who loomed most magnificently at the table, had a sauce-boat launched upon the capacious lap of a silver-sprigged muslin gown, by the manoeuvring of a little politick frenchman, who was dexterously attempting to make a lodgement under the covered way of a chicken-pie—Human nature could not bear it!—the lady bounced round, and, with one box on the ear, drove the luckless wight to utter annihilation.

But these little cross accidents are amply compensated by the great variety of amusements which abounds at this charming resort of beauty and fashion. In the morning the company, each like a jolly bacchanalian, with glass in hand, sally forth to the Spring; where the gentlemen, who wish to make themselves agreeable, have an opportunity of *dipping* themselves into the good opinion of the ladies: and it is truly delectable to see with what grace and adroitness they perform this ingratiating feat. Anthony says that it is peculiarly amazing to behold the quantity of water the ladies drink on this occasion, for the purpose of getting an appetite for breakfast. He assures me he has been present when a young lady of unparalleled delicacy, tossed off in the space of a minute or two, one and twenty tumblers and a wine-glass full. On my asking Anthony whether the solicitude of the bye-standers was not greatly awakened as to what might be the *effects* of this *debauch*; he replied, that the ladies at Ballston had become such great sticklers for the doctrine of *evaporation*, that no gentleman ever ventured to remonstrate against this excessive drinking, for fear of bringing his philosophy into contempt. The most notorious water-drinkers in particular, were continually holding forth on the surprising aptitude with which the Ballston waters *evaporated*; and several gentlemen, who had the hardihood to question this female philosophy, were held in high displeasure.

After breakfast, every one chooses his amusement—some take a ride into the pine woods, and enjoy the varied and romantick scenery of burnt trees, post and rail fences, pine flats, potatoe patches, and log huts—others scramble up the surrounding sand hills, that look like the abodes of a gigantick race of ants—take a peep at other sand hills beyond them—and then—come down again; others who are romantick (and sundry young ladies insist upon being so whenever they visit the Springs, or go any where into the country) stroll along the borders of a little swampy brook that drags itself along like an alexandrine, and that, so lazily, as not to make a single murmur—watching the little tadpoles, as they frolick right flippantly in the muddy stream, and listening to the inspiring melody of the harmonious frogs that croak upon its borders. Some play at billiards, some play the fiddle, and some— play the fool—the latter being the most prevalent amusement at Ballston.

These, together with abundance of dancing, and a prodigious deal of sleeping of afternoons, make up the variety of pleasures at the Springs—a delicious life of alternate lassitude and fatigue, of laborious dissipation, and listless idleness, of sleepless nights, and days spent in that dozing insensibility which ever succeeds them. Now and then, indeed, the influenza, the fever-and-ague, or some such pale-faced intruder may happen to throw a momentary damp on the general felicity; but on the whole, Evergreen declares that Ballston wants only six things; to wit, good air, good wine, good living, good beds, good company, and good humour, to be the most enchanting place in the world—excepting Botany-bay, Musquito Cove, Dismal Swamp, and the Black-hole at Calcutta.

The following letter from the sage Mustapha, has cost us more trouble to decypher and render into tolerable english, than any hitherto published. It was full of blots and erasures, particularly the latter part, which we have no doubt was penned in a moment of great wrath and indignation. Mustapha has often a rambling mode of writing, and his thoughts take such unaccountable turns that it is difficult to tell one moment where he will lead you the next. This is particularly obvious in the commencement of his letters, which seldom bear much analogy to the subsequent parts—he sets off with a flourish, like a dramatick hero—assumes an air of great pomposity, and struts up to his subject, mounted most loftily *on stilts.*

L. LANGSTAFF.

FROM MUSTAPHA RUB-A-DUB KELI KHAN,
To Asem Hacchem, principal slave-driver to
his highness the Bashaw of Tripoli.

Among the variety of principles by which mankind are actuated, there is one, my dear Asem, which I scarcely know whether to consider as springing from grandeur and nobility of mind, or from a refined species of vanity and egotism. It is that singular, although almost universal, desire of living in the memory of posterity; of occupying a share of the world's attention, when we shall long since have ceased to be susceptible either of its praise or censure. Most of the passions of the mind are bounded by the grave—sometimes, indeed, an anxious hope or trembling fear, will venture beyond the clouds and darkness that rest upon our mortal horizon, and expatiate in boundless futurity: but it is only this active love of fame which steadily contemplates its fruition, in the applause or gratitude of future ages. Indignant at the narrow limits which circumscribe existence, ambition is forever struggling to soar beyond them—to triumph over space and time, and to bear *a name,* at least, above the inevitable oblivion in which every thing else that concerns us must be involved. It is this, my friend, which prompts the patriot to his most heroick achievements; which inspires the sublimest strains of the poet, and breathes ethereal fire into the productions of the painter and the statuary.

For this the monarch rears the lofty column; the laurelled conqueror claims the triumphal arch, while the obscure individual, who moved in an humbler sphere, asks but a plain and simple stone to mark his grave, and bear to the next generation this important truth, that he was born, died—and was buried. It was this passion which once erected the vast numidian piles, whose ruins we have so often regarded with wonder, as the shades of evening—fit emblems of oblivion!—gradually stole over and enveloped them in darkness—It was this which gave being to those sublime monuments of saracen magnificence, which nod in mouldering desolation as the blast sweeps over our deserted plains.—How futile are all our efforts to evade the obliterating hand of time! As I traversed the dreary wastes of Egypt, on my journey to Grand Cairo, I stopped my camel for a while, and contemplated, in awful admiration the stupendous pyramids—An appalling silence prevailed around; such as reigns in the wilderness when the tempest is hushed, and the beasts of prey have retired to their dens. The myriads that had once been employed in rearing these lofty mementoes of human vanity, whose busy hum once enlivened the solitude of the desart—had all been swept from the earth by the irresistible arm of death—all were mingled with their native dust—all were forgotten! Even the mighty names which these sepulchres were designed to perpetuate, had long since faded from remembrance; history and tradition afforded but vague conjectures, and the pyramids imparted a humiliating lesson to the candidate for immortality.—Alas! alas! said I to myself, how mutable are the foundations on which our proudest hopes of future fame are reposed. He who imagines he has secured to himself the meed of deathless renown, indulges in deluding visions, which only bespeak the vanity of the dreamer. The storied obelisk—the triumphal arch—the swelling dome shall crumble into dust, and the names they would preserve from oblivion shall often pass away, before their own duration is accomplished.

Yet this passion for fame, however ridiculous in the eye of the philosopher, deserves respect and consideration from having been the source of so many illustrious actions; and, hence, it has been the practice in all enlightened governments to perpetuate by monuments, the memory of great men, as a testimony of respect for the illustrious dead, and to awaken in the bosoms of posterity an emulation to merit the same honourable distinction. The people of the american logocracy, who pride themselves upon improving on every precept or example of antient or modern governments, have discovered a new mode of exciting this love of glory—a mode by which they do honour to their great men, even in their life time!

Thou must have observed by this time, that they manage every thing in a manner peculiar to themselves; and doubtless in the best possible

SALMAGUNDI

manner, seeing they have denominated themselves "the most enlightened people under the sun." Thou wilt therefore, perhaps, be curious to know how they contrive to honour the name of a living patriot, and what unheard of monument they erect, in memory of his achievements—By the fiery beard of the mighty Barbarossa, but I can scarcely preserve the sobriety of a true disciple of Mahomet while I tell thee!—Wilt thou not smile, oh, mussulman of invincible gravity, to learn that they honour their great men by *eating*, and that the only trophy erected to their exploits, is a *publick dinner!* But trust me, Asem, even in this measure whimsical as it may seem, the philosophick and considerate spirit of this people is admirably displayed. Wisely concluding that when the hero is dead, he becomes insensible to the voice of fame, the song of adulation, or the splendid trophy, they have determined that he shall enjoy his quantum of celebrity while living, and revel in the full enjoyment of a nine days immortality. The barbarous nations of antiquity immolated human victims to the memory of their lamented dead, but the enlightened americans offer up whole hecatombs of geese and calves, and oceans of wine in honour of the illustrious living; and the patriot has the felicity of hearing from every quarter the vast exploits in gluttony and revelling that have been celebrated to the glory of his name.

No sooner does a citizen signalize himself in a conspicuous manner in the service of his country, than all the gormandizers assemble and discharge the national debt of gratitude—by giving him a dinner—not that he really receives all the luxuries provided on this occasion—no my friend, it is ten chances to one that the great man does not taste a morsel from the table, and is, perhaps, five hundred miles distant; and, to let thee into a melancholy fact, a patriot, under this *economick* government, may be often in want of a dinner, while dozens are devoured in his praise. Neither are these repasts spread out for the hungry and necessitous, who might otherwise be filled with food and gladness, and inspired to shout forth the illustrious name, which had been the means of their enjoyment—far from this, Asem—it is the rich only who indulge in the banquet—those who pay for the dainties are alone privileged to enjoy them; so that, while opening their purses in honour of the patriot, they, at the same time, fulfill a great maxim, which in this country comprehends all the rules of prudence, and all the duties a man owes to *himself*—namely, *getting the worth of their money.*

In process of time this mode of testifying publick applause, has been found so marvellously agreeable, that they extend it to events as well as characters, and eat in triumph at the news of a treaty—at the anniversary of any grand national era, or at the gaining that splendid victory of the tongue—an *election*.—Nay, so far do they carry it, that certain days are set apart when the guzzlers, the gormandizers, and the

wine bibbers meet together to celebrate a *grand indigestion*, in memory
of some great event; and every man in the zeal of patriotism gets
devoutly drunk—"as the act directs." Then, my friend, mayest thou
behold the sublime spectacle of love of country, elevating itself from a
sentiment into an *appetite*, whetted to the quick with the cheering prospect of tables loaded with the fat things of the land. On this occasion
every man is anxious to fall to work, cram himself in honour of *the day*,
and risk a surfeit in the glorious cause. Some, I have been told, actually
fast for four and twenty hours preceding, that they may be enabled to
do greater honour to the feast; and certainly, if eating and drinking are
patriotick rites, he who eats and drinks most and proves himself the
greatest glutton, is, undoubtedly, the most distinguished patriot. Such,
at any rate, seems to be the opinion here; and they act up to it so
rigidly, that by the time it is dark, every kennel in the neighbourhood
teems with illustrious members of the sovereign people, wallowing in
their congenial element of mud and mire.

   These patriotick feasts, or rather national monuments, are patronized
and promoted by certain inferior *Cadis*, called ALDERMEN, who are
commonly complimented with their direction. These dignitaries, as far
as I can learn, are generally appointed on account of their great
talents for eating, a qualification peculiarly necessary in the discharge
of their official duties. They hold frequent meetings at taverns and
hotels, where they enter into solemn consultation for the benefit of
lobsters and turtles—establish wholesome regulations for the safety
and preservation of fish and wild-fowl—appoint the seasons most proper
for eating oysters—inquire into the economy of taverns, the characters
of publicans, and the abilities of their cooks, and discuss, most learnedly,
the merits of a bowl of soup, a chicken-pie, or a haunch of venison: in
a word, the alderman has absolute control in all matters of eating, and
superintends the whole police—of the belly. Having in the prosecution
of their important office, signalized themselves at so many public festi-
vals; having gorged so often on patriotism and pudding, and entombed so
many great names in their extensive maws, thou wilt easily conceive
that they wax portly apace, that they fatten on the fame of mighty
men, and that their rotundity, like the rivers, the lakes and the mountains
of their country, must be *on a great scale!* Even so, my friend; and when
I sometimes see a portly alderman, puffing along, and swelling as if
he had the world under his waistcoat, I can not help looking upon him
as a walking monument, and am often ready to exclaim—"Tell me, thou
majestick mortal, thou breathing catacomb!—to what illustrious character, what mighty event, does that capacious carcass of thine bear
testimony?"

   But though the enlightened citizens of this logocracy *eat* in honour of their friends, yet they *drink* destruction to their enemies.—Yea, Asem, woe unto those who are doomed to undergo the publick vengeance, at a publick dinner. No sooner are the viands removed, than they prepare for merciless and exterminating hostilities. They drink the intoxicating juice of the grape, out of little glass cups, and over each draught pronounce a short sentence or prayer—not such a prayer as thy virtuous heart would dictate, thy pious lips give utterance to, my good Asem— not a tribute of thanks to all bountiful Allah, nor a humble supplication for his blessing on the draught—no, my friend, it is merely a *toast,* that is to say, a fulsome tribute of flattery to their demagogues—a laboured sally of affected sentiment or national egotism; or, what is more despicable, a malediction on their enemies, an empty threat of vengeance, or a petition for their destruction; for toasts thou must know are another kind of missive weapon in a logocracy, and are levelled from afar, like the annoying arrows of the tartars.

Oh Asem! couldst thou but witness one of these patriotick, these monumental dinners—how furiously the flame of patriotism blazes forth—how suddenly they vanquish armies, subjugate whole countries, and exterminate nations in a bumper, thou wouldst more than ever admire the force of that omnipotent weapon the tongue. At these moments every coward becomes a hero, every raggamuffin an invincible warrior; and the most zealous votaries of peace and quiet, forget for a while their cherished maxims and join in the furious attack. Toast succeeds toast—kings, emperors, bashaws, are like chaff before the tempest; the inspired patriot vanquishes fleets with a single gun-boat, and swallows down navies at a draught, until overpowered with victory and wine, he sinks upon the field of battle—dead drunk in his country's cause—Sword of the puissant Khalid! what a display of valour is here!—the sons of Africk are hardy, brave and enterprising; but they can achieve nothing like this.

Happy would it be if this mania for *toasting,* extended no farther than to the expression of national resentment. Though we might smile at the impotent vapouring and windy hyperbole, by which it is distinguished, yet we would excuse it as the unguarded overflowings of a heart, glowing with national injuries, and indignant at the insults offered to its country. But alas, my friend, private resentment, individual hatred, and the illiberal *spirit of party,* are let loose on these festive occasions. Even *the names of individuals,* of unoffending fellow-citizens, are sometimes dragged forth, to undergo the slanders and execrations of a distempered herd of revellers.*—Head of Mahomet!—how vindictive,

NOTE, BY WILLIAM WIZARD, ESQ.
*It would seem that in this sentence, the sage Mustapha had reference to a *patriotick* dinner, celebrated last fourth of July, by some *gentlemen* of Baltimore,

how insatiably vindictive must be that spirit, which can drug the mantling bowl with gall and bitterness, and indulge an angry passion in the moment of rejoicing!—"Wine," say their poets, "is like sunshine to the heart, which under its generous influence expands with good will, and becomes the very temple of philanthropy."—Strange, that in a temple consecrated to such a divinity, there should remain a secret corner, polluted by the lurkings of malice and revenge—strange, that in the full flow of social enjoyment, these votaries of pleasure can turn aside to call down curses on the head of a fellow-creature. Despicable souls! ye are unworthy of being citizens of this "most enlightened country under the sun"—rather herd with the murderous savages who prowl the mountains of Tibesti; who stain their midnight orgies with the blood of the innocent wanderer, and drink their infernal potations from the sculls of the victims they have massacred.

And yet trust me, Asem, this spirit of vindictive cowardice is not owing to any inherent depravity of soul, for, on other occasions, I have had ample proof that this nation is mild and merciful, brave and magnanimous—neither is it owing to any defect in their political or religious precepts. The principles inculcated by their rulers, on all occasions, breathe a spirit of universal philanthropy; and as to their religion, much as I am devoted to the Koran of our divine prophet, still I cannot but acknowledge with admiration the mild forbearance, the amiable benevolence, the sublime morality bequeathed them by the founder of their faith. Thou rememberest the doctrines of the mild Nazarine, who preached peace and good will to all mankind; who, when he was reviled, reviled not again; who blessed those who cursed him, and prayed for those who despightfully used and persecuted him! what then can give rise to this uncharitable, this inhuman custom among the disciples of a master, so gentle and forgiving?—It is that fiend POLITICKS, Asem— that baneful fiend, which bewildereth every brain, and poisons every social feeling; which intrudes itself at the festive banquet, and like the detestable harpy, pollutes the very viands of the table; which contaminates the refreshing draught while it is inhaled; which prompts the cowardly assassin to launch his poisoned arrows from behind the social board; and which renders the bottle, that boasted promoter of good

---

when they righteously drank perdition to an unoffending individual, and really thought "they had done the state some service." This amiable custom of "eating and drinking damnation" *to others*, is not confined to any party:—for a month or two after the fourth of July, the different newspapers file off their columns of *patriotick* toasts against each other, and take a pride in showing how brilliantly their partizans can blackguard publick characters in their cups—"they do but jest—poison in jest," as Hamlet says.

fellowship and hilarity, an infernal engine, charged with direful combustion!

Oh Asem! Asem! how does my heart sicken when I contemplate these cowardly barbarites—let me, therefore, if possible, withdraw my attention from them forever. My feelings have borne me from my subject; and from the monuments of antient greatness, I have wandered to those of modern degradation. My warmest wishes remain with thee, thou most illustrious of slave-drivers; mayest thou ever be sensible of the mercies of our great prophet, who, in compassion to human imbecility, has prohibited his disciples from the use of the deluding beverage of the grape—that enemy to reason—that promoter of defamation—that auxiliary of POLITICKS.

ever thine,

MUSTAPHA.

SALMAGUNDI NO. XVII

NO. XVII]   *Wednesday, November 11, 1807.*

AUTUMNAL REFLECTIONS.

BY LAUNCELOT LANGSTAFF, ESQ.

When a man is quietly journeying downwards into the valley of the shadow of departed youth, and begins to contemplate in a shortened perspective the end of his pilgrimage, he becomes more solicitous than ever that the remainder of his wayfaring should be smooth and pleasant, and the evening of his life, like the evening of a summer's day, fade away in mild uninterrupted serenity. If haply his heart has escaped uninjured through the dangers of a seductive world, it may then administer to the purest of his felicities, and its chords vibrate more musically for the trials they have sustained—like the viol, which yields a melody sweet in proportion to its age.

To a mind thus temperately harmonized, thus matured and mellowed by a long lapse of years, there is something truly congenial in the quiet enjoyment of our early autumn, amid the tranquillities of the country. There is a sober and chastened air of gaiety diffused over the face of nature, peculiarly interesting to an old man; and when he views the surrounding landscape withering under his eye, it seems as if he and nature were taking a last farewel of each other, and parting with a melancholy smile; like a couple of old friends, who having sported away the spring and summer of life together, part at the approach of winter, with a kind of prophetick fear that they are never to meet again.

It is either my good fortune or mishap, to be keenly susceptible to the influence of the atmosphere, and I can feel in the morning, before I open my window, whether the wind is easterly. It will not, therefore, I presume, be considered an extravagant instance of vain-glory when I assert, that there are few men who can discriminate more accurately in the different varieties of damps, fogs, scotch-mists, and north-east storms, than myself. To the great discredit of my philosophy I confess, I seldom fail to anathematize and excommunicate the weather, when it sports too rudely with my sensitive system; but then I always endeavour to atone therefor, by eulogizing it when deserving of approbation. And as most of my readers—simple folk!—make but one distinction, to wit, rain and sunshine—living in most honest ignorance of the various nice shades which distinguish one fine day from another, I take the trouble, from time to time, of letting them into some of the secrets of nature—so will they be the better enabled to enjoy her beauties, with the zest of connoisseurs, and derive at least as much information from my pages, as from the weather-wise lore of the almanack.

Much of my recreation, since I retreated to the Hall, has consisted in making little excursions through the neighbourhood which abounds in the variety of wild, romantick, and luxuriant landscape, that generally characterizes the scenery in the vicinity of our rivers. There is not an eminence within a circuit of many miles but commands an extensive range of diversified and enchanting prospect.

Often have I rambled to the summit of some favourite hill, and thence, with feelings sweetly tranquil as the lucid expanse of the heavens that canopied me, have noted the slow and almost imperceptible changes that mark the waning year. There are many features peculiar to our autumn, and which give it an individual character. The "green and yellow melancholy" that first steals over the landscape—the mild and steady serenity of the weather, and the transparent purity of the atmosphere speak not merely to the senses, but the heart—it is the season of liberal emotions. To this succeeds a fantastick gaiety, a motley dress which the woods assume, where green and yellow, orange, purple, crimson and scarlet, are whimsically blendid together, like the hues in Joseph's coat of many colours.—A sickly splendour this!—like the wild and broken-hearted gaiety that sometimes precedes dissolution— or that childish sportiveness of superannuated age, proceeding, not from a vigorous flow of animal spirits, but from the decay and imbecility of the mind. We might, perhaps, be deceived by this gaudy garb of nature, were it not for the rustling of the falling leaf, which, breaking on the stillness of the scene, seems to announce in prophetick whispers the dreary winter that is approaching. When I have sometimes seen a thrifty young oak, changing its hue of sturdy vigour for a bright, but transient, glow of red it has recalled to my mind the treacherous bloom that once mantled the cheek of a friend who is now no more; and which, while it seemed to promise a long life of jocund spirits, was the sure precursor of premature decay. In a little while, and this ostentatious foliage disappears; the close of autumn leaves but one wide expanse of dusky brown, save where some rivulet steals along, bordered with little strips of green grass—the woodland echoes no more to the carols of the feathered tribes that sported in the leafy covert, and its solitude and silence is uninterrupted, except by the plaintive whistle of the quail, the barking of the squirrel, or the still more melancholy wintry wind, which rushing and swelling through the hollows of the mountains, sighs through the leafless branches of the grove, and seems to mourn the desolation of the year.

To one who, like myself, is fond of drawing comparisons between the different divisions of life, and those of the seasons, there will appear a striking analogy which connects the feelings of the aged with the decline of the year. Often as I contemplate the mild, uniform, and genial lustre with which the sun cheers and invigorates us in the month of October, and the almost imperceptible haze which, without obscuring, tempers all the asperities of the landscape, and gives to every object a character of stillness and repose, I cannot help comparing it with that portion of existence, when the spring of youthful hope, and the summer of the passions having gone by, reason assumes an undisputed sway, and lights us on with bright, but undazzling lustre adown the hill of life. There is a full and mature luxuriance in the fields that fills the bosom with generous and disinterested content. It is not the thoughtless extravagance of spring, prodigal only in blossoms, nor the languid voluptuousness of summer, feverish in its enjoyments, and teeming only with immature abundance—it is that certain fruition of the labours of the past—that prospect of comfortable realities, which those will be sure to enjoy who have improved the bounteous smiles of heaven, nor wasted away their spring and summer in empty trifling or criminal indulgence.

Cousin Pindar, who is my constant companion in these expeditions, and who still possesses much of the fire and energy of youthful sentiment, and a buxom hilarity of the spirits, often, indeed, draws me from these half-melancholy reveries, and makes me feel young again by the enthusiasm with which he contemplates, and the animation with which he eulogizes the beauties of nature displayed before him. His enthusiastick disposition never allows him to enjoy things by halves, and his feelings are continually breaking out in notes of admiration and ejaculations that sober reason might perhaps deem extravagant:—But for my part, when I see a hale, hearty old man, who has jostled through the rough path of the world, without having worn away the fine edge of his feelings, or blunted his sensibility to natural and moral beauty, I compare him to the evergreen of the forest, whose colours, instead of fading at the approach of winter, seem to assume additional lustre, when contrasted with the surrounding desolation—such a man is my friend Pindar—yet sometimes, and particularly at the approach of evening, even he will fall in with my humour; but he soon recovers his natural tone of spirits, and, mounting on the elasticity of his mind, like Ganymede on the eagle's wing, he soars to the ethereal regions of sunshine and fancy.

One afternoon we had strolled to the top of a high hill in the neighbourhood of the Hall, which commands an almost boundless prospect; and as the shadows began to lengthen around us, and the distant mountains to fade into mist, my cousin was seized with a moralizing fit. "It seems to me," said he, laying his hand lightly on my shoulder, "that there is just at this season, and this hour, a sympathy between us and the world we are now contemplating. The evening is stealing upon nature as well as upon us—the shadows of the opening day have given place to those of its close, and the only difference is, that in the morning they were before us, now they are behind, and that the first vanished in the splendours of noonday, the latter will be lost in the oblivion of night—our 'May of life' my dear Launce, has forever fled, our summer is over and gone—But," continued he, suddenly recovering himself and slapping me gaily on the shoulder,—"but why should we repine?—what though the capricious zephyrs of spring, the heats and hurricanes of summer, have given place to the sober sunshine of autumn—and though the woods begin to assume the dappled livery of decay—yet the prevailing colour is still green—gay, sprightly green.

"Let us then comfort ourselves with this reflection, that though the shades of the morning have given place to those of the evening—though the spring is past, the summer over, and the autumn come—still you and I go on our way rejoicing—and while, like the lofty mountains of our Southern America, our heads are covered with snow, still, like them, we feel the genial warmth of spring and summer playing upon our bosoms."

BY LAUNCELOT LANGSTAFF, ESQ.

In the description which I gave sometime since, of Cockloft-hall, I totally forgot to make honourable mention of the library; which I confess was a most inexcusable oversight, for in truth it would bear a comparison, in point of usefulness and eccentricity, with the motley collection of the renowned hero of La Mancha.

It was chiefly gathered together by my grandfather, who spared neither pains nor expense to procure specimens of the oldest, most quaint, and insufferable books in the whole compass of english, scotch, and irish literature. There is a tradition in the family that the old gentleman once gave a grand entertainment in consequence of having got possession of a copy of a phillipick by archbishop Anselm, against the unseemly luxury of long toed shoes, as worn by the courtiers in the time of William Rufus, which he purchased of an honest brick-maker in the neighbourhood, for a little less than forty times its value. He had, undoubtedly, a singular reverence for old authors, and his highest eulogium on his library was, that it consisted of books not to be met with in any other collection, and as the phrase is, entirely out of print. The reason of which was, I suppose, that they were not worthy of being re-printed.

Cousin Christopher preserves these relicks with great care, and has added considerably to the collection; for with the hall he has inherited almost all the whim-whams of its former possessor. He cherishes a reverential regard for ponderous tomes in greek and latin, though he knows about as much of these languages, as a young bachelor of arts does, a year or two after leaving college. A worm-eaten work in eight or ten volumes he compares to an old family, more respectable for its antiquity than its splendour—a lumbering folio he considers as a duke—a sturdy quarto, as an earl, and a row of gilded duodecimoes, as so many gallant knights of the garter. But as to modern works of literature, they are thrust into trunks, and drawers, as intruding upstarts, and regarded with as much contempt, as mushroom nobility in England; who, having risen to grandeur, merely by their talents and services, are regarded as utterly unworthy to mingle their blood with those noble currents that can be traced without a single contamination through a long line of, perhaps, useless and profligate ancestors, up to William the bastard's cook, or butler, or groom, or some one of Rollo's freebooters.

WILL WIZARD, whose studies are of a most uncommon complexion, takes great delight in ransacking the library, and has been, during his late sojournings at the hall, very constant and devout in his visits to this receptacle of obsolete learning. He seemed particularly tickled with the contents of the great mahogany chest of drawers mentioned in the beginning of this work. This venerable piece of architecture has frowned in sullen majesty from a corner of the library, time out of mind, and is filled with musty manuscripts, some in my grandfather's hand-writing, and others evidently written long before his day.

It was a sight, worthy of a man's seeing, to behold Will, with his out-landish phiz, poring over old scrawls that would puzzle a whole society of antiquarians to expound, and diving into receptacles of trumpery, which, for a century past, had been undisturbed by mortal hand. He would sit for whole hours, with a phlegmatick patience unknown in these degenerate days (except, peradventure, among the high dutch commentators) prying into the quaint obscurity of musty parchments, until his whole face seemed to be converted into a folio leaf of black-letter; and occasionally, when the whimsical meaning of an obscure passage flashed on his mind, his countenance would curl up into an expression of gothick risibility, not unlike the physiognomy of a cabbage leaf wilting before a hot fire.

At such times there was no getting Will to join in our walks, or take any part in our usual recreations—he hardly gave us an oriental tale in a week, and would smoke so inveterately that no one else dared enter the library under pain of suffocation. This was more especially the case when he encountered any knotty piece of writing; and he honestly confessed to me that one worm-eaten manuscript, written in a pestilent crabbed hand, had cost him a box of the best spanish cygarrs, before he could make it out, and after all, it was not worth a tobacco-stalk. Such is the turn of my knowing associate—only let him get fairly in the track of any odd, out of the way whim-wham, and away he goes, whip and cut, until he either runs down his game, or runs himself out of breath—I never in my life met with a man, who rode his hobby-horse more intolerably hard than Wizard.

One of his favourite occupations for some time past, has been the hunting of black-letter, which he holds in high regard, and he often hints that learning has been on the decline ever since the introduction of the roman alphabet. An old book printed three hundred years ago, is a treasure; and a ragged scroll, about one half unintelligible, fills him with rapture. Oh! with what enthusiasm will he dwell on the discovery of the Pandects of Justinian and Livy's history; and when he relates the pious exertions of the Medici in recovering the lost treasures of greek and roman literature, his eye brightens, and his face assumes all the splendour of an illuminated manuscript.

Will had vegitated for a considerable time in perfect tranquillity among dust and cobwebs, when one morning as we were gathered on the piazza, listening with exemplary patience to one of cousin Christopher's long stories about the revolutionary war, we were suddenly electrified by an explosion of laughter from the library.—My readers, unless, peradventure they have heard honest Will laugh, can form no idea of the prodigious uproar he makes. To hear him in a forest, you would imagine (that is to say if you were classical enough) that the satyrs and the dryads had just discovered a pair of rural lovers in the shade, and were deriding, with bursts of obstreperous laughter, the blushes of the nymph and the indignation of the swain:—or if it were suddenly, as in the present instance, to break upon the serene and pensive silence of an autumnal morning, it would cause a sensation something like that which arises from hearing a sudden clap of thunder in a summer's day, when not a cloud is to be seen above the horizon. In short, I recommend Will's laugh as a sovereign remedy for the spleen; and if any of our readers are troubled with that villanous complaint—which can hardly be, if they make good use of our works—I advise them earnestly to get introduced to him forthwith.

This outrageous merriment of Will's, as may be easily supposed, threw the whole family into a violent fit of *wondering;* we all, with the exception of Christopher, who took this interruption in high dudgeon, silently stole up to the library, and bolting in upon him, were fain at the first glance to join in his inspiring roar. His face—but I despair to give an idea of his appearance—and until his portrait, which is now in the hands of an eminent artist, is engraved, my readers must be content— I promise them they shall one day or other, have a striking likeness of Will's indescribable phiz, in all its native comeliness.

Upon my inquiring the occasion of his mirth, he thrust an old, rusty, musty, and dusty manuscript into my hand, of which I could not de-cypher one word out of ten, without more trouble than it was worth. This task, however, he kindly took off my hands, and in little more than eight and forty hours, produced a translation into fair roman letters; though he assured me it had lost a vast deal of its humour by being modernized and degraded into plain english. In return for the great pains he had taken, I could not do less than insert it in our work. Will informs me that it is but one sheet of a studendous bundle which still remains uninvestigated—who was the author we have not yet discovered; but a note on the back, in my grandfather's handwriting, informs us that it was presented to him as a literary curiosity, by his particular friend, the illustrious RYP VAN DAM, formerly lieutenant-governor of the colony of NEW AMSTERDAM, and whose fame if it has never reached these latter days, it is only because he was too modest a man ever to do any thing worthy of being particularly recorded.

CHAP. CIX.
OF THE CHRONICLES OF THE RENOWNED
AND ANTIENT CITY OF GOTHAM.

How Gotham city conquered was,
And how the folk turned apes—because.   LINK. FID.

Albeit, much about this time it did fall out, that the thrice renowned and delectable city of GOTHAM did suffer great discomfiture, and was reduced to perilous extremity, by the invasion and assaults of the HOP-PINGTOTS. These are a people inhabiting a far distant country, exceeding pleasaunte and fertile—but they being withal egregiously addicted to migration, do thence issue forth in mighty swarms, like the Scythians of old, overrunning divers countries, and commonwealths, and committing great devastations wheresoever they do go, by their horrible and dreadful feats and prowesses. They are specially noted for being right valorous in all exercises of the leg; and of them it hath been rightly affirmed that no nation in all Christendom, or elsewhere, can cope with them in the adroit, dexterous, and jocund shaking of the heel.

This engaging excellence doth stand unto them a sovereign recommendation, by which they do insinuate themselves into universal favour and good countenance; and it is a notable fact that, let a Hoppingtot but once introduce a *foot* into company, and it goeth hardly if he doth not contrive to flourish his whole body in thereafter. The learned Linkum Fidelius in his famous and unheard-of treatise on man, whom he defineth, with exceeding sagacity, to be a corn-cutting, tooth-drawing animal, is particularly minute and elaborate in treating of the nation of the Hoppingtots, and betrays a little of the pythagorean in his theory, inasmuch as he accounteth for their being so wonderously adroit in pedestrian exercises, by supposing that they did originally acquire this unaccountable and unparalleled aptitude for huge and unmatchable feats of the leg, by having heretofore been condemned for their numerous offences against that harmless race of bipeds—or quadrupeds—(for herein the sage Linkum Fidelius appeareth to doubt and waiver exceedingly) the frogs, to animate their bodies for the space of one or two generations. He also giveth it as his opinion, that the name of Hoppingtots is manifestly derivative from this transmigration. Be this, however, as it may, the matter (albeit it hath been the subject of controversie among the learned) is but little pertinent to the subject of this history, wherefore shall we treat and consider it as naughte.

Now these people being thereto impelled by a superfluity of appetite, and a plentiful deficiency of the wherewithal to satisfy the same, did take thought that the antient and venerable city of *Gotham*, was, peradventure, possessed of mighty treasures, and did, moreover, abound with all manner of fish and flesh, and eatables and drinkables, and such like delightsome and wholesome excellencies withal. Whereupon calling a council of the most active heeled warriors, they did resolve forthwith to put forth a mighty array, make themselves masters of the same, and revel in the good things of the land. To this were they hotly stirred up, and wickedly incited by two redoubtable and renowned warriors, hight PIROUET and RIGADOON, ycleped in such sort, by reason that they were two mighty, valiant, and invincible little men, utterly famous for the victories of the leg which they had, on divers illustrious occasions, right gallantly achieved.

These doughty champions did ambitiously and wickedly inflame the minds of their countrymen, with gorgeous descriptions, in the which they did cunninglie set forth the marvellous riches and luxuries of Gotham—where Hoppingtots might have garments for their bodies, shirts to their ruffles, and might riot most merrily every day in the week on beef, pudding, and such like lusty dainties. They (Pirouet and Rigadoon) did likewise hold out hopes of an easy conquest; forasmuch as the Gothamites were as yet but little versed in the mystery and science of handling the legs, and being, moreover, like unto that notable bully of antiquity, Achilles, most vulnerable to all attacks on the heel, would doubtless surrender at the very first assault.—Whereupon, on the hearing of this inspiriting council, the Hoppingtots did set up a prodigious great cry of joy, shook their heels in triumph, and were all impatience to dance on to Gotham and take it by storm.

The cunning Pirouet and the arch caitiff Rigadoon, knew full well how to profit of this enthusiasm. They forthwith did order every man to arm himself with a certain pestilent little weapon, called a fiddle—to pack up in his knapsack a pair of silk breeches, the like of ruffles, a cocked hat of the form of a half moon, a bundle of cat-gut—and inasmuch as in marching to Gotham, the army might, peradventure, be smitten with scarcity of provision, they did account it proper that each man should take especial care to carry with him a bunch of right merchantable onions. Having proclaimed these orders by sound of fiddle, they (Pirouet and Rigadoon) did accordingly put their army behind them, and striking up the right jolly and sprightfull tune of *Ca Ira,* away they all capered towards the devoted city of Gotham, with a most horrible and appalling chattering of voices.

Of their first appearance before the beleaguered town, and of the various difficulties which did encounter them in their march, this history saith not, being that other matters of more weighty import require to be written. When that the army of the Hoppingtots did peregrinate within sight of Gotham, and the people of the city did behold the villanous and hitherto unseen capers, and grimaces, which they did make, a most horrifick panick was stirred up among the citizens; and the sages of the town fell into great despondency and tribulation, as supposing that these invaders were of the race of the Jig-hees, who did make men into baboons, when they achieved a conquest over them. The sages, therefore, called upon all the dancing men, and dancing women, and exhorted them with great vehemency of speech, to make *heel* against the invaders, and to put themselves upon such gallant defence, such glorious array, and such sturdy evolution, elevation, and transposition of the foot as might incontinently impester the legs of the Hoppingtots, and produce their complete discomfiture. But so it did happen by great mischance, that divers light-heeled youth of Gotham (more especially those who are descended from three wise men so renowned of yore, for having most venturesomely voyaged over sea in a bowl) were from time to time captured and inveigled into the camp of the enemy; where being foolishly cajoled and treated for a season with outlandish disports and pleasauntries, they were sent back to their friends, entirely changed, degenerated, and turned topsy-turvy; insomuch that they thought thenceforth of nothing but their heels, always assaying to thrust them into the most manifest point of view—and, in a word, as might truly be affirmed, did forever after walk upon their heads, outright.

And the Hoppingtots did day by day, and at late hours of the night, wax more and more urgent in this their investment of the city. At one time they would, in goodly procession, make an open assault by sound of fiddle, in a tremendous contra-dance—and anon they would advance by little detachments and manoeuvre to take the town by figuring in cotillons. But truly their most cunning and devilish craft, and subtilty, was made manifest in their strenuous endeavours to corrupt the garrison, by a most insidious and pestilent dance called the *Waltz*. This, in good truth, was a potent auxilliary, for by it were the heads of the simple Gothamites most villanously turned, their wits sent a woolgathering, and themselves on the point of surrendering at discretion, even unto the *very arms* of their invading foemen.

At length the fortifications of the town began to give manifest symptoms of decay, inasmuch as the breastwork of decency was considerably broken down, and the curtain works of propriety blown up. When that the cunning caitiff, Pirouet beheld the ticklish and jeopardized state of the city—"Now by my leg," quoth he—(he always swore by his leg, being that it was an exceeding goodlie leg) "Now by my leg, quoth he, but this is no great matter of recreation—I will show these people a pretty, strange and new way forsooth, presentlie, and will shake the dust off my pumps upon this most obstinate and uncivilized town." Whereupon he ordered, and did command his warriors, one and all, that they should put themselves in readiness, and prepare to carry the town by a GRAND BALL. They, in no wise to be daunted, do forthwith, at the word, equip themselves for the assault, and in good faith, truly, it was a gracious and glorious sight, a most triumphant and incomparable spectacle to behold them gallantly arrayed in glossy and shining silk breeches, tied with abundance of ribbon; with silken hose of the gorgeous colour of the salmon—right goodlie morocco pumps, decorated with clasps or buckles of a most cunninge and secret contrivance, inasmuch as they did of themselves grapple to the shoe without any aid of fluke or tongue, marvellously ensembling witchcraft and necromancy. They had withal, exuberant chitterlings which puffed out at the neck and bosom, after a most jolly fashion, like unto the beard of an antient he-turkey—and cocked hats, the which they did carry not on thir heads, after the fashion of the Gothamites, but under their arms, as a roasted fowl his gizzard.

Thus being equipped, and marshalled, they do attack, assault, batter and belabour the town with might and main—most gallantly displaying the vigour of their legs, and shaking their heels at it most emphatically. And the manner of their attack was in this sort—first, they did thunder and gallop forward in a *contre temps*—and anon, displayed column in a cossack dance, a fandango, or a gavot. Whereat the Gothamites, in no wise understanding this unknown system of warfare, marvelled exceedinglie, and did open their mouths, incontinently, the full distance of a bow shot (meaning a cross-bow) in sore dismay and apprehension. Whereupon, saith Rigadoon, flourishing his left leg with great expression of valour, and most magnifick carriage—"my copesmates, for what wait we here—are not the townsmen already won to our favour—do not their women and young damsels wave to us from the walls in such sort that, albeit there is some show of defence, yet is it manifestly converted into our interests?" so saying, he made no more ado, but leaping into the air about a flight-shot, and crossing his feet six times after the manner of the Hoppingtots, he gave a short *partridge run,* and with mighty vigour and swiftness did bolt outright over the walls with a *somerset.* The whole army of Hoppingtots danced in after their valiant chieftain, with an enormous squeaking of fiddles, and a horrifick blasting, and brattling of horns, insomuch that the dogs did howl in the streets; so hideously were their ears assailed. The Gothamites made some semblance of defence, but their women having been all won over into the interest of the enemy, they were shortly reduced to make most abject submission, and delivered over to the coercion of certain professors of the Hoppingtots, who did put them under most ignominious durance, for the space of a long time, until they had learned to turn out their toes, and flourish their legs after the true manner of their conquerors. And thus, after the manner I have related, was the mighty and puissant city of Gotham circumvented, and taken by a *coup de pied,* or as it might be rendered, by *force of legs.*

The conquerors showed no mercy, but did put all ages, sexes, and conditions, to the fiddle and the dance, and, in a word, compelled and enforced them to become absolute Hoppingtots. "Habit," as the ingenious Linkum Fidelius, profoundly affirmeth, "is second nature." And this original and invaluable observation, hath been most aptly proved and illustrated, by the example of the Gothamites, ever since this disastrous and unlucky mischaunce. In process of time, they have waxed to be most flagrant, outrageous, and abandoned dancers; they do ponder on naughte but how to gallantize it at balls, routs, and fandangoes, insomuch that the like was and in no time or place ever observed before. They do, moreover, pitifully devote their nights to the jollification of the legs, and their days forsooth to the instruction and edification of the heel. And to conclude their young folk, who whilome did bestow a modicum of leisure upon the improvement of the head, have of late utterly abandoned this hopeless task, and have quietly, as it were, settled themselves down into mere machines, wound up by a tune, and set in motion by a *fiddle-stick!*

SALMAGUNDI NO. XVIII

NO. XVIII]   *Tuesday, November* 24, 1807.

THE LITTLE MAN IN BLACK.
BY LAUNCELOT LANGSTAFF, ESQ.

The following story has been handed down by family tradition for more than a century. It is one on which my cousin Christopher dwells with more than usual prolixity; and, being in some measure connected with a personage often quoted in our work, I have thought it worthy of being laid before my readers.

Soon after my grandfather, mr. Lemuel Cockloft, had quietly settled himself at the hall, and just about the time that the gossips of the neighbourhood, tired of prying into his affairs, were anxious for some new tea-table topick, the busy community of our little village was thrown into a grand turmoil of curiosity and conjecture; (a situation very common to little gossiping villages) by the sudden and unaccountable appearance of a mysterious individual.

The object of this solicitude was a little black looking man of a foreign aspect, who took possession of an old building, which having long had the reputation of being haunted, was in a state of ruinous desolation, and an object of fear to all true believers in ghosts. He usually wore a high sugar-loaf hat, with a narrow brim, and a little black cloak, which, short as he was, scarcely reached below his knees. He sought no intimacy or acquaintance with any one; appeared to take no interest in the pleasures or the little broils of the village, nor ever talked; except sometimes to himself in an outlandish tongue. He commonly carried a large book, covered with sheepskin, under his arm; appeared always to be lost in meditation, and was often met by the peasantry, sometimes watching the dawning of day, sometimes at noon seated under a tree poring over his volume, and sometimes at evening, gazing with a look of sober tranquility at the sun as it gradually sunk below the horizon.

The good people of the vicinity beheld something prodigiously singular in all this—a profound mystery seemed to hang about the stranger, which, with all their sagacity they could not penetrate, and in the excess of worldly charity they pronounced it a sure sign "that he was no better than he should be"—a phrase innocent enough in itself, but which, as applied in common, signifies nearly every thing that is bad. The young people thought him a gloomy misanthrope, because he never joined in their sports—the old men thought still more hardly of him, because he followed no trade, nor even seemed ambitious of earning a farthing—and as to the old gossips, baffled by the inflexible taciturnity of the stranger, they unanimously decreed that a man who could not or would not talk, was no better than a dumb beast. The little man in black, careless of their opinions, seemed resolved to maintain the liberty of keeping his own secret; and the consequence was that, in a little while, the whole village was in an uproar—for in little communities of this description, the members have always the privilege of being thoroughly versed, and even of meddling in all the affairs of each other.

A confidential conference was held one Sunday morning after sermon, at the door of the village church, and the character of the unknown fully investigated. The schoolmaster gave as his opinion that he was the wandering Jew—the sexton was certain that he must be a free-mason from his silence—a third maintained, with great obstinacy, that he was a high german doctor, and that the book which he carried about with him, contained the secrets of the black art; but the most prevailing opinion seemed to be that he was a *witch*—a race of beings at that time abounding in those parts; and a sagacious old matron from Connecticut proposed to ascertain the fact by sousing him into a kettle of hot water.

Suspicion, when once afloat, goes with wind and tide, and soon becomes certainty. Many a stormy night was the little man in black seen by the flashes of lightning, frisking and curveting in the air upon a broomstick; and it was always observed that at those times the storm did more mischief than at any other. The old lady in particular, who suggested the humane ordeal of the boiling kettle, lost on one of these occasions a fine brindled cow; which accident was entirely ascribed to the vengeance of the little man in black. If ever a mischie-

The Little Man in Black

Woodcut by Alexander Anderson (1775–1870), the first American wood engraver, for the second American edition of *Salmagundi* (D. Longworth: New York, 1814).

vous hireling rode his master's favourite horse to a distant frolick, and
the animal was observed to be lame and jaded in the morning—the
little man in black was sure to be at the bottom of the affair, nor could
a high wind howl through the village at night, but the old women
shrugged up their shoulders and observed "the little man in black was
in his *tantrums*." In short he became the bugbear of every house, and
was as effectual in frightening little children into obedience and hys-
tericks, as the redoubtable Raw-head-and-bloody-bones himself; nor
could a house-wife of the village sleep in peace, except under the
guardianship of a horse-shoe nailed to the door.

The object of these direful suspicions remained for some time totally
ignorant of the wonderful quandary he had occasioned, but he was
soon doomed to feel its effects. An individual who is once so unfortunate as to incur the odium of a village, is in a great measure outlawed
and proscribed; and becomes a mark for injury and insult—particularly
if he has not the power or the disposition to recriminate. The little
venomous passions, which in the great world are dissipated and
weakened by being widely diffused, act in the narrow limits of a country
town with collected vigour, and become rancorous in proportion as
they are confined in their sphere of action. The little man in black
experienced the truth of this—every mischievous urchin returning from
school, had full liberty to break his windows; and this was considered
as a most daring exploit, for, in such awe did they stand of him, that
the most adventurous schoolboy was never seen to approach his threshold, and at night would prefer going round by the cross-roads, where
a traveller had been murdered by the indians, rather than pass by
the door of his forlorn habitation.

The only living creature that seemed to have any care or affection
for this deserted being, was an old turnspit—the companion of his lonely
mansion and his solitary wanderings—the sharer of his scanty meals,
and, sorry am I to say it—the sharer of his persecutions. The turnspit,
like his master, was peaceable and inoffensive; never known to bark
at a horse, to growl at a traveller, or to quarrel with the dogs of the
neighbourhood. He followed close at his master's heels when he
went out, and when he returned stretched himself in the sunbeams at
the door, demeaning himself in all things like a civil and well disposed
turnspit. But notwithstanding his exemplary deportment he fell likewise
under the ill report of the village, as being the familiar of the little man
in black, and the evil spirit that presided at his incantations. The old
hovel was considered as the scene of their unhallowed rites, and its
harmless tenants regarded with a detestation, which their inoffensive
conduct never merited. Though pelted and jeered at by the brats of
the village, and frequently abused by their parents, the little man in

black never turned to rebuke them, and his faithful dog, when wantonly assaulted, looked up wistfully in his master's face, and there learned a lesson of patience and forbearance.

The movements of this inscrutable being had long been the subject of speculation at Cockloft-hall, for its inmates were full as much given to *wondering* as their descendants. The patience with which he bore his persecutions, particularly surprised them—for patience is a virtue but little known in the Cockloft family. My grandmother, who it appears was rather superstitious, saw in this humility nothing but the gloomy sullenness of a wizard, who restrained himself for the present, in hopes of midnight vengeance—the parson of the village, who was a man of some reading, pronounced it the stubborn insensibility of a stoick philosopher:—my grandfather, who, worthy soul, seldom wandered abroad in search of conclusions, took a data from his own excellent heart, and regarded it as the humble forgiveness of a christian. But however different were their opinions as to the character of the stranger, they agreed in one particular, namely, in never intruding upon his solitude; and my grandmother, who was at that time nursing my mother, never left the room, without wisely putting the large family bible in the cradle—a sure talisman, in her opinion, against witchcraft and necromancy.

One stormy winter night, when a bleak north-east wind moaned about the cottages, and howled around the village steeple, my grandfather was returning from club, preceded by a servant with a lantern. Just as he arrived opposite the desolate abode of the little man in black, he was arrested by the piteous howling of a dog which, heard in the pauses of the storm, was exquisitely mournful; and he fancied now and then, that he caught the low and broken groans of some one in distress. He stopped for some minutes, hesitating between the benevolence of his heart and a sensation of genuine delicacy, which in spite of his eccentricity he fully possessed—and which forbade him to pry into the concerns of his neighbours. Perhaps too, this hesitation might have been strengthened by a little taint of superstition; for surely, if the unknown had been addicted to witchcraft, this was a most propitious night for his vagaries. At length the old gentleman's philanthropy predominated; he approached the hovel and pushing open the door—for poverty has no occasion for locks and keys—beheld, by the light of the lantern, a scene that smote his generous heart to the core.

On a miserable bed, with pallid and emaciated visage and hollow eyes—in a room destitute of every convenience—without fire to warm, or friend to console him, lay this helpless mortal who had been so long the terror and wonder of the village. His dog was crouching on the scanty coverlet, and shivering with cold. My grandfather stepped softly and hesitatingly to the bed side, and accosted the forlorn sufferer in his usual accents of kindness. The little man in black seemed recalled by the tones of compassion from the lethargy into which he had fallen; for, though his heart was almost frozen, there was yet one chord that answered to the call of the good old man who bent over him—the tones of sympathy, so novel to his ear, called back his wandering senses and acted like a restorative to his solitary feelings.

He raised his eyes, but they were vacant and haggard—he put forth his hand, but it was cold—he essayed to speak, but the sound died away in his throat—he pointed to his mouth with an expression of dreadful meaning, and, sad to relate! my grandfather understood that the harmless stranger, deserted by society, was perishing with hunger!—With the quick impulse of humanity he dispatched the servant to the hall for refreshment. A little warm nourishment renovated him for a short time—but not long; it was evident his pilgrimage was drawing to a close, and he was about entering that peaceful asylum, where "the wicked cease from troubling."

His tale of misery was short and quickly told; infirmities had stolen upon him, heightened by the rigours of the season: he had taken to his bed without strength to rise and ask for assistance—"and if I had," said he, in a tone of bitter despondency, "to whom should I have applied? I have no friend that I know of in the world!—the villagers avoid me as something loathsome and dangerous; and here, in the midst of christians, should I have perished without a fellow-being to soothe the last moments of existence, and close my dying eyes, had not the howlings of my faithful dog excited your attention."

He seemed deeply sensible of the kindness of my grandfather, and at one time as he looked up into his old benefactor's face, a solitary tear was observed to steal adown the parched furrows of his cheek—poor outcast!--it was the last tear he shed—but I warrant it was not the first by millions! My grandfather watched by him all night. Towards morning he gradually declined, and as the rising sun gleamed through the window, he begged to be raised in his bed that he might look at it for the last time. He contemplated it for a moment with a kind of religious enthusiasm, and his lips moved as if engaged in prayer. The strange conjectures concerning him rushed on my grandfather's mind: "he is an idolator!" thought he, "and is worshipping the sun!"—He listened a moment and blushed at his own uncharitable suspicion—he was only engaged in the pious devotions of a christian. His simple orison being finished, the little man in black withdrew his eyes from the east, and taking my grandfather's hand in one of his, and making a motion with the other, towards the sun—"I love to contemplate it,"

said he, "tis an emblem of the universal benevolence of a true christian—
and it is the most glorious work of him, who is philanthropy itself!"
My grandfather blushed still deeper at his ungenerous surmises; he
had pitied the stranger at first, but now he revered him—he turned
once more to regard him, but his countenance had undergone a
change—the holy enthusiasm that had lighted up each feature
had given place to an expression of mysterious import—a gleam of
grandeur seemed to steal across his gothick visage, and he appeared
full of some mighty secret which he hesitated to impart. He raised the
tattered nightcap that had sunk almost over his eyes, and waving his
withered hand with a slow and feeble expression of dignity,—"In me,"
said he, with laconick solemnity—"In me you behold the last descendant
of the renowned Linkum Fidelius!" My grandfather gazed at him with
reverence, for though he had never heard of the illustrious personage
thus pompously announced, yet there was a certain black-letter dignity
in the name, that peculiarly struck his fancy and commanded his respect.

"You have been kind to me," continued the little man in black, after
a momentary pause, "and richly will I requite your kindness, by making
you heir to my treasures! In yonder large deal box are the volumes of my
illustrious ancestor, of which I alone am the fortunate possessor. Inherit
them—ponder over them—and be wise!" He grew faint with the exertion
he had made, and sunk back almost breathless on his pillow. His hand,
which, inspired with the importance of his subject, he had raised to
my grandfather's arm, slipped from its hold and fell over the side of the
bed, and his faithful dog licked it, as if anxious to soothe the last
moments of his master, and testify his gratitude to the hand that had
so often cherished him. The untaught caresses of the faithful animal
were not lost upon his dying master—he raised his languid eyes—turned
them on the dog, then on my grandfather, and having given this silent
recommendation—closed them forever.

The remains of the little man in black, notwithstanding the objections
of many pious people, were decently interred in the church-yard of
the village, and his spirit, harmless as the body it once animated, has
never been known to molest a living being. My grandfather complied
as far as possible with his last request—he conveyed the volumes of
Linkum Fidelius to his library—he pondered over them frequently—but
whether he grew wiser the tradition does not mention. This much is
certain, that his kindness to the poor descendant of Fidelius, was amply
rewarded by the approbation of his own heart, and the devoted attachment of the old turnspit, who transferring his affection from his deceased
master to his benefactor, became his constant attendant, and was father
to a long line of runty curs that still flourish in the family. And thus was

the Cockloft library first enriched by the invaluable folioes of the sage
LINKUM FIDELIUS.

LETTER
FROM MUSTAPHA RUB-A-DUB KELI KHAN,
*To Asem Hacchem, principal slave-driver to
his highness the bashaw of Tripoli.*

Though I am often disgusted, my good Asem, with the vices and
absurdities of the men of this country, yet the women afford me a
world of amusement. Their lovely prattle is as diverting as the chattering
of the red-tailed parrot; nor can the green-headed monkey of Timandi
equal them in whim and playfulness. But, notwithstanding these valuable
qualifications, I am sorry to observe they are not treated with half the
attention bestowed on the before mentioned animals. These infidels put
their parrots in cages and chain their monkeys; but their women, instead
of being carefully shut up in harams and seraglioes, are abandoned to
the direction of their own reason, and suffered to run about in perfect
freedom, like other domestick animals:—this comes, Asem, of treating their
women as rational beings and allowing them souls. The consequence of
this piteous neglect may easily be imagined—they have degenerated into
all their native wildness, are seldom to be caught at home, and at an
early age take to the streets and highways, where they rove about in
droves, giving almost as much annoyance to the peaceable people, as the
troops of wild dogs that infest our great cities, or the flights of locusts,
that sometimes spread famine and desolation over whole regions of
fertility.

This propensity to relapse into pristine wildness, convinces me of the
untameable disposition of the sex, who may indeed be partially domesti-
cated by a long course of confinement and restraint, but the moment
they are restored to personal freedom, become wild as the young partridge
of this country, which, though scarcely half hatched, will take to the
fields and run about with the shell upon its back.

Notwithstanding their wildness, however, they are remarkably easy
of access, and suffer themselves to be approached, at certain hours of the
day, without any symptoms of apprehension; and I have even happily
succeeded in detecting them at their domestick occupations. One of the
most important of these consists in thumping vehemently on a kind of
musical instrument, and producing a confused, hideous, and indefinable
uproar, which they call the description of a battle—a jest, no doubt, for
they are wonderfully facetious at times, and make great practise of passing jokes upon strangers. Sometimes they employ themselves in painting
little caricatures of landscapes, wherein they will display their singular

drollery in bantering nature fairly out of countenance—representing her tricked out in all the tawdry finery of copper skies, purple rivers, calico rocks, red grass, clouds that look like old clothes set adrift by the tempest, and foxy trees, whose melancholy foliage, drooping and curling most fantastically, reminds me of an undressed periwig that I have now and then seen hung on a stick in a barber's window. At other times they employ themselves in acquiring a smattering of languages spoken by nations on the other side of the globe, as they find their own language not sufficiently copious to supply their constant demands, and express their multifarious ideas. But their most important domestick avocation is to embroider on satin or muslin, flowers of a non-descript kind, in which the great art is to make them as unlike nature as possible—or to fasten little bits of silver, gold, tinsel and glass, on long strips of muslin, which they drag after them with much dignity whenever they go abroad —a fine lady, like a bird of paradise, being estimated by the length of her tail.

But do not, my friend, fall into the enormous error of supposing, that the exercise of these arts is attended with any useful or profitable result— believe me, thou couldst not indulge an idea more unjust and injurious; for it appears to be an established maxim among the women of this country that a lady loses her dignity when she condescends to be useful; and forfeits all rank in society the moment she can be convicted of earning a farthing. Their labours therefore, are directed not towards supplying their household but in decking their persons, and—generous souls!—they deck their persons, not so much to please themselves, as to gratify others, particularly strangers. I am confident thou wilt stare at this, my good Asem, accustomed as thou art to our eastern females, who shrink in blushing timidity even from the glances of a lover, and are so chary of their favours that they even seem fearful of lavishing their smiles too profusely on their husbands. Here, on the contrary, the stranger has the first place in female regard, and so far do they carry their hospitality, that I have seen a fine lady slight a dozen tried friends and real admirers, who lived in her smiles and made her happiness their study, merely to allure the vague and wandering glances of a stranger, who viewed her person with indifference and treated her advances with contempt—By the whiskers of our sublime bashaw, but this is highly flattering to a foreigner! and thou mayest judge how particularly pleasing to one who is, like myself, so ardent an admirer of the sex. Far be it from me to condemn this extraordinary manifestation of good will—let their own countrymen look to that.

Be not alarmed, I conjure thee, my dear Asem, lest I should be tempted by these beautiful barbarians to break the faith I owe to the three-and-twenty wives from whom my unhappy destiny has perhaps severed me for ever—no, Asem; neither time nor the bitter succession of misfortunes that pursues me, can shake from my heart the memory of former attachments. I listen with tranquil heart to the strumming and prattling of these fair syrens—their whimsical paintings touch not the tender chord of my affections; and I would still defy their fascinations, though they trailed after them trains as long as the gorgeous trappings which are dragged at the heels of the holy camel of Mecca: or as the tail of the great beast in our prophet's vision, which measured three hundred and forty-nine leagues, two miles, three furlongs, and a hand's breadth in longitude.

The dress of these women is, if possible, more eccentrick and whimsical than their deportment, and they take an inordinate pride in certain ornaments which are probably derived from their savage progenitors.—A woman of this country, dressed out for an exhibition, is loaded with as many ornaments as a circassian slave when brought out for sale. Their heads are tricked out with little bits of horn or shell, cut into fantastick shapes, and they seem to emulate each other in the number of these singular baubles—like the women we have seen in our journeys to Aleppo, who cover their heads with the entire shell of a tortoise, and thus equipped are the envy of all their less fortunate acquaintance. They also decorate their necks and ears with coral, gold chains, and glass beads, and load their fingers with a variety of rings; though, I must confess, I have never perceived that they wear any in their noses—as has been affirmed by many travellers. We have heard much of their painting themselves most hideously, and making use of bear's-grease in great profusion; but this, I solemnly assure thee, is a misrepresentation, civilization, no doubt, having gradually extirpated these nauseous practises. It is true, I have seen two or three of these females, who had disguised their features with paint; but then it was merely to give a tinge of red to their cheeks, and did not look very frightful—and as to ointment, they rarely use any now, except occasionally a little grecian oil for their hair, which gives it a glossy, greasy, and (as they think) very comely appearance. The last mentioned class of females, I take it for granted, have been but lately caught and still retain strong traits of their original savage propensities.

The most flagrant and inexcusable fault however, which I find in these lovely savages, is the shameless and abandoned exposure of their persons. Wilt thou not suspect me of exaggeration when I affirm—wilt thou not blush for them most discreet mussulman, when I declare to thee, that they are so lost to all sense of modesty as to expose the whole of their faces from the forehead to the chin, and that they even go abroad with their hands uncovered!—Monstrous indelicacy!—

But what I am going to disclose, will doubtless appear to thee still more incredible. Though I cannot forbear paying a tribute of admiration to the beautiful faces of these fair infidels, yet I must give it as my firm opinion that their persons are preposterously unseemly. In vain did I look around me on my first landing, for those divine forms of redundant proportions which answer to the true standard of eastern beauty—not a single fat fair one could I behold among the multitudes that thronged the streets; the females that passed in review before me, tripping sportively along, resembled a procession of shadows, returning to their graves at the crowing of the cock.

This meagreness I at first ascribed to their excessive volubility; for I have somewhere seen it advanced by a learned doctor, that the sex were endowed with a peculiar activity of tongue, in order that they might practise talking as a healthful exercise, necessary to their confined and sedentary mode of life. This exercise, it was natural to suppose, would be carried to great excess in a logocracy—"Too true" thought I "they have converted, what was undoubtedly meant as a beneficent gift, into a noxious habit that steals the flesh from their bones and the roses from their cheeks—they absolutely talk themselves thin!"—judge then of my surprise when I was assured not long since, that this meagreness was considered the perfection of personal beauty, and that many a lady starved herself, with all the obstinate perseverance of a pious dervise—into a fine figure!—"Nay more," said my informer, "they will often sacrifice their healths in this eager pursuit of skeleton beauty, and drink vinegar, eat pickles and smoke tobacco to keep themselves within the scanty outlines of the fashion."—Faugh! Allah preserve me from such beauties, who contaminate their pure blood with noxious recipes; who impiously sacrifice the best gift of heaven, to a preposterous and mistaken vanity.— Ere long I shall not be surprised to see them scarring their faces like the negroes of Congo, flattening their noses in imitation of the Hottentots, or like the barbarians of Ab-al Timar, distorting their lips and ears out of all natural dimensions. Since I received this information I cannot contemplate a fine figure, without thinking of a vinegar cruet; nor look at a dashing belle, without fancying her a pot of pickled cucumbers! What a difference, my friend, between these shades, and the plump beauties of Tripoli—what a contrast between an infidel fair one and my favourite wife, Fatima, whom I bought by the hundred weight, and had trundled home in a wheel-barrow!

But enough for the present; I am promised a faithful account of the arcana of a lady's toilette—a complete initiation into the arts, mysteries, spells and potions, in short the whole chemical process by which she reduces herself down to the most fashionable standard of insignificance; together with specimens of the strait waistcoats, the lacing, the bandages and the various ingenious instruments with which she puts nature to the rack, and tortures herself into a proper figure to be admired.

Farewel, thou sweetest of slave drivers! the echoes that repeat to a lover's ear the song of his mistress, are not more soothing than tidings from those we love. Let thy answers to my letters be speedy; and never, I pray thee, for a moment cease to watch over the prosperity of my house, and the welfare of my beloved wives. Let them want for nothing, my friend; but feed them plentifully on honey, boiled rice and water gruel, so that when I return to the blessed land of my fathers (if that can ever be!) I may find them improved in size and loveliness, and sleek as the graceful elephants that range the green valley of Abimar.

Ever thine.

MUSTAPHA.

SALMAGUNDI NO. XIX

NO. XIX]   *Thursday, December* 31, 1807.

FROM MY ELBOW CHAIR.

Having returned to town, and once more formally taken possession of my elbow chair, it behoves me to discard the rural feelings, and the rural sentiments, in which I have for some time past indulged, and devote myself more exclusively to the edification of the town. As I feel at this moment a chivalrick spark of gallantry playing around my heart, and one of those dulcet emotions of cordiality, which an old bachelor will sometimes entertain toward the divine sex, I am determined to gratify the sentiment for once, and devote this number exclusively to the ladies. I would not, however, have our fair readers imagine that we wish to flatter ourselves into their good graces; devoutly as we adore them, (and what true cavalier does not) and heartily as we desire to flourish in the mild sunshine of their smiles, yet we scorn to insinuate ourselves into their favour; unless it be as honest friends, sincere well wishers, and disinterested advisers. If in the course of this number they find us rather prodigal of our encomiums, they will have the modesty to ascribe it to the excess of their own merits—if they find us extremely indulgent to their faults, they will impute it rather to the superabundance of our good nature, than to any servile and illiberal fear of giving offence.

The following letter of Mustapha falls in exactly with the current of my purpose. As I have before mentioned, that his letters are without dates, we are obliged to give them irregularly, without any regard to chronological order.

The present one, appears to have been written not long after his arrival, and antecedent to several already published. It is more in the familiar and colloquial style than the others. Will Wizard declares he has translated it with fidelity, excepting that he has omitted several remarks on the *waltz*, which the honest Mussulman eulogizes with great enthusiasm; comparing it to certain voluptuous dances of the seraglio. Will regretted exceedingly that the indelicacy of several of these observations compelled their total exclusion, as he wishes to give all possible encouragement to this popular and amiable exhibition.

LETTER

FROM MUSTAPHA RUB-A-DUB KELI KHAN,

to MULEY HELIM AL RAGGI, (*surnamed the agreeable*
Ragamuffin) *chief mountebank and buffa-dancer to*
his highness.

The numerous letters which I have written to our friend the *slave driver*, as well as those to thy kinsman THE SNORER, and which doubtless were read to thee, honest Muley, have in all probability awakened thy curiosity to know further particulars concerning the manners of the barbarians, who hold me in such ignominious captivity. I was lately at one of their publick ceremonies, which at first perplexed me exceedingly as to its object; but as the explanations of a friend have let me somewhat into the secret, and as it seems to bear no small analogy to thy profession, a description of it may contribute to thy amusement, if not to thy instruction.

A few days since, just as I had finished my coffee, and was perfuming my whiskers preparatory to a morning walk I was waited upon by an inhabitant of this place, a gay young infidel, who has of late cultivated my acquaintance. He presented me with a square bit of painted pasteboard, which he informed me would entitle me to admittance to the CITY ASSEMBLY. Curious to know the meaning of a phrase, which was entirely new to me, I requested an explanation; when my friend informed me that the assembly was a numerous concourse of young people of both sexes, who, on certain occasions, gathered together to dance about a large room with violent gesticulation, and try to out-dress each other.—"In short," said he, "if you wish to see *the natives* in all their glory, there's no place like the *City Assembly;* so you must go there, and sport your whiskers."—Though the matter of *sporting my whiskers*, was considerably above my apprehension, yet I now began, as I thought, to understand him. I had heard of the war dances of the natives, which are a kind of religious institution, and had little doubt but that this must be a solemnity of the kind—upon a prodigious great scale. Anxious as I am to contemplate these strange people in every situation, I willingly acceded to his proposal, and to be the more at ease, I determined to lay aside my turkish dress, and appear in plain garments of the fashion of this country—as is my custom whenever I wish to mingle in a crowd, without exciting the attention of the gaping multitude.

It was long after the shades of night had fallen, before my friend appeared to conduct me to the assembly. "These infidels," thought I, "shroud themselves in mystery, and seek the aid of gloom and darkness to heighten the solemnity of their pious orgies." Resolving to conduct myself with that decent respect, which every stranger owes to the customs of the land in which he sojourns, I chastised my features into an expression of sober reverence, and stretched my face into a degree of longitude suitable to the ceremony I was about to witness. Spite of myself, I felt an emotion of awe stealing over my senses as I approached the majestick pile. My imagination pictured something similar to a descent into the cave of Dom-Daniel, where the necromancers of the east are taught their infernal arts. I entered with the same gravity of demeanour that I would have approached the holy Temple at Mecca, and bowed my head three times, as I passed the threshold. "Head of the mighty Amrou!" thought I, on being ushered into a splendid saloon, "what a display is here! surely I am transported to the mansions of the Houris, the elysium of the faithful!"—How tame appeared all the descriptions of enchanted palaces in our arabian poetry!—wherever I turned my eyes, the quick glances of beauty dazzled my vision and ravished my heart—lovely virgins fluttered by me, darting imperial looks of conquest, or beaming such smiles of invitation, as did Gabriel when he beckoned our holy prophet to heaven. Shall I own the weakness of thy friend, good Muley?—while thus gazing on the enchanted scene before me, I for a moment forgot my country; and even the memory of my three-and-twenty wives faded from my heart—my thoughts were bewildered and led astray by the charms of these bewitching savages, and I sunk for awhile into that delicious state of mind where the senses, all enchanted, and, all striving for mastery, produce an endless variety of tumultuous, yet pleasing emotions. Oh, Muley, never shall I again wonder that an infidel should prove a recreant to the single solitary wife allotted him, when even thy friend, armed with all the precepts of Mahomet, can so easily prove faithless to three-and-twenty!

"Whither have you led me?" said I at length to my companion, "and to whom do these beautiful creatures belong? certainly this must be the seraglio of the grand bashaw of the city, and a most happy bashaw must he be to possess treasures which even his highness of Tripoli cannot parallel." "Have a care," cried my companion, "how you talk about seraglioes, or you'll have all these gentle nymphs about your ears; for seraglio is a word which, beyond all others, they abhor;—most of them," continued he, "have no lord and master, but come here to catch one—they're *in the market*, as we term it."—"Ah, hah!" said I, exultingly, "then you really have a fair, or slave-market, such as we have in the east, where the faithful are provided with the choicest virgins of Georgia and Circassia?—by our glorious sun of Africk, but I should like to select some ten or a dozen wives from so lovely an assemblage! pray, what would you suppose they might be bought for?"—

Before I could receive an answer, my attention was attracted by two or three good looking middle sized men, who being dressed in black, a colour universally worn in this country by the muftis and dervises, I immediately concluded to be high priests, and was confirmed in my original opinion that this was a religious ceremony. These reverend personages are entitled *managers*, and enjoy unlimited authority in the assemblies, being armed with swords, with which I am told they would infallibly put any lady to death, who infringed the laws of the temple. They walked round the room with great solemnity, and with an air of profound importance and mystery put a little piece of folded paper in each fair hand, which I concluded were religious talismans. One of them dropped on the floor, whereupon I slily put my foot on it, and watching an opportunity, picked it up unobserved and found it to contain some unintelligible words and the mystic number 9. What were its virtues I know not, except that I put it in my pocket, and have hitherto been preserved from my fit of the lumbago, which I generally have about this season of the year, ever since I tumbled into the well of Zim-zim on my pilgrimage to Mecca. I enclose it to thee in this letter, presuming it to be particularly serviceable against the dangers of thy profession.

Shortly after the distribution of these talismans, one of the high priests stalked into the middle of the room with great majesty, and clapped his hands three times; a loud explosion of musick succeeded from a number of black, yellow and white musicians perched in a kind of cage over the grand entrance. The company were thereupon thrown into great confusion and apparent consternation. They hurried to and fro about the room, and at length formed themselves into little groupes of eight persons, half male and half female—the musick struck into something like harmony, and in a moment to my utter astonishment and dismay, they were all seized with what I concluded to be a paroxysm of religious phrenzy, tossing about their heads in a ludicrous style from side to side and indulging in extravagant contortions of figure—

now throwing their heels into the air, and anon whirling round with
the velocity of the eastern idolators, who think they pay a grateful
homage to the sun by imitating his motions. I expected every moment
to see them fall down in convulsions, foam at the mouth, and shriek
with fancied inspiration. As usual the females seemed most fervent in
their religious exercises, and performed them with a melancholy expression of feature that was peculiarly touching; but I was highly gratified
by the exemplary conduct of several male devotees, who, though their
gesticulations would intimate a wild merriment of the feelings, maintained throughout as inflexible a gravity of countenance as so many
monkeys of the island of Borneo at their anticks.

"And pray", said I, "who is the divinity that presides in this splendid
mosque?"—"The divinity!—oh, I understand—you mean the *belle* of the
evening; we have a new one every season; the one at present in fashion
is that lady you see yonder, dressed in white, with pink ribbons, and a
crowd of adorers around her." "Truly," cried I, "this is the pleasantest
deity I have encountered in the whole course of my travels—so familiar,
so condescending, and so merry withal—why, her very worshippers take
her by the hand, and whisper in her ear."—"My good mussulman," replied
my friend with great gravity, "I perceive you are completely in an error
concerning the intent of this ceremony. You are now in a place of publick
amusement, not of publick worship—and the pretty looking young men
you see making such violent and grotesque distortions, are merely indulging in our favourite amusement of dancing." "I cry you mercy,"
exclaimed I, "these then are the dancing men and women of the town,
such as we have in our principal cities, who hire themselves out for the
entertainment of the wealthy—but, pray who pays them for this fatiguing
exhibition?"—My friend regarded me for a moment with an air of
whimsical perplexity, as if doubtful whether I was in jest or earnest.—
"'Sblood, man," cried he, "these are some of our greatest people, our
fashionables, who are merely dancing here for amusement."—*Dancing
for amusement!*—think of that, Muley—thou, whose greatest pleasure is
to chew opium, smoke tobacco, loll on a couch, and doze thyself into
the region of the Houris!—*Dancing for amusement!*—shall I never cease
having occasion to laugh at the absurdities of these barbarians, who are
laborious in their recreations, and indolent only in their hours of business?—*Dancing for amusement!*—the very idea makes my bones ache, and
I never think of it without being obliged to apply my handkerchief to
my forehead, and fan myself into some degree of coolness.

"And pray," said I, when my astonishment had a little subsided, "do
these musicians also toil for amusement, or are they confined to their
cage, like birds, to sing for the gratification of others?—I should think
the former was the case, from the animation with which they flourish

their elbows." "Not so," replied my friend, "they are well paid, which is no more than just, for I assure you they are the most important personages in the room. The fiddler puts the whole assembly in motion, and directs their movements, like the master of a puppet-show, who sets all his pasteboard gentry kicking by a jerk of his fingers:—there now—look at that dapper little gentleman yonder, who appears to be suffering the pangs of dislocation in every limb—he is the most expert puppet in the room, and performs, not so much for his own amusement, as for that of the bye-standers."—Just then, the little gentleman, having finished one of his paroxysms of activity, seemed to be looking round for applause from the spectators. Feeling myself really much obliged to him for his exertions, I made him a low bow of thanks, but nobody followed my example, which I thought a singular instance of ingratitude.

Thou wilt perceive, friend Muley, that the dancing of these barbarians is totally different from the *science* professed by thee in Tripoli; —the country, in fact, is afflicted by numerous epidemical diseases, which travel from house to house, from city to city, with the regularity of a caravan. Among these, the most formidable is this dancing mania, which prevails chiefly throughout the winter. It at first seized on a few people of fashion, and being indulged in moderation, was a cheerful exercise; but in a little time, by quick advances, it infected all classes of the community, and became a raging epidemick. The doctors immediately, as is their usual way, instead of devising a remedy, fell together by the ears, to decide whether it was native or imported, and the sticklers for the latter opinion traced it to a cargo of trumpery from France, as they had before hunted down the yellow-fever to a bag of coffee from the West-Indies. What makes this disease the more formidable, is that the patients seem infatuated with their malady, abandon themselves to its unbounded ravages, and expose their persons to wintry storms and midnight airs, more fatal in this capricious climate than the withering Simoom blast of the desert.

I know not whether it is a sight most whimsical or melancholy to witness a fit of this dancing malady. The lady hops up to the gentleman, who stands at the distance of about three paces, and then capers back again to her place—the gentleman of course does the same—then they skip one way, then they jump another—then they turn their backs to each other—then they seize each other and shake hands—then they whirl round, and throw themselves into a thousand grotesque and ridiculous attitudes—sometimes on one leg, sometimes on the other, and sometimes on no leg at all—and this they call *exhibiting the graces!*—By the nineteen thousand capers of the great mountebank of Damascus, but these *graces* must be something like the crooked backed dwarf Shabrac, who is sometimes permitted to amuse his highness by imitating the tricks of a monkey. These fits continue at short intervals from four to five hours, till at last the lady is led off, faint, languid, exhausted, and panting, to her carriage—rattles home—passes a night of feverish restlessness, cold perspirations and troubled sleep—rises late next morning (if she rises at all) is nervous, petulant, or a prey to languid indifference all day—a mere household spectre, neither giving nor receiving enjoyment—in the evening hurries to another dance—receives an unnatural exhiliration from the lights, the musick, the crowd, and the unmeaning bustle—flutters, sparkles, and blooms for awhile, until, the transient delirium being past, the infatuated maid droops and languishes into apathy again—is again led off to her carriage, and the next morning rises to go through exactly the same joyless routine.

And yet, wilt thou believe it, my dear Raggi, these are rational beings; nay, more, their countrymen would fain persuade me they have souls!—Is it not a thousand times to be lamented that beings, endowed with charms that might warm even the frigid heart of a dervise—with social and endearing powers, that would render them the joy and pride of the haram—should surrender themselves to a habit of heartless dissipation, which preys imperceptibly on the roses of the cheek—which robs the eye of its lustre, the mouth of its dimpled smile, the spirits of their cheerful hilarity, and the limbs of their elastick vigour—which hurries them off in the spring-time of existence; or, if they survive, yields to the arms of a youthful bridegroom a frame wrecked in the storms of dissipation, and struggling with premature infirmity. Alas, Muley! may I not ascribe to this cause the number of little old women I meet with in this country, from the age of eighteen to eight-and-twenty?

In sauntering down the room, my attention was attracted by a smoky painting, which on nearer examination I found consisted of two female figures crowning a bust with a wreath of laurel. "This, I suppose," cried I, "was some famous dancer in his time?"—"Oh, no," replied my friend, "he was *only* a general."—"Good; but then he must have been great at a cotillion, or expert at a fiddle-stick—or why is his memorial here?"—"Quite the contrary," answered my companion, "history makes no mention of his ever having flourished a fiddle-stick, or figured in a single dance. You have, no doubt, heard of him—he was the illustrious WASHINGTON, the father and deliverer of his country; and as our nation is remarkable for gratitude to great men, it always does honour to their memory, by placing their monuments over the doors of taverns or in the corners of dancing-rooms."

From thence my friend and I strolled into a small apartment adjoining the grand saloon, where I beheld a number of grave looking persons with venerable grey heads, (but without beards, which I thought very unbecoming) seated around a table, studying hieroglyphicks;—I approached them with reverence, as so many *magi*, or learned men, endeavouring to expound the mysteries of egyptian science: several of them threw down money, which I supposed was a reward proposed for some great discovery, when presently one of them spread his hieroglyphics on the table, exclaimed triumphantly "two bullets and a bragger!" and swept all the money into his pocket. He has discovered a key to the hieroglyphicks, thought I—happy mortal! no doubt his name will be immortalized. Willing, however, to be satisfied, I looked round on my companion with an inquiring eye—he understood me, and informed me that these were a company of *friends*, who had met together to win each other's money, and be agreeable. "Is that all?" exclaimed I, "why then, I pray you, make way, and let me escape from this temple of abominations, or who knows but these people, who meet together to toil, worry and fatigue themselves to death, and give it the name of pleasure —and who win each others money by way of being agreeable—may some one of them take a liking to me, and pick my pocket, or break my head in a paroxysm of hearty good-will!"

thy friend.

MUSTAPHA.

BY ANTHONY EVERGREEN, GENT.

Nunc est bibendum, nunc pede libero
Pulsanda tellus.   HOR.

Now is the tyme for wine and myrtheful sportes,
For daunce, and song, and disportes of syche sortes.

LINK FID.

The winter campaign has opened. Fashion has summoned her numerous legions at the sound of trumpet, tamborine and drum, and all the harmonious minstrelsy of the orchestra, to hasten from the dull, silent, and insipid glades and groves, where they have vegetated during the summer, recovering from the ravages of the last winter's campaign. Our fair ones have hurried to town eager to pay their devotions to this tutelary deity, and to make an offering at her shrine of the few pale and transient roses they gathered in their healthful retreat. The fiddler rosins his bow, the card-table devotee is shuffling her pack, the young ladies are industriously spangling muslins, and the tea-party heroes are airing their *chapeaux bras* and pease-blossom breeches, to prepare for figuring in the gay circle of smiles, and graces, and beauty. Now the fine lady forgets her country friends in the hurry of fashionable engagements, or receives the simple intruder who has foolishly accepted her thousand pressing invitations, with such *politeness* that the poor soul determines never to come again—now the gay buck who erst figured at Ballston and quaffed the pure spring, exchanges the sparkling water for still more sparkling champaign, and deserts the *nymph* of the fountain, to enlist under the standard of jolly Bacchus. In short, now is the important time of the year in which to harangue the bon-ton reader, and like some ancient hero in front of the battle, to spirit him up to deeds of noble daring, or still more noble suffering, in the ranks of fashionable warfare.

Such, indeed, has been my intention; but the number of cases which have lately come before me, and the variety of complaints I have received from a crowd of honest and well-meaning correspondents, call for more immediate attention. A host of appeals, petitions, and letters of advice are now before me; and I believe the shortest way to satisfy my petitioners, memorialists, and advisers will be to publish their letters, as I suspect the object of most of them is merely to get into print.

TO ANTHONY EVERGREEN, GENT.

SIR,

As you appear to have taken to yourself the trouble of meddling in the concerns of the beau monde, I take the liberty of appealing to you on a subject, which though considered merely as a very good joke, has occasioned me great vexation and expense. You must know I pride myself on being very *useful* to the ladies; that is, I take boxes for them at the theatre, go shopping with them, supply them with boquets, and furnish them with novels from the circulating library. In consequence of these attentions I am become a great favourite, and there is seldom a party going on in the city without my having an invitation. The grievance I have to mention, is the exchange of hats which takes place on these occasions; for, to speak my mind freely, there are certain young gentlemen who seem to consider fashionable parties as mere places to barter old clothes, and I am informed that a number of them manage by this great system of exchange to keep their crowns decently covered without their hatter *suffering* in the least by it.

It was but lately that I went to a private ball with a new hat, and on returning in the latter part of the evening, and asking for it, the scoundrel of a servant, with a broad grin informed me, that the new hats had been dealt out half an hour since, and they were then on the third quality; and I was in the end obliged to borrow a young lady's beaver rather than go home with any of the ragged remnants that were left.

Now I would wish to know, if there is no possibility of having these offenders punished by law—and whether it would not be advisable for ladies to mention in their cards of invitation, as a postscript, "stealing hats and shawls positively prohibited." At any rate, I would thank you mr. Evergreen, to discountenance the thing totally by publishing in your paper, that *stealing a hat is no joke.*

Your humble servant,

WALTER WITHERS.

My correspondent is informed that the police have determined to take this matter into consideration, and have set apart Saturday mornings for the cognizance of *fashionable larcenies.*

MR. EVERGREEN,

SIR,

Do you think a married woman may lawfully put her husband right in a story, before strangers, when she knows him to be in the wrong, and can any thing authorize a wife in the exclamation of—"lord, my dear, how can you say so!"

MARGARET TIMSON.

DEAR ANTHONY,

Going down Broadway this morning in a great hurry I ran full against an object which at first put me to a prodigious non plus. Observing it to be dressed in a man's hat, a cloth overcoat, and spatterdashes, I framed my apology accordingly, exclaiming "my dear *sir,* I ask ten thousand pardons—I assure you, *sir,* it was entirely accidental—pray excuse me *sir,* &c." At every one of these excuses, the thing answered me with a downright laugh; at which, I was not a little surprised until, on resorting to my pocket glass I discovered that it was no other than my old acquaintance Clarinda Trollop—I never was more chagrined in my life, for being an old bachelor I like to appear as young as possible, and am always boasting of the goodness of my eyes. I beg of you, mr. Evergreen, if you have any feeling for your cotemporaries, to discourage this hermaphrodite mode of dress; for really, if the fashion take, we poor bachelors will be utterly at a loss to distinguish a woman from a man. Pray let me know your opinion, sir, whether a lady who wears a man's hat and spatterdashes before marriage, may not be apt to usurp some other article of his dress afterwards.

Your humble servant,

RODERICK WORRY.

DEAR MR. EVERGREEN,

The other night, at Richard the Third, I sat behind three gentlemen, who talked very loud on the subject of Richard's wooing Lady Ann directly in the face of his crimes against that lady. One of them declared

such an unnatural scene would be hooted at in China. Pray, sir, was that
mr. Wizard?   SELINA BADGER.

P. S. The gentleman I allude to, had a pocket glass, and wore his
hair fastened behind by a tortoise shell comb, with two teeth wanting.

MR. EVERGRIN,

SIR,
Being a little curious in the affairs of the toilette, I was much interested by the sage Mustapha's remarks in your last number, concerning
the art of manufacturing a modern fine lady. I would have you caution
your fair readers, however, to be very careful in the management of
their machinery, as a deplorable accident happened last assembly, in
consequence of the architecture of a lady's figure not being sufficiently
strong. In the middle of one of the cotillions the company was suddenly alarmed by a tremendous crash at the lower end of the room,
and on crouding to the place, discovered that it was a fine figure which
had unfortunately broken down, from too great exertion in a pigeon-
wing. By great good luck I secured the *corset,* which I carried home in
triumph, and the next morning had it publickly dissected and a lecture
read on it at Surgeon's Hall. I have since commenced a dessertation on
the subject, in which I shall treat of the superiority of those figures
manufactured by steel, stay-tape and whale-bone, to those formed by
dame nature. I shall show clearly that the Venus de Medicis has no
pretension to beauty of form, as she never wore stays, and her
waist is in exact proportion to the rest of her body. I shall inquire into
the mysteries of compression, and how tight a *figure* can be laced
without danger of fainting; and whether it would not be adviseable for
a lady when dressing for a ball, to be attended by the family physician, as culprits are when tortured on the rack—to know how much
more nature will endure. I shall prove that ladies have discovered the
secret of that notorious juggler who offered to squeeze himself into a
quart bottle, and I shall demonstrate to the satisfaction of every fashionable reader, that there is a degree of heroism in purchasing a preposterously slender waist at the expense of an old age of decrepitude and
rheumaticks. This dissertation shall be published as soon as finished,
and distributed gratis among boarding-school madams, and all worthy
matrons who are ambitious that their daughters should sit straight, move
like clockwork, and "do credit to their bringing up." In the mean time,
I have hung up the skeleton of the corset in the Museum, beside a
dissected weazel and a stuffed alligator, where it may be inspected by
all those naturalists who are fond of studying the "human form divine."
                                                        Yours, &c.
                                                   JULIAN COGNOUS.

P. S. By accurate calculation I find it is dangerous for a fine figure, when full dressed, to pronounce a word of more than three syllables. Fine figure, if in love, may indulge in a gentle sigh, but a sob is hazardous. Fine figure may smile with safety, may even venture as far as a giggle, but must never risk a loud laugh. Figure must never play the part of a *confidante;* as at a tea-party some five evenings since, a young lady whose unparalleled impalpability of waist was the envy of the drawing-room, burst with an important secret, and had three ribs [of her corset] fractured on the spot.

MR. EVERGREEN,

SIR,

I am one of those industrious gemmen who labour hard to obtain currency in the fashionable world. I have went to great expense in little boots, short vests, and long breeches—my coat is regularly imported per stage from Philadelphia, duly insured against all risks, and my boots are smuggled from Bond-street. I have lounged in Broadway with one of the most crooked walking-sticks I could procure, and have sported a pair of salmon coloured small-clothes and flame coloured stockings, at every concert and ball to which I could purchase admission. Being affeared that I might possibly appear to less advantage as a pedestrian, in consequence of my being rather short and a little bandy, I have lately hired a tall horse with cropped ears and a cocked tail, on which I have joined the cavalcade of pretty gemmen, who exhibit bright stirrups every fine morning in Broadway, and take a canter of two miles per day, at the rate of 300 dollars per annum. But, sir, all this expense has been laid out in vain, for I can scarcely get a partner at an assembly, or an invitation to a tea-party. Pray sir inform me what more I can do to acquire admission into the true stylish circles, and whether it would not be advisable to charter a curricle for a month and have my cypher put on it, as is done by certain dashers of my acquaintance.

Yours to serve,

MALVOLIO DUBSTER.

TEA,

A POEM.

FROM THE MILL OF PINDAR COCKLOFT ESQ.

and earnestly recommended to the attention of all maidens of a certain age.

Old time, my dear girls, is a knave who in truth
From the fairest of beauties will pilfer their youth;

MALVOLIO DUBSTER.

Woodcut by Alexander Anderson (1775–1870), the first American wood engraver, for the second American edition of *Salmagundi* (D. Longworth: New York, 1814).

Who by constant attention and wiley deceit
For ever is coaxing some grace to retreat;
And, like crafty seducer, with subtle approach,
The further indulged, will still further encroach.
Since this "thief of the world" has made off with your bloom,
And left you some score of stale years in its room—
Has deprived you of all those gay dreams that would dance,
In your brains at fifteen, and your bosoms entrance,
And has forced you almost to renounce in despair
The hope of a husband's affection and care—
Since such is the case, (and a case rather hard!)
Permit one who holds you in special regard,
To furnish such hints in your loveless estate
As may shelter your names from detraction and hate.
Too often our maidens grown aged, I ween,
Indulge to excess in the workings of spleen;
And at times, when annoyed by the slights of *man*-kind,
Work off their resentment by *speaking their mind;*
Assemble together in snuff taking clan,
And hold round the tea-urn a solemn divan,
A convention of tattling—a *tea party* hight,
    Which, like meeting of witches, is brewed up at night:
Where each matron arrives, fraught with tales of surprize,
With knowing suspicion and doubtful surmize,
Like the broomstick whirl'd hags that appear in Macbeth,
Each bearing some relick of venom or death,
"To stir up the toil and to double the trouble,
That fire may burn, and that cauldron may bubble."
    When the party commences, all starched and all glum,
They talk of the weather, their corns, or sit mum:
They will tell you of cambrick, of ribbons, of lace,
How cheap they were sold—and will name you the place.
They discourse of their colds, and they hem and they cough,
And complain of their servants to pass the time off;
Or list to the tale of some doating mamma
How her ten weeks old baby will laugh and say *taa!*
    But *tea*, that enlivener of wit and of soul
More loquacious by far than the draughts of the bowl,
Soon unloosens the tongue and enlivens the mind,
And enlightens their eyes to the faults of mankind.
It brings on the tapis their neighbours defects,
The faults of their friends or their wilful neglects;
Reminds them of many a good natured tale,

About those who are stylish or those who are frail,
Till the sweet tempered dames are converted by tea,
Into character manglers—Gunaikophagi.*

'Twas thus with the Pythia who served at the fount,
That flowed near the far famed parnassian mount:
While the steam she inhaled of the sulphuric spring,
Her vision expanded, her fancy took wing,
By its aid she pronounced the oracular will,
That Apollo commanded his sons to fulfill.
But alas! the sad vestal performing the rite
Appeared like a demon—terrifick to sight,
E'en the priests of Apollo averted their eyes,
And the temple of Delphi resounded her cries.
But quitting the nymph of the tripod of yore,
We return to the dames of the tea-pot once more.
   In harmless chit-chat an acquaintance they roast,
And serve up a friend, as they serve up a toast,
Some gentle *faux pas*, or some female *mistake*,
Is like sweetmeats delicious, or relished as cake;
A bit of broad scandal is like a dry crust,
It would stick in the throat, so they butter it first
With a little affected good-nature, and cry
"No body regrets the thing deeper than I."
Our young ladies nibble a good name in play
As for pastime they nibble a biscuit away:
While with shrugs and surmises, the toothless old dame,
As she mumbles a crust she will mumble a name.
And as the fell sisters astonished the scot,
In predicting of Banquo's descendants the lot,
Making shadows of kings, amid flashes of light,
To appear in array and to frown in his sight.
So they conjure up spectres all hideous in hue,
Which, as shades of their neighbours, are passed in review.
   The wives of our cits of inferior degree,
Will soak up repute in a little *bohea*;
The potion is vulgar, and vulgar the slang
With which on their neighbours' defects they harangue.
But the scandal improves, (a refinement in wrong)

---

*I was very anxious that our friend Pindar, should give up this learned word,
as being rather above the comprehension of his fair readers; but the old gentleman,
according to custom, swore it was the finest point in his whole poem—so I knew it
was in vain to say any more about it.   W. WIZARD.

As our matrons are richer and rise to *souchong*.
With *hyson*—a beverage that's still more refined,
Our ladies of fashion enliven their mind,
And by nods, inuendos, and hints, and what not,
Reputations and tea send together to pot.
While madam in cambricks and laces arrayed;
With her plate and her liveries in splendid parade,
Will drink in *imperial* a friend at a sup,
Or in *gunpowder* blow them by dozens all up.
Ah me! how I groan when with full swelling sail,
Wafted stately along by the favouring gale,
A China ship proudly arrives in our bay,
Displaying her streamers and blazing away.
Oh! more fell to our port, is the cargo she bears,
Than granadoes, torpedoes, or warlike affairs:
Each chest is a bombshell thrown into our town
To shatter repute and bring characters down.
    Ye Samquas, ye Chinquas, ye Chouquas, so free,
Who discharge on our coast your cursed quantums of tea,
Oh think as ye waft the sad weed from your strand,
Of the plagues and vexations ye deal to our land.
As the Upas' dread breath o'er the plain where it flies,
Empoisons and blasts each green blade that may rise,
So wherever the leaves of your shrub find their way,
The social affections soon suffer decay:
Like to Java's drear waste they embarren the heart,
Till the blossoms of love and of friendship depart.
    Ah ladies, and was it by heaven designed,
That ye should be merciful, loving and kind!
Did it form you like angels, and send you below
To prophesy peace—to bid charity flow!
And have ye thus left your primeval estate,
And wandered so widely—so strangely of late?
Alas! the sad cause I too plainly can see—
These evils have all come upon you through *tea*:
Cursed weed that can make our fair spirits resign
The character mild of their mission divine,
That can blot from their bosoms that tenderness true,
Which from female to female forever is due!
Oh how nice is the texture—how fragile the frame
Of that delicate blossom, a female's fair fame!
Tis the sensitive plant, it recoils from the breath
And shrinks from the touch as if pregnant with death.

How often, how often, has innocence sigh'd;
Has beauty been reft of its honour—its pride;
Has virtue, though pure as an angel of light,
Been painted as dark as a demon of night:
All offer'd up victims, an *auto de fe,*
At the gloomy cabals—the dark orgies of tea.
    If I, in the remnant that's left me of life,
Am to suffer the torments of slanderous strife,
Let me fall I implore in the slang-whangers claw,
Where the evil is open, and subject to law.
Not nibbled and mumbled and put to the rack
By the sly underminings of tea party clack:
Condemn me, ye gods, to a newspaper roasting,
But spare me! oh spare me a tea table toasting!

SALMAGUNDI NO. XX

NO. XX]   *Monday, January* 25, 1808.

FROM MY ELBOW-CHAIR.
Extremum hunc nihi concede laborem. VIRG.
"Soft you, a word or two before we part."

In this season of festivity when the gate of time swings open on its
hinges, and an honest rosy-faced New-Year comes waddling in, like a
jolly fat-sided alderman, loaded with good wishes, good humour and
minced pies—at this joyous era it has been the custom, from time immemorial, in this antient and respectable city, for periodical writers,
from reverend, grave, and potent essayists like ourselves, down to the
humble but industrious editors of magazines, reviews, and newspapers,
to tender their subscribers the compliments of the season, and when
they have slily thawed their hearts with a little of the sunshine of flattery, to conclude by delicately dunning them for their arrears of subscription money. In like manner the carriers of newspapers, who undoubtedly belong to the antient and honourable order of literati, do
regularly at the commencement of the year, salute their patrons with
abundance of excellent advice, conveyed in exceeding good poetry, for
which the aforesaid good-natured patrons are well pleased to pay them
exactly twenty-five cents. In walking the streets, I am every day saluted
with good wishes from old grey-headed negroes, whom I never recollect

to have seen before; and it was but a few days ago, that I was called out to receive the compliments of an ugly old woman, who last spring was employed by mrs. Cockloft to white-wash my room and put things in order: a phrase which, if rightly understood, means little else than huddling every thing into holes and corners, so that if I want to find any particular article, it is, in the language of an humble but expressive saying—"looking for a needle in a haystack." Not recognizing my visitor, I demanded by what authority she wished me a "Happy New-Year?" Her claim was one of the weakest she could have urged, for I have an innate and mortal antipathy to this custom of *putting things to rights*— so giving the old witch a pistareen, I desired her forthwith to mount her broomstick, and ride off as fast as possible.

Of all the various ranks of society, the bakers alone, to their immortal honour be it recorded, depart from this practice of making a market of congratulations; and, in addition to always allowing thirteen to the dozen, do, with great liberality, instead of drawing on the purses of their customers at the New-Year, present them with divers large, fair spiced cakes, which, like the shield of Achilles, or an egyptian obelisk, are adorned with figures of a variety of strange animals, that in their conformation, out-marvel all the wild wonders of nature.

This honest grey-beard custom of setting apart a certain portion of this good-for-nothing existence, for purposes of cordiality, social merriment, and good cheer, is one of the inestimable relicks handed down to us from our worthy dutch ancestors. In perusing one of the manuscripts from my worthy grandfather's mahogany chest of drawers, I find the new year was celebrated with great festivity during that golden age of our city, when the reins of government were held by the renowned Rip Van Dam, who always did honour to the season, by *seeing out the old year*, a ceremony which consisted of plying his guests with bumpers, until not one of them was capable of seeing. "Truely," observes my grandfather, who was generally of these parties—"Truely, he was a most stately and magnificent burgomaster, inasmuch, as he did right lustily carouse it with his friends, about new-year; roasting huge quantities of turkies; baking innumerable minced pies, and smacking the lips of all fair ladies the which he did meet, with such sturdy emphasis that the same might have been heard the distance of a stone's throw." In his days, according to my grandfather, were first invented those notable cakes, hight *new-year cookies*, which originally were impressed on one side with the honest burley countenance of the illustrious Rip, and on the other with that of the noted St. Nicholas, vulgarly called Santaclaus— of all the saints in the kalendar the most venerated by true hollanders, and their unsophisticated descendants. These cakes are to this time given on the first of January, to all visitors, together with a glass of cherry-bounce, or raspberry-brandy. It is with great regret, however, I observe that the simplicity of this venerable usage has been much violated by modern pretenders to style, and our respectable new-year cookies, and cherry-bounce, elbowed aside by plumb-cake and outlandish liqueurs, in the same way that our worthy old dutch families are out-dazzled by modern upstarts, and mushroom cockneys.

In addition to this divine origin of new-year festivity, there is something exquisitely grateful to a good-natured mind, in seeing every face dressed in smiles—in hearing the oft repeated salutations that flow spontaneously from the heart to the lips—in beholding the poor for once, enjoying the smiles of plenty, and forgetting the cares which press hard upon them, in the jovial revelry of the feelings—the young children decked out in their sunday clothes, and freed from their only cares, the cares of the school, tripping through the streets on errands of pleasure—and even the very negroes, those holiday-loving rogues, gorgeously arrayed in cast-off finery, collected in juntoes at corners, displaying their white teeth, and making the welkin ring with bursts of laughter, loud enough to crack even the icy cheek of old winter. There is something so pleasant in all this, that I confess it would give me a real pain, to behold the frigid influence of modern style, cheating us of this jubilee of the heart, and converting it, as it does every other article of social intercourse, into an idle, and unmeaning ceremony. 'Tis the annual festival of good-humour—it comes in the dead of winter, when nature is without a charm, when our pleasures are contracted to the fire-side, and where every thing that unlocks the icy fetters of the heart, and sets the genial current flowing, should be cherished, as a stray lamb found in the wilderness, or a flower blooming among thorns and briers.

Animated by these sentiments, it is with peculiar satisfaction I perceived that the last new-year was kept with more than ordinary enthusiasm. It seemed as if the good old times had rolled back again, and brought with them all the honest, unceremonious intercourse of those golden days, when people were more open and sincere, more moral, and more hospitable than now—when every object carried about it a charm which the hand of time has stolen away, or turned to a deformity—when the women were more simple, more domestick, more lovely, and more true; and when even the sun, like a hearty old blade, as he is, shone with a genial lustre, unknown in these degenerate days:— in short, those fairy times when I was a mad-cap boy, crowding every enjoyment into the present moment—making of the past an oblivion—of the future a heaven; and careless of all that was "over the hills and far away." Only one thing was wanting to make every part of the celebration accord with its antient simplicity.—The ladies, who (I write it with the most piercing regret) are generally at the head of all domestick innovations, most fastidiously refused that mark of good will, that chaste and holy salute which was so fashionable in the happy days of governor Rip and the patriarchs.—Even the miss Cocklofts, who belong to a family that is the last entrenchment behind which the manners of the good old school have retired, made violent opposition; and whenever a gentleman entered the room, immediately put themselves in a posture of defence;—this Will Wizard, with his usual shrewdness, insists was only to give the visitor a hint that they expected an attack, and declares he has uniformly observed, that the resistance of those ladies, who make the greatest noise and bustle, is most easily overcome. This sad innovation originated with my good aunt Charity, who was as arrant a tabby as ever wore whiskers; and I am not a little afflicted to find that she has found so many followers, even among the young and beautiful.

In compliance with an antient and venerable custom, sanctioned by time and our ancestors, and more especially by my own inclinations, I will take this opportunity to salute my readers with as many good wishes, as I can possibly spare; for in truth, I have been so prodigal of late, that I have but few remaining. I should have offered my congratulations sooner, but to be candid, having made the last new-year's campaign, according to custom under cousin Christopher, in which I have seen some pretty hard service, my head has been somewhat out of order of late, and my intellects rather cloudy for clear writing. Beside, I may allege as another reason, that I have deferred my greetings until this day, which is exactly one year since we introduced ourselves to the publick; and surely periodical writers have the same right of dating from the commencement of their works, that monarchs have from the time of their coronation, or our most puissant republick, from the declaration of its independence.

These good wishes are warmed into more than usual benevolence, by the thought that I am now perhaps addressing my old friends for the last time. That we should thus cut off our work in the very vigour of its existence, may excite some little matter of wonder in this enlightened community. Now though we could give a variety of good reasons, for so doing, yet it would be an ill-natured act to deprive the publick of such an admirable opportunity to indulge in their favourite amusement of conjecture—so we generously leave them to flounder in the smooth ocean of glorious uncertainty. Beside, we have ever considered it as beneath persons of our dignity, to account for our movements or caprices—thank heaven we are not like the unhappy rulers of this enlightened land, accountable to the mob for our actions, or dependant on their smiles for support:—this much, however, we will say, it is not for want of subjects that we stop our career. We are not in the situation of poor Alexander the Great, who wept, as well indeed he might, because there were no more worlds to conquer; for, to do justice to this queer, odd, rantipole city, and this whimsical country, there is matter enough in them, to keep our risible muscles, and our pens going until doomsday.

Most people, in taking a farewel which may perhaps be forever, are anxious to part on good terms, and it is usual in such melancholy occasions, for even enemies to shake hands, forget their previous quarrels, and bury all former animosities in parting regrets. Now because most people do this, I am determined to act in quite a different way; for as I have lived, so should I wish to die in my own way, without imitating any person, whatever may be his rank, talents, or reputation. Besides, if I know our trio, we have no enmities to obliterate, no hatchet to bury, and as to all injuries—those we have long since forgiven. At this moment, there is not an individual in the world, not even the Pope himself, to whom we have any personal hostility. But if, shutting their eyes to the many striking proofs of good-nature displayed through the whole course of this work, there should be any persons so singularly ridiculous as to take offence at our strictures, we heartily forgive their stupidity, earnestly intreating them to desist from all manifestations of ill-humour, lest they should, peradventure, be classed under some one of the denominations of recreants, we have felt it our duty to hold up to public ridicule. Even at this moment, we feel a glow of parting philanthropy stealing upon us—a sentiment of cordial good will towards the numerous host of readers that have jogged on at our heels during the last year; and in justice to ourselves, must seriously protest, that if at any time we have treated them a little ungently, it was purely in that spirit of hearty affection, with which a schoolmaster drubs an unlucky urchin, or a humane muleteer his recreant animal, at the very moment when his heart is brim-full of loving kindness. If this is not considered an ample justification, so much the worse; for in that case I fear we shall remain forever unjustified—a most desperate extremity, and worthy of every man's commisseration!

One circumstance in particular, has tickled us mightily, as we jogged along; and that is, the astonishing secrecy with which we have been able to carry on our lucubrations! Fully aware of the profound sagacity of the publick of Gotham, and their wonderful faculty of distinguishing a writer by his style, it is with great self-congratulation we find that suspicion has never pointed to us as the authors of Salmagundi. Our grey-beard speculations have been most bountifully attributed to sundry smart young gentlemen, who, for aught we know, have no beards at all; and we have often been highly amused, when they were charged with the sin of writing what their harmless minds never conceived, to see them affect all the blushing modesty and beautiful embarrassment of detected virgin authors. The profound and penetrating publick, having so long been led away from truth and nature by a constant perusal of those delectable histories, and romances, from beyond seas, in which human nature is for the most part wickedly mangled and debauched, have never once imagined this work was a genuine and most authentick history—that the Cocklofts were a real family dwelling in the city— paying scot and lot, entitled to the right of suffrage, and holding several respectable offices in the corporation.—As little do they suspect that there is a knot of merry old bachelors seated snugly in the old-fashioned parlour of an old-fashioned dutch house, with a weathercock on the top, that came from Holland; who amuse themselves of an evening by laughing at their neighbours, in an honest way, and who manage to jog on through the streets of our antient and venerable city, without elbowing or being elbowed by a living soul.

When we first adopted the idea of discontinuing this work, we determined, in order to give the criticks a fair opportunity for dissection, to declare ourselves, one and all, absolutely defunct; for it is one of the rare and invaluable privileges of a periodical writer, that by an act of innocent suicide he may lawfully consign himself to the grave, and cheat the world of posthumous renown. But we abandoned this scheme for many substantial reasons. In the first place, we care but little for the opinion of criticks, who we consider a kind of freebooters in the republick of letters; who, like deer, goats, and divers other graminivorous animals, gain subsistence by gorging upon the buds and leaves of the young shrubs of the forest, thereby robbing them of their verdure, and retarding their progress to maturity. It also occurred to us that though an author might lawfully, in all countries, kill himself outright, yet this privilege did not extend to the raising himself from the dead, if he was ever so anxious; and all that is left him in such a case, is to take the benefit of the metempsychosis act, and revive under a new name and form.

Far be it, therefore, from us, to condemn ourselves to useless embarrassments, should we ever be disposed to resume the guardianship of this learned city of Gotham, and finish this invaluable work, which is yet but half completed. We hereby openly and seriously declare that we are not dead, but intend, if it pleases providence, to live for many years to come—to enjoy life with the genuine relish of honest souls, careless of riches, honours, and every thing but a good name, among good fellows; and with the full expectation of shuffling off the remnant of existence, after the excellent fashion of that merry grecian, who died laughing.

TO THE LADIES.

BY ANTHONY EVERGREEN, GENT.

Next to our being a knot of independent old bachelors, there is nothing on which we pride ourselves more highly, than upon possessing that true chivalrick spirit of gallantry, which distinguished the days of king Arthur, and his valiant peers of the Round-table. We cannot, therefore, leave the lists where we have so long been tilting at folly, without giving a farewel salutation to those noble dames and beauteous damsels who have honoured us with their presence at the tourney. Like true knights, the only recompense we crave is the smile of beauty, and the approbation of those gentle fair ones, whose smile and whose approbation far excels all the trophies of honour, and all the rewards of successful ambition. True it is that we have suffered infinite perils, in standing forth as their champions, from the sly attacks of sundry arch caitiffs, who in the overflowings of their malignity have even accused us of entering the lists as defenders of the very foibles and faults of the sex.—Would that we could meet with these recreants hand to hand—they should receive no more quarter than giants and enchanters in romance.

Had we a spark of vanity in our natures, here is a glorious occasion to show our skill in refuting these illiberal insinuations—but there is something manly, and ingenuous, in making an honest confession of ones offences when about retiring from the world—and so, without any more ado, we doff our helmets and thus publickly plead guilty to the deadly sin of GOOD NATURE; hoping and expecting forgiveness from our good natured readers—yet careless whether they bestow it or not. And in this we do but imitate sundry condemned criminals; who, finding themselves convicted of a capital crime, with great openness and candour, do generally in their last dying speech make a confession of all their previous offences, which confession is always read with great delight by all true lovers of biography.

Still, however, notwithstanding our notorious devotion to the gentle sex, and our indulgent partiality, we have endeavoured, on divers occasions, with all the polite and becoming delicacy of true respect, to reclaim them from many of those delusive follies and unseemly peccadilloes in which they are unhappily too prone to indulge. We have warned them against the sad consequences of encountering our midnight damps and withering wintry blasts—we have endeavoured, with pious hand, to snatch them from the wildering mazes of the waltz, and thus rescuing them from the arms of strangers, to restore them to the bosoms of their friends—to preserve them from the nakedness, the famine, the cobweb muslins, the vinegar cruet, the corset, the stay tape, the buckram, and all the other miseries and racks of a *fine figure*. But above all we have endeavoured to lure them from the mazes of a dissipated world, where they wander about careless of their value, until they lose their original worth—and to restore them before it is too late, to the sacred asylum of home, the soil most congenial to the opening blossom of female loveliness, where it blooms and expands in safety in the fostering sunshine of maternal affection, and where its heavenly sweets are best known and appreciated.

Modern philosophers may determine the proper destination of the sex—they may assign to them an extensive and brilliant orbit in which to revolve, to the delight of the million and the confusion of man's superior intellect; but when on this subject we disclaim philosophy, and appeal to the higher tribunal of the heart—and what heart that had not lost its better feelings, would ever seek to repose its happiness on the bosom of one, whose pleasures all lay without the threshold of home—who snatched enjoyment only in the whirlpool of dissipation, and amid the thoughtless and evanescent gaiety of a ball room. The fair one who is forever in the career of amusement, may for a while dazzle, astonish and entertain; but we are content with coldly admiring and fondly turn from glitter and noise, to seek the happy fire side of social life there to confide our dearest and best affections.

Yet some there are, and we delight to mention them, who mingle freely with the world, unsullied by its contaminations; whose brilliant minds, like the stars of the firmament, are destined to shed their light abroad, and gladden every beholder with their radiance—to withhold them from the world, would be doing it injustice—they are inestimable gems, which were never formed to be shut up in caskets; but to be the pride and ornament of elegant society.

We have endeavoured always to discriminate between a female of this superior order, and the thoughtless votary of pleasure; who, destitute of intellectual resources, is servilely dependant on others for every little pittance of enjoyment; who exhibits herself incessantly amid the noise, the giddy frolick and capricious variety of fashionable assemblages; dissipating her languid affections on a crowd—lavishing her ready smiles with indiscriminate prodigality on the worthy, or the undeserving; and listening, with equal vacancy of mind, to the conversation of the enlightened, the frivolity of the coxcomb, and the flourish of the fiddlestick.

There is a certain artificial polish—a common place vivacity acquired by perpetually mingling in the *beau-monde*; which, in the commerce of the world, supplies the place of natural suavity and good humour, but is purchased at the expense of all original and sterling traits of character. By a kind of fashionable discipline, the eye is taught to brighten, the lip to smile, and the whole countenance to emanate with

the semblance of friendly welcome—while the bosom is unwarmed by
a single spark of genuine kindness, or good will. This elegant simulation
may be admired by the connoisseur of human character, as a perfection
of art; but the heart is not to be deceived by the superficial illusion:
it turns with delight to the timid retiring fair one, whose smile is the
smile of nature; whose blush is the soft suffusion of delicate sensibility;
and whose affections, unblighted by the chilling effects of dissipation,
glow with all the tenderness and purity of artless youth. Her's is a
singleness of mind, a native innocence of manners, and a sweet timidity,
that steal insensibly upon the heart and lead it a willing captive—though
venturing occasionally among the fairy haunts of pleasure, she shrinks
from the broad glare of notoriety, and seems to seek refuge among her
friends, even from the admiration of the world.

These observations bring to mind a little allegory in one of the
manuscripts of the sage Mustapha, which being in some measure
applicable to the subject of this essay, we transcribe for the benefit of
our fair readers.

Among the numerous race of the Bedouins, who people the vast tracts
of Arabia Deserta, is a small tribe, remarkable for their habits of
solitude and love of independence. They are of a rambling disposition,
roving from waste to waste, slaking their thirst at such scanty pools
as are found in those cheerless plains, and glory in the unenvied
liberty they enjoy. A youthful arab of this tribe, a simple son of nature,
at length growing weary of his precarious and unsettled mode of life,
determined to set out in search of some permanent abode. "I will seek"
said he "some happy region, some generous clime, where the dews of
heaven diffuse fertility—I will find out some unfailing stream, and
forsaking the joyless life of my forefathers, settle on its borders, dispose
my mind to gentle pleasures and tranquil enjoyments, and never
wander more."

Enchanted with this picture of pastoral felicity, he departed from the
tents of his companions, and having journeyed during five days, on the
sixth, as the sun was just rising in all the splendours of the east, he
lifted up his eyes and beheld extended before him, in smiling luxuriance,
the fertile regions of Arabia the Happy. Gently swelling hills, tufted
with blooming groves, swept down into luxuriant vales, enamelled
with flowers of never withering beauty. The sun, no longer darting his
rays with torrid fervour, beamed with a genial warmth that gladdened
and enriched the landscape. A pure and temperate serenity, an air of
voluptuous repose, a smile of contented abundance pervaded the face
of nature, and every zephyr breathed a thousand delicious odours. The
soul of the youthful wanderer expanded with delight—he raised his
eyes to heaven, and almost mingled with his tribute of gratitude a

sigh of regret, that he had lingered so long amid the sterile solitudes of the desart.

With fond impatience he hastened to make choice of a stream where he might fix his habitation, and taste the promised sweets of this land of delight. But here commenced an unforseen perplexity; for, though he beheld innumerable streams on every side, yet not one could he find which completely answered his high raised expectations. One abounded with wild and picturesque beauty, but it was capricious and unsteady in its course; sometimes dashing its angry billows against the rocks, and often raging and overflowing its banks. Another flowed smoothly along, with out even a ripple or a murmur; but its bottom was soft and muddy, and its current dull and sluggish. A third was pure and transparent, but its waters were of a chilling coldness, and it had rocks and flints in its bosom. A fourth was dulcet in its tinklings, and graceful in its meanderings; but it had a cloying sweetness that palled upon the taste; while a fifth possessed a sparkling vivacity, and a pungency of flavour, that deterred the wanderer from repeating his draught.

The youthful Bedouin, began to weary with fruitless trials and repeated disappointments, when his attention was suddenly attracted by a lively brook, whose dancing waves glittered in the sunbeams, and whose prattling current communicated an air of bewitching gaiety to the surrounding landscape. The heart of the wayworn traveller beat with expectation; but on regarding it attentively in its course, he found that it constantly avoided the embowering shade, loitering with equal fondness, whether gliding through the rich valley, or over the barren sand—that the fragrant flower, the fruitful shrub, and worthless bramble were alike fostered by its waves, and that its current was often interrupted by unprofitable weeds. With idle ambition it expanded itself beyond its proper bounds, and spread into a shallow waste of water, destitute of beauty or utility, and babbling along with uninteresting vivacity and vapid turbulence.

The wandering son of the desert turned away with a sigh of regret, and pitied a stream which, if content within its natural limits, might have been the pride of the valley, and the object of all his wishes. Pensive, musing and disappointed, he slowly pursued his now almost hopeless pilgrimage, and had rambled for some time along the margin of a gentle rivulet, before he became sensible of its beauties. It was a simple pastoral stream, which, shunning the noonday glare, pursued its unobtrusive course through retired and tranquil vales—now dimpling among flowery banks and tufted shrubbery; now winding among spicy groves, whose aromatick foliage fondly bent down to meet the limpid wave. Sometimes, but not often, it would venture from its covert to stray through a flowery meadow, but quickly, as if fearful of being seen, stole back again into its more congenial shade, and there lingered with sweet delay. Wherever it bent its course, the face of nature brightened into smiles, and a perennial spring reigned upon its borders. The warblers of the woodland delighted to quit their recesses and carol among its bowers; while the turtle-dove, the timid fawn, the soft-eyed gazel, and all the rural populace who joy in the sequestered haunts of nature, resorted to its vicinity.—Its pure transparent waters rolled over snow-white sands, and heaven itself was reflected in its tranquil bosom.

The simple arab threw himself upon its verdant margin—he tasted the silver tide, and it was like nectar to his lips—he bounded with transport, for he had found the object of his wayfaring. "Here," cried he, "will I pitch my tent—here will I pass my days; for pure, oh fair stream, is thy gentle current; beauteous are the borders; and the grove must be a paradise that is refreshed by thy meanderings!"

> Pendent opera interrupta.   VIRG.
> The work's all aback.   LINK FID.

"How hard it is" exclaims the divine Con-fut-sé (better known among the illiterate by the name of Confucius) for a man to bite off his own nose! At this moment I, William Wizard, esq. feel the full force of this remark, and cannot but give vent to my tribulation at being obliged through the whim of friend Langstaff, to stop short in my literary career when at the very point of astonishing my country, and reaping the brightest laurels of literature. We daily hear of shipwrecks, of failures and bankruptcies, they are trifling mishaps which from their frequency excite but little astonishment or sympathy; but it is not often that we hear of a man's letting immortality slip through his fingers, and when he does meet with such a misfortune, who would deny him the comfort of bewailing his calamity?

Next to the embargo laid upon our commerce, the greatest publick annoyance is the embargo laid upon our work: in consequence of which the produce of my wits like that of my country must remain at home, and my ideas, like so many merchantmen in port or redoubtable frigates in the Potomac, moulder away in the mud of my own brain. I know of few things in this world more annoying than to be interrupted in the middle of a favourite story, at the most interesting part, where one expects to shine; or to have a conversation broken off just when you are about coming out with a score of excellent jokes, not one of which but was good enough to make every fine figure in corsets literally split her sides with laughter.—In some such predicament am I placed at present;

and I do protest to you, my good-looking and well-beloved readers, by the chop-sticks of the immortal Josh, I was on the very brink of treating you with a full broadside of the most ingenious and instructive essays, that your precious noddles were ever bothered with.

In the first place, I had with infinite labour and pains, and by consulting the divine Plato, Sanconiathon, Appollonius Rhodius, sir John Harrington, Noah Webster, Linkum Fidelius and others, fully refuted all those wild theories respecting the first settlement of our venerable country; and proved, beyond contradiction, that America, so far from being, as the writers of upstart Europe denominate it, *the new world*, is at least as old as any country in existence, not excepting Egypt, China, or even the land of the Assiniboils, which, according to the traditions of that antient people, has already assisted at the funerals of thirteen suns, and four hundred and seventy thousand moons!

I had likewise written a long dissertation on certain hieroglyphicks discovered on those fragments of the moon which have lately fallen, with singular propriety, in a neighbouring state—and have thrown considerable light on the state of literature and the arts in that planet— showing that the universal language which prevails there is high dutch— thereby proving it to be the most antient and original tongue, and corroborating the opinion of a celebrated poet, that it is the language in which the serpent tempted our gandmother Eve.

To support the theatrick department, I had several very judicious critiques, ready written wherein no quarter was shown either to authors or actors; and I was only waiting to determine at what plays or performances they should be levelled. As to the grand spectacle of Cinderella, which is to be represented this season, I had given it a most unmerciful handling: showing that it was neither tragedy, comedy, nor farce; that the incidents were highly improbable, that the prince played like a perfect harlequin, that the white mice were merely powdered for the occasion, and that the new moon had a most outrageous copper nose.

But my most profound and erudite essay in embryo, is an analytical, hypercritical, review of these Salmagundi lucubrations; which I had written partly in revenge for the many waggish jokes played off against me by my confederates, and partly for the purpose of saving much invaluable labour to the Zoiluses and Dennises of the age, by detecting and exposing all the similarities, resemblances, synonimies, analogies, coincidences, &c. which occur in this work.

I hold it downright plagiarism for any author to write or even to think in the same manner with any other writer that either did, doth, or may exist. It is a sage maxim of law—*"Ignorantia neminem excusat"*— and the same has been extended to literature: so that if an author shall publish an idea that has been ever hinted by another, it shall be no exculpation for him to plead ignorance of the fact. All, therefore, that I had to do was to take a good pair of spectacles, or a magnifying-glass, and with Salmagundi in hand and a table full of books before me, to mouse over them alternately, in a corner of Cockloft library: carefully comparing and contrasting all odd ends and fragments of sentences. Little did honest Launce suspect, when he sat lounging and scribbling in his elbow-chair, with no other stock to draw upon than his own brain, and no other authority to consult than the sage Linkum Fidelius— little did he think that his careless, unstudied effusions, would receive such scrupulous investigation.

By laborious researches, and patiently collating words, where sentences and ideas did not correspond, I have detected sundry sly disguises and metamorphoses of which, I'll be bound, Langstaff himself is ignorant. Thus, for instance—The Little Man in Black, is evidently no less a personage than old Goody Blake, or goody something, filched from the Spectator, who confessedly filched her from Otway's "wrinkled hag with age grown double." My friend Launce has taken the honest old woman, dressed her up in the cast-off suit worn by Twaits in Lampedo, and endeavoured to palm the imposture upon the enlightened inhabitants of Gotham. No further proof of the fact need be given, than that Goody Blake was taken for a witch, and the little man in black for a conjuror, and that they both lived in villages, the inhabitants of which were distinguished by a most respectful abhorrence of hobgoblins and broomsticks—to be sure the astonishing similarity ends here, but surely that is enough to prove that the little man in black is no other than Goody Blake in the disguise of a white witch.

Thus, also, the sage Mustapha, in mistaking a brag-party for a convention of Magi studying hieroglyphicks, may pretend to originality of idea and to a familiar acquaintance with the black-letter literati of the east—but this tripolitan trick will not pass here—I refer those who wish to detect his larceny to one of those wholesale jumbles, or hodge-podge collections of science, which, like a tailor's pandimonium, or a giblet-pie, are receptacles for scientifick fragments of all sorts and sizes. The reader, learned in dictionary studies, will at once perceive I mean an encyclopoedia. There, under the title of magi, Egypt, cards, or hieroglyphicks, I forget which, will be discovered an idea similar to that of Mustapha, as snugly concealed as truth at the bottom of a well, or the misletoe amid the shady branches of an oak:—and it may at any time be drawn from its lurking-place, by those hewers of wood and drawers of water, who labour in the humbler walks of criticism. This is assuredly a most unpardonable error of the sage Mustapha, who had been the captain of a ketch, and of course, as your nautical men are for the most part very learned, ought to have known better. But this is not the only blunder of the grave mussulman who swears by the head of Amrou, the beard of Barbarossa, and the sword of Khalid, as glibly as our good christian soldiers anathematize body and soul, or a sailor his eyes and odd limbs. Now, I solemnly pledge myelf to the world, that in all my travels through the east, in Persia, Arabia, China and Egypt, I never heard man, woman, or child, utter any of these preposterous and new fangled asseverations; and that, so far from swearing by any man's head, it is considered throughout the east, the greatest insult that can be offered to either the living or dead, to meddle in any shape even with his beard. These are but two or three specimens of the exposures I would have made—but I should have descended still lower, nor would have spared the most insignificant *and*, or *but*, or *nevertheless*, provided I could have found a ditto in the Spectator or the dictionary—but all these minutiae I bequeath to the lilliputian literati of this sagacious community, who are fond of hunting "such small deer," and I earnestly pray they may find full employment for a twelvemonth to come.

But the most outrageous plagiarisms of friend Launcelot, are those made on sundry living personages. Thus; Tom Straddle has been evidently stolen from a distinguished *Brumagem* emigrant, since they both ride on horseback—Dabble, the great little man, has his origin in a certain aspiring counsellor, who is rising in the world as rapidly as the heaviness of his head will permit—Mine Uncle John will bear a tolerable comparison, particularly as it respects the sterling qualities of his heart, with a worthy yeoman of Westchester-county;—and to deck out Aunt Charity and the amiable Miss Cocklofts, he has rifled the charms of half the antient vestals in the city. Nay, he has taken unpardonable liberties with my own person—elevating me on the substantial pedestals of a worthy gentleman from China, and tricking me out with claret coats, tight breeches, and silver-sprigged dickeys, in such sort that I can scarcely recognize my own resemblance— whereas I absolutely declare that I am an exceeding good-looking man, neither too tall nor too short, too old nor too young, with a person indifferently robust, a head rather inclining to be large, an easy swing in my walk; and that I wear my own hair, neither queued, nor cropped, nor turned up, but in a fair, pendulous, oscillating club, tied with a yard of ninepenny black ribband.

And now having said all that occurs to me on the present pathetick occasion—having made my speech, wrote my eulogy, and drawn my portrait, I bid my readers an affectionate farewel; exhorting them to live honestly and soberly—paying their taxes and reverencing the state, the church and the corporation—reading diligently the bible, the almanack, the newspaper and Salmagundi—which is all the reading an honest citizen has occasion for—and eschewing all spirit of faction, discontent, irreligion and criticism.

which is all at present,
from their departed friend,
WILLIAM WIZARD.

EDITORIAL APPENDIX

Historical and Explanatory Notes by
Bruce I. Granger

Textual Commentary,
Discussions, and Lists by
Martha Hartzog

HISTORICAL NOTE

At this distance it is impossible to be certain whether James Kirke Paulding or Washington Irving initiated the *Salmagundi* papers, though Paulding seems the more likely candidate. Forty years later he recollected: "We were both under twenty, when one day in a frolicksome mood, we broached the Idea of a little Periodical merely for our own Amusement, and that of the Town, for neither of us anticipated any further circulation. We each without concert, prepared an introductory Paper, and I think mine was taken as the basis, with Mr. Irving's for the Superstructure. The first number, though it seemed to su[r]prise the Town, astonished us still more. In short it circulated throughout the United States, and most unquestionably did much to awaken the genius of the Country, by exciting emulation. It was the work in fact of two Boys, and when I chance to look into it now, I am surprised at its faults more than its beauties."[1] For his part WI was turning over in his mind characters and ideas that would appear shortly in *Salmagundi*.[2] Whichever of the two conceived the idea, they interested William Irving in the venture and would probably have enlisted Peter Irving, too, had he not recently gone to Europe.

David Longworth, who agreed to publish the work, had been displaying his wit and whimsy in the New York City Directories for more than a decade. The Directory for 1806 concluded with this characteristic flourish: "David Longworth has provided at the Shakespeare Gallery, fifth house south of the Theatre, a repast adapted to the palates of gentlemen possessing literary taste. At this his Sentimental Epicure's Ordinary (in the vernacular, termed a Book Store) he has constantly on hand a collection of the most dainty articles, suited to an entertainment in every variety of style, 'either tragedy, comedy, history, pastoral, pastoral-comical, historical-pastoral, scene-individual, or poem unlimited.'" The frontispiece to the Gallery, according to the 1802 Directory, "represented SHAKESPEARE seated upon a rock, between *Poetry* and *Painting*." Longworth was not one to hide his light. "We recommend David Longworth," announced the 1805 Trade Directory, "for having

1. *Letters of Paulding*, p. 426.
2. In an undated notebook at the New York Public Library there occur early descriptions of Will Wizard and ideas that would find expression in the Mustapha letters on logocracy in Nos. VII and XIV, especially the notion that "the slang whangers may be considered as so many slave drivers" (p. 2).

published a number of Belles Lettres works in a style of elegance and correctness superior to any other in this city. To him America is chiefly indebted for the many good editions now daily publishing; for by the spirited manner in which his books were executed he gave a different tone to the mode of printing, and created that emulation now so prevalent throughout the United States." John W. Francis recalled that Longworth "waged a war of extermination against almost every capital in the case, and this curious deformity is found in many of his publications, as *british america*, and *london docks*."[3] Salmagundi was no exception. "Oddly enough," writes Evert A. Duyckinck, "the man who was so grandiloquent himself would not allow New York its appropriate capitals. It must be written new-york, and portly philadelphia must dwindle in lower-case."[4] Paulding must have been thinking of alterations of this sort when he remarked that Longworth had "taken the liberty to add some of his own nonsense occasionally."[5] On learning of Longworth's death in 1838, Paulding reminded WI of the "excellent hot cakes, the which he dispensed So liberally in his little Back room."[6]

The *Salmagundi* authors might well have said after Sterne, "I write a careless kind of a civil, nonsensical, good-humoured *Shandean* book, which will do all your hearts good" (*Tristram Shandy*, book VI, chap. 17). Webster defines *salmagundi* as "a mixed dish, as of chopped meat and pickled herring, with oil, vinegar, pepper, and onions. Hence a heterogeneous mixture; a medley; potpourri." The Irvings and Paulding were not the first to use the name. In 1791 George Huddesford an Englishman, had published *Salmagundi, A Miscellaneous Combination of Original Poetry: consisting of Illusions of Fancy; Amatory, Elegiac, Lyrical, Epigrammatical, and Other Palatable Ingredients.* Thomas Green Fessenden, a rival editor at New York, facetiously implied that the *Salmagundi* authors stole Huddesford's poem "in some of their rambles, and thus gained a *legal* claim to the wit it contains."[7]

The first paper-covered number of *Salmagundi* appeared January 24, 1807; succeeding numbers were published at irregular intervals, the twentieth and final number appearing January 25, 1808. At the outset Launcelot Langstaff, the chief persona in the series, apportioned the duties among himself and his two bachelor associates, naming fashion as Anthony Evergreen's department and criticism as Will Wizard's,

3. *International Magazine* 5 (February, 1852), 261.
4. *Salmagundi* (New York: G. P. Putnam, 1860), p. xi.
5. *Literary Life of Paulding*, p. 39. The importance of Longworth's influence on the text of *Salmagundi* is discussed in more detail in the Textual Commentary.
6. *Letters of Paulding*, p. 222.
7. *Weekly Inspector*, February 21, 1807, p. 299.

reserving for himself the freedom to range at large. The second number introduced Pindar Cockloft, from whose mill the poetry in the series would issue. Mustapha Rub-A-Dub Keli Khan, captain of a ketch and at the moment a prisoner at New York, made his appearance in the third number, supplying the first of nine foreign-visitor letters to friends back in Tripoli. The traveler Jeremy Cockloft, who would entertain the reader with his tours of New Jersey, Pennsylvania, and Broadway, was introduced in the fourth number. By the sixth number it was clearly established that the social center of the world of *Salmagundi* was Cockloft Hall, where Langstaff's cousin, Christopher Cockloft, dwelt with his wife and three children, Barbara, Maggie, and Jeremy, and where Langstaff, Evergreen, and Wizard were permanent house guests.

The question as to which of the three *Salmagundi* authors had the major hand in composing each part cannot be settled absolutely. The following are the editor's assignments of authorship, the argument for which is to be found in the Assignments of Authorship discussion, pp. 327–36. William Irving wrote all the poetry, the Mustapha letters in Nos. V and XIV, and probably those in Nos. VII and IX. Paulding wrote the Publisher's Notice and Elbow-Chair essay in No. I, "Mr. Wilson's Concert," "Character of Pindar Cockloft," and "Advertisement" in No. II, the Mustapha letter, "Wise Conjectures of the Town," and possibly "——How now mooncalf!" in No. III, "The Stranger in New Jersey" in No. IV, "Notes, by William Wizard" in No. VII, "Letter from Demy Semiquaver" in No. X, "Mine Uncle John" in No. XI, the Elbow-Chair essay and "The Stranger at Home" in No. XII, probably "A Retrospect" in No. XIII, "Sketches from Nature" in No. XV, "Style at Ballston" in No. XVI, "Autumnal Reflections" in No. XVII, the Mustapha letter in No. XVIII, probably the Anthony Evergreen essay in No. XIX, and probably the Elbow-Chair essay in No. XX. WI wrote the "New-York Assembly" and probably "Theatrics" in No. I, the Elbow-Chair essay in No. II, "Fashions" in No. III, the Elbow-Chair essay in No. IV, "Will Wizard at a Ball" in No. V, the Elbow-Chair essay and "Theatrics" in No. VI, "Character of Launcelot Langstaff," "On Style," and "Answer to Certain Meddling Correspondents" in No. VIII, "My Aunt Charity" in No. IX, "The Stranger in Pennsylvania" in No. X, the Mustapha letter in No. XI, the Elbow-Chair essay and "Plans for Defending Our Harbor" in No. XIII, "Cockloft Hall" and "Theatrical Intelligence" in No. XIV, probably "On Greatness" in No. XV, the Mustapha letter in No. XVI, "Chronicles of the City of Gotham" in No. XVII, "The Little Man in Black" in No. XVIII, the Mustapha letter in No. XIX, and probably "To the Ladies" and the Will Wizard essay in No. XX.

The *Salmagundi* authors broke off after the twentieth number, but not because their fund of information was exhausted. "It is not for want of subjects that we stop our career," explained Langstaff. "We are not in the situation of poor Alexander the Great, who wept, as well indeed he might, because there were no more worlds to conquer; for, to do justice to this queer, odd, rantipole city, and this whimsical country, there is matter enough in them, to keep our risible muscles, and our pens going until doomsday" (305.43–306.6). In fact, it had been WI's intention to extend "these papers by carrying out the invention and marrying Will Wizard to the eldest Miss Cockloft—with, of course, a grand wedding at Cockloft Hall."[8] The Salmagundi authors were piqued with the publisher Longworth who, when they refused to follow his advice and take out a copyright, took it out himself, as was his right, and so ran off with the profit. "The immediate cause of their abrupt retirement on the twentieth number was his advancing the price to one shilling."[9]

The first American edition of Salmagundi (New York, David Longworth, 1807–08) exists in a number of new settings or subeditions representing stages of revision by its collaborators. David Longworth labeled these new settings "editions" and issued them to satisfy the unexpected demand for additional copies of the series. Only a fragment of the manuscript is extant, the first paragraph of WI's "Cockloft Hall" essay in No. XIV (236.39–237.20). Since the first setting of each number of the first American edition represents the version closest to the manuscript, it was chosen as copy-text. WI may have helped Longworth prepare the second American edition of 1814 for publication and certainly prepared the Paris edition of 1824. Toward establishing a critical text these two editions, together with the new settings or subeditions of the first American edition, were collated against the copy-text. The Textual Commentary, pp. 379–429, describes the complete collational pattern followed and provides a discussion of Salmagundi's textual history, with especial reference to the complex first American edition.

The critical reception of Salmagundi began with Thomas Green Fessenden's unfavorable reaction in The Weekly Inspector in February and March, 1807. (See Explanatory Note on 97.30–98.28.) The influential Joseph Dennie, on the other hand, declared that Salmagundi "bears the stamp of superior genius, and indicates its unknown authours to be possessed of lively and vigorous imaginations, a happy turn for ridicule, and an extensive knowledge of the world."[10]

8. Evert A. and George L. Duyckinck, Cyclopaedia of American Literature (New York, 1856), II, 47.
9. Algernon Tassin, The Magazine in America (New York, 1916), p. 113.
10. The Port Folio, n.s. 3 (March 21, 1807), 127. This issue reprinted the

John Lambert, an English traveler who carried a copy of *Salmagundi* back to England, praised the work in 1810: "It possesses more of the broad humour of Rabelais and Swift, than the elegant morality of Addison and Steele, and is therefore less likely to become a classical work; but as a correct picture of the people of New York, and other parts of the country, though somewhat heightened by caricature, and as a humorous representation of their manners, habits, and customs, it will always be read with interest by a native of the United States."[11] In his Introductory Essay to the first English edition of 1811 he added: "Though wit, humour, and satire, are its principal ingredients, yet the thoughts and language are clothed in the most chaste and modest habiliments. It is also as free from dulness, pedantry, and affectation, as it is from indecency and immorality" (p. xxxviii). An anonymous reviewer of the first English edition (1811) hailed the work "as the fore-runner of a species of writing in America, that above all tends to cultivate the taste and improve the morals of a nation," though he deplored the absence of a good style throughout, "the aukward attempts at a display of meagre quotations, and the unclassical mistakes in the quantity and even the meaning of Latin words." He praised the *Salmagundi* authors for excelling "in an adroit species of irony which leaves something to the imagination of the reader beyond what is expressed," citing as an example "The Stranger in New Jersey." Singled out for its humor is "Letter from Demy Semiquaver," wherein "the grand instrumental piece, called 'the Breaking of the Ice in the North River,' admirably exposes that style which substitutes noise for the expression of passion, and difficulty of execution for genuine harmony."[12]

In 1819 Richard H. Dana regarded "the good papers of Salmagundi, and the greater part of Knickerbocker," as superior to *The Sketch Book*. *Salmagundi*, he declared, "had to do with the present and real, not the distant and ideal. It was exceedingly pleasant morning or after-dinner reading, never taking up too much of a gentleman's time from his business and pleasures, not so exalted and spiritualized as to seem mystical to his far reaching vision. It was an excellent thing in the rests between cotillions, and pauses between games at cards; and

---

Mustapha letter in No. III, the issue of May 16 the Mustapha letter in No. VII, and the issue of May 30 the Mustapha letter in No. IX and "The Stranger in Pennsylvania" in No. X.

11. *Travels Through Canada, and the United States of North America, in the Years 1806, 1807, & 1808* (London, 1810), II, 98.

12. *Monthly Review* 65 (August, 1811), 418-23 passim. See the Textual Commentary, pp. 398-401, for a discussion of the *Review*'s impact on the revisions WI made for the second American edition (1814).

answered a most convenient purpose, in as much as it furnished those
who had none of their own, with wit enough for six-pence, to talk out
the sitting of an evening party." "Mr. Irving's style in his lighter productions, is suited to his subject.... He is full, idiomatic and easy to
an uncommon degree; and though we have observed a few grammatical
errors, they are of a kind which appear to arise from the hurry in
which such works are commonly written. There are, likewise, one or
two Americanisms. Upon the whole, it is superior to any instance of the
easy style in this country, that we can call to mind.... Though its wit
is sometimes forced, and its serious style sometimes false, upon looking
it over, we have found it full of entertainment, with an infinite variety
of characters and circumstances, and with what amiable, good natured
wit and pathos, which show that the heart has not grown hard while
making merry of the world."[13]

After Thomas Tegg's unauthorized London edition of *Salmagundi*
appeared late in 1823, the work was noticed in several of the British
reviews of the day. "There is a juvenile spirit—a freshness, an audacity
about these nefarious acts of humour and pathos perfectly intolerable,"
wrote one reviewer. "The author is not satisfied to take our sensibilities
by surprise, or entrap us into smiles; but, without the slightest regard
to our stoical dignity, he storms sword in hand the citadel of our hearts,
demolishes our gravity by a single blow; stretches our risible muscles
almost to cracking; and despite of our critical, crocodile, and unmelting
mood, he makes us as amiably lachrymose as 'the Arabian trees,' &c."[14]
Another reviewer was most impressed by the depiction of American
manners and customs, "the watering-places, balls, elections, reviews, and
coteries... in a style of unsparing and broad humour"; also "the
scurrility of their hireling editors,... the pretensions of catamaran-
projectors, and the manoeuvres of electioneering jobbers,... and even
Mr. President Jefferson himself, with his windy proclamations, red
breeches, and black sultana."[15] John Neal displayed greater acumen:
"The papers of Paulding are more sarcastic, ill-natured, acrimonious—
bitter, than those of Irving; but quite as able:... as a whole, the work
is quite superior to anything of the kind, which this age has produced."
The following month he added: "No two writers could be more thoroughly opposed, in everything—disposition—habit—style—than were Irving
and Paulding. The former was cheerful; pleasant; given to laughing at

13. *North American Review* 9 (September, 1819), 323-45 passim.
14. *London Literary Museum and Register*, December 20, 1823, p. 805. Tegg
published at least three further issues dated 1824; see the Textual Commentary,
p. 402.
15. *Quarterly Review* 31 (March, 1825), 474.

whatever he saw—not peevishly—satirically or spitefully—but in real good humour: the latter—even while he *laughed*—as Byron says of Lara—*sneered.* Irving would make us love human nature—wish it well—or pity it: Paulding would make us ashamed of it; or angry with it. One looks for what is good—in everything; the other, for what is bad."[16]

In 1827 an anonymous reviewer at Paris, assessing WI's literary achievement, said of *Salmagundi:* "Les auteurs ne s'entre-tiennent que de leur propre importance; et tous les numéros sont remplis du bruit qu'ils font. Et cependant ces essais ne surpassent en rien tous les ouvrages qui, depuis *le Spectateur* et *le Bavard,* ont été publiés dans ce goût. Ils ont même cette verve grossière des magasins anglais, qui est très éloignée de la décence et du bon goût. Mais ce livre est precieux comme un miroir des moeurs américaines à cette époque."[17] "The work was a brilliant success from the start," wrote the Duyckincks in 1856. "The humors of the town were hit off with a freshness which is still unexhausted to the readers of an entirely different generation. It disclosed, too, the literary faculties of the writers, both very young men, with a rich promise for the future, in delicate shades of observation, the more pungent traits of satire, and a happy vein of description which grew out of an unaffected love of nature, and was enlivened by studies in the best school of English poetry."[18] Finally, William Cullen Bryant said of *Salmagundi* shortly after Irving's death: "Its gaiety is its own; its style of humor is not that of Addison nor Goldsmith, though it has all the genial spirit of theirs; nor is it borrowed from any other writer. It is far more frolicsome and joyous, yet tempered by a native gracefulness. 'Salmagundi' was manifestly written without the fear of criticism before the eyes of the authors, and to this sense of perfect freedom in the exercise of their genius the charm is probably owing which makes us still read it with so much delight. Irving never seemed to place much value on the part he contributed to this work, yet I doubt whether he ever excelled some of those papers in *Salmagundi* which bear the most evident marks of his style, and Paulding, though he has since acquired a reputation by his other writings, can hardly be said to have written anything better than the best of those which are ascribed to his pen."[19]

After the appearance of Duyckinck's edition for Putnam in 1860, *Salmagundi* was subsequently reprinted in various formats and/or com-

16. *Blackwood's Edinburgh Magazine* 17 (January-February, 1825), 61, 199.
17. *Le Globe, Journal Philosophique et Littéraire* 4 (March 31, 1827), 522.
18. *Cyclopaedia of American Literature,* II, 2.
19. *A Discourse on the Life, Character and Genius of Washington Irving* (New York, 1860), pp. 15-16.

binations of volumes in such various Putnam impressions as the Knickerbocker Edition (1869), the People's Edition (1874), the Spuyten Duyvil
Edition (1881), the Hudson Edition (1856–1889), the Author's Auto-
graph Edition (1897), another Knickerbocker Edition (1897), and
another Hudson Edition (1902). On the other hand, the post–1860
English editions of Bell and Daldy use the same plates and are derived
from the 1814 New York and 1824 Tegg editions. The fact that *Salmagundi* was kept in print in America and England for a century after its
first appearance testifies to its ongoing popularity among WI's writings.

ASSIGNMENTS OF AUTHORSHIP

The assignments of authorship presented in the first column of the chart below, headed PMI, are from Pierre M. Irving's *Life and Letters of Washington Irving* (New York, 1862), I, 176–210. The second column, headed L&B, contains the assignments of W. R. Langfeld and P. C. Blackburn in *Washington Irving: A Bibliography* (New York, 1933), p. 10. The third column, headed STW, contains those of Stanley T. Williams, *The Life of Washington Irving* (New York, 1935), II, 271–72. The fourth column, headed ALH, contains those of Amos L. Herold, *James Kirke Paulding* (New York, 1926), pp. 34–37. The fifth column, headed JB, contains penciled notations of assignments in volume one of a presentation copy of the 1814 New York edition of *Salmagundi*, inscribed "from J. K. Paulding to R. McCall," now in the Berg Collection, New York Public Library, as transcribed by Jacob Blanck, "The Authorship of 'Salmagundi,'" *Publishers Weekly* 130 (November 28, 1936), 2101; it is Blanck's opinion, and one in which the editor concurs, that Paulding himself made the notations. Also appearing in the fifth column are Blanck's own assignments for some of the parts in Nos. X–XX, recorded in *Bibliography of American Literature*, V (New Haven, 1969), 3–9. The sixth column, headed RSO, contains the assignments of Robert Stevens Osborne, "A Study of Washington Irving's Development as a Man of Letters to 1825" (Ph.D. diss., University of North Carolina, 1947), pp. 121–64. In the seventh column, headed BG, are the editor's own assignments. Of those who have made earlier attributions greatest weight is attached to Paulding's notations in the presentation copy of the 1814 New York edition and next greatest to Osborne who has made the fullest and most persuasive argument for attribution of any scholar to date. The *Salmagundi* authors are identified in this chart by the following initials: P—Paulding; WI—Washington Irving; WmI—William Irving. Titles supplied for the untitled pieces and explanatory titles are in brackets.

No. I (January 24, 1807)	PMI	L&B	STW	ALH	JB	RSO	BG
[Advertisement]							
Publisher's Notice	P&WI	P&WI				P	P
From the Elbow-Chair	P	P	P(&WI) P	P	P	P	
Theatrics	WI	WI	WI		P	P	WI?
New-York Assembly	WI	WI			WI	WI	WI

No. II (February 4, 1807)	PMI	L&B	STW	ALH	JB	RSO	BG
From the Elbow-Chair	WI	WI			WI	WI	WI
Mr. Wilson's Concert	P	P		P	P	P	P
[Character of Pindar Cockloft]	P	P		P	P	P	P
To Launcelot Langstaff	WmI	WmI	WmI	WmI	WmI	WmI?	WmI
Advertisement	WI	WI			P	P	P

No. III (February 13, 1807)							
From My Elbow-Chair			P(&WI)		WI		WI
Mustapha Letter	P	P	P	P	P	P	P
Fashions					WI	WI	WI
[Wise Conjectures of the Town]					P	P	P
"——How now, mooncalf!"							P?
Mill of Pindar Cockloft	WmI	WmI	WmI	WmI	WmI	WmI	WmI

No. IV (February 24, 1807)							
From My Elbow-Chair					WI	WI	WI
The Stranger in New Jersey					P	P	P
From My Elbow-Chair							
Flummery	WmI	WmI	WmI	WmI		WmI	WmI?
General Remark							
Notice							
Card							

No. V (March 7, 1807)							
Mustapha Letter	WmI	WmI	WmI	WmI	WmI	WmI	WmI
Anthony Evergreen							
[Will Wizard at a Ball]					WI	WI	WI
To the Ladies	WmI	WmI	WmI	WmI	WmI	WmI	WmI

No. VI (March 20, 1807)							
From My Elbow-Chair				P	WI	WI	WI
Theatrics			WI		WI	WI	WI

No. VII (April 4, 1807)							
Mustapha Letter	WI	WI	WI	WI	WmI	WmI	WmI?
Mill of Pindar Cockloft	WmI	WmI	WmI	WmI	WmI	WmI	WmI
Notes, by William Wizard					P	P	P

No. VIII (April 18, 1807)							
Anthony Evergreen,							
[Character of Launcelot Langstaff]	WI			WI	WI	WI	WI
On Style				P	WI	WI	WI
[Answer to Certain Meddling Correspondents]					WI	WI	WI

No. IX (April 25, 1807)							
From My Elbow-Chair							
[My Aunt Charity]			P&WI	P(&WI)	WI	WI	WI
Mustapha Letter	WI	WI	WI	WI	WmI	P	WmI?
Mill of Pindar Cockloft	WmI	WmI	WmI	WmI	WmI	WmI	WmI

	PMI	L&B	STW	ALH	JB	RSO	BG
No. X (May 16, 1807)							
From My Elbow-Chair and							
Letter from Demy Semiquaver					P	P	P
The Stranger in Pennsylvania	WI	WI			WI	WI	WI
No. XI (June 2, 1807)							
Mustapha Letter	WI	WI	WI	WI	WI	WI	WI
Mine Uncle John	P	P	P(&WI)	P	P	P	P
No. XII (June 27, 1807)							
From My Elbow-Chair			P(&WI)	P		P?	P
The Stranger at Home			WI			P	P
Mill of Pindar Cockloft	WmI	WmI	WmI	WmI	WmI	WmI	WmI
No. XIII (August 14, 1807)							
From My Elbow-Chair						WI	WI
Plans for Defending Our Harbour			WI			WI	WI
A Retrospect				P		WI?	P?
To Readers and Correspondents							
No. XIV (September 19, 1807)							
Mustapha Letter	WmI	WmI	WmI	WmI		WmI	WmI
Cockloft Hall				P	WI	WI?	WI
Theatrical Intelligence			WI			WI	WI
No. XV (October 1, 1807)							
Sketches from Nature			P&WI	WI		P	P
On Greatness				P			WI?
No. XVI (October 15, 1807)							
Style at Ballston				P		P	P
Mustapha Letter	WI	WI	WI	WI	WI	WI	WI
No. XVII (November 11, 1807)							
Autumnal Reflections			P	P		P	P
Chronicles of the City of Gotham			WI	WI		WI	WI
No. XVIII (November 24, 1807)							
The Little Man in Black			WI	WI		WI	WI
Mustapha Letter	P	P	P	P	P	P	P
No. XIX (December 31, 1807)							
Mustapha Letter	WI	WI	WI	WI	WI	WI	WI
Anthony Evergreen							P?
Tea	WmI	WmI	WmI	WmI	WmI	WmI	WmI
No. XX (January 25, 1808)							
From My Elbow-Chair	P			P	P	P	P?
To the Ladies						WI?	WI?
[Will Wizard]						WI	WI?

Any discussion of the authorship of *Salmagundi* must begin and end
with a recognition that the work was a collaboration throughout its
length. To assign each of the parts to one or other of the authors, as
the chart above has done, is perhaps to do no more than identify the
major hand among the two or even three that composed it. "The thoughts
of the authors were so mingled together in these essays, and they were
so literally joint productions," cautions Paulding in the Preface to the
1835 New York edition, "that it would be difficult, as well as useless,
at this distance of time, to assign to each his exact share." In a letter of
March 31, 1846, to Rufus W. Griswold, Paulding further warmed, "Our
ideas are so Dovetailed in with each other, that it is impossible to
separate them."[1]

One contemporary writer speculated, "All the poetry, and two of
the prose articles [presumably the Mustapha letters in Nos. V and XIV],
were from the hand of William Irving; the rest were furnished, in about
equal parts by Washington Irving and J. K. Paulding."[2] Granting that
Salmagundi was a joint production, it behooves an editor to try to
determine which of the three authors had the major hand in composing
each part. The editor will consider in turn the authorship of the poetry
and six series of prose writings: those by Launcelot Langstaff, Anthony
Evergreen, and Will Wizard, the Cockloft essays, the tour essays, and
the Mustapha letters. Earlier scholars are unanimous in assigning all
the poems from the Mill of Pindar Cockloft to William Irving. The
editor is inclined to accept such unanimity; if any of the poetry in
Salmagundi was composed jointly, it was most likely "Flummery" in
No. IV and the pseudo-erudite notes accompanying it. William Irving
had a reputation as a writer of light verse. In later years his brother
Washington furnished the Duyckincks with a copy of one of these
poems, "a trifle in allusion to an absurdity in the whisker line of the
fops in the early years of the century."[3]

Of the three principal personae in *Salmagundi* Paulding chose instinctively to identify himself with Langstaff; a preference hinted at,
though after the fact, by Evergreen's declaration in the thirteenth
number of *Salmagundi, Second Series*, "Almost all the fatigues of
conducting the work have fallen upon our worthy principal Launcelot
Langstaff."[4] On the other hand, WI felt drawn to Evergreen and Wizard
who represent a splitting of the character of Jonathan Oldstyle, the one

1. *Letters of Paulding*, p. 426.
2. *New-York Mirror*, March 17, 1832, quoted in STW, II, 271.
3. *Cyclopaedia of American Literature*, II, 52.
4. *Salmagundi. Second Series* (New York, 1835), II, 289. Hereafter quotations
from this edition will be identified by volume and page in the body of the text.

discoursing on fashion, the other on theatrical criticism.[5] William Irving appears to have taken no major part in the composition of any of these three series of essays. Earlier scholars are unanimous in assigning the Elbow-Chair essay in No. I to Paulding, an essay centrally important since its apportions the duties among the three bachelor associates, sets the tone, and determines the format of Salmagundi. (Paulding's Introduction to the Second Series functions in much the same manner.) Thus Paulding, who would initiate the Cockloft and tour essays and the Mustapha letters, emerges as the guiding spirit behind Salmagundi, a work which counted for more in his literary career than it did in WI's. Little wonder that he complained years later, "My Countrymen have done me great injustice, in assigning the work to Mr. Irving alone."[6] In "Wise Conjectures of the Town" in No. III, also assigned to Paulding, the Spectator-like character of Langstaff, who is described as a "listening incog." (96.11), becomes apparent. The argument for assigning the Elbow-Chair essay in No. XII to Paulding, as Paulding himself and Osborne do, is circumstantial but convincing. It is most unlikely that WI, who wrote Paulding from Richmond on June 22, 1807, "I shall endeavor to send you more for another number, as soon as I can find time and humor to write it in; at present I have neither,"[7] could have supplied copy for the twelfth number which appeared five days later. Moreover, in the Second Series Paulding would portray two beaux who resemble the Birmingham agent Tom Straddle: Jack Dandy in No. IV and Randie Dandie in No. XII. "A Retrospect" in No. XIII is a comprehensive backward glance over what the Salmagundi authors had written to date. In tentatively assigning it to Paulding, the editor is influenced by evidence elsewhere that his was the controlling hand where the character of Langstaff was concerned and the probability that, having written the Langstaff essay in the first number, he rather than WI would have written this intermediate one. Of the remaining Langstaff essays, there is little doubt that WI wrote "The Little Man in Black" in No. XVIII, a tale which anticipates "The Stout Gentleman" in Bracebridge Hall. He may also have written "On Greatness" in No. XV, which he revised for the 1824 Paris edition and which Paulding omitted from the 1835 New York edition.

5. What lends weight to the argument that Will Wizard was largely WI's creation are early descriptions of him in an undated notebook at the New York Public Library, especially the mention of Will's "old fashioned brocaded vest—broad backed coat or tight small clothes" (p. 12), which anticipates Anthony Evergreen's more detailed description of Will's dress for a ball in No. V.

6. Letters of Paulding, p. 426.

7. PMI, I, 194.

As for the Evergreen essays, there is unanimity in assigning the "New-York Assembly" in No. I to WI, to whom the Mustapha Letter in No. XIX on the same subject is also assigned. Evergreen's Sternean phrase, "the grumbling smellfungi of this world" (75.37), echoes WI's 1804–1806 European journal. There is likewise unanimity in assigning "Mr. Wilson's Concert" in No. II to Paulding. "Fashions" in No. III is assigned to WI who, having alluded to Madame Bouchard and Mrs. Toole in the "New-York Assembly," now dwells on these New York milliners at length; in a letter of October 26, 1805, from London, WI had written his brother William of the contrast between French and English women in a way very like that which appears in this essay.[8] "Will Wizard at a Ball" in No. V is assigned to WI, an attribution strengthened by the mention of "Sophy Sparkle" (126.21), a pseudonym for Mary Fairlie with whom he was corresponding at this time. Moreover, the old-fashioned bachelor Will calls to mind Jonathan Oldstyle at the theater. "Character of Launcelot Langstaff" in No. VIII is generally assigned to WI; WI having made the acquaintance of Joseph Dennie on a visit to Philadelphia in the spring of 1807, Dennie recognized the portrait of Langstaff in this number as bearing a likeness to himself (especially 156.18–39). Osborne bases his attribution of "Sketches from Nature" in No. XV to Paulding on the fact that this essay reads like an extension of "Mine Uncle John," known to have been written by him. It might further be argued in support of this attribution that though Paulding tended in the Second Series to be perfunctory in his description of the Cockloft family, in the fifth number he dwells at length on Old Caesar. Moreover, if a distinction be drawn between the sentimental and the picturesque—picturesqueness marking WI's style from an early date as it clearly did not Paulding's—"Sketches from Nature" is sentimental rather than picturesque. There is some basis for attributing the Evergreen essay in No. XIX to Paulding: one of the letters in it is signed "Walter Withers" (296.4), a signature Duyckinck says Paulding used in his contributions to the Morning Chronicle about 1805;[9] there is also a reference to Ballston (295.2), which essay in No. XVI Paulding is thought to have written. "To the Ladies" in No. XX is assigned to WI by Osborne, who says, "There is no justification for this assignment except the probability that Irving would write the last number of a series in which he had had the major part."[10]

8. See Journal of the Rutgers University Library 10 (December, 1946), 23–24.
9. "Memoranda of the Literary Career of Washington Irving," MS, New York Public Library.
10. "Study of Washington Irving's Development," p. 127, n. 53.

Langstaff informs his readers in the first number that "in the territory of criticism, WILLIAM WIZARD, esq. has undertaken to preside" (71.31–32), meaning theatrical criticism, which had been the chief topic of the *Oldstyle* letters. Will is also a judge of fashion, however, and soon begins encroaching on Anthony Evergreen's territory. There is disagreement about the authorship of "Theatrics" in No. I; although Osborne, who assigns it to Paulding, says, "The Wizard writings of the first volume are of the conventional type and could have been written by any one of the three writers,"[11] this essay sounds like "Theatrics" in No. VI, which is unanimously assigned to WI. In tone and topic "Theatrics" in No. VI resembles the *Oldstyle* letters, especially in its criticism of actors; here too, as later in WI's "Stranger in Pennsylvania," the punning proclivity of Philadelphians is alluded to (138.19–20). Paulding is probably to be honored over Herold in assigning "On Style" in No. VIII to WI, not himself; here for the first time Will encroaches on Anthony's territory. Stanley Williams' convincing argument for assigning "Plans for Defending Our Harbour" in No. XIII to WI is based on the fact that he dealt with this subject at length in the 1809 *History of New York*.[12] What helps confirm the assignment of "Theatrical Intelligence" in No. XIV to WI is the fact that he composed verses for the reopening of the Park Theater on September 9, 1807;[13] that is to say, the reopening was a matter of some importance to him. What lends some weight to attributing "Style at Ballston" in No. XVI to Paulding is the following description in the *Second Series*: "The ladies from the east and south meet on the bloody field of Ballston and Saratoga, to marshal their crapes and muslins in battle array, and stare at each other like cats in a strange garret" (IV, 32). (It should not be forgotten, however, that WI described Ballston in his 1803 New York journal and that the essay "On Style" in No. VIII is probably by him.) The evidence for attributing the "Chronicles of the City of Gotham" in No. XVII to WI is strong; for example, the mock battle between the Hoppingtots and the Gothamites anticipates the mock-heroic battle before the wall of Fort Christina in the 1809 *History* (VI, vii). This whimsical essay differs sharply from Paulding's caustic tone in *The Diverting History of John Bull and Brother Jonathan* (1812). Finally, the Will Wizard essay in No. XX, attributed to WI by Osborne, seems correctly assigned; the pantomime

11. *Ibid.*, p. 152.
12. *A History of New York* (New York: Inskeep and Bradford, 1809), book VII, chap. viii. Hereafter references to and quotations from this edition will be identified by book and chapter in the body of the text.
13. See *Bulletin of the New York Public Library* 34 (November, 1930), 766–69.

Cinderella here alluded to (313.26–32) had been described at length in "Theatrical Intelligence" in No. XIV (243.16–32, 244.36–245.6).

As for the Cockloft essays, scholars are unanimous in assigning to Paulding the portrait of Pindar Cockloft in No. II, a short essay introducing the poetry which issued thereafter from Pindar's mill. The essay on the Cockloft family in No. VI, which established what steadily becomes the social center of the world of *Salmagundi*, seems to have been written by WI, who would share with Paulding the authorship of the Cockloft series; confirming this attribution are references to Prince Madoc and the Dutch tiles depicting biblical scenes, details which would reappear in the 1809 *History* (I, iii; III, iii). It seems clear that WI had a larger stake in the Cockloft series than Paulding. Cockloft Hall and its inhabitants anticipate *Bracebridge Hall*. Conversely, after the Introduction to the *Second Series* Paulding scarcely mentions the Cockloft daughters, although at the end of No. XIII, he announced the marriage of Barbara Cockloft and Will Wizard. There is general agreement in assigning "My Aunt Charity" in No. IX to WI. There is unanimity in assigning "Mine Uncle John" in No. XI to Paulding; in contrast to the satiric tone of earlier Cockloft essays, this one is sentimental, as though Paulding were nostalgically recalling his youth in Westchester County. The only surviving manuscript of *Salmagundi* is the first paragraph of "Cockloft Hall" in No. XIV, in WI's hand; this sentimental and whimsical extension of the essay on the Cockloft family in No. VI is in effect a recollection of Mount Pleasant, Gouverneur Kemble's home near Newark. The description in this essay of the fat little German caught by the chin on the back of Barbara Cockloft's chair where "he dangled and kicked about for half a minute, before he could find terra firma" (239.20–21) anticipates the burlesque hyperboles that are so plentiful in the 1809 *History*. There is general agreement that Paulding wrote "Autumnal Reflections" in No. XVII; in tone it is of a piece with "Mine Uncle John" and "Sketches from Nature," though there is less narrative and more description than in them; indeed, it is the least whimsical and most sentimental essay in the Cockloft series.

Osborne follows Paulding in assigning to him the first of the three tour essays, "The Stranger in New Jersey" in No. IV. In view of Paulding's later writings in answer to the way British travelers misrepresented the United States, it seems logical that he would have been the *Salmagundi* author to start parodying travel books by Sir John Carr and other Englishmen. What helps confirm this attribution is the following speculation in the *Second Series*: "Observing this mysterious personage occasionally very busily occupied in making memorandums, I set him down in my own mind as a compiler of travels, or, in other words, a gentleman travelling for the purpose of making up a book about our country, to suit the present English market, as per contract with the London bookseller. Every thing he saw or heard was forthwith transferred to his memorandum-book, and destined for immortality" (IV, 37). But since the essay introducing the traveler Jeremy Cockloft in No. IV was probably by WI, this series should be thought of as a joint undertaking. The most conclusive testimony for assigning "The Stranger in Pennsylvania" in No. X to WI is his letter of June 22, 1807, to Paulding, wherein he says of the tenth number of *Salmagundi*, "I wrote the greatest part of it myself, and that at hurried moments."[14] Moreover, WI's letter of March 17, 1807, to Mary Fairlie anticipates his observations about the "*pun* mania" (185.24). This essay, which is critical of the rival city of Philadelphia, would be dropped from the 1814 New York edition and from all subsequent editions in WI's lifetime, as one that apparently did not satisfy him. As in the case of the Elbow-Chair essay in No. XII, the strongest argument for assigning "The Stranger at Home" to Paulding is the improbability that WI, who was in Richmond, would have had time to compose anything for this number. The editor finds plausible, too, Osborne's argument that "The Stranger at Home," being a parody of Samuel Mitchill's *Picture of New York* (1807), resembles that other parody, "The Stranger in New Jersey," much more closely than it does "The Stranger in Pennsylvania," which is a general satire on the people of Philadelphia.[15]

Nowhere else in Salmagundi is the joint nature of the undertaking so evident as in the case of the nine Mustapha letters. It is demonstrable that each of the three authors had a leading hand in composing two or more of them: William those in Nos. V and XIV, Paulding those in Nos. III and XVIII, WI those in Nos. XI, XVI, and XIX; the letters in Nos. VII and IX seem to have been written by William, although Osborne assigns that in No. IX to Paulding. There is general agreement that Paulding initiated the series. Whereas WI never again used the foreign-visitor device after his participation in this series (and did not begin contributing to this one until it had been developed by Paulding and William Irving), Paulding created King Cornelius Taykaonta of the Oneida Indians in the *Second Series*, who visited England and France and sent letters back home. In addition to Goldsmith's *Citizen of the World*, which influenced all three authors but Paulding in particular, there were also American examples of this convention immediately available to the Salmagundi authors, notably Benjamin Silliman's *Letters of Shahcoolen* (1802) and William Wirt's *Letters of*

14. PMI, I, 194.
15. "Study of Washington Irving's Development," p. 131.

the British Spy (1803). There is unanimity in assigning the Mustapha letters in Nos. III, V, XI, XIV, XVI, XVIII, and XIX to one or other of the authors. The Mustapha letter in No. XI, assigned to WI, echoes the language as well as the sentiment of a letter he sent Mary Fairlie on May 2, 1807, wherein he declared, "We have toiled through the purgatory of an Election,"[16] alluding to the statewide election in New York just concluded. The Mustapha letters in Nos. III and XVIII are assigned to Paulding; both treat of American women. The Mustapha letter in No. XIX, assigned to WI, returns to the subject of the City Assembly, which he had described more briefly in the first number. The two Mustapha letters whose authorship is in dispute are those on logocracy in No. VII and economy in No. IX. Tentatively the editor assigns them both to William Irving, who as an established business leader in New York would presumably have felt freer than his much younger associates to speak his mind on such inflammatory topics.

16. PMI, I, 186.

EXPLANATORY NOTES

The numbers before all notes indicate page and line respectively. Chapter numbers, chapter or section titles, epigraphs, author's chapter or section summaries, text quotations, and footnotes are included in the line count. Only running heads and rules added by the printer to separate the running head from the text are omitted from the count. The quotation from the text, to the left of the bracket, is the matter under discussion.

Whenever notes in editions of *Salmagundi* later than the first American, which is serving as copy-text, are quoted, they are identified in this manner: "1811 London ed." refers to the first English edition, prepared by John Lambert and published at London by J. M. Richardson in 1811.

68.12 "by the pricking of our thumbs"] Adapted from *Macbeth*, IV, i, 44.

68.26 "Town,"] A short-lived literary journal which ran through only five numbers at New York, January 1, 3, 7, 9, 12, 1807. The editor announced that while "neither politics nor commerce are ever to be mentioned, ... Criticism of the Stage will never be disregarded. Every species of elegant public amusement will receive similar attention. The remainder of the paper will be occupied by poetry, and by miscellaneous literature in general, and by scientific and literary information."

71.13 Kissing-bridge] "In the way there is a bridge, about three miles distant from New York," writes Andrew Burnaby, "which you always pass over as you return, called the Kissing Bridge; where it is a part of the etiquette to salute the lady who has put herself under your protection" (*Travels Through the Middle Settlements in North America, in the Years 1759 and 1760* [London, 1798], p. 87). This bridge spanned a creek in the Bowery, a little to the south of the present Chatham Square.

71.16–17 old Vauxhall] The Old Vauxhall, on what is now Greenwich Street, between Warren and Chambers Streets, facing the Hudson River, was at various times in the eighteenth century a tavern, bowling green, garden, and place of public resort.

71.17 Bull's-head] An important tavern on Bowery Lane.

72.5 mr. COOPER] The Englishman Thomas Abthorpe Cooper (1776–1849) was the leading actor and manager at the Park Theater. "Endowed with great genius, and the highest qualifications in face, voice, and person," writes John Bernard, "he had little or no art, which he never strove to acquire, being content to cover its want by his impulse and freshness. . . . Still, with all his defects, I look back to his youth as displaying a power which I can only rank second to the greatest I have seen. I still think his Macbeth was only inferior to Garrick's, and his Hamlet to Kemble's; while his Othello, I think, was equal to Barry's itself" (*Retrospections*, pp. 267, 268).

72.5 mrs. OLDMIXON] A singing actress who emigrated from England to America in 1797.

72.6 mrs. DARLEY] Mrs. John Darley (1779–1848) was born Ellen Westray and played under that name until 1801.

72.32–33 will fight "till from our bones the flesh be hackt"] Adapted from *Macbeth*, V, iii, 32.

73.17 "Bardolph, Peto, and I"] In *Henry IV, Part 1*, II, ii, Sir John Falstaff, Bardolph, and Peto, having robbed the travelers on Gadshill and bound them, are in turn robbed and chased away by the disguised Prince Hal and Pointz. The above quotation does not appear in the play, however.

73.30 MACBETH] Performed at the Park Theater on January 5, 1807, with Thomas Cooper in the title role.

73.33 KEMBLE] Of the English actor John Philip Kemble WI wrote his brother William from London on October 26, 1805: "Kemble is the 'grand Colossis' of Tragedy in London. . . . tho at present I decidedly give him the preference yet were Cooper to be equally studious & pay equal attention to his profession I would transfer it to him without hesitation" (*Journal of the Rutgers University Library* 10 [December, 1946], 25, 26). And yet WI, who became an intimate friend of Cooper in New York, wrote Henry Brevoort from Birmingham on December 28, 1815: "I shall never forget Cooper's acting in Macbeth last spring, when he was stimulated to exertion by the presence of a number of British officers. I have seen nothing equal to it in England" (*Letters of Washington Irving to Henry Brevoort*, ed. George S. Hellman [New York, 1918], pp. 150–51).

73.41 *Chow-Chow*] Probably fictitious.

73.41 Roscius] Quintus Roscius (126?–?62 B.C.), Roman comic actor.

74.10 MRS. VILLIERS] Mrs. Villiers, formerly Miss Elizabeth Westray, played Lady Macbeth in the performance of January 5, 1807, at the Park Theater. Studying the roles of the two sisters, Mrs. Darley and Mrs. Villiers, Odell concludes that though they "divided the leading business, Mrs. Darley generally had the better of it, except when very heavy tragedy was involved" (*Annals*, II, 276).

74.21 *Glumdalca*]   A captive queen of the giants in Henry Fielding's *Tom Thumb* (1730), a play performed at the Park Theater several times in this period.

74.31 "this is a *sorry sight*"]   Criticizing Mrs. Villiers' interpretation of the line, "A foolish thought, to say a *sorry* sight," *The Town* said: "She seems not to understand, that *sorry* here signifies *sad*. We presume that she interprets it, *a sight to cause repentance*; but the meaning is, *a sight sad or melancholy*. Lady Macbeth says that this is a foolish thought, because, in her estimation, the sight is joyful" (1 [January 1, 1807], 3).

74.43 Nat Lee]   The Restoration playwright Nathaniel Lee (1653?–1692) lost his reason and was confined in Bedlam from 1684 to 1689.

75.9 *Monterio Cap*]   A Spanish hunter's cap, having a spherical crown and a flap capable of being drawn over the ears (*OED*). See *Tristram Shandy*, bk. 5, chap. 24.

75.10 NEW YORK ASSEMBLY.]   Having visited the Assembly in 1807 at the City Hotel, Broadway, the Englishman John Lambert writes: "I did not perceive any thing different from an English assembly, except the cotillons, which were danced in an admirable manner, alternately with the country dances. Several French gentlemen were present, and figured away in the cotillons with considerable taste and agility. The subscription is two dollars and a half for each night, and includes tea, coffee, and a cold collation. None but the first class of society can become subscribers to this assembly" (*Tarvels Through Canada, and the United States*, II, 99).

75.16 Herschell]   Sir William Herschel (1738–1822) discovered the planet Uranus.

75.25 WILL HONEYCOMB]   The fashion-conscious, aging member of the Spectator Club, "very ready at that sort of Discourse with which Men usually entertain Women. He has all his Life dressed very well, and remembers Habits as others do Men" (*Spectator* No. 2).

75.28 Mrs. TOOLE and madame BOUCHARD]   Two fashionable milliners. See also note at 93.30.

75.35 mr. Jefferson's ⁕⁕⁕⁕⁕]   "These Shandean stars mean neither more nor less than the late President's *breeches*, which are of *red* velvet; and, it is said, were always worn by him on levee-days, and other particular occasions" (Note, 1811 London ed.). John Randolph of Roanoke declared, "I cannot live in this miserable undone country where as the Turks follow their sacred standard, which is a pair of Mahomet's green breeches, we are governed by the old red breeches of that Prince of Projectors, St. Thomas of *Canting*bury; and surely Becket himself never had more pilgrims at his shrine than the saint of Monticello" (Hugh A. Garland, *The Life of John Randolph of Roanoke* [New York, 1890], II, 346).

75.35–36 Tom Paine's nose] "In earlier life," writes Moncure D. Conway, "Paine drank spirits, as was the custom in England and America; and he unfortunately selected brandy, which . . . partly produced the oft-quoted witness against him—his somewhat red nose. His nose was prominent and began to be red when he was fifty-five" (*The Life of Thomas Paine* [New York, 1892], II, 395).

75.37 grumbling smellfungi] Smelfungus was the name by which Sterne in *A Sentimental Journey* designated Smollett on account of the captious tone of the latter's *Travels Through France and Italy*. Speaking of French inns, WI wrote: "There is nothing I dread more than to be taken for one of the Smellfungii of this world. I therefore endeavor to be satisfied with the things round me when I find there is no use in complaining . . . (*Journals and Notebooks*, I, 86).

76.6 cockney] In the Introductory Essay to the 1811 London edition of *Salmagundi* John Lambert writes: "Frequent mention is made in these Essays of the word *Cockney*. This phrase is not meant merely for a Londoner, but is intended to designate those consequential gentlemen from England, who cross the Atlantic on the strength of a consignment from Birmingham or Liverpool. . . . Disappointed, however, at not attracting that notice, and causing that degree of astonishment which they fondly expected, they speak with contempt of every thing that is American" (pp. xlii–xliii). See especially "The Stranger in New Jersey" in *Salmagundi* No. IV and the portrait of Tom Straddle in No. XII.

76.21 Duport] Pierre Landrin Duport was director of a dancing academy in New York.

76.23 Chilton] Longworth's *New-York Directory* for 1805 lists a George Chilton as "philosophical lecturer."

76.25 "North-river society."] "An imaginary association," WI later explained, "the object of which was to set the North-river (the Hudson) on fire. A number of young men of some fashion, little talent, and great pretension, were ridiculed as members" (Note, 1824 Paris ed.). Before it was done away with in the alterations of the Park Theater in the summer of 1807, "the Society used to meet in the old lounging room which they had consecrated as a *Temple to Dullness.*—A large Franklin stove was their altar, round which they assembled, each sapient phiz illumined by a segar, and offered up libations to their *long-eared deity*" (*Daily Advertiser*, November 14, 1807). After this alteration "they invaded the Theatre and then spent the rest of the evening bragging and drinking in a coffee house" (*Daily Advertiser*,

November 19, 1807). This organization seems to have been the same as the North River Company, described by Paulding in 1802 as having "Contracted to deliver at the Bear market by the middle of September, as many Smoked, roasted, and Broiled fish, as will supply the City for one whole week" (*The Letters of James Kirke Paulding*, ed. Ralph M. Aderman [Madison, 1962], p. 17). See also 200.21–22, 263.25.

77.19–20 roses . . . lilies] "The beauty of the American women partakes more of the lily than the rose, though the soft glow of the latter is not unfrequently met with. Their climate, however, is not so favourable to beauty as that of England, in consequence of the excessive heat, and violent changes of the weather, peculiar to America. Fair complexions, regular features, and fine forms, seem to be the prevailing characteristics of the American fair sex" (Note, 1811 London ed.).

80.7 Dilworth] Probably a reference to Thomas Dilworth's *Schoolmaster's Assistant* (New York, 1793), a reader in use at Josiah Henderson's school in John Street when WI attended it in 1797.

80.35 JOSSELIN] John Josselyn, an English scientific writer who visited New England, wrote *New-England Rarities Discovered* (1672) and *An Account of Two Voyages to New-England* (1674), works which combine botanical and historical lore, much of it fictitious. Robert Osborne believes that "the name Josselyn became a symbol in Irving's mind for gullibility and belief in witches" (Robert Stevens Osborne, "A Study of Washington Irving's Development as a Man of Letters to 1825" [Ph.D. diss., University of North Carolina, 1947], p. 128, n.).

81.24 lord Burleigh nod] In Richard Sheridan's *The Critic*, III, i, Lord Burleigh appears briefly, says nothing, shakes his head, and exits. Puff explains: "Why, by that shake of the head, he gave you to understand that even tho' they had more justice in their cause and wisdom in their measures—yet, if there was not a greater spirit shown on the part of the people—the country would at last fall a sacrifice to the hostile ambition of the Spanish monarchy." Dangle replies, "Ah! there certainly is a vast deal to be done on the stage by dumb show, and expression of face, and a judicious author knows how much he may trust to it."

81.26 "thereby *hangs a tale*."] *As You Like It*, II, vii, 28.

81.37–38 the new City-Hall] The cornerstone of the new City Hall, situated in the park between Chatham Row and Broadway, was laid in 1803; the building was completed in 1812.

82.4 mr. WILSON] J[oseph?] Wilson, pianist, singer, and later proprietor of a music store in Maiden Lane, gave a concert at the City Hotel on January 20, 1807, which "enlisted a full band, Riley, Wilson

(piano), Wheatall (in song), Mrs. Clark, and Weldon (piano). Curious
features were three waltzes, played by a combination of piano, flute,
triangle and tambourine, Weldon, Wilson, Master Wilson, Taylor
and Master Taylor, the performers (except David at the flute), shifting
instruments from waltz to waltz" (Odell, *Annals*, II, 285–86).

82.14 Paff's musical tree]   Michael and John Paff kept a music store
at the City Hotel. On a poplar in front of the shop hung the complete
genealogy of music.

82.21–22 that unfortunate saint]   Probably St. Simon Zelotes, one of the
Twelve Apostles, who is represented in art with a saw in his hand.
He is supposed to have suffered martyrdom by being sawn asunder.
See S. Baring-Gould, *The Lives of the Saints* (Edinburgh, 1914),
XII, 673.

82.38 "make a bow, Johnny—Johnny make a bow!"]   "That expression
is repeatedly made use of by the gods, at the New-York Theatre,
whenever, on the change of scenes, the livery servants come on the
stage to carry off the chairs and tables" (Note, 1811 London ed.).

83.2 M'Sychophant]   Sir Pertinax MacSycophant is the ambitious Scottish politician in Charles Macklin's comedy, *The Man of the World*
(1781), first performed in New York in 1803.

83.18 "knight of the burning lamp,"]   In *Henry IV, Part 1*, III, iii, 24–27,
Falstaff addresses Bardolph, "Do thou amend thy face, and I'll amend
my life: thou art our admiral, thou bearest the lantern in the poop,—
but 'tis in the nose of thee; thou art the Knight of the Burning Lamp."

83.30 neat yellow cover]   "The numbers of Salmagundi were originally
published in this form" (Note, 1824 Paris ed.).

86.2 grograms]   Grogram is a coarse fabric made of silk and mohair, or
of coarse silk, often stiffened with gum; also, a garment.

86.6 bishop'd]   Furnished with a bishop or a bustle (*DA*).

86.9 O'Brallagan's mistress]   Charlotte Goodchild in Charles Macklin's
Love à-la-mode (1759), whose successful suitor is the Irish soldier,
Sir Callaghan O'Brallaghan.

87.16 Sappho, (who changed to a swan;)]   In *Spectator* No. 233 Addison
expands on the legend that the Greek poet, in despair over her un-
requited love for the boatman Phaon, leaped to her death from the
rock of Leucas off the coast of Epirus, relating that some who were
present affirmed "that she was changed into a Swan as she fell, and
that they saw her hovering in the Air under that Shape."

88.33 good-natured villainy]   "The manuscript had characterized [the
Salmagundi authors'] satirical pleasantries as 'good-natured raillery,'
which last word, by an expressive blunder, the printer converted into
'villainy.' Whether the blunder was felicitous or not, there was some-

thing waggishly descriptive in the epithet which hit the humor of
Washington, and he resolved at once to retain it. The adopted misprint, 'good-natured villainy,' has stood from that day to this to characterize the merry mischief of their labors" (PMI, I, 177).

90.17–18 a ragged regiment of tripolitan prisoners]   On February 25,
1805, seven Tripolitan prisoners arrived in New York aboard the U.S.S.
John Adams, having been taken prisoner during the action off Tripoli
in August, 1804; four of them were "captains said to have commanded
in the Bashaws Service" (*Naval Documents Related to the United
States Wars with the Barbary Powers* [Washington, D.C., 1944], V,
374, 143). The prisoners attended a performance of *Blue Beard* at
the Park Theater on March 6, 1805, the advertisement identifying
them as "Mustaffa, Captain of the Ketch, Abdullah, Captive of the
Gun Boat taken on the 3rd of August, 1804," etc. (Odell, *Annals*, II,
229). The *Evening Post* of March 29, 1805, announced that "at the
request of several Gentlemen, a Benefit will be given to the Turkish
Captives, for the purpose of accommodating them with additional
cloathes; they have at present no other apparel than what they had
on at the time they were made prisoners of war."

90.29 Psalmanazar]   George Psalmanazar (1679?–1763), a Frenchman
whose real name is unknown, was a literary imposter who came to
London in 1703 and presented Bishop Compton with the catechism
in "Formosan" (his invented language). His *Memoirs* appeared post-
humously in 1764, containing an account of the imposture. The title
page of *Salmagundi* carries lines ascribed to him.

92.21–22 He is chosen . . . by the people]   At this time candidates for
the presidency were nominated by members of Congress.

92.24–28 The present bashaw . . . to a post.]   The Federalist community
was highly critical of Jefferson's republican simplicity. "He makes it
a point," declared the *New York Evening Post*, April 20, 1802, "when
he has occasion to visit the Capitol to meet the representatives of the
nation on public business, to go on a single horse, which he leads into
the shed and hitches to a peg." WI wrote Mary Fairlie from Washington on July 7, 1807, that her letters are "perhaps the mere method by
which you *delassitude* yourself after the fatigues of an evenings campaign, like the illustrious Jefferson who, after toiling all day in deciding
the fates of a nation, retires to his closet and amuses himself with
impaling a tadpole" (holograph, Yale University Library).

93.30 **Fashions,**]   "Methought I could discern a pretty *Democrat* à la
mode Françoise," writes John Lambert, "and a sweet *Federalist* à la
mode Angloise. I know not whether my surmises were just; but it is
certain that Mrs. Toole and Madame Bouchard, the two rival leaders

of fashion in caps, bonnets, feathers, flowers, muslin, and lace, have each their partisans and admirers: one because she is an English-woman, and the other because she is French; and if the ladies are not really divided in opinion as to politics, they are most unequivocally at issue with respect to dress" (*Travels Through Canada, and the United States*, II, 91–92). Longworth's *New-York Directory* for 1805 lists a Susannah Toole, "mantuamaker and milliner, 138 Broadway," but no Madame Bouchard.

94.38–39 *nudity* being all the rage] Simeon Baldwin wrote to his wife from Washington on January 12, 1805: "Young Bonaparte & his wife were here last week. I did not have an opportunity to inspect her charms but her dress at a Ball which she attended has been the general topic of conversation in all circles—Having married a Parissian [*sic*] she assumed the mode of dress in which it is said the Ladies of Paris are clothed—if that may be called clothing which leaves half of the body naked & the shape of the rest perfectly visible—Several of the Gent[n] who saw her say they could put all the cloaths she had on in their vest pockett—& it is said she did not appear at all abashed when the inquisitive Eyes of the young Galants led them to chat with her tete a tete.— Tho' her taste & appearance was condemned by those who saw her, yet such fashions are astonishingly bewitching & will gradually progress, & we may well reflect on what we shall be when fashion shall remove all barriers from the chastity of women" (*Life and Letters of Simeon Baldwin*, ed. Simeon E. Baldwin [New Haven, (1918?)], p. 345).

95.25 Dat . . . Columbas] Juvenal, *Satires*, II, 63: "Our censor absolves the raven and passes judgment on the pigeons."

96.28 little Teucer] Homer relates how in battle with the Trojans Teucer hid behind the shield of his half-brother Ajax and when he spied his chance shot arrows at the enemy (*Iliad*, VIII, 266–74).

97.24–25 the wool-clad warriors of Trapoban] In Part 1, book 3, chap-ter 4, Don Quixote mistakes two flocks of sheep for opposing armies, the one led by the pagan emperor Alifamfaron, lord of the island of Trapobana, the other by the Christian king, Pentapolin. He sets spurs to Rosinante and begins to lance among the former flock, where-upon the shepherds sling stones at him until he falls down off his horse. Thinking they have slain him, the shepherds gather their flock together, including the dead muttons, and leave the scene in haste.

97.25 puppets of the itinerant showman] In Part II, chapter 26, Don Quixote is so incensed by a puppet-show depicting Moorish knights pursuing the Catholic Don Gayferos and his wife Melisendra that he unsheathes his sword and beheads, maims, and cuts the knights to pieces.

97.30–98.28 "———— *How now, mooncalf!*"...a monster."] In *The Tempest*, II, ii, 126, Trinculo asks Stephano: "How now, moon-calf! How does thine ague?" The second number of *Salmagundi* (February 4, 1807) carried the following couplet: "As to dull Hudibrastic, so boasted of late,/ The doggrel discharge of some muddle brain'd pate" (87.7–8). Thomas Green Fessenden (1771–1837) chose to interpret these lines—and undoubtedly he was right!—as a reference to his poem *Terrible Tractoration* (1804), wherein he had used the pen name "Christopher Caustic" and took unfavorable notice of *Salmagundi* in his New York newspaper, *The Weekly Inspector*. "Pray, Messrs. Caterers of Salmagundi," he declared on February 7, "give us a little *bubble and squeak*, or *topsy-turvy*, by way of variety, or a little plain plum-pudding, if you have it at hand. But, in the name of all the gods of gormandizing, spare us your whipped syllabub, if you have nothing but *flummery* to substitute" (pp. 275–76).

The word "*flummery*" was ill chosen, for in *Salmagundi* No. III (February 18) the authors promised to serve "Dr. Christopher Costive" "a plentiful dish of flummery from his own shop, whenever he thinks fit to demand it, and garnished with a little Salmagundi for sauce" (98.8–10). Fessenden retorted in *The Weekly Inspector* on February 21: "We have to beg pardon of the public for the too favourable notice which we have given of 'Salmagundi.'... America has not hitherto proved a very kindly soil to the shoots of genius.... when like 'Salmagundi,' it turns out a *bramble*, and pricks and scratches without discrimination every thing within its reach, we naturally ask, why encumbereth it the ground?" (p. 298). "If the town still profess a fondness for this riff-raff mixture," he concluded, "we shall be forced to conclude, that a farrago of hob-nails and flint stones, peppered with a little grit from a grind-stone, is the most proper food for the many-headed monster.... we would beg leave to give them a new and more appropriate name, which conveys a correct idea of the 'treat' with which they feast our dainty citizens.... SILLY-KICKABY.... It consists of a sow's stomach, filled with a composition of learned *calve's brains*, gander's eggs, garlic, rue, ginger, aniseed, lovage, guinea pepper, and syrup of poppies" (p. 298–99).

On February 27, in *Salmagundi* No. IV, appeared the promised Hudibrastic poem, "Flummery," obviously parodying that of Fessenden. Fessenden, who was to have the last word in this verbal war, retorted in *The Weekly Inspector* on March 6: "Dr. Caustic declares, that he will bet any sum, from one mill to three cents, that he can blow the conductor of a certain liliputian journal, through a goose quill, out of the top of the tallest chimney. This he can perform forty-nine times in one ninety-ninth part of less than no time at all, any day in the year, and all day long 'OLDSTYLE'" (p. 30). For further details on this controversy, see Porter Gale Perrin, *The Life and Works of Thomas Green Fessenden* (Orono, Maine, 1925), pp. 117–20, 131.

98.11 Dr. Lampedo] A comic character in John Tobin's *The Honey Moon* (1805).

99.4 Dyde's] A public house in the London Hotel, operated by Robert Dyde and situated on Park Row near the theater.

101.24 Pliny the elder] Pliny the Elder died of asphyxiation on August 24, 79 A.D. while observing the eruption of Vesuvius. Although he wrote many historical works, only his *Naturalis Historia* survives.

101.35 our university] Columbia College.

102.7 Lacedemonian black broth] In his "Life of Lycurgus" Plutarch, describing the Spartan custom of taking meals in common, writes: "The 'black broth' was the most esteemed of their luxuries, insomuch that the elder men did not care for any meat, but always handed it over to the young, and regaled themselves on this broth. It is related that, in consequence of the celebrity of this broth, one of the kings of Pontus obtained a Laconian cook, but when he tasted it he did not like it. His cook thereupon said, 'O king, those who eat this broth must first bathe in the Eurotas'" (*Plutarch's Lives*, trans. Aubrey Stewart and George Long [London, 1916], I, 78).

102.19 *senior wrangler*] The head of the first class of those who are successful in the Mathematical Tripos at Cambridge University (*OED*). Hence, one who graduates with first honors.

103.1 MEMORANDUMS] "The Stranger in New Jersey," together with "The Stranger in Pennsylvania" in No. X and "The Stranger at Home" in No. XII, comprises the *Salmagundi* authors' satirical response to the unfavorable accounts of the United States written by English and European travelers in America. "An affectation of contempt for America," complained Charles Jared Ingersoll, "is one of the only prejudices in which all the nations of Europe seem to concur" (*Inchiquin, The Jesuit's Letters* [New York, 1810], p. 164).

103.22 *skilly-pots*] The skilly-pot or skilpot is the red-bellied terrapin.

103.31–32 toll man . . . pence table, &c.] The editor did not find any such description in Carr's *Stranger in Ireland*.

103.34–35 sting through the thickest boot] "General Washington told me," writes Weld, "that he never was so much annoyed by musquitoes in any part of America as in Skenesborough, for that they used to bite through the thickest boot" (*Travels Through the States of North America*, p. 164).

103.35 *Gallynipers*] "One of the local peculiarities of Virginia," writes John Bernard, "was an improved breed of mosquitoes, termed galli-nippers, in size and sting not much inferior to wasps. The origin of their name I could never precisely discover. This class of natives were, in general, most sedulous in their attentions to foreigners, but the gallinippers, perhaps with a more refined taste, specially preferred Frenchmen; and while the common mosquito appeared capable of adapting himself to every local variation of the country, being found on clayey or marshy soils, rocks or rivers, this species, with more of the air of an hereditary peerage, traced their extraction solely to swamps. Round the brink of these strongholds they lay in wait for their prey like the old robber knights; and, in hot weather, their thirst was not fastidious as to the color of the skin. Imagine the situation of a luckless wight journeying along a road of transverse trees, where expedition would be annihilation, seated, perhaps, on the bottom of a wagon, which bobbed him up like a parched pea—a jolt a second— while the sun streamed fire upon his caput, finding himself suddenly in the grasp of these sanguinary marauders, each of whom, however active in the defence, was sure to sheathe his blade in him at the same instant. What was an ancient martyrdom in comparison? What would not Nero have given for such auxiliaries" (*Retrospections*, pp. 169–70).

103.35 Archy Gifford] Identified as a tavernkeeper at Newark, N.J., in James Kirke Paulding's *Lay of the Scottish Fiddle* (New York, 1813), pp. 6, 7.

103.36 Carr's Stranger in Ireland] An examination of Sir John Carr's *The Stranger in Ireland: or, A Tour in the Southern and Western Parts of that Country, in the Year 1805* (Hartford, 1806) failed to turn up the phrase, "the man in the moon." This allusion, and several that follow, may be spurious.

103.37 Weld] An examination of Isaac Weld's *Travels Through the States of North America and the Provinces of Upper and Lower Canada During the Years 1795, 1796, and 1797*, 2d ed. (London, 1799) failed to turn up any "hints to travellers about packing their trunks."

104.1–2 a knowing traveller . . . waiters] Not found in any of the sources given.

104.16–18 Rahway-River . . . hay vessels?] This passage reflects New York resentment that the gunboats of 1804 were built to defend the Mississippi River rather than the eastern seaports.

104.38 Moore . . . Parkinson . . . Priest] John Moore, *A View of Society and*

Manners in France, Switzerland and Germany (London, 1781); Richard Parkinson, *A Tour in America in 1798, 1799, and 1800* (London, 1805); William Priest, *Travels in the United States of America; Commencing in the Year 1793 and Ending in 1797* (London, 1802).

104.40 The Sentimental Kotzebue] Augustus von Kotzebue (1761–1819) wrote countless domestic plays, many of which William Dunlap adapted and staged at the Park Theater, especially in the period 1799–1801, for audiences who responded enthusiastically to their sentimentality and glorification of the middle class.

105.16 man planting cabbages] Not found in Carr's *Stranger in Ireland*.

105.22–23 Philadelphians gave the preference to racoon] William Priest says of Philadelphians, "At two they dine on what is usual in England, with a variety of american dishes, such as bear, opossum, racoon, &c." (*Travels in the United States*, p. 33).

105.23 splac-nuncs] In the Voyage to Brobdingnag Lemuel Gulliver is announced by the town crier as "a strange creature to be seen at the Sign of the Green Eagle, not so big as a *splacknuck* (an animal in that country very finely shaped, about six foot long) and in every part of the body resembling an human creature, could speak several words, and perform an hundred diverting tricks" (*Gulliver's Travels*, pt. 2, chap. 2).

105.29–30 El Dorado . . . Thundertentronck] Voltaire's Candide, a young man living in the castle of Baron of Tunder-ten-tronckh of Westphalia, listens to the lessons of Doctor Pangloss, the greatest philosopher in the world. The baron, discovering Candide and his daughter Cunegonde making love one day, expels the young man. In the course of his journeys Candide witnesses the Lisbon earthquake from aboard ship and visits El Dorado.

105.34 country finely diversified with sheep and haystacks] While this can be inferred from reading Carr's *Stranger in Ireland*, Carr nowhere discusses sheep and haystacks in the same sentence or even in the same paragraph.

105.36 Carr and *Blind Bet!*] Carr describes Blind Bet as "stone blind, but a fine, cheerful, healthy woman; by the bounty of travellers, and the sale of gloves and stockings, the manufacture of her own hands, she maintains an infirm mother, and a train of little brothers and sisters." Having quoted the lines of "Poor Blind Bet" which found their way into his pocketbook on her quitting him, Carr concludes, "Poor Blind Bet's misfortunes and her virtues excite distinguished respect and admiration in the breasts of her neighbours" (*The Stranger in Ireland*, pp. 19–20).

106.12–13 languishing state of literature in this country] The Irish poet

Thomas Moore (1799–1852), having visited the United States in 1803–1804, included in his *Epistles, Odes, and Other Poems* (London, 1806) a section entitled "Poems Relating to America." One poem in particular, "To the Honourable W. R. Spencer," focuses on the low state of literature in America; herein the Muse of Nature "whispers round, her words are in the air, / But lost, unheard, they linger freezing there, / Without one breath of soul, divinely strong, / One ray of mind to thaw them into song" (lines 55–58). One American magazine was quick to reply: "Moore used to ask where were our poets? had we any? We had scarce a songster among us. He was afraid to look at the terrible Trumbull, with his 'sword trenchant.' Dwight's *ode* voice was too strong to whisper imbecilities to the flaxen ear locks of ideal beauty. Barlow would have rolled him in one corner of Manco Capae's white robe, to screen his frail form from the warring winds of the Andes; and Humphrey's would have sent him sailing adrift in little toy ships to sing songs to the fishes in the waters of his western world" (*Literary Magazine and American Register* 6 [1806], 219). And yet there was a measure of truth in Moore's charge. An anonymous American writer offered the following reasons for the mediocrity of American literature at this time: "the love of gain," deficiencies in collegiate education, "the small number of distinguished scholars in whom the candidate for literary fame may find competitors," the failure to reward writers adequately, and "the scarcity of *books*, and the difficulties of procuring them" (*Monthly Magazine, and American Review*, 1 [1799], 15).

106.19–20 only wants a castle . . . Naples] A parody of Carr's description of the bay of Dublin: "On the right was the rugged hill of Howth, with its rocky bays, wanting only a volcano to afford to the surrounding scenery the strongest resemblance, as I was well informed, to the beautiful bay of Naples" (*The Stranger in Ireland*, p. 28).

106.23 Justice Bridlegoose] Rabelais' Judge Bridlegoose settled lawsuits by the throw and hazard of dice. See *Gargantua and Pantagruel*, III, 39–40.

106.26 all the american ladies . . . have bad teeth] "This is certainly a fair subject for American severity. The ladies of the United States have no reason to be gratified with the remarks of English travellers; if truth would not have permitted the latter to hide the imperfections of the fair, gallantry might, at least, have prompted them to soften the asperity of their remarks; but, in fact, these gentlemen have not truth on their side; their representations are not only ungenerous but ill-founded, when applied generally to the American females, and to them in particular. The men are much more liable to loss of teeth than the women; indeed, I do not believe there are more instances of that misfortune among the latter than are to be met with in England, making allowance for the numerical difference in population" (Note, 1811 London ed.).

106.26–27 Anacreon Moore's opinion] Thomas Moore's *Odes of Anacreon.* See also note at 128.3.

106.36 fill up my book like Carr] In the later chapters of *The Stranger in Ireland* Carr quotes extensively, offering for example extracts from Dean Kirwan's sermons (chapter 20), Grattan's speeches (chapter 21), and Mr. Curran's speeches (chapter 22).

106.37 Carr's learned derivation of *gee* and *whoa*] Carr writes: "The Irish drivers set their horses in motion much in the same way as we do, by the word 'gee,' an important word which, as well as that of 'whoe,' have been too much in constant use to have had much illustration. Dr. Johnson defines the accelerating word 'gee' to be 'a term amongst waggoners, to make their horses go faster;' but does not recur to the radical word. Ge, or geh, seems to be the imperative of the German verb gehen, to go; a word by which, with an accompanying stroke of the whip, a horse thoroughly understands that he is to advance. The retarding word 'who,' we are told, was formerly applied to valorous knights and combatants in armour, or *harness*, as it was called, and hence degraded to horses *in harness.* When the king, as president at tilts and tournaments, threw down his baton as the signal of discontinuance, the heralds cried out, in the Danish language, to the combatants, 'ho,' that is, stop" (*The Stranger in Ireland*, pp. 34–35).

107.1–2 Saw a democrat ... democrats] In a note to Epistle 2, "To Miss M——e. From Norfolk, in Virginia, November 1803," Thomas Moore says of this town, "It is in truth a most disagreeable place, and the best the journalist or geographer can say of it is, that it abounds in dogs, in negroes, and in democrats" (*Epistles, Odes, and Other Poems,* p. 21, n.).

107.2 superfine sentiment] Not found in Carr's *Stranger in Ireland.*

107.3 Joe Miller] Joe Miller (1684–1738), a comic actor at Drury Lane, was said to be so grave in his demeanor off the stage that he never uttered a joke. It became the custom to ascribe every new joke to him, and soon after his death there appeared *Joe Miller's Jests: or, the Wit's Vade Mecum* (1739).

107.3 piggin] A small wooden pail or tub with an upright stave as handle.

107.18 a seventh ward politician] Of New York's nine wards, numbered north from the Battery, the seventh was the most populous in 1807. The southernmost first four wards stood apart from the northern as socially better, wealthier, and Federalist. The newer northern wards contained a larger alien element, notably the recently arrived Irish, and were Republican in sympathy.

112.7 SEARSON] John Searson, a Philadelphia poet, author of *Mount Vernon* (1800).

115.9 LLOYD] From Robert Lloyd's "A Familiar Epistle. To a Friend Who Sent the Author a Hamper of Wine," lines 181–84, where the first word is "Or," not "All."

115.34 "People's Friend."] *The People's Friend & Daily Advertiser*, a daily newspaper published at New York, September 1, 1806, to August 3, 1807.

116.2 "THE ECHO"] Satirical poems by Theodore Dwight, Richard Alsop, Lemuel Hopkins, E. H. Smith, and Mason Cogswell, published originally in the (Hartford) *American Mercury* (1791–1805) and then in book form at Hartford in 1807. In his Introductory Essay to the 1811 London edition of *Salmagundi* Lambert says that the volume "met with considerable applause, not only from the federal party, but also from many who were of an opposite way of thinking" (p. xxxiv).

116.28–29 spendid review] At the close of the American Revolution the last British troops left New York on November 25, 1783, an event celebrated annually thereafter. On November 12, 1806, the Common Council "ordered that the usual quantity of powder be furnished to the military," and on December 8 David King was ordered paid $654.87 for the "anniversary Dinner November 25, and sundries" (*Minutes of the Common Council of the City of New York, 1784–1831* [New York, 1917], IV, 292, 314). On such occasions the militia assembled at the Battery. "The troops do not amount to more than 600," writes Lambert, "and are gaudily dressed in a variety of uniforms, every ward in the city having a different one; some of them, with helmets, appear better suited to the theatre than the field. The general of the militia and his staff are dressed in the national uniform of blue and buff. They also wear immense cocked hats and feathers, which, with their large gold epaulets, have a very showy appearance" (Note, 1811 London ed.). In the 1809 *History of New York* WI describes the semiannual militia reviews which Stuyvesant conducted (V, v).

117.25–29 *wooden* bulwarks ... *warm fire*] In the 1809 *History of New York*, III, v, WI has Diedrich recall "that remarkably cold winter, in which our sagacious corporation, in a spasm of economical philanthropy, pulled to pieces, at an expense of several hundred dollars, the wooden ramparts [on the Battery], which had cost them several thousand; and distributed the rotten fragments, which were worth considerably less than nothing, among the shivering poor of the city—

never, since the fall of the walls of Jericho, or the heaven built battlements of Troy, had there been known such a demolition—nor did it
go unpunished; five men, eleven old women and nineteen children,
besides cats, dogs and negroes, were blinded, in vain attempts to
smoke themselves warm, with this charitable substitute for firewood,
and an epidemic complaint of sore eyes was moreover produced, which
has since recurred every winter; particularly among those who undertake to burn rotten logs—who warm themselves with the charity of
others—or who use patent chimnies" (I, 159–60).

117.29–30 ECONOMY . . . nation] The Jeffersonian administration had
worked steadily to achieve economy, trying to discharge the public
debt and at the same time lower internal taxes. Here, and again in
the Mustapha letter in No. IX, the *Salmagundi* authors satirized these
efforts. WI did so again in the 1809 *History of New York*, IV, iv: "Not
to keep my reader in any suspence, the word which had so wonderfully arrested the attention of William the Testy . . . is no other than
economy—a talismanic term, which by constant use and frequent
mention has ceased to be formidable in our eyes, but which has as
terrible potency as any in the arcana of necromancy" (I, 230).

119.10 The grand bashaw of the city] Apparently Marinus Willett,
mayor of New York.

119.42–120.2 rulers . . . discipline] "When he became President," writes
Pete Kyle McCarter, Jefferson "argued that to maintain a large standing
army and navy would be to invite war with a foreign power; in this
manner were his economy and his naval policy closely interrelated
with his pacificism. The Federalists argued that preparation for war
was the best guaranty of peace" ("The Literary, Political, and Social
Theories of Washington Irving" [Ph.D. diss., University of Wisconsin,
1939], p. 303).

122.22 Leonidas] Heroic king of Sparta, who perished with his 300
men at Thermopylae (480 B.C.).

122.28–29 "none but the brave deserve the fair!"] Dryden's "Alexander's
Feast," line 15.

122.29 the immortal Amrou] Probably a reference to Amru Ibn al Aass
(594–664), Arab general and statesman mentioned in Irving's *Mahomet*,
p. 236, and elsewhere.

122.43 "the soldier tired of war's alarms,"] First line of a song in the
opera *Artaxerxes* by the eighteenth-century English composer, Dr.
Thomas Arne; reprinted in *A Collection of Favorite Songs*, arr. A.
Reinagle (Philadelphia, [1789?]). See Sonneck, *Bibliography of Early
Secular American Music*, p. 388.

123.22 Waller's Sacharissa] After the death of his first wife Edmund

Waller (1607–1687) paid unsuccessful court to Lady Dorothy Signey, whom he celebrated in poems as "Sacharissa."

124.17 *Nang-Fou*] Probably fictitious.

125.16 Dessalines] Jean Jacques Dessalines (ca. 1785–1806), born in Guinea and imported into Haiti as a slave, was bought by a French planter, whose name he assumed. He was created governor of Haiti in January, 1804, and on October 8 was crowned emperor as Jean Jacques I. But his cruelty and debauchery soon alienated even his firmest adherents, and while trying to repress a revolt he was cut down by Henri Christophe, who succeeded him.

126.21 miss SOPHY SPARKLE] Miss Mary Fairlie of New York, celebrated for her wit and beauty, with whom WI corresponded during the spring and summer of 1807. In 1812 she married the actor Thomas Cooper.

127.31 To whirl the modest waltz's rounds] Of the waltz, a German dance introduced in the post-Revolutionary period and taught by French refugees, it has been written: "American young women were extremely fond of dancing, in which they indulged freely, and in which they excelled.... Quadrilles and cotillions were the favorite form of this amusement; the waltz gained headway, but slowly because of the charge of indelicacy that was brought against it. These scruples prevailed longer in New England than in the South, where waltzing came to be very much in vogue" (Jane Louise Mesick, *The English Traveller in America, 1785–1835* [New York, 1922], p. 95).

127.36 Meetz] Probably Raymond Meets, who kept a music store in New York in 1818 and is listed two years later as being a music teacher. See *A Register of Artists, Engravers, Booksellers, Bookbinders, Printers & Publishers in New York City, 1633–1820,* comp. George L. McKay (New York, 1942), p. 49.

128.3 dapper volume] Undoubtedly Thomas Moore's *Odes of Anacreon* (1800), a metrical translation completed at Trinity College, Dublin, a few years earlier. The *Edinburgh Review* 4 (July, 1803), 476, dismissed the work as "calculated for a bagnio."

128.36 Ausonia's] Italy's.

130.1 prince Madoc] Madog ab Owain Gwynedd (d. 1169), legendary Welsh prince and subject of Southey's poem, *Madoc* (1805), according to legend sailed to America and established a colony on the southern branches of the Missouri. In the 1809 *History of New York,* I, iii, WI writes, "Nor shall I investigate the more modern claims of the Welsh, founded on the voyage of Prince Madoc in the eleventh century, who having never returned, it has since been wisely concluded that he must have gone to America, and that for a plain reason—if he did

not go there, where else could he have gone?—a question which most
Socratically shuts out all further dispute" (I, 30).

130.32 Hogarth] William Hogarth (1697–1764), English painter and
engraver.

133.13–14 fire-place . . . dutch tiles . . . scripture pieces] In the 1809
History of New York, III, iii, WI, describing the Golden Age of
Wouter Van Twiller, writes, "As to the gentlemen, each of them
tranquilly smoked his pipe, and seemed lost in contemplation of the
blue and white tiles, with which the fire-places were decorated;
wherein sundry passages of scripture, were piously pourtrayed" (I, 150).

134.11 soup-maigre] Thin soup, made chiefly from vegetables or fish
(*OED*).

136.39 Cinderella] An English play. See note at 243.17.

136.39 Valentine and Orson] Thomas John Dibdin's *Valentine and
Orson* (1804), based on an ancient Italian romance, was first performed in America on April 15, 1805, at the Park Theater, and often
thereafter. Charles Brockden Brown's *Literary Magazine and American
Register* 7 (February, 1807), 144–45, carried an "Account of the
Splendid Melodrama called Valentine and Orson, now Performing at
the New Theatre," that is, the Chestnut Street Theater, Philadelphia.

136.39 Blue Beard] George Colman the Younger's *Blue Beard* (1798)
was adapted by William Dunlap for the Park Theater and first played
there on March 5, 1802. "The piece satisfied a craving for Gothic
thrills, and for a spectacle of oriental magnificence" (Odell, *Annals*,
II, 133).

137.16 Little RUTHERFORD] The *Theatrical Censor* said of Rutherford
as Davidson in *Mary, Queen of Scots* at the Chestnut Street Theater
on January 15, 1806, He "takes more pains with his feet than with his
head" and "always appears to be preparing for a minuet" (quoted in
Reese Davis James, *Cradle of Culture 1800–1820: The Philadelphia
Stage* [Philadelphia, 1957], p. 77). Rutherford first appeared at the
Park Theater on January 2, 1807, in the title role of George Lillo's
George Barnwell (1731); the next day *The Town* said of his performance, "It was free from rant, but it wanted vigour." Rutherford
remained for a while with the company at the Park.

137.30–31 Herodotus . . . hair] Herodotus writes: "For it is plain to
see that the Colchians are Egyptians; and this that I say I myself
noted before I heard it from others. When I began to think on this
matter, I inquired of both peoples; and the Colchians remembered
the Egyptians better than the Egyptians remembered the Colchians;
the Egyptians said that they held the Colchians to be part of Sesostris'
army. I myself guessed it to be so, partly because they are dark-

skinned and woolly-haired; though that indeed goes for nothing, seeing that other peoples, too, are such; but my better proof was that the Colchians and Egyptians and Ethiopians are the only nations that have from the first practised circumcision" (*History*, bk. II, line 104, trans. A. D. Godley [London, 1920], I, 391–93). William Beloe's translation of the *History*, which first appeared in 1790 or so and from which Knickerbocker quotes the first few lines in the 1809 *History of New York*, II, xv, carried the following note by Volney on this passage: "The ancient Egyptians were real negroes, of the same species with all the natives of Africa: and though, as might be expected, after mixing for so many ages with the Greeks and Romans, they have lost the intensity of their first colour, yet they still retain strong marks of their original conformation" (*The Ancient History of Herodotus*, trans. William Beloe [New York, 1855], p. 163, n.). In the 1809 *History*, I, ii, WI writes: "The negro philosophers of Congo affirm, that the world was made by the hands of angels, excepting their own country, which the Supreme Being constructed himself, that it might be supremely excellent. And he took great pains with the inhabitants, and made them very black, and beautiful; and when he had finished the first man, he was well pleased with him, and smoothed him over the face, and hence his nose and the nose of all his descendants became flat" (I, 14–15).

137.35 Fennel] James Fennell (1766–1816), author of *The Wheel of Truth* (1803), the afterpiece described in *Oldstyle* No. VII, was an English actor who came to America in 1794. William Dunlap writes: "Tall, handsome in person, specious in manner, well educated, and ever courteous, Fennell as a gentleman at this time stood high. He lived splendidly, and far beyond his income, courted the world, and was courted in return. Cooper's character and conduct was as opposite as possible" (*History of the American Theatre*, I, 351). During the 1806–1807 season at the Park Theater Fennell appeared with Cooper in many "star" engagements at Cooper's request, playing among other roles Richard III to Cooper's Richmond, Othello to Cooper's Iago, and King Henry to Cooper's Hotspur. "As an actor," writes Bernard, "he certainly laid small claim to genius, being rather what is known as an excellent reader; but he had great cultivation; and in particular characters, where his coldness and person were equally needed, such as Brutus and Zanga, he could exhibit great force, and tower at moments into positive grandeur" (*Retrospections*, p. 267).

137.4 the Lyceum] The Chestnut Street Theater in Philadelphia, where in the spring of 1806 "engagements with Fennell and Cooper were

making possible the performance of eight of Shakespeare's plays"
(James, *Cradle of Culture*, p. 80).

138.1–2 Scarcely... nose] At the beginning of book 4 of *Tristram
Shandy* Slawkenbergius tells a tale of a stranger with an immense
nose who entered the town of Strasburg one sultry August day on
his way to Frankfort and said he would be back at Strasburg a month
from that day. The whole town, upon his departure, was in an uproar,
some calling it a false, others a true nose. The stranger's nose troubled
their dreams and roused their curiosity. The two universities of
Strasburg divided about the nose, the Lutheran becoming Nosarian
and the Papist Antinosarian. In their curiosity the Strasburgers ventured out onto the road to Frankfort, whereupon the French marched
in and won the town.

138.6 Cocker's Arithmetic] Edward Cocker (1631–1675) was the author
of several arithmetical works. *Cocker's Arithmetick* (London, 1678)
went through many editions.

138.14 WOOD and CAIN] William B. Wood (1779–1861) was a comedian
and at this time co-manager of the Chestnut Street Theater. Alexander
Cain was "for some time considered the rival of Mr. Wood" (Dunlap,
History of the American Theatre, II, 231). "Mr. Wood is very respectable in genteel comedy," writes the Censor. "Mr. Cain, possessed of
a good figure and voice, might, by care and study, recover the favor
of the public, which, if he continue much longer in the careless track
he has taken, he must inevitably lose: his walk is sentimental comedy"
(*Theatrical Censor* 8 [January 16, 1806], 70).

139.24–28 Theobald, Hanmer,... Johnson] Lewis Theobald (1688–
1744) wrote *Shakespeare Restored* (1726) and Sir Thomas Hanmer
(1677–1746), *The Works of Shakespear... Revised and Corrected*
(1744); Samuel Johnson published his edition of Shakespeare in 1765.
All three works made restorations and emendations in the text.

139.27 General Washington's life] John Marshall's five-volume *Life of
George Washington* (1804–1807) was hastily written and badly pro-
portioned, focussing more heavily on eighteenth-century military and
civil history than on Washington himself.

139.37–38 a predilection... day] An allusion to the story that Jefferson
kept a Negro mistress, which seems to have originated in 1802 in
James Thompson Callender's Richmond newspaper, *The Recorder*,
whence it spread over the country in the opposition press.

143.27 editors or SLANG-WHANGERS] In the 1809 *History of New York*,
IV, iii, the trumpeter Anthony Van Corlear twangs "his trumpet
in the face of the whole world, like a thrice valorous editor daringly
insulting all the principalities and powers—on the other side of the

Atlantic" (I, 216). At his death (VII, vii) he leaves behind two or three dozen "fine, chubby, brawling, flatulent little urchins, from whom, if legend speak true, (and they are not apt to lie) did descend the innumerable race of editors, who people and defend this country, and who are bountifully paid by the people for keeping up a constant alarm—and making them miserable" (II, 226).

143.37–40 There has been a civil war ... in his stead.] From the time of the campaign of 1800 there had been a reléntless attack on Jefferson in the opposition press, most notably for his acceptance of much French deistic thought. "No calumny was too black to circulate about the terrible atheist," writes Howard Mumford Jones. "He was a *sansculotte*, a red-legged Democrat; and Gallatin, his secretary of the treasury, was Genevan by birth, a Frenchman in accent, a Jesuit in morals" (*America and French Culture, 1750–1848* [Chapel Hill, 1927], p. 553). A defender of the principle of freedom of the press, Jefferson wrote on February 11, 1807: "I have therefore never even contradicted the thousands of calumnies so industriously propagated against myself. But the fact being once established that the press is impotent when it abandons itself to falsehood, I leave to others to restore it to its strength by recalling it within the pale of truth" (quoted in Frank Luther Mott, *American Journalism* [New York, 1941], p. 171).

144.8–9 a professed *anti-deluvian* from the gallic empire] On March 18, 1801, Jefferson wrote Thomas Paine, then at Paris waiting for means of conveyance to America: "You expressed a wish to get a passage to this country in a public vessel. Mr. Dawson is charged with orders to the captain of the 'Maryland' to receive and accommodate you with a passage back, if you can be ready to depart at such short warning" (quoted in Henry Adams, *History of the United States of America* [New York, 1891], I, 316). The opposition press attacked this invitation so vehemently that Jefferson "apologized by making the matter appear an act of charity" (Conway, *Life of Thomas Paine*, II, 298).

144.28 langrage] A type of shot formerly used in battle at sea, for tearing sails and rigging.

145.12 blustering windy assembly] The 1809 *History of New York*, VII, v, describes the debate of the "grand divan of the councillors and robustious Burgomasters" of New Amsterdam (II, 204–10).

146.3 "all talk and no cider;"] Much talk but no results (*DAE*).

147.9–11 Does a foreign invader.... utters a *speech*.] On December 31, 1806, James Monroe and William Pinkney signed an agreement with Great Britain adjusting certain Anglo-American diplomatic issues. Because the agreement left British impressment of American sailors and indemnities for previous ship and cargo seizures at issue, Jefferson refused to submit the treaty to the Senate, but sought to utilize it as a base for further negotiation. In this he was rebuffed by Canning, British Foreign Secretary.

147.14–15 Is a peaceable citizen...power] On April 25, 1806, the *Leander*, one of three British frigates then blockading the port of New York, fired a shot across the bow of a merchant vessel in order to bring it to; the "passing vessel happened by an unlucky chance to be in line with a coasting sloop far behind," and the shot "killed one John Pierce, brother of the coaster's captain" (Henry Adams, *History of the United States*, III, 199).

147.16–23 Does an alarming insurrection. . . . out of existence.] Warned by General James Wilkinson, commander of American forces in the West, of Aaron Burr's plans to lead an expedition against Spain on the Lower Mississippi, President Jefferson, without naming Burr, issued a proclamation on November 27, 1806, declaring that "information has been received that sundry persons—are conspiring and confederating together to begin—a military expedition or enterprise against the dominions of Spain," and "warning and enjoining all faithful citizens who have been led without due knowledge or consideration to participate in the said unlawful enterprise to withdraw from the same without delay" (Thomas Perkins Abernethy, *The Burr Conspiracy* [New York, 1954], p. 190).

147.36 the british islanders...every thing] "An Englishman without his *dinner* is like a mechanic without his tools. Even our very charities are subservient to *eating* and *drinking*; for heart and purse are both open to the cheerful glass. As to the Americans, they are certainly as much inclined to eating and drinking as Englishmen; nay, I am of opinion they are much greater epicures in the modern acceptation of that term than even ourselves. But, with respect to *talking* and drinking of *toasts* they are far beyond us. Indeed, take them either as an *eating* or a *windy* nation, or both together, we are by no means a match for them" (Note, 1811 London ed.).

148.32 MAN-SOUL] In John Bunyan's *The Holy War* (1682) the town of Mansoul, built by Shaddai, is overwhelmed by Diabolus. Shaddai's son, Emmanuel, recovers and new-models the town and holds it against the repeated assaults of Diabolus.

148.38 CLELIA] Clelia, in the legendary history of Rome, was a Roman maiden, one of the hostages given to Porsena. She made her escape from the Etruscan camp by swimming across the Tiber. She was sent back by the Romans, but Porsena not only set her at liberty for her gallant deed, but allowed her to take with her a part of the hostages. Mlle. de Scudéry took this story as the framework for her celebrated romance *Clélie*, published in ten volumes (1654–1660).

150.4 MORSE] Mr. Morse made his first appearance on the stage as Pierre in Thomas Otway's *Venice Preserved* at the Park Theater on November 28, 1806. The son of a Massachusetts yeoman, "he lacked the ease of a gentleman at the time of his debut" (Dunlap, *History of the American Theatre*, II, 242).

151.27 the HORNET] Probably a reference to the 16-gun brig which cruised on the Atlantic coast, November 1805, to February, 1806, under Master Commandant Isaac Chauncey, and in the Mediterranean, May, 1806, to 1807, under Master Commandant John H. Dent. Possibly, though, a reference to the 10-gun sloop of the same name which had participated in General Eaton's attack on Derne, April, 1805, during the Tripolitan War and returned to Philadelphia, August 9, 1806, much damaged by a gale, where it was sold September 3, 1806. See *Register of Officer Personnel United States Navy and Marine Corps and Ships' Data 1801–1807* (Washington, D.C., 1945), pp. 73, 74.

151.42 *Fair Penitent*] Nicholas Rowe's *The Fair Penitent* (1703), very popular on the New York stage, was performed at the Park Theater on February 18, 1807, with Mrs. Warren as Calista. "Never have we seen Mrs. Warren play so well, or with so much effect," declared the *Evening Post*, February 20. It seems likely that Cooper, who had played the role earlier, appeared as Lothario in this production.

152.17–20 "In . . . thee."] These four lines appeared in *Spectator* No. 68, being a translation of Martial, *Epigrams*, XII, 47, who imitated Ovid, *Amores*, III, 11, 39.

153.3 "a most villanous congregation of vapors."] See "a foul and pestilent congregation of vapours" (*Hamlet*, II, ii, 314–15).

153.28–29 a striking likeness of my friend] A reference to the woodcut at the head of *Salmagundi* No. VIII in the first American edition of 1807–1808.

157.22–23 STYLE . . . *Johnson*.] A compression of four of the seven definitions of *style* given in Samuel Johnson's *Dictionary of the English Language* (1755), which read as follows: "1. Manner of writing with regard to language"; "3. Title; appellation"; "6. Any thing with a sharp point, as a graver; the pin of a dial"; "7. The stalk which rises from amid the leaves of a flower."

157.29 Blair's lectures] Hugh Blair (1718–1800) was an influential rhetorician in his day and for a century thereafter. Fifteen of the 47 lectures he delivered repeatedly at the University of Edinburgh for twenty-four years (1759–1783) were on Style (Nos. 10–24), four of those being a critical examination of Addison's *Spectator* papers and one an examination of Swift's writings. They were published as *Lectures on Rhetoric and Belles Lettres* (London, 1783).

161.1 lodoiska] John Philip Kemble's musical spectacle, *Lodoiska*, was first performed at Drury Lane on June 9, 1794, and long esteemed in America. The earliest New York performance recorded in Odell is that of June 13, 1808.

162.3 Linkum Fidelius] Emended to "Lithgow" in the 1824 Paris edition. William Lithgow (1582–1645?), a Scottish traveler, was author of *Nineteen Years Travels Through the Most Eminent Places in the Habitable World* (1632). The quotation in question reads, "For my part, what I have reaped, is by a dear bought knowledge, as it were, a small contentment, in a never contenting subject, a bitter pleasant taste, of a sweet-seasoned sowre, and all in all, what I found was more than ordinary rejoycing, in an extraordinary sorrow of delights" (*Nineteen Years Travels*, 10th ed. [London, 1692], p. 12). A piece attributed to WI by Martin Roth in *The Corrector* for April 11, 1804, contains the following passage: "[Ebenezer] went away, as honest Lithgow says, 'rejoicing in an extraordinary sorrow of delights'" (*Washington Irving's Contributions to the Corrector*, p. 70).

164.4–5 the lady . . . in the lobster] The calcareous structure in the stomach of a lobster, serving for the trituration of its food; fancifully supposed to resemble the outline of a seated female figure (*OED*). In *The Battle of the Books* Swift describes Dryden's helmet as "nine times too large for the head, which appeared situate far in the hinder part, even like the lady in a lobster, or like a mouse under a canopy of state, or like a shrivelled beau, from within the penthouse of a modern periwig."

164.36 poor old *Acco*] Zenobius writes, "Acco was a woman celebrated for foolishness, who, they say, while she looked at herself in a glass talked with the image as though with another person" (*Corpus Paroemiographorum Graecorum*, ed. E. L. von Leutsch and F. G. Schneidewin [Hildesheim, 1958], I, 21).

165.21–22 latonian feat] Latona (or Leto), the mother of Apollo, would have thrown herself into a small pool by the wayside (in her wanderings) to refresh herself, but was prevented by Juno.

165.32 Whitfield] George Whitefield (1714–1770), English Methodist revivalist.

166.3 *yerb*] Obsolete or dialect for herb (*OED*).

166.17 american philosophical society] The first scientific society in America, founded at Philadelphia in 1743.

166.18 *Hutchin's improved*] In 1752 John Nathan Hutchins, who had published almanacs for many years, wrote the first number of what was after 1759 entitled *Hutchins Improved*. In 1756 he was described as a "teacher of mathematicks in New-York" (Hugh Alexander Morrison, *Preliminary Check List of American Almanacks: 1639–1800* [Washington, D.C., 1907], p. 80). In 1807 the office of *Hutchins' Almanack* was 104 Water Street. See McKay, *Register*, p. 38.

168.4 *bidets*] Vessels on low, narrow stands, which can be bestridden for bathing purposes (*OED*).

169.10 "Fire in each eye—and paper in each hand."] Pope's "Epistle to Dr. Arbuthnot," line 5.

171.34–36 the grand bashaw ... *by the day*] "The salaries paid to the president and the government officers are not very great," writes Lambert, "though quite enough, perhaps for every good purpose in a republic. The president receives about £5,300 sterling;—Vice-president, £1060;—Speaker of the House of Representatives, 12 dollars per diem during his attendance. The members of the Senate, and House of Representatives, 6 dollars each for every day's attendance, as well as for every twenty miles travelling to and from the seat of government. The chief justice of the United States has £850 per annum—the rest in proportion" (Note, 1811 London ed.).

172.13–15 they were ... their meetings] On December 15, 1806, Jefferson informed Congress that he had been unable to ready the south wing of the Capitol for the present session. On February 5, 1807, Joseph Lewis, Jr., a Virginia Representative and member of the committee to whom the presidential message had been referred, introduced a bill "making appropriations for finishing the south wing of the Capitol, and for other purposes." In the House debate which ensued on February 13, Benjamin H. Latrobe, appointed surveyor of public buildings by Jefferson in 1803, pointed out that if the $25,000 which Lewis moved be appropriated for this purpose ($20,000 of this amount for the Chamber) "were not granted and repairs made, the walls would tumble down." Another Virginia Representative, John Jackson, "was unable to conceive how twenty thousand dollars could be wanted to furnish one room. ... Mr. J. was in favor of economy, not of the economy of the last eight or ten years, but that of old times." Shortly "Mr. Lewis observed, that he had no particular concern in this subject. Perhaps he should never have again the honor of a seat in the House, and if he did he should, he believed, be as willing to sit on a stool as other gentlemen." On March 3 Lewis' motion was approved. See *The Debates and Proceedings in the Congress of the United States ... Ninth Congress—Second Session* (Washington, D.C., 1852), pp. 456, 496, 1272.

173.7–9 an illustrious warrior . . . at Derne]   William Eaton, United States
   Navy Agent for the Barbary Regencies in Egypt, cooperating under
   Commodore Barron with Hamet Karamanli, exiled Bashaw of Tripoli,
   entered into a convention on February 23, 1805, to reestablish Hamet
   in possession of his sovereignty of Tripoli. As "general and commander-
   in-chief" of the land forces operating against the usurping bashaw,
   Eaton marched at the head of an international army of 400 men across
   the Libyan Desert to Derne, a coastal city some 600 miles distant.
   On April 27, acting in concert with American naval forces, he stormed
   Derne and in the weeks that followed withstood several Tripolitan
   efforts to recapture the town. See Gardner W. Allen, *Our Navy and
   the Barbary Corsairs* (Boston, 1905), chap. 14.
173.30 sorry little gun-boats]   The economy-minded administration of
   Jefferson steadily sought to reduce appropriations for the navy, even
   as the worsening situation in Europe posed a threat to American
   commerce. Gunboats were preferred to other naval armament, including frigates. In 1807 "the United States Navy owned sixty-nine
   of these horrid little two-gun scows, which at high tide loved to
   float up into cornfields and mud" (STW, II, 168). At the end of the
   year a bill to build 188 more gunboats was introduced and passed
   by an enormous majority.
174.14 *in querpo*]   In undress; without clothing (*OED*).
179.16 a nine days wonder]   An event of temporary interest (*OED*).
180.17–18 the American Ticket . . . *dished.*]   Republicans scornfully referred to the Federalist slate in the New York state election of 1807
   as the "American Ticket." On April 30 Daniel D. Tompkins, DeWitt
   Clinton's choice for governor and the official Republican candidate,
   defeated the coalition candidate, Morgan Lewis, by over 4,000 votes.
   WI wrote Mary Fairlie on May 2, "We have toiled through the
   purgatory of an Election—and 'may the day stand for aye accursed
   on the Kalender,' for never were poor devils more intollerably beaten
   & discomfitted than my forlorn brethren the federalists" (holograph,
   Yale University Library).
181.2 Amphion]   The son of Zeus and Antiope who, according to
   Greek legend, built Thebes by the music of his lute, which was so
   melodious that the stones danced into walls and houses of their
   own accord.
181.3 Arion]   Arion, once returning to Corinth from Sicily and finding
   his life threatened by the sailors who were greedy for his property,
   gained permission to delight himself with his music, sang and played
   upon his lyre, and threw himself into the sea. The song-loving dolphins
   carried him safely to land.

182.13–14 The house of assembly breaks up] In 1807 the New York Assembly adjourned on April 7.

182.24 Polopoy's island] This may be "Polepel's-Island" in the Hudson near West Point, listed in Longworth's *New-York Directory* for 1806.

182.42 Solomon Lang] John Lang, a printer who became associated with the *New-York Gazette* in 1797, and its proprietor in 1799. "For some forty or more years," recollects John W. Francis, "Lang's *Gazette* was recognized as the leading mercantile advertiser, and the patronage which it received from the business world was such as doubtless secured ample returns to its proprietor. . . . unconscious of the penury of his intellectual powers, [Lang] at times, unwittingly became the pliant agent of designing individuals, and from the blunders into which he was led, his baptismal name, John, seemed easily converted into that of Solomon, by which specification much of his correspondence was maintained. He bore the pleasantry with grateful composure" (*International Monthly Magazine* 5 [February, 1852], 258).

183.1 "Nose, nose, jolly red nose"] In Beaumont and Fletcher's *The Knight of the Burning Pestle*, I, 334–35, Old Merri-thought sings, "Nose, nose, jolly red nose, / And who gave thee this jolly red nose?"

183.2 Communipaw] An early name for Jersey City.

185.1–2 a play . . . Philadelphia] *The Fox Chase*, a sentimental comedy by the Philadelphian Charles Breck (1782–1822), published by David Longworth at New York in 1808, "as performed at the theatres Philadelphia and Baltimore."

185.24 *pun* mania] On March 17, 1807, during a visit to Philadelphia, WI wrote Mary Fairlie: "The Philadelphians do absolutely 'live and move, and have a being' entirely upon puns— . . . I absolutely shudder with horror—think what miseries I suffer—me to whom a pun is an abomination—is there any thing in the whole volume of the 'miseries of human life' to equal it. I experienced the first attack of this forlorn wit on entering philadelphia—it was equal to a twinge of the gout, or *a stitch in the side*—I found it was repeated at every step. . . . I hastened home prodigiously indisposed, took to my bed and was only roused therefrom by the sound of the breakfast bell. I have suffered more or less ever since, but, thank heaven it is a complaint of which few die, otherwise I should be under no small apprehension" (holograph, Yale University Library).

186.3 *Licentia punica*] There appears to be no such phrase in Horace or, so far as the editor can discover, in any other classical Latin writer. The *Salmagundi* authors may have been thinking of *perfidia plus quam Punica*, an expression that occurs in Livy, XXI, iv, 9.

186.13 F. S. A.] Fellow of the Society of Antiquaries.

186.19 *doup*]   *Doop* means baptism and, by extension, something sopped (as bread is in milk) or dipped (as a biscuit is in tea).

187.29–30 tomb . . . colossus of Rhodes]   The tomb of Mausolus, king of Caria, and the Colossus at Rhodes were two of the Seven Wonders of the World.

187.41–42 Trim's argument]   In *Tristram Shandy*, book 8, chapter 19, Uncle Toby observes: "Bohemia being totally inland, it could have happened no otherwise—It might, said Trim, if it had pleased God—." Thus Philadelphia might have stood where New York is if it had pleased God.

188.15–16 a name utterly impossible to pronounce]   "The Philadelphians call it *belly-guts*" (Note, 1811 London ed.).

190.7 AN ELECTION]   On May 2, 1807, WI wrote Mary Fairlie, describing the city election just concluded: "I got fairly drawn into the vortex and before the third day was expired, I was as deep in mud & politics as ever a moderate gentleman would wish to be—and I drank beer with the multitude, and I talked handbill fashion with the demagogues, and I shook hands with the mob—whom my heart abhorreth. . . . Oh my friend I have been in such holes and corners—such filthy nooks and filthy corners, sweep offices and oyster cellars! . . . I shall not be able to bear the smell of small beer or tobacco for a month to come. . . . Truly this serving one's country is a nauseous piece of business— and if patriotism is such a dirty virtue—prythee, no more of it—I was almost the whole time at the Seventh Ward—as you know—that [*sic*] the most fertile ward in mob—riot, and incident—and I do assure you the scene was exquisitely ludicrous—Such haranging & puffing & strutting among all the little great men of the day—Such shoals of unfledged heroes from the lower Wards, who had broke away from their mammas and run to electioneer with a slice of bread and butter in their hands. Every carriage that drove up disgorged a whole nursery of these pigmy wonders, who all seemed to put on the brow of thought, the air of bustle & business, and the big talk of general committee men" (holograph, Yale University Library). See the portrait of Timothy Dabble in No. XV.

190.15 fast of Ramazan]   Ramazan or Ramadan is the ninth month in the Mohammedan year, on each day of which, from dawn to sunset, strict fasting is practiced.

190.25 mumpers]   Beggars; those who sponge on others (*OED*).

192.39 *old continentals*]   Veterans of the Continental Army.

194.33–34 a number of hand-bills]   "At elections, hand-bills, containing particular speeches of celebrated characters, under the title of the Ghost of Washington, Franklin, Hamilton, &c. are distributed among the crowd, with a view to influence them in favour of the respective candidates of either party" (Note, 1811 London ed.).

195.8 the British islands] "The Federalists and Democrats never enter the lists against each other, even on the most trifling occasion, without introducing the crimes of France and the outrages of England into their disputes.—In every political discussion it may truly be said that they play at foot-ball with these poor nations:—if it were not for France and England I really think the Americans would have nothing to keep their tongues on the wag" (Note, 1811 London ed.).

195.40 MINE UNCLE JOHN.] Paulding's model for this sketch was his father's younger brother, John Paulding (1755–1847). On August 31, 1825, he wrote WI: "Our worthy Uncle John is waxing old and infirm, and no more aspires to buxom widows, or blooming maidens. Yet he still admires a pretty girl" (*Letters of Paulding*, p. 82).

196.34 anti——] Anti-Federalist.

197.7 The brook, or *river* as they would call it in Europe] "This is a sly rap of the knuckles for those consequential gentlemen who look with contempt on America, and who consider every thing in that part of the world as diminutive and degenerate, when compared with Europe; in artifical [*sic*] endowments it is certainly inferior; but, in natural qualifications, it is equal, and, in some respects, superior.— Compared with America, our rivers are brooks, and our mountains mole-hills" (Note, 1811 London ed.). WI repeated these sentiments in *The Sketch Book*.

197.19 Eclipse colt] "During the sun's eclipse in 1764, the mare Spiletta dropped a chestnut foal by Marske, a great-grandson of the Darley Arabian, on the Duke of Cumberland's estate. The foal was named Eclipse.... he had speed, the most dazzling speed of his age.... The saying was, 'Eclipse first, the rest nowhere.'... Go to Saratoga in August when the great night *vendues* are held. You may hear a hard-boots trainer say, as a yearling with mincing steps is led into the ring: 'I like that colt—he's got Eclipse blood in him'" (Charles B. Parmer, *For Gold and Glory* [New York, 1939], pp. 23, 24, 26).

200.2 the Mechanic Society] "This society was instituted by the mechanics and tradesmen of New York, for charitable purposes, under an act of the legislature, in 1792. A large hotel at the corner of Robinson-Street, in Broadway, belongs to the society, and is called Mechanic-Hall" (Note, 1811 London ed.).

201.34 Heliogabalus] Of Heliogabalus (218–222), the first Roman emperor of Asiatic extraction, Edward Gibbon writes: "The richest wines, the most extraordinary victims, and the rarest aromatics, were profusely consumed on his altar.... The confused multitude of women, of wines, and of dishes, and the studied variety of attitudes and sauces, served to revive his languid appetite" (*The Decline and Fall of the Roman Empire*, chap. 6).

201.34 mrs. Glasse] Longworth's *New-York Directory* for 1805 lists a "Sarah Glass, widow," but does not give her trade.

202.22 Catch-club] The word *catch* is specially applied to rounds in which the words are so arranged as to produce ludicrous effects, one singer catching at the words of another (*OED*).

202.23 ringing bob-majors] In bell-ringing *bob* denotes certain changes in the working of the methods by which long peals of changes are produced, a bob major being rung upon eight bells (*OED*).

202.25 Spouting-club] A society meeting for the purpose of practising recitation, declamation, or oratory (*OED*).

202.27 Abel Drugger ... Major Sturgeon] In Ben Johnson's *The Alchemist* Abel Drugger, a tobacconist, is robbed of his goods and money by Face and the alchemist Subtle. There is no reference to Major Sturgeon (who is a character in Samuel Foote's *The Mayor of Garratt*), though Drugger does "play the Fool" (IV, iv).

203.15 Guthrie's Geography] William Guthrie (1708–1770) was author of *A New Geographical, Historical and Commercial Grammar, and Present State of the Several Kingdoms of the World* (London, 1770), a geography long used in American schools.

203.26 *quiz*] A jest or witticism.

204.31 like Philip's ass, laden with gold] Plutarch says of Philip of Macedon, "When he was desirous of capturing a certain stronghold, his scouts reported that it was altogether difficult and quite impregnable, whereupon he asked if it were so difficult that not even an ass laden with money could approach it" (*Moralia*, trans. F. C. Babbitt [London, 1927], III, 45–47).

206.2–3 a race of people who ... "are hated by gods and men."] The term "hated by gods and men" is a cliché; Cicero has it several times, e.g., *Philippics*, VIII, iii, 10. In *De Officiis*, I, 150, he so describes the trade of moneylending. Tacitus, *Histories*, V, iii, 1, speaks of the Jews as being a race hated by the gods. If WI really had a classical source in mind, he was quoting very loosely, perhaps combining several texts.

206.30–31 "*who ... hay*"] In the course of a nonsense speech the Fool tells King Lear, "'Twas her brother that, in pure kindness to his horse, buttered his hay" (II, iv, 126–28).

207.1 "a Picture of New-York,"] Dr. Samuel L. Mitchell's *Picture of New York*, published at New York on May 2, 1807, is the handbook

that WI set out to parody two years later in A History of New York.
207.16–18 Louis Keaffee . . . Staten-Island] "The quarantine-ground is
situated in this island, and a short distance from thence is Signal-
Hill, where a number of poles are erected to display the public and
private signals, which may be seen from the battery at New York.–
Every merchant has a particular signal, to inform him of the arrival
of his vessels long before they come in sight of the town" (Note,
1811 London ed.). There is no such name as Keaffee, by any of its
many spellings, in Longworth's New York Directories for 1805–1808.
207.36–208.8 Conjectures . . . wrong?] In the 1761 London edition of
Journal of a Voyage to North America, reprinted by Louise Phelps
Kellogg (Chicago, 1923), Charlevoix writes: "Augustine Torniel is
of opinion, that the descendents of Chem and Japhet have passed
to America, and from thence to the countries lying to the southward
of the streights of Magellan, by way of Japan, and the Continent, to
the Northward of the Archipel, or cluster of islands. . . . The Fries-
landers have likewise had their partisans with respect to the origin
of the Americans. Suffridus Petri and Hamconius assert, that the
inhabitants of Peru and Chili came from Friesland. James Charron
and William Postel do the same honour to the Gauls, Abraham Milius
to the antient Celtae, Father Kirker to the Egyptians, and Robert
Le Comte to the Phenicians; every one of them at the same time
excluding all the rest" (I, 5). "Lescarbot leans somewhat more towards
the sentiment of those who have transported into the new world the
Canaanites, who were driven out of the promised land by Joshua. . . .
[De Laet] justly remarks, that if the Canaanites sacrificed their children
to their idols [one of Lescarbot's arguments], we, however, read in
no place of the scripture of their being Anthropophagi" (I, 13–14).
"Edward Brerewood, a learned Englishman, after having refuted the
ill-grounded opinion, which makes all the Tartars descend from the
Israelites, and after showing that the ignorance of the true etymology
of the name Tartar, which comes neither from the Hebrew nor the
Syriack, but from the river Tartar, will have the New World to have
been entirely peopled from this numerous nation" (I, 15). "If we
may credit the learned Dutchman [Grotius], excepting Yucatan, and
some other neighbouring provinces, whereof he makes a class apart,
the whole of North America has been peopled by the Norwegians,
who passed thither by way of Iceland, Greenland, Estotiland and
Norembega" (I, 16). Paulding, who probably wrote "The Stranger
at Home," may have introduced WI to Charlevoix, since a passage
similar to this one in Salmagundi appears in the 1809 History, I, iv
(I, 36–37).

208.22 Custom-house] "The old government-house facing Bowling Green, built for the President of the United States, afterward the residence of George Clinton and John Jay" (Note, 1860 New York ed.).

208.30–31 Dr. Johnson . . . a flea] When asked which was the better poet, Derrick or Smart, Johnson replied, "Sir, there is no settling the point of precedence between a louse and a flea" (*Boswell's Life of Johnson*, ed. G. H. Hill [Oxford, 1934], IV, 192–93).

208.33–34 the academy of arts] The New York Academy of Fine Arts was founded December 3, 1802, with Mayor Edward Livingston as its first president and Peter Irving as secretary. "A number of paintings and statues were obtained for the instruction of artists; the former were placed in a large room at the custom-house, and the latter, which consist of copies in plaster from some of the finest pieces of antient sculpture, were obliged to be put in a cellar under the state-house, where they remain locked up for want of a convenient building to exhibit them in" (Note, 1811 London ed.).

209.27 City-hall] The old City Hall, situated in Wall Street.

209.35–40 Story of Quevedo . . . the truth.] In the first of the *Visions* by the Spanish novelist and poet, Francisco Gómez de Quevedo y Villegas (1580–1645), entitled "The Alguazil: or, Catchpole Possessed," the spirit that troubles the man exclaims, "To tell you the truth, we devils never enter into the body of a Catchpole but by compulsion; and therefore you should not say a Catchpole be-deviled, but a Devil be-catchpoled" (*The Works of Don Francisco de Quevedo* [Edinburgh, 1798], I, 4).

210.4–5 *otium cum dignitate*] Cicero, *Pro Sestio*, xlv, 98: "peace with honor."

210.35 Areskou] Areskoui (or Agreskoui), a Huron-Iroquois demon.

211.29–30 my lord Coke's] Sir Edward Coke (1552–1634), English jurist.

211.32 Hogg's porter-house] John Hogg (1770–1813), proprietor of a porter house at 11 Nassau Street, advertised that he would "make it his duty to keep a choice assortment of all such Liquors and other refreshments and conveniences, as the public expect in a well kept house of this sort" (*Evening Post*, June 28, 1804). For fifteen years (1797–1812) he appeared in a wide variety of comic roles at the Park Theater.

212.2–4 Napoleon . . . family] "If report speaks true, the quondam family of brother Jerome are really provided for, remittances being annually made from Europe for that purpose, and paid through the medium of a French agent residing in the United States. This settlement, it is said, was only made on condition that Madame Jerome Bonaparte should renounce her second husband, whom she had espoused after Jerome's marriage with the Princess of Wirtemberg" (Note, 1811 London ed.).

212.6 the famous *Peach war*] This incident, which occurred in 1655, is recounted by Edmund Bailey O'Callaghan in his *History of New Netherland; or, New York under the Dutch* (New York, 1848), II, 290–91: "A party of savages, Mohegans, Pachamis, with others from Esopus, Hackingsack, Tappaan, Stamford and Onkeway, as far east as Connecticut, estimated by some to amount to nineteen hundred in number, from five to eighteen hundred of whom were armed, landed suddenly before daybreak, in sixty-four canoes, at New Amsterdam, and whilst the greater part of the inhabitants were still buried in sleep, scattered themselves through the streets, and burst into several of the houses, on pretence of looking for 'Indians from the North,' but in reality to avenge the death of a squaw, whom Van Dyck, the late Attorney-general, had killed for stealing a few peaches from his garden. The Council, magistrates and principal citizens assembled in the fort, and calling the chief Sachems before them, enquired the cause of this irruption. They succeeded in prevailing on them to quit the place by sundown, and to retire to Nut Island. Instead, however, of observing their promise, when evening arrived they became bolder, shot Van Dyck in the breast with an arrow, and felled Captain Leendertsen to the ground with an axe. 'The hue and cry of murder now rang through the streets.' Urged on by Van Tienhoven, the military and burgher corps rushed from the fort, attacked the Indians, and forced them to take to their canoes, leaving three of their men dead on the shore. The Dutch lost Cornelis Van Loon and Jan de Vischer. Three others were wounded. The savages now crossed over to the western side of the river. 'In a moment a house at Hoboken was on fire, and the whole of Pavonia was wrapt in flames.' With the exception of Michel Jansen's family, every man was killed, together with all the cattle. A large number of women and children were taken prisoners. Elated by success and maddened by an increased thirst for blood, the savages next passed over to Staten Island, the population of which now amounted to ninety souls, by whose industry eleven bouweries had been brought into a high state of cultivation. Of all these sixty-seven escaped." WI alludes to the Peach War in the 1809 *History*, II, v (I, 114).

216.19 the late *fracas* at Canton] At this time sailors were sometimes taken from American ships in the ports of Macao and Canton by British warships and impressed into naval service. Isaac Chauncey, master of the *Beaver*, an American ship engaged in the China Trade, "spent some days late in December, 1806, while at Canton, in correspondence concerning the impressment from the *Beaver* of a seaman, variously known as William Bryant or James Briant. Although this sailor claimed to be an American citizen, the British captain declined to give him up." The *Beaver* returned to New York in June, 1807. See Kenneth Wiggins Porter, *John Jacob Astor: Business Man* (Cambridge, Mass., 1931), p. 140.

216.22 some new outrage at Norfolk] An allusion to the *Chesapeake–Leopard* affair, over which American humiliation and anger were then runnnig high. On June 22, 1807, off Hampton Roads, the American frigate *Chesapeake* was stopped by the British ship *Leopard*, whose commander demanded the surrender of four seamen, claiming them to be deserters. Upon the refusal of the American commander, Captain James Barron, to give up the men, the *Leopard* opened fire. The American vessel was unprepared for battle. After suffering great damage to his ship and losses to the crew of three men killed and twenty wounded, Barron surrendered. The British boarding party recovered only one deserter, the others having left the *Chesapeake*; but three American seamen were also removed by force. The British captain refused to accept the *Chesapeake* as a prize but forced her to creep back into port in her crippled condition. "The mob at Norfolk," writes Henry Adams, "furious at the sight of their dead and wounded comrades from the 'Chesapeake,' ran riot, and in the want of a better object of attack destroyed the water-casks of the British squadron.... all Virginia was aroused, an attack on Norfolk was generally expected, the coast was patrolled by an armed force, and the British men-of-war were threatened by mounted militia" (*History of the United States*, II, 27, 28). Subsequently Barron was court-martialed and suspended from the navy for five years without pay.

217.8 Lavater] Johann Kaspar Lavater (1741–1801), Swiss physiognomist, theologian, and poet.

218.8–10 shout of the romans ... into the Campus Martius] When Titus Quintius Flamininus, after defeating Philip V of Macedon, announced to the crowd assembled at the Isthmian games that Greece was now free, a joyous shout went up so incredibly loud that ravens which chanced to be flying overhead fell down dead into the stadium. See *Plutarch's Lives*, trans. Bernadotte Perrin (London, 1921), X, 351–53.

218.16 PLANS FOR DEFENDING OUR HARBOUR.] Among the innumerable plans suggested for the defense of New York harbor was the submarine developed by Robert Fulton. On July 20, 1807, he failed twice to sink a 200-ton brig, anchored between Governor's and Ellis Islands for the experiment, finally succeeding on the third attempt. The next day the *Commercial Advertiser* stated: "No machinery like this which requires the manager to proceed in full view, within 30 or 50 yards of the vessel to be destroyed, can ever in any degree succeed. A thousand of them, with the managers and their boats, could be blown from the surface of the water, before they could approach so near as to do the least injury to a hostile fleet" (I. N. P. Stokes, *The Iconography of Manhattan Island* [New York, 1926], V, 1463).

218.30 the *poplar worm*] "The foot-paths of Broadway, and some other streets, in New York, are planted with poplars, which afford an agreeable shade from the sun in summer. In 1806, the inhabitants were alarmed by a large species of caterpillar, or worm, which bred in great numbers on the poplars, and were supposed to be venomous. Various experiments were tried; and cats and dogs were made to swallow them. It was reported that many of the animals died in consequence; but the whole proved to be a false alarm, though the city, for some time, was thrown into as great a consternation as we have frequently been in this country mad dogs" (Note, 1811 London ed.).

219.22–23 the fat inn-keeper in Rabelais] Not found in Rabelais.

221.8 Toujoursdort and Grossitout] Possibly fictitious.

221.14 *chevaux-de-frises*] Pieces of timber or an iron barrel from which iron-pointed spikes, spears, or pointed poles project five or six feet long, used in warfare to defend a passage (*OED*).

22.16 *Bohan upas*] "A tree in the Island of Java, which is said to possess such a poisonous quality as to destroy every thing that comes within reach of its destructive atmosphere. The wonderful stories, however, related of this 'hydra tree of death' are now generally disregarded" (Note, 1811 London ed.).

224.1 *in Baroco*] In logic a mnemonic word, representing by its vowels the fourth mood of the second figure of syllogisms, in which the premises are a universal affirmative and particular negative, and the conclusion is a particular negative (*OED*).

225.25–27 Noah Webster... Dilworth] Thomas Dilworth's *New Guide to the English Tongue* (1740) held undisputed command in the teaching of orthography in American schools until successfully challenged by Noah Webster's spelling book, which first appeared in 1783 as Part 1 of the *Grammatical Institute*. In 1859 Dr. John W. Francis, a younger schoolmate of WI's at Josiah Henderson's seminary in 1797, recalled: "There was a curious conflict existing in the school between the principal and his assistant-instructor: the former a legitimate burgher of the city, the latter a New England pedagogue. So far as I can remember, something depended on the choice of the boy's parents in the selection of his studies; but if not expressed otherwise, the principal stuck earnestly to Dilworth, while the assistant, for his section of instruction, held to Noah Webster" (*Irvingiana*, ed. Evert A. Duyckinck [New York, 1860], p. xxxiii).

225.31 "baseless fabrick!"] *The Tempest*, IV, i, 151.

227.38–39 is neither the age of gold, silver, iron, brass, chivalry, or pills] Not found in Carr's *Stranger in Ireland*.

227.41 Smollett's honest pedant] In *The Adventures of Peregrine Pickle*, chapter 27, the governor of Oxford undertakes to prove by geometrical principles that if Peregrine pursues his intrigue with Miss Emily Gauntlet, it will tend to his disgrace and ruin. Peregrine "interrupted the investigation with a loud laugh, and told him that his *postulata* put him in mind of a certain learned and ingenious gentleman, who undertook to disprove the existence of natural evil, and asked no other *datum* on which to found his demonstration, but an acknowledgment that *every thing that is, is right.*"

228.1 like Hannibal's application of vinegar to rocks] In his account of how Hannibal's soldiers constructed a road across an Alpine cliff, Livy writes: "Since they had to cut through the rock, they felled some huge trees that grew near at hand, and lopping off their branches, made an enormous pile of logs. This they set on fire, as soon as the wind blew fresh enough to make it burn, and pouring vinegar over the glowing rocks, caused them to crumble" (*Ab Urbe Condita*, trans. B. O. Foster [London, 1929], V, 109).

228.9 "ignorance is bliss,"] Gray's "Ode on a Distant Prospect of Eton College," line 99.

232.36–37 "neither . . . pocket."] In 1785 Jefferson wrote: "The legitimate powers of government extend to such acts only as are injurious to others. But it does me no injury for my neighbour to say there are twenty gods, or no god. It neither picks my pocket nor breaks my leg" (*Notes on the State of Virginia*, ed. William Peden [Chapel Hill, 1955], p. 159).

233.18–19 "in . . . moveth."] "out of the abundance of the heart the mouth speaketh" (Matt. 12:34).

238.41 shingles] "Shingles are made generally of cedar wood, cut much in the same form and size as slates; and are nailed on the roof in the same manner. They sell from 12 to 15 shillings per 1000" (Note, 1811 London ed.).

239.25 summer-house] See Evert A. Ducykinck's long note in the 1860 New York edition of *Salmagundi*, pp. 290–91.

239.41 London particular] A special quality of Madeira wine as imported for the London market (*OED*). In the 1824 Paris edition "London particular" is changed to "Madeira." See also 19.17–18.

241.11 stock] Stocking.

243.9 Vauxhall-Garden] "This fashionable place of resort," writes Samuel Mitchill, "is in the Bowery road, not quite two miles from the city-hall. The garden is laid out with taste. The walks are agreeably disposed, and strewed with gravel. Their sides are adorned with shrubs, trees, busts and statues. In the middle is a large equestrian figure of Washington. The orchestra is built among the trees, gives to the band of music and singing voices, a charming effect on summer evenings. Within this enclosure, the large apparatus for fire-works, the artificial mound of earth to view them from, the numerous booths and boxes for the accommodation of company, refreshments of every kind, and above all, the buildings and scenery for public entertainment during the suspension of dramatic exercises in the great theatre at the park, are all of them proofs of Mr. Delacroix's zeal and success to gratify the public" (*Picture of New York*, pp. 156–57).

243.17 Cinderella] *Cinderella; Or, The Little Glass Slipper*, an allegorical pantomime imported from Drury Lane and performed January 1, 1806, at the Chestnut Street Theater in Philadelphia, was given at the Vauxhall Garden Theater, New York, on August 17, 1807. It was the first great hit of the year 1808 at the Park Theater and was published in New York the same year.

243.33 The theatre opened on Wednesday last] The Park Theater was closed during the summer of 1807 for extensive alterations to the interior. It reopened September 9, on which occasion Thomas Cooper spoke verses composed by WI. See Dunlap's *History of the American Theatre*, II, 245–47, for a detailed description of the remodeling.

245.13 mr. Ciceri] Charles Ciceri, longtime scene painter and machinist at the Park Theater.

245.15 Signior Da Ponte] Lorenzo Da Ponte, Italian teacher in New York, best remembered as librettist of Mozart's *Don Giovanni*.

245.17 Dunderbarrack] Dunderberg, a mountain in Rockland County, New York.

248.20 Peter Pindar's magpie] John Wolcot (1738–1819), who wrote under the pseudonym Peter Pindar, in his poem "Magpie and Robin Red-breast, pictures the magpie resting atop a baronial castle looking "dev-lish knowing, with his head, / Squinting with connoisseurship glances" (*The Works of Peter Pindar* [Dublin, 1795], II, 288).

250.17 THE HERO ROSE.] Alexander Pope's translation of Homer's "'Αχιλλεὺς ωρτο" (*Iliad*, XVIII, 203).

251.5–6 a note of one of the little New-England banks] "In the United States there are bank-notes for *half dollars*; these, however, are current for their full value only in the state where they are created; in all the rest they either will not pass at all or are current only at a very considerable discount" (Note, 1811 London ed.).

256.3 STYLE AT BALLSTON.] If as seems probable Paulding wrote this essay, he must surely have been influenced by WI who, having visited Ballston Spa near Saratoga in 1803, wrote in his journal on August 3: "Mrs. Smith is an original in ⟨look⟩ appearance & manners[.] she dresses ⟨in the⟩ ↑with the↓ most outrageous extravagance. part old & part new fashion. . . . Mrs Smiths dress for the Ball was of muslin with large gold sprigs. A gold ribbon round her waist her hair turnd up over a cushion powderd pomatomed and covered with lace & trinkets. She ⟨carried⟩ was surrounded with an atmosphere of perfume" (*Journals and Notebooks*, I, 7, 8).

In *The Literary Picture Gallery, and Admonitory Epistles to the Visitors of Ballston Spa* (Ballston-Spa, N.Y., 1808), a duodecimo magazine, occur further intimate glimpses of the world at Ballston. Thus, in "Admonitory Epistle No. II" Simeon Senex writes: "I myself have been annoyed at a dinner table of 100 persons, with a fellow on my right snatching up my fork and carelessly pricking his teeth with it; and when turning to rebuke him pop came a lady's glass in my eye. . . . The practice of swearing, in ladies is to be sure shocking. . . . I should think if ladies were to confine themselves to a single G——d d——n it would be quite sufficient. . . . It is now become *notoriously genteel to laugh at merit*. In publick readings or when songs are singing, ladies should always make a noise to show a contempt of the authour or reader."

258.27 feast of the Centaurs and the Lapithae] Peirithous, king of the Lapithae in Thessaly, invited the Centaurs to his marriage feast. A bloody conflict ensued, in which the Centaurs were defeated by the Lapithae.

258.36 longed] An obsolete form of "lunged" (*OED*).

262.5 the mighty Barbarossa] Frederick I, Holy Roman emperor (1152–1190).

263.18 ALDERMEN] In the 1809 *History of New York*, VI, vi, occurs the following simile: "Like as a mighty alderman, when at a corporation feast the first spoonful of turtle soup salutes his palate, feels his impatient appetite but ten fold quickened, and redoubles his vigorous attacks upon the tureen, while his voracious eyes, projecting from his head, roll greedily round devouring every thing at table— so did the mettlesome Peter Stuyvesant, feel that intolerable hunger for martial glory, which raged within his very bowels, inflamed by the capture of Fort Casimer, and nothing could allay it, but the conquest of all New Sweden" (II, 126).

265.12 Tibesti] The northernmost and largest province in the north-central African nation of Chad, inhabited by the nomadic Tibbu people. Tibesti includes the highest summit of the Sahara, the volcanic massif of Emi Koussi, which reaches 11,204 feet.

269.8–9 like Ganymede on the eagle's wing] Ganymede, son of Tros, was carried off by the gods (*Iliad*, XX, 234–35) or, according to later writers, by the eagle of Zeus or by Zeus himself, his great-great-grandfather, on account of his beauty, to be cupbearer to Zeus.

270.6 a phillipick by archbishop Anselm] On February 23, 1094 (Ash Wednesday), as William II at the head of an army assembled to invade Normandy waited at Hastings for favorable winds, Anselm, archbishop of Canterbury, solicited him "for the relief of the churches which were daily going to ruin, for the revival of the Christian law which was being violated in many ways, and for the reform of morals which every day and in every class of people showed too many corruptions" (*The Life of St. Anselm Archbishop of Canterbury by Eadmer*, ed. R. W. Southern [London, 1962], p. 69).

270.31 Rollo's freebooters] Rollo or Hrolf (860–?931), Norse chieftain; but WI's reference may be to Kotzebue's *Pizarro in Peru; or, The Death of Rolla* (1800), which he had many opportunities to see during the Kotzebue vogue on the New York stage.

272.30 RYP VAN DAM] On July 1, 1731, Governor John Montgomerie died of the smallpox then raging and Rip Van Dam, president of the council, was appointed acting governor. His term of office lasted thirteen months. Under his prudent administration "the fierce political contests of the colony . . . ceased: there was no longer any apparent cause of enmity between the governor and the governed" (James Grant Wilson, *The Memorial History of the City of New-York* [New York, 1892], II, 209).

272.34–36 CHAP. CIX. . . . GOTHAM.] This essay by WI anticipates the 1809 *History of New York*, notably the mock-heroic battle before the walls of Fort Christina in VI, vii (II, 135–51).

275.28 curtain works] A veil or the overhanging shade of a bonnet (*OED*).

277.15 THE LITTLE MAN IN BLACK.] This character is a variation on Goldsmith's "man in black," a disappointed bachelor in the *Citizen of the World* who in Letter XXVII tells his history. WI may have picked up hints for the present story from "The Old Man and His Dog," a sentimental tale which appeared in Charles Brockden Brown's

Literary Magazine and American Register in May, 1807. Subtitled "A Parisian Story," it relates how "a poor old man had a dog, which he had reared from a puppy, and with which he had daily shared the parsimonious morsel that was scarcely sufficient for the subsistence of both. By age and scantiness of food, his strength declined so fast, that he could no longer procure enough to keep his dog and himself alive." Whereupon he took the dog "in his arms, tied a stone to one end of a string, and the other end round the neck of the dog, carried him to one of the bridges, wept over him, kissed him, and plunged him into the river." Immediately he felt remorse, telling a neighbor who was passing by: "I am a miserable and guilty wretch. . . . there was but one creature in the world that loved me, and him I have this minute destroyed. . . . I had no longer any food to give him, without fasting myself; and for that I had not courage." The neighbor informs him that his son Antoine whom he had supposed fallen at Toulon was in fact "taken prisoner, has made his escape, and is now waiting at home, impatient to embrace his father." At this moment the dog "Fidel came running up. . . . The stone had slipped out of the noose."

281.16–17 "the wicked cease from troubling."] "There the wicked cease from troubling, and there the weary be at rest" (Job, 3:17).

284.4 foxy] Marked by excessive predominance of reddish tints; over-hot in coloring (*OED*).

289.20 the cave of Dom-Daniel] The abode of evil spirits, gnomes, and enchanters, somewhere under the "roots of the ocean," near Tunis.

294.6 "two bullets and a bragger!"] In brag, a cardgame like poker, bullets are aces, nine-spots and knaves are called braggers. The highest hand is three white (or real) aces, the next highest is "two bullets and a bragger" (*DA*).

294.22–23 *Nunc . . . tellus.*] Horace, *Odes*, I, xxxvii, 1–2: "Now is the time to drain the flowing bowl, now with unfettered foot to beat the ground with dancing."

296.36 Richard the Third] *Richard III* was performed many times at the Park Theater in this period, most recently on November 27, 1807, starring Cooper.

298.34 TEA.] On May 24, 1806, WI wrote Gouverneur Kemble: "Present my particular remembrance to your sister [Gertrude, future wife of Paulding], and tell her she occupies three long sentences in my prayers, whether French or English; in return for which, I only beg that she will take particular notice of the different kinds of tea they drink in Philadelphia, their several effects; whether it is still the fashion there to give grand perspirations; whether the young ladies are still educated in the market place as the best means of preparing them *for the market*; whether Hyson, Gunpowder, or Cat-nip is the rage; and any other information that may be of service to me in my folio dissertation on tea." Two days later, in another letter to Kemble, he declared: "The lads of Kilkenny are completely scattered; and, to the riotous, roaring rattle-brained orgies at Dyde's, succeeds the placid, picnic, picturesque pleasures of the tea-table. We have resigned the feverish enjoyments of Madeira and Champagne, and returning with faith and loyalty to the standard of beauty, have quietly set down under petticoat-government" (PMI, I, 170, 171).

299.27–28 "To ... bubble."] Variant on *Macbeth*, IV, i, 10–11 *et seq.*

302.18 *Extremum ... laborem*] Adapted from Vergil, *Eclogues*, X, 1: "My last task this—vouchsafe me it, Arethusa!" "Nihi is a misprint for "mihi."

312.16 *Pendent opera interrupta.*] Vergil, *Aeneid*, IV, 88: "The works are broken off."

312.30 the embargo] Congress passed the Embargo Act on December 22, 1807, forbidding clearances to foreign ports and limiting the coasting-trade in the United States.

313.6–7 Sanconiathon, Appollonius Rhodius, sir John Harrington] Sanchuniathon is the name under which Philon of Byblos (A.D. 64–161) appears to have published Φοινικικα, a work in nine books which treats cosmogony, the rise of human society, theogony, and Phoenician cult-practice. Apollonius Rhodius, Greek scholar and epic poet, was appointed librarian at Alexandria in 196 B.C. Sir John Harington (1561–1612) was an English writer, godson to Elizabeth I.

313.12 Assiniboils] Variant spelling of Assiniboins, an American Indian tribe in the northern Plains, of Siouan affiliation.

313.37 Zoiluses and Dennises] Both Zoilus, a fourth-century B.C. Greek rhetorician, and the Englishman John Dennis (1657–1734) gained reputations as carping critics, Zoilus for his severe criticism of Homer, Dennis for his *Reflections, Critical and Satirical* (1711), a reply to Pope who in the *Essay on Criticism* had satirized his tragedy *Appius and Virginia* (1709) for its bombast.

313.42 "*Ignorantia neminem excusat*"] An elliptical form of the expression, *Ignorantia legis neminem excusat.*

314.16 old Goody Blake] In *Spectator* No. 117 Addison relates how the Spectator, while walking with Sir Roger de Coverley near one of his woods, was stopped by an old beggar woman whose dress and figure put him in mind of the description in Thomas Otway's *The Orphan* of the "wrinkled hag, with age grown double" (II, i, 245). Sir Roger explains that the old woman is named Moll White and that she has the reputation throughout the county of being a witch.

314.19 Twaits in Lampedo]   The English actor William Twaits (1781–
1814) played the role of Lampedo at the Park Theater on November 5,
1806. See note at 52.21.

314.40–41 hewers of wood and drawers of water]   Josh. 9:21.

TEXTUAL COMMENTARY

Salmagundi presents its editor with unusually complex problems; indeed, it has been observed that *Salmagundi* is not only one of the most interesting, but also one of the most irritating problems for a bibliographer.[1] Rather than appearing as a unified literary product, it was published as a short-lived periodical at irregular intervals. As such, its composition and publication were subject to informal and often careless treatment by its three author-collaborators, William and Washington Irving and James Kirke Paulding, and by its publisher-printer, David Longworth. The unexpected popularity of *Salmagundi* made it necessary to print additional copies of certain of the numbers and gave the authors opportunity for revisions, so that the twenty numbers of the first American edition (1807–1808) exist in a bewildering proliferation of settings and variant states. Unfortunately no manuscript—except one paragraph in Washington Irving's hand from No. XIV—survives; in the absence of a manuscript, the original setting of each of the twenty numbers, representing the earliest version of the text, has been chosen as copy-text. Compounding the editor's problem, Washington Irving soon regretted his role in the series. In the second American edition (1814) and to an even greater degree in the first French edition (1824), Irving attempted to edit out much of the material he considered juvenile, careless, or in bad taste. Irving continued to regard *Salmagundi* as an embarrassment and attempted to deny it a place in his canon by refusing to include it in his Author's Revised Edition (1848–1851). The editor's task has been threefold; determining the order of revisions in the first edition (1807–1808), evaluating Irving's subsequent revisions (1814 and 1824), and selecting the revisions to incorporate in the Twayne edition.

THE TEXTS

The following symbols are used to identify the texts in the Textual Commentary, the Discussions of Adopted Readings, the List of Emendations, and the List of Rejected Substantives.

MS   A manuscript fragment of a portion of Washington Irving's "Cockloft Hall," from No. XIV

1. Jacob Blanck, "Salmagundi and its Publisher," *Papers of the Bibliographical Society of America* 41 (1947), 1; hereafter cited as PBSA.

1A¹⁻⁷	The first American edition (1807–1808), published by David Longworth, including its many settings and variant states described and explained below (pp. 383–97)
1E	The first English edition (London, 1811), prepared by John Lambert
2A	The second American edition (New York, 1814), published by David Longworth, who was probably aided by Washington Irving
3A	The third American edition (New York, 1820)
2E	The second English edition (London, 1824), an unauthorized publication by Thomas Tegg
1F	The first French edition (Paris, 1824), published under the double imprint of Galignani and Baudry, was an English language edition revised by Washington Irving
3E	The third English edition (London, 1824), like 2E, an unauthorized publication of Thomas Tegg's, but incorporating some of the revisions from 1F
2F	The second French edition (Paris, 1834) published by Baudry, Volume I of *The Complete Works of Washington Irving*
4A	The fourth American edition (New York, 1835), Volumes I–II of James Kirke Paulding's *Works*
NY1860	An edition prepared by Evert A. Duyckinck for G. P. Putnam
T	Twayne edition

The ten significant editions of *Salmagundi* are discussed in detail in the pages that follow. A number followed by a capital letter identifies the edition: the capital letter indicates the country of publication, the number places the edition in chronological sequence within the country, e.g., first American edition is 1A. Customarily, number sequences are not assigned editions published a long time after a work's first appearance in print or to editions of collected works (4A is an exception since it was not an edition of Irving's works, but of Paulding's).

The first setting of each number of the first American edition (1A¹) was chosen as copy text. Subsequent settings of the numbers (see pp. 383–97 for an explanation) provide the most important textual variations. The second American edition (2A), which more than likely Irving helped prepare, and the first French edition (1F), which he is known to have revised, supply further textual variations. Also of interest are the fourth American edition (4A), prepared by James Kirke Paulding,

Table 1

MS
A fragment of the Cockloft
Hall essay in No. XIV

1A
*Salmagundi; or the Whim-Whams and Opinions of Launcelot
Langstaff, Esq. and Others.* New York: David Longworth,
1807–1808.

*2A New York: David Longworth, 1814. Probably revised by Washington Irving.	***1E** London: J. M. Richardson, 1811. Prepared by John Lambert.
3A New York: Thomas Longworth, 1820.	**2E** London: Thomas Tegg, 1824. Unauthorized.
	*1F Paris: A. & W. Galignani, 1824. Revised by Washington Irving.
	*3E London: Thomas Tegg, 1824. Based on Irving's French revisions. Unauthorized.
4A New York: Harper, 1835. Volumes I–II of his *Works*.	**2F** Paris: Baudry, 1834. In *The Complete Works of Washington Irving in One Volume.*

*NY1860
New York: G. P. Putnam,
1860. Prepared by Evert
A. Duyckinck.

382   SALMAGUNDI

and the New York edition of 1860 (NY1860), edited by Evert A. Duyckinck. Five other editions are of historical importance: the first English edition (1E), Thomas Longworth's edition (3A), Tegg's two unauthorized editions (2E and 3E), and Baudry's reprint of the first French edition (2F).[2] Table 1 (p. 381) illustrates the relationships of the ten editions. Significant later printings collated with the copy-text are marked with a star.

MS: First paragraph of the Cockloft Hall Essay, No. XIV.

Because of the serial and collaborative nature of *Salmagundi*, it is not surprising that only one manuscript page and no proof sheets (if there were any) survive. The only known extant manuscript portion is the first paragraph of the Cockloft Hall Essay (236.40–237.21).[3] By fortunate chance it is in Washington Irving's hand. The original of this manuscript page is in the Clifton Waller Barrett Library of the University of Virginia. The surviving manuscript represents a very small part of pages—and exhibits the work of only one of the three authors. Nevertheless, it is the sole source of information for the kinds of changes the original manuscripts of the several authors must have undergone as they were prepared for print in 1807–1808. The results of collating the manuscript with the copy-text (1A¹) are tabulated below (substantive variants are entered as well in either the List of Emendations or the List of Rejected Substantives at the end of the volume). The collation shows that commas were added and subtracted, a few spellings were altered to agree with the publisher's house style (237.7, 20, 21), and several words were changed (237.6, 13). A misreading of the manuscript by the printer, not corrected until the second American

2. The Tegg editions of 1824 (2E and 3E), although pirated, are included because they are relevant to the textual history of *Salmagundi*. Other editions published during Irving's lifetime are: London, J. Limbird, 1824; London, John Bumpas, 1825; London, T. Tegg, 1825 and 1839; London, C. Daly, 1841; London, H. G. Bohn, 1850; and G. P. Putnam, 1857. Listed in Stanley T. Williams' and Mary Ellen Edge's *A Bibliography of the Writings of Washington Irving: A Check List* (New York, 1936), these editions are either reprints of previous texts or unauthorized publications of little textual or historical interest.

3. Page and line references to the text of *Salmagundi* are to the Twayne (T) edition, except in a few instances where reference was to material not found in the Twayne text. In special instances 1A page and line references are given. The roman numeral indicates the number to which the reference belongs (e.g., the manuscript is from No. XIV).

edition of 1814 (2A), occurs at 237.17, where "the lowing of the castle" should have read, as the manuscript does, "the lowing of the cattle." A caret ∧ after a word indicates a mark of punctuation was left out.

T	1A[1]	MS
236.41	multitude,	multitude∧
237.6	has	thus
237.7	sun-set	sunset
237.7	romantick	romantic
237.13	senses	feelings
237.13	zephyr	zephyr,
237.16	abound,	abound∧
237.17	castle	cattle
237.17	bells,	bells∧
237.18	woodman's	woodmans
237.20	rustick	rustic
237.21	musick	music

1A: New York, David Longworth, 1807–1808. BAL 10097[4]

Immediately in the first number of *Salmagundi* the three authors establish their insouciant tone, stating: "We beg the public particularly to understand, that we solicit no patronage. . . . We have nothing to do with the pecuniary concerns of the paper, its success will yield us neither pride nor profit—nor will its failure occasion to us either loss or mortification" (68.16–20). In the same number, Launcelot Langstaff announces in his Elbow Chair essay: "so soon as we get tired of reading our own works, we shall discontinue them, without the least remorse, whatever the public may think of it" (70.13–15). In fact they abandoned *Salmagundi* after twenty numbers, because of a disagreement with David Longworth.

On March 6, 1807, after the popularity of the series was established, Longworth took out the copyright on *Salmagundi*, despite the statement in the Publisher's Notice to No. I: "The publisher professes the same sublime contempt for money as his authors" (69.3–4). The three authors, believing it would not be worthwhile, had earlier refused Longworth's suggestion that they take out a copyright. All they cared was to cover the expense of paper and printing; indeed, financial success was not the usual fate of small magazines of the period. After the

4. This is the number assigned the edition in the section on Washington Irving in Jacob Blanck's *Bibliography of American Literature*, Vol. V (New Haven, 1969), pp. 2–86; hereafter cited as BAL.

sensation *Salmagundi* created, however, the authors began to be resentful of the profits Longworth, as holder of the copyright, was making.[5] On June 22, 1807, after No. X had been published and Washington Irving was in Richmond, Virginia, on business, he wrote Paulding asking "What arrangement have you made with the Dusky [Longworth] for the profits? I shall stand much in need of a little sum of money on my return."[6] According to Pierre M. Irving, all the money the authors ever received from Longworth "was a hundred dollars apiece, although at the time the original copyright expired in 1822," Paulding conjectures in a letter to Ebenezer Irving, "[Longworth] had made by all accounts ten or perhaps fifteen thousand dollars out of it."[7] The sum may have been exaggerated, but it is undoubtedly true that Longworth made a considerable profit on *Salmagundi* while the authors did not. Because of the financial instability of American publishing in the first half of the nineteenth century, it was standard practice for an author to assume all or part of the risk of publishing his work. It is possible, however, that publisher Longworth may have underwritten the cost of *Salmagundi* himself; in that case the actions of this publisher-printer-bookseller were perhaps justifiable.

According to Pierre M. Irving, the real reason *Salmagundi* was discontinued was a disagreement "between themselves [the Irvings and Pauldings] and their publisher, who had put the price at a shilling, and was disposed to limit somewhat dictatorially for these novices in authorship the quantity of matter for each number."[8] This suggests that Longworth wanted to control not only the finances of *Salmagundi*, but also to some extent its content. The man who added doggerel verses to the *New York Directory*—perhaps the best-known product of his press—may have had some literary aspirations of his own.[9] In suggesting to Irving in February, 1822 (after Longworth's copyright expired), that they revise the work, Paulding gave as one of his reasons that the publisher had "taken the liberty to add some of his own nonsense occasionally." Specifically Paulding claimed that Longworth "was debauching it with blunders, and vile pictures, &c., that were a disgrace to any decent publication."[10] Then there is the matter of the lowercase proper nouns found in *Salmagundi*. In his edition

5. Pierre M. Irving, *The Life and Letters of Washington Irving* (New York, 1862–1864), I, 179; hereafter cited as PMI.

6. PMI, I, 194.

7. PMI, I, 179.

8. PMI, I, 210–11.

9. PBSA, p. 10.

10. From a letter Paulding wrote Ebenezer Irving, partially quoted in William I. Paulding's *Literary Life of James Kirke Paulding* (New York, 1867), p. 39.

of *Salmagundi*, Evert Duyckinck describes Longworth's capitalization preferences: "In the original edition of some of his books, proper names are spelt with small initial letters. Oddly enough, the man who was so grandiloquent himself would not allow New York itself appropriate capitals. It must be written new-york and portly philadelphia must dwindle in lower-case" (NY1860, p. xi). Indeed, in one of the two house styles used in the first edition of *Salmagundi*, proper nouns such as names of cities, prominent among them New York and Philadelphia, are lowercase. If more were known about Longworth's role in *Salmagundi*'s production, the series' textual and bibliographical oddities might be better understood. Longworth's name for his Shakspeare Gallery was modeled after a popular and distinguished English counterpart, the Shakspeare-Press, established in London by John Boydell and George Nicoll in 1790. Clearly Longworth ran an idiosyncratic and egocentric operation. The Publisher's Notice to 1F (1824)—possibly written by Irving himself—provides a charming description of Longworth's establishment—"DAVID LONGWORTH, an eccentric bookseller . . . had filled a large apartment with the valuable engravings of 'Boydell's Shakspeare Gallery,' magnificently framed, and had nearly obscured the front of his house with a huge sign—a colossal painting, in *chiaro scuro*, of the crowning of Shakspeare" (1F, p. 7).[11]

Although all copies bearing the imprint "New York, David Longworth, 1807–1808," or a variation thereof, are identified as the first American edition (1A), this identification considerably oversimplifies a complex textual and bibliographical situation. The so-called first edition of *Salmagundi* was actually issued in two well-defined stages, the only difference between the two stages being the binding. In the first stage, each of the twenty numbers appeared separately at irregular intervals between January 24, 1807, and January 25, 1808, as wrappered numbers. These numbers went through a quantity of separate editions or subeditions during 1807 and 1808, which represent fresh settings of the text. In the second stage, the individual numbers were gathered together and bound up as a two-volume book.[12]

11. Jacob Blanck describes David Longworth and his Shakspeare-Gallery in the article previously cited (PBSA, 41), but does not add to our knowledge of Longworth's role in *Salmagundi*.

12. The Twayne edition significantly increases the textual and bibliographical information about 1A. In doing so, it proves incorrect some longheld assumptions. It has been generally assumed (1) that copies labeled "editions" were merely reprints of the original text and not genuine editions, (2) that Longworth simply added "second edition," "third edition," and so forth to the top of the first page of the so-called reprints, (3) that the text of 1A remained virtually the same throughout the new settings, and (4) that if there were textual changes, they

The series proved more popular than anticipated, and in the words of Pierre M. Irving: "The sensation increased with every issue [he means "number"], and eight hundred numbers [he means "copies"] were once disposed of in a day."[13] Not enough copies of the early numbers were printed to meet the public demand. For additional copies of a number the type had to be reset. Since stereotype plates were not yet in common use in the United States, after the first printing of a number the original type would have been broken up and distributed for reuse. The first thirteen numbers were reset and reissued at least once and in the case of the earlier numbers three times or more (see Table 2, pp. 390–91). With only a few exceptions Longworth labeled the new settings "second edition," "third edition," etc. For these settings, which represent new editions or subeditions, Longworth retained the format, the continuous pagination, and the text-to-page relationship of the original subedition of each number. Possibly he anticipated the time when the series would be issued in book form (the second stage).[14] This meant that any combination of settings or subeditions of the numbers could be used to make up the two-volume issue. What complicates the situation for the textual editor is the fact that every time a number was reset, the text was revised or altered, the alterations ranging from small corrections and minor improvements to

---

were minor. In 1933 Langfeld and Blackburn correctly observed that many of the reprints represent new editions: "Many copies bear at the top of the first page the words 'second edition,' 'third edition,' etc. It has been claimed that there was only one edition and that this notation was printed on some copies merely to create the impression of popularity. A comparison of the different editions, however, proves this opinion to be incorrect, since such comparison reveals variations in text, in the typesetting, number of words to the line, etc." (*Washington Irving, A Bibliography* [New York, 1933], p. 6). But they gave no indication of the kind or extent of the variations, which were especially significant in Nos. X and XII. In 1969 Jacob Blanck persisted in calling the subeditions "reprints," while recognizing that textual differences existed: "Parts bearing reprint notices . . . vary textually from earlier printings but for the purpose of this entry such marked reprints have been all but ignored and are neither listed nor described" (BAL, no. 10097, p. 2). This did little to clarify the status of Longworth's editions, which are here called subeditions. A lack of consistency in terminology also clouded the textual history of 1A: the terms "part," "number," and "issue" were used interchangeably for the numbers; and the subeditions were called "issues," "editions," and "reprints."

13. PMI, I, 179.

14. One of the subeditions at least fails to maintain the continuous pagination: In No. IV, the first subedition ($1A^1$) ends on 1A, p. 124, and No. V begins 1A, p. 125; however, the second subedition ($1A^2$) of No. IV ends on 1A, p. 126; the third subedition ($1A^3$) restores the continuous pagination.

extensive revisions. The successive new settings or subeditions have been sequentially labeled 1A², 1A³, etc. What emerges is a major textual and bibliographical puzzle.[15]

After the periodical series was discontinued (or perhaps before) *Salmagundi* appeared in its second stage—a two-volume issue, ten numbers per volume.[16] The bound issue was planned from the beginning: No. I facetiously declares that the series "will be a small neat duodecimo size, so that when enough numbers are written, it may form a volume sufficiently portable to be carried in old ladies' pockets and young ladies' work bags" (68.39–41). Rather than representing the same subedition for each number, the two-volume issue is actually a random collection of the numbers that were originally printed to be issued separately. It is extremely unlikely that any two-volume copy contains the same subeditions and variant states per number. A general title page dated 1808 and a table of contents (which becomes an index in the second volume) were bound in with the numbers.[17] There is evidence that initially more than twenty numbers were planned. Writing to Paulding June 22, 1807, Washington Irving complains "I am much disappointed at your having concluded the first volume at No. 10. Besides making an insignificant baby house volume, it ends so weakly at one of the weakest numbers of the whole."[18] According to Pierre M. Irving, his uncle had ideas for future numbers: "he had designed, among other plans in embryo, a marriage of William Wizard with one of the Miss Cocklofts, and had amused himself in idea with

15. *Salmagundi*'s printing history as well as its literary character can be compared to the earlier *Tatler*. Both were carelessly printed; and like the errata in the *Tatler*, *Salmagundi*'s revisions improve grammar, correct mistakes, and make stylistic corrections. For a discussion of a parallel but not perfectly analogous textual-bibliographical situation the reader is directed to William B. Todd's "Early Editions of *The Tatler*," *Studies in Bibliography* 15 (1962), 121–33.

16. A few copies have been seen which are two volumes bound in one; they do not differ in any other respect from copies of the two-volume issues and may have been bound by someone other than Longworth. Since the bulk of bound issues examined have been two volumes, reference is always to these, rather than to the single, twenty number volume.

17. Testifying to the extreme irregularity of bibliographical evidence pertaining to *Salmagundi*, BAL cautions: "A bound volume has been seen with an 1807 title-page bound together with a table of contents taken from an 1808 printing. Unfortunately, the list of such frauds appears endless" (BAL, No. 10097, p. 2). According to a letter Irving wrote Paulding June 22, 1807, Paulding ended Volume I at No. X, so that one volume of the two-volume issue at least could have come out in 1807 (PMI, I, 193–94).

18. PMI, I, 193–94. Irving refers to the fact that No. X contains his "Stranger in Pennsylvania" which never satisfied him.

a description of their queer nuptials."[19] In the opening article of No. XX Paulding states that "it is not for want of subjects that we stop our career" (305.43–306.1). In 1A, part way through No. XII, at the bottom of the page, can be found "END OF THE FIRST VOLUME," which either is a typesetter's error or else means that twelve numbers per volume were at one time contemplated.

In unsnarling the textual and bibliographical sequences of 1A, it must be kept in mind that *Salmagundi* was a periodical series and not a book. As such, it cannot be made to conform exactly to definitions such as "edition," "state," "issue"—terms designed to describe the printing history of books. Strictly speaking, *Salmagundi* was not issued in book form and cannot be considered a book until 1E (the first English edition, 1811). As a magazine, much of it was prepared hastily (especially the early numbers which came out almost weekly), and the series is highly variable in both text and printing. Its printing history is not composed of precisely defined, distinct and separate sequences, but of highly variable composites. Each of the twenty numbers is an independent unit with a unique printing sequence. The designation 1A includes all of Longworth's subeditions of each number and both the wrappered and the bound issues of 1807–1808. It would be difficult to apply strictly the term "edition" to the *Salmagundi* that was published during 1807–1808. Each of the twenty numbers would have to be considered separately, and Longworth's subeditions (true editions in every case, representing new settings and always involving text changes) would have to be counted for each number. That would mean a different number of editions for most of the twenty numbers— an impossible situation to carry over to the succeeding American editions (2A, 3A, etc.). The two-volume issue is not a new edition. It was not made up of numbers specifically printed to be included in book form but rather was made up of randomly selected copies of numbers at hand.[20] Numbers so bound do not need to be distinguished and really cannot be distinguished from the numbers printed to be issued separately, because the bound issues are but the separate numbers bound

19. PMI, I, 210.

20. There is of course an exception to this: a completely new typesetting which does not follow the text-to-page relationship of the original or its format has been found in one two-volume copy for Nos. XI–XX. As BAL explains it, "In 1808 (?) Longworth had a stock of unsold parts and in order to make complete sets, reset and printed needed parts. These reprints (see notes on *Parts 11–12*) are not signed or folded as individual parts but as parts of a larger whole" (BAL, No. 10097, pp. 2–3). At some point during 1808 Longworth apparently ran out of copies for several of the later numbers. Since he no longer intended to publish the parts separately, there was no further need to duplicate

with title page and table of contents/index added. Numbers so bound are treated the same as wrappered numbers.[21]

Table 2, Subeditions and Variant States of 1A, sets forth the highly complex printing sequence for each number. "Longworth's edition" column lists the label the publisher gave the subedition. Subeditions are identified by a number and variant states by a lowercase letter. Since Longworth did not always label his subeditions, and since there are several instances of more than one subedition within one of Longworth's "editions," there is sometimes no correspondence between the edition and the subedition columns. Always the original setting or subedition is bracketed, since it was never labeled "first edition." Some unlabeled subeditions do not represent the original settings and are indicated by "[unidentified]." The copy-text for *Salmagundi* is 1A[1] (the first subedition or setting of 1A) or, when more than one variant state of 1A[1] exists, 1A[1]a.[22]

---

the original format or follow its text-to-page relationship and continuous pagination. Longworth reset a few of the numbers, but it was done as a matter of expediency, not design.

21. It is possible that two two-volume issues (or even two wrapped sets) might contain an identical assemblage of subeditions and variant states, but it would be a surprising occurrence (none of the approximately twenty-five sets examined for this edition did so). Collectors of American literature have assembled sets of unlabeled, wrappered "first editions," but that was usually accomplished by deliberately searching for the numbers separately.

22. Subeditions and variant states of the numbers of *Salmagundi* were established by comparing some twenty-five sets against the copy-text. In every case, a subedition represents a completely new typesetting of a number. Most subeditions were confirmed by comparison of copies via Hinman collator (a simple and ingenious device which uses mirrors to superimpose the image of one page onto the image of another, revealing the smallest alterations in type, type alignment, etc.). Variant states of a subedition (also confirmed for the most part via Hinman Collator) represent copies with limited typographical, lineation, and textual changes from the basic setting. These were usually created by partial resettings of type or stop press alterations. Occasionally, major substantive changes were introduced at these points. Variant states also represent composites or conglomerates of settings, having been created by mixing sheets or gatherings from two or more subeditions.

Given the widespread use of the *Bibliography of American Literature* (BAL) as a standard and a guide, it is inevitable that the findings of this edition as represented in Table 2, Subeditions and Variant States of 1A, will be compared against those in BAL (V, 2–13). Of the fifty-five subeditions and variant states of 1A[1] listed in the Table for the twenty numbers of *Salmagundi* (BAL being concerned only with the original subeditions), BAL notes only twenty-five subeditions and variant states. This must be an approximate figure because the comparison is not a simple one: often BAL notes the presence of "intermediate states," but does not specify the textual or bibliographical variants; often it

TABLE 2
Subeditions and Variant States of 1A

No.	Longworth's Edition	Subedition & Variant State	No.	Longworth's Edition	Subedition & Variant State
I	[first]	1a	IV	[first]	1a
		1b			1b
	second	2a			1c
		2b		second	2
	third	3		third	3
	fourth	4		third	4a
	fourth	5			4b
	fifth	6			
	fifth	7			
II	[first]	1a	V	[first]	1a
		1b			1b
		1c			1c
		1d			1d
	second	2		second	2
	third	3		third	3
	fourth	4		third	4a
	fourth	5			4b
					4c

mentions a variant state, but does not record all of its variants; and sometimes the variant state BAL records is really another state. BAL of course provides discussions regarding the variant state designations. Since these are of a bibliographical nature, similar descriptions will appear in an expanded Table of Subeditions and Variant States of 1A in the Bibliography, the final volume of the Twayne edition.

It is very difficult to precisely define the variant states, since so often they are not distinct and separate sequences, and since they are so highly variable. Some of the variant states now existing may have been created by zealous booksellers who made up a complete copy of a number by combining two or more incomplete copies. *Salmagundi*'s bibliographical states are complicated by the fact that it has been so widely collected by American literature enthusiasts. It must be emphasized that the Table of Subeditions and Variant States does not represent a final rendering of the bibliographical complexities of 1A. To do that would probably require a collation of each copy produced by Longworth. Since *Salmagundi* proves itself endlessly variable, Jacob Blanck's comment (made first in PBSA, p. 11, then repeated in BAL, V, 3) also applies to the Twayne edition: "It would be nice to assert that this description is final and definitive; but with so comparatively few copies to work with ... anything remotely resembling finality is impossible. However, some progress toward that devoutly-to-be-wished end has been made."

No.	Longworth's Edition	Subedition & Variant State	No.	Longworth's Edition	Subedition & Variant State
III	[first]	1	VI	[first]	1a
	second	2			1b
	third	3			1c
	[unidentified]	4		second	2
	fourth	5a		third	3a
		5b			3b
				third	4a
					4b
VII	[first]	1a	XI	[first]	1a
		1b			1b
	second	2			1c
	second	3a		[unidentified]	2
		3b		second	3
VIII	[first]	1a	XII	[first]	1a
		1b			1b
		1c			1c
		1d		second	2
	second	2		second	3
	second	3			
IX	[first]	1	XIII	[first]	1
	second	2		[unidentified]	2
	second	3			
X	[first]	1	XIV	[first]	1a
	second ...	2a			1b
	corrected	2b			
	second ...	3			
	corrected				
XV	[first]	1a	XVIII	[first]	1a
		1b			1b
		1c			1c
		1d			1d
		1e			
		1f			
XVI	[first]	1a	XIX	[first]	1a
		1b			1b
		1c			1c
XVII	[first]	1a	XX	[first]	1a
		1b			1b
					1c

In order to illustrate the kinds of textual variations on which the subeditions and variant states were established, No. II will be examined in detail. No. II is representative of the kinds of substantive alterations which took place in 1A.[23] These were composed of small corrections for the most part and stylistic changes. At 79.20–21 "their mothers were equally anxious that we would show no quarter" ($1A^1$–$1A^4$) was changed to ". . . should show no quarter" ($1A^5$); and at 78.28–29 "The old folks" ($1A^1$–$1A^3$) was changed to "The old folk" ($1A^4$–$1A^5$) a recurring alteration in *Salmagundi* (it also occurs at 102.24; 108.30; and 187.3), perhaps part of the self-conscious use of quaint expressions and archaisms. The remaining three substantives (87.26; 87.40; 87.40) are also small stylistic changes. Compositor's errors, exasperatingly frequent in *Salmagundi* and often uncorrected, occasionally are created when the type was reset for a new subedition. The change at 85.7–9 from "Time, though it has dealt roughly with his person, has passed lightly over the graces of his mind, and left him in full possession of all the sensibilities of youth" to "Time, though it has dealt lightly with his person, has passed roughly over the graces of his mind . . ." simply does not make sense and must be due to the compositor's transposing the two phrases.

Though it is sometimes difficult to determine whether a punctuation or a word change is due to compositor's error or to deliberate revision, "readers" ($1A^1$a,d) to "reader" ($1A^1$b–c, $1A^2$–$1A^4$) at 78.6 and "retinues" ($1A^1$–$1A^3$) to "retinue" ($1A^4$–$1A^5$) at 88.28 belonging in the uncertain category, out of the twenty cruxes for No. II, three are clearly compositor's errors (83.18; 85.7; 85.8); three more may have originated with the compositor (78.6; 81.30; 88.28); six are matters of house styling and not attributable to the authors (1A II, 21.head; II, 21.10–11; II, 21.13; II, 23.head; 81.31; and 38. pi); one is a change in punctuation (82.6); another is a minor spelling change (81.32). These last two also may have been the work of the printer or the house editor (if there was one), rather than the authors. That leaves five substantive changes attributable to the authors, and all of them involve minor alterations (78.29; 79.21; 87.26; 87.40; 87.40 again).[24]

23. Here and in the sequel, textual variants are classified as substantives when they affect meaning (i.e., word change) and as accidentals when they affect form (e.g., spelling and punctuation). Most differences between the subeditions and variant states of the twenty numbers can be deduced from the List of Emendations and the List of Rejected Substantives.

24. The accidental changes here transcribed are only those that prove a variant state. In fact there were in all some 150 accidental changes between the five subeditions and the four variant states of No. II. For a breakdown of

Table 3, Collation Table for No. II, includes the substantives and accidentals which signify the subeditions and variant states of No. II. Entries in the table are numbered for the reader's convenience. Page references are to T and to 1A. When significant, a slash / indicates the end of a line. Notice that in many cases, 1A page reference alone signals a resetting of type. The first three entries comprise (1) Longworth's edition label, (2) four words appearing in the mock quotation, (3) the dateline. All of these appear as part of the short title, which is also the first page of text of each number. The sixth entry is a number identification added to the running head in subeditions subsequent to the first. The final entry is the printer's imprint, a constant characteristic of the numbers, and like the first three entries, varying from subedition to subedition and sometimes within subeditions.[25] A swung (wavy) dash ~ means that the word cited in the previous subedition or variant state remains the same, but the punctuation following is different. A caret $_\wedge$ indicates that a mark of punctuation was left out. Information supplied appears in caret brackets. The symbol n/a means there is no Twayne equivalent for the entry.

Additional examples of the small textual changes in *Salmagundi* can of course be taken from the other numbers. At 89.19 the relative pronoun "whom" referring to a nightingale ($1A^1$–$1A^2$) was changed to "which" ($1A^3$–$1A^5$); at 73.13, in the phrase "honor of his editors," the word "editors" ($1A^1$–$1A^2$, $1A^4$) was corrected to "authors" ($1A^3$, $1A^5$–$1A^7$). Some long phrases were added for amplification; at 71.41 "porcelaine. He" ($1A^1$–$1A^4$) became "porcelane, and particularly values himself on his intimate knowledge of the buffalo, and war dances of the northern indians. He" ($1A^5$–$1A^7$). Already there is a tendency, continued in later editions (2A and 1F specifically) to make *Salmagundi* more genteel. At 108.16 the phrase "can tell what the devil tune" ($1A^1$–$1A^2$) became "can make out what tune" ($1A^3$–$1A^4$). Euphemisms were substituted for mild profanities; at 1A 202.34 "d——n" ($1A^1$) became "bullied" ($1A^2$–$1A^3$). A fastidiousness about the parts of the body was exhibited: at 113.3 "paunch" ($1A^1$–$1A^2$) became "waist" ($1A^3$). Some earlier colloquialisms and spellings were modified. The most notable example appears at 100.35–36, when the following lines

---

these changes, see footnote 71. The complete accidental lists are on deposit at the University of Texas.

25. Assuming various forms, Longworth's imprint appears on the paper wrappers and at the end of each of the twenty numbers. The two most common versions are "New-York, Printed and Published by D. Longworth" and "Printed & Published by D. Longworth, at the Shakspeare-Gallery," both usually but not always in italics.

TABLE 3
Collation Table for No. II

T		1A¹a	1A¹b	1A¹c	1A¹d
n/a	1)	⟨21⟩.head	⟨none⟩		
n/a	2)	⟨21⟩.10–11	broil'd, stew'd, boil'd, smoak'd		
78.2	3)	⟨21⟩.13	NO. II] *Wednesday, February 4, 1807.*		
78.6	4)	⟨21⟩.18	his readers	4) ⟨21⟩.18 his reader		4) ⟨21⟩.18 his readers
78.29	5)	22.22	folks			
n/a	6)	23.head	⟨none⟩			
79.21	7)	23.30	would			
81.21	8)	27.12	*what-d'ye-callums*			
81.30	9)	27.25	dregs and draining of the ancient			
81.31	10)	27.26	entirely			
81.32	11)	27.28	naiades			
82.6	12)	28.22	audience,	12) 28.22 ~;		
83.18	13)	30.32–33	knight of / of ⟨typo⟩		13) 30.32–33 knight / of ⟨corrected⟩	
85.7	14)	34.3	dealt roughly			
85.8	15)	34.4	passed lightly			
87.26	16)	37.9	I warrant			
87.40	17)	37.27	into a passion			
87.40	18)	37.27	having been			
88.28	19)	38.26	retinues			
n/a	20)	38.pi	⟨none⟩			

No.	T	IA²	IA³	IA⁴	IA⁵
		(second edition)	(third edition)	(fourth edition)	
1)	n/a ⟨21⟩.head	⟨21⟩.head	⟨21⟩.head	⟨21⟩.head	
2)	n/a ⟨21⟩.10-11	broil'd, stew'd, boil'd, smok'd		⟨21⟩.10-11 broiled, stewed, boiled, smoked	
4)	78.6 ⟨21⟩.18	his reader			
5)				22.22 folk	
6)				23.head NO. 2]	
7)				23.31 ⟨text same⟩	23.31 should
8)	81.21 27.12	what-d'ye‿callums	27.13 what-d'ye-call'ms		27.14 what-d'ye-call-ms
9)	81.30 27.26	⟨text same⟩		27.26 dregs and drainings of the ancient	27.27 ⟨text same⟩
10)	81.31 27.27	⟨text same⟩	27.27 intirely		27.28 ⟨text same⟩
11)	81.32 28.1	⟨text same⟩	27.29 ⟨text same⟩		27.30 niades
12)	82.6 28.22	audience,	28.22 ~;		
13)	83.18 30.15	⟨text same⟩	30.33 ⟨text same⟩		
14)	85.7 33.17	⟨text same⟩	34.5 ⟨text same⟩		34.4 dealt lightly
15)	85.8 33.18	⟨text same⟩	34.6 ⟨text same⟩		34.5 passed roughly
16)	87.26 36.21	⟨text same⟩	37.6 I'll warrant		
17)	87.40 37.6	⟨text same⟩	37.23 ⟨text same⟩		37.23 in a passion
18)	87.40 37.6	⟨text same⟩	37.24 ⟨text same⟩		37.24 being
19)	88.28 38.3	⟨text same⟩	38.22 ⟨text same⟩	38.24 retinue	
20)	n/a 38.pi	New-York, Printed and Published by D. Longworth / ⟨rule⟩	38.pi ⟨same as IA² except: rule precedes imprint⟩		38.pi ⟨rule⟩ / Printed by D. Longworth, at the Shakspeare Gallery.

in dialect from "Proclamation, from the Mill of Pindar Cockloft, esq."
are changed. " 'Vhat shtops,' as he says, 'all de peoples vhat come /
'Vhat schmiles on dem all, and vhat peats on de trum' " (1A¹) were
revised to read " 'What shtops,' as he says, 'all de people what come: /
'What smiles on dem all, and what peats on de trum' " (1A³–1A⁵).

Unlike the other numbers, X and XII were extensively rewritten. The
revised subeditions of No. X (1A²–1A³) which differ only slightly from
each other were labeled "Second edition, revised and corrected," the
only subedition to advertise its revisions. In the original subedition
(1A¹) of No. X, in James Kirke Paulding's "The Breaking up of the
Ice in the North-river" (180.20–184.10), Demi Semiquaver wrote to
Launcelot Langstaff about Anthony Evergreen's "terrible phillipic against
modern music in No. II" (180.22–23). Semiquaver describes a piece
of modern music *he* has composed about the New York Assembly at
Albany and the North-river Society's attempt to set the Hudson on fire.
The prose is in a notebook style similar to the travel notes by Washington Irving later in the same number. In the revision (1A²–1A³) Semiquaver's note on modern music was changed to more formal prose, and
near the conclusion of the piece (183.20–21) an entirely new satirical
paragraph aimed at the amateur musical and dramatic audiences of New
York was added to make the satire more pertinent. Directly following
is Washington Irving's "The Stranger in Pennsylvania" (184.12–189.17)
by Jeremy Cockloft—a satire on Philadelphia and on travel pieces so
popular at the time. It also was revised from a rough notebook style
filled with numerous ellipses and dashes (1A¹) into something closer
to connected discourse (1A²–1A³). In the revision an introductory
paragraph was added in the voice of Langstaff, explaining that Jeremy's
travel notes in No. IV ("The Stranger in New Jersey," 103–108.16) were
so well received by the Cockloft family that Jeremy "put his whole
budget of memorandums into my hand, with full powers to make use
of them as I pleased" (1A²–1A³). Jeremy's comments on Pennsylvania
follow in 1A²–1A³, but in the third person instead of the first person.
The original version reads:

Part II.—GREAT THAW.—This consists of the most *melting*
strains, following so smoothly, as occasion a great overflowing of
scientific rapture—air—"One misty moisty morning."—The house
of assembly breaks up—air—"The owls came out and flew about"—
Assemblymen embark on their way to New-York—air—The ducks
and the geese they all swim over, fal, de ral, &c.—

And is quite changed in 1A²–1A³ to read:

My second part opens with a grand musical experiment, which is nothing less than to perform a GREAT THAW!—Talk to me of your hail–storms and snow-storms, and thunder and lightning—here is something that will out-do them all—such melting airs, such soft flowing strains:—

There are also two subeditions of the revisions in No. XII, and like the two in No. X, these differ principally in minor details. William Irving's satirical poem, "From the Mill of Pindar Cockloft, Esq." (213.3–215.40) was· revised in 1A²–1A³ to direct it more specifically at young coxcombs. For instance, in 1A¹ the opening couplet reads: "How often I cast my reflections behind, / And call up the days of past youth to my mind" (213.5–6); 1A²–1A³ changed this to "Full oft I indulge in reflections right sage, / And ease off my spleen by abusing the age." Some of the changes merely altered lines or phrases: for example at 215.14 "Receiving and claiming the vows of the heart" (1A¹) became "Receiving the homage and vows of the heart" (1A²–1A³).

1E: London, J. M. Richardson, 1811.   BAL 10225

Although it had always been planned to bind up the individual numbers and issue *Salmagundi* in book format, Stanley Williams is correct when he observes "The beginning of [*Salmagundi's*] history as a book was in 1811."[26] The first English edition was prepared by John Lambert, the English traveler, who explained in the preface dated April 8, 1811: "Just before my departure from the United States the essays were discontinued, and I had an opportunity of procuring a complete copy of the whole. On my return to this country I published a work entitled 'Travels through Lower Canada and the United States of North America, in the years 1806, 1807, and 1808' in three volumes, in which I introduced a few of the Salmagundian Essays, as a specimen of American literature" (1E, p. i–ii). In addition to the preface, Lambert wrote a long Introductory Essay and made extensive efforts to mollify the then rampant British prejudice against the United States: "Should I have the good fortune to be instrumental to the removal of one single prejudice against the Americans, or, in any way, tend to conciliate the minds of my countrymen in favour of a people whose character has been grossly misrepresented, I shall feel myself amply rewarded for my trouble, and consider such a change of sentiment to have arisen more

26. Stanley T. Williams, *The Life of Washington Irving* (New York, 1935), II, 269.

from the liberal opinions of my readers than from any feeble effort of mine" (1E, pp. iii–iv).

The "complete copy of the whole" Lambert procured must have consisted of later subeditions of the numbers, for 1E is made up of the revised instead of the original texts of the numbers. Included were the two reworked features (1A²–1A³) in No. X, "The Breaking up of the Ice in the North-river" and "The Stranger in Pennsylvania"; also included was the rewritten version (1A²–1A³) of "From the Mill of Pindar Cockloft, Esq." in No. XII. Lambert's edition was carefully edited. He did not follow the 1A texts slavishly, but corrected some typographical errors not caught in the particular subedition or variant state of 1A he used as printer's copy: "principal" was corrected to "principle" (102.2) and "laying" corrected to "lying" (102.38). Nor did Lambert accept typographical errors introduced into the particular subedition or variant state he used as printer's copy. Thus although he followed 1A⁴ for No. III, at 96.31 he corrected the error "conscious struck" which appeared in subedition 1A⁴ to "conscience struck."

2A: New York, David Longworth, 1814.   BAL 10102

In 1814 David Longworth published "A New and Improved Edition, with Tables of Contents and a Copious Index," using woodcuts and plates by the American engraver Alexander Anderson. Longworth added a brief table of contents and a section summarizing each essay or feature. The text of the second American edition (2A) is based on a mixture of subeditions and variant states of 1A. Compared to the amount of revisions that took place in 1A, 2A introduces few new readings. While it corrects certain minor errors in 1A and makes small stylistic "improvements," the edition is chiefly notable because it removed entire features from 1A, namely, the several attacks on Thomas Green Fessenden: the one at 97.30–98.28 entitled "——— How now, mooncalf!" (Perhaps written by Paulding), and five features from No. IV— "From My Elbow-Chair" (authorship not known), "Flummery" (perhaps by William Irving), "General Remark," "Notice," and 'Card" (all of whose authorship is unknown), at 107.5–116.23.[27] Also deleted from 2A was Washington Irving's "The Stranger in Pennsylvania" at 184.12– 189.17, which had always displeased Irving. Material which by 1814 may have seemed offensive, unnecessary, or perhaps ill-considered was struck. For example, the following unflattering description of the interior of the Park Theatre which Irving wrote for the "Theatrics" section of No.

27. Assignments of authorship for each piece are discussed in pp. 327-36.

VI (137.9–12) was removed: "As the house was crowded, we were complimented with seats in Box No. 2, a sad little rantipole place, which is the strong hold of a set of rare wags, and where the poor actors undergo the most merciless tortures of verbal criticism." Deleted from Paulding's "The Stranger at Home" was the reference to Trinity Church and its congregation at 209.22–27: "New brick church! . . . what a pity it is the corporation of Trinity church are so poor! . . . if they could not afford to build a better place of worship, why did they not go about with a subscription? . . . even I would have given them a few shillings rather than our city should have been disgraced by such a pitiful specimen of economy." Also deleted was the similarly unflattering reference to the corporation of Bowling Green at 209.9–14. Most of the political satire, personal and general, was left untouched; however, two sentences describing the deadly warfare between the "holeans" and the "anti-holeans" were dropped at 172.28–35. Clearly there was an attempt to make the style more "genteel" and less colloquial: "*dished*" became "thrown out" at 180.18 and "twaddle" became "worry" at 192.33. Omitted were the indelicate "and chafe" at 192.34, "or nozzle" at 83.15–16, and "got a tremendous *flea in his ear*" at 200.15–16.

While David Longworth, the holder of the copyright on *Salmagundi*, may well have been responsible for some of the substantive alterations in 2A, it may be that one or more of the three authors added to their original revisions of six years earlier. To be sure, by 1814 the Lads of Kilkenny had scattered, and the convivial mood which had found ready expression in the *Salmagundi* of 1807–1808 had passed. As early as 1809 Paulding told a friend, "Our Club has undergone a dispersion, to which that of the Tower of Babel was a mere breaking up of the Congregation of a village Church."[28] It is most unlikely therefore that the three authors collaborated in revising the 1814 edition. William Irving would probably have had no time to spare for such a task since he was now a financial leader in New York and would serve in Congress from 1814 to 1819. James Kirke Paulding was contentious early in his career, as witness his caustic *Diverting History of John Bull and Brother Jonathan* (1812) and the vigor he displayed in entering the paper war against England with his *United States and England* (1815). It is doubtful, therefore, that in 1814 he would have been the one to replace phrases or delete offensive passages such as the attacks on Fessenden in Nos. III and IV.

Irving is the most likely candidate of the three original authors to make such revisions, for he would have wished to avoid giving offense.

28. Paulding and John Markoe, May 17, 1809, in *The Letters of James Kirke Paulding*, ed. Ralph M. Aderman (Madison, 1962), p. 27.

As early as 1809 he wrote his brother William, "Whatever I may write in future I am determined on one thing—to dismiss from my mind all party prejudice and feeling as much as possible, and to endeavor to contemplate every subject with a candid and good-natured eye."[29] There is corroborative evidence of a more concrete nature that Irving revised Longworth's edition. On December 16, 1812, while in Washington, Irving wrote Longworth, saying, "I expect to be home in about eight days, when I will attend to the second edition of Salmagundi."[30] The deletion from No. X of Irving's article, "Stranger in Pennsylvania," which according to Pierre M. Irving[31] failed to satisfy his uncle (perhaps the reason it was revised in $1A^2$–$1A^3$), also argues for Irving's having revised Longworth's edition. Evidence Irving approved of the revised text is the fact that he used 2A as printer's copy for 1F, which he revised for Galignani ten years later, in 1824.

Irving, but probably not Longworth, would have been sensitive to the critical reception of *Salmagundi*. A number of the revisions in 2A may have been occasioned by a review of 1E (John Lambert's English edition of 1811), which appeared in *The Monthly Review*.[32] Writing to his brother William, Irving remarks "Salmagundi has been reviewed in the London Monthly Review, and much more favorably than I expected. The faults they point out are such as I had long been sensible of, and they seem particularly to attack the quotations and the Latin interwoven in the poetry, which certainly does halt most abominably in the reading."[33] It may have been the criticisms in the *Review* that led Irving to decide to help Longworth prepare 2A. The reviewer called *Salmagundi* "A literary curiosity."[34] And though praising its prose and its value as a description of the American character, the reviewer sharply criticized the "vulgarisms, or at best provincialisms, which we forbear to mention, but hope we may not see repeated in similar compositions."[35] The revisions in 2A which attempt to make the style less colloquial may reflect those observations. "The aukward attempts at a

29. Washington Irving to William Irving, February 9, 1811, quoted in PMI, I, 271.

30. Holograph letter, The Clifton Waller Barrett Library at the University of Virginia.

31. PMI, I, 195.

32. 65 (May–August, 1811), 418–424. The editor is indebted to Martin Roth for calling attention to this cause and effect in a letter dated July 14, 1970.

33. PMI, I, 213; the letter was written from Washington but PMI gives no date.

34. *Monthly Review*, 65, 418.

35. *Ibid.*, p. 419.

display of meagre quotations"[36] the reviewer railed against were deleted: the adjective "atlean" in the phrase "atlean burthen of Salmagundi" at 96.19; the "*Di majorum gentium*," "*Dii penates*" reference in "From the Mill of Pindar Cockloft" at 215.11–12; the mention of Gunaikophagi" in the poem "Tea" at 300.3 and 300.39–42; and the lines from Juvenal and Linkum Fidelius at 95.25–29. Perhaps to soften the edge in *Salmagundi*'s description of the English traveler the following was also omitted: "Now Straddle knew that the savages were fond of beads, spike-nails and looking-glasses, and therefore filled his trunk with them" (203.18–20).

3A: New York, Thomas Longworth, 1820.   BAL 10229

By the time Thomas Longworth[37] published the third American edition in 1820 (3A), Irving had achieved an international reputation, a circumstance which caused him to wish *Salmagundi* had been allowed to go out of print. In 1819 Paulding had written additional numbers in the style of the original *Salmagundi*. These (dated May, 1819, to August, 1820) were published by Moses Thomas under the title *Salmagundi, Second Series*. Paulding's *Second Series* may have prompted Thomas Longworth to reissue the original *Salmagundi*. Alluding to Paulding's *Second Series*, Irving wrote Henry Brevoort from England July 10, 1819: "I am sorry that Paulding has undertaken to continue Salmagundi without consulting me. He should have done so as I am implicated in the first series. I think it a very injudicious thing. The work was pardonable as a juvenile production and has been indulgently received by the public. But it is full of errors, puerilities & impertinences which James should have had more judgment than to guarantee at his maturer age. I was in hopes it would gradually have gone down into oblivion; but it is now dragged once more before the public & subject to a more vigorous criticism."[38] On August 12, 1819, he adds: "I have looked through James Ps first number of Salmagundi & am pleased with some parts of it—but cannot but regret he had not suffered the old work to die a natural death."[39]

Evidently Paulding hoped that Irving would come to feel more kindly toward *Salmagundi*, for "In February, 1822," writes Paulding's son, "the original copyright [held by David Longworth] having expired,

36. *Ibid.*, p. 419.
37. In a letter to Irving, July 30, 1838, Paulding refers to "that most amiable rascal, his [David Longworth's] Son Tom" (Paulding, *Letters*, p. 222).
38. George S. Hellman, ed., *Letters of Washington Irving to Henry Brevoort* (New York, 1918), pp. 311.
39. *Ibid.*, pp. 322–23.

Mr. Paulding proposed to his friend (through his brother Ebenezer), that they should revise the work and republish it for their joint benefit; observing that it still had a good sale, and adducing as an additional reason for the course suggested, that the publisher had 'taken the liberty to add some of his own nonsense occasionally'; and that 'it would therefore be desirable even on that account to get the work out of his diabolical clutches if possible.' "[40] William I. Paulding then remarks, "I find no answer to this proposition at that time." Granting that Paulding's son was not always a reliable biographer, it seems that the attitude Irving expressed to Brevoort three years earlier remained unchanged. In view of such strong feelings, it is not surprising that thirty years later Irving would take care to exclude *Salmagundi*, along with *Oldstyle*, from the revised edition of his writings, although he had in the meantime allowed himself to be persuaded by Galignani to supervise 1F (Paris, 1824). Paulding, on the other hand, remained enthusiastic about *Salmagundi* and on several occasions in years following wrote Irving about plans to reissue the series.

Thomas Longworth's edition (3A), almost without exception, followed the text of 2A. It did not, however, change "Linkum Fidelius" to "Linkum" at 74.2–3 and 84.43 as had 2A, and it corrected a few of the errors in 1A that 2A had not caught; for instance, at 102.2 "principal" became "principle," an error also corrected by 1E.

2E: London, Thomas Tegg, 1824.   Not recorded by BAL

The second English edition is dated 1824 (2E), but appeared late in 1823. Perhaps designed for the Christmas trade, it was reviewed in December by several journals, notably the *London Literary Museum and Register*.[41] Based on 2A, this edition of Tegg's was the first of a series of versions issued by him in 1824, all of them unauthorized, pirated editions. On December 22, 1823, Irving wrote John Murray from Paris: "I am sorry to see that Tegg has been republishing a little work in which I had a share in my very young days. It is full of crudities and puerilities and I had hoped would have remained unnoticed & forgotten."[42]

1F: Paris, A. and W. Galignani, 1824.[43]   BAL 10113

At first Irving refused Galignani's offer to publish an edition of *Salmagundi*. On December 21, 1823, Irving records in his Paris journal:

40. William I. Paulding, *Literary Life of James Kirke Paulding* (New York, 1867), p. 39.

41. December 20, 1823, p. 805.

42. Holograph letter to Murray in the Carl Pforzheimer Library, New York City.

43. 1F also appeared under the imprint "Paris: Printed by Jules Didot, Sen.

"Young Galignani wishes to know if I have objection to their republishing Salmagundi & upon my saying I had he promises not to publish it."[44] Seventeen days later on January 7, 1824, he had changed his mind: "Call this morng at Galignanis agree to correct Salmagundi for him."[45] By February 4, 1824, he was finished with his revisions, and on February 8, 1824, Irving wrote Charles R. Leslie: "I am sorry to see *Salmagundi* is published at London, with all its faults upon its head. I have corrected a copy for Galignani, whom I found bent upon putting it to press. My corrections consist almost entirely in expurging words and here and there an offensive sentence."[46] By March 20, 1824, 1F was listed in *Bibliotheque Francaise*.[47] In agreeing to let Galignani publish the work, Irving may have been influenced by Tegg's edition and by the recollection of Sir Walter Scott's encouraging words five years earlier: "I am certain the Sketch Book could be published here with great advantage; it is a delightful work. Knickerbocker and Salmagundi are more exclusively American, and may not be quite so well suited for our meridian. But they are so excellent in their way, that if the public attention could be once turned on them I am confident that they would become popular; but there is the previous objection to overcome."[48] It is possible, too, that Galignani paid Irving for his assistance.

Although Irving requested a copy of the first English Edition (1E), possibly for use as a copy-text,[49] a comparison of the three texts proves that 1F is based on the text of 2A. The Publisher's Notice to the Paris edition states: "The present edition has been submitted to the revision of one of the authors, who, at first, contemplated making essential alterations. On further consideration, however, he contented himself with correcting merely a few of what he termed the most glaring errors and

---

for Baudry, Rue de Coq. No. 9 MDCCC XXIV" (BAL, p. 24). The comparative publishing relationship between Baudry and Galignani is discussed in Giles Barber's "Galignani and the Publication of English Books in France from 1800 to 1852," *The Library*, 5th ser. (1961), 267–76.

44. *Journals and Notebooks*, III, 260.

45. *Ibid.*, p. 266.

46. PMI, II, 186. An Englishman born of American parents, Leslie illustrated both *History of New York* and *Sketchbook*; in 1820 he painted Irving's portrait. Later he illustrated Scott's Waverly novels and became an Associate of the Royal Academy.

47. BAL, 10013.

48. PMI, I, 443–44.

49. At least he wrote to John Howard Payne on January 7, 1824: "I wish you to procure for me . . . a copy of the London Edition of Salmagundi published several years since—and forward it to me—care of Galgnani" (Holograph in the Columbia University Library).

flippancies, and judged it best to leave the evident juvenility of the work to plead it own apology" (1F, p. vii). Irving may have written the Publisher's Notice himself, for it includes the original Publisher's Notice from 1A, prefaced by the following explanation: "LONGWORTH had an extraordinary propensity to publish elegant works, to the great gratification of persons of taste, and the no small diminution of his own slender fortune. He alludes ironically to this circumstance in the present notice" (1F, p. vii). The Publisher's Notice is referring to Longworth's statement in No. I: "The publisher professes the same sublime contempt for money as his authors" (69.3–4). The observation about Longworth must have been meant as ironic, since Longworth realized substantial monies from the sale of Salmagundi, while the authors received very little.

As further evidence that Irving still resented Longworth's financial handling of Salmagundi in 1807–1808, references to the casual attitude of the authors and the publisher toward the sale of Salmagundi (at that time) were either deleted or repositioned in 1F. And he omitted the statement by the authors: "We have nothing to do with the pecuniary concerns of the paper, its success will yield us neither pride nor profit— nor will its failure occasion to us either loss or mortification. We advise the public therefore, to purchase our numbers merely for their own sakes" (68.18–22). Irving added footnotes explaining certain references in Salmagundi he felt would be obscure to the European reader. For instance, in No. I he added a note on the magazine "Town" (1F, p. 4), on Kissing Bridge (1F, p. 16), on the milliners Mesdames Toole and Bouchard (1F, p. 21), on Thomas Jefferson's red slippers (1F, p. 22), and on the North-River Society (1F, p. 24).

Irving's instinctive fastidiousness and sense of propriety, more deeply ingrained in 1824 than when he collaborated on Salmagundi seventeen years earlier, explain some of his revisions in 1F; for instance, the deletion of the final half of this sentence after "ridicule": "It is not in our hearts to hurt the feelings of one single mortal, by holding him up to public ridicule, and if it were, we lay it down as one of our indisputable facts, that no man can be made ridiculous but by his own folly" (88.1–4). Irving seemed especially conscious of references to noses and tobacco. He softened "snout" to "musical feature" (83.20); omitted in the same number "Snout, the bellowsmender, never tuned his wind instrument more musically; nor did the celebrated 'knight of the burning lamp,' ever yield more exquisite entertainment with his nose" (83.16–19); omitted "and turn their noses to the south when the wind blows" (104.4–5); in two instances "tobacco-box" became "snuff-box" (138.17 and 216.12), "quid" became "pinch" (216.14), "and smoke tobacco" (286.24) was omitted. In addition to the pieces deleted from 2A, he omitted from 1F the poem "To the Ladies" at 126.38–129.28, which contained lines critical of Thomas Moore, and he revised lines referring to the "lascivious" poetry of Thomas Moore at 148.28–29, no doubt because he had in the meantime befriended Moore. He also omitted critical references to a concert at the City Hotel at 82.23–28, and to Columbia College at 102.19–22.

In an attempt to make the text less wordy, Irving took out many of the adjectives in *Salmagundi*. The Mustapha Letter in No. XIV, written by William Irving, which concerned logocracy and politics, was tightened by the removal of many of the modifiers and redundant phrases, and the satire was somewhat sharpened. More extensive here than in 2A was the excision of political references, especially those relating to Thomas Jefferson. Thus a slur on Jefferson's gunboat policy (104.17–18), the rumor that he kept a Negro mistress (139.37), and passages critical of logocracy (146.7–20), economy (172.7–10), and mobocracy (195.14–36), were either omitted or revised.

Also removed from 1F was some of the whimsy present in the original; for example, the sentence from No. IV: "I should have said Jeremy Cockloft *the younger*, as he so styles himself by way of distinguishing him from Il Signore Jeremo Cockloftico, a gouty old gentleman who flourished about the time that Pliny the elder was smoked to death with fire and brimstone of Vesuvius, and whose travels, if he ever wrote any, are now lost forever to the world" (101.21–26).

3E: London, Thomas Tegg, 1824.   BAL 10243

Soon after Galignani's edition appeared listed in *Bibliotheque Francaise* March 20, 1824, Thomas Tegg marketed another edition. This was 3E, Tegg's second edition dated 1824. 3E incorporates some, but not all, of the revisions of 1F, and like 2E is based on 2A. Three title pages are recorded for this edition: one without reference to its being a new edition, one designated as a "New Edition," and the other "New Edition, Corrected and Revised by the Author." These issues have been called respectively 3Ea, 3Eb, and 3Ec. The last issue is the only one to advertise its unauthorized relationship to 1F. The Prefatory Notice in 3Ea and 3Eb is expanded in 3Ec to a Publisher's Notice, which is clearly patterned after the Publisher's Notice of 1F and quotes directly from it, without attribution of course.

The 3E texts are curious productions: they include many revisions new in 1F, but not all of them. Obviously a certain selectivity was exercised by Tegg in adopting Irving's revisions. A large number of the adjectives and phrases Irving removed in 1F were retained; also,

the passage critical of the City Hotel in No. II (82.23–28), a reference
to noses in the same number (83.16–19) and passages mentioning
Linkum Fidelius in No. IV (104.13, 104.16) were allowed to stand.
When 3E does not follow the 1F revisions, it reverts to the 2A text
rather than to 1A. There is a tendency to incorporate more 1F revisions
as the sequence of issues progresses. This is particularly evident when
comparing 3Ea and 3Eb with 3Ec, which after all advertised itself as
"Revised by the Author."

Irving's Journal provides the following amusing anecdote, dated
August 7, 1824. On a visit to Davison's, Irving caught Tegg in the act
of pirating 1F: "After breakfast, go down to Mr. Davidsons. Find a
man there whom I suspect to be Tegg—who was busy with Davidson
about a book which I see to be Salmagundi—Takes up the book in
confusion."[50]

In the decade following the publication of Galignani's French edition
(1F), no known new editions of Salmagundi were published, though
pirated editions appeared.[51] In 1824 Irving and Paulding talked of creat-
ing additional sketches for a new edition of Salmagundi. On March 20,
1824, Paulding wrote to Irving, "I approve your plan of a new edition
of Salmagundi, and will set about my part as soon as the spirit moves
me. I anticipate much barrenness in my attempts, having almost
exhausted myself in this line" (a reference to Paulding's Second Series,
1819–1820). He continues, expressing his sanguine view of Salmagundi's
merits: "I don't hold this early bantling of ours in such utter contempt
as you do, and can't help viewing it in the light of a careless popular
thing that will always be read in spite of its faults, perhaps in consequence of these very faults."[52] Certainly a better assessment of Salmagundi than Irving's low opinion of the work.

On July 7, 1824, Irving, perhaps encouraged by the sale of the
recent Paris and London editions (1F, 2E, and 3E) and fearful lest
the pirates make off with all the profits, wrote his brother Peter: "I
have promised Murray to prepare a corrected edition of Salmagundi
for him, with additions, such as you and I had talked of; and have
written to Paulding to hasten the essays he is to contribute. I have
materials enough for my part of the job lying by me in half-formed
sketches, that I should otherwise have probably made no use of. It will,

50. Journals and Notebooks, III, 378.

51. Pirated editions of Salmagundi were published in London by: Limbird
(1824), Tegg (1824, 1825, 1839), Bumpas (1825), Daly (1841), and Bohn (1850).

52. Paulding, Letters, p. 70.

therefore, cost me scarce any trouble, and will pay me handsomely."[53] Nothing came of the project, and the tantalizing question of which "half-formed essays" he intended to include remains unanswered.[54]

Nine years later, in 1833, a further project to reissue *Salmagundi* was contemplated. On March 7 of that year Paulding wrote to Irving: "Messrs. Conner & Cooke who are about commencing the Publication of a Series of American Works, under the title of A National Library, have applied to me on the Subject of Old Salmagundi, which they wish to commence with. . . . Would you . . . be willing to contribute a few articles, according to the plans you suggested to me while in Paris several years ago? . . . I know You hold this Old Bantling of ours rather deaf, as authors like other parents, are very apt to pet their Youngest children, but I have always told you it had been and always will be, one if not the most popular of our works."[55] Nothing came of this project either, despite Paulding's persuasive tone. It can only be surmised that Irving's reluctance was the cause; perhaps he was too much immersed in his Western books to devote any more time to this early literary "bantling."

2F: Complete Works, Paris, Baudry, 1834.   BAL 10280

In 1834 *The Complete Works of Washington Irving in One Volume* appeared in Paris; *Salmagundi* was the lead work in this volume of Baudry's European Library. A spot check reveals 2F to be a reprint of 1F, the Paris edition published in 1824 under the double imprint of Galignani and Baudry. 2F is interesting as being one of the two editions used by Evert A. Duyckinck in preparing his edition of 1860.

4A: New York, Harper, 1835, Volumes I–II of James Kirke Paulding's Works.   BAL 10147

On February 28, 1834, when Paulding was arranging with Harper for the publication of a uniform edition of his works, he wrote Irving: "I know you consider Old Sal as a sort of saucy flippant trollope, belonging to nobody, and not worth fathering, and therefore venture to ask if you have any objection to have her again presented to the public in connexion with the continuation, and for our joint benefit. It can be reprinted from the Paris edition [of 1814] which I have,

---

53. PMI, II, 202–3.

54. Henry A. Pochmann, in a note to the editor (Spring, 1970) regarding an earlier version of this commentary, suggests: "Very possibly some of the 'American Essays' (later destroyed) were part of this series."

55. Paulding, *Letters*, pp. 129–30.

and without any further sanction of the authors than that indicates."[56] Of this letter by his father William I. Paulding says, "Mr. Irving rejoins the next day, according permission, but . . . depreciating the work somewhat in the spirit of a respectable elderly gentleman when called upon to harvest the wild oats of his youth." Paulding then quotes from Irving's letter: " 'These, however, are excusable in a juvenile production; as such, therefore, I wish it to be considered, and for that reason am disinclined to any additions or modifications that may appear to give it the sanction of our present taste, judgment, and opinions.' "[57]

Paulding, however, did not heed Irving's advice. Harper published the new edition (4A) as Volumes I and II of Paulding's *Works,* Volumes III and IV being Paulding's *Second Series* originally published 1819–1820. Paulding reprinted the Publisher's Notice of 1F, rewording it in the plural to make it appear that Irving sanctioned Paulding's revisions. Although Paulding based his edition (as he said he would) on 1F, he felt free to make some major changes. He replaced Irving's Mustapha Letter in No. XI (189.20–195.38) with a new one of his own. Irving's letter described a city election, whereas Paulding's spoke in general about the "great bashaw" and the constitution, and represented himself as impressed by the order that coexists with liberty. Thus Paulding softened and generalized the political satire of the original letter. In addition, he replaced the essay "On Greatness" in No. XV (250.14–255.34), a political attack on great men of the logocracy like Timothy Dabble, tentatively ascribed to Irving, with an essay about a gentleman who married four times and each time discovered that he had made a mistake, a much tamer and wholly social satire. Following Malvolio Dubster's letter in No. XIX (298.10–33), he added seven paragraphs in which the editors commented on the letters addressed to Anthony Evergreen. Although Paulding had been vitriolic and satiric at the beginning of his literary career, he had long before abandoned much of his youthful contentiousness. As early as when he wrote the *Second Series* (1819–1820), he had one of Langstaff's correspondents complain "that we take no part in politics" (*Works,* III, 253). In 1835 he was engaged in a political career and had become even more sensitive to the political overtones in *Salmagundi* than Irving had been in 1824. By 1835 Paulding had served in the Navy Department for twenty years and would shortly become Martin Van Buren's Secretary of the Navy. He deleted references in 4A to Thomas Paine and to Jefferson (105.31–32 and 232.5–6) and especially to Jefferson's naval policy (146.30–147.6; 173.30–32; and 174.26–27).

56. *Ibid.,* p. 142.
57. *Literary Life of James Kirke Paulding,* pp. 40–41.

NY1860: New York, Putnam, 1860.   BAL 10369

As often happens when an author dies, Irving's death on November 28, 1859, "only served to increase the sale of his books."[58] The following April his publisher, George Putnam, who had profited handsomely from the revised edition of Irving's *Works* (ARE, 1848–1851, from which *Salmagundi* was excluded), brought out Evert A. Duyckinck's edition of *Salmagundi*. Duyckinck apparently never sought Irving's consent or advice in the project begun before Irving's death. In his Preface Duyckinck speculates, perhaps trying to justify the edition, "The book would probably have been included by Mr. Irving in the revised edition of his works, had it been wholly his own" (NY1860, p. vii). It is unlikely that Irving, who was working against time to complete the *Life of Washington*, had any knowledge of Duyckinck's plans for the edition, or that he would have agreed in 1860 to a revised edition of *Salmagundi*, a work that from the 1820's on he regarded as a trivial publication.[59]

Irving held Duyckinck's abilities as an editor in high regard. On January 22, 1856, shortly after publication of the *Cyclopaedia of American Literature*, Irving wrote Charles Scribner that it was "executed with culture, critical insight and amiable spirit."[60] Duyckinck did not always respect Irving's wishes, however; for example, although Irving asked that the paragraph on his brother Dr. Peter Irving be omitted from the bibliographical notice of Washington Irving that Duyckinck prepared for the *Cyclopaedia*, Duyckinck let it stand unchanged.

In the preface to the 1860 edition of *Salmagundi*, Duyckinck explained, "The text of this edition is that of the original work as it was first published by Longworth. In the subsequent reprints, several papers of interest were dropped, which are now restored" (NY1860, p. xiv). Notably, the 1860 edition retained the attacks on Fessenden in Nos. III and IV, the poem "To the Ladies" in No. V, and "The Stranger in Pennsylvania" in No. X. Duyckinck also noted, "A few verbal corrections have been made, following the Paris edition of Irving's works of

58. George E. Mize, "The Contributions of E. A. Duyckinck to the Cultural Development of Nineteenth Century America" (Ph.D diss., New York University, 1955), p. 102.

59. Entries in Duyckinck's Diary, now in the Manuscript Division of the New York Public Library, make frequent mention of Irving, especially of Duyckinck's visits to Sunnyside in the late 1850's, but never to the edition Duyckinck was preparing (NY1860). A typical entry is that for June 24, 1859: "Mr. Irving seemed more interested for the day in his gardners children than in any thing else."

60. Mize, "Contributions of E. A. Duyckinck," p. 224.

1834, which had more or less of the author's supervision" (NY1860, p. xiv), suggesting that he was either unacquainted with the Paris edition of 1824 (1F), or else had no ready access to a copy.[61]

EMENDATION OF THE TEXT

In establishing the necessary critical text, the Twayne edition, unlike previous editions of *Salmagundi*, takes into consideration the revisions in 1A (1807–1808) presumably made by all three authors, and those made by Irving for 2A (1814) and for 1F (1824). To determine the kind and extent of revisions in all significant editions, the copy-text (1A^1 or 1A^{1}a, if more than one variant state of the first subedition exists for the number under discussion) was sight read against the lateral texts (subeditions and variants states subsequent to 1A^{1}a); then against the vertical texts (1E, 2A, 3A, 1F, 2E, 3E, 4A, and NY1860).[62] Search for copy-text was complicated and difficult because *Salmagundi* was originally published as twenty individual numbers of a periodical series and no one collection or set of twenty numbers has been found to represent the same subedition and variant state for each number. A copy of *Salmagundi* originally owned by Evert Duyckinck now in the New York Public Library was found to be made up of the original subeditions for Nos. II–XX. For No. I a copy at the University of Texas was used. Together, these two copies served as copy-text, and all collations were made against them. Seven other copies of 1A

61. While it is not perfectly clear that Duyckinck means Baudry's 1834 edition of Irving's *Works*, he does specify "works"; furthermore, there is no record of another edition published in Paris in that year, either in the *Bibliographe de la France* or the *Catalogue General des Livres Imprimes de la Bibliotheque Nationale, Autheurs* (BAL, p. 24). Textual evidence suggests that Duyckinck may have used 2A as well as 1A and 2F to prepare his edition. When Duyckinck rejects a revision in 2F (which duplicates the text of 1F), he reverts to the subedition of 1A that 2A used as printer's copy for that number: for example, at 93.14 Duyckinck rejects the 1F/2F revision "have met not less." But instead of following the original version "have not met with less" (1A^1–1A^2), Duyckinck uses "have met with not less" the revision in later subeditions (1A^3–1A^5, 2A). Subedition 1A^3 was probably used as copy-text for No. III of 2A. A Xerox of a copy of *Salmagundi* from Duyckinck's library (copy D) was used as the original collation copy for Nos. II–XX of the present edition. There are handwritten notations in copy D which compare the text of 1A to the 1F/2F revisions.

62. Sight collation (as distinct from machine collation with the aid of the Hinman Collator) is required when two editions (in this case subeditions of 1A) are involved, since the editions represent different settings of type. Impressions of the same edition can be more accurately collated by machine.

were sight read or machine collated against the copy-text, and some twenty-five copies were checked for substantives and accidentals.[63] Two copies of 2A and one of 1F were collated against 1A^1; the re-

63. The Duyckinck copy (New York Public Library, Rare Book Room), provided printer's copy for Nos. II–XX. Once owned by Evert A. Duyckinck, D contains interesting notations comparing it to the revisions Irving made for 1F. An example of a two-volume issue with title pages dated 1808, D contains early subeditions of the numbers; it collates as follows:

No. I (*second edition*) ⟨3⟩–20, ⟨A^9⟩ signed ⟨A, A$_1$⟩ A$_{2-4}$ ⟨A$_{5-8}$⟩;
No. II ⟨21⟩–38, ⟨A^9⟩ signed ⟨A,A$_1$⟩ A$_{2-4}$ ⟨A$_{5-8}$⟩;
No. III ⟨39⟩–56, ⟨A^9⟩ signed ⟨A, A$_1$⟩ A$_{2-4}$ ⟨A$_{5-8}$⟩;
No. IV ⟨57⟩–82, ⟨A^9⟩ A^4 signed ⟨A, A$_1$, A$_2$⟩ ⟨A$_3$ signed A$_4$⟩ A$_4$ ⟨A$_{5-8}$⟩ A ⟨A$_{2-4}$⟩;
No. V ⟨83⟩–104, ⟨A^9⟩ B^2 signed ⟨A, A$_1$⟩ A$_{2-4}$ ⟨A$_{5-8}$⟩ B ⟨B$_2$⟩;
No. VI ⟨105⟩–124 ⟨A^9⟩ B^1 signed ⟨A, A$_1$⟩ A$_{2-4}$ ⟨A$_{5-8}$⟩ B;
No. VII ⟨125⟩–142, ⟨A^9⟩ signed ⟨A, A$_1$⟩ A$_{2-4}$ ⟨A$_{5-8}$⟩;
No. VIII ⟨i–ii⟩ ⟨143⟩162, frontispiece caption ⟨A^{11}⟩ signed ⟨+1 fs⟩ ⟨A, A$_1$⟩ A$_{2-4}$ ⟨A$_{5-9}$⟩
No. IX ⟨163⟩–188, ⟨A^9⟩ B^4 signed ⟨A, A$_1$⟩ A$_{2-4}$ ⟨A$_{5-8}$⟩ B ⟨B$_{2-4}$⟩;
No. X ⟨189⟩–206, ⟨A^9⟩ signed ⟨A, A$_1$⟩ A$_{2-4}$ ⟨A$_{5-8}$⟩;
No. XI ⟨207⟩–228, ⟨A^9⟩ ⟨B^2⟩ signed ⟨A, A$_1$⟩ A$_2$, A$_8$, A$_4$ ⟨A$_{5-8}$⟩ ⟨B$_{1-2}$⟩;
No. XII ⟨229⟩–254, ⟨A^9⟩ B^4 signed ⟨A, A$_1$⟩ A$_{2-4}$ ⟨A$_{5-8}$⟩ B ⟨B$_{2-4}$⟩;
No. XIII ⟨255⟩–280, ⟨A^9⟩ B^4 signed ⟨A, A$_1$⟩ A$_{2-4}$ ⟨A$_{5-8}$⟩ B ⟨B$_{2-4}$⟩;
No. XIV ⟨281⟩–306, ⟨A^9⟩ B^4 signed ⟨A, A$_1$⟩ A$_{2-4}$ ⟨A$_{5-8}$⟩ B ⟨B$_{2-4}$⟩;
No. XV ⟨307⟩–324, ⟨A^9⟩ signed ⟨A, A$_1$⟩ A$_{2-4}$ ⟨A$_{5-8}$⟩;
No. XVI ⟨325⟩–342, ⟨A^9⟩ signed ⟨A, A$_1$⟩ A$_{2-4}$ ⟨A$_{5-8}$⟩;
No. XVII ⟨343⟩–360, ⟨A^9⟩ signed ⟨A, A$_1$⟩ A$_{2-4}$ ⟨A$_{5-8}$⟩;
No. XVIII ⟨361⟩–378, ⟨A^9⟩ signed ⟨A, A$_1$⟩ A$_{2-4}$ ⟨A$_{5-8}$⟩;
No. XIX ⟨379⟩–404, ⟨A^9⟩ B^4 signed ⟨A, A$_1$⟩ A$_{2-4}$ ⟨A$_{5-8}$⟩ B ⟨B$_{2-4}$⟩;
No. XX ⟨405⟩–430, ⟨A^9⟩ B^4 signed ⟨A, A$_1$⟩ A$_{2-4}$ ⟨A$_{5-8}$⟩ B ⟨B$_{2-4}$⟩;

Longworth's nine-leaf gatherings are further testimony to his eccentricity. For more detailed bibliographical description of 1A, see BAL, V, No. 10097 and the Bibliography, the final volume of the Twayne edition, which will treat (as BAL does not) the subeditions of 1A. The present descriptions serve only to identify the copies used and make no attempt to record such varying elements as the printer's imprint, the short-title, the wrappers, the copyright notice, the table of contents, or the index to the two-volume issue; these will be thoroughly described in the Bibliography.

A University of Texas at Austin copy (Humanities Research Center no. 60–1601), provided printer's copy for No. I. The numbers are separately bound in cream paper, not original wrappers, edges trimmed and gilt, boxed in red Morocco, with general title pages dated 1808. The Texas copy collates the same as the D copy, except: No. I ⟨3⟩–20, ⟨A^9⟩ signed ⟨A, A$_1$⟩ A$_{2-4}$ ⟨A$_{5-8}$⟩; No. VIII ⟨i–ii⟩ ⟨143⟩–162, frontispiece has no caption, ⟨A$_{11}$⟩ signed ⟨+1 fs⟩ ⟨A, A$_1$⟩ A$_{2-4}$ ⟨A$_{5-9}$⟩.

Other copies sight read or machine collated were one from the Smithsonian Institute (no call number) and three from the University of Texas at Austin (Humanities Research Center: Jr86/1808se; no call number; no call number).

The remainder of the 1A copies were spot checked for variants. These copies were from Harvard University (Houghton Library: AF 1968.602*; AL 1968.600*),

maining vertical texts (1E, 3A, 2E, 3E, 4A, NY1860) were sight read for substantives.[64]

The task of establishing a critical text was complicated by (1) the absence of manuscript or prepublication states, (2) the variety and degree of revisions in 1A, (3) *Salmagundi's* triple authorship, and (4) the unknown extent to which Longworth influenced the text of 1A. In the first place, *Salmagundi* was truly a collaborative venture. Though Washington Irving has been identified as the author of twenty-six of the pieces, Paulding twenty-one, and William Irving twelve, it has not been possible to identify positively the author for each piece (see Assignments of Authorship, pp. 327–36). There was by all accounts a close collaboration between Irving and Paulding on most of the prose pieces. In the Preface to Volume I of his *Works* (4A) Paulding states: "The thoughts of the authors were so mingled together in these essays, and they were so literally joint productions, that it would be difficult, as well as useless, at this distance of time, to assign to each his exact share" (*Works*, I, 11). And it may well be impossible to determine which of the authors made the revisions in each feature.[65] To complicate matters, it is clear from Paulding's remarks to Irving (previously quoted, p. 384) that Longworth had some effect on the text and even contributed his own whimsy to it.[66] Even if some of the revisions in 1A

Yale University (Beinicke Library: Za/Ir8/807/copy 1; Za Ir8/807b/v. 1; Za/Ir8/807bb/v. 1; Za/Ir8/807bb/v. 1, 2; Za/Ir8/807c/v. 1, 2.) University of North Carolina (Rare Book Room: T814/172s/V.1, 2; T814/172s/1808); New York Public Library (Arents: labeled Ar1, Ar2, Ar3); Ralph Aderman Collection (labeled Ad); Lily Library: PS 2064/.A1/1807a; PS 2064/.A1/1807b v.1; PS 2064/.A1/1807–1808; PS 2064/.A1/1808.

64. Copies for these vertical collations are identified by library name and call number or name of the present owner, together with whatever identifying marks can be noted: 1E (Rare Book Room, New York Public Library); 2A (New-York Historical Society); 2A (Rare Book Room, New York Public Library); 3A (University of Texas, call no. Ir8s; blind stamped on upper fly "CHAS. MILLER'S BOOK HIVE"); 1F (Alderman Library, University of Virginia); 2E (University of Texas, call no. Ir8s1); 3E (University of Texas, call no. Ir8s2 with bookplate of William Leigh; and another copy from the University of Texas, call no. Bartfield, bookplates of Edward Chatterton-Orpen and Mabel Hill).

65. William L. Hedges describes the collaboration between Paulding and Irving thus: "what one wrote initially the other usually revised" (*Washington Irving*, [Baltimore, 1965], p. 48).

66. Longworth "was debauching it with blunders, and vile pictures, &c., that were a disgrace to any decent publication" (*Literary Life of James Kirke Paulding*, p. 39). Even the typesetters made free with the text of *Salmagundi*: the manuscript of No. II "had characterized their satirical pleasantries as 'good-natured raillery,' which last word, by an expressive blunder, the printer converted into

were made by Longworth, it must be assumed that the three authors agreed to them at the time, whatever their subsequent feelings, and raised no effective objections. Revisions in 1A—since presumably they represent the concerted desire of the three original authors, the two Irvings and Paulding—should be given greater consideration than the revisions in 2A and 1F—the work of Irving alone. In revising 2A (again, Longworth's role is not known), and 1F, Irving altered and sometimes rewrote not only his own pieces, but also those of William, his brother, and of Paulding. Irving's attitude proved a great obstacle to achieving a critical text. As early as 1819, in a letter to Brevoort (quoted earlier, p. 000), Irving expressed regret at having collaborated on *Salmagundi*. The revisions he undertook for 2A and 1F were made reluctantly; and those he made in 1F, especially, represent a bowdlerizing which substantially reduces the vigor and charm of the original. Since *Salmagundi* was not Irving's alone, it could perhaps be argued that only those changes in 2A and 1F which Irving made on his own works should be taken into account. Unlike Irving, Paulding was fond of *Salmagundi* and remained active in trying to keep the work alive. It could also be argued that when Paulding's revisions for 4A (1835) affect his work, they should be considered.

In view of these complications, the Twayne edition has made few changes in the copy-text (1A^1), incorporating only those revisions found in 1A, 2A, and 1F, which correct errors or otherwise clarify the text without altering its spirit. In this way, the original whimsy of the work is maintained—a product of collaboration among the three authors—and Irving's delightful early satirical style is unchanged.

TREATMENT OF SUBSTANTIVES

The unexpected popularity of *Salmagundi*, at a time when periodical magazines in America regularly failed to build a sustained readership, created a demand for more copies of the first numbers than were printed. To supply the additional copies, the numbers had to be reset. Many of the pieces have the air of having been dashed off hastily (as could be expected in a magazine), and the necessity for resetting the type gave the authors an opportunity to revise their work during 1807 and 1808. As the numbers progressed toward twenty and the

---

'villainy.' Whether the blunder was felicitous or not, there was something waggishly descriptive in the epithet which hit the humor of Washington, and he resolved at once to retain it. The adopted misprint, 'good-natured villainy,' has stood from that day to this to characterize the merry mischief of their labors" (PMI, I, 177).

printer began to guess more accurately how many copies to print of a number, the subeditions per number decline sharply (see Table 2, Subeditions and Variant states of 1A, p. 390–91) and so do the number of revisions. The Twayne edition has resisted the tendency to accept revisions which "improve" the style of the copy-text. When the authors' substantive revisions correct or clarify the text, they have been accepted, but when they fail to correct, or when they censor, soften, or otherwise change *Salmagundi*'s tone, they have been rejected. The same principle has been applied to new readings and revisions in 2A (1814) and 1F (1824), only more strictly.

It was tempting to adopt revisions made in 1A when the text of 2A and 1F were in agreement with them, on the grounds that if 2A and 1F kept the 1A revision, it must represent Irving's wishes. Conversely, it was tempting to question and reject emendations in 1A not backed by the authority of 2A or 1F. However, the agreement of 2A and 1F with a particular 1A reading does not necessarily indicate that Irving favored that reading. The copy-text for 2A was probably chosen arbitrarily and represents a random assemblage of subeditions and variant states of 1A for each number. It seems highly unlikely that Irving (or Longworth) consciously chose one subedition over another for each of the twenty numbers: No. I represents subedition $1A^5$, No. II is $1A^1b–c$, No. III is subedition $1A^3$. Irving is known to have been careless about details when reading proof or preparing printer's copy. Since most of the revisions in 2A are small ones (the exception being those in Nos. X and XII, discussed below), it seems doubtful that Irving would have remembered each of them, especially in prose pieces and poems written by Paulding or William Irving. After all, some six years had elapsed since the original revisions were made. In turn, 1F, prepared sixteen years after 1A, used 2A as its copy-text rather than a copy of 1A. 1F follows 2A readings found in the subeditions and variant states for each number that 2A was based on. Often errors in a particular subedition of 1A were not corrected in 2A or 1F, probably a testimony to Irving's reliance on his printer's copy. For example, at 96.31, 2A and 1F retain the incorrect "conscious struck" ($1A^2–1A^5$) instead of the original and correct "conscience struck" ($1A^1$) because 2A used $1A^3$ as copy-text for No. III. At 196.14, 2A repeats the original but incorrect "even" ($1A^1–1A^2$) instead of the corrected "ever" ($1A^3$) because 2A used $1A^1$ as copy-text for No. XI; 1F however corrects the error. To repeat the point, the agreement of 2A and 1F with a particular 1A reading does not necessarily indicate Irving approved the reading.

Because of the character of the revisions, it is difficult to arrive at the exact number of substantive changes made in the 1A, 2A, and 1F texts combined. Not only were single words and phrases altered, but several pieces were deleted, two were completely rewritten, and often the same passage was revised in more than one of the three editions.[67] Discounting the features deleted and those that were completely revised, there were approximately 698 substantive revisions. Of these, some 219 occurred in 1A, 75 in 2A, and 404 in 1F. Only 29 of the 698 were adopted in the Twayne edition. Of these, only one was introduced by 2A, three by 1F, and the remainder by 1A. No emendations were made silently.

Most substantive differences among the subeditions and variant states of 1A range from corrections of printer's errors or of word choice, to slight alterations in wording, to substitutions of more genteel language. Many of the small alterations in wording seem carelessly done and either fail to make a great deal of difference to the text or else destroy a stylistic felicity. In a few instances new material is added and several pieces are reworked. Among the corrections made in 1A and accepted in the Twayne edition is the substitution at 73.13 of "authors" ($1A^3$, $1A^5$–$1A^7$) for "editors" ($1A^1$–$1A^2$, $1A^4$) in the phrase "honor of his editors," since the subject is the three authors. Another correction accepted is "loses" ($1A^2$–$1A^3$) in place of "looses" ($1A^1$) at 183.28. Others are recorded in the List of Emendations.

Examples of the small alterations in style which seem to have little effect on the text and which were rejected, are the deletion of "its" ($1A^2$–$1A^7$) from "on its delivery" ($1A^1$) at 69.3, and the change of wording from "by being experienced" ($1A^1$–$1A^4$) to "from his long experience" ($1A^5$–$1A^7$) at 70.43. A good example of a revision which seems ill-considered is the change from "the shoe" ($1A^1$–$1A^2$) to "your shoe" ($1A^3$–$1A^5$) at 99.37, which destroys the parallelism the original had with "the head." Other instances of these kinds of changes can be found in the List of Rejected Substantives. Alterations were often complicated, going through several versions. For example, at 68.28–29 the long phrase in $1A^1$ "exchange of civilities; he shall furnish us with notices of epic poems" was shortened in subedition $1A^2$ to "exchange of epic poems."

67. A further complication in arriving at the number of substantives arises from the difficulty to distinguish always between substantive variants involving changes of words that affect meaning, and accidental variants involving spelling, punctuation, and the like. One category of changes difficult to categorize are apostrophes used to form the possessive. A change in the possessive from plural to singular, like that at 106.30, when "sturgeons'" ($1A^1$–$1A^2$) becomes "sturgeon's" ($1A^3$–$1A^4$) may have substantive effect, but may have been the result of a compositor's error and not a deliberate substantive revision. Hence the List of Emendations includes both accidentals and substantives and the List of Rejected Substantives includes certain accidentals which have substantive effect on the text.

This may represent a compositor's error rather than an authorial change, because $1A^3$–$1A^5$ restored the original reading; $1A^6$–$1A^7$ continued the original reading, but altered the spelling of "epic" to the perhaps consciously archaic "epick" in order to conform to a change in house style which had taken place throughout *Salmagundi* by the time $1A^6$ was set in type.

An interesting sequence of revisions occurs in No. XVI. In 1A the text read: "This was too much for the patience of old Crusty; he longed his fork into the partridge, whipt it into his dish" (258.35–37). 1E (Lambert's edition of 1811) changed "longed," a variant of "lunged" to "lunged"; then in 2A (1814) Irving altered "longed" to "lodged" which sacrifices the notion of movement forward, but does express the fact that the fork was put into the partridge. Both 1E and 2A change only one letter of the original "longed." In 1F (1824) Irving decided to express the notion of movement, rejecting the original word, and changed "long" to "thrust." Here the decision was to respect the copy-text by rejecting both revisions.

The revisions of "The Breaking up of the Ice in the North-river" by James Kirke Paulding and "The Stranger in Pennsylvania" by Washington Irving, both in No. X, are so extensive that it seems they must have been authorial. Also surely the author's work were the revisions, not quite so thorough, of William Irving's poem, "From the Mill of Pindar Cockloft, Esq." in No. XII. It could be argued that since these revisions surely represent the wish of the authors, the Twayne edition should present the revised versions of the pieces in question. However, the decision is not easy to make. Washington Irving should have remembered the changes; but both 2A and 1F, editions prepared by Irving, publish the unrevised versions ($1A^1$) of "The Breaking up of the Ice in the North-river" and "From the Mill of Pindar Cockloft, Esq.," instead of the revised versions ($1A^2$–$1A^3$). And Irving omitted altogether his "The Stranger in Pennsylvania" from 2A and 1F. Apparently he had been unhappy with his sketch from the very beginning. In a letter to Paulding dated June 22, 1807, he complains that Paulding has concluded Volume I of *Salmagundi* at No. X, and alludes to "The Stranger in Pennsylvania": "At least it is a number which is not highly satisfactory to me, perhaps because I wrote the greatest part of it myself, and that at hurried moments. I had intended concluding it in style, and commencing Vol. 2 with some eclat."[68] The revisions in the "second edition, revised and corrected" of No. X must have been an attempt to conclude the number with "some eclat," but the number was still not satisfactory to Irving. In preparing 4A (1835), Paulding, who

68. PMI, I, 194.

also should have remembered the revisions, followed 1F and published the 1A¹ versions of his "Breaking up of the Ice" and of William Irving's "From the Mill" (including, however, the small changes Irving made in 1F); respecting Irving's wishes, Paulding did not republish the "Stranger in Pennsylvania." There is the possibility that the choice of the unrevised versions of "The Breaking up of the Ice" and "From the Mill" for 2A was not so much deliberate choice as it was done out of convenience. Perhaps the set of *Salmagundi* used as copy-text for 2A happened to contain the unrevised versions, and Irving made no attempt to find the revised ones. Furthermore, Paulding, who told Irving he would use 1F for his edition (4A), may have merely followed suit rather than making an independent editorial decision. Whatever the case, however, it seemed the wisest course to reprint the original versions of the three pieces. The revised versions are of course transcribed in full in the List of Rejected Substantives (pp. 445-82).

Out of the approximately seventy-five new readings introduced by 2A, only one, a correction of error, was incorporated into the Twayne edition. It occurs at 117.4. The copy-text *"centinal"* (1A¹–1A²), an incorrect spelling, was changed to *"sentinel"* in 1A³–1A⁴, and to *"centinel"* in 2A. The 2A revision was chosen over 1A³–1A⁴ because "sentinel," though a valid correction of the original misspelling, is not as close to the copy-text as is the 2A version. Irving's revisions in 2A which try to make *Salmagundi* genteel and which delete sections Irving now found embarrassing or not to his taste, have been rejected. For example, he took out "or nozzle" at 83.15–16, and "who Evergreen whimsically dubs my *Tender*" at 244.21, phrases he considered indelicate; and he deleted unflattering references to Thomas Green Fessenden (97.30–98.28; 107.5–116.23), and Thomas Jefferson (104.16–18), and passages critical of the Park Theatre (137.9–12), of the Corporation of Bowling Green (209.9–14) and of the Corporation of Trinity Church (209.22–27). Also rejected by the Twayne edition are his deletions, probably made in response to the criticisms voiced in the *Monthly Review*,[69] of classical references (96.25–29; 96.19; 215.11–16; 299.39–300.3; and 300.39–42). While his use of the unrevised version of "From the Mill of Pindar Cockloft, Esq." was respected, his revisions of William Irving's poem at 213.33, 214.22–23, and 215.11–16 were rejected as unnecessary. Although he removed "The Stranger in Pennsylvania" which he wrote, from No. X, probably because he was never satisfied with it, it has been retained because it is an integral part of the copy-text.

Three instances of the 404 alterations introduced in 1F are adopted

69. 65 (May–August, 1811) pp. 418–24.

by the Twayne edition, and like 2A, these are confined to corrections. Perhaps the most difficult kind of decision whether or not to emend occurs in that category of revisions which border on being either corrections or clarifications. The one at 205.10 is a good example: the copy-text "talked to" (1A) is revised to "talked of" (1F). The sense of the passage seems to be that Straddle is talking "of his horses," while the people are talking "of Straddle," until it is not known whether Straddle or his horses are the more admired. The emendation was accepted because if Straddle was talking "to his horses," the parallel between himself and his horses would not be clear. Also, Straddle, as a man of fashion, would not confine himself to talking "to his horses," but would talk "of" them in order to bolster his own reputation.

Irving made significant changes in the text of 1F at several points. He rewrote part of William Irving's Mustapha Letter in No. XIV. Certain of Irving's revisions improve the letter's satirical thrust. For instance, at 235.24 he substituted "in this nation of quick tongues" for the less pointed "here." While it was often difficult to resist incorporating some of the changes, they represent a too extensive revision of the copy-text and so were rejected. The remainder of Irving's 1F revisions rejected in the Twayne edition consist of words, sentence elements, sentences, paragraphs, and whole sections which he deleted from the text and which had the effect of making the style of *Salmagundi* less colloquial and more genteel, less vivid, and, especially in the case of the Mustapha letters, less appropriate. He took out "with his feet on the massy andirons, and smoke his cigarr" at 134.33, and "I should have said Jeremy Cockloft *the younger*, as he so styles himself by way of distinguishing him from IL SIGNORE JEREMO COCKLOFTICO, a gouty old gentleman who flourished about the time that Pliny the elder was smoked to death with the fire and brimstone of Vesuvius, and whose travels, if he ever wrote any, are now lost forever to the world" (101.21–26). He also deleted references to Linkum Fidelius, like the one at 104.13 "according to Linkum Fidelius." And at 82.9 and elsewhere throughout the text, he transformed the two cockneys, Snivers and 'Sbidlikens, into one, 'Sbidlikens. Irving also took out William Irving's poem "To the Ladies" (126.38–129.28). The copy-text has been respected in all these and similar instances; they are recorded in the List of Rejected Substantives.

TREATMENT OF ACCIDENTALS

In its punctuation and spelling, as in all else, *Salmagundi* is inconsistent and eccentric. Although there were three (and counting Longworth and his printer, five) sources for the text's accidentals, it is still possible to generalize about its punctuation and spelling. Happily, most of these generalizations apply to Irving's preferences as established in his later works. *Salmagundi's* long and clause-laden sentences are punctuated according to a rhetorical feeling or intuition, with punctuation chosen and positioned to signal pauses or create emphasis. Some mark of punctuation—usually a semicolon, a comma, or a dash—appears after almost every phrase. A good example of *Salmagundi's* style is this rambling sentence in No. I from Will Wizard's "Theatrics" probably written by Irving: "Mrs. Villiers, however, is not by any means large enough for the character; lady Macbeth having been, in our opinion, a woman of extraordinary size, and of the race of the giants, notwithstanding what she says of her 'little hand,' which being said in her sleep, passes for nothing" (74.16–20). As this sentence illustrates, *Salmagundi* conforms to the late eighteenth- and early nineteenth-century preference for close or heavy punctuation. The semicolon after "character" signals a longer pause than would a comma and divides the sentence into two parts, one with Mrs. Villiers as the center, the other with Lady Macbeth. The comma after "size" intervenes between two parallel prepositional phrases and is placed there to emphasize "and of the race of the giants." The following summarizes *Salmagundi's* (often eccentric) punctuation and spelling: (1) Commas are used, but not always, to set off introductory clauses, or phrases that contain a verb form. (2) Often, but not in every case, commas appear after short introductory clauses and phrases and before adverbial phrases and clauses which follow the principal clause, where modern usage finds them unnecessary. (3) Commas usually, but not always, set off nonrestrictive modifiers, whether phrases or clauses. (4) Commas are also used, but not always, to separate restrictive modifiers whether phrases or clauses. (5) Commas frequently, but not always, separate elements of a compound structure—compound subjects, predicates, prepositional phrases—again a custom found unnecessary in modern usage. (6) Commas often separate subject and predicate. (7) Commas usually appear before "that" introducing a relative clause—a habitual practice of Irving's. (8) Commas often set off introductory infinitive phrases—another example of Irving's usages. (9) Commas sometimes do and sometimes do not appear before the conjunction in an *a, b,* and *c* series. (10) While commas are often used to set off modifying constructions, contrasting phrases, or for emphasis, in many instances the first or last of intended pairs of commas is omitted. (11) Commas often appear after coordinating conjunctions such as "but," and usually before some element of the sentence that appears after "but." (12) Semicolons are often used where modern usage finds commas sufficient, and occasionally a comma appears where a semicolon seems more appropriate. (13) Commas are not consistently employed in connection with parenthetical expressions. (14) Commas are used inconsistently to set off direct as well as indirect discourse. (15) Quotation marks are carelessly employed: often the first or last of an intended pair is omitted, or there may be no quotation marks at all when they are called for. (16) Dashes are frequently used to set off a construction, for emphasis or to create a rhythm. The dash was one of Irving's favorite marks of punctuation, especially in his early writings. (17) Hyphens are inconsistently used, and often their appearance and disappearance can be attributed to faulty printing, common in *Salmagundi*. (18) Spelling is eccentric and inconsistent; the text is laced with conscious archaisms and puns.

Those accidentals not attributable to individual decision on the part of Longworth or the authors come under the category of house style. Thorough collation of the various settings or subeditions of 1A reveals that 1A was composed in two house styles. The first house style normally follows American spelling and uses uppercase letters to begin proper nouns; the second, more obviously eccentric and perhaps utilizing conscious archaisms, conforms more nearly to British spelling; it also presents certain kinds of proper nouns (inhabitants of cities or countries and titles of address) in lowercase. In Table 4, 1A House Styles, common examples of each kind of house-style change are given.[70]

TABLE 4
1A House Styles

Usage Shift	First	Second
SPELLING		
-ic to -ick	public	publick
-or to -our	humor	humour
-os to -oes	pianos	pianoes
-ice to -ise	practice	practise
-ize to -ise (n.)	surprize	surprise
-ize to -ise (v.)	to sympathize	to sympathise
-ze to -se	phraze	phrase

70. The shift in the house styles is apparent in more than accidentals: a running head specifying the number appears on odd-numbered pages of most subeditions after the first; the style of the dateline, the quotation on the first page of each number, and the printer's imprint, also changed (see Table 3, Collation Table for No. II, pp. 394-95).

-edge to -ege	alledge	allege
-tient to -cient	antient	ancient
-tion to -sion	pretention	pretension
-eable to -able	adviseable	advisable
-cede to -sede	supercede	supersede
en- to in-	entirely	intirely

CAPITALIZATION

geographic place names and adjectives derived from them; religious denominations: cap to lc	Philadelphian	philadelphian
titles of address: cap to lc	Mr.	mr.
cap and small caps to small caps	Oldmixon	oldmixon
second word in a compound place name: cap to lc	Spank-Town	Spank-town

The first subeditions of Nos. I through XII follow the first house style; the subsequent subeditions for Nos. I through XII, and all subeditions for Nos. XIII through XX follow the second house style. It seems that Longworth or the three authors made a continuing effort to arrive at a consistent house style and that ultimately such a style was adopted. The two house styles were not consistently adhered to, however; nor was there a distinct point at which the shift was made from the first to the second house style. Rather, as Table 5 illustrates, the changeover was gradual and never complete. A subedition sometimes reverts to an earlier style spelling, and changes in spelling sometimes occur early in one instance and later in another. In the table, page and line citations refer to T. Lack of entry for an item indicates that the style did not change for that subedition.

TABLE 5
House Style Shift for No. IV

SPELLING		$1A^1$	$1A^2$–$1A^3$	$1A^4$
-ic to -ick	102.14	mechanics		mechanicks
-or to -our	105.27	favorite	favourite	
	106.14	inferior		inferiour

en- to in-	111.19	entirely	intirely	
-ice to -ise	103.20	practice		practise
-ize to -ise	107.26	surprized		surprised

CAPITALIZATION

proper names:

personal	101.18	Cockloft Family	Cockloft family	
institutions	104.10	Legislature	legislature	

geographic:

adjectives	102.7	Lacedemonian	lacedemonian	
names	103.22	Philadelphians		philadelphians
titles:	105.26	Sir Christopher Hatton		sir Christopher Hatton
	108.27	Mr. Hunt	mr. Hunt	
hyphenated	104.11	Bridge-Town	Bridge-town	
names:	103.27	Rattle-snake Hill		Rattle-Snake Hill
caps:	101.20	Mr. JEREMY COCKLOFT		MR. JEREMY COCKLOFT
	101.21	Mr. CHRISTOPHER COCKLOFT		mr. Christopher Cockloft
	107.7	WILL WIZARD	Will Wizard	

There are one hundred subeditions and variant states of 1A discovered to date, with approximately 2,460 accidental revisions. The first thirteen numbers, which were reset at least once, provide the bulk of these totals. Each time there was a new setting or subedition of a number, its accidentals (and to a lesser extent its substantives) were revised. After comparing approximately twenty-five copies of *Salmagundi*, it was discovered that Nos. I through XII average from ten to fifteen accidental revisions per page of 1A text.[71] Many of the revisions seem

71. To return to the revisions in No. II; in its eighteen pages of text there were approximately 150 accidental differences in its five subeditions and four variant states. That averages eight accidentals per page. Forty-three of these were house-style changes; fifteen commas were added where there had previously been no comma; forty commas were subtracted; fifteen commas became semicolons; four semicolons became commas; eight dashes were omitted, often when there was an accompanying mark of punctuation; and one dash was added; one colon became a semicolon; two semicolons became colons; ten hyphens were added; and two subtracted; two quotation marks were added; and nine nonhouse-style spellings were changed.

The figures given here and in other accidental or substantive counts derived from collations (whether in precise or approximate figures) are intended only as suggestive summaries of information. Since certain variants can be classified and counted in more than one way, it is possible to work out other relationships based

to have been deliberate attempts to correct or improve the text, but a substantial number are either unnecessary or redundant, and in a few instances confusing. There is much worn type, and frequently the type seems carelessly set. Many of the punctuation changes appear arbitrary, as if when the text was reset, it was pointed according to the typesetter's whim. Taken as a whole, the accidental revisions have an uncanny way of canceling each other out, as though the changes made actually had little effect on the text. The quality and kind of revisions vary widely from number to number and even from feature to feature. Textual content occasionally determines which kinds of changes were the most frequent. For example, No. IV, badly type set, contains the travel piece by Jeremy Cockloft, "The Stranger in New-Jersey," which makes many references to inhabitants, to specific persons, and to titles of learned texts. As could be expected its most common accidental change is capitalization, in this case a change attributable not to deliberate revision but to a shift in the publisher's house style.

It has been generally assumed that the eccentric house styles and punctuation of 1A were imposed on the text by the publisher, David Longworth. Although both house styles exhibit orthographic peculiarities, probably Longworth instigated the second house style, since it follows his known preferences in spelling and capitalization more closely than does the first house style. An Anglophile (his publishing house was modeled after one in London), Longworth would no doubt have preferred the -*our* spelling of the second house style over the American -*or* of the first, a spelling rather recently endorsed by Noah Webster in his innovative *Compendious Dictionary of the English Language* (1806). The manuscript fragment in Irving's hand, though brief and the work of only one of three authors, follows the spelling form -*ic*, found in the first house style. When the manuscript for No. XIV was prepared for print, the second house style was in effect, and Irving's "romantic" was changed to "romantick" at 237.6. Irving did

---

on lists of emendations and of variants. In addition, it is not always possible to strictly decide whether a misprint or faulty impression is owing to broken, damaged, or dropped type, or to faulty inking, or whether an irregularity represents an error of commission (authorial or compositional), or ordinary type wear and damage.

Compounding the difficulty in arriving at precise figures for the revisions is the fact that the typesetters "seem to have operated with a fair degree of editorial license" (PBSA, p. 6); also, "the work is so very badly printed that punctuation is often absent from the printed pages. This factor must be considered in checking transcriptions" (BAL, No. 10097, p. 3).

not begin consistently to Anglicize his spelling style until he went to England in 1815. As the following quotation from Duyckinck indicates, Longworth preferred lowercase in place of capitals for certain proper nouns: "Oddly enough, the man who was so grandiloquent himself would not allow New York itself appropriate capitals. It must dwindle in lower-case" (NY1860, p. xi).

The remaining nonhouse style accidentals, which involve punctuation and spelling, are difficult to assess. Did Longworth, his printer, or the authors make the many accidental revisions in the subeditions and variant states of 1A? If there were only accidental revisions, but no substantives, it would be easier to assign all responsibility to Longworth or his printer. If the authors were responsible, were they equally responsible? Irving is known for his exasperating carelessness about accidentals; he normally left their regularization up to his editors. (Whether or not the accidental revisions in 1A, which vary in effectiveness from feature to feature, will provide a source of additional information about the individual authorship of the prose pieces and poems is at present open to investigation.) Even though the accidental revisions must be assumed to have authorial sanction, the source of the revisions cannot now be determined.

For these reasons it seemed best to respect the accidentals in the copy-text (1A^1). Out of the approximately 2,460 accidental revisions occurring in the one hundred subeditions and variant states of 1A, only a very small number, 101, were adopted in the text of the Twayne edition. Only those revisions in 1A which correct an error or make readable an otherwise confused sentence have been adopted. No attempt was made to make the spelling, punctuation, or styling regular or consistent. Not only would that involve too large a number of emendations—using not only 1A revisions but requiring many editorial emendations in order to regularize the text—but it would presume the authors wished their whimsical effort to be consistent. House styles were left as they appear in the copy-text (1A^1): Nos. I through XII remain in the first house style, and Nos. XIII through XX in the then prevailing second house style. None of the punctuation or house styling from 2A and 1F was adopted. Not only do these accidentals represent an attempt to regularize and make consistent the original text, but they also represent the wishes of only one of the three authors. In addition, it is doubtful that Irving even concerned himself with 2A and 1F accidentals.

There are two reasons for emending the copy-text: one is to correct errors, the other is to clarify confused passages. The correction of errors represents the largest group of emendations made in the Twayne edition. The corrections usually involve (1) errors in spelling, (2) omission or misplacement of quotation marks around direct quotations, (3) omission of one of a pair of quotation marks, (4) omission of one of a pair of commas, (5) correction of broken or damaged type. Most of this class of emendations were taken out of revisions appearing in the subeditions and variant states of 1A. But a few, fourteen out of the 101 accidental emendations, had to be made by the editor. These are identified by a "T." It is difficult, perhaps impossible, to determine whether the errors in 1A were compositorial or whether the manuscript copy the printer was using was faulty or unclear. For the resettings, the compositor for 1A used previous subeditions of the number as a guide, for the most part hewing to the same end-of-the-line text distribution on the page. Typographical errors occur so frequently that it can only be concluded that the compositor was careless and/or in an incredible hurry. While many errors in the copy-text are corrected by revisions in subsequent settings and variant states, new errors are also introduced, surely the result of careless printer's work.

Emending for clarity of text is the second rationale for emendations in the Twayne edition. One example of such a change introduced in the text is the following from No. I: the copy-text reads, "He likewise remembers the time when ladies paid tea-visits, at three in the afternoon and returned before dark, to see that the house was shut up and the servants on duty" (71.13–16). The emendation removes the comma after "tea-visits" and adds one after "afternoon." Sometimes editorial emendations were necessary when the adopted revision in a later subedition of 1A was only partially acceptable. For instance, at 203.4 the word "satisfaction" appears incorrectly as "satisfac-/faction" in 1A^1. The typographical error is corrected in 1A^2–1A^3 to "satisfac-/tion", but a comma is introduced after the corrected word. Since the comma is an unnecessary addition to the copy-text, an editorial emendation was unavoidable, and the entry in the List of Emendations reads:

satisfaction] T; satisfac-/faction 1A^1; satisfac-/tion, 1A^2–1A^3

It should be recalled that out of the approximately 2,460 accidental revisions in the subeditions and variant states of 1A, only a very small number, some 101 were accepted. The revisions in the following typical sentence from *Salmagundi* involves commas, semicolons, hyphens, and an indiosyncratic spelling. These revisions are representative of the kinds of revisions rejected in the Twayne edition. The sentence reads: "He can tell a crotchet at first sight, and like a true englishman, is delighted with the plumb-pudding rotundity of a semi-breve; and, in short, boasts of having incontinently climbed up Paff's musical tree, which hangs every day upon the poplar, from the fundamental-concord, to the fundamental major discord, and so on from branch to branch, until he reaches the very top, where he sung 'Rule Britannia,' clapped his wings, and then—came down again" (82.11–17). The semicolon after "semi-breve," which seems gratuitous to the modern eye, is here noted because of its use to indicate a longer pause than a comma, typical of *Salmagundi*. There are five revisions in the eight subeditions and variant states of No. II which affect this sentence. (1) A second semicolon was added after "top" in 1A⁵, probably to divide the sentence into three parts; this was rejected as unnecessary, and the comma retained. (2) A comma was added after the first "and" in 1A⁴–1A⁵ to set off "like a true englishman"; this revision was also unnecessary. (3) The spelling of "plumb-pudding" in 1A¹–1A³ was changed to "plum-pudding" in 1A⁴–1A⁵; since the copy-text spelling is an acceptable variant spelling of "plum-pudding" the revision was rejected. (4) "Semi-breve" in 1A¹–1A³ was changed to "semibreve" in 1A⁴–1A⁵; it too was rejected as unnecessary. (5) "Major discord" in 1A¹–1A³ has a hyphen added in 1A⁴–1A⁵; all additions and/or deletions of hyphens in *Salmagundi* had to be treated as suspect, since no consistent pattern could be determined. Deletions were as likely due to type wear or careless impression of type on the paper as to deliberate revision, and additions of hyphens were quite inconsistent. The final revision was also rejected.

An important large category of revisions taking place in the subeditions and variant states of 1A which were rejected are those which unnecessarily destroy the rhetorical style of *Salmagundi*. For example, take the removal in 1A⁶–1A⁷ of the comma after "avow" in the following phrase from No. I: "but this reason we candidly avow, would not hold good with ourselves" (67.24–25). The comma, appearing in subeditions 1A¹–1A⁵, is placed at a natural pause; there is no reason to delete it and every reason not to delete it. Or take the sentence also from No. I: "We beg the respectable old matrons of this city, not to be alarmed at the appearance we make" (69.39–40). The comma after "city" in 1A¹–1A⁶, again at a natural pause, is removed in 1A⁷. It is a comma placement so characteristic that to delete it would be to tamper with an essential feature of *Salmagundi's* style.

Eccentric and inconsistent spelling—meant to be archaic, semiliterate, or simply ludicrous—contribute to *Salmagundi's* impudent tone and overall texture and have not been changed. Revisions in the subeditions and variant states of 1A that bring spellings into standard forms were not adopted unless the original seems to be a typographical error or mars the sense, in which case the correction was adopted.[72] Thus the revision at 79.10 of "facinating" ($1A^1$) to "fascinating" ($1A^2$–$1A^5$) and at 105.24 "dessertation" ($1A^1$) to "dissertation" ($1A^2$–$1A^4$) were adopted. Likewise the change from the archaic "cotemporary" ($1A^1$–$1A^2$) to the modern "contemporary" ($1A^3$–$1A^4$), at 104.36 and again at 114.31, were rejected.

One category of spelling changes difficult to treat consistently is foreign words or foreign words that have been Anglicized, since it is hard to know whether an idiosyncratic spelling was intended or accidental. Such a case is the original "musselmen" ($1A^1$) subsequently changed to "mussulmen" ($1A^3$–$1A^5$) at 91.38–39. Since no confusion would result from the original it was retained. Neither was the change from "friccazeed" ($1A^1$–$1A^2$) to "fricasseed" ($1A^5$–$1A^7$) at 70.3, accepted. There is of course a fine line of judgment in treating this category of changes, and the deciding factor has been whether or not the words left uncorrected are unusual ones or ones with amusing and/or satirical connotations.

Contractions often appear in the copy-text without apostrophes, or words are unexpectedly contracted at unusual places. Unless the sense seemed endangered, the copy-text version was retained. As previously stated, hyphens are very unreliable: they appear to have been added and subtracted at the compositor's whim. Since it is especially difficult to determine whether the absence or presence of a hyphen is a conscious choice or not, no changes in hyphenation were adopted in the Twayne edition.

Quotation marks were carelessly treated in *Salmagundi*: either one of a pair were missing or else the quotation marks were left out entirely. When necessary, that is, when comma errors absolutely necessary for sense were left uncorrected in 1A subeditions and variant states, the editor has added them. When the subeditions and variant states of 1A correct the situation the revision has been adopted.

Certain features in the text, presumably introduced by the publisher and normally the publisher's responsibility and/or the choice of the printer, were rejected by the Twayne edition as nonauthorial, or if retained, were not reproduced exactly. Within this category are the changes in format, the alteration of type on the page from subedition

72. Noah Webster's *A Compendious Dictionary of the English Language* (Hartford, 1806) and John Walker's *A Critical Pronouncing Dictionary and Expositor of the English Language* (London, 1797), were consulted for spelling forms, since they were dictionaries the three authors would have had access to or would have been familiar with. Webster and Walker were also consulted in preparing the List of Compound Words Hyphenated at End of Line.

to subedition, the precise arrangement of the titles of prose and poetry, the pagination and lineation, the running heads, and the footnotes. The short-title, which appears on the first page of text of each number in 1A (with small variations from subedition to subedition) has been retained only once in the Twayne edition—immediately preceding the text of No. I (p. 67). The dateline, which appears immediately after the short-title head in 1A (and, like the short-title, varies among subeditions) has been retained in a standardized form at the beginning of each number. The printer's imprint, appearing at the end of almost every number of 1A (also with small variations from subedition to subedition) has been deleted; as have such notices as those announcing the appearance of the second edition of No. I (occurring at the end of No. III) and the end of Volume I (occurring at the end of No. XII).

Because of the complexity of the revision patterns between 1A, 2A, and 1F, certain problems arose in the transcription of entries in the List of Emendations and the List of Rejected Substantives. One of these problems was whether or not to reproduce in the lists the accidental differences, house styling, and punctuation, between 1A and the Irving-revised 2A and 1F editions, when 2A and 1F do not contain substantive revisions but merely follow a particular subedition of 1A in its substantives. Since the accidentals in 2A and 1F were most likely nonauthorial, they were not recorded in the lists in this instance. Of course when 2A or 1F revised 1A, care was taken to reproduce the accidentals in each of the texts. Another transcription problem involves accidental revisions occurring among the subeditions and variant states of 1A, when the 1A text was revised in 2A or 1F, but remained substantially the same in the 1A subeditions and variant states. So pervasive were accidental changes among the 1A subeditions that their occurrence is inevitable for the longer 2A and 1F revised passages; it would be impossible however to transcribe each 1A subedition or variant state for the longer entries. For instance, the following passage in No. I was retained in 2A but repositioned in 1F: "We beg the public particularly to understand that we solicit no patronage. We are determined on the contrary, that the patronage shall be entirely on our side" (68.16–18). The repositioning of the sentences in 1F is described in the List of Rejected Substantives by an editorial note; and the accidental differences between 1A and 2A and 1F are ignored. But there is an accidental change which occurs in the later subeditions of 1A: Two sentences become one. The period at 68.17 after the first "patronage" in subeditions $1A^1$–$1A^5$ is changed to a dash in $1A^6$–$1A^7$; and the "We" in $1A^1$–$1A^5$ is decapitalized in settings $1A^6$–$1A^7$. In such cases, and there are many, the copy-text, the first subedition or its variant state ($1A^1$ or $1A^1a$) only is represented in the Lists.

The only accidental variations that appear in the List of Emendations and List of Rejected Substantives occurs when 1) there is an accidental emendation among the subeditions and variant states of 1A which involve substantive revision; or 2) when a 2A or 1F substantive revision is transcribed in full.

The text of *Salmagundi* has been faithfully and critically rendered by the Twayne edition. The Historical Note, the Textual Commentary, and the accompanying Discussions of Adopted Readings, together with the List of Emendations, the List of Rejected Substantives and the List of Compound Words Hyphenated at End of Line, are designed to provide the reader with all the data needed to reconstruct the copy-text and to follow the steps by which the Twayne text of *Salmagundi* was established. The assembled evidence is designed not only to enable the reader so minded to examine and consider the bases on which all editorial decisions were made, but to reconsider them, if he chooses, and in the process to see the relationships that exist among the several revised states of 1A produced by the three authors together, and the revisions Irving made in 2A and 1F.

DISCUSSIONS OF ADOPTED READINGS

In the following, which discusses decisions to emend or not to emend, as well as describes and explains the more complicated revisions in authorized texts of *Salmagundi*, the following symbols are used to designate the texts.

MS	A manuscript fragment of a portion of Washington Irving's "Cockloft Hall," from No. XIV
1A$^{1-7}$	The first American edition (1807–1808), including its many subeditions and variant states, identified by superscript numbers and lowercase letters (see Table 2, pp. 390-91)
1E	The first English edition (1814), prepared by John Lambert and published by J. M. Richardson
2A	The second American edition (1814), published by David Longworth, who was probably assisted by Washington Irving
1F	The first French edition (1824), an English language edition published by Galignani and Baudry and revised by Washington Irving
T	Twayne edition
Walker	*A Critical Pronouncing Dictionary and Expositor of the English Language* (London, 1797)
Webster	*A Compendious Dictionary of the English Language* (Hartford, 1806)

The page and line figures locating the entry in the Twayne edition are keyed to a word or words in the text to which the discussion or comment refers. A bracket separates the key word or words from the comment that follows.

68.16–18 We. . . . side.] When preparing 1F Irving revised the author's notice to No. I; part he placed in the Elbow-chair Essay (here and at 168.22–23) and part he omitted (68.18–22).

63.35–69.8 PUBLISHER'S NOTICE.] For 1F Irving repositioned the Publisher's Notice of 1A to the end of Galignani's Publisher's Notice.

69.9–13 It . . . essay.] When Irving repositioned the original Publisher's Notice at 68.35 (which may have been written by Longworth), he omitted this authorial note from the text of 1F, perhaps because he felt it called unnecessary attention to the publisher.

71.14   tea-visits] The comma appears to have been set after the wrong word. This emendation, with the one following at 71.14 adding a comma after "afternoon," corrects the error.

72.13   corps,] This emendation, and the one at 72.15 adding a comma after "breeches," are both in accord with postcopy-text versions, and make a confused sentence readable.

72.34   subjects] The change from the copy-text "subjects" (1A¹–1A⁶, 2A, 1F) to "objects" (1A⁷) is probably a compositorial error or whim, especially since "objects" appears in only one of the several 1A subeditions. Revisions which clearly correct printer's errors (and are thus adopted in T) and revisions like this one which create such errors (and are thus rejected) are not discussed unless circumstances seem unusual.

73.13   authors] As the context makes clear, the copy-text "editors" (1A¹–1A², 1A⁴) is an error which was later corrected to "authors" (1A³, 1A⁵–1A⁷, 2A). 1F rejects a larger passage (73.10–14) of which this is a part, since it had to do with the authors' indifference to "pecuniary matters"—by 1824 a somewhat sensitive subject for Irving.

74.25   occurences,] Commas in Salmagundi often set off asides, parenthetical or contrasting phrases, and delineate natural pauses. The omission of the comma after "occurences" in the copy-text (1A¹) was clearly an error corrected in subsequent subeditions (1A²–1A³, 1A⁵–1A⁷). Similar emendations occur at 115.35 and 139.20.

75.27   humor] "Humor of a lady" (1A¹) is probably used in the sense of Ben Johnson's humour comedies; thus the copy-text is retained and the revisions "humors" (1A²–1A⁴, 2A) and "humours" (1A⁵–1A⁷, 1F) rejected.

77.17   mountebank] The "mounteback" change (1A⁶) from the copy-text "mountebank" (1A¹–1A³, 1A⁵, 1A⁷, 2A) is probably a compositorial error, considering it appears only in a single 1A subedition; however, it could have been a bawdy jest made by the author, or possibly the compositor. The overparticular Irving deleted the entire "mountebank" phrase from 1F. Compare this revision, which creates a bawdy pun, to the ones at 190.4–5 and 192.33 which change the original bawdy "horeback" (1A¹) to "horseback" (1A²–1A³, 2A, 1F). Both changes were rejected.

78.6   reader] The context of the sentence requires the revised singular form "reader" (1A¹b–c, 1A²–1A⁵, 2A, 1F) to agree with "him," instead of the original plural "readers" (1A¹a, d).

78.15   divan;] Compound sentences in Salmagundi are almost always divided by a comma or a semicolon; so the lack of any punctuation after "divan" in the copy-text ($1A^1$–$1A^2$) was surely an oversight. 1A revisions offered two choices: a comma ($1A^3$–$1A^4$) or a semicolon ($1A^5$). Since both are characteristically used in such situations and since there are three commas in the sentence, the semicolon was selected.

79.10   fascinating] Here is an example of a spelling correction adopted by T. The original "facinating" ($1A^1$) seems to be a misprint rather than an attempt at a humorous spelling.

82.9   SNIVERS] The identical revision from "Snivers" to " 'Sbidlikens" was made in 1F at 83.14; 136.38; 136.41; 137.5; 137.21; 137.22; 138.35; 139.11; 139.24; 139.34; 140.10; 162.7. This is because in 1824, when preparing 1F, Irving decided to make the two Cockneys in *Salmagundi*—"Snivers" and " 'Sbidlikens"—into one person.

82.26   reverberations] The *OED* gives "reverbating," but not "reverbations" ($1A^1$–$1A^2$), so the revision ($1A^3$–$1A^5$) was accepted.

89.6   traveller] Since the sentence already contains the word "strangers," the copy-text "stranger" ($1A^1$–$1A^2$) was emended to "traveller" ($1A^3$–$1A^5$, 2A, 1F).

89.12   sand-flat, than] The revision which adds "rather" between "sand-flat" and "than" ($1A^3$–$1A^5$, 2A, 1F) is a good example of the often careless and/or unnecessary small revisions which occur in later subeditions of 1A. It destroys the parallelism created by the simple "than" ($1A^1$–$1A^2$), repeated in structure somewhat later in the sentence, namely, "sand-flat, than plod" and "knife grinder, than endure."

90.32   trammels] According to Webster, "trammels" were either shackles for a horse or long nets; "hangers," the 1F revision, were short broad swords or irons. Since both were used to describe handwriting flourishes, the reading in 1A and 2A was respected.

96.31   conscience] The random copy of *Salmagundi* Irving and/or Longworth used as copy-text for 2A, seems likely to have been the $1A^3$ subedition for No. III, since 2A follows the $1A^3$ text in every instance but one (see note to 97.24). 2A even includes the incorrect "conscious struck" of the third subedition ($1A^3$), instead of the original and correct "conscience struck" of the first subedition ($1A^1$). Irving carried the error through 1F. Perhaps it should be emphasized at this point that the agreement of 2A and 1F with a particular 1A version does not mean that Irving consciously chose that reading over another. On the contrary, he relied on a copy of 1A representing a random collection of subeditions when he prepared 2A, and he then prepared 1F using 2A.

97.24 wool-clad warriors] The revision "wood-clad warriours" (1A²–1A⁵) is a compositorial error, possibly caused by "wooden warriors" which appears three lines above. (Notice the house-style spelling change from *-or* to *-our*.) Since this is an error of literary fact (see the Historical Note at p. 322), Irving or Longworth would have caught the error when preparing 2A. That is why in this single instance 2A deviates from the 1A³ setting.

102.2 principle] Here the English edition of 1811 (1E) was the first to correct a misprint in 1A, changing "principal" to "principle." 2A, not as carefully prepared as John Lambert's 1E, fails to make the correction. Irving or his editors caught the mistake and corrected it for 1F.

103.37 *vide*] The revision (1A³–1A⁴) conforms with the style of all other footnotes in this feature which lack punctuation after "*vide.*"

104.13 Linkum Fidelius] The references to Linkum Fidelius here and at 141.16 and 144.38 omitted in 1F, are retained. Elsewhere, at 74.2–3 and 84.43, both 2A and 1F change "Linkum Fidelius" to read simply "Linkum"; these revisions were also rejected.

106.20 Naples—‡] The dagger was misplaced before "only" in the copy-text (1A¹–1A²).

106.30 sturgeon's] Although Jeremy Cockloft had been talking about sturgeons (plural), the original "sturgeons' nose capital for tennis-balls" (1A¹–1A²) seems unnecessarily awkward. "Sturgeons' noses" would have been an acceptable emendation had it been made, but "sturgeon's nose" (1A³–1A⁴, 1F) seems to be the reading originally intended

107.5–116.23 FROM.... dog!] 2A and 1F delete five features from No. IV: "From My Elbow-Chair," "Flummery," "General Remark," "Notice," and "Card," all satirizing Thomas Green Fessenden. That is why there are no 2A and 1F entries in the Lists for pp. 107.5–116.23.

109.38 Dr. Costive] Since "Dr. Costive" is used in every other instance in the poem "Flummery" as a wordplay on "Dr Caustic"—the well-known pseudonym of Thomas Green Fessenden whose style the poem satirizes—the copy-text reading "Dr. Caustic" (1A¹) has been emended to "Dr. Costive" (1A²–1A⁴).

110.38 "*Wintry*"] like "Salmagundi," "Whim whams," and "Will Wizard" previously cited in the immediate text, and all quoted from No. III, "*Wintry*" requires quotation marks. The omission appears to have been an unintentional oversight.

111.16 Terrible Tractoration] At 111.6 the title was capitalized.

111.22 "pleader's guide"] It was tempting to adopt the emendation of the fourth subedition (1A⁴) "Pleader's Guide." Proper names are usually capitalized in the notes to "Flummery" (though they are

often represented as lowercase in subeditions that adhere to the
second house style). However, since there is no precedent (as there
was at 111.22), the emendation follows the revision in the second
and third subeditions (1A²–1A³) and merely supplies the omitted
quotation mark before "pleader's guide."

112.1   *I wont*] Webster gives "wunt" as a second choice in pronouncing "won't," which would provide the rhyme with "Hunt." Thus,
although the parenthetical addition after "*I wont*" is parallel with
the phrase in parentheses the last line of the quatrain, i.e., "(or Lousy
anee.),", the change from the copy-text "I wont" (1A¹-1A²) is
unnecessary.

112.4   (*or Lousy anee.*)] The revision corrects a typographical error
in the copy-text. The phrase is perhaps a pun on "lousy" for "bug-
infested" Annie.

112.30   *hangman,*] The reference to line sixteen of "Flummery" was
incorrectly quoted as "*hangmen*" in the copy-text (1A¹a).

117.4   *centinel*] The 2A/1F reading "*centinel*" was chosen over "*sentinel*" (1A³–1A⁴) because it is closer to the copy-text "*centinal*" than
the 1A³–1A⁴ version.

130.32   *runty*] There are recurring patterns of omission in the 1F
text, usually of adjectives Irving took out because he thought they
made *Salmagundi* too wordy. "Runty" is one of these and is omitted here
and at 132.36 and 282.43. Other examples of words or phrases consistently removed are recorded in the List of Rejected Substantives.

131.39   buttocks] The revision of "buttocks" (1A¹–1A², 2A) to the
more delicate "flanks" (1A³–1A⁴) is a good example of the recurring
attempts to make *Salmagundi* fit for sensitive eyes and ears. Although
the revision could be said to be more precise, since the reference
made is to a horse rather than to a person, like the other attempts
to make *Salmagundi* genteel, it was rejected. Irving deleted the entire
phrase in which the offending word appears when revising 1F.

144.5   excepting] Although the variant reading "excepting" (1A¹a)
has been seen in only one copy of *Salmagundi*, the remainder of subeditions and variant states reading "except" (1A¹b–1A³, 2A, 1F), there
seems to be no compelling reason to change the copy-text.

145.5   ⟨*Paragraph*⟩ While] In the copy-text (1A¹) the line preceding
"While" contains only nine letters, indicating that the next line
beginning with "While" should be the first word in a new paragraph.
And since the context corroborates a new paragraph, the 1A²–1A³
version was adopted.

146.1   fact,] There is a space at the end of the line after "fact" in the copy-text, suggesting that the comma fell off after the line was set. Such instances of damaged type are common in *Salmagundi*.

149.28–29 lore . . . MOORE.] 1F revises the original couplet which called Moore's poetry lascivious. The copy-text version was retained.

152.21 nor] The 1F revision "or" was rejected because the correct reading is "nor" (1A, 2A); see the *Spectator*, No. 68.

152.32–33 rise and sink] The compositor probably reversed the original and idiomatic "rise and sink" (1A^1) to "sink and rise" (1A^2–1A^3, 2A, 1F). Since in No. VIII, 2A was based on a 1A^2 or 1A^3 subedition, 2A and 1F continue the reversal of the original phrase.

153.20 grum] Since according to the *OED*, "grum" of the copy-text (1A, 2A) means the same as "glum" (1F), the revision was rejected.

153.28–34 Annexed . . . humorist.] This passage, deleted in 1F, refers to a woodcut of Launcelot Langstaff by Alexander Anderson which appeared at the head of No. VIII in earlier editions. See illustration following p. 68.

154.20 esq.,] Following "esq." is a long independent clause introduced by "for." The rejected 1A^3 revision, rather than simply adding a comma after "esq." begins a new sentence by capitalizing "For"; then adds an unnecessary comma after "for" to set off "as Langstaff never made a confidant on these occasions." The 1A^3 emendation slightly changes the meaning of the original. The editor's addition of the comma after 'esq." provides a simple solution to the problem of whether or not to accept the overcomplicated and perhaps careless revision in 1A.

157.29 subject] While "article" (1A^2–1A^3, 2A, 1F) avoids the repetition of "subject" (1A^1), it seems likely from the context that the second "on the subject" was the one meant to be changed to "on this article"; the revision was not adopted.

158.12 lord] Although the revision replacing the vague "a lord" (1A, 2A) with the specific "an earl" (1F) fits better with the other two specific ranks in sequence—"baronet" and "duke"—the revision was rejected because unnecessary.

162.3 Linkum Fidelius] The lines identified as Linkum's are actually from William Lithgow's *Nineteen Years Travels* (see the Historical Note, p. 321), but since it was a common humorous device in *Salmagundi* to quote lines from a legitimate source and ascribe them to a fictitious person, Irving's revision in 1F correcting the source of the lines to "Lithgow" was rejected.

165.22 which] According to Webster, "recover" may be used without "from" to mean "to get the better of." Thus the addition of "from" in 1F was rejected as unnecessary. A similar rejection occurs at 274.18.

166.3 fingers'] The singular possessive "finger's ends" ($1A^1$, $2A$) seems
unidiomatic for "The whole catalogue of *yerb* teas was at her
fingers' ends"; so the revision ($1A^2-1A^3$, $1F$) was adopted. Irving,
the author of this feature, was notoriously unreliable about apostrophes. In fact, misplaced apostrophes are common throughout
Salmagundi.

171.13 pray,"] Quotation marks are often treated carelessly in *Salmagundi*, being either left out entirely, or misplaced, or one of a pair
omitted, as in this instance. The $1A^2$ correction was adopted. It was
necessary in several cases for the editor to supply quotation marks
(see 249.11). Other examples can be found in the List of Emendations.

180.14–15 cherubims and seraphs] Neither of the two revisions of the
copy-text were acceptable: "cherubims and seraphims" ($1A^2-1A^3$) and
"cherubim and seraphim" ($1F$). According to Webster there is a
general confusion about the plural forms. Cherubim and seraphim—
the Hebrew plurals of cherub and seraph—have sometime erroneously
been treated as singular. Thus the *s* was added to the forms in $1A^2$–
$1A^3$. The English plurals are cherubs and seraphs, the latter form
used by $1A^1$ and $2A$. Although the copy-text mixes the Hebrew (and
an incorrect form of the Hebrew plural at that) and the English
forms of the plural, the copy-text was retained over the incorrect
$1A^2-1A^3$ revision and the correct, but perhaps too formal, $1F$ version.

181.36 ⟨Paragraph⟩ The piece] From this point on until the end of the
feature, the copy-text version of "Breaking up of the Ice in the North-
river," part of the Letter from Demy Semiquaver written by James
Kirke Paulding, was thoroughly revised in subeditions $1A^2$ and $1A^3$,
both of which were labeled "second edition, revised and corrected."
So completely revised was the feature that no line-by-line or passage-
by-passage comparison is possible between $1A^1$ and $1A^2-1A^3$. Both the
original and the revised version are reproduced in full in the List of
Rejected Substantives. Since there are only minor accidental and substantive differences between $1A^2$ and $1A^3$, the earliest revised version
($1A^2$) is reproduced in the List. Whether through intent or indifference, $2A$ was based on $1A^1$ rather than on $1A^2-1A^3$, and Irving chose
to follow suit when he prepared $1F$. He did make minor substantive
revisions in the original when preparing $1F$ (182.39, 182.39–41, and
182.42). The T edition retains the copy-text version, and has not
adopted any of Irving's $1F$ changes. For $4A$ Paulding also used the
original $1A^1$ version.

183.20 doctors.] Between "doctors" and the paragraph beginning "In
my warm," $1A^2-1A^3$ adds a paragraph about music, dramatists, and
audiences, not incorporated into T.

184.11 THE STRANGER] Immediately following Paulding's "Breaking up of the Ice" is "The Stranger in Pennsylvania" written by Washington Irving. Like Paulding's piece Irving's is extensively revised in 1A²–1A³. Chapter I (184.14–185.22) was completely rewritten and both versions are reproduced in the List of Rejected Substantives. Chapter II (185.24–189.17), however, was only spot-revised, so its revisions can be represented by single entries. In 1F Irving substituted a three-page note by the publisher in place of "Stranger." Identified as "Extracted from 'The Mirror of the Graces,'" it had previously appeared as the publisher's note at the beginning of ediition 2A. The T edition retains the copy-text version.

186.41 quicksilver,] This comma and that added at 186.41 after "eccentric" are placed after elements in two long series. The editorial emendation at 186.41 was necessary because the house style spelling of "eccentric" shifted from -ic to -ick in subeditions 1A²–1A³, which contain the adopted emendation.

187.24 separate] In this entry an error in spelling in 1A¹–"seperate"– was corrected in 1A² and reintroduced in 1A³. It is remarked as yet another example of the idiosyncratic and offhanded nature of *Salmagundi's* accidentals.

190.15 fast] See the Historical Note for p. 321.

192.1 puffs] Since the subject of the sentence is a dog, the substitution of "yelps" (1A²–1A³) for "puffs" (1A¹, 2A) was a tempting emendation. Irving must have been unhappy about the phrase in 1824, for he removed it altogether from 1F. However, to adopt "yelps" when "puffs" is acceptable seemed too much an attempt to improve the text, so the revision in 1A²–1A³ and the deletion in 1F were rejected.

192.22 doughty] "Doubty," the revision in 1A², is a common error in spelling "doughty" and carries an opposite meaning.

196.14 ever] Although "even" (1A¹–1A², 2A) could have been the original intent of the passage, it seems much more likely that "even" was a misreading for "ever" (1A³, 1F): "if we have ever lost (and who has not!)—an old friend." Consequently the revision was adopted.

207.21 beer,] The copy-text comma after "peanuts" (1A¹) was misplaced and should have followed "beer"—as the revision (1A²–1A³) corrects it.

208.22 merchandize–] In this notebook style whose primary mark of punctuation is the dash (much favored by Irving in his earlier years) or a dotted rule (perhaps used when the compositor ran out of dashes), the dash after "merchandize" added by 1A²–1A³ is stylistically consistent and required for clarity. Also, "merchandize" appears at the end of the line in 1A, a position where it is easy to forget to put in punctuation or where the punctuation may have fallen out.

211.22   blocks] The reason variant state 1A^{1}c follows subedition 1A^2–1A^3 from this entry to the end of the number is because when 1A^{1}c was bound up, signature B from subedition 1A^2 was used in combination with signature A from subedition 1A^1.

213.5   How often] Most of the remaining revisions in No. XII are from subeditions 1A^2–1A^3, in which William Irving's "From the Mill of Pindar Cockloft" was revised. William Irving's later feelings about his poem are not known, since he did not contribute to any edition of *Salmagundi* subsequent to 1A. 2A makes a few revisions in 1A^1 (213.11; 214.22–23; 215.11–16) which it follows, rather than the revised 1A^2–1A^3. Irving, preparing 1F, follows 2A, but adds a few more changes (213.11; 213.21–22; 213.33; 214.12; 214.24). 1A^2 and 1A^3 differ only in accidentals. The 1A^2 text is reproduced in the List of Rejected Substantives. The T edition retains the copy-text version of the poem.

234.7   oracles.] When preparing 1F, Irving rewrote much of William Irving's Mustapha Letter in No. XIV. In a few instances (for example, 234.11 and 243.13–15), Irving improved the satire. But the bulk of his changes (as could be observed of the 1F revisions as a whole) merely serve to tighten the text and make it more genteel. The copy-text version has been retained. The sentence Irving added between "oracles" and "True" was taken from the 1A text (see 234.15–23).

237.16   cattle] The manuscript "cattle" was misread by the compositor who typeset "castle" instead. The error went uncorrected until 2A.

252.6   Diogenes] The parenthetical "(like Diogenes his tub)" found in 1A and 1F means that the *Tumbler* rolls its little ball laboriously along in the same way that Diogenes rolled his tub along. The *OED* under "like" describes this use of "like" as introducing a clause with the verb suppressed. The suppressed verb in this case is "rolled." When the verb is suppressed, "like" is used; when the verb is not suppressed, "as" is used. There seems no reason to emend, but the emendation in 2A, "Diogenes in his tub," is not wrong, for Diogenes, according to legend, did live in his tub. Most of the revisions in No. XV made by Irving for 1F affect his essay "On Greatness" (250.14–255.34).

257.9   Springs] The "Springs campaign" refers to Ballston Springs, a popular watering resort (see Irving's *Journals and Notebooks*, I, 3, 5–8, for a description of his visit to the Springs). The 2A revision appears to be a correction of the 1A "spring."

286.43   strait] The revision (1A¹c–d) of "strait" from the copy-text "straight" (1A¹a–b, 2A) is probably a correction made by the authors, since "strait waistcoat" meaning "straight jacket" exactly makes the point in this description of a lady's "instruments of torture."

LIST OF EMENDATIONS

In this list of changes made in the copy-text ($1A^1$ or $1A^1a$) the following symbols are used to designate the sources of the readings:

MS	A manuscript fragment of a portion of Washington Irving's "Cockloft Hall" from No. XIV
$1A^{1-7}$	The first American edition (1807–1808), including its many subeditions and variant states identified by superscript numbers and lowercase letters (see Table 2, pp. 390–91)
2A	The second American edition (1814), published by David Longworth, who was probably assisted by Washington Irving.
1F	The first French edition (1824), an English language edition published by Galignani and Baudry and revised by Washington Irving.
T	Twayne edition

These notes, keyed to the Twayne edition, identify all emendations of the copy-text. Titles of features, the dateline on the first page of each number, chapter headings, notes, and footnotes are included in the line count; running heads, however, are not counted.

The reading to the left of the bracket represents an accepted reading that differs from the copy-text. Usually this accepted reading was chosen from revisions occurring in the subeditions and variant states of 1A, and less frequently from revisions introduced by 2A and 1F, which are represented in the substantive entries only. Occasionally the editor of the Twayne edition (T) has emended on his own authority, or a change in house style in the accepted revision made an editorial change necessary. The source of the emendation is identified by symbol after the bracket.

The reading after the semicolon is the rejected reading of the copy-text and any other text in which that reading occurs; when there are additional textual alternatives, they are recorded following the copy-text reading, all separated by a semicolon.

The swung (wavy) dash ~ represents the same word, words, or characters that appear before the bracket, and is used in recording punctuation variants; the caret ∧ indicates that a mark of punctuation is omitted.

Decisions to emend or not to emend, including emendations made on authority of the editor, are explained in the Discussions of Adopted Readings. Entries there discussed are identified in the List of Emendations by an asterisk (*).

71.14	tea-visits] 1A⁶–1A⁷; ~, 1A¹–1A², 1A⁵
71.14	afternoon,] 1A⁵–1A⁷; ~ᴧ 1A¹–1A²
72.13	corps,] 1A⁵–1A⁶; ~ᴧ 1A¹–1A², 1A⁷
72.15	breeches,] 1A², 1A⁵–1A⁷; ~ᴧ 1A¹
*73.13	honor of his authors] 1A³, 1A⁵, 1A⁷, 2A; honor of his editors 1A¹–1A², 1A⁴; honour of his authors 1A⁶; *omitted* 1F
*74.25	*occurences,*] 1A²–1A³, 1A⁵–1A⁷; ~ᴧ 1A¹
75.28	fashion, Mrs. Toole] T; fashion. Mrs. Toole 1A¹; fashion, mrs. Toole 1A², 1A⁵–1A⁷; fashion, mrs. Toole 1A³
75.28	Bouchard,] 1A²–1A³, 1A⁵; ~ᴧ 1A¹; Bouchard 1A⁶–1A⁷
77.13	dress! he then] 1A²–1A³, 1A⁵–1A⁷; dress he! then 1A¹
*78.6	his reader] 1A¹b–c, 1A²–1A⁵, 2A, 1F; his readers 1A¹a, d
*78.15	divan;] 1A⁵; ~ᴧ 1A¹–1A²; ~, 1A³–1A⁴
78.35	be] 1A³–1A⁵; he 1A¹–1A²
*79.10	fascinating] 1A²–1A⁵; facinating 1A¹
*82.26	reverberations] 1A³–1A⁵; reverbations 1A¹–1A²
83.18	of the] 1A¹c–1A⁵; of of the 1A¹a–b
84.39	woman,] 1A⁴–1A⁵; ~ᴧ 1A¹–1A³
*89.6	traveller] 1A³–1A⁵, 2A, 1F; stranger 1A¹–1A²
93.7–8	perhaps,] 1A⁴–1A⁵; ~ᴧ 1A¹–1A³
*102.2	principle] 1F; principal 1A, 2A
*103.37	*vide*ᴧ] 1A³–1A⁴; ~, 1A¹–1A²
105.24	dissertation] 1A²–1A⁴; dessertation 1A¹
106.10	men's] 1A³–1A⁴; men's 1A¹–1A²
*106.19–20	state—only . . . Naples—‡] 1A³–1A⁴; state—‡only . . . Naples— 1A¹–1A²
*106.30	sturgeon's] 1A³–1A⁴, 1F; sturgeons' 1A¹–1A²
109.1	(11)] 1A¹c–1A⁴; (11ᴧ 1A¹a–b
*109.38	Dr. Costive] 1A²–1A⁴; Dr. Caustic 1A¹
*110.38	"Wintry"] 1A⁴a; Wintry 1A¹; "wintry" 1A², 1A⁴b
*111.16	Terrible Tractoration] 1A²–1A⁴; terrible tractoration 1A¹
*111.22	"pleader's guide"] 1A²–1A³; ᴧpleader's guide" 1A¹; "Pleader's Guide" 1A⁴
111.30	allusion] 1A²–1A⁴; illusion 1A¹
*112.4	(*or Lousy anee.*)] 1A¹c; (*ro Lousy anee.*) 1A¹a–b; (*or Lousy-anee.*) 1A²–1A⁴

*112.30 $hangman,$] $1A^1b$–$1A^4$; $hangmen,$ $1A^1a$

113.18   a stave] $1A^1b$–$1A^4$; astave $1A^1a$

113.32   our] $1A^1b$–$1A^4$; out $1A^1a$

114.15 $Rump\text{-}fed$] $1A^2$–$1A^4$; $rump\text{-}fed$ $1A^1$

114.20 $rump\text{-}fed$] $1A^2$–$1A^4$; $rump_\wedge fed$ $1A^1$

114.26   man,] $1A^1b$–$1A^4$; $\sim_\wedge$ $1A^1a$

115.30   heretofore] $1A^1b$–$1A^4$; hertofore $1A^1a$

115.34   "People's Friend."] $1A^4$; $_\wedge\sim$ $\sim._\wedge$ $1A^1$; "$\sim$ $\sim_\wedge$" $1A^2$

115.35 $fraternity,$] $1A^1b$–$1A^4$; $\sim_\wedge$ $1A^1a$

115.39   its] $1A^1b$–$1A^4$; its $1A^1a$

116.11   english. Will] $1A^1b$–$1A^4$; english, Will $1A^1a$

116.21 $weakly$] $1A^2$–$1A^4$; "$\sim$ $1A^1$

*117.4 $centinel$] 2A, 1F; $centinal$ $1A$–$1A^2$; $sentinel$ $1A^3$–$1A^4$

117.36   unfor-/tunately] $1A^2$–$1A^4$; unfor-/tnnately $1A^1$

120.29   eleven.] $1A^2$–$1A^4$; $\sim_\wedge$ $1A^1$

126.19   have taken] $1A^1c$–$1A^4$, 2A, 1F; have took $1A^1a$–b

130.32   odd,] $1A^3b$–$1A^4$; $\sim_\wedge$ $1A^1$–$1A^2$

131.4   calvinist] $1A^2$, $1A^4$; calvanist $1A^1$, $1A^3b$

133.8   mahogany] $1A^2$, $1A^3b$–$1A^4$; mahogony $1A^1$

134.13   to be] $1A^2$–$1A^4$; to her $1A^1$

138.43   manual] $1A^3b$–$1A^4$; manuel $1A^1$–$1A^2$

139.20   say,] $1A^2$, $1A^3b$–$1A^4$; $\sim_\wedge$ $1A^1$

140.37   happens] $1A^1c$–$1A^4$; pappens $1A^1a$–b

141.12   bull's] $1A^1b$–$1A^4$; bull's $1A^1a$

141.15   country;] $1A^4b$; $\sim,$ $1A^1$–$1A^2$, $1A^3b$–$1A^4a$

142.24   above-mentioned,] $1A^2$–$1A^3$; $\sim_\wedge$ $1A^1$

143.24   accommodated] $1A^3$; accomodated $1A^1$; accommadated $1A^2$

*145.5   ⟨Paragraph⟩ While] $1A^2$–$1A^3$; ⟨no paragraph⟩ $\sim$ $1A^1$

145.21   arise] 1F; arises 1A, 2A

*146.1   fact,] $1A^3$; $\sim_\wedge$ $1A^1$–$1A^2$

147.38   thine,] $1A^2$–$1A^3$; $\sim.$ $1A^1$

150.8   head!] $1A^2$–$1A^3$; $\sim?$ $1A^1$

151.7   bewitching] $1A^2$–$1A^3$; bewithing $1A^1$

154.10–11   by a proposition of one of his] $1A^1c$–d; by a proposition of one his $1A^1a$–b; at a proposition of one of his $1A^2$–$1A^3$, 2A, 1F

*154.20   esq.,] T; $\sim._\wedge$ 1A

158.24   of the window] $1A^3$, 1F; of window $1A^1$–$1A^2$, 2A

159.10   rival, a red shawl,] $1A^1b$, $1A^2$–$1A^3$; $\sim_\wedge$ $\sim$ $\sim$ $\sim_\wedge$ $1A^1a$, c–d

159.17   and] $1A^2$–$1A^3$; aud $1A^1$

159.26	caprices;] 1A¹b–c, 1A²–1A³; ∼, 1A¹a, d
162.19	mrs. ———,] 1A³; ∼. –ᴧ 1A¹–1A²
163.20	falsehood] 1A³; falshood 1A¹–1A²
*166.3	fingers'] 1A²–1A³, 1F; finger's 1A¹, 2A
166.33	expression] 1A²–1A³; expresion 1A¹
169.27–28	situation,] 1A²–1A³; ∼ᴧ 1A¹
169.33	Kʜᴀɴ] T; Kᴀʜɴ 1A¹; Kʜᴀɴ 1A²–1A³
*171.13	pray,"] 1A²–1A³; ∼,ᴧ 1A¹
171.25	My] T; "∼ 1A
171.36	day,"] 1A²–1A³; ∼.ᴧ 1A¹
173.36	re-/quire] 1A²–1A³; re-/require 1A¹
175.6	land.] 1A²–1A³; ∼, 1A¹
176.24	breathe] 1A²–1A³; 2A, 1F; breath 1A¹
178.42	aim] 1A¹b–1A³; omitted 1A¹a
181.21	trampling] 1A²–1A³; trampiing 1A¹
182.3	&c."] T; ∼ᴧ 1A
182.35	ferry."] T; ∼.ᴧ 1A
183.28	loses] 1A²–1A³, 2A, 1F; looses 1A¹
186.41	quicksilver,] 1A²–1A³; ∼ᴧ 1A¹
186.41	eccentric,] T; ∼ᴧ 1A¹; eccentrick, 1A²–1A³
186.42	villanous] 1A²–1A³; ∼ᴧ 1A¹
*187.24	separate] 1A²; seperate 1A¹, 1A³
188.17	them] 1A²–1A³; then 1A¹
189.15	brick-bats:"] T; ∼:ᴧ 1A
189.27	discordant] 1A³; discordent 1A¹–1A²
189.31	disorganization,] 1A²; disorgani-/tion, 1A¹; disorgani-/zationᴧ 1A³
191.26	fact] 1A²–1A³; ∼, 1A¹
192.2	betters.] 1A³; ∼." 1A¹–1A²
192.9	logocracy] 1A²–1A³; logogracy 1A¹
192.12	country.] 1A²–1A³; ∼," 1A¹
192.15	detachments] 1A²–1A³; detatchments 1A¹
192.24	"At] 1A²–1A³; ᴧ∼ 1A¹
192.42	which] 1A³; ∼, 1A¹–1A²
193.18	intriguing] 1A³; intrigueing 1A¹–1A²
193.34	persuade,] 1A²–1A³; ∼ᴧ 1A¹
195.22	nations, barbarous] 1A²–1A³; ∼ ∼, 1A¹
*196.14	ever] 1A³, 1F; even 1A¹–1A², 2A
196.23	end."] 1A²–1A³; ∼ᴧ" 1A¹
201.35	me;] 1A²–1A³; ∼, 1A¹
201.36	family,] 1A²–1A³; ∼; 1A¹

202.25   Spout-/ing-club] 1A^{1}c; Spout-/in-gclub 1A^{1}a–b; spout-/ing-club 1A^2–1A^3

203.4   satisfaction] T; satisfac-/faction 1A^1; satisfac-/tion, 1A^2–1A^3

205.10   talked of] 1F; talked to 1A, 2A

207.12   country,] 1A^2–1A^3; ~$_\wedge$ 1A^1

*207.20–21   peanuts and beer,] 1A^2–1A^3; ~,~ ~ 1A^1

207.33   toiling assiduity,] 1A^{1}b–1A^3, 2A, 1F; toiling, assidulously 1A^{1}a

*208.22   merchandize–] 1A^2–1A^3; ~$_\wedge$ 1A^1

208.34   couldn't] 1A^3; could'nt 1A^1; couldn$_\wedge$t 1A^2

208.38–39   though, poor wench,] 1A^2–1A^3; ~$_\wedge$ ~ ~$_\wedge$ 1A^1

209.4   CHAPTER] 1A^{1}b–1A^3; CHAPTFR 1A^1

210.8   at] 1A^2–1A^3; at at 1A^1

211.7   across] 1A^2–1A^3; a cross 1A^1

211.41   Napoleon] 1A^{1}c–1A^3; Napolean 1A^{1}a–b

212.2   Napoleon] 1A^3; Napolean 1A^1–1A^2

212.11   Napoleon] 1A^3; Napolean 1A^1–1A^2

212.16–17   dudgeon./FROM MY ELBOW CHAIR.] T; dudgeon./END OF THE FIRST VOLUME./FROM MY ELBOW CHAIR. 1A

214.34   weakness] 1A^{1}c–1A^3; weaknes 1A^{1}a–b

219.6   guarantee] 1A^2; gaurantee 1A^1

*237.18   cattle] MS, 2A, 1F; castle 1A

249.11   "Poor] T; $_\wedge$~ 1A

*257.9   Springs] 2A; spring 1A; Springs' 1F

257.42   couples,] T; couple 1A^{1}a–b; ~, 1A^{1}c

259.24   philosophy,] 1A^{1}c; ~$_\wedge$ 1A^{1}a–b

259.24   were] T; where 1A

270.30   ancestors] 1A^{1}b; ancsetors 1A^{1}a

272.4   is] T; is is 1A

281.37   sun!"] T; ~!$_\wedge$ 1A

282.11   dignity,–] T; ~.– 1A

285.5   fascinations]1A^{1}b–d; facinations 1A^{1}a

285.26   misrepresentation,] T; ~$_\wedge$ 1A, 2A; mis-statement 1F

*286.43   strait] 1A^{1}c–d; straight 1A^{1}a–b, 1A^2

296.12   exclam-/ation] 1A^{1}c; exclam-/tion 1A^{1}a–b

305.19   truth] T; ruth 1A

306.15–16   At this] T; Att his 1A

309.31   exhibits] 1A^{1}c, 2A, 1F; exhibit 1A^{1}a–b

316.6   WIZARD.] T; WIZARD./END OF VOLUME II. 1A

LIST OF REJECTED SUBSTANTIVES

This list provides an historical record of substantive variants in the manuscript fragment and authorized texts which appeared during Irving's lifetime, but which were not adopted for the Twayne edition. The following symbols were used to designate the sources of the readings.

MS	A manuscript fragment of a portion of Washington Irving's "Cockloft Hall" from No. XIV
1A$^{1-7}$	The first American edition (1807–1808), including its many subeditions and variant states identified by superscript numbers and lowercase letters, as set forth in Table 2, pp. 390–91
2A	The second American edition (1814), published by David Longworth, who was probably assisted by Washington Irving
1F	The first French edition (1824), an English language edition published by Galignani and Baudry and revised by Washington Irving
T	Twayne edition

The List of Rejected Substantives, like the List of Emendations, is keyed to the Twayne edition. The reading to the left of the bracket is the copy-text; to the right of the bracket are the rejected revisions from 1A, 2A, or 1F. Accidental differences between 1A, 2A, and 1F are recorded only if substantive revisions were involved. Entries identified by an asterisk *, appear in the Discussion of Adopted Readings. Brackets occurring in the text of *Salmagundi* are represented in bold face to differentiate them from the brackets which set off the reading accepted for the Twayne edition. Editorial notes within the entries are set off by caret brackets ⟨ ⟩.

67.20	was] 1A^1; were 1A^2–1A^3, 1A^5–1A^7, 2A, 1F
68.3	that] 1A^1; *omitted* 1A^2–1A^7, 2A, 1F
*68.16–18	We beg the public particularly to understand, that we solicit no patronage. We are determined on the contrary, that the patronage shall be entirely on our

side.]   1A, 2A; ⟨repositioned to the Elbow-Chair essay
(69.31) between "contempt" and "The public"⟩ IF

68.18–22   We have nothing to do with the pecuniary concerns of
the paper, its success will yield us neither pride nor
profit—nor will its failure occasion to us either loss or
mortification. We advise the public therefore, to purchase our numbers merely for their own sakes—] 1A,
2A; *omitted* 1F

68.22–23   if they do not, let them settle the affair with their
consciences and posterity.] 1A, 2A; ⟨repositioned to
the Elbow-Chair essay (69.39) between "paper" and
"We beg" with the addition of "own" before "consciences"⟩ 1F

68.28–29   exchange of civilities; he shall furnish us with notices
of epic] 1A^1, 1A^3–1A^5, 2A, 1F; exchange of epic 1A^2;
exchange of civilities; he shall furnish us with notices
of epick 1A^6–1A^7

*68.35–69.8   PUBLISHER'S NOTICE. / This work will be published
and sold by D. Longworth. It will be printed on hot-
prest vellum paper, as that is held in highest estimation
for buckling up young ladies' hair—a purpose to which
similar works are usually appropriated; it will be a
small neat duodecimo size, so that when enough numbers are written, it may form a volume sufficiently
portable to be carried in old ladies' pockets and young
ladies' work bags. ⟨*Paragraph*⟩ As the above work will
not come out at stated periods, notice will be given
when another number will be published. The price
will depend on the size of the number, and must be
paid on its delivery. The publisher professes the same
sublime contempt for money as his authors. The liberal
patronage bestowed by his discerning fellow-citizens
on various works of taste which he has published, has
left him no *inclination* to ask for further favors at their
hands, and he publishes this work in the mere hope
of requiting their bounty] 1A, 2A; ⟨repositioned to
the end of Galignani's Publisher's Notice⟩ 1F

69.3   its] 1A^1; *omitted* 1A^2–1A^7, 2A, 1F

*69.9–13   It was not originally the intention of the authors to
insert the above address in the work; but, unwilling
that a *morceau* so precious should be lost to posterity,
they have been induced to alter their minds. This will

account for any repetition of idea that may appear in the introductory essay.] 1A, 2A; *omitted* 1F

69.30 philosophical wiseacres] 1A, 2A; philosophers 1F

70.15 it] 1A^1–1A^3, 1A^5, 2A, 1F; us 1A^4, 1A^6–1A^7

70.16 shall] 1A, 2A; will 1F

70.25 a more than] 1A; more than a 2A, 1F

70.25 guardian] 1A, 2A; golden 1F

70.38 stupid] 1A, 2A; sapient 1F

70.39 miss ———'s] 1A, 2A; Mrs ———'s 1F

70.43 by being experienced] 1A^1–1A^4; from his long experience 1A^5–1A^7, 2A, 1F

71.1 tea-parties] 1A, 2A; routes 1F

71.11 sleigh-riding] 1A, 2A; a sleigh-riding 1F

71.34–35 or Cambridge] 1A^1–1A^5, 2A, 1F; at Cambridge 1A^6–1A^7

71.40 and] 1A^1–1A^4; *omitted* 1A^5–1A^7, 2A, 1F

71.41 porcelaine. He] 1A^1–1A^4; porcelane, and particularly values himself on his intimate knowledge of the buffalo, and war dances of the northern indians. He] 1A^5–1A^7, 2A, 1F

72.17–19 shall . . . shall] 1A, 2A; will . . . will 1F

72.18 well] 1A, 2A; *omitted* 1F

72.25 attempts] 1A^1; attempt 1A^2–1A^3, 1A^5–1A^7, 2A, 1F

72.26 shall] 1A^1–1A^2, 1A^4; should 1A^3, 1A^5–1A^7, 2A, 1F

72.28 are] 1A^1; be 1A^2–1A^7, 2A, 1F

*72.34 subjects] 1A^1–1A^6, 2A, 1F; objects 1A^7

72.39 recommend] 1A^1, 1A^3, 1A^5–1A^7, 2A, 1F; commend 1A^2

72.40–42 daughters, who will be taught the true line of propriety, and the most adviseable method of managing their beaux. We advise all daughters to purchase them for the sake of their mothers, who shall be initiated] 1A, 2A; daughters, who will be initiated 1F

*73.10–14 As we have before hinted, that we do not concern ourselves about the pecuniary matters of our paper, we leave its price to be regulated by our publisher; only recommending him for his own interest, and the honor of his authors, not to sell their invaluable productions too cheap.] 1A, 2A; *omitted* 1F

73.35 that there] 1A^1; there 1A^2–1A^3, 1A^5–1A^7, 2A, 1F

74.2–3 Linkum Fidelius] 1A; Linkum 2A, 1F

74.8 recorded] 1A, 2A; reported 1F

74.11 given greater] 1A^1–1A^2, 1A^4; given a greater 1A^3, 1A^5–1A^7, 2A, 1F

74.23	likewise] 1A, 2A; also 1F
74.28	daggers] 1A, 2A; dagger 1F
74.30	rather] 1A^1–1A^4; *omitted* 1A^5–1A^7, 2A, 1F
74.34	doubts] 1A^1–1A^2, 1A^4; doubt 1A^3, 1A^5–1A^7, 2A, 1F
75.5	rise up in] 1A, 2A; rise in 1F
*75.27	humor] 1A^1; humors 1A^2–1A^4, 2A; humours 1A^5–1A^7, 1F
77.14	this wonderful] 1A^1–1A^3, 1A^5–1A^6, 2A, 1F; his wonderful 1A^7
*77.17	or a mountebank] 1A^1–1A^3, 1A^5, 1A^7, 2A; or a mounteback 1A^6; *omitted* 1F
77.38	precaution] 1A^1, 1A^3, 1A^5–1A^7, 2A, 1F; precautions 1A^2
78.7	showing] 1A; conducting 2A, 1F
78.29	folks] 1A^1–1A^3, 2A, 1F; folk 1A^4–1A^5
79.11	modestly] 1A, 2A; *omitted* 1F
79.21	would] 1A^1–1A^4, 2A, 1F; should 1A^5
80.41	stopped] 1A, 2A; stepped 1F
81.5	a corner] 1A, 2A; the corner 1F
81.30	draining] 1A^1–1A^3, 2A, 1F; drainings 1A^4–1A^5
*82.9	Snivers] 1A, 2A; 'Sbidlikens 1F
82.23–28	The concert was given in the tea-room, at the City-Hotel; an apartment admirably calculated by its dingy walls, beautifully marbled with smoke, to show off the dresses and complexions of the ladies, and by the flatness of its ceiling to repress those impertinent reverbations of the music, which, whatever others may foolishly assert, are, as Snivers says, "no better than repetitions of old stories."] 1A, 2A; *omitted* 1F
83.8	scowls] 1A, 2A; and scowls 1F
83.8–9	and grins every little trembling] 1A; as though he would grin every 2A, 1F
83.14	Snivers] 1A, 2A; 'Sbidlikens 1F
83.15–16	or nozzle] 1A; *omitted* 2A, 1F
83.16–19	Snout, the bellows-mender, never tuned his wind instrument more musically; nor did the celebrated "knight of of the burning lamp," ever yield more exquisite entertainment with his nose;] 1A, 2A; *omitted* 1F
83.20	snout] 1A, 2A; musical feature 1F
84.43	Linkum Fidelius] 1A; Linkum 2A, 1F
85.7	dealt roughly] 1A^1–1A^4, 2A, 1F; dealt lightly 1A^5
85.7	passed lightly] 1A^1–1A^4, 2A, 1F; passed roughly 1A^5
86.28	all] 1A; will 2A, 1F
86.31	blaze] 1A, 2A; show 1F

87.9	its] 1A, 2A; true 1F
87.26	I warrant] 1A^1–1A^2; I'll warrant 1A^3–1A^5, 2A, 1F
87.27	living!] 1A, 2A; powers! 1F
87.41	into] 1A^1–1A^4, 2A, 1F; in 1A^5
87.41	having been] 1A^1–1A^4, 2A, 1F; being 1A^5
88.2–4	and if it were, we lay it down as one of our indisputable facts, that no man can be made ridiculous but by his own folly] 1A, 2A; *omitted* 1F
88.28	retinues] 1A^1–1A^3, 2A, 1F; retinue 1A^4–1A^5
*89.12	sand-flat, than] 1A^1–1A^2; sand-falt, rather than 1A^3–1A^5, 2A, 1F
89.19	whom] 1A^1–1A^2; which 1A^3–1A^5, 2A, 1F
89.25–26	masters] 1A^1–1A^3, 1A^5, 2A, 1F; master 1A^4
90.1	two] 1A, 2A; *omitted* 1F
90.26	in Tripoli] 1A^1–1A^2; at Tripoli 1A^3–1A^5, 2A, 1F
*90.32	trammels] 1A, 2A; hangers 1F
91.10	necks] 1A^1–1A^3, 2A, 1F; neck 1A^4–1A^5
91.15	nobody] 1A^1–1A^2; no one 1A^3–1A^5, 2A, 1F
92.5	we] 1A, 2A; was 1F
92.11	were they] 1A; they were 2A, 1F
92.24	vessel, which] 1A^1–1A^3, 2A, 1F; vessel that 1A^4–1A^5
92.41	wives do they make! what] 1A^1–1A^2; wives they make. What 1A^3–1A^5, 2A, 1F
93.14	have not met with less] 1A^1–1A^2; have met with not less 1A^3–1A^5, 2A; have met not less 1F
93.16	with] 1A, 2A; *omitted* 1F
94.16	any] 1A^1–1A^2; *omitted* 1A^3–1A^5, 2A, 1F
95.12	newspaper] 1A^1; newspapers 1A^2–1A^5, 2A, 1F
95.25–29	Dat veniam corvis, vexat censura Columbas. / JUV. / A, *was an archer and shot at a frog, / But missing his aim shot into a bog.* / LINK. FID. vol. CIII. chap. clv.] 1A; *omitted* 2A, 1F
95.35	clutches] 1A^1–1A^2; grasp 1A^3–1A^5, 2A, 1F
95.36	its] 1A, 2A; his 1F
96.2	cent] 1A, 2A; farthing 1F
96.13	sleeves] 1A^1; sleeve 1A^2–1A^5, 2A, 1F
96.19	atlean] 1A; *omitted* 2A, 1F
96.23	these] 1A, 2A; those 1F
*96.31	conscience] 1A^1; conscious 1A^2–1A^5, 2A, 1F
96.37	sure] 1A, 2A; soon 1F
*97.24	wool-clad warriors] 1A^1, 2A, 1F; wood-clad warriors 1A^2; wood-clad warriours 1A^3–1A^5

97.30–98.28   "——— *How ... monster.*"] 1A; *omitted* 2A, 1F
98.39   mistresses'] 1A¹; mistress' 1A³–1A⁵, 2A, 1F
99.6   whoe'er] 1A, 2A; whome'er 1F
99.37   the shoe] 1A¹–1A²; your shoe 1A³–1A⁵, 2A, 1F
100.7   a wintery] 1A¹; a chill wintry 1A²–1A⁵, 2A, 1F
100.34   b——h of an] 1A, 2A; queer-looking 1F
100.35–36   "Vhat shtops," as he says, "all de peoples vhat come /
              "Vhat shmiles on dem all, and vhat peats on de
              trum."] 1A¹; "What shtops," as he says, all de people
              what come; / "What shmiles on dem all, and what
              peats on de trum." 1A²; "What shtops," as he says,
              all de people what come: / "What smiles on dem all,
              and what peats on de trum." 1A³–1A⁵
101.21–26   I should have said Jeremy Cockloft *the younger*, as he
              so styles himself by way of distinguishing him from
              IL SIGNORE JEREMO COCKLOFTICO, a gouty old gentle-
              man who flourished about the time that Pliny the elder
              was smoked to death with the fire and brimstone of
              Vesuvius, and whose travels, if he ever wrote any, are
              now lost forever to the world.] 1A, 2A; *omitted* 1F
101.23   him] 1A¹–1A², 2A; himself 1A³–1A⁴
102.3   cat, worried] 1A¹–1A², 2A, 1F; rat, worried 1A³–1A⁴
102.5–6   thundering] 1A, 2A; detonating 1F
102.11   fingers'] 1A¹, 1A⁴, 1F; finger's 1A²–1A³, 2A
102.19–22   By this sketch, I mean no disparagement to the abilities
              of other students of our college, for I have no doubt
              that every commencement ushers into society, lumi-
              naries as brilliant as *Jeremy Cockloft, the younger.*]
              1A, 2A; *omitted* 1F
102.24   folks] 1A¹–1A², 2A, 1F; folk 1A³–1A⁴
102.38   laying] 1A, 2A; lying 1F
103.35   Archy] 1A; Archer 2A, 1F
104.2–3   all fat as] 1A¹–1A³, 2A, 1F; as fat as 1A⁴
104.4–5   and turn their noses to the south when the wind blows]
              1A, 2A; *omitted* 1F
°104.13   according to Linkum Fidelius] 1A, 2A; *omitted* 1F
104.16–18   Linkum as right as my left leg—Rahway-River—good
              place for gun-boats—wonder why Mr. Jefferson dont
              send a *river fleet* there, to protect the hay vessels?] 1A,
              2A; *omitted* 1F
104.31   sleep] 1A, 2A; sleep in 1F
105.15   and pensive] 1A, 2A; *omitted* 1F

105.23	and splac-nuncs] 1A, 2A; *omitted* 1F
105.39	§*vide* Carr.] T; †*vide* Carr. 1A; *omitted* 2A, 1F
106.19	capital] $1A^1$–$1A^3$, 2A, 1F; capital $1A^4$
106.38	†Moore.] 1A, 2A; *omitted* 1F
*107.5–116.23	FROM.... dog!] 1A; *omitted* 2A, 1F
107.39	*Moore.] 1A, 2A; *omitted* 1F
108.16	can tell what the devil tune] $1A^1$–$1A^2$; can make out what tune $1A^3$–$1A^4$
108.30	folks] $1A^1$–$1A^3$; folk $1A^4$
109.33	idea] $1A^1$–$1A^3$; ideas $1A^4$
111.27	the doctor's] $1A^1$–$1A^3$; his $1A^4$
111.29	we say] $1A^1$; we may say $1A^2$–$1A^4$
111.34	paunch] $1A^1$–$1A^2$; waist $1A^3$
*112.1	*I wont*] $1A^1$–$1A^2$; *I wont* (*or wunt*) $1A^3$; *I wont or* (*wunt*) $1A^4$
112.34	or no,] $1A^1$; or no$_\wedge$ $1A^2$; or not, $1A^3$; or no$_\wedge$ $1A^4$a; or not, $1A^4$b
112.41	*vide* Costive.] $1A^1$; Costive. $1A^2$–$1A^4$
113.24	*prospects*] $1A^1$–$1A^4$a; *prospect* $1A^4$b
116.31	in honorable] $1A^1$; in the honourable $1A^2$–$1A^4$, 2A, 1F
116.36–37	this being what I understand by *military foppery.*] 1A; *omitted* 2A, 1F
117.9	a wave] $1A^1$; the wave $1A^2$–$1A^4$, 2A, 1F
117.12	infernal] 1A, 2A; *omitted* 1F
117.14	tranquil] 1A, 2A; *omitted* 1F
118.18	very active] $1A^1$–$1A^2$, 2A, 1F; were active $1A^3$–$1A^4$
119.6	most] 1A, 2A; *omitted* 1F
119.12	to single] $1A^1$–$1A^3$, 2A, 1F; to a single $1A^4$
119.16	splendid] 1A, 2A; *omitted* 1F
119.22	or stun] $1A^1$–$1A^3$, 2A, 1F; and stun $1A^4$
120.33–34	hooting, hubbub and combustion] 1A, 2A; hooting and hubbub 1F
120.35	fascinating] 1A, 2A; *omitted* 1F
121.2	kettle] 1A, 2A; *omitted* 1F
121.9	paddle] 1A, 2A; pass 1F
121.15	magnanimous] 1A, 2A; *omitted* 1F
121.19	kettle-drummers] 1A, 2A; drummers 1F
121.29	breeches] 1A, 2A; leather breeches 1F
121.31	and poke hole] 1A, 2A; *omitted* 1F
122.1–2	This is a sage truism, and I trust, therefore, it will not be disputed.] 1A, 2A; *omitted* 1F

122.20–21   they fly in showers like the arrows of the parthians] 1A,
                 2A; *omitted* 1F
122.21–22   like the intrepid followers of Leonidas,] 1A, 2A; *omitted*
                 1F
122.31   share] 1A¹–1A³, 2A, 1F; have 1A⁴
122.35   as unwieldy, and cumbrous, as] 1A¹–1A³, 2A, 1F; as
                 cumbrous and unwieldy as 1A⁴
122.39   all] 1A¹–1A³, 2A, 1F; *omitted* 1A⁴
123.9   grade] 1A, 2A; rank 1F
123.16   in itself] 1A¹–1A³, 2A, 1F; of itself 1A⁴
123.32   stuck] 1A, 2A; shut 1F
124.6   frizzed] 1A¹; frizzled 1A²–1A⁴, 2A, 1F
124.19   remarkable] 1A, 2A; perfect 1F
124.20   larger] 1A¹–1A², 2A, 1F; longer 1A³–1A⁴
124.33   pictures] 1A¹–1A², 1A⁴, 2A, 1F; picture 1A³
124.41   to] 1A¹; into 1A²–1A⁴, 2A, 1F
125.22   tails] 1A, 2A; tail 1F
125.30   kettle] 1A, 2A; bottle 1F
125.38   perpetual] 1A, 2A; perfect 1F
126.12   on his] 1A¹; on the 1A²–1A⁴, 2A, 1F
126.38–129.28   TO. . . . fault.] 1A, 2A; *omitted* 1F
129.36   coming into] 1A¹–1A², 2A, 1F; went into 1A³b–1A⁴
129.36–130.1   Wales, became] 1A¹–1A², 2A, 1F; Wales, where he
                 became 1A³; Wales; where he became 1A⁴
130.8   rule for] 1A¹–1A², 1A³b, 2A, 1F; rule of 1A⁴
130.12   starting] 1A¹–1A³, 2A, 1F; striking 1A⁴
130.17   was] 1A, 2A; were 1F
130.18–19   mr. Christopher Cockloft, or to do him justice,] 1A, 2A;
                 omitted 1F
130.27   both to be] 1A; to be both 2A, 1F
130.30   of a] 1A¹–1A³, 2A, 1F; in a 1A⁴
*130.32   *runty*] 1A, 2A; *omitted* 1F
130.41   who] 1A, 2A; whom 1F
131.3   argument] 1A, 2A; arguments 1F
*131.39   and with large goggle eyes in their buttocks] 1A¹–1A²,
                 2A; and with large goggle eyes in their flanks 1A³–
                 1A⁴; *omitted* 1F
132.6   asserting] 1A; asserted 2A, 1F
132.14   codger of an] 1A, 2A; *omitted* 1F
132.36   runty] 1A, 2A; *omitted* 1F
132.37   bells ring] 1A¹–1A², 2A, 1F; bell rings 1A³–1A⁴
133.11   set] 1A¹–1A²; sit 1A³–1A⁴, 2A, 1F

133.15–16   them as he does poison, for] $1A^1$–$1A^2$, 2A, 1F; them most cordially for $1A^3a$; them most cordially, for $1A^3b$; them most cordially, for, $1A^4$

133.19   had] $1A^1$, $1A^3$–$1A^4$, 2A, 1F; has $1A^2$

133.25   sunshine] 1A, 2A; sunshiny 1F

133.30   unfeelingly] $1A^1$, $1A^3$–$1A^4$; unreasonably $1A^2$, 2A, 1F

133.37–38   forgotten, or remembered, only with a kind of tender respectful pity by] $1A^1$–$1A^2$, 2A, 1F; either entirely unnoticed or passed over with indulgence by $1A^3$; either intirely unnoticed or passed over with indulgence by $1A^4$

133.43   around] 1A; round 2A, 1F

134.5   majority] $1A^1$, $1A^3$; majesty $1A^2$, $1A^4$, 2A, 1F

134.11   soup-maigre] $1A^1$–$1A^2$, 2A, 1F; soup-meagre $1A^3$–$1A^4$

134.21   smile] $1A^1$–$1A^2$, 2A, 1F; sneer $1A^3$–$1A^4$

134.32   family, and] $1A^1$–$1A^2$, 2A, 1F; family. He $1A^3$–$1A^4$

134.33   set] 1A; sit 2A, 1F

134.33–34   with his feet on the massy andirons, and smoke his cigarr,] 1A, 2A; *omitted* 1F

134.38   "goody graciouses,"] 1A, 2A; *omitted* 1F

135.13   half a dozen] $1A^1$, $1A^3$–$1A^4$; half dozen $1A^2$, 2A, 1F

135.22   to be the] $1A^1$–$1A^2$, 2A; is the $1A^3$–$1A^4$, 1F

135.30   like old Tommy Fizgig,] 1A; *omitted* 2A, 1F

135.32   and strive] 1A; striving 2A, 1F

135.36   an old] 1A, 2A; a 1F

136.21   in the rear] $1A^1$, $1A^3$–$1A^4$; in rear $1A^2$, 2A, 1F

136.23   cleaned] 1A, 2A; cleansed 1F

136.38   Snivers] 1A, 2A; 'Sbidlikens 1F

136.41   Snivers] 1A, 2A; 'Sbidlikens 1F

137.2   corresponds] $1A^1$–$1A^2$, 2A, 1F; correspond $1A^3$–$1A^4$

137.4   have] 1A, 2A; has 1F

137.5   Snivers] 1A, 2A; 'Sbidlikens 1F

137.9–12   As the house was crowded, we were complimented with seats in Box No. 2, a sad little rantipole place, which is the strong hold of a set of rare wags, and where the poor actors undergo the most merciless tortures of verbal criticism.] 1A; *omitted* 2A, 1F

137.21   Snivers] 1A, 2A; 'Sbidlikens 1F

137.22   Snivers] 1A, 2A; 'Sbidlikens 1F

137.34   red hot] 1A, 2A; *omitted* 1F

138.9   greatest] $1A^1$, $1A^3$–$1A^4$; greater $1A^2$, 2A, 1F

138.17   tobacco-box] 1A, 2A; snuff-box 1F

138.24–25   once, on a visit which he made from the Button manu-
               factory to *Lunnun*,] 1A, 2A; *omitted* 1F
138.27   backside] 1A, 2A; back 1F
138.35   Snivers] 1A, 2A; 'Sbidlikens 1F
139.11   Snivers] 1A, 2A; 'Sbidlikens 1F
139.20   our friend] 1A¹, 1A³–1A⁴; our old friend 1A², 2A, 1F
139.24   Snivers] 1A, 2A; 'Sbidlikens 1F
139.28   bottle-holder] 1A, 2A; ally 1F
139.34   Snivers] 1A, 2A; 'Sbidlikens 1F
139.37   might possibly] 1A¹–1A², 2A, 1F; possibly might 1A³–1A⁴
139.38   like a certain philosophical great man of our day] 1A,
               2A; *omitted* 1F
140.10   argument] 1A¹, 1A³–1A⁴; arguments 1A², 2A, 1F
140.10   Snivers] 1A, 2A; 'Sbidlikens 1F
140.41   gentleman] 1A¹a, 1A², 1A³b–1A⁴, 2A, 1F; gentlemen 1A¹c
140.43   he should] 1A¹a; she should 1A¹b-c, 1A³–1A⁴; they
               should 1A², 2A, 1F
141.2   most potent] 1A, 2A; *omitted* 1F
141.14   own] 1A, 2A; *omitted* 1F
141.16   by the great Linkum Fidelius] 1A, 2A; *omitted* 1F
141.24   that he] 1A¹a, c, 1A², 1A³b–1A⁴, 2A, 1F; he that 1A¹b
141.24   blow] 1A¹–1A⁴a, 2A, 1F; wound 1A⁴b
141.28–29   if that was a dozen years ago] 1A, 2A; even though
               that were a dozen years since 1F
142.7   and proper character] 1A, 2A; *omitted* 1F
142.32   arabs, who] 1A¹; arabs, that 1A²–1A³, 2A, 1F
143.12   well knowest] 1A, 2A; must know 1F
143.19   are] 1A; is 2A, 1F
143.25   incessant brawlers] 1A, 2A; *omitted* 1F
*144.5   excepting] 1A¹a; except 1A¹b–1A³, 2A, 1F
144.15   upon each] 1A¹; on each 1A²–1A³, 2A, 1F
144.38   either by Linkum Fidelius, or] 1A, 2A; *omitted* 1F
145.14   to find out wisdom] 1A¹; to find wisdom 1A²–1A³, 2A, 1F
146.7–20   This has been the case more than once, my friend; and
               to let thee into a secret, I have been told in confidence,
               that there have been absolutely several old women
               smuggled into congress from different parts of the em-
               pire, who having once got on the breeches, as thou
               mayst well imagine, have taken the lead in debate,
               and overwhelmed the whole assembly with their gar-
               rulity; for my part, as times go, I do not see why old
               women should not be as eligible to public councils

as old men, who possess their dispositions—they certainly are eminently possessed of the qualifications
requisite to govern in a logocracy. ⟨*Paragraph*⟩ Nothing,
as I have repeatedly insisted, can be done in this
country without talking, but they take so long to talk
over a measure, that by the time they have determined
upon adopting it, the period has elapsed, which was
proper for carrying it into effect.] 1A, 2A; *omitted* 1F

146.22	put in] 1A^1; put into 1A^2–1A^3, 2A, 1F
146.33	like an Atlas] 1A, 2A; *omitted* 1F
146.36	nonsense] 1A, 2A; wisdom 1F
148.22	set] 1A^1; sit 1A^2–1A^3, 2A, 1F
149.16	windings] 1A^1–1A^2, 2A, 1F; winding 1A^3
°149.28–29	lore, / To the lascivious rhapsodies of MOORE.] 1A, 2A; lines, / Each now for soft licentious verse declines. 1F
149.35	smutty] 1A, 2A; ribald 1F
150.5	days] 1A, 2A; day 1F
151.9	intertwine] 1A^1; intwine 1A^2–1A^3, 2A, 1F
151.14	have] 1A^1; has 1A^2–1A^3, 2A, 1F
151.23	should] 1A^1; would 1A^2–1A^3, 2A, 1F
151.26–27	and above all, from the disagreeable alternative of send- ing an *apology* by the HORNET,] 1A, 2A; *omitted* 1F
151.33	toast] 1A, 2A; roast 1F
°152.21	nor] 1A, 2A; or 1F
°152.32–33	rise and sink] 1A^1; sink and rise 1A^2–1A^3, 2A, 1F
°153.20	grum] 1A, 2A; glum 1F
°153.28–34	Annexed to this article, our readers will perceive a strik- ing likeness of my friend, which was taken by that cunning rogue Will Wizard, who peeped through the key-hole, and sketched it off, as honest Launcelot sat by the fire, wrapped up in his flannel *robe de chambre*, and indulging in a mortal fit of the *hyp*. Now take my word for it, gentle reader, this is the most auspi- cious moment in which to touch off the phiz of a genuine humorist.] 1A, 2A; *omitted* 1F
154.13	tremendous] 1A, 2A; *omitted* 1F
154.15–16	is ... is] 1A, 2A; be ... be 1F
154.41	cooped] 1A, 2A; served 1F
154.41	poets'] 1A^1; poet's 1A^2–1A^3, 2A, 1F
155.10	sweep] 1A^1–1A^2, 2A, 1F; speed 1A^3
155.16	forbid] 1A, 2A; forbade 1F

155.18–19	however most unluckily happened to be rather] 1A, 2A; turned out 1F
155.21	most] 1A, 2A; *omitted* 1F
156.40	Launcelot] 1A¹–1A², 2A, 1F; Langstaff 1A³
157.1	care] 1A¹–1A², 2A, 1F; desire 1A³
157.15	than the] 1A, 2A; than in the 1F
157.17	of excellent] 1A¹a–b; of most excellent 1A¹c–1A³, 2A, 1F
°157.29	the subject] 1A¹; this article 1A²–1A³, 2A, 1F
°158.12	a lord] 1A, 2A; an earl 1F
158.40	lay] 1A, 2A; lie 1F
159.3	townswomen] 1A, 2A; townsmen 1F
159.10	fine] 1A, 2A; *omitted* 1F
159.17	gradations] 1A; gradation 2A, 1F
159.35–36	with a sneer] 1A¹; *omitted* 1A²–1A³, 2A, 1F
160.2	shavers] 1A, 2A; urchins 1F
160.17–18	and after a life of incessant self-denial, and starvation,] 1A, 2A; *omitted* 1F
160.28–29	I can liken their sudden *eclat* to nothing but] 1A, 2A; Their sudden *éclat* may be likened to 1F
160.35	tinsel] 1A, 2A; bustle 1F
161.15–16	they hired cooks, they hired fiddlers,] 1A, 2A; *omitted* 1F
161.36	their noses up in the wind] 1A, 2A; up their noses 1F
°162.3	Linkum Fidelius] 1A, 2A; Lithgow 1F
162.7	Snivers] 1A, 2A; Sbidlikens 1F
163.7	vociferously] 1A, 2A; *omitted* 1F
163.25–26	make an apology] 1A¹–1A²; make apology 1A³, 2A, 1F
165.22	which] 1A, 2A; from which 1F
165.31	lean] 1A, 2A; leaning 1F
165.41	sick] 1A, 2A; ill 1F
167.8	for] 1A, 2A; *omitted* 1F
167.13	calamities and] 1A, 2A; *omitted* 1F
168.30	confounded] 1A; *omitted* 2A, 1F
169.28	traveller like,] 1A, 2A; *omitted* 1F
169.37	departing] 1A¹–1A², 2A, 1F; departed 1A³
170.15	sublime and] 1A; *omitted* 2A, 1F
170.17	such ardent] 1A, 2A; *omitted* 1F
170.42	amazing] 1A, 2A; amazingly 1F
171.1	had] 1A, 2A; has 1F
°171.13	pray,"] 1A, 2A; pray, sir," 1F
172.3	was] 1A¹, 2A, 1F; were 1A²–1A³
172.7–10	The shrewd fellow would doubtless have valued himself

much more highly on his *economy,* could he have known that his example would one day be followed by the bashaw of America, and sages of his divan.] 1A, 2A; *omitted* 1F

172.28–35   ⟨*Paragraph*⟩ In the course of debate on this momentous question, the members began to wax warm, and grew to be exceeding wroth with one another, because their opponents most obstinately refused to be convinced by their arguments—or rather their *words.* The hole in the wall came well nigh producing a civil war of words throughout the empire; for, as usualy in all public questions, the whole country was divided, and the *holeans* and the *anti-holeans,* headed by their respective slang-whangers, were marshalled out in array, and menaced deadly warfare.] 1A; *omitted* 2A, 1F

172.36–39   when two rampant virginians, brim-full of logic and philosophy, were measuring tongues, and syllogistically cudgelling each other out of their unreasonable notions.] 1A, 2A; *omitted* 1F

172.42   hitting on] 1A, 2A; *omitted* 1F

173.2–3   As it happened, only a few thousand dollars were expended in paying these men, who are denominated, I suppose in derision, legislators.] 1A, 2A; *omitted* 1F

173.10   whole] 1A, 2A; *omitted* 1F

173.11   somniferous] 1A, 2A; profound 1F

173.11   about] 1A, 2A; upon 1F

173.12   like] 1A, 2A; as 1F

173.13   exerting] 1A, 2A; exert 1F

173.22   termed] 1A, 2A; called 1F

174.21   in] $1A^1$–$1A^2$, 2A, 1F; into $1A^3$

175.6   blessing] $1A^1$–$1A^2$; blessings $1A^3$, 2A, 1F

175.8   my] 1A, 2A; the 1F

175.38   her] 1A, 2A; their 1F

176.2   transports] 1A, 2A; feelings 1F

176.4   clasped] 1A, 2A; held 1F

176.22–23   Ten . . . six] 1A, 2A; Six . . . ten 1F

176.30   guileless] 1A; guiltless 2A, 1F

177.2   brilliance] 1A, 2A; freshness 1F

177.15   timorous] $1A^1$, 2A, 1F; timid $1A^2$–$1A^3$

177.28   dreams] 1A, 2A; dream 1F

177.30   your] 1A, 2A; its 1F

177.31   ah!] 1A, 2A; oft 1F

177.33   Still feels] 1A, 2A; will feel 1F

178.8–9   And as she found her stock enlarge, / Had stampt new
                graces on her charge.] 1A, 2A; *omitted* 1F

178.10   The fair] 1A, 2A; But now 1F

178.12   And flew] 1A, 2A; They'd flown 1F

178.34–37   Who hover round them as they glide / Down fashion's
                smooth deceitful tide, / And guard them o'er that
                stormy deep / Where Dissipation's tempests sweep:]
                1A, 2A; *omitted* 1F

179.2   beam] 1A, 2A; beams 1F

179.34   declared] 1A¹, 2A, 1F; expressed 1A²–1A³

*180.14–15   cherubims and seraphs] 1A¹, 2A; cherubims and sera-
                phims 1A²–1A³; cherubim and seraphim 1F

180.18   *dished*] 1A; thrown out 2A, 1F

181.24   mind, so as entirely to do away the necessity] 1A¹, 2A,
                1F; mind without the assistance 1A²–1A³

181.32   to prove to] 1A¹, 2A, 1F; to satisfy 1A²–1A³

181.33   the different] 1A¹, 2A, 1F; a few of the 1A²–1A³

*181.36–183.4   ⟨*Paragraph*⟩ The piece opens with a gentle andante
                affetuoso, which ushers you into the assembly-room,
                in the state-house at Albany, where the speaker ad-
                dresses his farewel speech, informing the members that
                the ice is about breaking up, and thanking them for
                their great services and good behaviour in a manner
                so pathetic as to bring tears into their eyes.—Flourish
                of Jacks a donkies.—Ice cracks—Albany in a hubbub—
                air, "Three children sliding on the ice, all on a sum-
                mer's day."—Citizens quarrelling in dutch—chorus of
                a tin trumpet, a cracked fiddle, and a hand-saw!—
                allegro moderato.—*Hard frost*—this if given with proper
                spirit has a charming effect, and sets every body's
                teeth chattering.—Symptoms of snow—consultation of
                old women who complain of pains in the bones and
                rheumatics—air, "There was an old woman tossed up
                in a blanket, &c.—allegro staccato—waggon breaks into
                the ice—people all run to see what is the matter—air,
                siciliano—"Can you row the boat ashore, Billy boy,
                Billy boy"—andante—frost fish froze up in the ice—
                air—"Ho, why dost thou shiver and shake. Gaffer
                Gray, and why does thy nose look so blue?"—Flourish
                of two-penny trumpets and rattles—consultation of

the North-river society—determine to set the North river on fire, as soon as it will burn—air—"O, what a fine kettle of fish." ⟨Paragraph⟩ Part II.—GREAT THAW.—This consists of the most *melting* strains, flowing so smoothly, as to occasion a great over-flowing of scientific rapture—air—"One misty moisty morning."—The house of assembly breaks up—air—"The owls came out and flew about"—Assembly-men embark on their way to New-York—air—"The ducks and the geese they all swim over, fal, de ral, &c.—Vessel sets sail—chorus of mariners—"Steer her up, and let her gang." After this a rapid movement conducts you to New-York—the North-river society hold a meeting at the corner of Wall-street, and deter-mine to delay burning till all the assemblymen are safe home, for fear of consuming some of their own members who belong to that respectable body.—Return again to the *capital.*—Ice floats down the river—lamenta-tion of skaiters—air, affetuoso—"I sigh and lament me in vain, &c."—Albanians cutting up sturgeon—air—"O the roast beef of *Albany*."—Ice runs against Polopoy's Island, with a terrible crash.—This is represented by a fierce fellow travelling with his fiddle-stick over a huge bass viol, at the rate of one hundred and fifty bars a minute, and tearing the music to rags—this being what is called *execution.*—The great body of ice passes West-Point, and is saluted by three or four dismounted cannon, from Fort Putnam.—"Jefferson's march"—by a full band—air—"Yankee doodle, with seventy-six vari-ations, never before attempted, except by the cele-brated eagle, which flutters his wings over the copper-bottomed angel at messrs. Paff's in Broadway.—Ice passes New-York—conch-shell sounds at a distance—ferryman calls o-v-e-r—people run down Courtlandt-street—ferryboat sets sail—air—accompanied by the conch-shell—"We'll all go over the ferry.—Rondeau—giving a particular account of BROM the Powles-Hook admiral, who is supposed to be closely connected with the North-river society.—The society make a grand attempt to fire the stream, but are utterly defeated by a remarkable high tide, which brings the pilot to light—drowns upwards of a thousand rats, and

occasions twenty robins to break their necks.*—Society
not being discouraged, apply to "Common Sense," for
his lantern—air—"Nose, nose, jolly red nose."—Flock of
wild geese fly over the city—old wives chatter in the
fog—cocks crow at Communipaw—drums beat on Governor's island. *Vide—Solomon Lang.—The whole to
conclude with *the blowing up of Sands' powder-house.*]
1A, 2A, 1F; The piece opens with a gentle andante
affetuoso, soft, sleepy, and monotonous, intended to
represent a discussion in the house of assembly at
Albany, which always breaks up at the same time with
the river; the speaker delivers his farewel address to
the tune of "oh must we part, to meet no more," and
the members wipe their eyes and blow their noses in
melodious symphony. This is followed by a *hard frost,*
which if given with proper fire and animation, will
make every body's teeth chatter, and their flesh creep
on their bones. It is to be managed by one of our
furious looking little fiddlers, flourishing his fiddlestick
at the rate of one hundred and fifty bars in a minute,
tearing an honest, portly, peaceable semibreve "to
tatters, to very rags," and throwing every real *amateur*
into an absolute ecstasy—this being what is called
execution. I also place great dependance for *effect,*
upon a quarrel among the albanians in *dutch.* To introduce a quarrel with perfect *harmony* and *concord,*
you may think rather extravagant; but have not our
enlightened audiences applauded the same, over and
over, in several of those musical monsters, called melo-
drames, wherein they even fight to a contra-dance,
stab with a crotchet, and die with a quaver! And as
to the dutch language, I have succeeded most happily
in imitating it, by the assistance of a tin trumpet, a
cracked fiddle and a handsaw. ⟨*Paragraph*⟩ My second
part opens with a grand musical experiment, which is
nothing less than to perform a GREAT THAW!—Talk to
me of your hail-storms and snow-storms, and thunder
and lightning—here is something that will out-do them
all—such melting airs, such soft flowing strains:—my
only apprehension is from our confounded fiddlers,
who have fallen of late into such an abandoned habit
of sawing, and strumming, and piping "to the very top

of the compass," that they can scarcely draw a fiddle-stick, without setting every nerve in your body in a tremour. Let them only acquit themselves in this part with the true *graziozo*, and they may afterwards indulge in their favourite noise to their heart's content; for afterwards comes the bustle, the hub-bub and the *effect* of my piece—then every catgut hero is at full liberty to scrape, and saw, and quaver, and bray, and rattle, and thunder, and produce a very tempest and whirlwind of *sweet sounds*. The ice shall crash, the sleigh-bells shall jungle, the drums shall beat on Governor's-Island, and the whole shall conclude with *the blowing up of Sands' powder house.* 1A²

182.39   remarkable] 1A¹, 2A; remarkably 1F

182.39–41   drowns upwards of a thousand rats, and occasions twenty robins to break their necks.*] 1A¹, 2A; *omitted* 1F

182.42   *Vide—Solomon Lang.] 1A¹, 2A; *omitted* 1F

*183.20–21   doctors. ⟨Paragraph⟩ In] 1A¹, 2A, 1F; doctors. ⟨Paragraph⟩ You will observe likewise, how admirably the musick of my piece is calculated to illustrate the subject—"Suit the *action* to the word, the word to the *action.*" Says Hamlet—"suit the *musick* to the *fact*, the *fact* to the *musick*," say I: and I'll be bound no melo-dramatist ever succeeded better than myself in achieving impossibilities.—Let me only have a few thorough going *amateurs* to back me, and to applaud every thing with true scientifick enthusiasm and credulity, and I have no doubt of a harvest of laurels.— Oh sir, your *men of gusto*—your men of gusto are invaluable! Dramatists, picture daubers, toad-eaters, poetasters, and musick manufacturers, might all starve or hang themselves, were it not for your *amateurs*— your *connoisseurs*, and your *men of gusto.* ⟨Paragraph⟩ In 1A²–1A³

183.40   immortality] 1A¹–1A², 2A, 1F; immorality 1A³

184.6   and never be at a loss to make himself understood.] 1A¹, 2A, 1F; as conveniently as a savoyard in France, a bag-piper in Scotland, or a musick grinder in America. 1A²–1A³

184.9–10   P. S. I forgot to mention that I intend to publish my piece by subscription, and dedicate it to the North-River Society. ⟨Space⟩ D.S.] 1A¹; *omitted* 1A²–1A³, 2A, 1F

*184.10–11   D. S. / THE STRANGER] 1A¹; D. S. FROM MY
               ELBOW-CHAIR. / ⟨Paragraph⟩ The memorandums
               which I published sometime since from the common-
               place book of mr. Jeremy Cockloft, were received with
               universal approbation throughout the Cockloft family,
               and were read with peculiar delight—by his mother
               and himself. Old Christopher likewise betrayed great
               symptoms of self-congratulation on this specimen of
               his son's genius, and declared he had no doubt Jeremy
               would make a great lawyer, for he had the *gift of the
               gab* to perfection. This is a common notion among
               parents, who generally devote their most pert and
               forward children to the law—and hence the ingenious
               sophistry, the verbose wrangling, the knowing finesse,
               and the superlative ventosity that give such brilliancy,
               froth and flummery to our bar. Jeremy was so de-
               lighted with the encomiums lavished upon him, and
               particularly with a compliment from Will Wizard, who
               declared that he was as sapient as a ten-pound justice—
               that he put his whole budget of memorandums into
               my hand, with full powers to make what use of them
               I pleased. ⟨Paragraph⟩ The notes which follow those
               already published are entitled THE STRANGER]
               1A²–1A³

*184.11–185.22 THE STRANGER IN PENNSYLVANIA. / BY JEREMY
               COCKLOFT, THE YOUNGER. / CHAPTER I. / ⟨Paragraph⟩
               Cross the Delaware—knew I was in Pennsylvania, be-
               cause all the people were fat and looked like the
               statue of William Penn—Bristol—very remarkable for
               having nothing in it worth the attention of the
               traveller—saw Burlington on the opposite side of the
               river—fine place for pigeon-houses—and why?—Penn-
               sylvania famous for barns—cattle in general better
               lodged than the farmers—barns appear to be built, as
               the old roman peasant planted his trees, "for posterity
               and the immortal gods." Saw several fine bridges of
               two or three arches built over dry places—wondered
               what could be the use of them—reminded me of the
               famous bridge at Madrid, built over no water—Cha-
               mouny—floating bridge made of pine logs fastened
               together by ropes of walnut bark—strange that the
               people who have such a taste for bridges should not
               have taken advantage of this river, to indulge in their

favorite kind of architecture!—expressed my surprise
to a fellow passenger, who observed to me with great
gravity, "that nothing was more natural than that
people who build bridges over dry places should
neglect them where they are really necessary"—could
not, for the head of me, see to the bottom of man's
reasoning—about half an hour after it struck me that
he had been quizzing me a little—didn't care much
about that—revenge myself by mentioning him in my
book. Village of Washington—very pleasant, and remarkable for being built on each side of the road—
houses all cast in the same mould—have a very quakerish appearance, being built of stone, plastered and
white-washed, and green doors, ornamented with brass
knockers, kept very bright—saw several genteel young
ladies scouring them—which was no doubt the reason
of their brightness. Breakfasted at the Fox-Chase—recommend this house to all gentlemen travelling for
information, as the landlady makes the best buckwheat-cakes in the whole world; and because it bears
the same name with a play, written by a young
gentleman of Philadelphia, which, notwithstanding its
very considerable merit, was received at that city with
indifference and neglect, because it had no puns in
it. Frankfort *in the mud*—very picturesque town, situate on the edge of a pleasant swamp—or meadow as
they call it—houses all built of turf, cut in imitation of
stone—poor substitute—took in a couple of Princeton
students, who were going on to the southward, to tell
their papas, (or rather their mammas) what fine manly
little boys they were, and how nobly they resisted
the authority of the trustees—both pupils of Godwin
and Tom Paine—talked about the rights of man, the
social compact, and the perfectability of boys—hope
their parents will whip them when they get home,
and send them back to college without any spending
money. Turnpike gates—direction to keep to the right,
as the law directs—very good advice, in my opinion;
but one of the students swore he had no idea of
submitting to this kind of oppression, and insisted on
the driver's taking the left passage, in order to show
the world we were not to be imposed upon by such
arbitrary rules—driver, who, I believe had been a

student at Princeton himself, shook his head like a
professor, and said it would not do. Entered Philadelphia through the suburbs—four little markets in
a herd—one turned into a school for young ladies—
mem. young ladies early in the market here—pun—
good.] 1A¹; "THE STRANGER IN PENNSYL-
VANIA." / The first chapter contains an account of
his route from Trenton to Philadelphia: It is, as usual,
much in the style of Carr, sweetened, now and then,
with a sentimental episode, in the manner of Kotzebue, or a picturesque description, *a la Radcliffe*,
wherein wood and water, and grove and rock, and
silver streams, and golden clouds are mixed up as
intelligibly as in a chinese landscape on a tea-board—
and now and then he bounces upon you of a sudden
with a downwright—cracker, as electrifying as those
of Weld, of Moore, of Parkinson or Janson. He is
extremely facetious at every tavern, and takes care
that his readers shall not lose a single good saying
that passed—he undertakes to explain, most learnedly,
why the pennsylvanian cattle are better lodged than
the farmers, and insists that they build their barns, as
the old roman peasant did his trees, "for posterity and
the immortal gods." In short, he writes twenty solid
pages so ingeniously that, although at first sight there
appears to be a world of information, yet the only
real article on which we are really instructed, is, that
he travelled from Trenton to Philadelphia, and scrib-
bled the whole way. The second chapter is written
the day after his arrival, and I shall give it in his
own words, as containing the very cream of a modern
traveller's observations on *men and manners*. 1A²–1A³;
omitted 2A, 1F

185.24–25   Very ill—confined to my bed with a violent fit of the
pun mania—strangers] 1A¹; MALADIES] Among the
most prevalent maladies, is the punning distemper.
It is a kind of mania which seizes all classes of people,
who forthwith become strangely diseased in mind,
and vent their fury upon the english language, committing the most unheard of barbarities. If not speedily
checked it is apt to become a confirmed complaint,
and to terminate in a complete mental debility.
Strangers 1A²–1A³

186.4   and was two days] 1A¹; and have been ever since 1A²–
               1A³

186.6   ⟨Paragraph⟩ Having] 1A¹; ⟨Paragraph⟩ NAME.] Having
               1A¹–1A²

186.11–12   PHILO DRIPPING-PAN,] 1A¹; PHILO DRIPPING-PAN,*
               1A²–1A³

186.12   Footnote omitted] 1A¹; *I defy any travel monger to
               excel friend Jeremy in forcing a derivation. ⟨Space⟩
               W. WIZARD. 1A²–1A³

186.24   vinegar.] 1A¹; vinegar; not that his idea is altogether
               erroneous, for I am informed that the fair sex have
               of late years taken a wonderful fancy to acids, whether
               to improve their health, their persons, or their dis-
               positions, is best known to themselves; but the effects
               are known to every body.—Mem. a severe hit at skin
               and bone, chalky faces, delicate stomachs, and tart
               tempers. 1A²–1A³

186.25   ⟨Paragraph⟩ The] 1A¹; ⟨Paragraph⟩ SITUATION.] The
               1A²–1A³

186.37   God help] 1A¹; heaven help 1A²–1A³

187.1   ⟨Paragraph⟩ The] 1A¹ ⟨Paragraph⟩ STREETS.] The 1A²–
               1A³

187.3   folks] 1A¹; folk 1A²–1A³

187.6–9   There is, however, one place which I would recommend
               to all my fellow-citizens, who may come after me as
               a promenade—I mean Dock-street—the only street in
               Philadelphia that bears any resemblance to New-
               York] 1A¹; In the course of my walk, however, I en-
               countered one crooked street, whereupon "I thanked
               my stars and thought it luxury!" It was Dock-street,
               the only street in Philadelphia that bears any resem-
               blance to New-York, and I recommend it to all my
               fellow-citizens, who come after me, as a promenade
               1A²–1A³

187.24   contemplations] 1A¹; contemplation 1A²–1A³

187.28   ⟨Paragraph⟩ Every body] 1A¹; ⟨Paragraph⟩ BANK.] Every
               body 1A²–1A³

187.32–35   The honest man has never seen the theatre in New-York,
               or the new brick church at the head of Rector-street,
               which when finished, will, beyond all doubt, be in-
               finitely superior to the Pennsylvania barns, I noted
               before.] 1A¹; but I never yet heard of a city that had
               not some grand architectural wonder. The people of

Rome point with triumph to the Church of St. Peter—
the parisian boasts of the Louvre, and the Thuilleries
—the cockney extols St. Paul's and the monument; and
the *cicerone* of one of our little villages entertained
me lately with the ingenious construction of a new
pillory and whipping-post. The poor citizens of New-
York, are the worst off in this particular; for though
no city in the union has expended more money on
publick buildings, yet no city has less to brag of; they
console themselves, however, with boasting of what
they will have—*some fifty years hence.* 1A²–1A³

187.36   ⟨*Paragraph*⟩ Philadelphia] 1A¹; ⟨*Paragraph*⟩ COMMERCE.]
             Philadelphia 1A²–1A³

188.4   ⟨*Paragraph*⟩ Of] 1A¹; ⟨*Paragraph*⟩ MANUFACTURES.] Of
             1A²–1A³

188.9–11   (if you can beg, borrow, or steal your molasses it will
             come much cheaper than if you buy it)—] 1A¹;
             omitted 1A²–1A³

188.15–16   but by the polite philadelphians, by a name utterly im-
             possible] 1A¹; but the polite philadelphians give it a
             name which my delicacy will not suffer me 1A²–1A³

188.17   ⟨*Paragraph*⟩ The] 1A¹; ⟨*Paragraph*⟩ FAIR SEX.] The 1A²–
             1A³

188.30   mem—*golden apple!*] 1A¹; mem.—Venus—Paris, and *gold-
             en apple.* 1A²–1A³

188.31–33   ⟨*Paragraph*⟩ The amusements of the philadelphians are
             dancing, punning, tea-parties, and theatrical exhibi-
             tions. In the first, they are far inferior to the young
             people of New-York, owing to the misfortune of their
             mostly preferring] 1A¹; ⟨*Paragraph*⟩ AMUSEMENTS.]
             The character of a people is often to be learnt from
             their amusements; for, in the hour of mirth the mind
             is unrestrained and takes its natural bent. The phila-
             delphians are fond of dancing—but in this accomplish-
             ment they are far inferior, as I am informed by sundry
             travellers of observation, to the beau monde of New-
             York. This may be ascribed to their stupidly preferring
             1A²–1A³

188.35   an infinite] 1A¹; a great 1A²–1A³

188.37   to the attainment of such trifling] 1A¹; thereto all those
             valuable 1A²–1A³

188.39–42   On the other hand they excel the new-yorkers in pun-
             ning, and in the management of tea-parties. In N.

York you never hear, except for some young gentleman
just returned from a visit to Philadelphia, a single
attempt at punning, and at a tea-party, the] 1A[1];
Now, this is what I call an absurdity—does not an
architect first attend to finishing his foundation, before
he thinks of decorating the attick story; and should
not the *heels*, which form the foundation of the human
frame, be attended to before the *head*, which is merely
the garret?—Maxim.—A bad figure will sometimes pass
for a good argument. Another amusement to which
the philadelphians are very much given, as has been
before hinted, is the celebration of tea-parties: as these
answer to european routs and *conversaziones*, they
are well worthy the attention of the curious, or *lounging* traveller, who has an evening on hands—which he
has no objection to waste. The philadelphians conduct
them with as much gravity and decorum, as they
would a funeral, and very properly too, for they celebrate the obsequies of many a departed reputation.
The 1A[2]–1A[3]

189.6   dangers] 1A[1]; deadly perils 1A[2]–1A[3]

189.11–17   ⟨*No paragraph*⟩ Some ladies who were present at this
declaration of the gallant officer, were inclined to
consider it a great compliment, until one, more knowing than the rest, declared with a little piece of a
sneer, "that they were very much obliged to him
for likening the company to a London mob, and their
glances to brick-bats:—the officer looked blue, turned
on his heel, made a fine retreat and went home, with
a determination to quiz the american ladies as soon
as he got to London.] 1A[1]; ⟨*Paragraph*⟩ Jeremy then
goes on to treat of the theatre, rope-dancing, *Spottee*
the learned horse, the taverns, the watch-house and
several other places of amusement and polite resort,
and ends this chapter with a most unmeasureable paragraph, entitled MYSELF. As an apology, he observes,
that Carr, Weld, Kotzebue, and other learned travellers, have scattered their innumerable egotisms
throughout their works, whereas he has thought proper
to collect his in a mass; and, author like, he flatters
himself that this will be more interesting and more
thumbed than any other portion of his narrative. To
do Jeremy justice, he has acquitted himself most ably,

considering he has written so much without stirring
beyond the precincts of his tavern; and he bids fair
to be ranked on a par with MOORE, who saw enough
of America from a stage-waggon, to damn the whole
of it—or with the elegant BRYDONE, who gives a sublime description of the top of Mount Etna, which he
never reached—or with the rhapsodical DUPATY, who
scampered, exclaiming, and apostrophising, and ah!-
ing, and oh!-ing all over Italy—adored every marble-
headed saint—deified every nameless scoundrel of a
torso—threw himself into an ecstasy before every
painting—and yet never stirred from his chamber the
whole time.—Oh, these travel-mongers! $1A^2$–$1A^3$

189.21	captain of a ketch,] $1A^1$–$1A^2$, 2A, 1F; *omitted* $1A^3$
189.25	passenger] 1A; passengers 2A, 1F
189.29	inmost] $1A^1$–$1A^2$, 2A, 1F; *omitted* $1A^3$
189.30–31	of confusion, of licentious disorganization,] 1A, 2A; *omitted* 1F
189.33	the puffers] 1A, 2A; *omitted* 1F
190.4–5	hore- / back] $1A^1$; horseback $1A^2$–$1A^3$, 2A, 1F
°190.15	fast] $1A^1$–$1A^2$, 2A, 1F; feast $1A^3$
190.18	substance] 1A, 2A; subject 1F
190.21–22	the decisive battle when] 1A, 2A; where 1F
190.31–32	such is the wonderful patriotism of the people,] 1A, 2A; *omitted* 1F
190.38	head workmen] 1A, 2A; leaders 1F
191.9	and perplexed] 1A, 2A; *omitted* 1F
191.12	talking their ribs quite bare] $1A^1$–$1A^2$, 2A, 1F; har-rangueing them $1A^3$
191.23	which are generally practised,] 1A, 2A; *omitted* 1F
191.34	head of Mahomet] 1A, 2A; *omitted* 1F
191.38	that] $1A^1$–$1A^2$, 2A, 1F; who $1A^3$
°192.1	worries, and puffs about] $1A^1$–$1A^2$, 2A; worries, and yelps about $1A^3$; worries about 1F
192.4	mammas] 1A, 2A; nursery 1F
192.9	nursery or] 1A, 2A; *omitted* 1F
192.20	ward] $1A^1$–$1A^2$, 2A, 1F; war $1A^3$
°192.22	doughty] $1A^1$–$1A^2$, 2A, 1F; doubty $1A^3$
192.28–29	with thundering vehemence] 1A, 2A; *omitted* 1F
192.30–31	miserable minion of poverty and ignorance] 1A, 2A; penniless patriot 1F
192.33	horeback] $1A^1$; horseback $1A^2$–$1A^3$, 2A, 1F
192.33	twaddle] $1A^1$–$1A^2$; hurry $1A^3$; worry 2A, 1F

192.34   and chafe] 1A; *omitted* 2A, 1F

192.43   extremely] 1A, 2A; rather 1F

193.1   true spirit of a genuine] 1A, 2A; *omitted* 1F

193.8   dirty looking persons] 1A, 2A; though self-important per-
              sonages 1F

*193.16–19   capable of distinguishing between an honest man and
              a knave, or even if they were, will it not always happen
              that they are led by the nose by some intrigueing
              demagogue, and made the mere tools of ambitious]
              1A, 2A; instructed in the high concerns of legislation,
              and capable of discriminating between the moral and
              political merits of statesmen? Will they not rather
              be too often led by the nose by intriguing demagogues,
              and made the mere puppets of 1F

193.20   resort] 1A, 2A; *omitted* 1F

193.21–26   I plainly perceive the consequence.—A man, who pos-
              sesses superior talents, and that honest pride which
              ever accompanies this possession, will always be sacri-
              ficed to some creeping insect who will prostitute him-
              self to familiarity with the lowest of mankind, and
              like the idolatrous egyptian, worship the wallowing
              tenants of filth and mire."] 1A, 2A; What will be the
              consequence where promotion rests with the rabble!
              He who courts the rabble will be most likely to suc-
              ceed. The man of superior worth and talents, will
              always be too proud to stoop to the low arts by which
              vulgar minds are won; he will too often, therefore,
              be defeated by the pliant sycophant or blustering
              demagogues who address themselves to the passions
              and prejudices, rather than to the judgments of the
              populace." 1F

193.27–32   ⟨Paragraph⟩ "All this is true enough," replied my friend,
              "but after all you cannot say but that this is a free
              country, and that the people can get drunk cheaper
              here, particularly at elections, than in the despotic
              countries of the east." I could not, with any degree
              of propriety or truth, deny this last assertion, for just
              at that moment a patriotic brewer arrived with a load
              of beer, which, for a moment, occasioned a cessation
              of argument.—] 1A, 2A; My friend appeared a little
              puzzled either by the logic or the length of my
              remark. "That is very true—very true indeed," said he,
              with some hesitation; "there is a great deal of force

in what you say—yet after all you cannot deny that
this is a free country, and that the people can get
drunk at a cheaper rate, particularly during elections,
than in the despotic countries of the East." ⟨*Paragraph*⟩
I confess I was somewhat staggered by the pertinency
of this rejoinder, and had not a word to say against the
correctness of its concluding assertion; for just at that
moment a cart drove up with a load of patriotic beer-
barrels, which caused a temporary cessation of all
further argument. 1F

193.27	is] 1A¹–1A², 2A; may be 1A³
193.27	friend, "but] 1A¹–1A², 2A; friend, who seemed inclined to shift the conversation; "but 1A³
193.28	that] 1A¹–1A², 2A; *omitted* 1A³
193.36	antipathies] 1A, 2A; hostilities 1F
193.40	most relished by] 1A, 2A; taste of 1F
193.43	its operation] 1A, 2A; to operate 1F
194.7	that] 1A¹–1A², 2A, 1F; who 1A³
194.10–11	help applauding] 1A¹–1A², 2A, 1F; enough applaud 1A³
194.16	the list] 1A¹, 1A³, 2A, 1F; a list 1A²
194.20	coach] 1A, 2A; carriage 1F
194.27	a] 1A, 2A; *omitted* 1F
194.28	with them in her rough way] 1A, 2A; in her rough way with her gentleman suitor 1F
194.28	but] 1A¹–1A², 2A, 1F; *omitted* 1A³
194.29	attempted to be familiar with her] 1A, 2A; presumed upon her favors 1F
194.38–39	"is it thus thy name is] 1A¹–1A², 2A, 1F; "must even thy name be 1A³
194.41	infernal] 1A, 2A; *omitted* 1F
195.14–17	The confusion was such as no language can adequately describe, and it seemed as if all the restraints of decency, and all the bands of law had been broken and given place to the wide ravages of licentious brutality.] 1A, 2A; *omitted* 1F
195.16	bands of law] 1A¹–1A², 2A; bonds of law 1A³
195.19	with] 1A, 2A; *omitted* 1F
195.21	their dominion over] 1A, 2A; on 1F
195.22–23	mass of the people, the *mob*] 1A, 2A; gross minds, the mob of the people 1F
195.23–24	but their tyranny will not be long] 1A, 2A; Even of tyrants their reign is shirt ⟨*sic*⟩ 1F
195.24	leader, having at first] 1A, 2A; minion having first 1F

195.25   will at length become] 1A, 2A; at length becomes 1F
195.26   former] 1A, 2A; original 1F
195.27–36   Yet, with innumerable examples staring them in the
                face, the people still bawl out liberty, by which they
                mean nothing but freedom from every species of legal
                restraint, and a warrant for all kinds of licentiousness:
                and the bashaws and leaders, in courting the mob,
                convince them of their power and by administering
                to their passions, for the purposes of ambition, at
                length learn by fatal experience, that he who worships
                the beast that carries him on its back, will sooner or
                later be thrown into the dust and trampled under foot
                by the animal who has learnt the secret of its power,
                by this very adoration.] $1A^1$–$1A^2$, 2A; But woe to the
                bashaws and leaders who gain a seat in the saddle
                by flattering the humours and administering to the
                passions of the mob. They will soon learn, by fatal
                experience, that he who truckles to the beast that
                carries him, teaches it the secret of its power, and will
                sooner or later be thrown to the dust, and trampled
                under foot. 1F
195.30   licentiousness: and the bashaws and leaders,] $1A^1$–$1A^2$,
                2A; licentiousness. The bashaws and leaders, more-
                over, $1A^3$
195.32   ambition, at] $1A^1$–$1A^2$, 2A; ambition, they at $1A^3$
196.1   left them at] $1A^1$–$1A^2$, 2A, 1F; allowed them $1A^3$
196.19   MY UNCLE JOHN] $1A^1$–$1A^2$, 1F; MINE UNCLE JOHN
                $1A^3$, 2A
196.38   "Well I] $1A^1$–$1A^2$, 2A, 1F; "Well, my boy, I $1A^3$
197.13   lost nothing of] $1A^1$–$1A^2$, 2A, 1F; retained $1A^3$
197.24   Daddy] $1A^1$–$1A^2$, 2A; Father $1A^3$, 1F
197.36   hill-top] 1A; hill-tops 2A, 1F
198.34   but] 1A, 2A; *omitted* 1F
199.1   *to doing*] 1A, 2A; *to do* 1F
199.23   set] 1A, 2A; sit 1F
199.36   most] 1A, 2A; *omitted* 1F
200.1   tradesman] $1A^1$a–b, $1A^2$, 2A, 1F; tradesmen $1A^1$c, $1A^3$
200.15–16   got a tremendous *flea in his ear*,] 1A; *omitted* 2A, 1F
200.20   who] 1A, 2A; whom 1F
200.30   will] 1A, 2A; would 1F
201.28   friends and] 1A, 2A; *omitted* 1F
202.30   given to] $1A^1$, 2A, 1F; given by $1A^2$–$1A^3$
202.34   d——n] $1A^1$, 2A, 1F; condemn $1A^2$–$1A^3$

203.5–6   walked or rode] 1A; passed 2A, 1F
203.6–7   occasion] 1A, 2A; excite 1F
203.9   of] 1A, 2A; *omitted* 1F
203.18–20   Now Straddle knew that the savages were fond of beads,
                   spike-nails and looking-glasses, and therefore filled his
                   trunk with them.] 1A¹; Now Straddle knew that the
                   savages were fond of beads, spike-nails and looking-
                   glasses, and therefore filled his trunk with these arti-
                   cles. 1A²–1A³; *omitted* 2A, 1F
203.24   good] 1A, 2A; *omitted* 1F
203.40   ridiculously] 1A, 2A; ridiculous 1F
204.22–23   nest of tea-boards] 1A, 2A; teaboard 1F
204.25   beer barrel] 1A, 2A; tun 1F
205.21   d——d] 1A¹a–b, 2A, 1F; bullied 1A¹c–1A³
206.9   persecutors] 1A; prosecutors 2A, 1F
206.15   gentlemen] 1A¹–1A², 2A, 1F; men 1A³
206.19   gentleman] 1A¹–1A², 2A, 1F; gentlemen 1A³
206.34–36   .....*Peregre rediit.* / *He is returned home from abroad.* /
                   DICTIONARY.] 1A; *omitted* 2A, 1F
208.7   moles] 1A, 2A; mules 1F
208.9   had] 1A, 2A; has 1F
208.10   of Europe, or] 1A; in Europe, or 2A; in Europe, or of 1F
208.11   a book] 1A¹, 2A, 1F; an essay 1A²–1A³
208.31   louse] 1A, 2A; l—— 1F
209.9–14   The pedestal still remains, because, there was no use
                   in pulling *that* down, as it would cost the corporation
                   money, and not sell for any thing...mem...a penny
                   saved is a penny got....If the pedestal must remain, I
                   would recommend that a statue of somebody, or some-
                   thing be placed on it, for truly it looks quite melan-
                   choly and forlorn....] 1A; *omitted* 2A, 1F
209.22–27   New brick church!...what a pity it is the corporation
                   of Trinity church are so poor!...if they could not afford
                   to build a better place of worship, why did they not
                   go about with a subscription?...even I would have given
                   them a few shillings rather than our city should have
                   been disgraced by such a pitiful specimen of econ-
                   omy....] 1A; *omitted* 2A, 1F
209.27   place] 1A, 2A; places 1F
209.31   common] 1A, 2A; *omitted* 1F
209.35–36   in being] 1A¹, 2A; on being 1A²–1A³, 1F
210.3   that emulated] 1A; emulated 2A; emulating 1F
210.4   inquiring] 1A, 2A; inquiry 1F

210.20   last] 1A¹–1A², 2A, 1F; *omitted* 1A³
210.36   though] 1A, 2A; *omitted* 1F
211.2   viz.] 1A¹, 2A, 1F; *i.e.* 1A²–1A³
*211.22   blocks] 1A¹a–b, 2A, 1F; block 1A¹c–1A³
211.25   cartmen] 1A¹a–b, 2A, 1F; cartman 1A¹c–1A³
211.34   empire] 1A¹a–b, 2A, 1F; emperor 1A¹c–1A³
211.37   the] 1A¹a–b, 2A, 1F; *omitted* 1A¹c–1A³
211.38   settle the] 1A, 2A; settle the affairs of the 1F
212.3   place] 1A¹a–b, 2A, 1F; places 1A¹c–1A³
212.12   Conclude] 1A¹a–b, 2A, 1F; wind up 1A¹c–1A³
212.24   words] 1A¹a–b, 2A, 1F; nods 1A¹c–1A³
*213.5–6   ⟨*Paragraph*⟩ How often I cast my reflections behind, /
              And call up the days of past youth to my mind!]
              1A¹a-b, 2A, 1F; ⟨*Paragraph*⟩ Full oft I indulge in
              reflections right sage, / And ease off my spleen by
              abusing the age; 1A¹c–1A³
213.9–10   When the foplings of fashion bedazzle my sight, / Be-
              wilder my feelings—my senses benight;] 1A¹a–b, 2A,
              1F; When *Style* with false splendour bedazzles my
              sight, / And scares all the cherubs of tranquil delight;
              1A¹c–1A³
213.11   the day] 1A; to day 2A; to-day 1F
213.19   sweet fopling] 1A¹a–b, 2A, 1F; smart coxcomb, 1A¹c–1A³
213.20   changeable] 1A¹a–b, 2A, 1F; frivolous 1A¹c–1A³
213.21–22   Proclaims him *a man* to the near and the far, / Can he
              dance a cotillion or smoke a cygarr.] 1A, 2A; *omitted*
              1F
213.25   beaux that] 1A¹a–b, 2A, 1F; youths who 1A¹c–1A³
213.29–34   —How the graces of person and graces of mind, / The
              polish of learning and fashion combined, / Till soft'ned
              in manners and strength'ned in head, / By the classical
              lore of the living and dead, / Matured in person till
              manly in size, / He then was presented a beau to our
              eyes!] 1A¹a–b; How wisdom once deign'd to enlighten
              our youth, / When instead of *the fashion,* they fol-
              lowed—the truth / Never threw by their rattles, till
              able to talk, / Nor quit nurse's arms—ere they knew
              how to walk; / How they studied their Euclid instead
              of Hoyle's rules, / And instead of tea-parties, attended
              their schools; / Till corrected in manners and
              strength'ned in head, / With the classical lore of the
              living and dead, / They entered the world without
              flutter or noise, / To figure as *men,* not to trifle as

boys. 1A¹c–1A³; ⟨*follows the 1A¹a–b version, except the fifth line reads*:⟩ Matured in his person till manly in size, 2A, 1F

213.37   circles] 1A¹a–b, 2A, 1F; parties 1A¹c–1A³

213.38   fledg'd in] 1A¹a–b; fledged from 1A¹c–1A³, 2A, 1F

213.39–214.7   Who propp'd by the credit their fathers sustain, / Alike tender in years, and in person and brain, / But plenteously stock'd with that substitute *brass*, / For true wits and critics would anxiously pass. / They complain of that empty sarcastical slang, / So common to all the coxcombical gang, / Who the fair with their shallow experience vex, / By thrumming forever their *weakness of sex*; / And who boast of *themselves*, when they talk with proud air / Of MAN's mental ascendancy over the fair.] 1A¹a–b, 2A, 1F; Who, though tender in years and full feeble in brain, / Yet, propp'd by the credit their fathers sustain, / And arm'd with good stock of invincible brass, / For criticks and men of discernment would pass. / Oh how lofty each strut-me-down magpie will talk! / Like a bantam, he'd fain be "the cock of the walk," / At tea table argument none can be greater, / —You'd think it was Solomon turn'd *petit maitre*! / Deeply versed in the would-be satirical slang, / So common amongst the coxcombical gang, / With his shallow pretensions each fair one he'll vex,/ And strum that trite subject—her *weakness of sex*; / And will puff off *himself*, while he talks with proud air / Of MAN's mental ascendancy over the fair. / Oh, shield me kind stars from these pinks of the nation, / These tea-party heroes—these *lords of creation*! 1A¹c–1A³

214.12–13   Tho' fated to shun with his dim visual ray, / The cheering delights, and the brilliance of day;] 1A¹a–b, 2A; Though fated by nature forever to shun / The splendour of day-light—the rays of the sun; 1A¹c–1A³; ⟨*follows the 1A¹a–b version, except the first line reads*:⟩ Tho' fated to shun with dim visual ray, 1F

214.15   For dull moping caverns] 1A¹a–b, 2A, 1F; And mope in drear caverns 1A¹c–1A³

214.16   strength of the] 1A¹a–b, 2A, 1F; vigour of 1A¹c–1A³

214.17   unwinking] 1A¹a–b, 2A, 1F; undazzled 1A¹c–1A³

214.20   sad evils] 1A¹a–b, 2A, 1F; annoyance 1A¹c–1A³

214.21   feeble and vain.] 1A¹a–b, 2A, 1F; empty and vain; 1A¹c–
                  1A³

214.22–23   Tis the common place jest of the nursery scape-goat, /
                  Tis the common place ballad that croaks from his
                  throat] 1A¹a–b; Tis your fate to be ever distress'd
                  with a crowd, / Who know not the merits with which
                  you're endowed; 1A¹c–1A³; *omitted* 2A, 1F

214.24–27   He knows not that nature—that polish decrees, / That
                  women should always endeavour to please: / That the
                  law of their system has early imprest / The importance
                  of fitting themselves to each guest;] 1A¹a–b, 2A; Who
                  know not the merits with which you're endowed; /
                  Who know not that bountiful heaven decrees / Your
                  sex should be ever ambitious to please, / That by
                  nature, with witching variety blest, / You've the art
                  of adapting yourselves to each guest; 1A¹c–1A³ ⟨*follows
                  1A¹a–b version except the first line reads:*⟩ They know
                  not that nature—that custom decrees: 1F

214.36   when in] 1A¹a–b, 2A, 1F; in a 1A¹c–1A³

214.40   will] 1A¹a–b, 2A, 1F; may 1A¹c–1A³

214.41   delicate] 1A¹a–b, 2A, 1F; whimsical 1A¹c–1A³

214.42   He may] 1A¹a–b, 2A, 1F; Or may 1A¹c–1A³

215.7   star] 1A; orb 2A, 1F

215.11–16   Nor e'er would he wish those fair beings to find / In
                  places for *Di majorum gentium* designed; / But as
                  Dii penates performing their part— / Receiving and
                  claiming the vows of the heart——Recalling affections
                  long given to roam, / To centre at last in the bosom
                  of HOME.] 1A; *omitted* 2A, 1F

215.12   In places] 1A¹a–b; In a place 1A¹c–1A³

215.14   and claiming the] 1A¹a–b; the homage and 1A¹c–1A³

216.12   tobacco-box] 1A, 2A; snuff-box 1F

216.14   quid] 1A, 2A; pinch 1F

217.40   horrible] 1A, 2A; horribly 1F

218.31   so much in] 1A¹, 2A, 1F; in so much 1A²

219.34   shall] 1A, 2A; may 1F

220.36   other words] 1A, 2A; common phrase 1F

221.40   tremendous] 1A, 2A; *omitted* 1F

222.1   and through] 1A, 2A; *omitted* 1F

222.41   retired] 1A, 2A; had retired 1F

222.43   into] 1A¹, 2A, 1F; in 1A²

223.6   absolute] 1A, 2A; *omitted* 1F

223.15   the door] 1A; his door 2A, 1F

223.24–25   and which so much resemble] 1A, 2A; resembling 1F
224.34–35   he who, like mynheer, has written a book "as tick as a
             cheese"] 1A; he who has made out to swell a folio
             2A, 1F
225.7   us] 1A, 2A; we 1F
225.23   abounds] 1A, 2A; abound 1F
225.37   Canton.] 1A, 2A; Canton arrived. 1F
226.29   caucus] 1A, 2A; council 1F
227.39   as sir John Carr asserts] 1A, 2A; whatever Sir John
             Carr may assert 1F
228.26   old] 1A; *omitted* 2A, 1F
228.29   criticisms] 1A^1, 2A, 1F; criticism 1A^2
228.38   hot] 1A, 2A; warm 1F
229.34   factor] 1A; benefactor 2A, 1F
230.18   addresses] 1A^1, 2A, 1F; addressed 1A^2
230.33–34   benignant] 1A, 2A; *omitted* 1F
230.35   weary] 1A, 2A; *omitted* 1F
231.15   distinguishing] 1A, 2A; distinguished 1F
231.19–20   to supply the perpetual motion] 1A, 2A; for the per-
             petual excercise 1F
232.5   chose to wear] 1A, 2A; had worn 1F
232.5–6   to entertain] 1A, 2A; had entertained 1F
232.23–24   wandering] 1A, 2A; *omitted* 1F
232.26   these] 1A, 2A; *omitted* 1F
232.26   extensive] 1A, 2A; *omitted* 1F
232.27   in this country] 1A, 2A; here 1F
232.35   discovered] 1A, 2A; asserted 1F
232.41   forlorn, abandoned] 1A, 2A; *omitted* 1F
232.42   lays] 1A, 2A; lies 1F
233.2–3   the dead level of] 1A, 2A; its 1F
233.3   and soften the wide extent of desolation–] 1A, 2A;
             omitted 1F
233.3–4   darkened] 1A, 2A; *omitted* 1F
233.5   to whom no blissful perspective opens beyond the
             grave;–] 1A, 2A; *omitted* 1F
233.14   british island] 1A, 2A; British islands 1F
233.23   as fast as possible] 1A, 2A; again 1F
233.30   mighty and distracted] 1A, 2A; *omitted* 1F
233.36–37   be in the unhappy state of a patient whose palate
             nauseates] 1A, 2A; nauseate 1F
233.37–38   best calculated] 1A, 2A; proper 1F
233.38   his] 1A, 2A; their 1F

233.38–39 seem anxious to continue in the full enjoyment of] 1A, 2A; to abandon themselves wilfully to 1F

233.40 like] 1A, 2A; as 1F

233.42 most agonizing] 1A, 2A; *omitted* 1F

*234.7 oracles. True] 1A, 2A; oracles. For in this country every man adopts some particular slang-whanger as his standard of judgment, and reads every thing he writes, if he reads nothing else; which is doubtless the reason why the people of this logocracy are so marvellously enlightened. True 1F

234.7 unfortunate] 1A, 2A; *omitted* 1F

234.8 this insatiable] 1A, 2A; the insatiable 1F

234.9 for intelligence,] 1A, 2A; of their disciples; 1F

234.11 to their disciples] 1A, 2A; *omitted* 1F

234.12–14 ⟨Paragraph⟩ When the hungry politician is thus full charged with important information, he sallies forth to give due exercise to his tongue, and tell all he knows to every body he meets.] 1A, 2A; ⟨Paragraph⟩ Politics is a kind of mental food that is soon digested; it is thrown up again the moment it is swallowed. Let but one of these quidnuncs take in an idea through eye or ear, and it immediately issues out at his mouth—he begins to talk. No sooner therefore is a politician full charged with the rumours I have mentioned, but his tongue is in motion: he sallies forth to give it exercise; and woe to every one he encounters. He is like one charged with electricity; present but a knuckle, and you draw a spark. 1F

234.15–23 as wise as himself, charged with the same articles of information, and possessed of the same violent inclination to give it vent, for in this country every man adopts some particular slang-whanger as the standard of his judgment, and reads every thing he writes, if he reads nothing else—which is doubtless the reason why the people of this logocracy are so marvelously *enlightened.* So away they tilt at each other with their borrowed lances, advancing to the combat with the opinions and speculations of their respective slang-whangers which in all probability, are diametrically opposite—here] 1A, 2A; as highly charged as himself; with the self-same rumors too; and fully as eager to give them vent. The only difference is, that as each goes according to the doctrine of his respective slang-whanger, their views of every subject are diametrically opposite. Here 1F

234.27 begins to wax wanton, other auxillaries become necessary] 1A, 2A; waxes wanton 1F

234.30 contemptible enemy] 1A, 2A; *omitted* 1F

234.35–36 ever after against the indulgence of political] 1A, 2A; against future 1F

234.41–42 of contention] 1A, 2A; *omitted* 1F

234.43–235.1 the scowling] 1A, 2A; an 1F

235.2 throe and pulsation] 1A; throb 2A, 1F

235.6 This theory] 1A, 2A; This in theory 1F

235.14 its] 1A, 2A; the 1F

235.18 as] 1A, 2A; will as 1F

235.19 are waging] 1A, 2A; wage 1F

235.22 and impetuous passions,] 1A, 2A; *omitted* 1F

235.23 commotions] 1A, 2A; contentions 1F

235.23 here] 1A, 2A; in this nation of quick tongues 1F

235.24 high sounding words] 1A, 2A; wordy riots 1F

235.24–25 or in the insidious assassination] 1A, 2A; in assassinations 1F

235.25–27 a restless propensity among the base to blacken every reputation which is fairer than their own.] 1A, 2A; what is termed "murder of the King's English." 1F

235.39 *their*] 1A, 2A; their own 1F

236.7 most] 1A, 2A; *omitted* 1F

236.9 and faring sumptuously every day] 1A, 2A; *omitted* 1F

236.12 same state as it] 1A; same state it 2A; state it 1F

236.12–14 except a ... who have ... there] 1A, 2A; A ... it is true, have ... otherwise there 1F

236.18 whom they] 1A, 2A; whom as usual they 1F

236.19 sterling] 1A, 2A; *omitted* 1F

236.21 trample under foot] 1A, 2A; pull down 1F

236.22 wise] 1A, 2A; *omitted* 1F

236.23 amused with straws, and] 1A, 2A; *omitted* 1F

236.25–26 and puff himself up] 1A, 2A; *omitted* 1F

236.31 yet] 1A; *omitted* 2A, 1F

236.33 nothing to do but] 1A, 2A; but to 1F

236.39 smoky circumference] 1A, 2A; smoke 1F

236.41 unmeaning and] 1A, 2A; *omitted* 1F

237.4 unsophisticated] 1A; clear 2A, 1F

237.5 has] 1A, 2A, 1F; thus MS

237.13 senses] 1A, 2A, 1F; feelings MS

237.21–24 ⟨*Paragraph*⟩ At such times I feel a sensation of sweet tranquility—a hallowed calm is diffused over my senses; I cast my eyes around and every object is serene, simple, and beautiful; no warring passion, no discordant string there vibrates to the touch of ambition, self-interest, hatred or revenge—] 1A; ⟨as for 1A except:⟩ time 2A; At such time I am conscious of the influence of nature upon the heart. I cast my eyes around, all is serene and beautiful; the sweet tranquility, the hallowed calm settle upon my soul. No jarring chord vibrates in my bosom; every angry passion is at rest; 1F

238.10	vagabond] 1A, 2A; devil 1F
238.14	populate] 1A, 2A; people 1F
238.16	redundant] 1A, 2A; *omitted* 1F
238.19	most 1A, 2A; *omitted* 1F
238.27	sweet] 1A, 2A; *omitted* 1F
238.28	unmeaning,] 1A, 2A; *omitted* 1F
239.41	or London particular] 1A, 2A; and Madeira 1F
239.42	teems] 1A, 2A; abounds 1F
240.3–4	with great satisfaction] 1A, 2A; find room to 1F
240.25–26	square set of portly well fed looking] 1A, 2A; set of square, portly, well fed 1F
241.28	the finery thus put on of a sudden] 1A, 2A; its transient finery 1F
241.33	venerable] 1A, 2A; *omitted* 1F
242.6	old] 1A, 2A; *omitted* 1F
242.32	happy] 1A, 2A; *omitted* 1F
243.4	universal] 1A, 2A; *omitted* 1F
244.10	store] 1A, 2A; office 1F
244.21	who Evergreen whimsically dubs my *Tender,*] 1A; *omitted* 2A, 1F
244.31	effects] 1A, 2A; affects 1F
245.36	scud] 1A, 2A; scudded 1F
247.16	erst] 1A, 2A; once 1F
248.1	lady widow] 1A, 2A; widow lady 1F
248.42	his] 1A, 2A; the 1F
249.29	mind] 1A, 2A; heart 1F
250.36	always] 1A, 2A; already 1F
251.15	on all-fours] 1A, 2A; *omitted* 1F
251.17	like very reptiles] 1A, 2A; *omitted* 1F
251.24	progress] 1A, 2A; ascent 1F
251.39–40	reduce him into servile obedience] 1A, 2A; render him obedient 1F

252.4   ignobly] 1A, 2A; *omitted* 1F
*252.6   Diogenes his] 1A, 1F; Diogenes in his 2A
252.9   plunges into that mass of obscenity] 1A, 2A; buries
                   himself in 1F
252.11   rogues, ignoramuses and blackguards.] 1A, 2A; the
                   vulgar. 1F
252.13–14   the land] 1A, 2A; society 1F
252.18   pollution] 1A, 2A; the dirt 1F
252.31–32   in full caucus] 1A, 2A; *omitted* 1F
252.37   sat] 1A, 2A; set 1F
253.27   between two planets] 1A, 2A; *omitted* 1F
253.39   only now and then make a great man laugh] 1A; only
                   now and then make a man laugh 2A; only make a
                   great man laugh now and then 1F
253.43   sometimes] 1A, 2A; *omitted* 1F
254.7   hungry] 1A, 2A; *omitted* 1F
254.12   *caucuses*] 1A, 2A; gatherings 1F
254.12–13   adapted his dress to a similitude of dirty raggedness]
                   1A, 2A; assumed a patriotic slovenliness of dress 1F
254.30   dead] 1A, 2A; *omitted* 1F
254.31–32   loathsome] 1A, 2A; *omitted* 1F
254.34   swinish] 1A, 2A; *omitted* 1F
255.7–8   dignitaries, and drinking out of the same pot with them
                   at a porter-house!!] 1A, 2A; dignitaries—during elec-
                   tions. 1F
255.14   got] 1A, 2A; been 1F
257.8   break] 1A, 2A; exhaust 1F
257.37   the rights and privileges of] 1A, 2A; *omitted* 1F
258.10   released] 1A, 2A; relieved 1F
258.14   incredible] 1A, 2A; *omitted* 1F
258.36   longed] 1A; lodged 2A; thrust 1F
258.37–38   "There, miss, there's more than you can eat—] 1A, 2A;
                   "Permit me, Miss, to help you," cried he, presenting
                   the morsel—then growling to himself, as he dispatched
                   the remainder 1F
259.11   peculiarly] 1A, 2A; *omitted* 1F
259.22   aptitude] 1A, 2A; quickness 1F
259.36   harmonious] 1A, 2A; *omitted* 1F
263.25   seasons] 1A, 2A; season 1F
263.26   characters] 1A, 2A; character 1F
264.14   missive] 1A, 2A; missile 1F
265.3   say their poets] 1A; says their poet 2A, 1F

265.32–33   which contaminates the refreshing draught while it is inhaled;] 1A, 2A; *omitted* 1F

265.34   cowardly] 1A, 2A; *omitted* 1F

265.41   blackguard] 1A, 2A; vilify 1F

266.31   amid the tranquillities] 1A, 2A; in the tranquillity 1F

267.34–35   like the hues in Joseph's coat of many colours] 1A; *omitted* 2A, 1F

270.32   most uncommon] 1A, 2A; whimsical 1F

271.9   wilting] 1A, 2A; shrivelling 1F

272.11   this] 1A; the 2A, 1F

272.13   inspiring] 1A; aspiring 2A, 1F

273.4   migration] 1A; migrations 2A, 1F

274.18   profit of] 1A, 2A; profit by 1F

277.5   was and in] 1A, 2A; was, in 1F

278.9   profound] 1A, 2A; *omitted* 1F

280.14   a data] 1A, 2A; datum 1F

280.26   piteous] 1A, 2A; *omitted* 1F

280.27   exquisitely] 1A, 2A; dismally 1F

281.25   dying] 1A, 2A; *omitted* 1F

282.43   runty] 1A, 2A; *omitted* 1F

283.15   and seraglioes] 1A, 2A; *omitted* 1F

283.41   will] 1A, 2A; *omitted* 1F

284.1–2   representing her tricked out in all the tawdry] 1A, 2A; tricking her out in the 1F

284.4   melancholy] 1A, 2A; *omitted* 1F

284.5   me] 1A, 2A; one 1F

284.5–6   that I have now and then seen hung] 1A, 2A; hanging 1F

284.9   supply their constant demands, and] 1A, 2A; *omitted* 1F

285.7   or as] 1A, 2A; nay, even though they equalled 1F

285.34   original] 1A, 2A; *omitted* 1F

286.17   roses] 1A; rose 2A, 1F

286.24   and smoke tobacco] 1A, 2A; *omitted* 1F

286.27   gift] 1A; gifts 2A, 1F

287.35   and illiberal] 1A, 2A; *omitted* 1F

288.10   seraglio] 1A, 2A; harem 1F

288.22   such ignominious] 1A, 2A; *omitted* 1F

289.3–4   upon a prodigious great scale] 1A, 2A; *omitted* 1F

293.20   mouth] 1A, 2A; cheek 1F

294.36–37   ladies are ... heroes are ... their] 1A, 2A; lady is ... hero is ... his 1F

294.37   pease-blossom] 1A, 2A; pea-blossom 1F

295.21   occasioned] 1A, 2A; caused 1F

295.41	stealing] 1A, 2A; exchanging 1F
299.41–300.3	It brings on the tapis their neighbours defects, / The faults of their friends or their wilful neglects; / Reminds them of many a good natured tale, / About those who are stylish or those who are frail, / Till the sweet tempered dames are converted by tea, / Into character manglers–*Gunaikophagi.**] 1A; *omitted* 2A, 1F
300.6	she] 1A; was 2A, 1F
300.39–42	⟨*Paragraph*⟩ * I was very anxious that our friend Pindar, should give up this learned word, as being rather above the comprehension of his fair readers; but the old gentleman, according to custom, swore it was the finest point in his whole poem—so I knew it was in vain to say any more about it. ⟨*space*⟩ W. WIZARD.] 1A; *omitted* 2A, 1F
301.19	quantums] 1A, 2A; cargoes 1F
301.24	your] 1A, 2A; this 1F
301.26–27	Like to Java's drear waste they embarren the heart, / Till the blossoms of love and of friendship depart.] 1A, 2A; *omitted* 1F
302.22	alderman] 1A, 2A; butler 1F
304.22	article] 1A, 2A; usage 1F
305.38	conjecture] 1A, 2A; conjecturing 1F
305.38–39	so we generously leave them to flounder in the smooth ocean of glorious uncertainty] 1A, 2A; *omitted* 1F
307.30	did] 1A, 2A; does 1F
308.6	peers] 1A[1]a; knights 1A[1]b–c, 2A, 1F
308.27–29	with great openness and candour, do ... offences] 1A, 2A; do ... offences, with great openness and candor, 1F
308.32	and our indulgent partiality] 1A, 2A; *omitted* 1F
308.36	our] 1A, 2A; *omitted* 1F
309.13	had] 1A, 2A; has 1F
309.19	happy] 1A, 2A; *omitted* 1F
310.3	by the connoisseur of human character] 1A, 2A; *omitted* 1F
310.8	all] 1A, 2A; *omitted* 1F
310.22	glory] 1A, 2A; glorying 1F
310.25	some] 1A, 2A; a more 1F
310.28	joyless] 1A, 2A; roving 1F
311.11–12	its bottom was soft and muddy, and] 1A, 2A; *omitted* 1F
311.12	dull and] 1A, 2A; was dull, turbid, and 1F
311.29	expanded] 1A, 2A; at length expanded 1F
311.33	wandering] 1A, 2A; *omitted* 1F

LIST OF COMPOUND WORDS
HYPHENATED
AT END OF LINE

List I includes all compound and possible compound words that are hyphenated at the end of the line in the copy-text. In deciding whether to retain the hyphen or to print the word as a single-word compound (without the hyphen) the editor has made the decision first on the use of each compound word elsewhere in the copy-text, taking into consideration the inconsistent hyphenation practice found there; and second on contemporary American usage, chiefly as reflected in Webster's dictionary of 1848. Because of the collaborative nature of the work and the uncertain authorship of many of the pieces, it seemed advisable not to rely on Irving's practice in other writings. Each word is listed in its editorially accepted form after the page and line numbers of its appearance in the T text.

List II presents all compounds, or possible compounds, that are hyphenated or separated as two words at the end of the line in the T text. They are listed in the form in which they would have appeared in the T text had they appeared in midline.

LIST I

67.33	undertake	102.9	cook-maid
68.7	understand	103.14	ferryman
71.19	*beaumonde*	105.12	gentlemen
74.4	air-drawn	106.31	tennis-balls
74.29	outrage	112.5	marrow-bones
76.2	byestanders	113.35	blackguard
77.10	cobweb	119.43	ill-befitting
81.4	quidnuncs	120.34	loop-hole
83.36	gentleman	121.1	ten-fold
90.22	iron-bound	125.21	top-knot
92.27	tadpoles	135.1–2	snuff-taking
94.35	castile-soap	143.36	waist-band
95.3	brimstone	144.8	*anti-deluvian*
96.16	hodge-podge	146.24	windmill
101.13	countrymen	147.25	farm-yard

152.32	weather-cock	225.15	husbandman
160.18	self-denial	225.24	iron-bound
160.38	shoe-maker	230.3	POCKETBOOK
161.9	high-places	231.17	wind-mill
164.30	fifty-ninth	234.2	stage-waggon
165.29	gentlemen	240.9	clothes-presses
165.32	love-feasts	240.13	long-waisted
166.5	hoarhound	243.37	shell-work
167.23	fortnight	248.39	church-yard
167.27	household	253.1	market-places
167.30	uppermost	254.22	ward-meetings
169.34	slave-driver	254.32	sunshine
170.42	forthwith	255.27	slang-whangers
171.17	slave-driver	263.28	chicken-pie
171.22	throughout	267.17	weather-wise
184.18	pigeon-houses	269.21	noonday
184.40	land-lady	270.8	brick-maker
188.22	tea-parties	270.23	duodecimoes
188.37	pigeon-wing	272.28	handwriting
188.40	tea-parties	275.3	light-heeled
189.22	slave-driver	277.33	sugar-loaf
189.34	*slang-whangers*	279.9	house-wife
190.26	bellows-blowing	280.35	gentleman's
199.40	chimney-sweeper's	280.43	grandfather
200.5	fortnight	283.38	uproar
202.13	hardware	297.37	clockwork
205.43	turn-pike	300.40	gentleman
208.24	Wholesale	305.36	ill-natured
210.30	Yankey-doodle	306.41	grey-beard
216.28	household	308.15	overflowings
221.42	half-sheets	309.6	sunshine
222.28	newspapers	314.3	magnifying-glass

LIST II

71.11–12	grand-mammas	97.37–38	sugar-candy
76.26–27	dancing-master	98.25–26	topsy-turvy
77.1–2	frenchman	104.10–11	inn-keepers
78.30–31	gentleman	110.10–11	*pumpkin-pie*
78.36–37	grandfathers	120.6–7	throughout
79.3–4	frenchman	122.22–23	splash-dash
84.31–32	ink-stand	123.32–33	steam-engine
89.10–11	blockhead	126.8–9	frenchman
96.9–10	horse-flesh	126.16–17	apple-pudding

131.24–25	beef-steaks		221.20–21	whim-whams
135.1–2	snuff-taking		223.6–7	house-keeper
144.31–32	slang-whanger		225.36–37	gunpowder-tea
151.37–38	tender-hearted		227.26–27	grandfathers
153.41–42	quarter-staff		228.27–28	*gentleman*
155.21–22	pericranium		234.7–8	slang-whangers
158.28–29	household		234.22–23	slang-whangers
165.1–2	looking-glass		234.39–40	fire-side
166.9–10	materia-medica		239.1–2	gentleman
169.6–7	sky-rocket		240.8–9	bed-steads
184.40–185.1	buckwheat-cakes		242.2–3	gentleman
190.4–5	hore-back		247.40–41	whim-wham
190.26–27	slang-whangers		257.40–41	out-riders
192.21–22	slang-whangers		271.5–6	black-letter
196.27–28	good-natured		292.33–34	gentleman
198.42–199.1	*harum-scarum*		297.16–17	pigeon-wing
200.30–31	overwhelm		303.43–304.1	cherry-bounce
217.37–38	fire-place		304.5–6	out-dazzled
221.14–15	nursery-garden			

103519